TREMONTAINE

TREMONTAINE

[season 1]

CREATED BY **Ellen Kushner**

WRITTEN BY
**Ellen Kushner, Alaya Dawn Johnson,
Malinda Lo, Joel Derfner,
Patty Bryant, Racheline Maltese,
Paul Witcover**

ILLUSTRATED BY **Kathleen Jennings**

SAGA PRESS

LONDON SYDNEY **NEW YORK** TORONTO NEW DELHI

SERIAL
BOX

SAGA PRESS
AN IMPRINT OF SIMON & SCHUSTER, INC.

1230 AVENUE OF THE AMERICAS, NEW YORK, NEW YORK 10020

SAGA PRESS and colophon are trademarks of Simon & Schuster, Inc.
For information about special discounts for bulk purchases, please contact Simon & Schuster Special Sales at 1-866-506-1949 or business@simonandschuster.com.
The Simon & Schuster Speakers Bureau can bring authors to your live event. For more information or to book an event, contact the Simon & Schuster Speakers Bureau at 1-866-248-3049 or visit our website at www.simonspeakers.com.
Also available in a Saga Press hardcover edition
Interior design by Greg Stadnyk
The text for this book was set in Berkeley Old Style.
The illustrations for this book were rendered in cut paper.
Manufactured in the United States of America
First Saga Press paperback edition May 2017
2 4 6 8 10 9 7 5 3 1
ISBN 978-1-4814-8559-3 (hardcover)
ISBN 978-1-4814-8558-6 (paperback)

31088100976958

To the memory of
David G. Hartwell,
the City's first champion,
and
for
Julian Yap,
who wanted to return there

CONTENTS

Episode One

ARRIVALS

Ellen Kushner

I n the highest room of their splendid family townhouse on the highest part of the Hill, Diane, Duchess Tremontaine, sat in a window seat and surveyed her city.

Below the sweeping lawns of Tremontaine House the river roiled under the dull gray skies of a windy, rainy day. Across the river, prosperous houses sent up trails of smoke from their many chimneys. But beyond them, in the older part of the City, only some of the ancient buildings of the University bore these flags of prosperity. Many students went cold for their learning. But for a clever man not born to land or riches, what else was there?

Diane smiled. Her husband the duke loved the University. He believed in clever men, and he had some pretensions to learning, as his extensive library testified. He served on the University's Board of Governors, and was happier there than in the halls of the Council of Lords. She didn't object. It gave him something to occupy his mind, while she occupied hers with weightier matters.

She clutched the sheaf of papers in her hand and craned her

slender neck, looking down the river past the Council buildings to the docks, where every day she hoped for her salvation.

The docks were impossible to see from the Hill, of course. The river bent through the City like a bow, crossed by bridges connecting the older side of the City to the new. And the *Everfair* was lost; the papers told her that, leaving no room for hope anymore. But there was a Kinwiinik Trader ship due in soon. There always was, this time of year, daring the first of the spring storms, bringing things exotic and delightful to the City's inhabitants: bright feathers, exotic spices, colorful cloth . . . and chocolate. These things were always welcome. But this time, the duchess had a particularly urgent use for them.

There were footsteps on the stairs. She shoved the papers under the generous folds of her skirts.

"Diane?"

Her husband knew she loved it up here. The servants had instructions not to trouble her when she was in her retreat—her "bower" William romantically called it or, sometimes, her "gentle falcon's nest." But he could visit when he liked.

The little door opened. She did not turn her head. Let him find her lost in thought, gazing dreamily out the window.

William Alexander Tielman, Duke Tremontaine, bent his long body to her. When his lips touched her neck, she arched it and smiled lazily, leaned into the warmth of his chest, then turned her lips up to his.

"I thought I'd find you here," he said. For a moment, they looked out over the City together. William rubbed her satin-clad arm. "It's gotten cold," he said gently. "Your fire is low, and you haven't even noticed."

"No," the duchess said. "I hadn't. What a good thing you came." She snuggled into his coat again. "So why are you here? Surely you can't be missing me already!" They had spent the better part of the morning sporting in bed for so long that their morning chocolate had grown cold, and they had to ring for new.

"Why should I not?" he said gallantly. "But I wouldn't disturb you for that. I just wanted you to look over my speech for tomorrow's Council. My man Tolliver's drafted it according to your notes, and I've tweaked it here and there . . . but I'm not quite certain yet. Will you . . . ?"

"With pleasure." She sat up briskly, folding her hands on her lap. "Read it to me, why don't you?"

But he made no move to produce notes from his pockets. "And there's something else," he said.

"Really?" She had to struggle to make it sound like a question. She'd known he wanted something else from the moment he'd entered.

"It's Honora." The duchess waited, expressing just the right mix of politeness and disinterest. "She's had another child."

"Already? It must be the country air."

On the subject of their married daughter, the duchess was intractable. But the duke pressed on: "It's a boy, this time. They've named him David—for the old duke, of course, the King Killer. The family hero." He risked a smile, inviting her to join him. "He's David Alexander Tielman."

". . . Campion," the duchess finished sharply. "Don't forget the *Campion*."

Duke William sighed. "You haven't forgiven her, have you?"

The duchess bit her lip and turned to look out the window. "No," she said, "I haven't."

"But Diane . . ." He stroked her shoulder. "Honora does seem happy in her new life. If you could find your way to—"

"I am very glad that she is happy, William. Truly." She did not try very hard to keep the rancor out of her voice. "In time, I am sure I will get over what she did to us."

"I'm sure you will," he said softly. His charm was in seeing the best in her, even when it wasn't there.

"Oh, William!" She threw her arms around him, allowing herself the luxury of tears. "I had such hopes! The years I spent, preparing to bring her out to make a good—a fine, an excellent—marriage! The alliances, the parties, the dresses we could ill afford . . ."

He stroked her carefully arranged curls, and she let him.

"And then, to fling it all in my face! To ruin every plan I had for repairing our fortunes! To run off with that ridiculous country nobleman, not even halfway through her first season!"

"Raymond Campion seems a decent man. His estates, though small, are in order."

"I'm sure they are, my dear. As far as they go." She lifted her head, wiped her nose, and patted her hair back into place. "It could have been worse, I suppose; she could be begging us to support her and some impecunious nobody." She looked at her husband with sudden suspicion. "She hasn't been asking you for money, has she?"

"What? Oh, no, no. Not money."

"What, then?" the duchess asked, more sharply than she had intended.

He sat by her side and took her hand. "Don't you think . . . a little visit . . . just to see the children . . ."

She did not pull away, but every part of her stiffened. "No. Absolutely not. Honora made her choice, and she must stand by it. She knew her marriage was critical to the future of Tremontaine."

"But surely—"

"She did not consider us; why should we consider her? I've no wish to see her, or to see what Raymond Campion begot on her."

That was not entirely true. If he lived, this baby boy would most likely be Duke William's heir, given Diane and her husband's unsuccessful attempts to produce a male themselves. But Honora's and that Campion fellow's boy was bound to be a disaster. She might have to take him in hand someday.

Diane stroked her husband's brocade sleeve. "I'm sorry, William. Of course they must be acknowledged. People have had a glorious time gossiping about the runaway Tremontaine daughter; it wouldn't do to have them talking about the babies, now, poor mites. Go ahead and send them something; silver, perhaps, with our swan on it. Something from the cabinets; we can't afford new, and anyway, it will seem more important if it's family silver, crested."

"Goblets?" He smiled. "Or rattles?"

"Whatever you like," she said warmly. "I trust to your selection."

Her husband squeezed her arm. "We'll come through, my love. It wasn't all on our daughter's shoulders." The duchess wisely held her tongue. He did not know about the wreck of the *Everfair*. Nor did he know what she had mortgaged to fund that expedition.

"Tremontaine's been leaking cash for years," the duke went on blithely. "But no tradesman in this city will refuse credit to us or to any other noble for that matter. Why, some of our friends—"

The duchess shuddered. "You know how I feel about credit, William. I do not like to owe anyone anything. And it does not become the House."

"Another loan, then . . . ?"

"And I know how *you* feel about loans!" She put her fine hand over his big one, gave it a squeeze. "When we put the Catullan vineyards up for security against that loan for the improvements at Highcombe, you didn't sleep a wink until they were completed, repaid, and the vineyards out of danger."

He looked down at both their hands. "Not a bit," he said softly. "I knew we'd made the right decision. Couldn't let my father's house go to ruin. I spent some happy years there. . . ." He smiled at something she couldn't see. "And then we got that phenomenal Catullan harvest, as you predicted—and what a laugh, to pay them back with profits from the very vineyards they were hoping to get their paws on if we failed!" He grinned at her, a boy's grin. "I'm only sorry I couldn't share the joke with everyone I know."

The duchess squeezed his hand harder. "But you know you mustn't, don't you? Not ever. For anyone to know we were taking out loans, much less putting up Tremontaine land for them . . ." He nodded. But she pressed on. "We can enjoy the joke together, the two of us, my darling—but that's as far as it goes."

He lifted her hand and kissed it. "You keep a most careful house."

"Because I must, William!" The duchess smiled ruefully. "The cook and the staff all hate me, because I make them do so very much with so very little. To their credit, they always come through. But the ball for Honora's presentation was a triumph of ingenuity over penury. And how I'm going to manage our Tremontaine ball this year, I do not know. I've got the musicians all hired at reasonable rates, but there's the invitations all to be handwritten and—"

"Why not have them printed? There are some fine engravers."

"William." She looked at him with her clear gray eyes, a tiny frown between them. "Tremontaine does not print invitations. To anything."

Her husband smiled. "Sometimes I think that you are more Tremontaine than I am."

His duchess chuckled. "You were born to it. You didn't care."

"I cared. But my father was such a dreamer. He wasn't at all practical. I think he spent his time longing for the old kings and the lost glories of Tremontaine."

His hand wandered up from her shoulder to stroke the exposed white stem of her neck. "But that was in my favor, in the end. If the old duke hadn't been so set on the family's glorious past, he would never have insisted that I marry the only remaining daughter of a dying branch: a very young girl, with very little fortune beyond her wit"—he kissed her ear—"her grace"—kissed her brow—"and her beauty."

Duke William tweaked one curl of his wife's perfectly coiffed head, careful not to disarrange anything. "I'm sure my mother objected to that match every bit as much as you do to Honora's. So you see? It's a fine old family tradition."

"Thank you, William." His duchess rested her head against his brocade-clad chest, despite what it did to her curls. "I am sure I do not deserve you."

Her husband kissed her nose. "And I am sure you deserve far more."

"Now," the duchess said briskly, "let us go downstairs. I shall get my maid to tidy me up, while you read me your lovely speech."

It was not difficult to slip the papers in her petticoat pocket, nor—when she got to her rooms—to close them in a cabinet drawer before her maid could find them.

Ixkaab Balam, first daughter of a first daughter of the House of Balam of the Traders of the Kinwiinik, stood on the dock enjoying the feel of the land still moving under her like a ship on the waves. She knew it was an illusion. A Trader and a daughter of Traders, she was used to ships. She could sail one herself, if she had to; she and her cousins had grown up coaxing the nimble river ships around the Ulua's turgid bends to their family's home in the mountains when the elders were occupied at sea, or at war.

She'd been at sea before, herself, though never for as long or as far as these ninety days past on the merchant ship *Wasp*, leaving the warm waters of Binkiinha behind for the cold north. She knew the sensation of rolling ground would pass and figured she might as well take pleasure in the contradiction while it lasted. Ixkaab hated to be bored.

She had tried not to be bored on the ship. She'd badly needed to be distracted on this voyage, while making sure that her particular skills did not rust. But there was very little of interest to glean on the *Wasp* about twenty-one gut-led Kinwiinik sailors, two Tullan outlaw runaways, a crippled old Xanamwiinik sailmaker, and a cook deaf in one ear, on a cargo ship full of feathers and parrots, spices and maize flour, and a king's daughter's ransom in processed cacao beans—along with five Traders, each of whom she was somehow related to. Besides the obvious facts that Uncle Koxol's sister's son's wife was pregnant, Mother's cousin Mukuy was already dyeing his hair, Father's cousin Chokan was sneaking twice his ration of tamales from the galley, and the captain wrote poetry to the cabin boy, what was there to learn?

And so Kaab had wisely applied herself to studying everything she could about these North Sea people, these Xanamwiinik, among whom she was bound to dwell for a while, at least until her part in the disastrous affair of the Tullan Empire mission had blown over.

It was a dismal prospect. This gray and smoky little backwater with its piddling river was hardly the broad, sunswept avenues of the Tullan capital, or even the flower-laced lanes of her sweet Binkiinha. Ixkaab set her jaw. All-knowing Chaacmul knew she'd seen uglier places—though not, so far, colder ones. As the *Wasp* had drawn nearer this side of the world, she had finally understood why everyone insisted she bring all her quilted clothing. *A damp cold,* Aunt Saabim used to write her mother, and now Kaab knew what she meant. Of course, there would be Local clothing to put on, better suited to the climate—she eyed the ship's agent's heavy wool jacket, which he wore unbuttoned in defiance of the chill. It looked scratchy. What kind of animal made wool like that? Would she be forced to wear it? Why hadn't her people tried importing decent fabric to this place—something with some color in it . . . *Spoken like a Trader, little bee,* her mother's voice said in her head. *Now, think like an agent.*

An agent whose wrists are bound by one mistake, Kaab argued with her mother. *What else is there to find out here?* Two generations of Kinwiinik Traders had surely learned everything there was to know.

She feared that there was nothing for her to *do* here.

". . . and that, milady, up there on the right, is our Hall of Justice."

She already carried the map of this new city in her head. But she let the kindly ship's agent explain it all to her anyway: "It was built in the days of the old kings, but is now the seat of our noble Council of Lords."

It was hard to understand his accent. Had he really said all the kings were old? She shook her head. Of course not. These people had no kings. He meant "old" as in "previously had been there but now were not."

Ixkaab badly needed to immerse herself in the daily speech of

Xanaamdaam. She had tried on the voyage, but her relatives spoke only basic merchant Xanam, preferring to remain among their own kind in the strange city that so loved cacao. Her many shipboard conversations with the toothless old Xanamwiinik sailmaker had given her seven fistfuls of curse words, a profound knowledge of what a Riverside prostitute would and would not do for money, and many ways to defend herself with a canvas sail needle (including where to slip it in to kill and leave no trace, which Kaab was too polite to say she knew already). She had also spent hours in her cabin reacquainting herself with their clever system of alphabet letters to make words, and she and Cousin Chokan had practiced some dance steps that the sailmaker swore were just what decent Xanamwiinik ladies did in public—even though this involved holding hands with men who were not their relatives.

It would come to her, she was sure. She just needed to talk with more Locals. Kaab was good at languages. As a child she had learned this one from a family servant who'd worked for Aunt Saabim here. Her mother had wanted her daughter's tongue to be as swift as one of the little chameleons that flitted across the sunny courtyard—her mother, who, Ixkaab realized now, had also been one of the great movers of the chocolate trade across the North Sea passage to this land. But her mother was gone to the houses beneath the earth. Instead, it was Ixmoe's younger sister Ixsaabim who dwelt here with her new husband, keeping the Balam family at the forefront of the northern chocolate trade. And here Kaab would stay, in the Balam family compound, until her father called her home.

"The old kings were terribly corrupt," the agent was saying.

"So now you are ruled by the Lords of Council."

"The Council of Lords!" The agent laughed with the patronizing amusement of one not used to hearing his language imperfectly understood. What a hick! "But here I keep you chatting, when I'm sure you are tired and would like to go home to your family."

"I am not in the least tired," Kaab said. "Pray, continue your most delicious explaining."

Because, in fact, Ixkaab Balam was not at all eager to arrive at Aunt Saabim and Uncle Chuleb's before they had had time to read her father's hastily written letter, the letter that had accompanied her on the *Wasp*, the letter explaining just what she was doing there, and why she had had to leave home in such a hurry.

"Your hair was perfect already," the Duke Tremontaine said, standing awkwardly against the passementerie on his lady's boudoir wall. It was one of the things she loved about him: the way he always seemed to feel out of place, no matter where he stood, everywhere except in his leather-filled library. When Diane had traveled here almost twenty years ago, a callow girl about to be married to the young heir to Tremontaine, she had been so afraid that he would turn out to be cold or arrogant or even dull. Duke William was none of those things. "I don't know why you must spend so much time on it."

The duchess's maid knew better than to smile. It was her lady's place to contradict her husband, when she chose.

Lucinda had had cozier employers: rich, titled ladies who wanted sympathy, gossip, or even mothering from the woman who tended to their looks, their clothes, and their personal comfort. But the lady's maid preferred to work in silence, paying perfect attention to each curl, each ribbon, each fall of lace; to the placement of each jewel on the shining bodice or tight-laced sleeve. And the duchess repaid her efforts: Diane de Tremontaine was the shining star of every social gathering. She had a certain something no one could safely imitate: a simultaneous air of fragility and confidence, of grace and poise and hesitance, the desire to please and the fullness of being pleased. . . .

The Duchess Tremontaine suited Lucinda very well. She made no demands other than to be turned out perfectly every time.

"Now, madam," the duke said, "since you are sitting quite still for the foreseeable future, would you be so good as to listen to the notes for my speech at this afternoon's Council meeting? You know I dread these things like a visit to the tooth surgeon's."

"I know you do." Diane nodded her approval of the second set of enameled hairpins Lucinda set before her. "But you always perform splendidly. I wish I could come and see you in the Council of Lords. I could watch from the gallery. But I must get dressed up and attend that dreadful chocolate party at dear Lady Galing's." Diane frowned down at her lap. "I don't know what I will wear; everyone's seen all my afternoon gowns so many times already!"

"They won't notice the gown; they'll be looking at you."

"You're a darling. Clara Galing will notice. She has an eye for such things." Diane turned a ruby ring on her finger, contemplative. "She isn't well, you know. Who can say how many more times we will be called upon to listen to harp music in that blue salon, while balancing those tiny saucers on our knees?" She snapped her fingers in annoyance. "If only Honora had held out, she might very well have been contracted to Galing, and have been lady to the Crescent Chancellor before she was twenty!"

"With a husband twice her age?" The duke, less than ten years his wife's senior, shook his head. "And anyway, Galing's besotted with Asper Lindley, now."

"Oh is he? With Lindley? I would have thought Asper a bit long in the tooth to attract Galing."

"Well, that's just it." William leaned back against the armoire, comfortably sure of his facts. "When we were boys, new come to town—thinking ourselves fine young men, of course—Galing took quite a fancy to Asper. But Asper wasn't having any 'dry old politician'—his very words, as I recall—he was too busy chasing other men's wives. Someone had told him they were easy, and he was . . . eager for experience."

Unable to nod under Lucinda's ministering hand, the duchess pressed her lips together in amusement. "And with that shock of gold hair, and that delicate mouth, I'm sure they were only too happy to oblige him. Land!" She laughed aloud. "What a pair you must have made! The scarecrow and the ivory god."

In the mirror, she saw her husband blush. Interesting. He'd been awkward on their wedding night, but not entirely ignorant. She'd made a point never to ask him how he'd learned, nor yet with whom. She covered her sigh with a yawn. Asper Lindley! Fancy that. Well, Lindley had her coloring, after all. No wonder William had been so enthusiastic when he met her. *What changed his mind now, I wonder?*

"His 'dry old politician' is not as old as he appeared to us then. And Galing is now the Crescent Chancellor of the Council of Lords. So Asper, having satisfied his taste for pretty girls (while still refusing to wed any, much to his mother's despair) . . . well, Asper has moved on to men of influence, while he still has power to attract them."

It all lined up, even her husband's slightly sarcastic tone: He wouldn't understand why a pretty boy would play with him and then move on. William loved deep, and William loved true.

"You should see the two of them in Council," he went on. "Sometimes I think the Crescent isn't paying attention to anything anyone's saying, he's so busy staring across the room at Asper Lindley's golden hair. I doubt he'd have looked twice at our Honora."

"Oh, darling. Galing looks twice at *everything*. I'm sure we could have arranged it." The languid duchess grew suddenly brisk. "Now, then, let's get your notes, shall we? If you can convince the Council to lower the tax on barley water, it will be very good for us. Our barley crop has done extremely well this year."

In the River Street Marketplace, a girl named Micah kept her eyes firmly on her turnip stall. It was a gray and muddy day—*the arse end of winter dragging its dirty tail behind it,* as Uncle Amos liked to say. Winter's end was mucky and messy enough at home on the farm; in the City it was worse. Not *ten* times worse—though that was what Aunt Judith always said. As if the multiple of "bad" was always ten! Micah liked people to be more precise. So, with the part of her that was not watching the stall, she calculated how much worse the City was, exactly.

On the farm, you pretty much knew what you were getting into, or how to avoid it—as long as you wore your clogs in the farmyard. You knew what season to plant things and when to put the chickens to bed. The way to the pasture didn't change, and the cows had worn a deep, clear rut over the years between it and the barnyard where they came to be milked.

The City, though, had streets tumbled about in no particular order. If cows had laid out the streets that wandered and crossed each other, Micah hoped never to meet them. And then there were the buildings, with their different shapes and sizes and ornaments: One was a house where people lived and one was a shop where people sold things and another was a place to get beer and another to get grilled meat, but because the shop had once been a tavern it still had those little windows taverns have, and somehow you were supposed to know what was what by the pictures hanging on boards over the doorways, though why a place with a horseman on the sign sold wine, while a sailing ship sold cloth. . . .

Micah did make a map of the streets in her head. She added new ones to it every time she went anywhere in the City. But she couldn't do anything about the houses.

In the City you couldn't always see the sky, and there were no trees at all. And underfoot lay all kinds of garbage that people tossed, not just dog or cow poop, and nobody saved it to put on the fields. Because there weren't any fields. Just a big open square where Micah and Cousin Reuben came every week to sell what the family grew, alongside lots of other farm folk from miles around, people who lived close enough to the City to make it there and back between sunrise and sunset. Micah's family was a little farther out, so they brought blankets to sleep in the cart overnight and leave for home the next day.

Weather-wise, Micah put the City at about four times worse than the country. In terms of the number of people, though, shouting and crowding, it was easily one hundred and ten times worse. So Micah kept her eyes on the stall, where all the bunches of sweet little turnips were arranged in the most beautiful patterns. By her. By Micah. Five on the bottom, then three, then two, then one. Eight rows like that.

And every time anyone bought some, she had to rearrange the whole thing. It kept her busy.

Kaab had convinced the agent to run her a little up the river in a skiff under the bridges, just to get oriented. Maps were all very well, but they didn't really show the details of a place: the height of a wall, the width of an alley. As it gave him a chance to show off his city and his knowledge to the exotic foreigner, the agent was happy to do it. A boatman did the rowing, of course, moving them northwest against the slow current.

Kaab pointed to the river's west side, on the opposite bank. "What are those funny—those pretty little roofs? With all the little chimneys?"

"Oh, that?" He looked away. "That's nothing."

"Nothing? But people live there . . . ?"

"Pay it no mind. It's called Riverside. A lawless place."

"Do you say so?" But Kaab knew all about Riverside. Her friend the sailmaker had many stories of the little island in the middle of the river, old in stone and old in mischief, the haunt of—

". . . thieves and pickpockets," the agent was saying, "fences and forgers, cardsharps and keen beggars, and, ah, very bad women."

Kaab shook her head sadly. It amused her no end to play the innocent stranger with him. "And swordsmen?" she asked doucely. "Are these famous fighters of yours there too?"

"The worst of them are," he said darkly. "These Riverside swordsmen are desperate men. Some do use their talents to move up to a better life, working as guards or duelists for the nobles. But the worst of them . . . well, they kill each other on the street just to try their blades."

"I did not know this city was so perilous."

"Oh, only in Riverside, lady." He hastened to assure her. "Don't you think of setting foot there! Why, the City Watch doesn't even go there. But anywhere else, you're safe as houses."

She let the funny phrase pass; his tone and his earnest face made the meaning clear. Like everywhere else she'd ever been, it was a *nice* city, they said, a *good* city, run by decent people. You'd only get in trouble if you did something stupid. Or failed to follow the 733 unspoken rules of conduct that of course anyone should simply know. Fortunately, Ixkaab Balam was a quick study.

"But must we all cross this terrible Riverside to get to the Middle City on the other bank?" she asked. "The very fine shops are there, no? And then one may climb to the Hill, with its stunning houses of the great nobles of the land."

He chuckled. "Never you fear, milady! You need never set foot in Riverside. There is a modern bridge upstream, just past the University, that will take you to the new side of the river, where the shops and the people are very fine, indeed. It is a bridge so wide, mark you, that two carriages may pass each other on it!"

"Stunning," Kaab murmured. It seemed to be the right answer to everything.

She wondered how quickly she could shake this fool and get to Riverside.

"Micah!" Cousin Reuben wanted her. "C'mere, boy!" She had to let him call her "boy" when they were in the City, because that way people wouldn't bother her. She even wore boys' clothes and had her hair cut short. Aunt Judith had put a big bowl over her head and cropped around it. Once she got used to the feel of nothing covering her neck, though, Micah liked it; long hair was a big nuisance to take care of and sometimes tickled you when you didn't want it to.

A woman with a basket was buying turnips, and Cousin Reuben was trying to count change. He wasn't very good at it.

"It's clear as the nose on your face!" the woman with the basket was saying. "I give you a quarter silver for these, and you give me seventeen brass minnows back."

"Eighteen," Micah said.

Reuben didn't seem happy. "You don't even know what she bought!"

"Yes, I do. A bunch of the little ones. Right there. I've got them in order, so I know. It would be seventeen minnows," she told the woman, "but you took the littlest ones, so we owe you eighteen instead. Did you want bigger? It would be seventeen, then."

The woman smiled. "You're an honest lad. Not like some of them kids. Yes, give me the bigger ones."

Carefully, Micah rearranged the stall to get the right bunch and put the wrong ones back. The woman stamped and blew on her fingers. "Hurry up," said Reuben, but the woman said, "No, take your time, honey. I know you'll pick a good bunch out for me."

"They're all good," said Micah, "but these ones cost more." The woman didn't say anything else. But Cousin Reuben managed to give her the right change.

"Well, she was a prize," Reuben grumbled. He looked at the sky. "Sun setting in a bit. Get ready for the oh-no-I-forgot-dinner rush."

"If we sell everything," Micah asked, "can we go home tonight?"

"Naw, sugar. Too dark to see, this time of year. You don't want old Rhubarb breaking her leg, do you?" He patted the head of the roan plow horse, who doubled as wagon puller. "That would make you sad."

"Yes, it would. I love Rhubarb. The horse, that is, not the plant. I like rhubarb pie, but that's about it. Sally likes fresh rhubarb dipped in honey, but—"

"Dear gods! Turnips!" A voice like a trumpet sounded in their ears. "You don't know what this means to me! You saved my job— possibly my life. Yes, my life for sure." The speaker was a big man with a beard tucked into his belt, who hardly paused for breath. "How much? See, I'm not even bargaining. I'll take everything you've got."

Micah looked at her piles. "Six and a half silver and thirty-two brass minnows."

"Why don't we make it a straight six?"

"Because that's not what they cost. If we sold every single bunch, we would get six and a half silver and thirty-two brass min—"

"My boy's real good at numbers," Reuben said, ruffling her hair. "It's all right, master. You can have the lot for six. And then we can go home, eh, Micah?"

"Not if Rhubarb breaks her leg! We can't go home in the dark, Reuben, you said—"

"Now, now, no one's going home in the dark."

The big man looked at all the turnips. "I shall have to make two trips. Unless . . . ?"

Reuben looked at Micah. Micah nodded.

"No trouble, mister; my boy will be glad to help you." He winked at Micah, which meant *be sure to ask for a tip*. And to her he said: "You just help the nice man carry them all home, and I'll stay right here and take care of Rhubarb, make sure she gets fed and rubbed down, and make us a nice, cozy bed in the cart for the night. And then we'll head out at first light, and be home by noontide."

"Well." The man drummed his fingers. "That's very kind of you. Offering help, I mean. It's not far—just down River Street and into the University." Reuben started putting their stock in sacks, while the man explained, "I'm Harcourt Onophrion, cook to the Horn Chair of History. A great man, Doctor Fleming, and he's throwing a little feast for some other University magisters tonight.

Something about some dead poet, and they all get drunk and sing and recite. I had a splendid meal all planned for them—not that they notice what they're eating once the Ruthven red starts flowing—but a very good meal. I was just going over the menu with Doctor Fleming—and he nearly burst a blood vessel when he saw I didn't have mashed turnips on it. Who knew? Turns out you can't properly celebrate Dead Poet without Mashed Turnips. Won't be made a fool of in front of his colleagues. Swears he explained all this to me, but I am here to tell you, he may remember ancient history, but he's clueless about two days ago. Thank you . . . Yes, yes, that's very good. I'll use some greens for salad tomorrow, and pickle the rest of them."

Reuben filled one sack and started on another. "I had to come myself," Master Onophrion explained. "My boy is down with the quinsy, and I wouldn't trust Fleming's manservant to find a black cat in a snowstorm, much less the right kind of turnip. I really am very grateful."

"That's all right. Micah, you take these—not too heavy for you, are they?—and just follow the gentleman. You'll find your way back, right?"

"Right," said Micah. "I've been to the university. Last time was fifty-nine days ago, when we made that carrot and potato delivery to Nan's Cookshop. I remember that way. And if this one is different, I'll put it on my map."

"Good boy."

"Come, then," said the cook. "Dead Poet won't wait forever!"

Back on the dock, Ixkaab thanked the agent profusely, pleased that she would never see him again.

Oh, don't thank me, always happy to help such a distinguished visitor, so pleased the first ship is in after a hard winter, please give your uncle my best regards and tell him it's a privilege to serve the Kin-Winny Trading fleet . . .

His words ran together in his enthusiasm, but she got the gist of it. Xamanek's light, was he never going to finish? He was like one of the beggars lining the flower-strewn road to Ixchel's temple. . . . Kaab smiled to herself as she figured it out. Of course he was.

"I will certainly tell my uncle when I see him." (And not my aunt? She'd heard these people undervalued women. Well, so much the better for her.) "But, sir, please allow the immediate expression of my gratitude for your kindness."

Kaab and the agent did the dance of protesting, insisting, protesting, insisting—she made note that, as with the Bakhim, it was the usual three times before he conceded. Kaab dug in her sash for her pouch of cacao and pressed a reasonable-size chunk on him.

He acted as if it were Nopalco gold and not just a common-variety bean, barely worth a hot bath back home. So she'd given him too much. But what of it? She raised her chin. The *Wasp* was full of cacao; and she was a first daughter of the House of Balam.

She let him bow to her one more time, waited until the agent's attention was once again turned to the unloading of cargo (as it should have been all along), and went to where her personal luggage sat awaiting transport.

Ixkaab was still wearing her shipboard travel dress: loose trousers and blouse under feathered vest under quilted jacket. Her thick, dark hair was decently wrapped atop her head, and she was grateful for the scarf that covered it all. Every piece of cloth kept you warmer here.

Traders, of course, were supposed to adopt the Local garb, to blend in. There would be plenty of time for that when she had presented herself at her family's compound. For now, let the Locals think of her what they would! She was not planning to go among decent people anyway. Before she settled into being the dutiful daughter of a house of prosperous foreign merchants here, convincing all her kinsfolk that she would never get into trouble again, she needed to test out her newest skill, acquired on the ship from the old crippled sailmaker who had once been a swordsman.

"There!"

The Duchess Tremontaine finished tearing the long, fine seam of her pale green silk skirt. Her maid was working on the other seam, but the duchess was not above putting her hand to fabric, if it would get the job done faster. And besides, the action of pulling the material apart, the sound of the careful stitches snapping under her hands, gave her satisfaction.

"Yes, good," she said. "All that green was getting vulgar. I'm going to wear dove colors this spring. They will look dreadful on poor Sarah Perry, but she won't dare try not to follow, not if Lady Davenant takes it up, and you know she will. Lady Sarah is about to marry her homely daughter to Rupert Vernay, who stands to inherit Lord Filisand's not inconsiderable estates someday. What a pity she'll have the choice of looking either stylish or corpsy at their wedding this spring. Now fetch me the gray satin underskirt."

"I fear I have not yet gotten the chocolate stains out of it, madam."

"Have you not?" The duchess rested her hands for a moment. But her tone was contemplative, not angry. "Have you not, indeed? Lucinda," she said with sudden briskness, "you will have to finish the task yourself. Run the seams up the green, so . . ." She bunched the fabric in her hands. "Yes, so it ruches naturally. You need not be precise. Just make sure it falls so that no one can see the chocolate stain on the gray." Her maid nodded, taking the green silk from her. "I will be writing letters in my closet. I am not to be disturbed."

"Yes, madam."

The duchess paused at the door. "Just remember—I want a sense of deliberate carelessness. The way you did my hair for the Lassiters' ball. A tumble of silk."

"Deliberate carelessness." Lucinda nodded, and a slow smile spread across her face. "Madam, no one will be able to copy you."

"Well, they can try," Diane said with the most piquant of little smiles, the one she had when something genuinely amused her. "They can certainly try."

The big man huffed and puffed as he walked with his sacks of turnips. He didn't want to talk. Which was good, because it meant Micah could really concentrate on remembering their route for her map because of the way the old cows had laid out the streets. It took some thought, but she could do it.

"Carry those for you, mister?" An enterprising boy tried to stop Master Onophrion, but: "No need," the big man huffed. "We're nearly there. You all right, then, little one?"

"Yes, I am," said Micah, without the breath to explain that she wasn't that little: She had strong shoulders and a broad waist. Cobby, Aunt Judith called her. Like a good plow horse. But compared to the cook, Micah was pretty little, so she guessed he could call her that if he wanted.

"Here we are." He fumbled with keys at the door of an old, old house and opened it. "Just drop them in here. Saaaaam!" he roared. "Come help me with these!" He turned back to Micah. "I'd offer you a hot drink, but I must get to work for the Turnip Poet. Here. Get yourself one at the Inkpot; it's close by."

He handed her a handful of brass. And then the door was shut, and she was alone, stamping her feet on the cold stones of the streets of the University.

It felt like a lot of brass. But her fingers were too cold to count it. She shoved the money deep into her pocket. A hot drink sounded like a really good idea. Micah started looking for the Inkpot.

The sun was still up, but the twisting streets were narrow, and the old houses hid most of the sky. Not too many people were about, and those that were were hurrying through the cold, their black scholars' robes clutched tight around them, their long scholars' hair flying behind.

"Ho-o-o-t taters!"

A boy stood by a big tin that held bright embers with baking potatoes nested in them. They looked good to Micah, and so did the warm tin.

"Get 'em while they're hot!"

She approached the fire and rubbed her hands at it.

"How many for you, friend?"

A potato would warm her hands, but if she was going to spend the money, it would be better to be indoors. And besides, the cook had told her to get a hot drink. People sometimes got mad if she didn't do exactly what they said. "Zero," Micah told the boy.

"*Zero?* 'Zat your name?"

"No. It is a number that is less than one. Less than one-half, even," she hastened to assure him, in case he got the wrong idea. She didn't like it when people tried to buy half a turnip, either.

"'Less than one' equals 'fuck off, kid.'"

"Can I just warm my hands a little?"

"No. Not if you're not paying any."

"Fair enough. Can you tell me how to get to a place called the Inkpot?"

"The Inkpot . . . hmm . . ." The boy stroked his chin, as if he had a beard. "'Zat where the poets hang out?" Micah didn't know, so she didn't say anything. "Let's see . . ."

The directions he gave were not very clear. He kept using street names—which wasn't useful because there weren't any signs—or else landmarks like "right by the bookseller's with the picture of the dog in the window," which was not that helpful either. But while he talked, Micah made all the turns a good pattern in her head, so when he finally finished, she thanked him politely and set off.

It was not as close as the cook man had said. Or else the potato boy was confused. When she got to where he had directed her, all she saw was a plain door, a door set in a wooden wall with a low shingle roof. Was this the Inkpot? It looked a lot like an old stable. But she could hear voices inside. Maybe it was a secret tavern. But where was the tavern sign? What if it was somebody's house? Micah was standing frozen when a young man in a black robe hurried up to the door. He stopped when he saw her.

"Don't be afraid, young'un. Doctor Padstow won't bite." He opened the door, motioning her in with him to a place full of voices and warmth. If they didn't have hot drinks, at least they had heat. Micah went in.

The little room was full of benches occupied by black-robed scholars with slates, all grouped around a hot brazier. In the middle, a man with black-banded yellow sleeves was drawing with a burned stick on the plaster wall.

Micah stared. It was an eight-sided shape, perfectly divided into eight triangles. Around the outside, each line was marked with a letter *a*. The sides that made up the triangles in the center were marked *b*. It made a fine pattern. But between each of these, a dotted line without a letter cut each triangle into two parts. Now, that was interesting.

"The question, gentlemen, is this," said the man with the burned stick. "What is the total length of the lines bisecting the triangles? *Bisecting*, as you will remember, Master Smith," he said pointedly to the student who had come in late with Micah and was clearly wrong about Doctor Padstow not being one to bite, "being the act of dividing in half . . ."

Bisecting, Micah murmured to herself. *What a wonderful word for it!*

". . . then: What is their total length, expressed in terms of *a* and *b*?"

The young men all scribbled furiously on their slates. "Doctor Padstow?" One raised his hand. "If we were to connect the eight *outside* points to create a circle . . ."

"It would create a very pretty picture, Master Elphinstone, but unfortunately, would not get you any nearer the answer." A bell started tolling, a huge, heavy sound on the air outside. "And so I'm afraid I will have to leave you to ponder the question until our next lesson."

Micah felt jumpy, as if she had to pee. She couldn't stop wriggling inside. She had to tell them, if they couldn't see. "Squares," she said loudly.

Doctor Padstow looked up sharply. "Who said that?"

"I think it was the kid."

"Because you've made the inside ones squares, and they're all the same, so to find out, you just add them all up!"

Everyone was staring at her. She really hated being stared at.

"Are you a geometer, boy?"

"No," Micah said. "I have to go!"

She turned and ran.

Now the streets were full of people, men of all ages in black robes, scurrying about as though they were rats set free from a trap. The big bell must have released them. They didn't see anything wrong with pushing to get where they were going, either. Micah really, really hated being pushed, or even being brushed, by strangers.

She tried going back the way she'd come, but the black-clad rats wouldn't let her. She was scared now. She counted backward from 215 by numbers divisible by three. That usually helped. But people kept bumping into her. She couldn't see where the street ended, so she couldn't tell where to turn. She was losing her numbers. She was losing her maps—

"You all right, kid?"

Micah looked up from where she was crouched in a doorway, her hands over her head. She didn't remember getting there.

"Don't touch me!" she said hoarsely.

It was a young scholar, almost as young as she was, maybe. "I won't." He drew back his hand. "Did somebody hurt you? Did your master beat you?"

"No." Micah felt in her pocket for the turnip cook's coins. They were all still there. "Nobody beat me. I just got lost."

The young scholar smiled. "I did too, my first month here. You're from the country, aren't you? I am too. Can I help you find your way?"

"The Inkpot?" Micah said without hope.

"I know it. Come on."

This boy did want to talk. But mostly he was telling her about himself. It didn't matter, anyway. The streets were a giant tangle of yarn, like when the cat got into Aunt Judith's basket. It would take her all night to untangle them. Eventually, Micah told herself, she'd find a street she knew, and she could start again. But she'd probably have to wait till dawn to find her way, unless she spent money to hire a torch to walk her through the night streets, and Cousin Reuben would be mad. She definitely had to have a hot drink first.

Riverside felt dangerous to an experienced hand like Ixkaab Balam. There were a million hiding places amid the close-together, leaning, old houses of stone, where anyone could be lurking.

But before she'd left her father's house, Kaab had taken a little memento from the wall of his accounting room. It was one of the curiosities her kinsfolk had sent back from foreign parts. Since his duties left him no chance to travel overseas, her father liked to line his workroom with exotica.

Her father might be annoyed to find the Xanamwiinik dueling sword gone, but surely he'd understand why she had carried it with her across the sea.

The blade was long and heavy and bright. The *Wasp*'s sail-maker had shown her how to keep it from rusting during those months at sea.

And he'd shown her how to use it, as well. His legs being as they were, he could no longer enact the moves, but by Ahkin, he could make Ixkaab dance! Up and down the deck, till the strange grip felt normal in her hand, and the weight of the sword on her arm. And then its silver tip up and down the mast-that-was-her-enemy, until Kaab was sure her enemy stood no chance. But when the sailmaker lifted a marlinespike and showed her what a clever blade could do to dance around her like a dragonfly in heat— Kaab smiled at the memory. It wasn't a toy, after all.

She was glad the Local sword hung at her hip now. There were very few people on the street, although it was nearly midday. But they had to be somewhere. Indoors, maybe? Few of the cunning, twisted chimneys gave forth smoke.

The Riverside stone still exuded coldness from the night, and, judging by how the houses nearly met across the narrow, filthy streets, the sun probably never reached between them long enough to warm them. On one street Kaab went down, most of the houses looked abandoned: wooden doors rotted, shutters and glass gone from the windows. Ancient staircases up to nowhere.

Kaab headed for a street where she could see wash lines hung across the road between houses. The sheets on them were yellowed, the underwear torn—but between them were bursts of color, like parrots roosting in a tree: a bright scarf, a frilled skirt, a stripy stocking . . . Poor people. But ones who liked some flash and dazzle.

Ixkaab counted dozens of mangy cats on the streets, the roofs, the doorways, cats of all sizes and colors—some new to her—all of them scrawny, many of them patchy and bitten, but she didn't see a lot of rats. *Good for you, kitties!* she thought.

"I know my love by his way of walking
And I know my love by his way of talking
And I know my love by his steel so true
And if one love leaves me, I'll seek a new!"

A woman was singing vigorously to herself, loud enough to be heard around the corner. Kaab slowed and took the side of a house, to see before she was seen.

The woman was leaning against a wall, catching a bit of sun on her pale, pale face. But her hair was aglow already. Kaab blinked. It was no trick of the light: The woman's hair was the color of clouds at sunset, of a good ripe mango, of a hunter's fire. If not for her face, she would be a creature of fire—but no: The woman heaved a long sigh, and her bosom rose like Ixel's pale twin moons from the top of her gown.

Kaab let her breath out slowly. Was this a Riverside prostitute, waiting for customers? Was her song some kind of signal to let people know? If so, where were they all? Why weren't the streets lined up five deep to taste the nectar of this woman's lips, bright and pink as the blush on her pale cheeks . . . to unbind those twin moons and let them sail the skies of pleasure. . . .

"I'm going to kill you, Ben!" the street goddess yelled up at a window above her.

A bright head popped out of it. "Not if I kill you first!" A young man's face, pretty and delicate as Chamwiinik porcelain, capped with tousled golden hair that just had to be fake. "You've hidden my best striped jacket!"

"I've pawned your ugly jacket!" Her hands on her hips, her head tilted up to the window, the sun-haired, moon-bosomed woman turned her back to Kaab. Her buttocks . . . well, there might be some padding under that skirt. Against the cold, maybe. But then, there might not.

"It wasn't funny the first time, Tess, and it isn't funny now! Come up and get me my goddamned jacket! Or I swear I'll—"

"Get it yourself," she sang. "It's under the bed, where you flung it last night sometime between when you got that message from your father, and when you finally stopped drinking."

"Very funny." But his head ducked back inside. The words wafted faintly out: "I *looked* under the— Oh."

"Oh." The woman Tess smiled to herself with those ripe guava lips. She leaned back against the wall, picked up a skein of her glorious hair, and started braiding it into tiny braids.

Kaab murmured a Tullan verse to herself: "'If I were your sweet sister, I would braid your night hair into as many strands as there are stars in the sky . . . and if it took all night, and the next night after that, then who could fault or interrupt us?'"

The door sprang open, revealing the gold-haired Ben in a fine, bold jacket of green and red stripes, buckling on a sword. *At last!* Kaab thought. *Some clothes with color!* But any approval she had for this Ben vanished when he seized Tess roughly by the arm.

"Let go of me, you sot!" she said.

Of course! He must be the man who sold her love, to pay for his vainglorious jackets. "Pimp," that was the word. Local custom or not, Kaab couldn't stand it. And hadn't he also just threatened to kill this glorious woman? She had come to Riverside to try her sword, and this was her perfect chance.

She stepped forth from the shadows.

"The brightest of mornings to the one of you, and a heap of trouble to the other." Kaab didn't know how these people issued a challenge, but the pimp could hardly mistake her meaning.

The man stared at her. And then he laughed. "Nice outfit, sister," he said, "but the Riverboaters' Masquerade was last month."

Masquerade? Oh, he meant her clothes. Kaab tightened her woven sash ostentatiously and showed him the scabbard at her side. "I do not joke."

"I do not care," he mocked.

"Shhh!" Tess pulled at his sleeve. "Ben, she's one of those *chocolate* people!"

He grinned. "Chocolate, huh? And does your rich Trader mama know you're out here in big bad Riverside, little girl?"

Kaab breathed in slowly through her nose. She had no trouble understanding Ben's language. His accent was like the sailmaker's, and he spoke as loud as a village priest.

"I will be clear," she said distinctly. "You trouble this lady. You insult my people, my mother, and my dress. You have a sword. I have a sword. Is more clearness needed?"

"'Is more clearness needed?'" He seemed to be mocking her accent. "Well, that depends." He put his hand on his hilt. At last. "I might need to see what color your blood is."

"Ben!" The glorious Tess was actually pulling on his arm. "That cart won't wait forever! Do you want to see your father before he dies, or not?"

"This won't take long." He shook his woman off.

Decency required that Kaab just let him go to attend his father's deathbed—but her liver-spirit was too stirred up to care. If he'd rather fight her, let him. She'd make short work of him and his insults. She drew her blade, all thoughts of formal challenge gone. And Ben drew his.

Like buzzards scenting meat, people were flocking to the space around them, making a rough circle for them to fight in, shouting incomprehensible things. It was crude, it was bizarre, it was outlandish—and Ixkaab Balam felt alive, for the first time in weeks.

Ben lunged at her at once—in a hurry to catch his cart, no doubt—but she knew this one; the sailmaker had taught her. Her wrist moved, and his blade slipped off hers with a grinding noise that made her grin. *Take that, you mangy little pimp!*

"She knows what she's doing, Ben!" Tess cried. "For godsakes, stop!"

Kaab's wrist finished the move, twirling her point around his to target his chest. But Ben was not to be had so easily. He stepped back, then came at her again, as if he couldn't believe it hadn't worked right the first time. Again she countered him, and this time her point reached closer to his chest.

The people kept yelling, again with no respect for the fighters, as if this duel were a servants' tavern brawl. Above them she heard Tess's voice blaring: "First blood! First blood!" What was she talking about? Kaab wasn't bleeding, and Ben wasn't either. "I'm the cause of the fight, and I'm calling it just to first blood!"

Circling Kaab, Ben growled, "Shut up. I'm going to kill her."

"No you're not! You haven't got time! Just pink her and go!"

Kaab's body was hot, but the fight was cooling her liver-spirit, and her head-spirit was reasserting itself. Ben was distracted. Maybe his woman was even doing it on purpose, to help Kaab rescue her from her pimp. It was the perfect time to try a special little play her shipboard friend had taught her, a trick he said would never fail: a fake thrust that led the enemy to aim for your shoulder, while you blithely went in straight to his heart.

It failed.

She felt a wasp sting her right arm. *"Rose-torn demons of hell!"* Kaab shouted, dropping her blade.

"First blood!" All around her, the people were crying it out, like an incantation. Kaab didn't trust them. Her sword had skidded west. She reached down for it—

A burly old man had his foot on the blade. "You know the rules," he told her. "Or if you don't, you shouldn't be here."

Kaab looked up at him. "Are you of honor?" It came out wrong, but the gray-head nodded.

"This is Riverside, honey. We know no honor but the sword."

He stepped back a pace.

"Now, pick up your blade and go back to whatever traveling sideshow you came from, girl. And if you ever want to come here again, I advise you to take a few more lessons first."

She risked a look across the circle. Ben stood there, panting and grinning. The perfidious Tess pulled at his arm. *"Now,* Ben!" She spoke to Kaab directly: "I'm sorry," she said. "He's mean when he's hungover."

"I was provoked!" Ben objected.

"Provoked to fight a girl?" someone jeered. So the sailmaker had been right. Women did not fight here.

"He'll tell you all about it," Tess said pointedly, "when he gets back from *visiting his dying father.*" She shooed people away like flies. "Stop gawking. Haven't you got anything better to do?"

But Kaab was a curiosity, now that the fight was over, and they would not depart. "Where you from, lady?" the voices came at her. "Where'd you get them clothes? What'll you take for that stripy head rag? Who taught you to fight?"

It was the kind of situation Kaab always enjoyed, Xamanek help her. A new city, a new role. She could tell them anything, and they'd most likely believe it as not.

She lifted her head, trying to look like the carving of Xkawkaw on a temple gate, and announced: "I came on a great ship from the west, on the Road of the Wind. An old god taught me to fight, and I honor him by shedding my blood on your soil. Lord Ben, you have served me well. I give you leave to depart."

She nodded imperiously at him. Much as he might like to, he would not attack her again; the glorious Tess would see to that. And indeed, she was rushing him off as quick as she could, berating him all the way.

Ixkaab Balam smiled. Her shoulder stung, but she'd had worse. It was a good first day in the new city.

Such a playactor! her mother's voice said fondly.

And the Riversiders parted to let her pass.

The Inkpot was a very nice place. It was pretty clean and not too crowded. There was a good fire going, and people were laughing and even singing in one corner of the room. Nobody seemed mad, and no one was looking at her. Lots of them were drinking things, mostly from pewter or earthenware mugs.

The boy who had guided her said, "I'll have one with you, if you like."

"All right," said Micah.

"Where's your brass?"

"In my pocket."

"Give it to me, then."

"Why?"

"So I can go get the drinks, you gubbins! What are you having?"

"I like hot cider," Micah said. "But you can't have my money. It's mine."

"They won't give me drinks without money! Don't be stingy. Didn't I bring you here? This place is for poets, and I'm a geographer."

"Don't call names," Micah said. He should at least be polite.

She looked around for someone selling drinks. She'd never actually been in a tavern by herself before, and Cousin Reuben always got the drinks.

"How much are they?" she asked the boy. When he told her, she nodded. She certainly had that much, and a little left over. "All right," Micah said. "I'll give you the money if you get the drinks." It seemed fair—or at least, a price worth paying so she didn't need to wade into the throng and figure it out herself. She counted out exactly the right amount and watched her helper head toward the bar.

"Come on!"

The voice behind her was loud and startling. Micah whirled; but they weren't shouting at her. Four young men sat at a round table, playing cards by candlelight in the low-roofed tavern, beer mugs at their elbows.

"Rafe, are you in or out?"

"I'm in." The tallest and darkest of them put some silver on the table.

Wow! Micah thought. They were betting with real money. She and her cousins only played with acorns.

Drawn to the game, she edged closer to the table, standing behind the dark-haired one, Rafe. She could see his cards. Not a bad hand, but it was more important to know what the others held. He couldn't bet against them if he didn't know. Each player had one card showing faceup on the table. The others had a Sun, a Comet, and a Two of Beasts. Rafe had a five, so at least they knew that. The betting went round again, and then another set was dealt.

The boy who had guided her handed Micah her drink, but she hardly noticed. She was following the patterns of the cards. She pretty much had them when Rafe laid more silver on the table and said, "All right. Everyone show."

They started laying their hands out, but she couldn't stand it. "Fold! Fold! What are you, stupid?"

Everyone was looking at her again. But she hardly even cared. How could he be so dumb?

Rafe turned a sharp face to her, and said kindly, "It's all right, young 'un; I've got a pair of Beasts, a pair of Crowns, and a Celestial. They can't beat that."

"Yes they can! It's so *obvious*!" She had that needing-to-pee feeling again, only it was needing to talk, to explain. "Look! He's got a Celestial showing, and he's got two cards down and he's betting high. There are only twenty-two cards left undealt, and the chance of one of them being a Celestial is five in a hundred, so that guy clearly has one more in his hand, which means he's got two and you lose!"

There was silence. Then, one by one, each man laid open his hand on the table.

"Holy Mother!"

She was right, of course. She always was. Her cousins wouldn't even play her anymore unless she played blindfolded.

"What's your name, son?" Rafe asked her, and she felt so sorry for him she didn't even bother to tell him she wasn't his son.

"Micah."

"Just come to town, have you?" She wasn't wearing a scholar's robe. And her hair wasn't even very long. But Rafe seemed to think she was one. "Well, Micah, would you like to join us for a hand or two?"

Five games later, Micah had a nice little pile of brass and silver in front of her. After the sixth, the other guys wanted to quit. "It's all right," Rafe told her. "We can go elsewhere. You're not tired, are you, Micah?"

"No," Micah said. This was fun. She'd already made four-sevenths of what she and Reuben had made all day selling turnips at the market.

"There's usually a good game going at the Gilded Cockatrice. Rich boys too. Do you play Constellations?"

"No. What's that?"

"I'll teach you later. It's a fancy game; you're right, not as much fun as Seven-Card Slap-Up. We'll go to the Blackbird's Nest instead. Full of historians who don't know a Celestial from a hole in their bum, and fancy themselves cardsharps. Easy pickings. And if there isn't a game going, we'll get one up."

They walked together through the twilight of the streets. Micah liked the way Rafe knew where he was going all the time. People just got out of his way.

In the Blackbird's Nest, she bought them both drinks, because that was what you did when people guided you somewhere, and she had plenty of money now. Rafe got a rum punch, and she got more hot cider, because it was the only thing she knew the name of that she liked.

Three men were playing Hole in the Corner. Rafe asked one of them, a man called Lawrence or possibly Larry, if he and his friend Micah could get in on the game. The other two were named Thaddeus and Tim. They moved aside on their benches for her and Rafe.

At first she hated betting her money, because once she had silver she wanted to keep it. But then she started getting some of theirs, and when they switched to Slap-Up she got even more.

"I'm out," said Tim. She didn't like Tim. He bluffed a lot, and she could never tell when people were bluffing. It didn't make sense. It was a crazy thing to do.

"What about you, Micah?" asked Rafe. "You getting tired?"

"No," she said. It was just getting good, really; she'd figured out that Rafe always thought that three of a kind would beat anything, even when it wouldn't. She felt bad about taking his money, but rules were rules.

Larry leaned forward. "Hey!" he said, but in a friendly way. "I remember you now. We went into Introduction to Geometry together this afternoon." He didn't look familiar to her, but all these men with long hair and black robes tended to look the same. "You're the one who knew about squaring triangles. Doctor Padstow wanted to meet you, but you ran away like the Hundred-Skin Maiden. Guess you realized you were in the wrong lecture, eh? You want a more advanced class."

"I like numbers," Micah muttered.

"Whose classes are you taking? Or don't you know yet?"

"I don't know yet."

"Well, we can help you. Thaddeus here did a lot of math before he realized he was a history man." Thaddeus had bought everyone another round. She'd had something that was like hot cider but with a special taste in it. It was good.

"And Tim can tell you where to get your robe for cheap, if you don't mind used."

"I don't mind."

"Your warmth is heart-melting," Rafe told his friend. "But we're here to play cards, Larry. You in?"

"Nope," Larry said cheerfully. "I'm the King of Losers in Loser City. If I lose any more, I'll lose my next term's fees, and then I'll be back to digging ditches for Lord Trevelyan like my dad."

"Me too." Thaddeus rose. "But another time, maybe. Your luck can't last, Micah. I'll win it all back from you, see if I don't."

"Do you want to bet?" Micah asked him. Back on the farm, she wasn't allowed to bet, but here at University nobody knew that.

Thaddeus leaned across the table. "Bet what?"

"Bet I can beat you eight games out of ten or better?"

"Eight hands, or eight full games? And why eight? Why not seven, or nine?"

"Because eight is—is the right number," Micah said.

Thaddeus rolled his eyes. "Mathematicians." He gathered up his books and wrapped a scarf around his neck. "I'll see you at home, then, Rafe. Don't stay out too late." He rapped his friend on the head in passing. "Or if you do, don't kick over the slop bucket and wake everyone—"

"I only did that once, you loser. And only because you and Joshua got drunk and left it in the middle of the floor."

"Because *you* were stone sober, of course . . . Where is Joshua, by the way? I thought he was supposed to keep you out of trouble."

"Off getting into trouble of his own, I hope."

"You need to find him some."

They were a lot like her big boy cousins.

After Larry went away, Thaddeus left too, and Rafe and Timothy started talking about stuff Micah wasn't interested in.

She counted the money in front of her again and gasped. Now it was more than twice what she and Cousin Reuben had made all day in the market, even including the turnip cook—

Then Micah gasped again. She'd forgotten all about Cousin Reuben.

She tugged on Rafe's black sleeve. "What is it?" he asked lazily. His breath smelled a little funny, like her cousins' at Year's End. She wondered if he'd had too much to drink. Drunk people didn't talk right and did bad things. Jackson on the farm down the road got drunk and beat his wife, and his children never had shoes. But Rafe was still perfectly clear and understandable, and still nice.

"I have to go back to the market," she said.

"The market's all closed up, kiddo," Timothy said. "Shops too, by now. What do you need?"

"I'll take care of him." Rafe swept a sleeve around her shoulders, and she let him because he didn't know any better about how she didn't like being touched, and she didn't want to hurt his feelings. "Micah's new in town. Come on, son; got all your winnings?"

Micah carefully put them in her pouch, tucked that inside her boys' breeches where Cousin Reuben told her nobody could lift it, and followed Rafe out of the tavern.

It was dark out. Really dark, except for the light from the torches stuck in brackets on the walls in front of all the taverns and cookshops that were still open, even this late.

Rafe leaned down to look into her face. "So what's this about the market?"

"My cousin is there. His name is Reuben. I came with him today. He'll be worried, and then he gets mad."

He peered at her in the flickering light. "What was he doing there?"

"Selling turnips. Only by now he might be asleep."

"You're a *farmer*?" Rafe kept looking, and then he slowly smiled. "But you found your way to Padstow's class. You want to study here, is that right?"

"I need to go find Reuben. He'll be mad, and I'll get yelled at."

Above their heads, the bell tolled. But the streets remained quiet and still, except for the noise from the tavern, spilling out the windows along with the bars of light.

"Look," Rafe said. "Micah. It's really, really late. You can't go running around the City at this hour. It's dangerous, see? There're bad people out."

"Oh," said Micah. "But where can I sleep, then?"

"In my rooms. You'd be welcome. There's three of us there already; one more won't matter, as long as you don't mind sleeping under the table."

"Well, all right. As long as I can tell Reuben in the morning. He's not stupid. He can see it's dark."

She trotted to keep up with Rafe. But at a low window along a twisty street, with good smells trickling out of it, he paused. "I haven't eaten. And I bet you haven't either."

It wasn't a real bet, because he'd been with her for hours. But Micah realized she was ravenous.

Rafe grinned. "Ever had tomato pie?"

Micah hadn't realized that cheese could be so good, all melty and drippy on top of tomato goop on top of flat bread baked in an oven. She usually hated goop, but this was so salty and chewy and, well, friendly, you couldn't mind it.

A barmaid brought them both beers. It was thin and nasty, nothing like the warm brown ale that Cousin Seth brewed each fall. Micah gave Rafe hers.

The barmaid came back. She had big titties, and she drooped them in Rafe's face, like a cow, which made Micah giggle.

The barmaid ignored her. "Anything else you need, Rafe? I gave you extra cheese."

"I know you did, Margery, and I'm grateful." Rafe tilted his stool back and looked off into the distance. "'Mannerly Margery, milk and ale.' That's a poem."

"A poem? For me?"

His stool came down with a *thunk*. "Thing is, Margery, I'm wedded to my studies. And Astronomy is a cruel mistress."

"Cold up there in the sky, is it? Maybe you need a nicer mistress, then."

"Probably. But I've got plans. Big plans. I—"

"Big plans." She snorted. "Big ones. Bigger than everyone else's? Right."

Margery went away. She wasn't interested anymore.

But Micah was. "What plans, Rafe?"

"Oh, Micah." Rafe spread his hands on the table. "Did you recognize the poem?"

"I don't know poems."

"There, see? I want everyone to know poems! Poems, and philosophy, and astronomy and geometry and mathematics and—and poems. Beauty. Complexity."

"How?"

He leaned forward, and his voice got lower. "I'm going to found a school. A school that's dedicated to teaching—to letting everyone learn beautiful, complex things! First in the City, and then, maybe, all over the Land."

"If you think farm people are stupid, we're not. We can read, and write, and cipher."

"Yes, and so can my father! He's a merchant, with ships and countinghouses. But he might as well be a farmer, for all he knows or cares about the finer things in life. A farmer of the sea, a farmer of coins and—and money." Rafe finished his beer and started on hers. "And will he support me in my venture? Hells, no. He wants me to study law, and accounting. To join him in his miserable little life of crates and bales."

"Will you?"

"Hells, no!" he said again. "I'm going to have to get a job, as soon as I become a Master. I'll need money, and lots of it, if I want to teach the poor." He was moving his hands around in the air. "Sure, I'll probably have to earn it tutoring some noble's kiddies at first, but I'm no climber. I won't be secretly hoping to be noticed by Lord Papa and raised to a secretarial position on his political staff, so I can help the nobles keep things the way they are. Not me!"

Micah stared, fascinated. "What, then?"

"I'll write pamphlets about my theories. Then people will come flocking to me—"

"Like sheep?"

"Yes! No! Not like sheep. Like . . . like . . . like true men and scholars! To spread knowledge throughout the Land." She didn't quite know what he meant, but he made it sound nice. "Micah." He leaned across the table to her, a little too close. "I want you to promise me something. You have a thirst for learning. I know it. Stay here. Stay here and learn."

"But I don't want to know poetry."

"Not poetry." He leaned back to wave his hands again, and she breathed a sigh of relief. "Mathematics. Start there. But not Padstow. Padstow's for beginners, and you're not one. I don't know who your tutor at home was, but there are magisters here more worthy of your knowledge. Men who can teach you something. Men you can study with. You have to join us here. You have to stay, and study what you love. Will you promise?"

She had never seen anyone whose face lit up as much as his. His eyes were like stars, like the first stars of evening that appeared while the low sky was still blue around the edges. Micah always wished on the first stars.

"Promise me," he said again. "Not just: *Sure, Rafe, anything you say, if you'll let me go.* Promise me you'll give it a chance, to dedicate yourself to learning with me."

"All right," she said breathlessly. How could she not? "But just for a week. Just till next market day, when Reuben comes back. Then I have to go home."

"Sure," Rafe said. "Sure, Micah, that's fine."

"I'll go see Cousin Reuben in the morning. He said he wasn't leaving right away."

"You could just write him a letter. You said he can read, right? I'll give you some paper, and there's always boys around who'll carry messages for a few minnows."

Micah was about to say she didn't have a few minnows, when she remembered she had more than that. "All right."

He gave her another starry smile. "And maybe you can teach us, too."

"How do you mean?"

"Your cards—the way you play, I mean. There's some kind of method, isn't there? You've figured something out?"

"Well, kind of. It's all in my head. But maybe I could draw you a chart. . . ."

"Could you?" He gripped her hands harder. "Would you? So I could start winning too? I could pay all my debts—buy all my friends food—stand the fees for my oral examinations . . . Oh, Micah! If you could do that for me! And I will help you. I swear it. You can bunk in our rooms, I'll help you find good classes, and find your way round. . . . You belong here. I promise."

He rose suddenly and slapped some coins on the table.

"Shouldn't I pay too?" Micah asked.

"Your first tomato pie? It is an honor."

That was so nice of him. When she had won all that money, even some of his. And he had shown her all around and found her card games. You should pay people for their help; she knew that.

Micah fished for her pouch. She'd give him 15—no, 17—percent of tonight's earnings. And in the morning, she'd start writing him up her likelies tables, so he could start winning too.

Facing her family was a lot harder than facing the Riverside swordsman.

They knew exactly who Ixkaab Balam was, and what she'd done, and there were no pretty stories to tell them.

Instead, Kaab let herself be scolded by Uncle Chuleb, and examined by Aunt Saabim, and fussed over by various older female relatives whose names she couldn't even remember—if she'd ever known them—but who all exclaimed about how she'd grown and how long her hair was and how much she resembled her mother (may she never be extinguished, may she never disappear) and laughed or tutted at the state of her clothes, according to their natures. The family's children wanted presents; the teens wanted to hear about the voyage; the older folk wanted the news from home. . . .

Finally, Uncle Chuleb had the sense or the courtesy to deliver the formal welcome: "The Sun shines upon your arrival, Ixkaab Balam, first daughter of my wife's sister."

Aunt Saabim picked up her cue: "In a week's time, we will feast your arrival. (Did your father remember the extra achiote I asked him for?) But now, we welcome you to the House of Balam in Xanaamdaam. It is your home as long as you respect the laws of gods and humans. Our life for your life."

Kaab placed her hand on her heart and bowed deeply. "And my life for yours."

"What you ask for shall be given, though we must walk the Road of the Sun to get it."

Everyone bowed to her now, even the littlest kids. Kaab looked around at them all, her people, old and young, women and men, some outlandishly dressed in Local clothing, but all with faces with the right expressions, skin the right color, eyes that knew her and welcomed her because she belonged to them.

She had to say something in response. But she was all out of words. She had been nearly ninety days at sea, and every day felt suddenly like a year.

"I would like . . ." Ixkaab Balam said. They nodded encouragingly at her, all smiles and welcome. She ought to ask to drink a welcome cup to toast them, or ask for prosperity on the house, or any number of things that meant nothing at all at the moment.

"I would like the longest, hottest, soapiest, scented bath it is within your power to provide."

The sound of their laughter welcomed her at last.

All eyes were upon the Duchess Tremontaine as she entered Lady Galing's drawing room. She was dressed in a marvelous confection of seafoam and lace that made her look like a water nymph, treading the land on little silver shoes, shoes with the smallest of bows and the sweetest curve of the heels. Instead of the elaborate jewelry of the other ladies, she wore a string of small pearls like bubbles of water and bracelets of fine silver. Individual pearls peeked from her hair, upswept save for the few fair curls that tumbled down her neck, caught by a silver ribbon.

The men who were in attendance this afternoon—younger sons not called to sit in Council, older men who thought that they could skip a day this once—felt that something had changed in the room, that the air they were breathing was suddenly cooler, like wind off the water; the day more like one from childhood in the country, finding a patch of wild mint. . . .

The ladies gasped at her splendor and audacity. Some sighed at Diane's ability to pull off something they could not. Even those who recognized the green dress from its previous incarnation could not but admire the effect. Some smiled at the sheer pleasure of seeing their art so well done.

And some did not.

"She looks like a window shade," Lady Davenant muttered to her friend Aurelia Halliday.

"She looks like a classical painting," Aurelia murmured in return.

"Something from the walls of Tremontaine House? I hear they're strapped for cash again. Maybe it's an advertisement," Lady Davenant said wickedly.

"Darling, everyone's strapped for cash. The harvest was bad or something; my husband explained it to me, but it doesn't really make sense. Why should a lack of grain mean I can't have a new carriage? It's not as though we sell the stuff!"

"But your tenants do. If they don't make money, how can you?" Lady Aurelia paled. Her friend patted her hand. "Don't worry, it's not as bad as all that. Ask him again."

"You explain it much better than he does." Aurelia pouted.

"Oh, not about the flour. About the carriage. Wear a low-cut bodice. They can't resist it."

"Can you?"

"Darling, it is all I can do not to ravish you before the chocolate is served. But I do require some sustenance. Biscuits and barley water just will not do. I wonder what Clara is waiting for? Afternoon chocolate is a serious affair."

Clara, Lady Galing, was seated in a carved chair of some magnificence, propped up with many cushions. Her skirts were quilted for more warmth, her head was wrapped in a turban of silk, pinned with an emerald ringed with diamonds, and around her shoulders were scarves in deep tones meant to make her color look less sickly and pallid. Lady Galing was indeed not well—in the less reputable gaming houses, bets were even being placed as to whether she would last out the year—but she took her position as wife to the Crescent Chancellor, head of the Council of Lords, very seriously and gloried in her chance to be an important hostess whose parties everyone wished to attend. If the *ladies* had been so vulgar as to bet on another's health, they would have bet that Lady Galing would drop dead presiding over one of her own musicales.

"My dear!" Lady Galing attempted to rise to greet the duchess. Her two manservants hurried to assist her, but before she could rise, Diane rushed to her hostess in a ripple of silk and took her hand.

"Lady Galing! How well you look! And how kind of you to provide us with delightful entertainment at this most dull season of the year."

The guests were standing around the room, talking, admiring the view from the tall windows onto the garden, flirting and chatting. It wasn't much of a view; the last of winter gripped the landscape, and much of the Galings' fine topiary was still wrapped up in burlap. But watery sunlight broke through the clouds from time to time, and here and there at the bases of statues peeped an impertinent crocus.

"It is the least I can do," Lady Galing said, twinkling, "when my husband keeps half your husbands locked up in the Council debating whatever urgent matter afflicts his mind today!"

"Indeed!" Diane laughed a musical laugh. "Without you, I don't know what we would do for amusement."

"Or for refreshment." Lord Asper Lindley was suddenly at her side.

Diane assessed him carefully. Lindley was one of those delicate blond men, a spun-sugar confection, whose appeal was obvious. But such men's beauty did not last. She thought he had very few years left before the delicacy began to sag.

"Ah! Asper!" Lady Galing turned to him with every appearance of delight. "I have been waiting chocolate on you. Now that you are here, we can begin."

Lindley raised his perfect eyebrows. "You will give me too great an opinion of myself, dear Clara. For the Duchess Tremontaine"—he bowed to Diane—"one waits chocolate. For me"—and he shrugged well-tailored shoulders—"well, all I can say, dear Clara, is that I am deeply honored."

It was a magnificent performance, thought the duchess, on both their parts. Poor Lady Galing! Asper and Lord Galing were having a spectacular affair—and the astute were aware that, throw as many parties as his lady pleased, the real way to the Crescent Chancellor's power and good opinion was through Asper Lindley now. Perhaps that was Lady Galing's strategy too?

Or perhaps she was one of those women who thought her dignity and status were best served, when faced with her husband's infidelities, by behaving as if they did not exist?

Lady Galing clapped her hands; the footmen bowed and hurried out to bring in the chocolate.

As Lady Davenant had said, chocolate was a serious affair. It was usually the first thing to pass anyone's lips as they lay in their great beds in the morning (or afternoon, if they were recovering from a particularly late-night ball or supper party or gambling or amorous adventure). Some people insisted on making it fresh themselves, but most were happy to be handed a pot of it by their maid or manservant, ready to pour into little china cups just the way they liked it.

But at an afternoon party, no noble would dream of drinking ready-made. Afternoon required the full regalia: the great pots of hot water, suspended over spirit flames. The chocolate itself, lifted with tongs and grated (with gloved hands) with silver graters made to look like fanciful creatures, into individual cups—or, at large parties, as in this case, smaller pots into which the hot water was poured, then whisked together with silver whisks until it foamed. Only then was the fragrant dark brew poured into the small cups and handed round to the guests, who each added sugar and cream to taste.

In the mornings, the Duchess Tremontaine took her chocolate black, but in the afternoon, she permitted herself a little sugar and a great deal of cream.

She watched to see how Asper Lindley took his and was rewarded with the sight of him being singularly honored by his hostess herself serving him with lump after lump of brown sugar.

"Thank you, Clara," he said. "I'll tell you when to stop."

She saw Clara Galing's hand shake as it returned to the silver sugar bowl again, saw her face, hidden for a moment from all but Diane, contort in rage and disgust.

The truth was plain. Lord Asper Lindley might as well have had a scroll above his head, written in Lord Galing's hand: *You will show him every courtesy.*

And Clara Galing obeyed to the letter. Out of love, out of fear, who knew? Lindley was a notorious gossip. Lady Galing's behavior concerning himself would be reported directly back to the Crescent Chancellor. Between the sheets, probably. Diane shuddered, ready to blame it on a chill from the window, if anyone asked.

"And how is dear William?" Lindley, with his sugary chocolate, had made his way to the duchess's side, not even bothering to offer to fetch her a cup. Fortunately, Lord Humphrey Devize had already claimed the privilege. He knew just how she liked it.

"My husband is well," the duchess said. "Although I think you see him as much as I do, being both so occupied in Council."

"Yes, we are quite grown-up now," said Lindley. "Grown-up and responsible." He gave her what was meant to be a charming smile. "We were boys together, or should I say young men, when our fathers first saw fit to bring us to the City and put a little town polish on us." He waited for her to say how much younger than that he looked. But she simply kept an expression of pleasant inquiry upon her face. "Would it be indiscreet of me to say that we discovered some of its more recondite pleasures . . . together?"

The duchess smiled. "No, as long as you don't enumerate them." Lindley's jibes were inexpressibly tedious. He was not a man of wit. It galled her to know that she could demolish him with a few well-chosen words, and that she must on no account do so. And it galled her to know that she must not only continue to endure his conversation as long as it pleased him to afflict her with it, but must pretend to enjoy the experience. Usually she found it restful, talking to idiots; it required so little of her actual attention. But Asper Lindley had a certain social cunning. He knew when he was being ignored; indeed, the duchess thought he needled largely to make sure that it never happened.

She looked Lindley in the eye, so that her peripheral gaze could scan the room for Humphrey with the chocolate, and said, "But, as you say, you are all grown-up and responsible now. And a credit to your houses. In truth, I am surprised to find you here this afternoon, Lord Asper. I know your great interest in politics."

"Ah," he said. People always said "ah" when they needed extra time to think. He was probably trying to figure out whether she'd insulted him or not. He must have decided not, since he went on. "Well, today the Council of Lords is set to discuss barley and shipping. My father's lands are mostly in cows and sheep, so I thought I might be spared for a little socializing. And besides, poor Clara . . . who knows how much longer we may have the pleasure of her company?"

Over his shoulder, Diane saw the rather large Lord Humphrey wheezing his way through the crowd, balancing her chocolate. It wouldn't be long now. But Lindley had time for a parting shot: "By the way, I love what you've made of that dress."

"Oh?" The duchess raised her delicately shaped eyebrows to give him time to wonder if she was going to take umbrage or not. "You don't think it's too much?"

Lord Humphrey caught the last of this. "Too much?" he blustered. "Never! Too much of you would still be not enough, sweetest lady!"

What an old dear he was. He flirted with her shamelessly. Diane turned her attention to him. "You've brought me chocolate! And just the way I like it too." She sipped delicately, and Asper Lindley took the hint. He bowed and went off to bother someone else.

Diane did not even look after him.

"And now, gentles!" Lady Galing coughed delicately into a handkerchief, drew a deep breath and announced: "Let us withdraw into the Blue Salon. Our dear Miss Sophronia Latimer has consented to soothe our cares and refresh our spirits with a little harp music."

Lord Humphrey had the pleasure of escorting Diane, Duchess

Tremontaine, into the Blue Salon. He was tremendously wealthy and had the Horned God's own luck with cards. She had been considering asking him for the cash to ransom Highcombe and put her back on her feet. He might do it just to be gallant. But men had hidden depths, even amiable men like Lord Humphrey. He was just as likely to expect her to sleep with him, and that she would not do. She had spent her life making sure she owed no one anything.

Diane de Tremontaine settled her green, foamy skirts around her in the small velvet salon chair and took her cup and saucer back from Lord Humphrey. The long harp recital would give her plenty of time to think. She took a sip of the thick, rich chocolate and considered the letter on her desk, waiting to be sent. It was either a good idea or merely a clever one. It was certainly a gamble. But the Duchess Tremontaine was very used to winning.

Episode Two

THE NORTH SIDE
OF THE SUN

Alaya Dawn Johnson

Ixkaab Balam, third of the name, first daughter of a first daughter of the greatest Trading family of the Kinwiinik, had been fully trained in the ways of the Locals, the Xanamwiinik. She had learned their language, their dances, their uncomfortable manner of dress.

She had learned these things over the course of years in the Balam family compound in Binkiinha, in between her more important studies of the five major Trading partners and her missions on behalf of her family. She had enjoyed their study, as the people across the sea to the north were profoundly different from those of the civilized world. But she had never expected to find herself actually stationed in this backwater, among the people with skin the color of ant eggs. What's more, even the elders of the family watched her with suspicion and exchanged rumors of the disaster that had chased her here.

It had been seven months since it had happened (she avoided thinking about the specifics as she would avoid passing too close to a sleeping jaguar), but she still hadn't accustomed herself to being in disgrace. She passed her nights embroidering ideas of how she could serve her family and regain their trust—but every morning, all such thoughts evaporated beneath the unblinking eye of reality, these people's weak and pallid sun.

Here, in the real world, there was to be a feast when the sun set tomorrow. Kaab had spent the last four hours stuffing dried maize husks and banana leaves with various preparations of maize dough and seasonings. It would not be a feast to dignify the family name without several thousand tamales. Her aunts and cousins and family servants had mostly kept their conversation among themselves. Or perhaps it was simply that Kaab, ignorant of the daily minutiae of their lives here, had no means of entering it. She wished that she had never gone on that mission to Tultenco. Or at least that soldiers of the Tullan hadn't been searching the coast for a woman of her description. Wishing so fervently for impossible things made her clumsy: She lost track of her hands and dropped wet, warm dough on her bare foot instead of on the banana leaf.

"Oh-ho," said one of the older women, a distant relation whose name Kaab hadn't quite managed to learn. "Tired, little bee? Or are you daydreaming? Found a boy you like here in just five days, already?"

The other women, including her aunt Ixsaabim, laughed and turned to Kaab, who went red-faced as she kicked the dollop of wasted dough to one of the hairless black dogs that lingered for scraps from the kitchen.

"Fast work, cousin!"

"From what I hear of our little bee, it's more likely a girl than a boy that has her tamales looking like crooked snakes."

Kaab looked down at the ones she had just finished. Her mother had trained her well: They looked even and plump, the same as the others. Perhaps she couldn't quite manage the seashell and bean decorations of the old women trained from birth for the kitchen, but she was hardly a daydreaming amateur!

Kaab raised her just-wrapped tamale, an indignant protest on her lips. But it died when she saw the friendly, laughing faces of the women around her. They were her family, even if she still couldn't tell her twin cousins apart or remember all of the elders' names. Aunt Ixsaabim reached across the great basket stacked with tamales ready for the steaming pots and rubbed Kaab's shoulder.

"Perhaps I have been a little distracted," Kaab said contritely. And then, with a flare of inspiration, she quoted, in Tullan-daan:

> "The woman I desire is a maize flower
> The morning after rain.
> Oh giver of life! Giver of rain!"

The elder aunt Ixnoom nodded in appreciation. "The great Tullan masters are good to know, child. Your mother—may she never be extinguished, may she never disappear—taught you well. I was married into the Nopalco court, you know. When my husband died, I returned home. Long ago. But I do remember the poetry."

The other women nodded, the older ones sadly. There had been a war with Nopalco just at the turn of the last century; they had rebelled against the demands of Tullan Empire tribute, and the poems said the river Amaxac had run red with their blood for thirteen years. Judging by her age, Aunt Ixnoom must have escaped that great massacre. She must have endured hardships that made Kaab shiver to imagine. And yet she had survived to be an elder, far away from home, but still with family. Perhaps by enduring, Kaab could redeem herself from the disaster that had made her father insist she leave home, without even a promise of return. Perhaps, even in this backwater, strategically important to family affairs but woefully lacking in any kind of refinement, she could find the means to honor her mother's spirit. Was she not the daughter of Ixmoe, legendary in her own time for her exploits among the peoples of the southern seas? Was she not dedicated from birth to the sacred art of trade—which was to say, the sacred art of intelligence gathering—and exploiting it for profit?

One of the young boys poked his head inside the doorway to the kitchen.

"Auntie Saabim," he said, "Uncle Chuleb asks to consult you about the Local dishes for the feast."

Saabim sighed and rolled her eyes. "Tell my dearest morning star that I will attend to his entirely unnecessary concern momentarily."

One of the younger women, a cousin by marriage, clucked loudly. "What husband tries to oversee his wife's kitchen?"

Aunt Ixnoom smiled. "He'll learn. You're still new in this marriage, Niece."

"Well, you're pregnant again, Saabim, so now is the time to tell your young husband to keep to his domain!"

At this, Kaab looked up sharply at her aunt. Saabim was pregnant? She was old to be having her first child with her second husband, but the embroidered blouse was loose enough to hide at least the first three months. Still, Kaab was disgusted with herself for not noticing. She had tried so hard not to let her observational skills unravel during her months on that tedious ship!

Saabim laughed and said, "You are all very kind to be concerned for me. But I'll have him in hand, don't you worry." She stood, stretched her back, and then stepped nimbly past the baskets and clucking women and cooking pots and scurrying maids to reach the exit. Kaab excused herself a moment later, making as if to use the privy (located inside the houses here, in what she considered a dubious use of technology). But instead of turning north down the hallway, she stepped lightly south, into the courtyard, taking care to keep herself in the shadow of a tall, box-cut shrub. The afternoon sunlight shocked her—she had been up and stumbling to the kitchen at the very first light of the morning star, and a bundle of hours had passed without her noting them.

"Husband," said Aunt Saabim, "I hope you have better matters to detain me with than my management of the kitchen?"

She wrapped her arms around Uncle Chuleb's neck and nibbled his bottom lip. Kaab suddenly and fiercely regretted her impulse to test her rusted skills on her own family. A woman as experienced as she should not forget what went on in marriage—but the fact was she often forgot to think of men that way. Unfortunately, the angle of the sun meant that her shadow would be immediately noticeable if she tried to return the way she had come. The sounds from the courtyard—oh how she wished she had stayed with the gossiping aunts in the steam-filled kitchen!—changed to cooing endearments, then wet smacking, and then, appallingly, soft grunting.

Kaab dared a glance past the shrub. Uncle Chuleb had one hand under Aunt Saabim's blouse and the other down the back of her skirt. For a horrible moment, Kaab imagined doing the same to that beauty from Riverside, Tess. She had to find a prudent exit. Perhaps her father was not entirely wrong when he accused her of being overconfident.

A good Trader, he had always said, *knows when to hide as well as when to fight.*

Recent events had taught her *that* lesson, at least. But she couldn't stand to hide here for another second. Why, they'd scare the dogs in a minute!

"Auntie!" she called, shuffling her feet pointedly on the flagstones and then emerging into the bright sunlight. Her aunt and uncle had managed to extricate themselves from each other, though Saabim's blouse fell half outside her wide, multicolored belt.

"Why—Kaab—what is it?"

Kaab smiled brilliantly. Uncle Chuleb regarded her as if he had just bit into a very young lime. Uncle Chuleb was not easily charmed.

"Aunt Ixnoom thought you were delayed in coming back. She asked me to ask you . . . why, what instructions dear Uncle has as to the preparations of Xanamwiinik food. Do we have all of their barbaric ingredients?"

Saabim looked somewhat bemused as she turned to her husband. "Dear?"

He cleared his throat. "Well. Let me see. We had nearly decided against serving that ridiculous gilded stuffed hare. To be honest, I thought it was a joke: To these Xanamwiinik, a hare is humble fare, fit only for a woodsman's pot. But apparently, if you stuff it with quince and walnut, and braise it with saffron, it becomes a dish fit for the Duchess Tremontaine's table. She served it at her last soiree, my Land agent tells me. The saffron turned the braised skin orange as a sunset." He turned to Kaab. "His words, Niece. I confess to being more interested in importing our own spices than trying a new one that costs nearly more than its weight in gold dust. But where the Duchess Tremontaine leads, the town follows, it seems. Those who can afford to. The omission on our part will be noted. And in any case, that lady has been . . ." He trailed off in a way that Kaab found distinctly curious and gave his wife a speaking glance. "Well. However events play out, it will do us no harm for the success of our feast to reach her ears."

Saabim gave Kaab a funny, knowing smile and kissed her husband on the cheek. "Then the expense must be borne, of course, my little thrush."

Chuleb reciprocated with nicknames that threatened to send the dogs scurrying for cover again, so Kaab intervened quickly. "Do we have the saffron? Would you like me to get it?"

He waved an impatient hand. "Oh, for the sake of the Nine Heavens, child, if it interests you so much! Try the Fenton compound first. They're in the spice trade and should have some on hand. We'll need—well, enough to braise forty hares. You might as well get the hares, too. I leave it in your care, Niece. I trust you will do the family honor."

This last was a formal phrase, meant to mark a charge given from an elder to an active family Trader. It had been seven months since someone had last said these words to Kaab, and her eyes pricked unexpectedly to hear them again, so far from home.

She touched her heart with her hand and bent her head. "As Ekchuah dives and Xamanek lights the way, this unworthy servant will give her precious water, her blood, that our honor may grow its roots into the earth."

Her reply was the ceremonial one, not generally given for common tasks. Her uncle blinked in surprise and then bowed his head briefly in reply. Aunt Saabim, who looked very much like Kaab's mother in this strong light, bowed her head as well.

"I'll be back soon!" Kaab said, before the tears that clogged the back of her throat came up any farther. "Can I use the good Caana chocolate for the trade?"

Chuleb sighed. "If you promise to be prudent. It's in the brown chest in—"

But Kaab was already heading to his offices, her bare feet sliding along the tiles of the peristyle. "I know," she called over her shoulder.

"Remember to wear Local clothes!" her aunt called after her. "And some shoes!"

Kaab allowed the maid to help her into the simplest bodice and skirts that her aunt had left in her closet. She nearly ignored Aunt Saabim's dictate about the shoes, but the maid reminded her about the appalling state of the streets in springtime (shit and mud were the least of it, apparently) and she reluctantly consented to the boots. Adopting Local customs was the Trader way, but her feet felt decidedly shackled in all but the simplest rubber-and-hide sandals. At home, women rarely went shod. But of course, at home the streets were swept meticulously clean every morning and night by phalanxes of war-captive slaves, and no one would dream of pissing in public. While living among the barbarians, Kaab reasoned, one had to make accommodations.

Once out on the street—a bag full of good chocolate on her arm and a modest amount of Local coin for any unforeseen circumstance—Kaab turned west and walked for several streets beneath tall, bare trees that had just begun to put out closed green buds. Kaab recalled the redolent purple jacarandas and the sunset spray of brush-tree flowers and felt her heart crack that much further. The walls were high in the merchants' neighborhood, and traffic minimal. Men and women whose clothing and demeanor marked them as servants brushed past her with hardly a glance sideways. Interesting. In Riverside and the neighborhoods in between she had been a curiosity as a foreigner. But clearly the merchants had long since grown accustomed to the presence of the Traders. And tomorrow evening, many of the most prominent Local merchant families would be arriving at the Balam compound to feast on a hundred delicacies that she and the other women had spent the last three days preparing. Fetching saffron might seem like a trivial task, but Kaab was prideful, not ignorant. A brilliant feast had the ability to help a family rise very far—just as an inferior one could bring down the curse of the gods, under whose purview such things rested.

Her uncle's directions to the Fenton compound had been mercifully clear—Kaab spoke two other languages which relied on the nonsensical left and right, but she had never been forced to live in the lands where they were common. She arrived a quarter hour after she had set out. The walls were an even-mortared limestone, solid, imposing, and unpainted. They rose three times her height, and above them tall spikes of greening iron deterred acrobatic thieves. The trees had been removed for ten yards on either side of the enormous, iron-braced doors. A cord hung on the west side, and, seeing no other option for gaining entry (aside from methods of which her uncle would surely not approve), she pulled it.

A small window in the door slid back, and an older man's face appeared. She explained that she was here on business of the Balam family. The man seemed dubious, but after a moment she heard several bolts sliding open. A small door eased back on deep hinges, and a large, rough hand emerged from the shadows as though from the underworld to help her through. She had to duck and step quite high—the weight and length of the unfamiliar skirts nearly sent her sprawling.

She emerged blinking and stumbling into an open courtyard

dominated by an unadorned building that she assumed was a storehouse and a stately, ornamented house of new construction.

"You can await Master Fenton's man of business inside the house, mistress," said the guard. He motioned for her to follow the path through the open garden. She hesitated, wondering if she should surrender her obsidian dagger, heavy and reassuring in her petticoat pocket, as a gesture of goodwill. But the guard had turned back to a game of cards with his companion and seemed entirely uninterested in her. The Xanamwiinik were worse than the Tullan, Kaab thought with hard amusement as she climbed the marble steps. They did not imagine women capable of killing a turkey, let alone a guard.

She repeated her request to the maid who answered the front door and was led to a small antechamber decorated with dark woods and tanned leathers and art from the remotest parts of the traded world. She spotted a cotton mantle embroidered and printed in the Bakhim style beside a small headdress of quetzal feathers, a kind only certain decorated warriors were allowed to wear at home. She wondered if her uncle Chuleb had traded these to Master Fenton, and if so, if he had explained their true use and origins. Kaab felt distinctly odd, standing here in her meticulous Local clothes, as if she herself could have been displayed on the walls if she hadn't bothered to change before she arrived.

She tensed at a sudden clamor of voices in the hallway outside, rapidly approaching.

"By god, he *will* see me now! If he had the nerve to summon me like some common accounting boy, he damned well can't expect me to wait when I get here."

"Master Rafe, I believe your father's letter instructed you to arrive in the morning—"

"Well, that bit of high-handed authoritarianism would have been impossible for me to comply with, even if I were the dutiful sheep of a son he wishes me to be!"

The owner of that deep voice—attempting to be imperious, but a little too piqued to manage—burst into the antechamber at that moment, swept his gaze across, noted the closed doors to what Kaab had presumed were the offices of Master Fenton and his man of business, and uttered several words that Kaab did not understand. She assumed they were not fit for polite company, judging by the deep blush of the trailing maid and pained wince of an older man with a pen in his hand.

"Master Rafe, there are ladies present."

The young man—Rafe—gave Kaab a cursory bow. "Apologies, madam. I did not see you standing there. Are you—goodness, you're one of the Balams!"

He seemed so disconcerted that she had to smile. "I just arrived," she replied. "I think that is why we never had the pleasure of meeting."

She put particular emphasis on *pleasure* and was rewarded with a flashing grimace.

"Madam," he said, and removed his hat and bowed. "My argument is with my father, not with you. And as my father isn't here to listen, I'm afraid I have been rude to no purpose."

"But you would be rude *to* a purpose?" she asked.

He blinked. "Well . . . of course. Even my enemies would grant me that."

"Then I say we have that in common, Rafe Fenton. I am Ixkaab Balam, and I'm here to trade for . . . two ounces of saffron from your family. At least, that's what I estimate. Any help you could give me on the matter of dressing forty hares I will appreciate."

"What the devil would I know of dressing hares? I'm a philosopher, madam. An acolyte to the ancient pursuit of higher knowledge. We don't generally concern ourselves with mundane affairs of the common man." He turned to one of the closed doors—presumably his father's—and hurled: "Particularly those related to trading and spices and *feasts!*"

Kaab muttered some choice words in her own language and turned to the trembling chain of servants who had followed the Fenton scion into the room.

"Would you please tell his man of business about the saffron?" she asked in their general direction.

"He'll be back soon, miss," said the maid who had opened the door. "But I expect you'll be needing at least four and a half or five ounces, for that many hares. If you'd like to do them in the Tremontaine style."

Kaab bestowed the maid with her most brilliant smile. "That is perfect. I thank you very much for your helpful information. Now I will sit here and await the man of business."

She selected the nearest leather chair and sat upon it. A very tiny embalmed head rested on a raised display cushion to her right. She did her best to ignore it.

Rafe sighed like a north wind, turned to her in a slouch, and regarded her under lowered lids.

"I expect this all-important feast is your fault."

"You expect correctly."

"You're the long-lost daughter."

"I've never been lost in my life!"

"It's a colloquial expression. And really, never?"

Kaab allowed herself a direct look. "I am a first daughter of a first daughter of the Balam. I have been trained from birth to the service. I do not get lost." *For very long,* she amended internally, for honesty's sake. Confusing left and north didn't count. Nor did a few dizzy, ill-fated nights in the company of the brilliant Citlali.

"Lucky you," he said.

Kaab hadn't felt lucky for seven months, but she couldn't very well contradict him. And perhaps he was right—she was alive, which was more than she could say for the relatives who had accompanied her on the mission.

"Why do you say so?"

He gave the shut door another moody glance and then cracked a bitter, self-deprecating smile. "Because you wish to do that which you have been born into. I am the first son of a trading family, and I wish to dedicate my life to science. My family is . . . merely tolerant. As if the movements of the very stars in the heavens are a delirium, a fever that will pass if they spoil me enough."

"I'm sure they have spoiled you sufficiently," she said dryly.

Rafe didn't catch the sarcasm. "They don't bother to understand a damned thing about my world! Take today. Father summons me home to attend your blasted feast—no offense intended—and this week of all weeks is when we must protest the Board of Governors before they vote to ruin the very institutions of higher learning! There are rumors that they'll meet at least once this week, and if I'm not on hand for the protests, I will never forgive myself."

Kaab knew that she should ask him about these protests and learn more of the local political situation, but the unquestioning arrogance of his manner made her itch to bait him, just a little.

"You're very important, then?"

Now Rafe noticed. "I'm—" He frowned at her. "Aren't you the little princess."

Kaab widened her eyes. "Do princesses here carry two pounds

of Caana chocolate to make trades with the spoiled sons of spice merchants?"

Rafe's bottom lip trembled even as the rest of his face struggled with outrage. His lip got the better of him and he let out a sweet, rueful chuckle. "Well, you're interesting, at least. What was that you said about two pounds of chocolate?"

Kaab lifted her bag to her lap and loosened the drawstring enough for the rich, bitter aroma of processed cocoa to drift in his direction. He swallowed.

"Five ounces of saffron, you said?"

She nodded. "And the hares."

"We're spice merchants, not butchers!"

"I'm sure you can manage it. Are you not a merchant's son?"

He looked at her sourly. "A scholar. As I said."

"I can," she said delicately, "of course, wait for his man of business. . . ."

He looked again at the bag, with its very valuable chocolate. Even more valuable, she gathered, to a scholar looking for status and leverage over his colleagues than to an established merchant who regularly bought from her family.

Rafe Fenton nodded with sudden determination. "I'll help you. This business might be significantly beneath me, but"—he cocked his head and gave her a little grin—"I can certainly get you forty goddamned hares. Do we have a deal?"

Kaab automatically put her hand over her heart. He did the same, and they exchanged bows. Only when she met his eyes again did she remember that these people clasped hands to make agreements. He tilted his head in that way he had, as if to say *don't underestimate me*. She laughed.

"I could come to like you, Rafe Fenton. I don't like everyone."

"Well neither do I, Princess Balam. Indeed, I'd lay good odds that I'm even more accomplished in the art of making enemies than you are."

Kaab quite believed him.

Visits home generally never netted Rafe more than a throat raw from arguing (*not* yelling, as his father loved to put it in that infuriatingly soft way of his) and a strong desire for strong wine, a strong man, and a bed sturdy enough to enjoy them. Depending on how impossible the visit, he had been known to forgo the latter in favor of whatever hard surface lay handy and tolerate Joshua—his best friend and long-suffering roommate—pulling the splinters from his chest the following morning. After receiving his father's summons to the bosom of the Fenton merchant empire, he'd spent the morning in the pub with Joshua, alternating complaints about the Board of Governors' proposed bylaw change with even more vociferous condemnations of the petty concerns of the so-aptly-termed petty merchant class.

"Thank the gods they won't actually vote until next month. Imagine, letting the university *doctors* dictate which students' committees they'll sit on! Choosing one's own committee has been the sacred right of examining students for . . . centuries, surely! How are we supposed to progress? Have new ideas? Break the goddamned status quo? I ask you! But still, I'm sure to get my slot in the next two weeks. They came too late to touch me."

Joshua, having heard this many times before, had patted his knee and looked decidedly bored. Micah had been playing cards for minnows and paid him no attention whatsoever. The boy did, however, look up when Rafe gathered his belongings to leave. Micah had handed him a letter, rather ingeniously folded and addressed to Cousin Reuben The Second Stall Past The Chicken Seller Fanoo The One With The Purple Cock.

Rafe had nearly choked on his beer. Micah took this to mean that perhaps she should come with him to the market, and Rafe had wasted five minutes assuring the boy (and walking gold mine) that it wouldn't be at all necessary.

But to his surprise, his visit home had yielded an unexpected opportunity: the new Balam girl, striding forcefully beside him in the inevitable ankle-deep muck of early spring. And as an added bonus, her presence had momentarily postponed the inevitable paternal confrontation. He had raided what stores of saffron he knew of in the house, which weren't quite enough to satisfy the order. So they were now headed to the market, where both hares and the rest of the saffron could be procured, and he could also deliver Micah's letter safely into the hands of the Cousin Who Must Not Take Him Away.

In the meantime, he had many reasons to be intrigued by the Balam girl's conversation. Provided that he could channel it to the proper theme. He had long suspected the Kinwiinik of having a much more enlightened grasp on celestial mechanics than those doddering Rastinites who liked to fancy themselves natural philosophers at the University. But the trouble with believing something truly radical—for instance, that the earth revolves around the sun—was that one needed to gather evidence. And where better to look than with those who regularly use the stars to guide them unimaginable distances across the sea?

"I expect that you arrived on the boat that put in just last week. The long-awaited chocolate shipment?"

"Oh," said the girl, with a sharp little smile, "I wasn't told what it was carrying. But if it's from home, it surely carried cacao. And other food, for the feast."

"Those peppers that could curl the hair of a sheepdog?"

"Many," she said. "The sun here isn't very strong, is it? You people, with your ant-egg skin, don't grow with much head-spirit."

Rafe had not the slightest idea what ant eggs looked like, nor what that had to do with his skin (or his head-spirit!), but he could tell from her eyes that she was challenging him. He straightened. "The consumption of peppers hot enough to constitute a form of torture is hardly an indication of strength!"

She looked at him steadily. "You would say so."

Rafe bit his lip on a nasty retort and took a deep, calming breath. He had a point here, and he would not let himself be diverted. He could subdue even his notorious temper in the pursuit of the sacrament of knowledge (as Nereau so eloquently put it).

"So what made you come here?" he asked with all the forced placidity of a tight curl beneath a hot iron.

"Saffron," she said.

Rafe grit his teeth. "I mean, what made you leave your home? Why travel here? Is your family looking for a husband for you?"

A vague shot, which landed very satisfyingly home. She stopped in the middle of the street and rounded on him. "I am dedicated to the service," she snarled, "and I may *never* marry if I do not choose. And I do not choose."

"Ah," said Rafe.

"What is that?" She resumed walking.

"What is what?"

"What you are thinking."

Rafe took his time to consider this. He smoothed down his ink-stained cuffs. "I think," he said, "that a Balam dedicated to the service would know the contents of the hold in the ship that had carried her from home."

She scowled at him, but the quivering right corner of her mouth ruined the effect. "I grant," she said, "that I might have been curious."

"And it did carry cacao?"

"Aren't you a merchant's son? You know well it did. Several very good varieties, including the most excellent Caana I have given your family in exchange for this saffron. Perhaps your father will be interested in discussing a larger purchase."

Rafe hadn't thought to leave his father any. But he supposed that the continued prosperity of the Fenton empire was in his most general interests. He could spare a few ounces. "How long was the journey?" he asked casually.

"Oh, three months, the way your people calculate them."

"So many! Is that normal?"

"If we sail straight through the North Sea. Sometimes the boats spend much time on the coast, and then on the islands of stone-cutters and basket makers."

"Is that part of your service, then? Sailing those great boats?" He took care not to appear too wide-eyed, merely curious. "Watch your step." He took her arm to keep her from slipping into a hole in the road. From the smell of it, the bums playing jacks nearby had used it for a latrine.

She shook him off gently. "Some are specialized for that service," she said. "And others . . . for other things."

"You have some of these other skills, I take it? I won't dare ask you what they are."

"Clever of you."

Rafe had to strangle a grin. "And those great journeys," he said as the market came into view. "You are guided by . . . maps? Charts? It must have taken your people many, many generations to find the way."

"Not so many," she said absently. "We follow the way of the Four Hundred Sibling Gods, who are the stars in the sky. The priests interpret their signs and give us the routes."

"And how long have your people known the earth is shaped as a sphere?"

She frowned. "It is—is it?"

"That's what we believe now. But moving across it is—"

She bared her teeth. "A complete mystery to me."

Oh damn. Perhaps he hadn't sounded as casually uninterested as he had thought.

"I just meant—"

"So where do we find the hares? Or should we look for saffron first?"

Their glance felt like a brief clash of blades—one which he summarily lost. He had always suspected that to navigate those great distances the Kinwiinik must have some knowledge of mathematics and natural philosophy which those at the University lacked. Given the proposed bylaw change, he had to sit his Master's exams within the month if he didn't want to find himself at the mercy of a handful of hidebound doctors who despised him (for entirely trivial reasons). If he could do so with some actual mathematics for his theories about the sun and the stars and the earth's place in the universe—if these could be bolstered by the truth of why navigators from the Land either foundered on unexpected shores or drowned in their attempts to traverse the large ocean distances that the Traders from the chocolate lands did as a matter of routine—

Well, even old hidebound curmudgeons like de Bertel couldn't fail to acknowledge the justice of his evidentiary methods.

But first he had to gain the Balam girl's confidence. So he elbowed his way through the milling crowd of bourgeois dowagers and scullery maids and potboys sniffing and cawing and bargaining for the winter's last root vegetables and the spring's first asparagus and peas. He had been going to this market since he was younger than those potboys, and while his merchant background was often a source of shame to him in the University, he could not help but hear the energetic clatter of a market day as a hum that warmed his veins and told him that here, too, was a home.

It is no longer, he told himself viciously. He could exploit his experience and contacts without quibbling over the implications. Knowing the fair price of sea bass on a spring morning after a storm did not make him a closeted merchant. It made him a young intellectual with *layers.* He sighed; he could practically see Joshua rolling his eyes.

The hares were duly selected and sent along to the Balam compound with the saffron via a boy. That only left the letter in his pocket.

"If you wouldn't mind," he told the Balam girl, "I have one last errand to attend to before we head back."

She inclined her head. Quite regally. *Damned princess,* he thought, more savagely than necessary. He was nervous about meeting Micah's cousin.

Cousin Reuben was unmistakable (and Micah's directions precise—Rafe did indeed note the purple cockerel). He had the family nose (flat) and the family jawline (square) and the family hair, precisely the shade of wheat before a harvest. He wore muddy breeches, fingerless gloves, and a well-kept leather hat with a large white feather that practically gleamed above the late-season rutabagas.

"What can I get for you today, son?"

Rafe scowled, realized this might not put the cousin entirely at ease, and forced a smile. "I have a letter," he said. "From your cousin Micah."

Cousin Reuben frowned. "I'll be damned. Another one? With another excuse, I'll bet. Well, let's have it."

He took the letter, looked over the folds, and took his time unpacking it. He read with his finger beneath the evenly spaced lines, pronouncing the words in a low voice.

"'Cousin Reuben this is Micah I have found many friends here especially Rafe Fenton who is showing me many things especially math. You remember how I like math'—Oh, don't I!—'and it turns out that here there is plenty of it so I think I'll stay another week. I'm very sorry for neglecting the garden I know it is time for asparagus because I had some soup last night and also because the rains have come. I promise I'll come back next week as soon as I solve these ek—eek—' What the hell word is this?"

"Equations, sir," Rafe said.

"'. . . as soon as I solve these equations they're very interesting. I'll tell you all about them next week. Love, Micah.'"

He peered over the letter. Rafe tried not to fidget. "You're the one who's taken our Micah, then?"

"Now hold on—I haven't *taken* him . . . he's a genius! He deserves to have his intellect planted in fertile soil! Not left out to rot in the country!"

Cousin Reuben looked a little worried. "Is he, now? Does he? And what if *he* isn't all you University types hope?"

"He absolutely is, sir." Rafe was very sincere. The Balam girl gave him a searching look.

Cousin Reuben sighed. "The kid does sound happy. *Math*." He shook his head. "I trust you to take care of our Micah, son. Fenton, eh? I've met your father."

Rafe couldn't tell if this was a threat or a statement of confidence, but he felt a momentary urge to take a potshot at the gleaming feather with one of the sandy turnips. Instead he made vaguely reassuring sounds and hurried away.

"What was that about?" the girl asked. She easily kept pace with his large strides; in fact, she seemed to glide beside him. His scowl deepened.

"I have his cousin in my rooms. A boy wonder. A mathematical genius. The key to all of my financial and academic worries! I just need to *keep* him."

"The cousin of the root-vegetable vendor?"

"I could hardly believe it myself."

"And why is he a key? Academically?"

Rafe turned to her. "Because he can put into practice my evidentiary theories! Our best theories demonstrate that the earth is round. But how does it move in the heavens? Rastin tells us that it doesn't move at all, merely anchors hooping planetary motions. But *that makes no sense*, and no one has the balls to say so. There are equations that no one has been able to solve—some don't even think they're worth solving! But this boy . . . Micah . . ."

"You think he can solve them?"

Had he said too much? But the girl only seemed mildly interested. He wanted to know how the Kinwiinik managed to travel such great distances without the help of any landmarks, but he had no idea if his equations (if *Micah's* equations) were related to their navigational techniques. And she was probably telling the truth about her unfamiliarity with that side of her family business. Who had ever heard of a woman mathematician?

"I do," Rafe said, after a moment. "I'm betting my career on it."

The girl considered this. "Do you know . . . I have been curious about your fine University ever since I arrived. Could you show me? And can I meet this remarkable boy?"

Rafe felt his smile spread like morning sunshine. "I would be delighted, my dear . . . er . . . what's your name again?"

"Kaab," said the Balam princess. "You may call me Kaab."

Micah sat at the same table in the Blackbird's Nest as she had the first time that Rafe brought her—in back, near the kitchens. It was a good table: away from the crowd by the bar and the rowdier gamblers. During an early afternoon on a market day, the low-roofed, tallow-lit room was full, but Micah could still think around the beer smells and kitchen noises and gamblers' patter. All she had to do was keep her eyes on the worn cards in her hand and the fascinating pattern of the ancient wood grain beneath them.

"Call," said the long-haired student sitting across from her. He tossed the last of his minnows casually on the pile at the center of the table. Micah calculated that the pot now held enough for two and a half tomato pies and two ginger beers. Or two tomato pies and three ginger beers. Micah frowned, trying to decide which she would prefer, and decided that it would depend on how hungry Rafe was. She had come here on her own today because all the money was gone from the chest in their rooms and she had wanted something more than a roasted potato. And now she could buy tomato pies for herself and Rafe, to thank him for the place to sleep. And the equations. The equations were very nice.

Micah didn't have a good hand—just a pair of Suns—but the long-haired student couldn't have any card higher than a Beast, and the older man in a dockworker's clothes had held a three-of-a-kind that would have beat either of their hands, but he had folded for reasons that still escaped Micah, though she had learned to accept them, like the weather.

"All right," Micah said, and held his gaze. Joshua had told her that this unnerved the other players, and so she had learned to do it for a few seconds at a time. She didn't much like it either, but they almost always looked away first.

The other players put down their cards. The student scowled at his hand while Micah busily arranged her winnings in stacks ordered by the size and value of the coins.

"Another hand," said the student, with a funny sort of lift in his voice. Micah decided that she should ask Joshua what it meant when their voices got tight like that, and their eyebrows started wandering up their foreheads like caterpillars. Joshua was better at that sort of thing than Rafe. Rafe was better at talking.

She was trying to decide if it was worth waiting out her next good hand when a crowd of students pushed in through the narrow front door.

"They're meeting now, the bastards!"

"Who's meeting, Dickson?"

"The governors! Word is they could even take the vote!"

Micah, putting the last five-minnow in its stack, had been trying to ignore the noisy intruders. But then the student with the wandering eyebrows stood abruptly and smacked his fist on the table, toppling her careful piles. The shouting grew very loud. In a sudden panic, Micah shoved the coins into the inside pocket of her jerkin. Losing the coins would be worse than jumbling them up, and she could put them in good order later. She was still very hungry. She should certainly leave. But when she looked up, all she saw was a smear, noise and high emotion blurring the angry faces before her into a mob.

Take a deep breath. That was what her grandfather had always told her to do when she was little and overwhelmed by the noises of the City on market day. She tried, but someone knocked into her and someone else held her up by her elbow so that she didn't fall and then the chanting grew louder, like a chisel between her ears. Her eyes watered. She didn't even have time to wipe them—the crowd swept her up like a saint on a feast day, and she was carried away.

"Freedom of the intellect!" was the chant, but they might as well have been speaking the language of the chocolate traders for all Micah understood them. She closed her eyes. An image of Cousin Reuben in his favorite feathered cap appeared behind her lids.

What have you done now, kid? said the cousin Reuben of her conscience.

Micah had been very excited about the cards and money and equations. But stumbling in the midst of a press of marching students, she began to think she would have been much better off keeping to her turnips.

Rafe's luck held: He and Kaab got there just as the students were flooding the University streets, tumbling from the pubs and classes and chocolate houses in all directions. They all gathered in front of the Great Hall, where the board had hoped to keep their meeting secret, and at the earliest possible opportunity Rafe climbed the base of the bronze statue of old Rastin and began a modest, stirring oratory he had composed while pushing through the crowd ahead of Kaab, who looked up at him now with amusement.

"If we let this gaggle of barely educated nobles dictate, for political ends, the course of our intellectual pursuits," called Rafe, aware that his black curls had fallen out of the leather tie, lending him a pleasingly raffish air in the current circumstances, "we might as well return to thinking that the stars have been painted on the cloth of the sky. We might as well tear down the lecture halls and burn the books. Because they will come for those next, if we say something that does not agree with the political aspirations of those lordlings on the Hill."

This got a satisfying cheer and another chant. He was just thinking of whether he should follow with a rather fine poem of Joshua's composition or something more traditional, when he heard his name called in a strangled voice, followed immediately by the somewhat sticky embrace at his knees of a young lad with a bowl cut and the family chin.

Rafe slid down the pedestal and only remained upright by dint of Micah's surprising strength.

"I didn't think I'd ever see you again!" said the boy.

"Goodness, no need to get apocalyptic. . . . Did you fall asleep in a beer keg? You smell like a bad amber wheat five days flat."

Micah sniffed. "I fell."

Some smart aleck from the crowd shouted, "Who's the sweetheart, Rafe?" and at least five others laughed. He glowered, but Kaab distracted him from identifying the culprits.

"Is this Micah?" she asked, peering at them both with that curious intensity of hers.

"Yes," he said shortly. "Talk amongst yourselves. I want to see the faces of those cowards when they walk out and have to face us."

The crowd that had gathered to hear him speak was now drifting toward the closed doors of the hall. The rumor was that the governors could even vote today, but after a few panicked moments Rafe had decided to discount it. The Board of Governors was, above all, a conservative body. The vote had been set for next month. Even student unrest was unlikely to make them move it up. Rafe did not want them to pass the bylaw change at all, of course, but provided that they did so safely after he sat his Master's exams, the outrage would give plenty of opportunity to intelligent men dedicated to the new modes of investigation. Once he had been accepted as a doctor, he would be able to open a school that would revolutionize the way a generation of scholars would think about natural philosophy. When he died, they might erect a statue of *him* beside natty old Rastin here in the Great Court. Not that he had mentioned that last ambition to anyone, even Joshua.

Despite the general air of expectation in the square, the doors remained stubbornly closed and barred. A few daring students attempted to rush them, but they had been built to withstand the dangers of a more volatile age. The aged oak and thumb-thick iron hasps would take more than a few students drunk on outrage to force open.

The meeting had been going on for hours, according to the latest rumors. They should have finished by now. Was the board *actually* voting? Rafe felt jittery, his throat full of bile or fire, his skin vibrating with the desire to *do* something, not just wait here like sheep in a defile. Was there another way out of the hall? Could those cowards be attempting an escape through the delivery entrance? Rafe elbowed his way back toward old Rastin, simultaneously pleased and worried that the crowd had grown so thick so quickly. Some kind of band blocked the most direct path to where he had left Micah and Kaab. The sound of pipe and tambour had never so offended him—what was this, a festival or a protest? If they didn't take themselves seriously, how could they expect the board to?

He was composing a few choice paragraphs on the subject when he reached the southern edge of the square. Here the crowd had thinned enough to finally let him beat his way back to Rastin's shit-stained shoulders. He shuddered to think of what he would tell Cousin Reuben if he managed to lose the boy. Micah did not do well in crowds. But, Rafe reasoned, he was with Kaab, who—for all that she was a woman and a foreigner new to the City—seemed like the sort who could keep her head at anything short of a chopping block.

A towheaded man, half a hand taller than most of those around him, composed as though by an artist of lean and elegant lines, rested against the retaining wall and looked nervously at the students still pouring in through the side streets and alleyways. Their eyes met and locked. The jittery feeling that had propelled Rafe away from his vigil by the entrance returned. Only now, that vague static seemed to align and gather force and move his feet and tongue as though of their own accord, so that he heard himself saying: "You look lost. Are you?"

The towheaded man looked down at him and shook his head with a twisted half smile that revealed a deep dimple in his left cheek.

"Am I so out of place, then?"

A voice as graceful as his carriage. Rafe did not like aristocratic men. He did not like men who towered over him. If they had to be fair, he preferred a bit of dirt to darken the blond. Rafe felt somewhat breathless.

"Oh, not at all," Rafe drawled. "You blend in like a vulture among crows. What are you looking for?"

The man raised his eyebrows. His eyes were blue as the poet's cornflowers. They crinkled in the corners, as though they were used to smiling. "I was hoping to hire a chair. I don't suppose it's possible in this mess."

"You'd have to walk the few turns to Chambers Street. Hire a chair, you say?" A terrible suspicion clawed its way through Rafe's consciousness. "Why, you're not here by chance at all! Are you one of their lackeys, attempting to help those dogs escape without facing the victims of their actions?"

The man *did* smile at this, with infuriating kindness. "You make it sound very dramatic. I was given to understand they were just reviewing a proposed change to the bylaws. Mundane stuff."

"The free pursuit of knowledge could never be mundane, and only someone whose livelihood depends on those spoiled wretches on the Hill could say such a thing!"

The lackey blinked. "Spoiled wretches on the Hill, you say?"

"What do they know of the intellectual life? Of dedication to knowledge? Why, hardly any of them even so much as take classes here."

"That doesn't preclude their having some knowledge of your activities, does it? They could read monographs and attend lectures. They could carry on correspondence. They could even, in a modest way, of course, contribute their own findings! Knowledge, surely, does not limit itself to one's physical presence in the pubs and chocolate houses on Chambers Street." He paused artfully, looked down, and seemed to notice for the first time a—quite small!—stain on Rafe's cravat. He rubbed it between thumb and forefinger. "Though no doubt you claim an extensive familiarity with *those* institutions of higher learning. At the very least."

Rafe felt dizzy. The lackey smelled of a light perfume: apricots and some darker spice—cloves or myrrh. His fingers were long and blunt at the ends, the nails meticulously clipped but not manicured. Blue ink lingered in the soft folds beneath the second and third joint of his index finger.

Rafe took a step forward. They stood only a hand apart now. "Just whose man are you?" His voice trembled.

Those fingers reached out again. They brushed back a long, dark curl, which had fallen slantwise across Rafe's face. The man's expression was unreadable, but the lips smiled. Rafe felt a sigh come through him like a summer storm.

"I am in the service of the Tremontaine family," the man said quite softly.

Rafe knew. As he had known he would be a scholar from the moment he first listened to de Bertel's lectures on the ascendance of man. As he had known he would follow evidentiary science when he had first read of the observations that proved the curvature of the earth.

This man, as beautiful as heartbreak, was the Duke Tremontaine himself. One of the most meddlesome members of the Board of Governors.

Rafe wiped his hands on his pants. "Oh hell's bells," he said. "Get the devil away from here before they hang you."

The cornflower eyes snapped up to scan the crowd behind Rafe again. "But you won't?"

"My name is Rafe Fenton, and I disagree with you in all the ways that matter. I expect you'll be hearing my name more often, if you insist on dictating the path of our intellectual pursuits. Because I will oppose you with everything I have in me. But I do not"—Rafe wiped his hands again—"approve of physical violence. So get out before you meet someone who does." His voice rasped. It was hard to hear over the running beat of his heart.

"Thank you, Rafe," said the duke. "I honor your passion and

commitment. And I hope you'll see that we share the same goal, in the end."

Rafe felt bleak, looking up at that earnest face that honestly believed what it was telling him. He was sure the conservative deans and department chairs, so eager to squash the new philosophies, had presented their terms in quite the flattering light.

"Go," Rafe said. "Redrun Alley will take you straight to Chambers Street. I don't know if anyone else might recognize you, but keep your head down just in case."

He turned to walk away, but the duke reached out and caught him by the shoulder. The fissure spreading through his middle split wider. He could have cried.

"Perhaps you might be persuaded to see the other side of the argument? By the time we meet again?" said the Duke Tremontaine.

"The sun is more likely to rise in the north than anyone succeed in persuading me of that. I doubt we shall see each other again, *dearest* Tremontaine."

An endearment wielded as an insult cuts sharpest of all. Rafe had made himself an expert in the technique. And yet, with this man, even sarcasm seemed to have turned on him. He felt sick.

The duke winced. "I suppose not. I . . ." He shook his head. "Good-bye, Rafe."

Rafe stared as the tall man threaded his way carefully through the crowd. He could follow his progress longer than he should have been able to: a head as bright as a new-minted coin—and a mind, and a heart.

Rafe had been gone for nearly half an hour before Kaab decided to look for him. The girl, Micah (she had asked her directly, and

Micah had seemed quite sure she was a girl, which made Rafe's confusion distinctly odd), seemed happy to climb the tall base of the statue of an old man with a broad cape and a fist in the air. He was three times human size and more than high enough to give them a good view of the main University square.

"I like it up here," Micah said when they had settled beside each other on the statue's shoulder and cape. "I can breathe better. There's lots of things in the City, but it doesn't smell good."

"No," Kaab agreed, still scanning the people surging below for a young man with a broad forehead and a mane of curling, ink-black hair. The students were still waiting by the closed wood-and-iron doors of the hall, but Kaab doubted they would get any satisfaction. If she were any judge, the guilty parties had long since escaped through one of several back entrances.

"How does it smell where you come from?" Micah asked.

"Like jacaranda flowers and cool springs and wet stone. Like tortillas on a *comal*."

"What are those?"

"A kind of pancake and a kind of stove. We eat tortillas at every meal."

"Does it taste good?"

"It's the food of the gods," Kaab said simply.

"And you're from very far away? I'm also from far away . . . well, a day's driving in the cart, but Rhubarb isn't a very fast horse. But you're from farther away than that." She sounded very sure.

Kaab thought she glimpsed Rafe, at the far edge of the square, near a retaining wall that backed onto some kind of garden.

"Much farther," she said absently. He was talking to a man now. Tall, with hair the color of golden maize. "Look." She pointed. "There's Rafe."

"Ah!" said Micah, smiling. "Yes, there he is. Rafe is very kind, I think. He's probably helping that man."

Kaab turned sharply to Micah, but there was nothing except innocent delight in her expression. "Do you . . . like him?" Kaab asked, wishing that her Xanamwiinik tutor had been more explicit in the nuances of such terms.

Micah nodded energetically. "Of course! He's like my cousins, only he doesn't care about gardens. He loves equations. And distances! I think you should talk to him about your home, and how far away it is. If it takes me a day from the farm, and the farm is twenty miles away . . . how long did it take you to travel here?"

"Ninety days," Kaab said.

Micah's eyes widened. "Then you're at least one thousand eight hundred miles away! If you were traveling by horse. But no, you came from the sea. I must ask Rafe how fast boats go. But you are from very far away! How did you travel so far? I'm sure he'd like to know."

"I'm sure he would," Kaab said dryly, thinking back to his clumsy interrogation earlier. This Rafe was very interested in things she was quite sure her family did not want him to know. Which made him a good person to stick close to. The Balams couldn't afford to have their monopoly on chocolate trade with the Land threatened. Not with things as they were back home, with the Tullan army just waiting for an excuse to attack.

"Who is he still helping over there?" she asked Micah, just for something to say.

Micah frowned. "I don't know. I think they're arguing now. But he is rubbing his hands on his thighs. Our friend Joshua says that he only does that when he wants to kiss someone."

Kaab laughed, but she felt an odd lurch. Even from this distance she could sense an intensity between the two men. Perhaps Micah was right.

"But why," Micah said, "does he want to kiss someone he's arguing with?" She sighed. "I like Rafe," she repeated. "But I don't think he makes very much sense sometimes."

Kaab thought of how many long months had passed since she had kissed anyone. Of the games she had played with Citlali, thinking that nothing too serious could come of them. She had seen quite a few pretty girls since she'd arrived (though she had to admit the University seemed remarkably devoid of that particular enticement). "He ought to kiss him," she said.

Micah wrinkled her nose. "Cousin Daniel tried to kiss me once. I hit him on the head with a turnip, and he never tried again."

Kaab laughed until she had to wipe her eyes. "I think that was very wise," she said.

Uncle Chuleb was waiting for Kaab when she returned home, kneeling with a brush and open codex upon a reed mat he had laid out in the courtyard garden. The gum trees, brought at great expense from home by the previous generation, were lit in the late evening chill by a series of oil lamps in sconces that hung from the trees on long ropes of finely braided henequen. A natural spring— almost certainly why her ancestors had bought the land here—fed a series of man-made streams and waterfalls that made the house feel like an oasis of home in a wide desert. Muscovy ducks and other waterfowl kept to the ponds and beneath overhanging rocks. Her uncle had arranged himself beside the largest waterfall, beside which grew the squat breadnut trees they kept wrapped in gauze throughout the long winter. He looked a picture of refined nobility, with his hair arranged in two loops beneath a stiff jade-beaded head cloth, and a mantle printed with the family pattern draped over his chest and left arm. She imagined he was reviewing the records of the recent shipment, but when she approached, she saw that he was in fact composing in the family book, the formal record of the history of the Balams.

"Niece," he said, when she had come close enough to acknowledge. "You took your time returning. Did you learn anything interesting?"

"Much, Uncle," she said, and knelt across from him. "What are you recording in red and black?"

Uncle Chuleb did not buy a note of her innocent tone, but it amused him. "Your arrival, dearest niece. For it comes to me that I might have cause to write more about you before long. And what did you learn?"

"That saffron costs a great deal, but in abundance smells of smelted copper and annatto."

Her uncle smiled. "You intrigue me. I look forward to the gilded hares at tomorrow's feast. And what else?"

"That there are great conflicts between the nobility and their intellectuals, who are not the same here. That some of their intellectuals are very interested in the mysteries of the Four Hundred Siblings and the secrets of moving great distances across the seas. I very much doubt that any of them have found it. But it seemed to me that if they do, there is a chance that their merchants might use such knowledge to take their own ships to our ports."

She did not spell out the rest of the implications. Chuleb, a minor Kinwiinik noble who had married into the family very young, understood them as well as she. With the monopoly broken by the Locals themselves, the other Trading families might use that to invalidate the Balam mandate to the port. And some of these

Trading families had lived for generations with the Tullan, whose insatiable political ambitions now threatened even the southern coastal cities of the Kinwiinik. Formally, all Traders owed their first loyalty to other Traders of all families. Practically, their relationships were more complex. Local ships in Trading waters had the potential to break the delicate political balance in the lands of the gods. It could bring a war that would destroy Balam power—and possibly the autonomy of the Kinwiinik themselves. She remembered the stories of Nopalco, the river that ran red for thirteen rotations of the great calendar wheel. And she thought—of course she did—of her role in bringing on this crisis. If her irresponsible actions contributed to the destruction of her people, her home . . .

She shook her head, a violent negation.

"It is good that you brought this to me, Niece. I take it that you met one of the students interested in this subject?"

"He's Fenton's son."

Chuleb did not look unduly surprised. "And perhaps you can continue to cultivate his acquaintance?"

"Of course, Uncle."

"Good. Just as a precaution, Niece. I have been aware of the current climate in the University, but the men in charge are conservative and easily threatened. They would rather eat stones than learn something new. As long as we encourage them, the few revolutionaries like young Fenton won't have enough support to make their new discoveries."

"Ah," Kaab said, and felt a little ill. It was best for her family, of course, to support the Board of Governors against the students. But she had felt Rafe and Micah's enthusiasm. Rafe, at least, would understand some of the implications of his discovery. Micah clearly lived for her equations and the joy of solving them. But what was necessary was not always just. Had her parents not struggled to make her understand that? Even sick with the illness that would kill her, Ixmoe had spoken to her daughter with the lessons of the elders: *Passion in excess is as much of a vice as passivity, my little bee. You must not recklessly waste the heat of your head-spirit, or you will attract the punishment of the gods for powers not held in sacred moderation.*

Her uncle noticed her preoccupation. "Are you well, Kaab?"

She smiled, with an effort. "I was recalling my mother."

"May she always walk the earth, may you always carry her." He paused thoughtfully, his eyes on the lights beyond her. "Before you go, I wonder what you make of this letter? It arrived the other day."

He took an object from behind the family book and held it across the mat. The paper was fine and thick, creamy. She turned it over and started to read. *Diane, Duchess Tremontaine* was the signature. Why did that name sound familiar? Ah yes. The lady who had first served the saffron hares. Rafe had been positively irascible on the way back home, and on his lips the name of the duke—this lady's husband, apparently—had nearly dripped poison. The duke sat on the Board of Governors.

The letter was short. It requested a meeting with Kaab's uncle to discuss matters of trade that would be beneficial to them both. It gently stressed her political connections through her husband, and her place in polite society.

"I thought the nobility here did not interest themselves in trade?"

"As did I, Niece. This letter is . . . quite unusual."

"Well, there can be no harm in seeing what she wants, can there? What does Aunt say?"

"She is inclined to agree with you."

"But?"

Uncle Chuleb looked out at the lamp-lit garden, accurate as a drawing of home by a Trader too long away. "The lady is not to be underestimated. Her husband is very influential, but I suspect that she personally exercises more political power than her peers believe. Her hand in anything is a reason to be cautious."

"How will you answer her?"

He shrugged. "I have petitioned Xamanek for guidance. May his star always guide us. And of course, I'll speak to your aunt. We will decide after the feast."

The doors to the courtyard thrown open, the arcaded peristyle draped in multicolored garlands of flowers sweet enough to coat the throat, the drums and flutes playing a song of welcome to the entering guests, a song of farewell to the flaming sun. The servants in mantles and draped loincloths of henequen carrying trays of wooden cups, filled with frothy chocolate prepared in the traditional style: cold, scented with honey and vanilla and blossoms of trees so exotic their names have yet to be made palatable to the Local tongue. The women of the house, as precious as flowers, as precious as jade in their skirts and blouses and wide belts stiff with precious jewels, multicolored embroidery whose meaning escapes the ant-egg-skin guests and sings its own song to the Traders far from home. The altars to Xamanek and Chaacmul on the north and west sides of the portico are laden with offerings of burning copal resin, wafting pleasantly among the guests, and with figurines of amaranth dough mixed with the blood, ritually let, of the girl called Ixkaab and her family.

The Balam family greets their guests in the courtyard, smiling broadly as the Locals cast wide eyes at the pleasing extravagance of the flowers bought for the occasion and of the formal attire of the hosts.

"By god that man has a rock the size of my thumb up his nose!"

"It's jade, dear. Inlaid with gold, if I'm not mistaken. A fine piece."

"How does he breathe around that thing?"

"How do you talk around yours?"

The guests move on, gently steered by discreet servants. Chocolate is held to be intoxicating among the Kinwiinik. Only certain classes are allowed to taste its refined, prized flavor, which even the gods are said to hold in esteem. The Traders are willing to sell the processed beans to the Locals to do with as they please, but not even the most plebeian of country squires would dare ask one of those smooth-faced servants for cream to cut the bitterness of the frothy brew being served tonight. And if he did, they would just as impassively pretend not to understand him.

Ixkaab is resplendent in shades of red and green. She embroidered the blouse herself on the long boat journey. Her thick hair has been bound in two braids, wrapped around the back of her head and gathered into two small points in front, at the height of her fine brown eyes. This is a sign of respect: Only married women and those dedicated to the service may bind their hair in this way. She is young, and so her jewels are modest, but Aunt Ixsaabim is a master of the art of personal adornment and they are brilliantly deployed. Her headdress is small, anchored to the back and shimmering with quetzal feathers that move in the brisk evening breeze like the river beneath the forest canopy: always green, but never quite the same shade. Her wide belt has been beaten with gold and layered with tiny jade beads in the motif of her father's family. Her brown skin glows a shimmering yellow, tinted with the cream of axin brought especially from home. Her uncle Chuleb and the male heads of the lesser Kinwiinik Trading families who also live and trade in this city wear more elaborate headdresses of hardened cloth that support their expertly layered feathers, the pure jade of the quetzal, the flaming ruby of the spoonbill, the opalescent clarity of the bottom feathers of a Muscovy duck, and the tail feathers of a white heron. Their mantles are the products of a hundred hours of hard labor with loom and needle, and advertise their status as much as their jewels. At home, they could not chance such a public display of wealth. At home, Traders must engage in the fiction that they are not as wealthy as the nobles they serve. Here in the Land, money and power have a more open relationship.

The bustle in the courtyard flows through an open passageway, lit warmly by torches burning fragrant pine, and into a large banquet hall. The ceiling is arched, and the high windows have all been thrown open. The servants lead the Local guests, somewhat stiff and hampered by stays and petticoats and starched linen, to the long table constructed in the Local manner, with sufficient height for its several dozen chairs. The Fenton patriarch notes that the table at the front of the hall is low to the ground and surrounded by woven reed mats and two squat chairs. The Kinwiinik guests who have been honored with invitations tonight remain standing near this low table. They appear content to wait. In their home, the Balams might occasionally be forced to prove their dominance over an upstart Trading family. In the land of the north, the great family maintains a careful, but unquestioned dominance.

Fenton's wife, among the stiffest of the Local women present—her stays have been pulled so tightly against the fat of her stomach that a nervous laugh escapes her every time she breathes too deeply—agrees with her husband about the odd stature of the table. She is the sort of woman who generally finds it prudent to agree with her husband. Rafe Fenton, who loves his mother very much, despises this about her.

"Do you suppose they eat standing up?" Mistress Fenton ventures.

"I suppose they eat squatting on the floor. Odd folk."

"They wear very fine cloth. And jewels. Rafe, dear, how do you think your sister would look with a few of those aquamarine feathers in her riding cap?"

"Like a ninny," Rafe says. "So, entirely appropriate."

"Oh, Rafe," sighs the Fenton matriarch. The words have the melody of a song she has sung many times before. Rafe, with the look of a man with other things on his mind, mumbles an apology.

The Balams enter once their Local guests have been seated. They and their Kinwiinik guests indeed kneel at the low table, though the graceful way they fold their legs beneath the rich fabric of their skirts and mantles make the Fenton patriarch's characterization of it as "squatting" seem satisfactorily churlish. To Rafe, at least. The lord and lady of the house occupy the two low stools and offer words of greeting to their assembled guests. The words, whatever they are, are lost on most listeners: The food has, at last, begun to arrive.

First comes a series of sauces studded with slices of meat only intermittently identifiable. "Salamander," come some shocked whispers down the long Local table. "Newt" and "crickets" and "dog!" But also venison and some kind of rich nut and mushrooms the color of ashes in the grate and a flavor at once sharp and earthy.

"Like a good Erlander cheese," says the head of the Greenglass family, one of the richest and most influential in the City. He asks the servants for more and mops it up with one of the two dozen kinds of maize pancakes in baskets placed at regular intervals along the table.

"Papa has a very fine palate," whispers a young lady to her dining companion, a broad-shouldered young man from a smaller

Trading family. "He's quite the gourmand." The young lady's whisper is not so soft as she imagines it to be. A wag replies: "He's quite the glutton!" and a few guests laugh more freely than strictly politic.

The chocolate poured from tall ceramic jugs has grown thicker and a little sour, not unpleasantly so. The addition of fermented agave nectar has begun to take its effect. At the Balam table, some of the men have switched out entirely for glasses of octli, dusted with a powder of chocolate. Kaab looks longingly at the jugs, but there is no time for the women to enjoy it.

"Come, Niece," says her aunt at a signal from one of the servants. "It's time."

The women of the family hasten to the kitchen. In honor of the Local guests, they have decided to modify the traditional serving of tamales. Kaab finds herself holding a copper tray on her shoulder and a basket heaped with ant-egg tamales in the crook of her other elbow.

"What if I drop it, Aunt?" Kaab asks very innocently.

"What if you—" Ixsaabim goes a little pale, peers at her niece, and laughs abruptly. "You little minx! You nearly had me! The great Ixkaab, dropping her food." She laughs again and gently touches the cotton ribbons woven into Kaab's braids. "How much you remind me of your mother, dear."

Kaab bites back sudden tears. She ducks her head. "Thank you, Aunt Saabim."

There's no time for any more. The flutes have begun to play in the hall and now the drums will start and the song begins at the front of the line of women, where Kaab takes the place of honor. This feast is—nominally, and, in some small way, actually—a celebration of her arrival.

"We bring tamales," she sings in the language of her childhood.

They don't mention the hares, because there is no word in Kindaan for saffron, and the Locals wouldn't understand in any case.

"Good god," blurts Master Greenglass when they dance into the room, smiling and spinning. "Are those saffron hares?"

"Won't the Duchess Tremontaine turn green when she hears of this!"

"Gracious, they're as orange as a sunset!"

"How poetic, darling. But I expect they've used some kind of dye. It'll be all turmeric, and bitter as an old radish."

"My sister had the good fortune to attend the Duchess Tremontaine's little soiree," says the young lady of the indiscreet whisper. "She married a noble, you know."

Her companion—indeed, the whole long table—knows.

"But did she truly use saffron?" asks Mistress Fenton, more tipsy than she realizes. "For it seems to me a very great expense for a house that has just suffered such a blow. Why, there were Tremontaine funds sunk into the *Everfair*, weren't there? The ship that foundered in the open seas and lost all hands in a storm?"

The doomed expedition to the Garay port, whose over-confident navigators had assured their own demise nearly a year previous, had been promoted and backed by Greenglass Imports. Master Greenglass, a prudent epicure, had invested in sufficient insurance to cover his losses. So he does not allow the implication that he convinced a noble family to participate in his ill-conceived scheme to spoil his dinner.

The golden hares are set before them, carved by the servants with a flourish, and served on fresh ceramic plates.

"It *is* saffron!" proclaims Master Greenglass over the sound of Fenton encouraging Mistress Fenton to speak more quietly. "I'll bet my cellar on it! By the Horned God, this must be enough saffron to dye the hair of twenty noblewomen. All over, if you know what I mean."

Kaab, passing behind him, does not know what he means. Rafe chokes on his chocolate.

"Well, taste that, dear. That isn't turmeric."

"I suppose not. And did you try those dumplings? What is that inside? Some kind of cheese?"

"I can't say that I know . . . and I'm afraid to find out, quite honestly!"

At the other end of the table, Mistress Fenton stares dreamily down at the remains of her ant-egg tamale.

"I dare say the whole Hill will be jealous when they hear of this. A true banquet from the chocolate lands! Oh, how happy I am that you brought me, Thelonious. And that you sold them all that saffron! Will it be very hard to get more?"

"Yes, it was quite clever of me," says Fenton with a pointed look at his son. "But I had a good man on hand to handle the negotiations."

The young Fenton raises his eyes to the ceiling, as if to pray for divine intervention.

The glow of success has finally descended upon the Balams, watching the contented jostling among their Local guests. No hares have been dropped, and quite a few have been picked clean. Ixsaabim turns to her young and handsome husband.

"Dearest, I think we should see what that woman wants."

She does not have to specify which woman.

Chuleb rubs his chin. "Fenton tells me there are rumors. You remember the ship last year? The *Everfair*?"

"The one their navigators took so far off course it sank within miles of the Garay coast and they didn't even realize it?"

"Many families lost their fortunes. And Fenton suggested Tremontaine might be one of them."

Saabim looks thoughtful. "That might be true, but the nobles here aren't like those at home. They can't be stripped of their positions for dishonorable actions. They all have debts, but so long as they keep their land no one seems to care. She'll have influence, my morning star. And influence is always valuable."

"She is very clever," he says. "And she likes to pretend that she isn't. It is a combination that worries me."

"Well, so am I clever, and so are you. So is Kaab for that matter, though she's impetuous enough that you can't always notice. I understand that this saffron woman might wish to use us for some political end, my precious flower, but we have our own tools at our disposal."

"True," says her husband. Kaab has vanished from the table— probably gone back to the kitchens.

"And the situation at home is too unstable. If the Tullan . . ." She can't finish. He puts a discreet hand on her stomach, where the baby has just started to show.

"I'll write her," he says. "I'll tell her to come here to us. She won't like it, but if she's serious, she will. I'll tell her to call three days hence."

Saabim squeezes her husband's hand beneath the table and gives him a quick, hard kiss. She looks around to see if anyone noticed and smiles, satisfied.

Someone in a modest headdress of shimmering feathers standing in the shadow of the kitchen hallway, within hearing distance of the head of the Balam table, did notice. And she smiles.

"Three days hence," says the spy under her breath, and walks back for more chocolate.

The spring storm spat rain like a drunk at a spittoon—wet and heavy and none too accurate. The river had swamped Riverside's inadequate levee again. Tess could hear the water gurgling through the streets two blocks over, the drunks cursing, the drunks laughing. It was nearly morning. This weather might have held Ben up. She wouldn't imagine anything worse happening to him, not until she had to.

She hadn't been able to sleep. She had tried, but it was cold and the rain was a nasty bedfellow. Tess and Ben kept a nice little place, the second floor above a washerwoman. Clean enough to discourage most of the roaches, shutters tight enough to keep out most of the wind and rain. On summer days she liked it enough to feel grateful. Her folks, rest them, had lived worse.

She held the fat tallow candle closer to the page, careful not to drip any wax and ruin the job. Routine stuff—a letter of recommendation for a Riverside girl, a former housebreaker, now getting old for the business, who wanted work as a chambermaid in the Middle City. The family seal at the bottom was real enough, though obscure. The girl's two years of loyal service, not so much. Tess sometimes had bigger jobs—credentials from foreign universities, arrest records—but this paid the bills. At least, it did with Ben's help. He had regular customers, the kind of men who paid him well for his time and could be counted on when there wasn't such a demand for good forgeries.

She wouldn't worry. Damn it, but she wouldn't.

Heavy steps up the stairs. Maybe his, if he were drunk, the bastard. The sound of a key fumbling in the lock. Definitely drunk. Or hurt? She ran to the door, had it open before she'd taken a full breath. If someone had wanted to kill her, she'd have been on the floor taking a bath in her own blood. You had to think about things like that in Riverside. But it was just Ben. He was drunk and grinning like clown. She frowned.

"What's the matter, sweet Tessie? You ain't happy to see me?"

"What happened? Did your father recover?"

Ben frowned and shrugged. "Naw. The old man's rotting six feet—well, three feet, at least—under."

Ben hadn't exactly been a dutiful son (and his bastard of a father hadn't deserved it), but this still seemed too callous for a man just returned from his father's graveside.

"What the hell's the smile for, then?"

Ben stepped into the room and locked the door behind them.

"Here," he said, and pulled from his waistcoat an oval locket on a long chain of linked gold. It was of an antiquated style, a master's workmanship. At a glance, not a forgery. At least, not a forgery that was passing off gilt for silver. She took the locket and opened it. She frowned.

"What is this, Ben?"

He was grinning again, leaning against the wall. "Our ticket out of here. The only good turn that son of a bitch ever did for me. We're going to be rich, Tessie."

Tess looked up at him, that baby face just a bit too beautiful to do him any good. He was grinning and humming to himself, an old song about going to the country. She looked back down at the locket, at the contents that meant nothing to her, and shivered. Ben's father had been a murdering lowlife. He wouldn't rest easy in his grave. And any gift he gave his son would be heavy with sin—the kind that came due.

Episode Three

HEAVENLY BODIES

Joel Derfner

Had the Duke Tremontaine noticed the anxious care with which his wife chose her gown that morning—silk the color of pale irises trembling open at the break of dawn, lace as fine as spider webs gathered at the cuffs, the bodice almost as exquisite as the collarbone it was cut to reveal—and the equal care she devoted to selecting the unutterably drab cloak with which she covered up all that silk and lace, it might, perhaps, have occurred to him to wonder exactly what impression she was trying to make, and why it was so vital that she do so. If he had seen her frown almost imperceptibly at the confusion her footman displayed when, rather than her own carriage, she bid him order an unmarked one from the hotelier in Napier Street, if he had overheard the strange address to which the driver was instructed to bear her, if he had observed the driver's respectful assertion that he must have mis-understood and her subsequent denial of that assertion, he might have taken a moment to ask himself with what urgent aim, as the carriage wheels began to click and then to clatter over the cobble-stones, she was leaving the ducal mansion.

111

Then again, he might not have. The duke had spent the better part of two decades not noticing things about his duchess, after all, and, unbeknownst to him, it had served him well.

Alas, that the good fortunes of men do not always remain so.

Someone was destroying Rafe's room.

It was giving him a headache.

"If you are going to insist," he said, burying his face as deeply into the tangle of bed linens and brown wool blanket as he could manage, "on entering my chamber in the middle of the night, by means of what blandishments do you suppose you might be prevailed upon to approach the task with slightly less *vigor*?"

"Develop a little talent for observation, pet." Ah, the baritone voice meant the situation was as he'd feared. Rafe heard the sound of the curtains being flung open and squeezed his eyes shut tight; they were in no condition to be assaulted by the cold morning light. "The University bells rang fully two hours ago."

"How barbaric. Have we been suddenly transported to Arkenvelt without my knowledge?"

"Oh, pigeon, do I have to do *everything* for you?"

Footsteps approached the bed. Rafe knew what was coming next, but moving quickly enough to prevent it would make his head hurt even worse. He therefore resigned himself to misery as he felt the bedclothes slip pitilessly off his naked body. He groaned and rolled onto his back, his arm flung over his eyes. "Besides," said the invader, "I want sausages."

"Joshua," said Rafe with all the patience he could muster, "this is Liberty Hall. You are most welcome to procure yourself as many sausages as you like, and, having done so, to insert them with gusto into your—"

"I see you're having one of *those* days again." His dear friend's voice was as smug as ever. "If you listened to my advice, you know, you'd have far fewer of them."

"If I wanted a big brother I would have asked—"

"Yes, yes, you would have asked your father for one long ago. As well you should have." A shuffle of foolscap pages. "'*On the Causes of Nature,*'" said Joshua. "You couldn't pick a drearier title for your book, pigeon?" This was unworthy of a reply. "My, you certainly have scratched these equations out savagely. I take it last night's measurements were of no more use than the rest?"

Rafe groaned.

"That bad, was it?" The groan grew more fervent and finally trailed into silence. "What was his name?"

"Matthew," said Rafe. Joshua was silent. "Anthony. Seth, Robert, Giles, the Horned God, your sister."

"Which one?"

"The giggly one. How in the Seven Hells should I know what his name was, when neither one of us asked and neither one of us offered? And how, for that matter, could you suppose I give a whore's left tooth about it in the first place, especially after all that port?"

"Well, you *should* give a whore's left tooth about it." Rafe could feel disapproval radiating from Joshua like heat from winter coals. "Go through every man in Riverside and half the dogs, Rafe, and I'll raise a glass to you. But sooner or later, when it happens with the same man a second time—"

"On the day the river flows uphill. Through what perversity do you still refuse to believe me when I tell you I have sworn an oath that such a thing will never come to pass?"

"Sooner or later," continued Joshua, as if Rafe had not spoken, "when it happens with the same man a second time, you won't know what to do with yourself. You're annoying enough as it is when you're not infatuated."

"I," said Rafe with extreme politeness, "am not the one who is being annoying." Joshua said nothing. "Aren't you going to ask me how he was?"

"How was he?"

"Satisfactory."

"Which college?"

This was enough to move Rafe to lift his arm from his face and open his eyes—in a squint, to be sure; there was, after all, only so much light the human body was designed to take in at this unfortunate hour. Through strands of hair so black it was almost blue, he saw his roommate standing over his bed far more judgmentally than was at all called for.

"You've gotten into the Fool's Delight again, haven't you?" said Rafe. "I've already had everybody in the other colleges worth having, and the few times I've been with anybody from Natural Science it's made me long for the disastrous night you and I spent together lo these many years ago."

"Good god. How awful for you."

"You have no idea." Rafe attempted to raise himself from the lumpy bed and had to close his eyes against the pain that blossomed in his head. "No, I've been going down to the docks for months. *Do* keep up." He opened his eyes again and sat up much more carefully.

"Pigeon," said Joshua, prim as new lace, "I gave up trying long ago. I can't count that high. Now get up, put on your robe, and let's go. Sausages. And chocolate. Then de Bertel."

"And what do you think either one of us could possibly have to learn from His Excrescence of the Swine?"

"Look, whether or not you've outstripped him in understanding as far as you've outstripped the rest of us—"

"Oh, much further."

"—you don't go to de Bertel's lectures to learn; you go because if you miss any more of them you'll offend the entire body of magisters so deeply they won't even let you sit your exams, much less pass them, and you'll never found your school."

Rafe assumed the expression he had developed to madden his father, his lips pressed tightly to one side. Joshua sighed and pushed back his hair, the color of good beer. *Oh gods, beer.* Even the thought of it—

"Ah," said Joshua. "Your I'm-unwilling-to-admit-you're-right face. I'll take one step more, then, and tell you not only to come to the lecture but also to keep your mouth shut while de Bertel is talking. After your performance last night you don't need to push him any further."

Oh dear. "What did I do last night?" Rafe's forehead creased helplessly, though it was a pose; any actual effort to remember would be doomed to failure.

Joshua's face was incredulous. "You can't be serious." He grinned. "I'm sorry to say, love, but you were in splendid fettle. He walked in just as you were reaching the climax of a woefully accurate impression of him. I sent Anselm over to stop you, but you bit him, so we left you be. Then, when you finally saw de Bertel, you called him a blind, mentally defective sloth who mistook shit for information and flung both at his students indiscriminately, which, you said, was an issue with most of the doctors at the University, but the problem with de Bertel was that his aim was so much more accurate with the shit."

Rafe sighed mournfully. "If only I weren't such a *perceptive* drunk."

"That's one way of looking at it. But please don't alienate him further, pigeon. You never know which way the Board of Governors is going to vote on the committee question."

"Don't be ridiculous; we've got weeks left before the vote, and with enough protests like last week's they'll have no choice but to vote it down."

"Oh, in the same way that de Bertel had no choice but to change his mind and agree with you about the movement of the heavenly bodies once you showed him your calculations?" Rafe did not dignify this with a response. "Come on, pigeon. Besides, I meant it about the sausages, so we'll need time to stop by the Eagle. Cheer up; we can get extra and throw them at de Bertel."

"How will we tell which is de Bertel and which the sausage?" With great effort and greater care, Rafe finally stepped out of bed, poured half a pitcher of cold water over his head, drank the rest, and toweled off with the edge of the bedsheet. He reached unsteadily for the robe hanging on the wall, black and clean enough for even the most respectable of scholars.

As he bent to dig for clean breeches, he felt Joshua's hand on his arm. "Your revolutionary school is a splendid idea, pigeon. But you'll need that doctor's robe if you want to acquire any students. Be careful. You tend to ruin things for yourself."

Rafe was silent for a moment and then nodded. "You needn't worry about me. I'll be fine."

"Good."

"Micah! Thad!" he called into the next room. By now Rafe was able to speak at a reasonable volume without fearing his head would split open. Sausages, too, would help. "You'd better hurry, or we'll be lucky enough to miss de Bertel's lecture entirely."

* * *

Xamanek's light, it was cold! If this was the spring, Kaab shuddered to think what the winters were like.

Are you ill, little bee? Her mother's voice in her head gave no quarter, cold or no. *Or have turkeys been coming in the night to peck at your head? Because otherwise I cannot think of a single reason you would consider doing again* exactly what you did in Tultenco, heading into the worst part of town seeking out trouble. The voice was as melodious as the River Ulua flowing into the sea, which only made the criticism sting the more sharply. *You have said you wish to work in the service. Why, then, are you risking everything on a whim? Make a mistake this time, and you will compel your father to choose between making your banishment permanent or calling you back home where you will be tossed out of the service for good.*

It would not help to object. Even from the houses beneath the earth, Ixmoe's spirit would have no patience with Kaab's protestations that this city would not see her repeat the errors she had made across the sea.

Kaab meant things to go well here. But she was coming to realize that it was one thing to learn about the natives of this land among the shining temples and plazas of Binkiinha thousands of miles away; quite another to come east across an ocean and be surrounded by them.

Oh, but if only Ixmoe could have seen them—the beautiful Local women with their strange, exotic skin the color of ant eggs, their thousand and one fascinating shades of hair—then, *then* she would have understood. Especially in Riverside, where Kaab stood now under the decaying houses bedecked with peeling paint and crumbling gaud. These women, unbound by the rules even of this city, behaved in ways that would shock her modest friends walking the white paved *sacbeob* ways of her homeland.

A clatter to the southeast. Kaab's hand flew to the hilt of her dagger, dark, reassuring obsidian in the hidden pouch she had sewn into the insufferable Local gown without which Auntie Saabim refused to allow her to leave the house. When she looked around for the source of the sound, she saw only a pair of young men, remarkably similar in face and dress, arms entwined, sauntering through the narrow streets of cracked and broken cobblestone, stepping lightly over murky brown puddles, paying no heed to anyone but each other.

She kept her hand on her dagger as they passed. A third man was coming down the street; when he was closer, she recognized him—a gold-headed wonder of lace and red velvet—as the man who had pinked her in her first duel last week, the day she arrived. What was his bizarre name again? Pem . . . no, Ben.

Kaab stepped quickly into the shadow of a narrow, twisted alley, lest he spot her. She needn't have worried; his mind was obviously on other matters as he ambled by, whistling something that he apparently thought of as a tune.

Curious, she followed him, watched him enter a tavern and leave again soon after, a black cloth tied around his arm. There was no harm in going in, was there?

Kaab opened the tavern door and breathed in the lingering perfume of stale alcohol. Other than the few scattered, ancient dere-licts seated among the mismatched jumble of chairs and the two comely barmaids bound up far too tightly in faded cotton wiping the battered tables, the place was empty. The girls, one a tall thing with hair the color of maize, the other short, stout, pale as peeled cassava, stopped their work when Kaab entered, but she had grown used to the staring by now. She waved the maize-haired girl over, ordered a beer she had no intention of drinking—not after her first taste a few days ago of the watery piss these people called beer—and touched the girl's hand when she brought it in a chipped red clay mug. The sight of her cheekbones filled Kaab with thoughts of Citlali, the girl with the divine . . . ah, but the disaster of Tultenco, the forged treaty, the treachery of the Nopalco court, the desperate flight before dawn—it was all too recent to bear thinking about.

"Haven't seen you around before," said the barmaid. She smelled faintly of sweat.

"That," said Kaab with a small, aloof smile, "is because I have not been around before."

"No, Cassie," one of the old men farther back in the tavern said, his voice heavy with drink despite—or perhaps because of—the early hour. "Don't you remember? Not a week ago this filly lost a duel to Ben over Tess the Hand right outside here." Kaab whipped her head around to look at him, her eyes narrow, ready to take umbrage. But he tipped in her direction, respectfully, an impossibly rumpled felt hat of an indeterminate shade, and she relaxed. "You made him work for it before he won, though," he said. "Never seen a girl with a sword do that."

"Tess the Hand?" said the girl, her eyes not leaving Kaab. "Then she's got good taste."

If the beautiful prostitute went by the name Tess the Hand, she was a beautiful prostitute worth discovering more about. "Tell me about her."

"Why, have you got custom for her?"

The Balam were the first family of Traders among the Kinwiinik. Kaab knew better than to appear too eager. "Perhaps."

"Well," said the girl, twirling a lock of her thick hair around her finger and giving Kaab a wink, "she's the best there is."

Kaab felt unaccountably warm, a thousand thanks be to Ahkin

in this miserable cold. "I am not surprised," she said. "She had the air of a talented woman."

"What do you want from her?"

Kaab thought for a moment. "Does she have particular specialties?"

"Oh, she does it all. Like I say, she's the best there is."

"And how much money does she ask for?"

"Depends on the job, really. You'd have to ask her."

This was growing more tedious than a game of Nine Bean with only three players. Really, a girl dressed like that in an establishment like this had no business being coy. "Oh? One deals with her directly, not with her—with the—" The idea the crippled sailmaker had explained on the voyage over still made no sense to her; no wonder she couldn't remember the word, either. "The man who manages her? Ben?"

The girl obviously had no idea what she meant. "What would you want to talk to Ben for? She can conduct her own business, thank you very much."

Well, that was a relief. "I am glad that at least some here do their prostitute work without the assistance of managers."

At this the girl threw back her head and gave herself over to full-throated laughter like a gibbon. "Is that what you think Tess— Oh, that's so—" But here she lost herself in hilarity again, while Kaab forced her fingers not to drum on the table. The girl gave a last chuckle and wiped her eyes. "Tess isn't a *whore*. She's a *counterfeiter*. And Ben's not her pimp; he's her protector. She's a talented woman, like you said. A lot of people would take advantage of her skill if they could. Ben's sword makes sure nobody does."

Far too basic an error to make, little bee. Kaab clenched her fists and restrained herself from banging one on the dented chestnut-brown surface of the table. "I see. That *is* an amusing misunderstanding. So Tess and Ben are lovers?"

"Hardly. He's not her flavor, nor she his, if you catch my drift."

Kaab's heart began to beat against the tight cage of her bodice like the wings of a hummingbird in flight.

"Though," said the barmaid uncertainly, "he'll indulge in any flavor he's asked so long as there's enough money in it."

"His preferences are not of interest to me," said Kaab. "But her—do you know where I might find her?" After all, if Tess—Tess the Hand—was a skilled counterfeiter, a closer acquaintance with her could be of use to Kaab's family.

"Not here, that's for sure, at least not till later tonight. She's out on a job. So's Ben, for that matter. He just ducked in here so I could tie on his mourning band—lost his father, you know—and he was dressed so fancy I couldn't help staring. 'Heading to the Hill, are you?' I said, and the Green God take me if he didn't say, 'Why, yes I am,' pretty as you please, and waltz out the door."

Kaab would have been happy to tarry longer, but she had promised Juub that she would demonstrate the swordplay she'd learned on the ship, and if she was any judge of adolescent boys, then the longer she kept her cousin waiting the more irksome he would be when she got back. "Thank you for your time, which I appreciate greatly," she said, standing and dropping a handful of minnows onto the table.

"What are the chances you'd take fifteen minutes and show me how much you appreciate it?"

Kaab looked her up and down, taking in the orange dress, the crimson petticoat underneath it, the blue eyes sparkling above it all. "Alas, lovely woman. In another place, at another time, I would cut your hair short for thinking fifteen minutes sufficient time to spend with me. But today my path leads toward other directions."

The girl grinned and shrugged. "She's lucky, whoever's in those directions."

Kaab grinned back, and out the door she went.

Her beer remained on the table, untouched.

The light streaming into the lecture hall from the high, leaded-glass windows dimmed, thank the gods, as it made its way down toward the students, and Rafe, fortified by sausages, found himself more than equal to it. There was Doctor de Bertel, waving his arms, eyes wide, stalking to this side of the podium and then that. "I see he's being subtle today," Rafe said as he walked in with Joshua and Micah, Thaddeus having preferred, wisely, to stay abed.

"Why don't you shout a little louder, pet?" said Joshua. "I don't think they can hear you in Chartil."

"What are you talking about?" said Micah, exasperated. "They wouldn't hear him in Chartil no matter how loud he talked."

"I don't know where you picked this one up," said Joshua to Rafe, who was failing to suppress a grin, "but I like him."

"Ah well," said Rafe, but he said it more quietly. "At least de Bertel is enjoying himself, the poor dear." The three settled themselves onto a sparsely populated bench in the back of the hall.

De Bertel, meanwhile, whose reputation as an entertaining lecturer not even Rafe could discredit, had worked himself into such a state he hadn't noticed their entrance. ". . . and thus the learned Chickering enters into a disquisition on the failings of Rastin—Rastin, of all people! This from a man who almost murdered his mother because of his grief over the death of his *dog*."

"There is another appropriate response," murmured Rafe, "to the death of one's dog?"

Alas, the snicker this elicited from Joshua finally caught de Bertel's attention, and his smile when he saw Rafe was uncomfortably reminiscent of something hungry. Rafe met his gaze long enough to communicate insolent disdain and then set about ostentatiously examining his fingernails.

De Bertel, for his part, seemed to be considering something. "But I think we shall depart from our intended subject," he said finally, "and discuss instead a set of even more extraordinary claims Chickering makes: that the earth itself—rather than being a fixed object at the center of the firmament around which the heavenly bodies rotate—that the earth itself *moves*." His voice was tinged with false wonder. "Now, after reading the second book of Rastin's *Considerations*, what might you say to a person who averred such a thing?" He nodded at a young man in the front row. "Master Pike?"

Pike, tall and gangly in his front-row seat, had already stood. "I should say, sir, that he was barking mad."

"And what proof might you offer, Pike, as demonstration of his lunacy?"

Rafe clucked his tongue. "Poor Pike. He couldn't even get through book one of the *Considerations*."

"Now, now, pet. Pike could have hidden depths."

Rafe sighed wearily. "I am in a position to be able to tell you with the utmost confidence, Joshua, that there is far less to Pike than meets the eye."

"We know, as a first principle," said Pike, apparently unaware of the spray of contumely behind him, "that a larger object falls more quickly than a smaller one."

Rafe snorted. "Yes, because we've investigated the question *so* closely."

"If the earth had the same kind of movement as other bodies," Pike continued—why, oh, *why* must he insist on speaking through his nose like that?—"then it would fall out of the heavens, leaving all other objects that rest and move on it, heavy and light, animals and humans, floating in the air."

De Bertel looked as pleased as if his dog had performed a trick correctly. "Quite so. But it pains me to have to say that the moving-earth crowd are hardly the worst offenders against the legacy of Rastin." Ah, so this was where he was heading. "Of late, an idea has arisen that makes Chickering look like Fontanus."

"And here we go," Rafe muttered.

"With what?" said Micah.

A few more of Rafe's classmates looked back at him to catch his expressive eye roll. "Those who espouse this new idea," continued de Bertel, "suggest not only that the earth moves, but that it moves around the sun—and that it therefore cannot be the center of the world." Gods, how thick was he going to lay the naïve amazement on?

De Bertel turned, of course, back to Pike. "What, Pike, are we to make of their claims?"

Pike said nothing; hardly surprising, as he hadn't read the answer in a book. But de Bertel was in a generous mood. "Don't worry, Pike, I won't keep you on the hook. I'd be disappointed, in fact, if you'd devoted enough time to such nonsense to be able to answer my question."

"No matter how well the scorned lover knows that scorn returned will avail him nothing," sighed Rafe, "he still finds himself powerless not to strike back."

"Someday you'll be a scorned lover, pigeon, and then you'll sympathize."

Rafe rolled his eyes. "On the day the sun declines to rise."

"Of course, such a notion is preposterous"—finally de Bertel was looking directly at Rafe, as were, for that matter, most of the others in the room—"an insult to thinking men everywhere, and its benighted adherents dreamers lost to reason who make mock of true scholarship."

"Oh, pigeon." Joshua's voice combined sympathy and regret. "I should have insisted Anselm try harder to stop your oration in the tavern."

"I would have just bitten him harder."

"I am grieved to know," de Bertel went on, looking more and more like a cockatrice with raised hackles, "that there is one among us who has so abandoned his senses as to subscribe to this feculence."

"Gods, how long is he going to take with this?"

Joshua patted his hand. "Come now, pigeon, you've had far worse beatings than this."

"Yes, and enjoyed them far more. I think I shall have to move things along at a somewhat quicker pace."

Joshua was a mother hen solicitous of her wayward chick. "Rafe . . ."

But there was Micah to consider. The boy didn't deal well with unpleasantness, and Rafe had no wish to unsettle him. "Remember how upset you got two days ago," he said, touching Micah's shoulder, "when Matthew and I fought about his absolutely ridiculous theory of circular motion?"

"Well," said Micah, "your theory was ridiculous too. But Matthew got really mad."

"The fight I'm about to have is going to be much worse."

"I'd better go, then." Like a shadow, Micah's small form moved along the wall and down the stairs.

De Bertel ignored him, caught up in his oration against the unnamed "one" who espoused such absurd notions of celestial place.

Rafe sat straight and gazed, expressionless, at the high-vaulted ceiling. "'O, how his hope-spent mother's heart would grieve,'" he said, his clear voice cutting effortlessly through de Bertel's gravelly one, "'to hear such wibber-wash as yon fool prateth!'"

All noise ceased at once, and it was not without satisfaction that Rafe noted every eye in the room on him.

De Bertel, for his part, had gone quite still. "You know, Fenton," he said casually, "I find myself recalling your perplexity a few days ago in the matter of—was it Chesney? Yes, I believe it was. You said you were utterly incapable of determining, after reading *Observations on the Nature of Heaviness and Lightness*, whether he was actually insane or simply a cow of dubious intelligence." He looked so pleased with himself that he had to be preparing a lightning bolt of no ordinary proportions. "Allow me to suggest that you should be the last among us to be perplexed by the question, since you have in fact shown yourself to be both." The class laughed, but Rafe felt the air in the room grow more charged.

"You have to admit, pigeon, that wasn't bad." Joshua sounded apologetic.

Rafe looked at the ceiling again. "He does have his moments. But then, so do I. And I've read more poetry than he has." He recited:

> "The cowherd told his talking bull, 'The day
> Thou best my wit, I die by mine own hand.'
> 'Then live,' the bull replied, 'thy wits unmatch'd.
> Debate thyself, whilst I attend thy wife.'"

De Bertel acknowledged the sally with a very slight bow. "Your wit, Fenton, admits of no equal." He assumed the air of a man who has just remembered something of mild interest. "You have your examination still to sit, don't you?"

"Indeed, sir, and never has a prisoner eyed his jailer's key ring with greater fervor."

"I have the honor of informing you that the Board of Governors met this morning and, piqued by the ill-advised and bombastic gathering last week, decided to vote on their proposal immediately."

"What?" Rafe stood so fast he almost fell, swayed, and threw his hand onto Joshua's shoulder for balance.

"Needless to say, it passed, by what I am given to understand was an overwhelming majority. And, now that it occurs to me, I realize I've been remiss in my duty to you and to the University. I'll have to make sure I'm one of your examiners. After the enlightening time we've spent together in my lectures, I shall enjoy testing your mettle to discover whether you're qualified to become a Master."

"My school—!" The color had vanished from Rafe's face. His hands were trembling.

"Oh, pigeon," whispered Joshua.

"I'm sure, Fenton," continued de Bertel pleasantly, "that you'll have no trouble whatsoever convincing each and every examiner of your qualifications."

Rafe finally found a response. "As *fascinating* as this lecture is, doctor," he said, his voice shaking only very slightly, "you'll understand if I decline to stay for the rest of it. I have a great deal of true scholarship still to make mock of, and I must go take the bull by the horns, lest I continue to be bested by intelligent bovines." He turned and, over his classmates' laughter—for they respected grace in defeat—left the room.

Disaster, calamity, ruin—language didn't contain the word that described this. His eyes brimmed. His school, the dream he'd cherished for years, his reason for being here, his reason for *living*. Gone. Forever out of his reach. Tears spilled over his lids and ran freely down his face as he careened out of the building into the light, headache be damned, walking, speeding up, running, heedless, over the flagstones and down the steps, right into the Duke Tremontaine.

This man was the last thing he needed. "Oh, for the Land's sake," he spat. "Out of the frying pan, into the imbecile."

"Now, now," said the duke, placing his hands on Rafe's shoulders. "And after you saved my life last week and then told me you wanted never to see me again."

"Get out of my way." Rafe's stomach clenched; he couldn't think.

"Or what?"

"I don't know! Or I'll hit you!" He hadn't hit anyone since his little sister broke his toy galleon.

"Won't that be fun!" Rafe looked for mockery, but the smile on Tremontaine's face was genuine. "Please, I insist." The duke stepped back and offered his face, all privilege and cream. Rafe shrugged off Tremontaine's hands and shoved past him.

He didn't get very far before he stopped in his tracks and turned around, his anger stopping the flow of his tears. "If you knew what you and your damned Board of Governors have just done," he cried, his voice hot and tight, "you wouldn't be issuing that invitation with quite so cavalier an air."

"Oh, you mean the examination committee decision?"

"You know damn well I mean the examination committee decision. Which way did you vote?"

"Why on earth should it matter?"

"Which way?"

"Come take chocolate with me and I'll tell you," said Tremontaine, and immediately looked startled, as if he'd said something completely different from what he'd expected to say.

Finally the duke made a gesture and spoke. "My carriage is this way." He paused. "If, that is, you're willing to enter it."

"I'd consider it," said Rafe savagely, and stalked toward the carriage.

Oh, Holy Ixchel, not the baby again.

As Kaab entered the room, Chuleb was once more on the floor, enraptured by the offspring of whatever cousin or aunt or sister the infant had come from. "Yes, widdle baby . . . where's the wattle now?"

Kaab smoothed the wide cotton belt she wore over her blouse, embroidered with the double-eagle pattern—Ixmoe's favorite— and thanked Xamanek that, if she had to face this scene, at least she could do so in civilized clothing.

"Where is it? Where's the wattle?" The creature's eyes widened as it began to search for the acacia-wood toy that Chuleb, chuckling, had moved just west of its line of sight. Making stupid faces, waving its fat little arms, it looked like nothing so much as a party guest playing Blinded Hunter. An *ugly* party guest. "Is it east? Southwest? Where's the wattle?"

Kaab looked up to the alcove in the red south wall at the goddess Ixchel, jade inlaid with cinnabar and feathered with gold, and repeated under her breath the blessing carved in intricate glyphs on the statue's forehead: *Protect us, Ixchel, from the spear by day and the jaguar by night. And,* she added, *babies.* She had no idea what mystical power they had to transform adults around them into drooling idiots, but she, for one, was relieved to be immune to it. Chuleb looked ridiculous.

Well, at least Auntie Saabim, at her dark cedar desk, a single *xukul nicte* flower over her east-facing ear, reading Trading records with the eye of a matriarch reviewing a treaty, seemed far enough away not to have succumbed.

The door to the room opened too forcefully and hit the wall behind it with a thud. The baby hiccupped. *Please,* Kaab thought, looking heavenward, *please do not begin wailing like a spider monkey.*

The baby, in its infinite mercy, deigned to grant her request.

But her uncle and aunt were looking at Dzan, standing in the doorway. "Forgive me, master. There is . . . a woman here to see you. She says she is the Duchess Tremontaine."

"Today?" Saabim exclaimed, and Kaab looked immediately in her direction. It was clear from the catch in Saabim's voice, the way Chuleb shifted his weight, the quick glance the two exchanged, that her aunt and uncle were surprised and, if not frightened, then unsettled at her arrival.

Chuleb rose, straightened the velvet of his Local-style doublet, white as the limestone stucco that covered Kaab's house in Binkiinha, and cleared his throat twice.

"She is waiting for you in your office, master."

"What does this woman want from us, Uncle?"

"That, Kaab, doesn't concern you," Aunt Saabim said.

"Forgive me, but as a first daughter of a first daughter of the Balam, I believe that a visit important to our interests here concerns me deeply. I would like to meet this duchess."

"Absolutely not," Chuleb said. "You made enough mischief in Tultenco. I think, for the moment, that you are safest here, watching the baby."

Ixchel preserve me. "But Uncle—"

"In our house, I think you'd best take our counsel." Kaab looked down, knowing when to stop. "Dzan, prepare chocolate."

Dzan grimaced. "I suppose you want me to ruin it by dumping it full of cream?"

"Cream?" said Kaab, mystified. "Why on earth would you put cream in chocolate?"

"Cream in a pitcher on the side," Saabim ordered from her desk, and then, to Kaab: "It is not our place to tell Locals what to do with the product we sell them."

Chuleb stepped to the western threshold of the room. "That," he said, turning back for a moment, "doesn't mean that I don't want to." And he closed the door behind him.

Kaab stood. Yes, she had made mistakes. But to prevent her from using her powers of observation to further the family's interests was nonsense. What could have so worried Chuleb and Saabim?

And she absolutely didn't want to watch the baby. She stood up.

Chuleb would be furious, but Kaab wasn't worth the maize it took to feed her if she let a trifle like that stop her, so after a quick change of clothes and a brief word with Dzan, reminding him of a certain indiscretion with Bapl the cook that she had witnessed a few days earlier and remarking on how unhappy Saabim would be were she to hear about it, she took a deep breath, held her arms out for the tray he carried, turned, and walked through the door.

". . . of course, my lady. Ah, this must be Dzan with the choco—" Chuleb stopped, his eyes widening almost imperceptibly and his lips pressing together only very slightly.

But she knew what her uncle looked like already. She was much more interested in the woman sitting across the desk from him, whose expression was so bland and impassive that it could only have been achieved under great control. This was not a woman to be underestimated.

Conversely, it would be quite wise to allow the woman to underestimate *her*.

"Forgive, master," Kaab said, thickening her accent until she sounded as she had when she was five, first encountering the spiky vowels of this language, "but Dzan been sent errand, warehouses. I serving chocolate instead." She deposited the tray on the north-wall table beside the niche altar to Xamanek, took hold of the chocolate grater, and turned to the duchess. "How you taking chocolate, mistress?"

The woman smiled at Chuleb as if he were the one who had spoken. "Since I am your guest, Master Balam, I should think it a wasted opportunity not to take chocolate in your people's own fashion. I understand that the merchants who banqueted with you recently were fortunate enough to do so."

"You are a kind woman," said Chuleb, "and a courageous one." The duchess inclined her head, and he turned to Kaab. "No cream. Chili, corn, and allspice."

The block of chocolate, solid in her hand, wove its odor through the sharp scents of the spices, filling Kaab with a sharp pang of longing for Binkiinha, which she might never see again, and for her mother, might they one day be reunited in the houses beneath the earth. But this was hardly the time for reverie. She served the duchess first, the cup delicate in her steady hand, and then Chuleb, looking him in the eye, neither of them betraying any emotion. Picking up the tray again, comforted by its weight, she went to stand by the door. The duchess paused, her cup halfway to her mouth, looked at Kaab, looked at Chuleb, raised a perfect eyebrow.

It would be much better if the duchess thought her incapable of understanding the implications of the gesture, but if she allowed her uncle to speak he would certainly send her out of the room, so she chose the smaller of two jaguars. "In our country, mistress, bad luck servant leave, chocolate not finished."

Chuleb's face was as impassive as the duchess's. "Have no fear, my lady," he said. "My servants are as silent as the grave." He looked over at Kaab mildly. "They know how severe my anger is when their foolishness leads them into error."

Her hand on her heart, she bowed to the duchess as Chuleb sipped his chocolate; the duchess gave a very small shrug and joined him.

The duchess took a sip of chocolate, shut her eyes. This woman could never have tasted a chili pepper in her life; the burning sensation in her mouth had to be frightening, and yet she smiled with satisfaction, as if the liquid pouring down her throat had exceeded all her hopes. No. Not a woman to be underestimated at all.

"Delicious," she said. "I must try serving chocolate this way at my next party." She put the cup down and breathed a barely audible sigh. "The duke was speaking to me the other day about some Council matter or other—a tedious subject between husband and wife, but he likes to try his thoughts aloud—when he happened to mention the crushing import tax burden under which you labor."

"Ah." Kaab admired Chuleb's composure. The tax was high, and the Kinwiinik had tried before, unsuccessfully, to get it lowered. The chocolate import tax ensured that it remained a luxury good in the City. But its inhabitants were developing more and more of a taste for it and would gladly buy more, if prices were reasonable. The Balam had had occasion to bewail how easy it would be to sell them a lower grade of chocolate for less; but Xanamwiinik taxes did not distinguish between the different varieties, and so all of it, from the rarest of Caana down to basic south coast street cacao, was priced accordingly.

"At first I was certain I had misheard him; it was the ridiculous number he gave that caught my attention to begin with. But when I asked him about it, he explained more thoroughly, and I must say I find it shocking."

"One might." Chuleb gave nothing away.

"And hardly a way to show courtesy to those who venture on the perilous seas to bring us such delights! As I say, I take no interest in politics, but I do think justice should be served. The duke has a great deal of influence in Council. I feel confident that, if I were to help him see how unjust the situation is, he would feel it his duty to exert that influence in an effort to do something about the tax."

This time it was Chuleb whose eyebrow rose. "That would be a feat indeed." The duchess's only reply was to incline her head. "If you were to extend such abundant courtesy to the Kinwiinik, as guests in your city we would be most grateful."

"It would be nothing. A matter, as I say, of justice."

"As you say." He toyed with a writing brush on the desk. "But in our country, a guest who is received with courtesy must show courtesy in return."

The duchess's eyes widened. "As if I would allow you to do anything in return!" Chuleb cocked his head, waiting. She took another sip of chocolate. "Yes," she said, "this drink is truly remarkable. But perhaps I was wrong about serving it at a party. I think few of my fellow nobles would appreciate this particular blend as I do."

"With all respect," Chuleb said, "I think you may be right."

Kaab kept her eyes on a mural celebrating the exploits of Kinwiinik heroines in the service. This was a game between two very skillful politicians. She must not betray herself.

"You come from far," the duchess said, "and have seen much of the world. I myself have never left these shores. Your knowledge of the ways of many peoples is much greater than mine. Tell me: How do folk in your country respond to gifts there?"

"That would depend on who the giver was. From a mother, a kiss! From a patron . . . good service."

"And from a friend?"

"Why, friendship in return. And a promise to share all other gifts equally, as good friends should."

"Ah." The duchess nodded. "I see your people, too, have a fine sense of justice. No wonder there is sympathy between us."

Chuleb leaned forward. "You honor me. I rejoice in it, and will speak of it tonight to my evening star, Ixsaabim."

"Oh?" A faint note of surprise suffused the duchess's voice.

"My wife." Chuleb was altogether too pleased with himself, Kaab thought. Love did strange things even to businessmen. "She is the second daughter of a first daughter of the Balam. I am but a minor noble in my own right, who had the fortune to marry into the first Trading family of the Kinwiinik. Ixsaabim is a woman well traveled, who knows the customs of many lands, and the value of friendship."

"She sounds delightful. I must take chocolate with her someday, your . . . evening star? What a poetic name. You must have many such endearments in your tongue. I'm sure our poor language cannot compare. Doubtless we could learn much from you."

Not a muscle in Kaab's face moved. But this was a slip. By one who could not possibly be given to slips. The duchess was very, very worried. About what, Kaab could not guess. Yet.

"Perhaps my lady will honor us with another visit someday?"

"I will await your invitation, Master Balam, and that of your people." To her credit, she drank the last of her fiery chocolate. Then, in a flurry of silk fine as a flower's petal, Duchess Tremontaine stood, setting the Kinwiinik cup down on the table beside her.

Uncle Chuleb rose with her. "It has been a very great honor to have you in my home, Madam Duchess."

"The honor has been mine. Few in the City have been so privileged as to taste chocolate of this singular quality."

Chuleb inclined his head, just like a Local. "To our great friends, we serve none but the finest of cacao."

"Then I hope," the duchess said, "that our friendship may long continue to prosper."

She looked around the room, her gaze passing over Kaab just as it passed over the furniture and the cotton feathered-serpent wall hangings. "It has been a delightful visit, Master Balam. Thank you for the invitation."

Kaab seized her opportunity, having no particular interest in being subjected to Chuleb's opinions of her subterfuge. "I show you door, mistress," she said.

"No," said her uncle. "Dzan has certainly returned from his errand by now. He will escort the duchess to the door. I wish to speak with you on another matter."

Kaab bowed again as the duchess walked through the door. Then she and Chuleb stood very still, looking at each other. The murmur of voices in the hallway, the opening and closing of the front door. How angry would he be? Silence. Stillness. This was becoming unbearable, but Kaab knew better than to move too soon. Ten more breaths. Ten more.

And then Chuleb exploded.

"What in the name of the gods and their parents were you thinking?" he shouted. "That woman is as subtle as a jaguar in the night! I invited her to come tomorrow, and she arrived today to catch me off guard. I have no idea what she really wants, but you can be certain that she would happily slit every Kinwiinik throat in the City if it suited her purpose."

"Which is why," Kaab countered, her chin high, "it was better that I be here."

"I have half a mind to expel you from the service and make you chief nursemaid to all the children for the rest of your life. If you've imperiled our trade here—"

This was not a serious threat. She knew it, and she knew that he knew she knew it. "Don't be ridiculous. If she saw me at all, she saw a barbarian servant. When it comes to dealing with her, you'll be better off with my help than without it. You appear, for example, not to have caught her mistake."

This brought him up short. "Which was?" he said after a pause.

"When you told her you would have to ask Auntie Saabim about her proposal, she began to chatter. She had not thought Kinwiinik women to have authority in our houses. And if she didn't bother to learn before she came that the Balam are nobility, then she believes us unimportant and more easily dealt with than is the case. She may be a jaguar, but she is not the jaguar you think she is."

Chuleb said nothing; he only stood, fuming.

"Fine," he snapped finally. "But if you're going to impersonate a servant then you can do so for the rest of the day. This office is a disaster. I want it as spotless by dinner as if Chaacmul had washed it with the sea."

It would not do to show her glee. She schooled her face until she resembled a statue guarding the royal tomb. "As you wish."

Micah was exhausted.

People kept getting angry at her. Sometimes it was when she told them why they were wrong. Sometimes it was when she asked them questions; sometimes it was when she *didn't* ask them questions. Sometimes it was when she answered their questions. Sometimes it was when she did what they'd told her to do. She wasn't acting any differently, but for some reason things that seemed to be fine on the farm were not fine here, and she often wanted to squeeze herself into a tiny ball in the corner and disappear.

But the exhaustion and the tension were worth it, because when they weren't getting mad at her for doing or saying the wrong thing, the people here were talking about numbers and calculations and shapes and patterns and all the incredible ideas that her family seemed not to care about at all—not just talking about them but loving them, respecting them, understanding how beautiful they were. And it turned out that those ideas, the things she spent all her time thinking about, had names! Seven-siders were actually called heptagons, for example, and twelve-siders were dodecagons, but that was just the beginning. The shapes and everything else made her mind move faster and faster and faster, until her body was filled with light. And if she had gained the key to so much in such a short time, how much would she learn if she stayed longer? In three days Uncle Amos would start sowing the early peas for spring, and she felt both that she wanted to be there to help and that she wanted to stay here, which was awful. That was another exhausting aspect of being here. Every time she tried to figure it out, her head started to throb in time with her heart, and she had to do numbers until she could calm herself down.

Micah reached for a pen and a sheet of foolscap.

Dear Aunt Judith and Uncle Amos, she wrote. *Sorry I'm not back yet I love it here even tho the people are confusing sometimes. Twelve-siders are actually called something I don't know how to spell yet, but they have a name and now I know it. Don't forget to plant the peas in three days I will see you soon. Love, Micah.*

"But if you despise him so," said the duke from the blue damask couch by the window, as Rafe paced around the library of Tremontaine House, his long stride made longer by impatience, "then why continue attending his lectures?"

"If I'd known I was going to have to pay for my chocolate by rehearsing my unpleasant and embarrassing career in the College of Natural Science, I don't think I would have stepped into your carriage, after all."

The chocolate had been amazing, better than the finest he'd ever tasted at his father's table. If this was what Tremontaine served to casual visitors, Rafe couldn't imagine what he brought out for special occasions. And somehow it had only made Rafe's mood worse.

"The chocolate is gratis. The rehearsal is entirely at your discretion."

Rafe stopped pacing and sighed. He was above rudeness for the sake of rudeness, or he ought to be. But he was distracted by the exquisite cut of the duke's black breeches against the deep red velvet of the couch. "He's brilliant, for one thing," he finally brought himself to say. "His take on planar geometry, his work on elliptical motion, his commentary on Delphin's mapping of the stars. He thought I was brilliant too, until I realized that the College's guiding principle—and his—was wrong." The delicacy of the man's hands as he brought his chocolate cup to his lips was extraordinary. Rafe turned away from Tremontaine to face the crackling fire. "He's also the only one left."

"Pardon?"

Rafe sighed, defeated. His shoulders slumped. He ought to turn back around and face the duke again, but for some reason he was reluctant to do so. "I started with de Bertel, when I first came to the University," he said to the fire, and rubbed his hands together. "Then I abandoned him for what seemed greener pastures. But gradually I've gone through most of the other magisters, breaking with each one as I grew more and more cognizant of their mistake. I ended up back with de Bertel, who forgave my betrayal at first, but now that I have the knowledge to back up my intuitions, it's worse with him than it ever was with any of the others. Today's fracas was the inevitable result of the last several years of my life."

"And what did it concern?"

He turned back to the duke, and his eyes suddenly filled with the sight of cheekbones. "The fact—not the idea, my lord, but the *fact*—that the earth revolves around the sun. I've been driving myself mad trying to prove it, but I can't. No matter how many observations I make, no matter how many measurements, the math never works out right." His hands had started moving again, in ever-larger sweeps and circles. "Or it does, but only because I add some lunatic number of epicycles, which simply compounds the problem I'm trying to solve."

"Which is?"

"Our current, stupid, *stupid* cosmology has the universe rotating horizontally with respect to the earth, but also moving on an epicycle oblique to that orbital rotation, so—" Rafe felt himself begin to step forward, thought better of it, stopped.

"Never mind. Go back to the magisters. You've worked with *most* of the others?"

"The ones whose lectures I never attended are idiots."

"Then I don't understand. How were you planning to find *anyone* to sit on your examination board who would pass you, let alone sponsor you for a mastership?" The duke turned over a questioning hand palm up, his wrist framed by elegant lace. "If every magister in Natural Science either hates you or is an idiot?"

"Oh, I had it all worked out," said Rafe, closing his eyes. "The examiners were going to be Chauncey, Martin, and Featherstone. Chauncey is an idiot, but I'm almost certain he agrees with me, alone of the magisters, though he wouldn't dare say it out loud. Martin is *also* an idiot, but he'd pass me if he thought it would increase his chances of getting me into his bed, which, by the by, it wouldn't; I may be free with my favors, but I don't do charity work. And Featherstone hates me, but he's a coward and invariably votes with the majority. He'd vote with the majority if they proposed to draw and quarter his daughter." He opened his eyes, only for them to be drawn again to the breeches. "Which means that if I had Chauncey and Martin, then I'd have him, too."

"I see. But with de Bertel on your committee—"

"Exactly! That was the *only* possible combination of magisters."

"And so you think your chances of passing the exam are shot."

Rafe emitted something that bore as little resemblance to a laugh as he could manage. "Oh, how delicately put." He couldn't keep the bitterness out of his voice. Finally he strode toward the duke, who stood as he approached the couch. "No, you oaf, I don't *think* it." He tossed his head. "That was the *only* permutation of examiners that would have allowed me to pass. And now you've made it impossible, and I'll never found my school, and my life is ruined, and it's *all your fault!*" He was standing quite close to Tremontaine now, breathing hard, his face crimson, his index finger stabbing the offending air.

The duke seemed poised to step forward. Rafe, filled with an inexplicable sense of alarm, immediately crossed to the other side of the library and made a careful inventory of the books on the shelves before him. He heard Tremontaine walk to the chair by the fire and settle himself. "Tell me about this school you want to found."

Rafe turned again but stayed where he was. "Describe your education, my lord."

"Why, I had a tutor until I was . . . I don't know, fourteen?" Tremontaine shrugged, the emerald green velvet of his doublet broadening his shoulders. "No, sixteen. When I came to the City. And since then I've merely read whatever has piqued my interest."

"And describe the education of your architect, say, or your portrait painter."

"Grammar school until twelve or so. If the parents are comfortable. Maybe even a tutor."

Rafe seemed unable to look away from the duke's shoulders. "And then?"

"Apprenticeship, I suppose. To learn a trade. To make a living."

"Well, what if his education continued?" Rafe wrenched his eyes from Tremontaine's shoulders to make a very close examination of the crown molding along the ceiling. "What if there were school at fifteen, at sixteen, seventeen? For people without tutors who wanted to keep learning without going to University? Or to be better prepared than most of the sluggards who start there now?" Rafe's head turned back to the duke. "And here's the beauty of it, the real point: If I got to them early enough, then the University's antiquated, stultifying point of view could never take hold in the first place, and educated men would finally approach the world with the proper perspective!"

"Which is?"

Rafe sighed, his hands beseeching, his face alight. "Oh, my lord, there isn't enough time left in the week! A new day is coming—has come! For hundreds of years, Natural Science has consisted of exactly two things, and two things only: Rastin, and commentaries on Rastin." The duke's eyes had darkened, Rafe noticed, his face limned by the fire behind him.

"Ah yes. I thought Chesney's *On the Velocity of Falling Bodies* was particularly ingenious."

Rafe snorted. "Certainly, if by 'ingenious' you mean 'putrescent.' Do you have it here?" The duke pointed, and Rafe crossed swiftly in front of him, scanning the books on the shelves as he approached them. He pulled a book out of the wall and gestured with it. "Chesney was *wrong*." He pulled out another book. "Fontanus *wrong*." Another. "Chickering was wrong too, though at least in an interesting direction."

"Say more." Tremontaine stood up and walked over to take the books from Rafe's hands. When their fingers brushed, Rafe drew his away with a hiss. Good god, were the man's hands iron pulled from a fiery forge?

Rafe crossed quickly to take a seat on another couch. "What's Rastin's central principle?" he said, looking toward the books on the shelves to his left.

"Oh my. It's been years since I've read Rastin. Let me see . . . It's the mind and the senses, yes? Nothing in the mind but what is in the senses . . . no, that's not right." Well, the Tremontaine library certainly had a varied collection. Trevor here. *Geographical Exotica* there. Delgardie. "Would you stoop to reminding a poor pupil?"

Rafe saw no reason to stop looking at the books. "Nothing exists in the world, my lord, that does not first exist in the mind and in the senses."

"Please be so good as to stop calling me that." Tremontaine sat on the other end of the couch. Rafe turned to face him but immediately cast his eyes on the space between them on the couch, where the blue of the damask shone vividly between violet stripes.

"Then what should I call you?" Rafe looked up. The duke's eyes were a deep cornflower blue. Rafe tried for lightness. "My friend Joshua calls me pigeon, but somehow I don't think that's right. Hawk, perhaps?"

"Most certainly not." Tremontaine's voice was almost offended, the curve in his lips slight. Rafe felt feverish. "Call me"—the duke cleared his throat and paused—"do you even know my first name?"

"You mean it isn't My?" No, the eyes weren't just deep blue. There was a touch of the green sea in them as well.

The smile broadened. "Would that I were so lucky. No. It's William."

"All right." Rafe shifted toward him on the couch. Why on earth should he feel a small thrill run through his chest? "*William.* So Rastin's point is that reason is our guide in the search for truth, and observation nothing more than her handmaiden." His hands illustrated his eloquence, animated, urgent. "The idea of isolating nature, of *experimenting*, to discover whether the conclusions to which reason has led us have anything to do with reality, is looked upon with horror. Observe nature out of its context, say Chesney and Chickering and Fontanus and all the rest of them, and it ceases to be either nature or an appropriate subject for Natural Science."

"And you feel differently."

Rafe swallowed. "How could any thinking man *not*?" His voice was thick with something that had to be frustration. "The earth orbiting the sun is only the beginning."

"But aren't you doing the same thing, coming up with an idea about the truth first and then using observation as its handmaiden?"

Rafe inhaled sharply. William smelled of apricots and cinnamon and something else he couldn't name. "Absolutely not. The endeavor I'm engaged in is completely different."

"Really?" William's voice was mild. "Because it sounds to me as if you were indulging in exactly the failure of logic you find in your university doctors."

Rafe's breath caught in his throat, and he sat up, very straight and very still. Suddenly Joshua's voice rang in his head. *You tend to ruin things for yourself.* But his tongue would not be held.

"As if you cared at all anyway," he said, his voice low, "about any of it. No, you just want to waltz on down to the University, slum it there until your moronic amusement is sated, stop for a moment and destroy the students, and come back to your fine house on the fine Hill to drink fine chocolate."

He stared at William, his nostrils flared. In one fluid motion, William reached out, put his hand on the back of Rafe's head, and drew their lips together.

For some time the spitting crackle of the fire was the only sound to be heard in the library of the Duke Tremontaine.

"I've always envied University men their hair," said William at last, softly, fingering the leather tie that sent Rafe's hair neatly down the nape of his neck. "I keep hoping that at some point long hair will come into fashion on the Hill."

"How long have you lived on the Hill?"

"Twenty of my last thirty-seven years."

"*Someone* is an optimist," said Rafe.

William's only response was to rearrange a stray lock of hair over Rafe's forehead. "This is not at all the direction I was expecting our conversation to turn."

"Nor I." Rafe's tone was casual, but he still felt as if he'd drunk far too much chocolate far too late in the day. "You still haven't told me which way you voted today."

"Other matters seemed more pressing."

Rafe shifted his balance and a slight gasp escaped William's mouth. "And now seem more pressing still." This earned him a chuckle. "Nonetheless, I would very much like to know."

"I suppose I could be persuaded to tell you."

"And how might I do that?" He repositioned his hand. "Would this help?"

"Oh, most definitely. But what would be even more persuasive would be to . . . yes, that. Oh yes."

And for a time Rafe was unable to speak, and then it was William's breath that had grown ragged. "But I am discomfiting you," said Rafe, his eyes wide and innocent. "Forgive me, good my lord. I don't know what could possibly have possessed me."

William's fingers moved to unbutton Rafe's robe and allow it to fall, to untie and toss his shirt to the floor, forgotten, to run smooth hands up and down his skin, caressing peaks of muscle and valleys of sinew.

Rafe leaned back on the couch, closed his eyes, and smiled the small smile of the cat who has come upon a dish it thought empty and found it full of milk. His pulse slowed and he breathed more easily, now that he was back on familiar ground; this was a pose that he knew well. Joshua would be scandalized and delighted in equal parts. To say nothing, of course, of how Rafe might make use of what was happening to influence the choice of magisters on his committee. This man could probably exclude de Bertel with a flutter of his little finger. Smiling, Rafe extended his arms above his head, his eyes half closed, as William's mouth found chest, collarbone, neck, throat, earlobe—

And then stopped. Rafe opened his eyes. William had pulled away from him.

"Where are you?" asked William.

"What do you mean?" Rafe, languid, pulled William's hand lazily to his mouth, tasting on his fingertips the slight, faint bitterness of the chocolate they had so recently grated. Rafe's eyes were heavy, his lids half closed, his face relaxed in an expression that frequent and effective use had made second nature. "I'm right in front of you."

William withdrew his hand and Rafe's brow creased. "No, you're not. This is somebody different. Where's the man who ran to my bookshelves two minutes ago to show me how putrescent my books were?" Rafe's skin felt warm, and his breath began to quicken. "He's the one I want to be with." William was looking at him with disapproval. "Not you."

Rafe jerked as if he'd been punched, his stomach tightening, his hands clenching. *"God!"* he said, and stood up, his lips twitching. *"Tell me how in the Seven Hells you voted!"*

"This," said William, "is much more to my taste," and enfolded him again, and this time the feeling was one with which Rafe was entirely unfamiliar. All thought of de Bertel and Joshua and the movement of the heavenly bodies left him, to be replaced by the greedy hands on his shoulders, on his back, lower, the wet breath quick between the two of them, the delicious sting of teeth on his lips.

And then he leaped back at William, devouring everything he could touch, as if he were starving, fast, quick, careless, lingering nowhere, taking in as much as possible, with an abandon that frightened him, fingers splayed, now standing, now lush carpet, soft as a kitten, on his back, skin hot as fever.

"This?" William's voice was quiet but steady.

"Yes."

"And here?"

Rafe stiffened. "I only—I'm always the one who—"

"Shh." William stroked his face. "Allow this."

And Rafe could only melt, and they moved together, and over the heat in his belly he started making sounds he'd never heard before, and William's arms tight around him always, keeping him safe and releasing him at the same time, and oh, the pain, so sweet in surrender, and finally he gave a small cry and shuddered and William stiffened and there was paradise and then again the room was silent except for the sound of the fire and of the breath of the two men as it gradually slowed.

After some minutes, William rolled over onto his side and caressed Rafe's face with the feathery touch of two fingers. "This school. How are you going to go about starting it?"

"Once I've figured out where to get the money to do it, I'll rent rooms somewhere."

"Who else will teach there? And how will people find out about it?"

"I don't know; they'll just . . ." When no answer came to him, he brought William's fingers to his lips instead.

"It's a compelling idea, but you seem to be somewhat vague on the specifics." Rafe said nothing. "Perhaps I can be of some assistance."

"Oh?"

"Well. I can't fund the whole thing myself, but I can certainly help. And the Tremontaine estates are not a school, but I do have some little experience managing things. For example, you—"

Rafe tried to focus on the school, but the odors of apricot and cinnamon and sweat in his nose made it impossible. "Time enough for that later."

"To be sure."

"In the meantime, is it possible *now* to tell me how you voted?" Flirtation rather than a real question; it was obvious the man with him had stood against the measure.

"Well," said William. A pause. Longer. Finally: "I voted for the measure." A sudden dizziness came upon Rafe even though he was lying down. He tried to sit up, failed. "I thought we couldn't trust the doctors produced by the University if they could manipulate their teachers like so many pieces in a game of Shesh." The words kept coming, tripping over themselves. "But after listening to you, I see I was wrong. I'll start working immediately to reverse the decision." William swallowed. "If I can." Silence. "The Board of Governors doesn't meet again until the fall, though." More silence. "So nothing will happen until at least next year."

Rafe finally stood, rigid. His mouth worked soundlessly for a moment until he was able to speak. "My lord." He reached for cold rage, fumbled for it in the whirling tumult of his emotions. Found anger of a sort, but only mixed with agitation, confusion, doubt. "I fear I must take my leave. I'm late for . . . I have a . . ." And without finishing the sentence, he put on his clothes and left the room.

He staggered down the grand stairs, the paintings on the wall of Tremontaines past in their gilded frames mocking him, the odor of salmon wafting up from the ducal kitchens, the smooth grain of the wood balustrade under his hand, the creaks and sighs of the ancient house settling mocking him. Oh, how great a fool he had been played for! His face tightened, his chest constricted, his skin hot, his breath unsteady, and he all but collided with a woman in silk and lace ascending the stairs.

"Pardon me," she said, and even he could hear the frost in her voice.

Rafe found the rage he'd been searching for. "I don't think I shall!" he cried. "Why should I? You're all the same, toying with our lives and then discarding us when you grow bored and going back to your damned *chocolate*! The world is changing, you know, and soon none of this"—he gestured wildly at the grandeur around them—"is going to matter at all! If it even lasts."

She paled, which only spurred him on.

"That would just serve you right, wouldn't it?" he said. "I hope you lose every last stick of furniture you have, I hope you have to wander the streets, begging for scraps of food like the rest of us, while the people with power turn *you* into *their* playthings, your hopes and dreams and desires nothing but cards in a tiresome game played for minnows!"

She swayed slightly on the stairs, her face completely white. A meaningless victory, but a victory nonetheless. Rafe grinned viciously, ran down the rest of the stairs and out the door into the street, where servants and coachmen looked curiously at him as he passed.

Her meeting with the awful student was not, to the sorrow of the Duchess Tremontaine, the most difficult moment she was to face this day. She was already on edge about what would happen to her resources, even to her marriage, should her efforts with the Kinwiinik fail to bear fruit: for to lose Highcombe, the great Tremontaine property she had staked as surety against her secret but substantial interests in the ill-fated trading ship *Everfair* would be a humiliation too great to contemplate.

But when her maid handed her the sealed paper a gentleman had given her, a gentleman waiting below, who had vowed that it would ensure that the duchess would wish also to see him, and Diane opened it, she was utterly unprepared for the shock of terror that ran through her body.

The gentleman—if one could call him that—was shown up. He was wearing a most vulgar striped jacket of which he seemed inordinately proud, but his bright hair, pretty face, and nonchalant manner made it clear that he expected to charm her, as he showed her a certain object that had long been in his family's possession; an object, he was sure, of the greatest interest to her.

The duchess held it in her hand. And in that moment she knew that, however precarious her previous position had been, she stood now on the edge of a blade sharper than that wielded by any swordsman. Before, she had been facing humiliation. What Diane de Tremontaine faced now was total destruction.

The gentleman asked one question, and, without hesitation, the duchess gave him the only answer possible.

And so it was with a light heart and a light step that Benjamin Hawke left Tremontaine House and walked in the direction of his own, whistling again the air that Ixkaab Balam had overheard earlier that day in Riverside.

But the Duchess Tremontaine, her hands trembling, sat frozen in a brocade chair that—along with every other part of a life that she cherished—she might very soon see for the last time.

Doctor Volney was talking about triangles, which were Micah's fourth-favorite regular shape, after octagons, hexagons, and triskaidecagons. Of course, she had a separate list for irregular polygons; you'd think that would go without saying, but then one day she had been drawing with a stick in the dirt out in front of the house and Aunt Judith had asked her whether she liked the regular heptagon better than the concave hexagon (of course, Aunt Judith hadn't known their names then, and neither had Micah) and had been absolutely unable to understand why it was a ridiculous question, so there you go.

"And so we see," said Volney, "that the ratio of the length of each side to the sine of its opposite angle is the same as the ratio of the length of each other side to the sine of *its* opposite angle. Which means what, in terms of our earlier discussion? Milner?"

"Given the derivations we've just been through, sir, the ratio of the length of any given side of the triangle to the sine of its opposite angle is twice the radius of the circumscribed circle."

"Good for you." Micah looked at Rafe on the bench beside her, about to grin, and then realized his mouth was still scrunched up and his eyebrows drawn together, just like when he'd walked into the room, and that meant he was upset about something.

She would ask him later what it was. Because right now she was just too happy to think about it. Of all the lectures Rafe had taken her to, Volney's delighted her the most, because it was Volney who talked most about the kinds of things she had always spent all her time thinking about. *Sine. Cosine. Tangent.* The very words tasted delicious.

"It should be clear, then, that, if we know the radius of the circumscribed circle, all we need to learn the length of any side is the angle opposite."

Circumscribed circle. This, *this* was why she was willing to put up with people who got upset with her. Amos and Judith and Seth never talked about circumscribed circles.

"Given that," Volney continued, "suppose a right triangle with an additional angle of sixty degrees. Suppose further that the radius of the triangle's circumscribed circle is seven and one part in two. Now, lay the triangle we have hypothesized on a sphere. What then is the length of the side of the triangle opposite the other angle?"

Silence as students around the room scratched on their slates. Micah caught sight of what Rafe was writing and was surprised to see that he was on the wrong track. She grunted softly and, when he looked up, gestured to his calculations and shook her head, at which point he stopped writing, his hand hovering in the air with the pen.

Finally a voice from somewhere in the room called out, "Three and three parts in four." Micah sighed: This was exactly the same error Rafe had been making.

"Just right, Pearson."

Micah's brows knit in consternation. Why was Doctor Volney teaching them something wrong?

"The trick here is in recognizing—since we started with a right triangle, a known radius, and an included angle—that the hypotenuse of a circumscribed right triangle is always equal to the circle's radius."

Micah began breathing hard. She pulled urgently on Rafe's sleeve, but she knew from the expression on his face—confusion was an easy one to recognize—that she was on her own. She felt an immense pressure somewhere deep within her. She knew this feeling well and she hated it fiercely, but she could never seem to control it. The pressure built and built and built. She had to do something. The pressure was almost crushing.

"Now, if we assume that—"

"No!" She knew it was the wrong thing to do, but she couldn't help herself. "That's wrong!"

And now everyone in the room was looking at her. She wanted to make herself tiny, or run away, or disappear into thin air. The horrible pressure was now joined by a hideous embarrassment. Her breath came even faster, and she began rocking back and forth very quickly, her eyes wide with fright.

Rafe put his arms around her and squeezed hard. "Want to do angles?" he said, and she nodded, grateful. "Tell me the angle in an equilateral triangle," he whispered in her ear.

"Sixty," she said at once, deeply grateful to have something else to focus on.

"In an equilateral pentagon."

"One hundred eight."

"Square."

"Ninety."

"Breathe, breathe slowly. Hexagon."

"One hundred twenty." She saw the shapes as he named them, and, though her breath was still heavy and her hands gripped the bench no less tightly, at least she was able to stop rocking.

"What, if I may be so bold to ask," said Doctor Volney, "is your name?" She knew the answer but somehow couldn't speak to say it.

"Octagon."

"One hundred thirty-five."

"Breathe. Decagon."

"One hundred forty-four." Micah remembered telling Rafe that this helped her. She also remembered that if she breathed deeply it helped her calm down, so she inhaled. Exhaled. Inhaled.

"Did I fail to speak clearly?" Doctor Volney again. She needed to answer him. "What is your name, boy?"

She could breathe again now, so she could speak. She shrugged Rafe off, and he stopped whispering. She could do this. "Micah, sir. Micah Heslop."

"And, Master Heslop, would you be so good as to honor us by explaining yourself?"

That one was easy too.

"Your conclusion. It's wrong." She was glad he had asked her. Immediately a small pulse of relief diminished her urge to rock.

You could have heard a feather fall. "Oh? How so?"

But she had to continue; speaking made it better. "How can you not *see* it?" She couldn't keep the frustration out of her voice. "The numbers you're talking about are right if the triangle is on a flat surface. But if you're on a sphere, the surface changes, and the number of angles in any triangle would have to add up to more than one hundred eighty, which is impossible. You can't lay a flat triangle perfectly on a sphere without breaking it somewhere, and then it's not a triangle anymore. The question doesn't even make *sense*."

There. She was still agitated, but her breathing, if fast, was at least even, and most of the pressure had gone. She looked up at Rafe and saw that his eyes had gone wide.

"Damn me for a dead swordsman's lover!" he said.

"In twenty years of teaching at this University," Doctor Volney said, his expression yet again altered, this time to something with narrowed eyes she found difficult to comprehend, "no student of mine has ever had the brazen effrontery to contradict me with such abysmal insults. You, Master Heslop, may take your leave, and you needn't bother to come to future lectures of mine."

This was confusing. "I'd rather stay. I mean, a lot of the things you talk about are pretty obvious, but there's also lots that I've never thought about before." She felt that something more was expected of her. "It's interesting to be here."

Without a word, the magister stalked down the aisle between the benches and out of the room.

Immediately, the silence in the room was broken by the rush of dozens of voices. The pressure she felt broke with it, mercifully, but people were still looking at her.

"Can you believe it?"

"What on earth was he talking about? Angles aren't different on spheres."

"Whether they are or no, Volney has had that coming for a long time."

It was all too loud, and she turned, mute, panicked, to Rafe.

"You," he said, with a grin on his face as wide as the river that flowed past Uncle Amos's farm, "are a prince among men—nay, a king, an emperor, a god. This calls for kidney pie. And a great deal of beer."

"No," said Micah.

"Oh?"

"Not kidney pie. Tomato."

"As long as the beer comes with it."

Kaab pushed open the dark, weathered tavern door. Chuleb's office was passably clean, but when she'd gone back to Riverside in search of Tess the Hand, the sun-haired girl had still been nowhere in evidence. "She might be up at the University buying paper," someone had said, so here Kaab was at the Inkpot. Not unlike a Riverside tavern: the same dark, heavy beams hanging overhead, the same tables scarred from years of abuse, though what littered these was not just mugs but also tiny bowls that looked to contain spices of various kinds: cumin, aniseed, fennel. This place was much fuller—only appropriate, given the time of day—and its clientele was composed almost entirely of long-haired young men wearing black robes in varying degrees of repair talking very, very seriously. The serving girls here were also less attractive.

Tess was nowhere to be seen, but there was the amusing boy, the merchant's son she had met the day before her welcome banquet a week earlier, along with his friend, the short, stocky, easily flustered girl Kaab remembered from the protest the same day.

"Ho, there, Kaab!" the boy called, and leaped up so enthusiastically as she walked to his table that he might have been a dancer at the Festival of the Silent Ones. "Micah has just answered the greatest conundrum of the age!"

Kaab slid onto the bench as Micah moved down to make room for her. "What's that? Discovering why you Landers prefer your food without flavor?" She looked around her. Two boys at the next table were staring at each other, rapt, and talking softly as if every word were a treasure. One of them had hair almost as red as that of Tess the Hand.

"Funny. No. He has solved the mystery of the heavenly bodies!" It still wasn't clear to Kaab why he might be referring to Micah as "he"—perhaps it involved some strange Xanamwiinik custom with which Kaab was unfamiliar.

"I do not understand."

"Well." Rafe's brow creased. "This will be difficult to explain."

"Try." *Without ordering me a beer,* she thought.

"All right," he said. "But you need a beer." Kaab sighed as he waved to the barmaid. "A beer for my friend!" He turned around, spoke to the boy at the next table who did not have red hair, accepted something he offered, turned back to her, and began to speak. "It may be hard to conceptualize," he said, holding up the orange he'd taken, "but, though we *seem* to be walking on flat ground, the earth itself, taken as a whole, is a three-dimensional body." He began turning the orange this way and that. "Now, my teachers at the University believe, as has been thought for three hundred years and more, that the sun is also such a body, and that it, along with the other fixed stars, orbits the earth. I have recently come to think, however, that—"

"I am sorry," she said. His words made no sense whatsoever. "You believe that the sun circles the earth?"

"Well, I don't," he said. "But everybody else. The idiots at the University."

Xamanek's light, how barbaric could he possibly think she was? "But *everyone* knows that the matter is exactly reversed."

His mouth dropped open so wide it looked like the lip of a small bean pot. He put the orange down next to his beer. "Everyone knows? You mean to say that heliocentrism is an *accepted tenet* in Kinwiinik society?" The boy with red hair threw his head back in joyous laughter.

The barmaid arrived with the beer and set it down in front of Kaab. Perhaps she could spill it. "The University is a center of learning, no?"

"According to the University."

And these people thought *her* home was uncivilized! "The University needs perhaps to reconsider its opinion of itself."

"You'll find no argument from me on that point." He shook his head in apparent wonder. "Anyway. I'm the only one here who believes what you say everybody in your land knows—even my friends think I'm a crackpot about this—and I've been trying to prove it, but I could never get the math to work out right. And now, because of my brilliant friend here and his geometrical insight, I know exactly what to do!"

"Well," said Micah as Rafe lifted his mug, "not *exactly*. All I said was that it couldn't be a triangle anymore. To know *exactly* what to do you'd have to figure out what it actually *was*, and if that's the same every time or not, so I guess you'd have to start by measuring the—"

"The details," said Rafe airily, "are immaterial. The point is, I've been doing all my calculations as if the heavenly bodies were revolving in a horizontal plane. But, cretin that I am, it never occurred to me to question the most basic assumption of Rastin's cosmology—but get rid of that and posit great circles that can start at any arbitrary point, and the numbers, at least those from last night, can be made to fit, because if you find the right oblique angle you can replicate the ecliptic! Now all we have to do is find that angle!" He glanced at Kaab's beer mug. "Don't you like it?"

Kaab brought the mug to her mouth and pretended to sip it. "It is delicious."

"The problem," said Rafe, "is that I could only make it work by positing another ecliptic, which—"

"I understand perfectly," said Kaab, not understanding at all. It was clear he was talking about the mysteries of the Four Hundred Siblings. But beyond that he was using too many words she didn't know and, she suspected, would never need to know.

Rafe shook his head. "I still can't believe it. *You* know the universe is heliocentric. Will wonders never cease?"

That was it. Evidently there was no end to these Xanamwiinik's arrogance. She would put him in his place. But first she would get rid of this disgusting drink. She reached for her beer and knocked it casually into her lap, making sure to start as the cold liquid hit her.

"Oh no! Here, I'll get you a new one."

"There is no need whatsoever." But as the beer began to run down the dress, and the petticoat against her legs grew sodden, she thought, *No more. Locals or no Locals, Auntie Saabim or no Auntie Saabim, I'm not going out dressed like this again.* "But as far as the earth circling the sun—of course we understand that. If we didn't, how do you think we would find our way here?"

The two boys had stopped talking entirely and were now only gazing, rapt, into each other's faces. Then Rafe began laughing and did not stop.

"What's so funny?" asked Micah.

"I must be drunk," he said finally.

"Why?" said Kaab.

"Because the first thing that occurred to me was that my father would be particularly interested in finding this out. And when I find myself caring about what my father would be particularly interested in, something has gone *dreadfully* wrong. Tell me how it works, navigating from there to here."

Kaab froze. How could she have been so stupid? This boy's father was a *merchant*. He made his living through people *sailing* places where he could buy and sell goods. And if these Xanamwiinik ever learned how to sail west, what would happen when they reached the shores of her homeland? When they found the cacao trees? What would that do to the Balam monopoly? Dear Chaacmul, what would it do to the Kinwiinik's ability to withstand the aggression of the Tullan Empire? She was a fool not to have considered this. She would be expelled from the service for sure, the Tullan would invade, and she would join Ixmoe in the houses under the earth far sooner than she'd expected.

"Oh," Kaab said hurriedly, "I do not know anything about the navigation. It is a matter only for the men of our people, the sailors. I have simply heard my father speak of such matters." Damn it!

The boy was too perceptive by half; his eyes had narrowed at her sudden discomfort. "And what, when he speaks of them, does he say?"

Xamanek's light! "I pay no attention. It doesn't interest me. I am sorry."

Rafe turned to Micah. "How difficult could it be, to understand how angles are affected when transferred from flat surfaces to spheres? What if we—"

Ah, here was something! If not a way out, then at least a stalling tactic. "Wait," she said, "your people think the earth is a *sphere?*"

Rafe and Micah stared at her. "You said the earth was round," said Rafe.

"Of course I did. To make sure you didn't think I believed it was flat. If you will forgive me, your people sometimes have very odd notions about mine. But of course, we Kinwiinik know it is a . . . Oh dear! I do not know the word. It's so complicated." She thought for a moment, took the orange from the table, and threw it hard at the ground, where it landed with a satisfyingly dull thud. She reached down, picked it up, and squeezed it in the middle to make something that looked like an egg. An orange egg, cracked and dripping juice. "It is like this." Would he believe her? *Protect me, Ixchel,* she thought, *from the spear by day and the jaguar by night. And from the consequences of my own folly.*

"*Ellipsoid?*" Oh, thank the immortal gods for the look of bemusement on his face! "The earth is ellipsoid?"

She shrugged apologetically. "That is what my father and the other men of the family say."

"Will wonders never cease?"

He believed her! Oh, thank Ahkin! She felt her heart began to slow.

Micah was looking at Rafe with fierce attention. "Ellipsoid? That's an ellipse in three dimensions?"

"It is." He drained his beer. The two boys at the other table had finally disappeared. She smiled to think what they must be doing. And what she would like to do if she ever found Tess.

"Well, Micah," Rafe said, "perhaps if the spirit takes you to discover how all this works, my father will finally have a son he's proud of." He stood up. "Thank you again, a thousand times. I'm off to take my nightly measurements." He grinned. "Now I'll actually be able to *use* them!" And with that, he was gone.

"I don't like Rafe's father," Micah said. "He sounds mean. Is your father nice?"

"Yes," Kaab said. She absently wrung out the beer in her skirt. But she'd have to make sure that neither Saabim nor Chuleb ever found out about this conversation.

Rafe stood at the dusty intersection, perplexed. He'd been standing there for some minutes, and he couldn't understand in the least why he wasn't turning left. In that direction, after all, lay his lodgings, his orrery, his measurements, his calculations, and ultimately the path to his school—now closer than ever, thanks to Micah's brilliance.

So why wasn't he moving?

It wasn't as if the time he had spent on the Hill earlier had been anything out of the ordinary—his partner's rank excepted; and he cared nothing for rank—until the hideous betrayal at the end. Nevertheless, there were other things to consider. If he played his hand carefully, he might so inflame the duke with desire for him—unfulfilled desire, after the afternoon's stab in the back—that neither de Bertel nor his father's unwillingness to help him set up his school would pose any further threat to his plans. In which case William should be unable to find him for at least a few days. There was, in other words, no reason whatsoever not to follow Joshua's instructions not to ruin this for himself. Besides, there was his oath to consider.

And yet here he stood.

Finally he sighed, set his shoulders, and turned right, toward the Bridge to the Hill.

"I wonder," he said when the door opened at his destination, "whether the duke is in."

Not far away—not far at all; in the same house, in fact—the Duchess Tremontaine sat in her boudoir.

A letter from the Trader Master Chuleb lay on her escritoire. *My lady,* it read. *My evening star shines bright upon our friendship. We long to share with you the finest cacao that friends can offer, as long as friends can share as equals. But you have stars of your own to consider. How brightly might they be convinced to shine down upon not only yourself, but upon those you honor with your friendship? And how should we know their light? Perhaps you can advise us, as strangers in your city, how we might draw nearer to its source, to know the pleasure of its light and favor?*

Nothing was easier; she had already begun making preparations to provide a spectacular answer to his question. The difficulty to which he provided the key, however, was now as nothing in comparison with the far greater one that had superseded it.

And so, as the sun sank beneath the horizon, sending indigo fingers creeping into the indulgent sky through which it passed, Diane, Duchess Tremontaine, decided upon a course of action. She summoned Reynald—among her house swordsmen, the one least likely to ask questions about an order he was given—and waited. When he came, she spoke a few words to him; he nodded, bowed deeply, and left the room.

Diane rose, stretched, and rang for Lucinda to dress her for dinner.

Much later that night, as Rafe was breaking an oath he had, up to that point, quite sincerely believed himself incapable of breaking, as Kaab pretended not to be annoyed at the bawling of her newest cousin, as Micah sat in her room and gazed, unseeing, at the wall, lost in the beauty of the ellipsoid that occupied her attention, as the Duchess Tremontaine sent the spray of her laughter over the other guests at the dinner table where she sat—on the other side of the City, in Riverside, something being carried slowly down the river caught a branch on the west bank and stuck, the calm flow of the current rippling softly around it as nearby crickets sang their children to sleep. Now fabric bobbed above the water, now leather.

Now flesh.

For the thing that had come out of the river was quite easily recognizable as the body of a man no longer among the living.

Or it would have been, had there been anyone there to see it.

Episode Four

A WAKE IN RIVERSIDE

Malinda Lo

I n the cool spring drizzle, Riverside was as gray as the surface of the river itself. Kaab made her way through the damp tangle of cobblestoned streets, where the buildings seemed to lean toward one another in an alarmingly casual manner, in search of the home of the red-haired forger named Tess.

Kaab remembered exactly where she had last seen her, almost two weeks ago, on the day of her arrival in the City. It felt like much more time had passed, but Kaab would not soon forget the site of her first Riverside duel. As the building came into view, Kaab noticed that the windows were all shuttered and the street was particularly quiet. Even the washerwoman's shop on the ground floor was dark. Perhaps the rain was keeping people inside, or perhaps it was still too early in the day for Riverside to be awake, but Kaab suspected that Tess was not at home. She approached the door that led up to Tess's apartment, where a boy covered in a ragged, patchwork cloak of faded green and russet brown huddled beneath the eaves. He emitted a faint snore, and Kaab reached out with a booted foot to gently nudge his ankle.

He started awake and mumbled, "Tess is out."

Kaab asked, "When will she return?"

The boy sat up and shot her a suspicious glance. "Who're you?"

Kaab pushed back the hood of her cloak and wondered what the boy would make of her. She found the Locals' reactions to be quite telling. They often stared, as this boy was doing, but she didn't mind, exactly. She understood his curiosity. Not only did she look different, with her coloring and hair twisted into unfamiliar braids, but this morning she had chosen to wear breeches she had tailored to fit herself and high boots she had acquired from a cobbler in the Middle City. She couldn't fathom how anyone could wear a sword while also wearing a dress—not to mention those stays, which were about as comfortable as donning a cactus—and she wasn't about to venture into Riverside unarmed. Luckily, she had managed to sneak out of the house without encountering Aunt Saabim. Kaab was supposed to be lying low here and deferring to her elders, not taking matters into her own hands the way she had done in Tultenco. But surely, Kaab had told herself that morning as she pulled on the unfamiliar and slightly stiff boots, she was perfectly capable of handling this small bit of intrigue on her own. There was no need to involve her aunt and uncle in such a simple little thing, even if it did require arming herself beforehand.

Kaab said to the boy, "My name is Ixkaab Balam. Can you tell me where she is?"

"She's not here," he said, still studying her face. "Do you want to leave a message? She pays me to take messages for her. I'll give it to her when she comes back."

Kaab ignored the light rain spattering on her head and asked, "Do you know when she will return? I must deliver my message in person."

The boy shook his head. "She didn't say, but if you ask me," he said slyly, "I think she'll be gone awhile."

Kaab recognized the boy's desire to spill a secret, and she obliged him by asking, "Really? Why?"

He leaned back casually against the door. "Well, she left after Tiny Pete came by with the news of that body that washed up on the riverbank." He looked off into the distance and said nonchalantly, "I bet she's gone to check it out."

Of all the reasons for Tess to be absent, this was certainly not one Kaab had anticipated. "A body?" she said, only slightly exaggerating her shock. "Who died?"

The boy shrugged. "Dunno. This kind of thing happens all the time, and someone has to go identify the body. Maybe Tess thought she knew him." He got a crafty look on his face. "Riverside's not a place for strangers, you know. You better be careful around here."

If the boy had been a couple of years older, his words might have come off as a threat, but he couldn't have been more than eleven, so Kaab found his warning rather sweet. She slipped a hand into the pocket of her cloak and pulled out a small package wrapped in brown paper. "You seem to be a smart boy—know your way around these parts."

The boy preened at the flattery. "I do. I was born not two blocks from here, raised on these streets. I know my way about. That's why Tess hires me to take messages for her. She knows I'll do it right."

"Then you must know where Tess went, in case you have to give her an urgent message." Kaab unwrapped the package to show him a good-size chunk of chocolate. It was of middling quality, but much better than anything he would be likely to taste. "I'll give you some of this if you tell me where she went," she said.

He gave the chocolate a glance that went rapidly from puzzlement to disgust. "What is that? Looks like a chunk of dried shit."

She was taken aback. "It's chocolate," she began indignantly. "Surely you—" She stopped at the expression on his face. He had never seen anything like it before and clearly did not know what he was missing. *Interesting,* she thought. "Never mind," she said, and folded the paper back over the chocolate before repocketing it. She made a mental note to inform her uncle that chocolate didn't seem to be known in Riverside. That was a market waiting to be broken open. "Will you tell me where Tess went?" she asked the boy again.

He gave her a measuring look that made him seem much older than eleven. "You want to know, it'll cost ya."

"Ah," she said. He might not understand chocolate, but he obviously understood money. She pulled out a few minnows and dropped them into his instantly outstretched hand.

"I have to feed my little brother, too! This won't even buy a leftover bowl of Lolly's week-old goat stew."

She could tell he was exaggerating, but the fact that a boy his age had to haggle over money for food made her drop two more minnows in his hand. *Soft-hearted idiot,* she could hear her mother saying fondly. *The service requires a sterner disposition than this. Next you'll be giving your own supper away. . . .*

Kaab pushed aside the sudden memory, forcing herself to focus once again on the dirty-faced boy in rags sitting on this cold gray doorstep in Riverside. "Where is Tess?"

He tucked the coins into one of the many invisible pockets of his patchwork cloak. "Down at the Three Dogs. That's where the body washed up."

"And how do I get to this Three Dogs? Is it a tavern?"

"Directions cost extra."

She had to give him credit for driving a hard bargain. She gave him one more minnow.

"It's a tavern on Sheaves Lane," he said, hiding the coin away. "Take a left on Bridgewater Street and a right at the sign of the Green Shears. Then you'll see the sign for the Three Dogs."

She groaned internally as he rattled off the directions. "Bridgewater Street's back there?" she confirmed, pointing in the direction she had come.

The boy nodded.

"Which direction do I turn? North or south?"

He shrugged and pointed north. "That way. You can't miss it. I bet there'll be a crowd there even in the rain. It's been a few weeks since a body washed up."

Kaab pulled the hood up over her damp hair and said, "Thanks. What's your name?"

"Jamie."

"I'll remember you next time I need information," she promised.

Jamie grinned. "You won't be sorry, miss."

Rafe's stomach rumbled as he draped one arm over the bare torso of William, the Duke Tremontaine, who was certainly the most noble man ever to be welcomed into Rafe's serviceable but slightly creaky bed.

"You're hungry," William observed, running his fingers over the pale skin of Rafe's back.

"If only we could call for servants to bring us some lunch," Rafe said, pressing his face into the hollow between William's shoulder and neck. He inhaled the scent of him: cloves, slightly spicy, over an undercurrent of fresh sweat.

"If you were in my home, we could," the duke said.

"You came here of your own accord," Rafe reminded him silkily. "There must have been something special to lure you here, given my lack of servants." *And it wasn't my cramped quarters and curious roommates,* Rafe thought. Indeed, Joshua's and Thaddeus's eyes had seemed to leap out of their skulls when the Duke Tremontaine had appeared on the landing outside the door to their rented rooms. Only Micah, his head bent as usual over a pile of calculations, had barely noticed. But Micah was like that.

William ran his hand lower, toward the small of Rafe's back, and Rafe shivered with delight. "Something special indeed," William said.

Rafe's stomach rumbled again—this time more urgently—and he groaned with frustration. "A moment," Rafe said, and rolled out of his bed. He had left a crust of bread and a wedge of cheese wrapped in some paper on his desk. The bread might be a bit stale, but he felt as if he could eat a horse about now. His room was chilly—the spring rain that pattered on the roof had brought a damp nip to the air—and he pulled a loose tunic over his head as he crossed the few feet from his bed to the battered scholar's desk, which had been an occupant of these rooms long before Rafe. "Aha," he said, digging the leftover bread and cheese out from behind a stack of books. He unwrapped it and examined the bread for signs of mold. Satisfied, he took the food back to bed, where William had propped himself up on one elbow to watch.

"Is that all you have?" William asked as Rafe slid back under the blanket.

"It'll tide me over till I can go out for a meat pie," Rafe said, biting into the bread. It was definitely stale and took some chewing. At least the cheese was still good. He offered a piece to the duke, who shook his head with a slight grimace. He was likely accustomed to much finer fare. "More for me then," Rafe said, and popped the bit of cheese into his mouth.

Rafe wasn't used to having his lovers in his room—it had happened a couple of times in the past, but those had been straightforward transactions that didn't involve any pillow talk—and he had the vague suspicion that he was being a terrible host. The duke seemed inclined to linger, and it made Rafe nervous. "Why did you drop by this morning, anyway?" Rafe asked abruptly. "When you arrived, I had the impression that you had some sort of business in mind—business other than getting in bed with me, that is."

The duke looked a bit pained by the sharpness in Rafe's tone. "This isn't business, Rafe."

Rafe glanced down at the small amount of bread and cheese he had left, clutched in his hands as if they were charms against— against what? A harmless conversation with his most recent lover? He forced himself to relax his grip. "Then what is this?" Rafe asked, feeling somewhat horrified by the fact that he was having this conversation at all—with the Duke Tremontaine, no less. And he still wasn't sure what he should call him. My Lord? Tremontaine? William? *Will.*

The duke sat up and leaned against the headboard, which squeaked. The bed had come with the room too (one reason Rafe had agreed to pay more for this room; the other was the fact that it had a door that could be bolted), and Rafe had tried to fix the damn squeaking before, to no avail.

"It's—it's something I've never experienced before," the duke said tentatively. He took one of Rafe's hands, still holding a lump of cheese, and kissed it. "I only know that I want to continue to experience it—to experience you. 'This wild boy / Whose lips sweeten my own.'"

Now the duke was quoting Audley at him! This was unheard of. Rafe disliked the strange fluttering he felt in his belly and tried to shrug it off. "I'm not from the Hill," he said, an edge to his voice. "Is that what you like about me? Perhaps you'd like it even better if we met down by the docks."

The duke let Rafe's hand go and made a frustrated noise. "Stop it. You are a brilliant man, Rafe. You are a scholar. This is what I admire about you! And you don't treat me like a noble to curry favors from, either. That is rare."

Rafe looked at the duke, whose face was turning red with emotion. It was endearing: this man with gray at his temples, complimenting him so fiercely. Impulsively, he threw the remaining bread and cheese onto the floor and kissed the duke again, pressing his mouth roughly against Will's, scraping the night's growth of his beard against the duke's cheek. Their kiss deepened, and Rafe slid his arms around the duke, beginning to press him down onto the thin mattress again, but Will said, "Wait. There's something I must say."

Rafe whispered, "What? What could be more important than this?" His hand slid down Will's body.

Will groaned but said, "Wait. Stop. Rafe, I can't stay. I'm sorry, but I've stayed too long already. I have an engagement this afternoon, and my wife will have my head if I miss it."

Rafe flopped onto his back with a bitter sigh. "The duchess."

"In a way, that's what I wanted to discuss with you," Will said seriously.

"The duchess?" Rafe said again, this time with surprise.

"Well . . . Tremontaine, I suppose." The duke winced. "It pains me to say this, but I have certain responsibilities that will prevent me from visiting you as often as I'd like. And I'd like to visit you often."

At that moment a drop of water plummeted from the ceiling directly onto the duke's forehead, causing the duke to start in surprise.

"Damn it," Rafe muttered. "That leak!" He glared up at the ceiling, noting that the piece of oilcloth he had tacked over the offending crack had come loose. He stood up on the bed, causing it to sway dangerously, and reached up to press the tack holding the oilcloth against the ceiling back in. He sat down again, pulling the sheets up. "You were saying?" he said, somewhat embarrassed.

The duke gave him a gentle smile. "My dear," he said softly.

Rafe's breath caught in his throat. *My dear?* Rafe tried to shake off the disturbingly warm feeling rising in his chest, but it was confoundedly difficult, especially when the duke was gazing at him with those blue eyes.

"I want to see you as much as possible," the duke continued. "Every day. But I cannot come here as often as I'd like, and you cannot simply visit Tremontaine House without a reason."

"I can think of a few reasons," Rafe said suggestively.

William smiled. "An acceptable reason."

"One that the duchess will accept?"

"That too."

Rafe scowled up at the oilcloth. He could already see the rainwater pooling in the center of it. He would have to move his bed over so that it blocked the desk again. Otherwise he'd have to sleep with a bucket on one side of the mattress, which he had done before and concluded was worse than having to sit on the bed rather than the chair to use the desk.

"Does the duchess object to me?" Rafe asked bluntly. He was a merchant's son, and his knowledge of nobles was largely limited to matters of business, but it was widely believed—or rumored, at least—that those who lived on the Hill viewed the bonds of matrimony a bit differently than Middle City types like Rafe's family. Rafe had assumed that Tremontaine was free to do as he wished with whom he wished, but now he wondered if the duchess had more influence than most noble women. Come to think of it, Rafe had heard of the Duchess Tremontaine recently, but he couldn't put his finger on where she had come up.

"I doubt my wife even knows about you," William responded, looking faintly horrified at the idea.

Rafe thought it best to avoid mentioning the fact that he had insulted the duchess in her own home a few days ago. "What would be an acceptable reason for me to come to Tremontaine House?" he asked.

William leaned toward him, a boyish delight suffusing his face with an eager glow. "My current secretary, Tolliver, has been with me my whole life—he was my father's secretary before me. He's begun to forget things—appointments and such—and he's simply not as sharp as he used to be. I need someone younger on my staff, and I think you would be perfect for the position. If you become my junior secretary, you can learn all the ins and outs of society, and we can be together every day. It wouldn't even be unheard of for you to have a small apartment at Tremontaine House, eventually."

Rafe was speechless. The idea of taking a job as a nobleman's secretary was something he had never considered. He had come to the University for the pursuit of knowledge, with the goal of eventually opening his own school. He had come here to avoid the life of a merchant—a life of bargaining and warehouses and waiting tensely for shipments to arrive or for word that those shipments had been lost. Rafe had a sudden vision of himself sitting at a secretary's desk in William's library, fingers stained with ink, as he wrote endless notes to various lords and Council members accepting this or declining that invitation. The thought of it was so strange that Rafe had no idea how he should feel about it.

He remembered, then, when he had last heard of the Duchess Tremontaine: at home, his parents had been talking about her. There had been something going around the countinghouses of the Middle City about the duchess's power to set fashions on the Hill, and what the Hill folk suddenly wanted, of course, affected the merchants. But was it that her influence was declining, or that it was on the rise? Rafe couldn't recall exactly what it was, and for once he cursed himself for not paying closer attention to merchants' gossip.

"What do you think?" William asked when Rafe continued to be silent.

"I—I don't know." If he became William's junior secretary, their relationship would change. Would it become a society-sanctioned, look-the-other-way affair, in which the Tremontaine servants would come to know the details of their trysts while keeping mum about them in public? If they did, surely the duchess would discover them sooner or later—and Rafe was inclined to believe it would be sooner.

"It would solve everything," the duke said. "We could be together. We could call for a proper luncheon to be made for us. In a few months you wouldn't have to live in these leaky rooms anymore. Come join my staff. You won't regret it."

"You're asking me to give up on my dreams," Rafe said.

The duke frowned. "No! I would never ask that of you. I share your dreams, Rafe."

"And what of your promise to convince the Board of Governors to reconsider that vote?" Rafe asked pointedly. "How is that coming along?"

The duke was taken aback. "I told you it would take some time."

"I don't have time!" Rafe snapped. "I've been working for this my whole life. I'm in the middle of something truly significant right now—it is the *end* of Rastin and his pigheaded regurgitators—it's going to be groundbreaking, and now I'm going to have to wait for *a year* while you attempt to force those idiots on the board to admit they made a mistake? What if you can't succeed? No one will attend a school founded by a second-rate University scholar with no connections."

William's face became increasingly gloomy. Unwilling to confront the duke's disappointment, Rafe threw off the sheet and swung his legs over the edge of the bed. "I'm sorry," he said. "I don't have time to be anyone's secretary."

The floor was cold and a bit scratchy beneath his bare feet. Rafe reached down for the pile of clothing he had discarded earlier that morning, when he had led William into his bedroom and shut the door between them and the rest of his roommates. He pulled on his shirt and breeches, tucked his shirt in before reaching for his scholar's robe. Behind him, he heard the duke dressing as well.

"You have connections," William said. "But you seem to have no faith in them."

Rafe turned to face the duke. He was so tall he made Rafe's room look as if it had been miniaturized. He did not fit here: He was all lean grace and aristocratic bearing. Rafe hated making this beautiful man look so glum.

"You don't understand," Rafe said miserably.

The duke took the few steps toward him and for a moment

Rafe thought he was going to kiss him, but he only reached for the handle of the door. "I'll see myself out," the duke said. "I hope you'll reconsider."

Sheaves Lane was even narrower than most of the Riverside streets Kaab had walked through on her way to the Three Dogs, and the overhanging buildings in combination with the drizzle made her feel as if she had stepped into twilight. There were only a few buildings on the crooked little lane, which dead-ended in a three-story house with a placard in the front bow window that advertised a price so low for one night's stay that Kaab was sure it was a front for some kind of vice.

Next to the house was the sign of the Three Dogs, which depicted, logically enough, three dogs cavorting around a pint of ale. One of the dogs was black, the second brown, and the third a color that might have once been red but had long since faded to rust. On the other side of the Three Dogs, separated by an alley, was a sagging, half-timbered building with shuttered windows. The Three Dogs itself had only one small window next to its front door, which was closed, and little could be seen through the dirty glass. It did not look like a place suitable for Tess; it looked like a den for thieves and criminals. Indeed, this entire street could have been plucked from any number of legends of Riverside that had fascinated Kaab on the long voyage across the sea. She itched to go inside, but she knew it would be smarter if she exercised the skills she had learned in the service to get a better lay of the land first. She well remembered her uncle Ahkitan's advice to avoid putting oneself in an unfamiliar and potentially dangerous place without first noting the locations of at least two exits. It was unlikely that the Three Dogs had only one entrance, and the alley looked promising. Without hesitating—because hesitation drew more suspicion than confidence—Kaab continued down Sheaves Lane and turned into the alley.

Though the street had been paved, the alley had not, and she skirted a couple of dank puddles that smelled as if someone had emptied their chamber pots into them. Wondering yet again why the people of this city allowed their streets to become so fouled, she was grateful for the thick soles of her new boots. She looked up and saw a couple of windows in the walls above, both dark, before the alley opened into an empty, muddy yard. It was hemmed in on two sides by the walls of neighboring buildings, but the rear of the yard overlooked the river itself. A broken iron railing leaned precariously over the edge, and steps descended from one corner.

Kaab approached the steps and peered over, seeing a steep, uneven flight of stone stairs. At the bottom a narrow wooden dock extended into the river, where a couple of small boats were moored. Across the steely expanse of the water the City rose into the misty midday. The dark stone towers and ancient, grand halls of the University were washed by the rain into shades of cloud and dusk and shining slate, while the river continued north in a wide, lazy curve.

Kaab turned back to the Three Dogs, where a lean-to at the rear of the tavern sheltered several canvas-covered cords of wood and the tavern's back door—her sought-after second exit—and a slightly less grimy window. She headed closer to see if she could get a look inside, and as she approached the lean-to, she noticed that one of the woodpiles didn't look quite right. In fact, it didn't look like a pile of wood at all. Kaab's pulse quickened as she knelt down inside the lean-to beside the suspicious-looking shape and reached out to pull back the canvas.

She was right: It was not a pile of wood. It was a body.

She uncovered the hand first—a man's hand—and then gently peeled the canvas back to reveal a torso dressed in a wet but otherwise unremarkable tunic, a sturdy neck, and a face that she recognized. It was Ben.

Kaab remembered him instantly. She recalled the gleam in his eyes and the grin on his lips as he fought her. Those lips were colorless slashes on a pale face now, his eyes half slit to reveal only the whites. Damp strands of hair clinging to his ghastly cheeks as well as his wet clothing suggested that his was the body that had been recovered from the river. This was the reason that Tess had come to this grim corner of Riverside. She had come for Ben.

Kaab wondered how he had died. Had he been killed in a fight? He was Tess's protector, after all, so that would make sense, but there were no signs of violence on his body. Had he taken an accidental tumble into the river and drowned? Kaab didn't know him well, but he had been light on his feet when they fought, and he was a healthy man who lived on an island in the middle of a river. She studied his body more closely. The shirt he wore was made of fine linen, the plentiful fabric bunched up in numerous folds and stained by the river water . . . which made it easy to overlook the small dark spot on his chest. She looked around, making sure the yard was still deserted, and then reached out and pushed up the shirt. The pale flesh of his chest was punctured by a small wound, as if someone had thrust a knife in through his back. Kaab's heartbeat quickened. She put her hands beneath Ben's body and heaved the stiff corpse on its side and then over to its stomach.

She peeled up the shirt to reveal a bigger wound: It was a thin, deep cut, clearly made by a dagger, judging by its shape. And it had been made with precision, angled in a way that would drive the blade up beneath Ben's ribs and straight into his heart.

At the end of last summer, Kaab had made a decision that put her in a lakeside Tullan courtyard under the light of a full moon. She could smell the cool, slightly damp scent of the night air in her nostrils even now, mixed with the jacaranda perfume that the women of that house wore. Instead of Ben's corpse on the ground before her, she saw the curved form of a woman crumpled on her belly. She felt the hard flat tiles beneath her knees as she knelt beside the body. The bright light of the moon silvered the wound on the woman's back, the exact shape of the obsidian daggers that Kaab and every person in the service carried with them. That had been an execution, and so was this.

How awful, and yet how horribly fitting: people killed in the same way here.

Kaab's stomach heaved as if she were aboard a ship on the open ocean during a storm. She swallowed thickly, and Ben's face swam into focus again. "May Ixchel guide you to the land of the dead," she whispered in Kindaan, and then adjusted Ben's shirt back into place before turning the corpse onto its back and re-covering it with the canvas.

The City was on the most distant edge of the Balams' trading empire; it was supposed to be a quiet little nothing of a place where she could be out of the way until the consequences of her ill-advised Tullan adventure faded into distant memory. *Listen to your aunt and uncle when you get there,* her father had said with a pained expression before she was hustled aboard the ship that would cross the great sea. *Follow the plan for once and don't get into trouble if you want to keep your place in the service.* Her aunt and uncle would not approve of what she was about to do, but Ixkaab Balam, first daughter of a first daughter of the greatest Trading family of the Kinwiinik, was not known for her prudence. She was known for her courage—or at least, her daring. She had learned from what had happened last autumn; she was wiser now, but she was still herself.

Kaab left the lean-to with its canvas-covered corpse behind and headed back out the alley toward the front door of the Three Dogs.

The problem with the figures Rafe had given her, Micah realized, was that the artificial number of unity was incorrect. It should be zero, not this unnecessarily huge and complicated number listed in the appendix. *That* number created an inordinate amount of complications, forcing all sorts of calculations that in turn caused a ridiculous percentage of error. Micah wondered why the mathematicians who had been so excited about this table hadn't been able to see this problem as clearly as she could. It reminded her of what had happened the other day at the lecture, when she had corrected the magister about the angles. In her mind, she could visualize the angles very clearly, like a curved slice out of the surface of a ball. It was beautiful, really, the way the angles would increase, like the crack in a doorway broadening bit by bit to let in more sunlight. And yet it seemed that the students in that class couldn't see it the way she could.

Micah was startled out of her mathematical reverie when the door to their rooms opened, smacking into the corner of the wooden table where she was working. The pen she had been holding scratched against the paper, accidentally turning a number seven into a two. Rafe came inside holding a meat pie wrapped in a bit of greasy, brown paper. "Hungry, son?" he asked, holding it out to her.

"Oh yes!" she cried, reaching for the pie with an ink-stained hand. She had been working on her calculations all morning and had been so absorbed in them she hadn't thought to eat, but as soon as she smelled the rich scent of lamb and gravy, her stomach growled. Before she took her first bite, though, she made sure to cross out the incorrect number two to prevent herself from making an error in the future.

Rafe nudged the door shut and sank down onto the chaise that served as Joshua's bed. The two rooms occupied by Rafe, Joshua, Thaddeus, and now Micah were on the third floor of a rickety residence around the corner from the Inkpot. They had long been rented out by University students, who tried to pack as many of themselves as they could into one lodging in order to save money. Micah was glad to have a place to sleep at night, even if it meant she had to sleep on a pallet under the table. She could use the table to work on during the day, putting up with Rafe and his roommates constantly going in and out. Rafe, as the senior roommate and longest tenant, had the second room, the one in back, which meant he was the only one with any privacy. Since he was helping her out voluntarily, Micah didn't complain about the constant disruptions, and she did find it deeply satisfying to solve the mathematical problems he presented to her.

As she bit into the meat pie, her gaze dropped down to her notes. She picked up her pen, dipped it back into the ink, and began to calculate again.

"How goes it?" Rafe asked, sliding over on the chaise to get a closer look at her careful columns of numbers.

"Very well," Micah said. "I've discovered the main problem with the table you gave me. How long have people been using it? It's so wrong!" She took another bite of the pie; it was only lukewarm, but the lamb and potatoes and carrots were quite tasty. She had a brief pang of longing, though, for Aunt Judith's pastry. This wasn't as flaky as hers.

Rafe picked up the thin booklet he had given her and turned back to the frontispiece. "Says here this was printed about twenty-five years ago. What's the problem?"

Micah launched into a detailed explanation of the issue, and as she spoke, Rafe studied her calculations. "It's relatively simple," she concluded. "Or it would be, if the artificial number of unity was zero, and then I could recalculate all the other figures. It would take a while, but I could do it."

"And if you did it, that would correct the errors?" Rafe asked.

Micah nodded enthusiastically. "Yes! I really don't know why it wasn't done this way in the first place. People must have gotten lost if they were using these figures to chart their course—isn't that what you said they were used for?"

"Yes." Rafe leaned back against the wall, an odd expression on his face. Micah wasn't exactly sure what it meant; he often had strange expressions that she couldn't read.

"Is something wrong?" she asked, having learned that it was beneficial to ask rather than to guess, since she often guessed incorrectly. Human emotions, of course, were not like math—which was why she enjoyed math so much. Everything made sense!

Rafe answered, "Not wrong, exactly—"

"Rafe, you old dog," cried Thaddeus, throwing open the front door, "what in the name of the Horned God possessed you to bring a nobleman into our rooms? Was that really the Duke Tremontaine?"

Rafe's face colored slightly. "Well . . . yes."

Thaddeus bounded into the room and pulled Rafe to his feet, patting Rafe's head and shoulders. "Let me check—I'm afraid you might have come down with an illness—no, no, you seem solid; nobody's smacked you on the head."

Rafe detached himself from Thaddeus with a disdainful frown, settling himself back into the corner of the chaise. "Thaddeus, I'm in the middle of—"

Joshua appeared in the doorway, saying, "You're back! What happened with the duke? I told you there would come a time when you'd find someone—"

Rafe dropped his head into his hands and groaned. "Will you both leave me alone? I'm trying to talk to Micah, here!"

Micah glanced at the three University students, Joshua and Thaddeus looking gleeful, Rafe hiding his face, and said seriously, "We were discussing the mathematical error in this table of artificial numbers. It's a problem."

"Yes, it is," Rafe agreed, his voice muffled.

Joshua closed the door, leaning against it as if to bar Rafe from exiting, and said, "You're not getting out of this, pigeon. What did he want? I mean obviously he wanted you—these walls are quite thin—but I heard you arguing at the end."

Thaddeus leaned toward Rafe with an expectant expression on his face. "Do tell. It's not every day that we're visited by the Duke Tremontaine. He's quite handsome, you know, for an older man."

"The more wealth a man has the handsomer he gets," Joshua quipped, sending Thaddeus into a paroxysm of laughter.

Rafe raised his reddened face and said glumly, "He wants me to be his secretary."

Joshua's eyebrows rose nearly to his hairline. "His secretary? But what about your school?"

Rafe winced. "Well . . ."

"Secretary to the Duke Tremontaine," Thaddeus said in an awed tone of voice. "You could do a lot with that."

Micah was puzzled. "Like what?"

"He could use the position to worm his way into the hearts of all those nobles on the Hill," Thaddeus said.

Joshua perched on the edge of the table where Micah was working. "That's a thought. So much for being true to your principles, though."

Rafe groaned. "My principles haven't gotten me very far."

Joshua cocked his head. "I suppose, if you're stuck with a hostile committee, you might as well consider the duke's offer."

Thaddeus bounced on the chaise next to Rafe. "Yes! Damn the degree, who needs it when you've got this on the table?"

"Got what on the table?" Micah asked, carefully moving her neat stack of papers out of the way of Joshua's bottom.

"The job offer," Rafe explained. "They seem to think I should take it."

"Does that mean you'd leave here?" Micah asked, suddenly concerned.

"I wouldn't leave *you* here," Rafe said quickly. "You're the brains behind this operation, Micah."

Micah wasn't entirely certain what he meant, but she liked the tone of his voice. "Well, do you want to know more about how I could solve these errors?"

"I do," Rafe said. "You say that if you made this correction, you could recalculate the figures in the table?"

"Yes. I would make it perfect," she said enthusiastically.

"How long do you think it would take?"

"Well, if I start from the beginning and go through each degree and minute . . ." She thought it through in her head and realized it would be quite an endeavor. "I don't know how long," she concluded, "but I would need some time."

"What if you had people to help you with the calculations?" Rafe asked. "Could that speed things up?"

Micah considered the options. "I would have to show them how to calculate these correctly, and then I would have to check their work, of course."

Joshua was leaning over her papers now, and he asked, "What is this you're working on, anyway?"

"It's a table of artificial numbers," Micah said.

"They're central to the problem of celestial navigation," Rafe said.

"Navigation," Thaddeus repeated. "Are you working on something for your father, Rafe?"

Rafe grimaced. "I don't know. Maybe. But what Micah's doing is—it's extremely important. It could affect not only trade but natural philosophy." He leaped to his feet and began to pace in the small room. "That's why I need that doctor's robe! How will I found my school without it? There's going to be an intellectual revolution, and I must be at the start of it."

"You do realize," Joshua said smoothly, "that working for the Duke Tremontaine could be a real lubricant for the wheels of revolution?"

Rafe halted and spun to face Joshua. "I—"

Joshua sighed. "You are so caught up in your intellectual revolution, Rafe, you can't see the easier path."

Thaddeus was nodding vigorously. "It's true. Joshua has a point."

Micah glanced at the three students, confused. Joshua and Thaddeus always seemed to speak in expressions that purposely hid the meaning behind their words. "What's the easier path?"

Joshua looked down at her and said, "If Rafe takes the job with the Duke Tremontaine, he'll be well positioned to influence many important people."

"Many *wealthy* people," Thaddeus said.

Rafe rolled his eyes. "Micah, they think that if I become the duke's secretary I can use my job to get what I want."

"And can you?" Micah asked.

Rafe blinked. "Well, I—I suppose it's possible."

Joshua went over to Rafe, put his hands on Rafe's shoulders, and looked him in the eye. "You have two options, Rafe. Stay here and bang your head against the wall trying to circumvent de Bertel and his cronies, or say yes to that lovely man and take the easier path toward your school." Joshua gestured toward Micah. "If you won't think of yourself, think of your protégé. You have young Micah locked up in a drafty room being constantly interrupted by me and you and Thaddeus, which I'm sure is horrible for intellectual progress."

Micah was pleasantly surprised that Joshua had noticed the interruptions were a problem.

Rafe came over to Micah and looked over the neat columns of numbers. "Tell me: Ideally, what would you need to fix these errors more quickly?"

Micah thought about it. "Paper, of course. Ink, and pens, and a place to do the work. A bigger desk would be wonderful! Of course, I like working here, and it's so very kind of you to let me stay with you, but Joshua is right—the interruptions make it harder. And, you know, I think this will take a few weeks, maybe more." The enormity of the task was beginning to sink in, and her eyes widened. "I thought I would only be here for a few days! I can't keep sending my cousins on the farm so many notes." She pulled the most recent note she had penned to Reuben from the top drawer of the desk, where she had put it for safekeeping until she could send it out, and passed it to Rafe. He glanced down at it, reading her brief words. *Dear Cousin Reuben, I'm still in the University staying with Rafe. I've started work on calculations that will be extremely useful, you know how good I am at numbers. I hope I will be able to come home in a day or two. Love, Micah.*

"It's almost time for planting, and it's my job to make sure we've got enough seed and to organize the storehouse. I should really go home," she concluded glumly.

"But you'd rather work on this, wouldn't you?" Rafe said, smiling at her.

"Oh yes," she said eagerly. "This is much more interesting."

Rafe ran his hands through his flyaway hair in agitation. "You must stay, Micah!" he declared. "This work you've done is too important. Other people can help out with the planting—your skills are required here."

"But what will I tell my cousin?" Micah asked, Rafe's enthusiasm beginning to make her feel giddy. "And should I go out to the tavern to get up a card game again? I might need to win some more money—"

"I will take care of it," Rafe said. "Joshua and Thaddeus are right."

"Oho!" Thaddeus said in delight. "That's a rarity coming from you."

Rafe continued to Micah: "I think I can make sure you'll have everything you need to solve these problems. And your new tables of—what do you call them?—tables of artificial numbers?"

"Yes, artificial numbers. Because they're not like natural numbers—"

"Yes, yes, exactly," Rafe interrupted in his excitement. "Your new, improved, and exceedingly accurate table of artificial numbers will be used to support celestial navigation—trade might come on board—natural philosophy—this is the answer!"

"You mean it will help people sail to new places without getting lost?" Micah asked.

"Precisely. *And* it will prove that I should have my own school." Rafe opened the door and added, "I'll be back soon. Meanwhile, continue on!"

"All right," Micah said. "Thank you for the meat pie!"

Rafe waved off her thanks and opened the front door again. "Wish me luck!"

"Good luck," she called out dutifully.

"Lucky bastard," Thaddeus said admiringly.

Joshua smirked. "Thaddeus, how about you and I head out for some chocolate and give Micah some quiet time for those calculations?"

"Lovely idea," Thaddeus agreed.

Once they left her alone, Micah pulled out a fresh sheet of paper, and began to draw out a new table.

The interior of the Three Dogs was dim, lit only by the small front window and a smoky oil lamp hanging over the bar on the far side of the room. As Kaab's eyes adjusted to the murk, she saw that a group of people was clustered there, and a man was talking, his booming voice cutting through the small space.

". . . a wild one from the beginning. We used to play in the Old Market, make a game of lifting little things from the stalls. Dangerous games, to be sure." The man chuckled. "Once Ben was caught by Crooked Nan, who gave him a bloody lip for making off with one of her kerchiefs."

"Nan was a hard one," a woman said. "I bet he learned from that!"

"True, Ben never stole from her again," the man said. "But I remember that day—after Crooked Nan smacked him, his father turned him over his knee and told him he never should've gotten caught in the first place!"

Everyone broke into laughter, and someone added, "His father was even harder, though. You don't hear of many highwaymen living as long as old Rupert Hawke did. Only just died, didn't he?"

"Yes, he did," said a different woman. "Ben had just got back from burying him."

Kaab thought she recognized the speaker. Was that Tess? Kaab stepped forward only to be confronted by a stocky figure about her own height, a hand on the dagger at his belt.

"Who're you?" came the voice—a woman's voice, though low and rough.

Kaab eyed her curiously. This was the first Local woman she'd seen dressed in trousers. Her face was pockmarked, her hair wiry and gray. Kaab lowered the hood of her cloak and saw the woman's eyes narrow on her foreign face. "I'm Ixkaab Balam."

"What kind of name is that? And what business do you have here?"

The small crowd grouped around the bar had overheard Kaab's arrival, and they were now all staring at her. Tess stood up, the light gleaming on her fiery hair. "I know her!" Tess exclaimed in surprise. "She challenged Ben, the day he left for his father's deathbed!"

A dozen hands reached for a dozen weapons; the sound of steel scraping against scabbards caused Kaab to say hastily, "And he defeated me fair and square. He was a good fighter, very honorable."

She had no idea if Ben had been honorable. From what little she'd heard when she entered the Three Dogs he probably hadn't been, but she was outnumbered and needed to defuse the situation. Praise generally did the trick.

"The finest," said a man in the crowd. He raised a tankard and added, "To Ben Hawke, one of Riverside's finest fighters!" Everyone joined in, dropping their weapons so they could raise their tankards and echo the toast.

A plump girl in a gown that exposed much of her bosom leaned over the bar, exposing even more of it, and called out, "Stranger, are you here to honor Ben?"

"Of course," Kaab agreed, since agreeing seemed to be the best option. "To honor Ben."

"Then you'd better drink to him," said the woman who dressed like a man. "Jenny, I'll buy this stranger a beer."

Jenny winked at Kaab before turning away to pull a tankard from beneath the bar. A moment later, Kaab had the tankard in hand, and everyone in the room, including Tess, was looking at her expectantly. Kaab thought quickly. Back home, honoring someone after their death involved fasting to show one's love for the departed, as well as leaving out carefully prepared food for the dead on feast days, when the path to the underworld was open to the spirits. Apparently, in Riverside, honoring someone involved drinking awful, watered-down, bitter beer. Kaab raised the tankard, some of the foaming substance splashing over the rim onto her hand, and said formally, "In honor of Ben Hawke, a strong and nimble fighter. May his life be remembered by all." She had considered translating a Kinwiinik saying into the Local language but wasn't sure if it would be appropriate.

"Hear, hear!" said Tess, who raised her tankard first. As the rest of the room followed suit, Kaab allowed herself to relax a tiny bit. Nobody had reached for a weapon, so she must have avoided insulting them. She took a sip of the beer, hiding her grimace at the sour taste.

"What was that they used to call Ben's father in his heyday?" someone asked, picking up the conversation where they'd left off.

"The Gentleman Robber," Tess said, though judging by the tone of her voice, she didn't love the name.

"Ah yes," said the same man who had told the story about stealing from Crooked Nan. "Rupert Hawke, Gentleman Robber, steals your money but spares your daughter!"

Scattered laughter and a few groans went through the tavern. A woman said, "I heard Hawke stole the Farnsleigh fortune from a close-guarded carriage, all on his own."

"I heard he robbed the ambassador from Arkenvelt, who was riding in a decoy carriage to elude highwaymen, but there was no fooling Hawke!"

"That's why he never teamed up with anyone. I heard that Wicked Thomas asked him to go in on a job but Hawke refused— said he worked alone."

"It probably saved him, because Wicked Thomas hanged— d'you remember? There was that street ballad about him. What was it?"

Jenny the barmaid sang in a sweet, clear voice:

> "Wicked Thomas is my name
> I left my home in search of fame.
> But though I found jewels and gold
> It wasn't in me to grow old.
> And though I'm only young and spry

I never was afraid to die.
Remember me, my heart was honest,
Even though I'm Wicked Thomas."

Applause filled the tavern when Jenny finished her song. Then someone said, "I remember now—after he turned down Wicked Thomas, didn't Hawke pull off that bloody caper involving the young ladies?"

"Yes, the story that gave him his nickname. It seems Hawke stopped a carriage that was coming to the City carrying two young noble girls, I think, from the North. He killed all the men—the driver, the footmen—made off with all the loot—there were jewels, silver, velvets, and all—but he let the two young ladies live out of the nobility of his heart."

"Rupert Hawke, Gentleman Robber, steals your money but spares your daughter," a woman repeated the doggerel, and everyone raised their tankards again.

"To Rupert Hawke, may his soul rest in peace!"

Kaab had never known Rupert Hawke, but it only seemed polite to join in. "Someone should write a ballad about Hawke," Jenny said.

"And Ben! It could be about the two of them. Why didn't Ben go into the family business?"

As the conversation continued, Kaab made her way toward the end of the bar, where she leaned against the scarred wood and sipped at her beer. Everyone in the Three Dogs seemed to know one another, and they had many stories to share about Ben Hawke and his father. Ben had also had a string of casual lovers, all men, who were mentioned in a series of ribald jokes that caused the crowd to snicker. No one mentioned the fact that Ben had been stabbed in the back, and Kaab wondered if they were refraining from talking about it out of respect for Tess, who joined in the storytelling only sporadically. It appeared that Ben had been her protector for several years now, and Tess thought of him as a brother. Every so often a story would cause her to break into tears, and someone would rub her back or squeeze her shoulder to comfort her. Kaab watched Tess go through a number of handkerchiefs, until her nose was almost as red as her hair.

By the time Kaab finished the tankard of beer she had been given, she had to admit the drink tasted a bit better than it had at the beginning. Perhaps the trick was to drink more than one. When Jenny approached and asked if she wanted another, Kaab agreed. She still wanted to talk to Tess, but it was clear she wouldn't have a moment alone with her until Tess was ready to leave, and it would look odd if she stood there in the corner without even a drink in her hand.

It wasn't until the light from the window darkened into dusk that the gathering began to break up. Tess was the last to leave, and Kaab overheard her talking with the tavern owner about arrangements for Ben's body to be transported for burial to a cemetery outside the City. As Tess turned to depart, reaching for her cloak, Kaab was waiting to help her put it on.

Tess looked worn out but not surprised. "I saw you were still here. Was there something you wanted from me?" She sounded somewhat curious, but reserved, as if she didn't know what to make of Kaab.

Kaab gestured toward the door. "May I walk you to your home? If Ben is no longer with you, you'll need protection."

"I'll be fine on my own for a fortnight," Tess said. "There's two weeks to mourn someone, here in Riverside, before anyone would even think to bother you." Then her curiosity seemed to win out over her reserve. "But sure, you can walk me home."

William, Duke Tremontaine, was ensconced in his study, reading through a series of extremely tedious notes on the taxation of foreign imports. He was supposed to be preparing for an upcoming Council session that his wife had insisted he propose, but his attention kept wandering to a certain young scholar in whom he had developed a sudden and increasingly intense interest. The duke wished that they had parted that afternoon on a better note.

The door to the library opened to reveal Tilson, the footman. "My lord, a Master Rafe Fenton has arrived. Shall I send him up?"

It was as if the gods could hear his thoughts! "Yes, bring him up, please, Tilson."

William hastily swept his papers into a ragged pile, then pushed the pile to one side. He adjusted the fall of his cravat and straightened his cuffs, feeling unusually nervous. Rafe would only come to him if his answer was yes, wouldn't he? Thankfully, it was only a few moments before the door opened again and Rafe appeared, looking a bit agitated.

"Good evening," William said formally, rising from his seat.

"My lord duke," Rafe said. He waited until the butler left them alone before continuing, "I've come to a decision."

"Have you?" The duke came around his desk but hesitated to approach the young scholar.

Rafe began to pace back and forth, his black robe fluttering behind him. "Yes. I realized that what you have offered me is quite significant. I—I am ashamed I did not understand this earlier today. I chalk it up to hunger." Rafe made a self-deprecating grimace. "I was too set on my scholarly ambitions without realizing

I can achieve them in more than one way. I have thought about it, and if—if you'll have me, I'd be very honored to be your junior secretary." Rafe took a shallow breath, took several swift steps across the intricately woven (and clearly imported, Rafe judged) rug, and took the liberty of grasping the duke's right hand. "Will," he said, loving the feel of the intimate name on his tongue. "Does your offer still stand?"

The duke gazed at the passionate young man before him, intoxicated by the gleaming dark pools of his eyes. He answered by pulling Rafe close and kissing him on the mouth.

Rafe returned the kiss hungrily, and he realized that though becoming the Duke Tremontaine's secretary had never been something he aspired to, it did come with some unmistakable benefits.

"My lady, would you like the peacock pin tonight or the pearl comb?"

Diane, Duchess Tremontaine, examined her reflection in her dressing room mirror while her lady's maid, Lucinda, waited by the jewel box. "The comb," Diane replied. "It's enough for a quiet supper at home, and I'll wear the peacock tomorrow when I call on Lady Godwin." Lucinda approached with the pearl-studded comb and began to place it expertly into Diane's blond hair. "I don't wear the peacock at home, unless there's a very special occasion," Diane said.

"I'll remember that, my lady."

As Lucinda put the finishing touches on her creation, Diane heard the door to her husband's study click shut. A low murmur of voices followed. The duchess's dressing room adjoined the duke's little upstairs study, and a rarely used door connected the two rooms. It was an odd arrangement for a couple with a townhouse as large as theirs, but Diane herself had suggested it, saying the light was better. It gave her an opportunity to keep an ear trained on her husband's business dealings, and bless his good-willed heart, he never seemed to have caught on to the fact that she might, at times, listen in.

The sound of voices next door briefly increased in volume, and Diane heard someone say "Will" in an unusually intense tone of voice. *Will?* Who called the duke by that name? Not even Diane. She found it extremely intriguing and not a little disturbing.

"That will be all for now, Lucinda."

The maid curtsied and backed out of the room. Diane rose from her dressing table and walked silently across the plush rug to the connecting door. It had a small latch that Diane kept well oiled, but she didn't need to open the door to hear. She simply pressed her ear to the crack and stood still.

She had done this before: not only here, but ages ago, as a girl. She remembered it suddenly with a sick lurch in her stomach. The whispers, the rustle of silk, the fear of being caught, all running in a hot, quick thrill through her veins.

She closed her eyes and took a shallow breath, her stays pressing into her sides as she locked those memories away once again. This was not the time nor the place for that. She was the Duchess Tremontaine, and some stranger was in the study with her husband.

She recognized the sounds she heard: the murmuring, the caught breath, the unmistakable smack of lips on skin, a low moan, a sharper one. A chill went through the duchess. She had heard them often, when the duke was with her. Judging by the answering sounds, the other was not a woman, but a man.

She had never known her husband to be unfaithful before. This was surprising, and Diane disliked surprises that she had not orchestrated herself.

She withdrew from the connecting door and took one last look at herself in the mirror. Her face was pale, powdered to perfection. Her lips were rouged into a bow, her hair swept up perfectly, the pearl comb gleaming in the candlelight. She heard a thump from her husband's study as something fell to the floor, followed by a brief laugh that was quickly silenced.

The chill that had gripped her seemed to harden and burn, as if frost had crackled across her skin. In the hallway, the clock struck the hour. It was time for supper.

Diane turned away from the mirror and proceeded downstairs to the dining room, her silk skirts swirling around her elegantly slippered feet.

Outside the Three Dogs, it had stopped raining at last, leaving a fresh, cool scent in the Riverside air. Houses spilled cheerful light from their windows, turning streets that had been gloomy tunnels during the day into cozy warrens filled with the scent of suppers cooking over hearth fires. Kaab said to Tess, "I am sorry about Ben."

"Thank you," Tess said quietly. "I am too."

"He had many friends," Kaab noted.

"Yes."

"That's the mark of a good man."

Tess snorted indelicately. "Well, he was too brash for his own good and yet not devious enough by half. But he was a good friend to me. I will miss him horribly, even his stupid little tricks." She sniffed and dabbed at her eyes with the edge of her sleeve.

Kaab found Tess's lack of self-consciousness distinctly charming. The girls back home were much less direct. Kaab had developed a knack for peeling back their layers of polite reserve, but she enjoyed the fact that the girls of Riverside were as forthright as she herself was.

"You haven't told me what brought you to the Three Dogs," Tess said. "It couldn't have been Ben—you hardly knew him."

"Few men have bested me in . . . well, in anything. I respect anyone who has." That won her a sly smile from Tess, and Kaab felt a flush of victory.

"What's your name?" Tess asked. "It was something unusual, wasn't it?"

"It's Ixkaab," she said, placing a hand over her heart and giving Tess a small bow. "You may call me Kaab."

"And where are you from, Kaab? What brings you to Riverside?"

"I am from Binkiinha, the greatest city in the land of the gods. My family is in the chocolate trade." She thought of the boy Tess paid to take messages and asked, "Do you know chocolate?"

"It's that fancy drink they love uptown, isn't it? I haven't had it."

"You've never had it!" Kaab exclaimed. She considered offering Tess the chocolate she carried with her for bartering, but she didn't want to give Tess something of such poor quality. She wanted, she realized, to impress this woman.

Tess shrugged. "I've had some pretty good wine, though."

"Wine is nothing compared with fine chocolate, expertly prepared. It is the drink of the gods."

"Well if you say it like that . . ." Tess teased.

Kaab grinned. "I will bring you some. I promise you will enjoy it."

"I'm sure I will," Tess said, sounding amused. She glanced sidelong at Kaab. "But you haven't told me what brings you to Riverside."

"I have heard of your many talents, and I wish to avail myself of your skill."

Tess seemed to enjoy the flattery. "Is that so?"

They had reached Bridgewater Street, and they turned down the lane that would bring them to Tess's home. The streets of Riverside were certainly livelier in the evening. Tess seemed to be known by many people who called to her as they passed. At that moment, a small, ragged boy approached them and tugged on her cloak. "Mistress Tess, Mistress Tess, spare a coin for my supper?"

Tess looked down at the boy's dirty face and said, "Oh, Tommykins, I don't have any money on me. Come by my house later?"

Kaab reached into her pocket and removed a few minnows. "Here you go," she said, pressing the coins into the boy's hand.

His eyes widened, and he bowed to her as if she were royalty. "Thank you, sir—ma'am—thank you!"

As the boy scampered off, Tess said, "That was kind of you."

"Those of us who are fortunate should help those who are not," Kaab said.

"Clearly you weren't raised on the Hill," Tess said dryly. "They chase beggars away there. Now tell me: What business do you have for me?"

Kaab said, "I would prefer to tell you in private. Will you allow me to come up to your office?"

Tess gave her a straightforward once-over, taking in Kaab's sword and clothing, and Kaab felt herself blushing. Tess seemed to like that, because she said, "I suppose your business is of a delicate nature?"

"It is," Kaab said.

"All right then, you can come up," Tess said. They had arrived at Tess's house now, and the boy Jamie, the one she paid to take messages for her, had fallen asleep with his head against the doorjamb.

Tess put a hand on his shoulder, and he woke with a start. Tess asked, "Any messages, Jamie?"

Jamie yawned and said sleepily, "Nothing all day, except some odd foreign woman came by." He hadn't spotted Kaab, who was standing a few paces behind Tess. "Not even Ben's been here. Where is Ben, anyway?"

Tess said gently, "Ben is dead."

At that, the boy's eyes snapped wide open. "Ben's dead? What did he do?" he asked loudly.

Tess pulled some keys out from the interior pocket of her cloak and began to unlock her front door. "Hush, now," she said. "Ben didn't do anything. Don't go spreading any rumors. Come inside and I'll pay you." She herded the boy inside, then gestured to Kaab to follow them up the dark stairs.

William was late for supper.

Diane ordered the servants to delay the food until the duke arrived. While she waited, she sat stiffly, her cool blue eyes moving over the polished silver, the delicate porcelain plates decorated with the Tremontaine swan. The household budget had been so tight lately that she had entertained the thought, however briefly, of selling the silver. The porcelain was out of the question—she would not sell anything with the Tremontaine crest on it—but the silver didn't bear the ducal swan and coronet. If anyone learned that she had stooped to selling silver, though, Tremontaine would be a laughingstock, and she couldn't have that. She had, instead, quietly parted with a landscape painting that had hung in the rose bedroom, and a marble statue of a nymph from the garden. In place of the statue, now, was an urn freshly planted with roses, and the painting had been replaced with a much less precious charcoal drawing that had been stored in the attic. The statue and painting had gone to a trader from Chartil, for whom they were exotic relics of a foreign land. For Diane, it meant that no one in the City would notice they were missing, and Tremontaine had enough funds for a little while, if she put off her creditors long enough for her plans with the Traders to come to fruition. She'd begin by redeeming the loan on the Highcombe estate—which made Diane's head pound every time she thought of it. Last night she had awakened from a nightmare, breathless with panic that William had failed to push the tax abatement through the Council as she had directed. It had taken every ounce of control she had not to shake him awake as well and demand to know what was delaying the passage of the measure.

Well, now she knew what was occupying his attention: Tilson had confirmed for her that the duke's guest was none other than that horribly rude young student who had nearly run her down on her own staircase the other day. She had considered telling the duke about the boy's insolence but decided he wasn't worth it. She was above being insulted by a University idiot, but apparently her husband wasn't above sleeping with one.

Finally, the duchess heard footsteps approaching the dining room, and a footman opened the door to admit the duke. His cravat was crooked and his waistcoat buttoned unevenly. Diane hid her rising irritation with a sweet smile. "My dear William, I hope you were not detained by bad news?"

His face was flushed, and he sat down hurriedly without kissing her. "I apologize. I had a last-minute visitor on business."

"Oh?" Diane took a sip of her wine. She had already drunk most of her goblet while waiting for her husband, and a footman came quickly to refill it. "Any business I should be aware of?"

Bowls of consommé were set in front of them, lukewarm now due to the delay. The duke picked up his spoon and answered, "It was a University man named Rafe Fenton. I've decided to hire him on as a junior secretary. Old Tolliver just can't keep up anymore."

Diane had some trouble swallowing her consommé. "This soup won't do," she said curtly to the footman behind her. "Take it back and tell the cook there's too much salt in it."

"Of course, madam," the servant murmured, and removed the soup bowl from her sight.

So William intended to lie to her about this Rafe. That was more upsetting than the affair itself. Men and women had needs, after all, and marriage was about more than physical desires. Did he not know she understood this? She wanted to demand that he tell her the truth, but he kept his gaze lowered to his bowl of soup and said nothing. He was a horrible liar.

She was not.

"My dear, of course the decision to hire a new secretary is yours to make, but are you intending to let Tolliver go?" she asked, barely a tremor in her voice. Given the loan against the country estate, not to mention the day-to-day demands of running the Tremontaine household in the manner it required, the expense of additional staff had to be carefully considered. Of course, her husband had no idea what dire straits they were in—and she intended to keep it that way.

"Certainly not," William said. "Tolliver has been with us so long it would be too much of a blow. And Rafe will be able to learn from him." Finally the duke met his wife's cool gaze. "You know, I've been horrible at remembering my appointments lately. I dare say it's partly because Tolliver can't remember them either. Rafe will keep me on track."

"I'm sure he will," Diane said. And when he finally let Tolliver go, there would be a comfortable pension to be paid out. . . . The duchess sighed inwardly. "When does Master Fenton begin?"

"Tomorrow," the duke answered brightly. "I'll ask him to share Tolliver's office for now, but I think we might be able to have the annex off the library—you know, the room I was thinking of using as my study—I could modify it to suit Rafe."

Diane took another sip of her wine. The anticipatory tone in her husband's voice set her nerves on edge. "Do you intend for Master Fenton to live in the house, my dear? Would you like me to have the servants prepare a room for him in the attic?"

The duke's face flushed slightly. "Oh, I don't want to trouble you."

She noted her husband's equivocacy, but chose to not press him for now. "If I may ask, what is Master Fenton's background? His course of study?"

"He's a brilliant scholar," the duke enthused. "He shares my interest in natural philosophy, and you know how much I enjoy my University work. Are you worried about his qualifications, my dear?"

She smiled prettily. "Oh, no, I'm sure you know better than I do whether he is qualified."

The duke returned the smile warmly. "I can assure you, he will be perfect for the job. He comes from a well-placed trading family. I'm not sure what sort of goods they specialize in, but I know how careful you are with household expenses. Perhaps Rafe can help you with that, too."

The very idea incensed the duchess. As if she would allow a stranger to have any knowledge of the Tremontaine finances, even if the knowledge related only to the price of turnips. "I wouldn't wish to burden him with details, my dear. But I appreciate knowing that he will be at my disposal if necessary."

The duke looked a bit nonplussed. "Of course, my love. Any secretary of mine is at your service as well."

She smiled at her husband again. Her cheeks hurt from it.

The footmen entered the dining room with the main course of roast pheasant and root vegetables in a cream sauce. Once the duchess had been served, she picked up her knife and fork and sliced evenly through the meat. It was beautifully seasoned, but she had little appetite. The fact that her husband was lying to her about this Rafe Fenton made her wonder if he would lie to her about other things as well. This was something she would not allow. It showed a lack of respect for her and all the work she had done—and was still doing—to maintain Tremontaine.

"How was your day, my dear?" the duke said, cutting into the silence. "Any news?"

"Great news!" she said with false brightness, to see if she could make him laugh, or even look at her as if she were really there. "I've accepted Lady Halliday's invitation to her garden party next week." She made a moue. "And I'm afraid you, too, are expected to attend, as the gentlemen will be there as well."

"I'll tell Rafe to make a note of it," the duke said, ignoring her completely.

He seemed quite hungry, polishing off his pheasant within minutes. The footman was waiting with more, and as her husband cut into his second portion, Diane forced herself to continue eating her own. The fury that had swelled inside her during supper seemed to coalesce in a hot lump lodged in her throat. The cream sauce was one of Cook's finest, but it was all Diane could do to swallow it.

"Rafe is on the verge of quite a revolutionary discovery," the duke said enthusiastically. "All he needs is a bit of time and space to finish his research. He lives over by the University in a positively ramshackle set of rooms that are surely horrible for intellectual cogitation. I was thinking . . . Highcombe is empty for the summer, is it not?"

Diane nearly dropped her knife and fork in shock. "Highcombe, my dear? Whatever made you think of that place? It hasn't been opened up in years."

"I spent time there when I was a boy; I remember early spring being especially glorious. I'm sure it would only take a week or two to make it habitable again," the duke said. "Of course, I know you're much too busy to leave town this season, but I could take Rafe with me out to the country, enjoy some fishing, maybe, and some riding, while he finishes his research. When he returns he can sit his exams, gain his degree, and then he can join my staff with the status of a full University doctor. Quite a coup for Tremontaine! Yes, yes, have Tolliver send a man out to Highcombe straightaway."

"My dear, I wish you would wait a bit on that," Diane said, ignoring the clammy chill that had risen on her skin. "I—I think there's been some trouble with—with mice at Highcombe. I know there was *something* wrong there, because, remember? We were speaking of letting it out this year. And they told me there was something— Of course, if you want it, it's yours, but let me send someone to take a look at it first, shall I?"

"If you insist, my love. In fact, I could go out and look myself!"

"No, no, you have the Council meeting to worry about. Let me handle the estates," Diane assured him, investing her voice with all the warmth she could muster—which, at the moment, was very little. No one must go to Highcombe, not until the estate was safely out of danger from the loan. Especially not William; she needed him here.

Diane continued to slice her pheasant into tinier and tinier bites, as it would not do for anyone to notice her lack of appetite. "My dear William," she said steadily, "tell me a bit more about these scholarly interests that Rafe Fenton has. I'm curious to know how they dovetail with your own."

The duke beamed at her and began to speak.

Tess Hocking's studio was warmly lit by a large oil lamp that shed a gentle, steady light over the rectangular sheet of paper that Kaab had given her. Tess leaned closer to the paper, studying the red and black signs and numbers, and reached out to touch the material. "This is not the kind of paper I normally see," she said.

"It is called *huun*," Kaab explained. "I have an extra piece for you to use." She unrolled another sheet of huun from the case she had secreted in the inner pocket of her cloak.

Tess took the sheet and said, "You want me to transcribe this . . . incorrectly?"

"Yes. Substitute this symbol for this one." Kaab turned the printed sheet of huun over and picked up one of Tess's ink pens to write out the substitutions.

"Hmm. Normally, when I'm hired, my clients want me to be accurate, not make mistakes." Tess gave Kaab a frankly curious glance. "Why? Are you really a chocolate merchant?"

The light turned Tess's skin rosy, and Kaab wanted to reach out and caress the soft curve of her cheek. "Yes, I am. My family, the Balam, were the first chocolate Traders ever to come to the City. But this is an unusual situation. Are you able to do it?"

Tess cocked her head to one side, her lips pursing.

Such kissable lips, Kaab thought, and almost leaned forward.

"It'll cost extra," Tess said, and smiled at her.

Kaab laughed. "Of course it will. How much extra?"

"You'll have to bring me some of that chocolate—the drink of the gods, you said?"

Kaab took one step closer and extended a hand to Tess. This was how the Locals struck deals, wasn't it? "The drink of the gods is yours," she said.

Tess took Kaab's proffered hand, and Kaab held it for a moment. The sturdy fingers were calloused and ink-stained with many colors: the mark of her profession. Tess flushed, her pale skin showing the rush of blood like a fire across her cheeks.

"Give me a week or two," Tess said, "and your mistake-riddled sheet of huun will be ready."

"I will." Kaab didn't want to leave, but she had to return home to the Balam compound; her aunt and uncle were surely wondering where she was. Tess picked up a small lamp to light Kaab's way down the stairs to the street, but before Kaab descended she turned back to Tess. "I should tell you about something I discovered today," Kaab said.

Tess's eyebrows drew together. "I don't like the sound of that."

"Before I went inside the Three Dogs, I looked at Ben's body outside."

Tess went stiff as a board. "What?"

"I'm sorry. He was murdered."

"How do you know that?" she demanded.

"He was killed in a way that showed it was deliberate."

Tess looked frightened. "How could you tell?"

"I've seen these things before."

Tess's gaze narrowed on her. "Where? Who are you, really?"

Kaab hesitated. She was attracted to Tess, that was true, but speaking to a beautiful girl of murder—with her protector lying cold and stiff nearby, no less—was certainly not the best way to seduce her. Finally Kaab said, "I'm no one to you, I know that, but I hope to be a friend."

Tess shook her head. "Why? You don't know me or Ben."

"If Ben was murdered, you might not be safe," Kaab said. "He could have been killed for protecting you. You do dangerous work."

"I told you before, I have a fortnight. No one in Riverside will harm me while I'm in mourning."

"What will you do when the fortnight is over?" Tess just shook her head. "And outside Riverside?" Kaab pressed her. "Across the Bridge? There is a whole great city out there right now, where even your mourning won't protect you."

Tess looked at her thoughtfully. "You really are worried, aren't you? You're a different one, Kaab. I don't think I've ever met anyone like you."

The way the lamplight turned Tess's skin into shades of strawberries and cream was simply irresistible. Kaab knew that she was about to ignore her father's instructions to stay out of trouble.

"I will find out why Ben was killed," Kaab said. Before Tess could do more than draw a single, startled breath, Kaab went to her and kissed her on the cheek: a brief, fleeting brush of her lips across Tess's heated skin. Kaab promised, "I will find out for you."

Episode Five

THE DAGGER AND THE SWORD

Alaya Dawn Johnson

The young foreigner had been fighting all challengers for the last two hours. She wasn't large for a woman, and yet gave the impression of height. Her hair, perhaps, which had begun in two thick braids wrapped curiously around her head and had long since transformed into two unraveling streamers that whipped about her face as she turned and tumbled and struck. She fought with rapier and dagger, handling the smaller blade with notably more assurance than the longer weapon. As a swordswoman, her skills stumbled on the bad side of mediocre—except at certain moments, when she would move like a snake in the water; then her challenger might find himself on the striking end of her dagger and be forced to concede the fight. The gathered crowd jeered the losers then. But they were fickle friends: They jeered the young woman plenty too.

Two hours into the spectacle, the press in the Old Market prevented all but the most determined drunkards from entering the Maiden's Fancy. So in this unseasonal dog-heat of early spring, the serving girls waded through the crowd with professional elbows to take orders in the square. Even to the jaded denizens of Riverside, training ground of the greatest swordsmen of the City, the sight of a foreign woman in tight-fitting men's clothes issuing challenges by the trash-filled mermaid fountain in the Old Market was a more than sufficient spectacle.

The foreign woman had long since kicked her fine leather boots to the edge of the space, a traditional Riverside challenge spot marked by a rough ring of broken and gapped cobbles.

A pair of hungry boys had eyed those fine-tooled shoes with professional avarice before a redheaded woman, gorgeous and plump, grabbed them herself and scowled at the boys. They shrugged and melted back into the crowd, eyes sharp for a hint of treasure. Just because Riversiders were poor didn't mean they had nothing to steal.

The redhead, now awkwardly clutching her friend's boots in addition to an overstuffed leather bag, seemed oddly distracted. After all, the fighting was being done in her name: Tess the Hand as they called her, the best forger in Riverside, both skilled and affordable. Her protector had been the pretty swordsman Ben, who hadn't looked so pretty when the clam women downriver, picking barefoot through the mud for the clams exposed at morning's low tide, discovered his body among their harvest. Two weeks ago that was, and Tess the Hand was on the market for a new protector with a strong arm who wouldn't expect sexual favors in exchange for the service.

A young man, soberly dressed in black and doeskin brown, whose measured stride still implied a swagger, edged through the crowd in a slow spiral. He had been among the first to pause and watch when the foreign woman issued her challenge.

"I go against any who dares cross blades with me," she had

called with a calm pride that lanced through the normal bustle of market day like a sword's thrust. "And I will choose the next protector of Tess the Hand from among those who best me." She spoke well, the foreign woman, like someone who had studied the language but was still accustoming herself to its shape on her tongue.

The young man had lived in Riverside for a time and made himself a reputation among those who cared about the sword. He was tall and lithe, brunet and not quite handsome, except for his eyes—green and gold and framed by curling pale lashes—which could have been his vanity, were he a man who cared less about the sword.

His name was Vincent Applethorpe, and watching the sweaty young woman fight so badly and so well in her unusually bare feet, he began to wonder if he had, at last, fallen in love.

Her latest opponent was one of the many swordsmen who frequented the Maiden's Fancy: Alaric, a short, heavyset Northerner capable of surprising bursts of speed. He was not clever, nor an artist, but he was vicious and not above foul play, provided he could get away with it. He was also fresh and well rested. He was dewy with the first ten minutes' exertion, but only because he was playing to the crowd, toying with his opponent. The foreigner seemed to know this. She kept her eyes on his sword. (*His face!* Vincent had wanted to shout more than once since the match had begun. *Watch his eyes; they'll tell you what his hands will do!*) She dodged Alaric's blows or blocked them as best she could. She seemed too tired to attack. Or perhaps she was waiting for a certain kind of opening, something that favored those enviably fluid foreign moves.

Alaric feinted left and right, and when that didn't so much as prompt her to move her blades, he aimed his next blow, without any fuss at all, at her exposed neck. The crowd had time for half a breath. The foreigner wouldn't have had time even for that. She raised her dagger for the parry at the last moment. She fell to one knee with a force that jarred those who knew what that cost her and then rolled to one side. She spat a few words in a language that Vincent didn't understand, though from their tone he gathered they were not polite.

The foreigner stumbled to her feet. "I concede!"

That should have been that, but she did not lower her weapon, which Vincent thought was only prudent, given that she had barely avoided a killing blow that Alaric had no business employing in a demonstration match.

Alaric laughed and advanced. "We go to first blood, remember?"

He gave the woman no time to reply. Each of his relentless blows could have killed her had they landed. The challenge had never been to blood—if it had, the woman would be bleeding in half a dozen places from the duels she had already found. Someone had to stop this fight.

Vincent pushed himself to the front of the crowd, near where the redheaded forger was standing.

"She conceded!" the redhead screamed, along with a number of supporters. But other, more bloodthirsty Riversiders seemed to appreciate the spectacle and sided with Alaric. This side shouted, "First blood!" as though this had ever been a fair fight.

"What's that, girl?" Alaric said as he hammered the foreigner. "You talk like you have marbles in your mouth. Speak civilized!"

"I concede!" the foreigner shouted again. Alaric lunged, and she slid beneath his attack in a move so chancy it struck Vincent as suicidal. She slashed his shoulder and danced back out again. Alaric's blade whistled through the air where she had been and threw sparks on the cobbles.

It was relief, Vincent thought later—and the shrieks of the crowd—that distracted him from anticipating Alaric's next move. No one would continue a duel when his opponent had yielded and then drawn blood in the same elegant breath.

No one but a certain Northern swordsman who would rather murder than let it be said he was bested by a woman.

The foreigner turned, exhausted but grinning. She saluted the blushing redhead, and Alaric swung his foot and kicked her in the back of her knees. The foreigner fell hard. Her rapier clattered on the stones. And Alaric moved in.

"Kaab!" the redhead screamed. "Help her, you gaping idiots!"

Vincent Applethorpe stepped forward.

72 hours earlier

"But this isn't right, Rafe," said Micah, not for the first time that afternoon.

Rafe looked down despairingly at his mug of half-drunk chocolate, the syrupy concoction of over-skimmed milk and dark sugar that might have once touched a few shavings of cacao, but not very good cacao, and not for very long. The Inkpot had perhaps the worst chocolate in the City.

"You have mentioned that," Rafe said, "a few times." He looked again at the pages of navigational tables written in a neat but crabbed hand, the sum of Micah's feverish work for the last two weeks. And, according to Micah, entirely wrong.

"Yes, four times, but I wasn't sure if you had heard me."

"I heard you."

"Oh." Micah looked nonplussed. The boy leaned forward and peered at Rafe, as though that could help him decipher the bland insouciance of Rafe's tone. Rafe rested his head on his open right palm, like a sunflower too heavy for its stem, and tried to focus on the details of Micah's latest discovery—if you could use a term so hopeful to describe the apparent failure of two whole weeks of work. Even using artificial numbers, Micah said, the tables came out wrong. There was some fundamental disconnect between the way that their people's navigators had always calculated distances and the reality of sailing a ship across the gently curved surface of the earth.

"Did you understand?" Micah tried.

He sighed. "More than you imagine. Your chocolate is getting cold."

Micah loved the chocolate at the Inkpot. The boy glanced back at his mug, blinked as though surprised to see it there, and finished the last of it in a single gulp of quiet ecstasy.

"Don't you want yours?" Micah asked.

Rafe pushed his mug toward Micah with the hand not occupied by his head. The Duke Tremontaine had good chocolate, he thought. Lately, it had been as good as anything Rafe's own father had been able to procure. Better than anything save the concoctions he had drunk at the feast of the Balam. That kind of chocolate was a tonic to the body and the spirit. The chocolate at the Inkpot, however, was an overpriced abomination, only fit to fuel late night arguments and hungover mornings. Rafe missed good chocolate. He missed, though he hated to admit it, the man who served it to him. Tremontaine. Will.

He hadn't seen Will for more than a passing moment in

days. Rafe didn't think the duchess had guessed the precise nature of his relationship with her husband, but neither did she trust him. And the feeling was mutual. She was an abomination, that woman, a small golden dagger with a poisoned hilt. Diane, Duchess Tremontaine, ran the entire household like a giant clock and had made of Will a clockwork duke, trotting out at the designated hours to do her bidding. The latest occasion had been some kind of discussion of arcane corners of tax import policy. Will had attempted to explain its importance to him, but the explanation had necessitated a distinct overuse of the word "Diane." Rafe had much preferred to kiss him, and one thing had led to another. Instead of working, they had enjoyed an afternoon romp on his secretary's desk. Papers were ruined. Rafe had no regrets—or he shouldn't have. But he had now passed three days without the duke's company, and he felt like his friend Thaddeus had looked a week into a cleansing regimen prescribed by some quack physician from Uru—haggard, snappish, held together with shoestring and spite.

"Will," he sighed, and his head fell from his hand to the table.

"Are you sick?" Micah asked.

"He's wasting his head-spirit," said Kaab Balam, finally returning with the popped maize and beer that recommended the Inkpot to budding natural philosophers far more than its insipid chocolate. "Look out, friend Rafe. If you aren't careful, it might escape you."

Rafe popped open an eye. "Escape me? My soul? What, are you planning to kill me with that fearsome black dagger of yours?"

She shook her head and sucked in her lips, which he had learned generally meant she was trying to find a way of explaining a difficult concept from her country to him. "You don't have *a* soul," she said, finally. "You have three. One of them is in your head—it is your power and your heat—and you waste it with such an un . . . an un—out of bounds? Out of normal behavior?"

"Unseemly?" he tried.

She brightened. "Yes! That! You waste it on an unseemly passion." Kaab settled back in her seat, nodded with ample self-satisfaction, and quaffed deeply from a tankard of the beer that she had very nearly spit on the floor the first time they'd come here.

"My perspicacious Kinwiinik princess," he said, pricked into raising his head, "are you speaking to me, by any chance, or to a mirror?"

"I . . ." She trailed off, choked by a visible internal struggle. "I am learning to moderate my excesses," she said stiffly.

"Pride chief among them!" Rafe plucked a sweet-salty maize kernel and tossed it into his mouth. He grinned. Kaab's scowl could have curdled fresh milk. He blew her a kiss.

"Rafe," Micah said, sounding puzzled. "Are you two arguing again?"

"Whyever would you think that, Micah? By the by, have you tried this popped maize? It's delicious."

"So glad we have something you approve of," Kaab said. "Go on, taste it, Micah. It's good!"

Micah picked up a puffy white kernel and split it open with his fingernail. He peered at the dried golden-brown lining, nibbled a corner, and looked suspiciously at Kaab.

"This isn't maize. We feed maize to the hogs."

"Hogs!" Kaab nearly spat out her beer. "Hogs? You don't feed this to hogs, Micah." Rafe watched, amused, as she suppressed her indignation. "Well, maybe you do. An inferior grade."

"Hardly worth the popping," Rafe added helpfully. She glared at him, so he took pity and explained, "This is special maize, Micah, newly brought from the same place as the chocolate. It costs more, but University students love it, and it's very fashionable right now." He took another handful.

Micah nodded. "Well, that's all right, then. Thank you, Rafe, but it tastes funny to me. Also, I need you to understand what's wrong with these tables."

"Arkenvelt isn't where it's supposed to be, you said."

"Not unless you use one of the corrections. But I recalculated the chart so we wouldn't need corrections! I thought the chart was wrong because I needed to use artificial numbers for it, but I did that and it still doesn't come out right. So now I think it must be something else, too."

"Why do the numbers have to be wrong at all?"

"Oh, they are! I explained before—"

"No, wait, never mind. What else must be wrong then?"

Micah scrunched his nose. "I don't know," he said. "I thought you might have an idea. Or Kaab, since her people travel so much."

The two of them turned to look at Kaab, busy studying her reflection in the bottom of her beer mug.

"I told you both already," she muttered, so low they had to lean in to hear, "I don't know much—anything—about the ways of navigation. They don't teach that to women."

"That's all right, Kaab. I don't need to know all about navigation," Micah said. "I just need to know, well, what does the earth look like? How do you move across it? I've been thinking about straight lines, Rafe." The young mathematician leaned in, so he could speak just inches from Kaab and Rafe. He looked at once panicked and excited. "I think that straight lines must be wrong."

Rafe stared at Micah's innocent brown eyes and tried to make sense of what he had just heard. "Straight lines? Good god, Micah, are you mad? Have you been eating too many tomato pies? No, it's this terrible chocolate. Inkpot chocolate, ruining your judgment as well as your palate!"

"It is terrible chocolate," Kaab agreed. "And of course straight lines exist. How else would we make buildings or roads or . . . anything?"

"No, not straight lines for normal things. *Straight lines on spheres!* Remember the problem in Doctor Volney's class? The one that was very wrong?"

"Volney didn't think so! He kicked you out for having the gall to contradict him."

Micah winced, as though the memory still hurt him. "But he was wrong, Rafe. They can't possibly be the same distance apart in three dimensions as on a plane. It's just not logical."

Rafe was about to object again when his eye caught on the mug Micah was drinking from.

"A straight line," he said slowly, imagining one traversing two arbitrary points on the glass, "on a curved three-dimensional surface."

Micah nodded vigorously. "Yes! Rafe, don't you see?"

"They're not straight. I'm not sure exactly how, but they must be . . . *longer?*"

"Yes!" Micah jumped a little in his chair. "I'm not sure exactly how either. I think the calculations might be difficult. But this seems clear to me."

Rafe felt dizzy. His hands tingled, and he could hardly feel the rest of his body. If Micah was right, then navigation required a complete change in the general understanding of geometry. At the very least, it would give him something worth arguing in his fellowship examinations!

"But in that case, the trouble is the earth," Rafe said. "Is it a sphere, as Rastin claims?"

"I don't know. Kaab said—" Micah glanced over at the foreign trader, who regarded them with a look so dark and inscrutable that Rafe scooted backward.

Micah hung his head. "I know you said not to tell."

Rafe gaped at Kaab. "Not to tell? Gods, I knew you were holding out on us! But you tell Micah, and not me? What is it?"

"You are . . . impossible to deal with . . . very frustrating . . . in—in—"

"Insufferable?"

Kaab nodded grimly. "I told Micah that I had seen some charts, maps of the stars and the earth for use by our navigators. My uncle has them."

"Why, Kaab! If your uncle has them, then surely you can just remove them for a few hours and let us look. In the spirit of the free exchange of knowledge. What harm could come of that?"

Rafe did know that, depending on what he and Micah could learn from the Kinwiinik star charts, a great deal of harm could come of it—at least, from the Kinwiinik traders' perspective. If traders from the Land, like his father, could adjust their navigational tables so that they were accurate, what would stop them from heading to Uru or Cham or the land of the Kinwiinik themselves and negotiating fairer prices at port? He felt a twinge of guilt at this, but excitement overrode his finer instincts.

Kaab was shaking her head slowly back and forth. "I don't think . . . I don't know . . ." She looked between her two companions and then back at her drink, and blinked to find it empty. She swallowed. "I might be able to. Just for a very short time. We could meet here again in a few days?"

Micah grinned and rocked a little in his chair. "Oh, Kaab!" he said. "This is very exciting! First we have to decide how to calculate the distances, Rafe. But after that I can do the tables again. I might be done in a month or two."

Rafe grinned. "And by then, I'll have figured some way out of this trouble with my committee—this new spherical approach to geometry might dazzle even de Bertel—and I'll be capable of promoting our theory among all scholars who now pretend to the study of natural philosophy!"

He grabbed an empty mug and clinked it with Kaab's and Micah's.

"This calls for a celebration," Rafe said, making a decision. "And I will leave you to it."

"Are you going somewhere, Rafe?" Micah asked.

Kaab raised an eyebrow, looking once again like her comfortable, competent self. "He returns to his duke. And he defies the duchess."

Kaab could sometimes be uncanny like that, knowing his thoughts a moment after he did. But right now he did not care at all. Rafe stood. He felt like spinning.

"I want," Rafe said, "very good chocolate."

Lying on the filthy cobbles of the Old Market, tripped by her dishonorable opponent, Kaab gasped like a fish pulled from a net. Some cold liquid, thankfully unidentifiable, seeped through her vest and tunic onto her lower back. Her sword, that unwieldy, overlong, beautiful, hateful weapon, had fallen from her numb and sweaty grip. All that remained was the dagger. She might get one chance, even at this extreme, to do her opponent enough damage to make him leave her alone. The alternative was to lie here and wait to be speared like a war captive on a foreign altar. Had she survived Tultenco only to die beside the trash-filled fountain of the Old Market on the dirty knife of a dishonorable warrior? And Tess had been almost sure that no one would try to kill her.

She heard the beautiful forger now, screaming. "Help her, you gaping idiots!"

Her opponent glanced around, startled. He took a slight step forward. Within striking range. She continued to gasp, though she had regained control of her breathing. From her position on the ground, she had a clear view of his dirty boots, cracked with mud and smelling of shit. Those would be tough to pierce. But his calf was merely covered by breeches, with none of the cotton padding that warriors from her lands used to protect themselves. It would be easy for her to lunge for that soft spot behind his knee, where there stretched a certain ligament that it would hurt him to lose.

She did not take more than a second to consider and make her decision. She was distantly aware of the surging crowd, the commotion and shouting outside the ring, but she did not take it into account. This was her fight, and she would finish it. The man growled an oath she didn't understand, something about a god of horns, and pivoted toward her with his sword raised. She rolled and lunged with the speed of a lifetime of training. Her blade went unerringly to his knee—

And she missed.

Momentum threw Kaab forward, and she caught herself with her hand. She had nicked the other man's skin, but no more. Certainly not the incapacitating blow that she had planned. Indignant, sweaty, and bruised, she heaved herself to her feet. A green-eyed man held her erstwhile opponent's arms behind his back. Tess stood right behind him, clutching her bag.

"Kaab, are you all right?" Tess looked furious and terrified, ready to slug her or kiss her. Her cheeks were nearly as red as her hair.

Suddenly, her exhaustion and bruises and near brush with death did not matter so much. Kaab grinned. "Quite well," she said, and bent to retrieve her fallen sword. "Even if I do have to fight cowards instead of honorable men."

The green-eyed man, who had been watching Kaab's performance since the beginning, pulled the swordsman's arms a little more firmly behind him. His captive yelped.

"Horned God's balls, Applethorpe, you bastard, let me go! This little bitch nearly hamstrung me!"

The green-eyed man, though the slighter of the two, did not seem preoccupied with the other man's struggles. He had an air of violence about him, honed to the edge of a fighting blade. He would know his own strength to the feather-weight. He would know how to exploit another man's weakness.

"Quiet, Alaric," he said mildly. "Or I'll let the lady finish what she started."

Alaric went very still.

"So," the green-eyed man asked Kaab, "where did you learn to fight so well with a dagger and so badly with a sword?"

"I learned the obsidian blade in my home in Binkiinha. And the sword I began on the ship here." She scowled at the object in her right hand. "It is a weapon more elegant to admire than to wield."

He laughed. "That depends on the wielder."

She acknowledged that with a wry grimace. This intriguing man might be the one they had hoped to flush out with this public display. Not a protector, as she had proclaimed from the beginning, but a murderer. Ben's murderer. Which meant that she and Tess needed to cast the bait.

Kaab glanced at Tess and nodded very slightly. Tess's wide lips quirked a little at the corners, and she reached casually into her bag.

"Oh no!" she said, not quite a shout, but with a quality to her voice that projected across the square. "They're gone! My drawings are gone! Someone must have taken them!" She spread the bag open for effect, empty but for a shawl.

"Did you drop them?" Kaab asked.

Tess raised an eyebrow. "They call me Tess the Hand and you think I'd lose track of a job?" But she took the hint and went back to where she had been standing beneath a portico, with a good view of the rest of the square. The curious and ghoulish crowded around her while she spun an elaborate tale of the very special forgery and the drawings she had made of it, as insurance against a dangerous client.

Kaab kept an eye on Alaric and the green-eyed man, but they were busy negotiating the terms of Alaric's release, speaking in low voices peppered like avocado soup with expletives and exhortations to their gods. They weren't paying the slightest attention to Tess. Not definitive proof, perhaps, but Kaab decided to trust her instincts and continue the hunt elsewhere.

She turned to the green-eyed man. "Will he kill me?" she asked.

He looked down speculatively. "I think the poison's out of him."

"Then let him go. I need a beer."

"I admire your priorities. I'm Vincent Applethorpe, at your service."

Kaab bowed, distracted by Tess's relatively subtle but persistent gestures for her to hurry up and move through the crowd. "Ixkaab Balam," she said.

He nodded. "Be good, Alaric," he said, and released the man

with a push. Alaric cursed and rubbed his shoulders. He tried to retrieve his weapons from the ground, but Applethorpe stopped him with a wagging finger.

"At the Fancy," he said, in the tone of a reminder, "a day hence. I promise to return them. You don't attack an opponent who has yielded, friend. And all the swordsmen will have heard of this by the end of day. I do this to spare you worse."

"You're a smug Southern pimp, you know that, Applethorpe?"

"Better than being a flaccid Northern boor. Now mosey on."

Alaric spat and hurried away in the direction of the Maiden's Fancy.

"Thank you for stopping him," Kaab said.

Applethorpe twirled Alaric's confiscated knife. "A matter of honor," he said. "Also, I've a mind to challenge you myself, and I needed you whole to do it."

At the thought, Kaab felt a strange exhilaration. This man would give her the fight of her life. But she had something to attend to first.

"Beer," Kaab said. "And rest. But then you may have your fight."

And she hurried into the crowd before he could respond, leaving him staring after her with bemusement and something else she couldn't quite name.

70 hours earlier

Kaab judged that she had played that quite well. The right amount of reticence and discomfort, a generous dollop of ignorance, and a sprinkling of devil-may-care recklessness, and she felt sure that she had pulled herself from the near disaster of that conversation in the Inkpot.

If she'd had any idea before how close Rafe and Micah were to a major discovery, she never would have so much as admitted to the location of the north star in the night sky. The idea that the safety of her family—and quite possibly of the Kinwiinik triple alliance itself—depended on her convincing a pair of provincial Locals that the earth was shaped more like an egg than a ball would have been a grand joke in other circumstances. That it had instead become a deadly serious game of wits made Kaab pull her hood over her head against the endless icy drizzle and hurry toward Riverside. Toward Tess.

The beautiful, wise-eyed redhead had told Kaab it would be two weeks until the forgeries she'd ordered were finished. But after witnessing Micah's disarming, razorlike intelligence slice open the heart of a problem that generations of Local sailors had not been able (or not bothered) to solve, Kaab knew she had to move quickly. She judged that she had a very narrow window remaining in which she'd still be able to influence Micah's future thinking on the topic. Even if she stopped Rafe and Micah permanently (and after Citlali, she wished never to see another assassination again), what was to stop some other Local scholar from reaching the same conclusions independently? On the other hand, if she could subtly misdirect Micah's investigation, Kaab might buy her family months—even years—to stabilize the situation at home and neuter the political and financial consequences of any potential discoveries in the Land.

Tess lived on a dead-end street just south of the old bridge. Kaab had memorized the way there as a matter of course the first time she visited. She found herself subject to a number of speculative stares now, as then, though the reason had clearly changed. In her Local dress, with her heavy skirts and the hood of a rain cloak pulled to shadow her face, they had no way of knowing her for a foreigner. But they knew her for a woman. Apparently just that was enough to make small boys stick dirty fingers in their mouths and whistle before laughing and running away. Old men smoking foul-smelling sticks in leaky porticos leaned forward in their rockers and called her things like "filly" and described how they'd like to "pierce her cheeks" as she hurried past them. The young men did not even bother with euphemism. This lack of respect infuriated Kaab, but she couldn't very well turn on each of them with her dagger, and so she tried instead not to listen.

And if this was what they did to *her*, how did a buxom, vivacious woman like Tess manage to walk the streets unmolested? Ben had died nearly two weeks ago. If the term "protector" had seemed abstract before, she understood its concrete purpose a little better by the time she climbed the stairs to Tess's apartment, obsidian blade in hand.

"Who is it?" Tess's voice sounded strained and tired. She spoke through the closed door and made no move to open it even a crack.

"It's Kaab," she said. "I wish to ask about the drawings—"

Kaab heard Tess push back two bolts before she unlocked and opened the door. She was wearing a long gown of white linen trimmed in ivory ribbon that looked very comfortable—no stays at all. Her sunset hair surrounded her face like the corona of an eclipse. Kaab felt undone, looking at her. She felt out of breath and full of fire. She thought of Citlali, months dead and as like this woman as the desert is like the sea, and could have cried.

"Are you planning to stick me with that pretty piece of black glass, or did you want to talk to me?"

Kaab realized that she still held the dagger in an open stance. She wrapped it in its sheath with hands that wanted very much to tremble and replaced it in her pocket.

"My apologies," Kaab said. "I received too much attention on the way here."

Tess laughed shortly. "Don't let the boys get to you," she said. "That's just how Riverside goes."

"It seems like a place fit for murderers and thieves."

Tess's cheeks quivered, as if she wanted to smile but couldn't. "It is," she said, and gestured for Kaab to enter. "So how is your inquiry going? Did you find out anything new about Ben?"

Kaab followed her inside, careful to keep her distance. She had hired Tess for a job, not for seduction. But she was starting to forget the difference.

"I'm sorry," Kaab said. "It's hard . . . it seems that no one will talk to a foreign girl about their murdered lover. He was a prostitute, your Ben?"

Tess sighed and walked over to her desk, where a fat tallow candle threw the brightest light in the small and curiously neat room. Tess's white dress billowed behind her knees.

"Prostitute, rent boy, paid companion, whatever you want to call him. Someone probably killed him over a stupid, reckless mistake he made. I don't know why I asked you. I don't know why I expected anything different."

Her reaction shocked Kaab. "But I told you, he was murdered from behind. It was no duel, no bar fight. He was your friend and protector. Don't you want to know what happened?"

Tess shook her head. "What happened is that we live in Riverside. How do you think men die around here? In feather beds, surrounded by weeping grandchildren?"

Kaab looked away—and saw what she should have seen the moment she walked in, had she not been so distracted by the beautiful Tess.

The room was too neat, the desk clear of all but a few sketches. Last time, it had been a comfortable warren of papers, wax seals, and colored inks. Kaab thought Tess's loose dress might be what she wore for sleeping. Yet she clearly hadn't slept for quite some time.

"Maize flower," Kaab said softly, in Kindaan. She continued in the Local tongue, "What has happened to you?"

Tess held herself very still for a moment. Then she lowered herself into the chair, dropped her head into her arms, and started to sob. Kaab rushed over and knelt.

"Someone ransacked the place," Tess said. "They came and went through every damn thing. Smashed half of my drawers for the hell of it. Pulled up floorboards, and I hope the mice ate them for their trouble. Went through all my work. My seals, my *Nobles' Almanack*—the latest edition! They destroyed most of my sketches. Tore them to shreds and left them around like snowflakes. All the ones I did for you are gone, Kaab. Destroyed."

Only Tess's continued sobs kept Kaab from rushing straight to the desk. She put her arm around the woman's shoulders and held her close.

"And the originals?" she said, trying to keep the panic from her tone. "The charts of my people I gave you to copy—to alter?"

"I had those with me. I'd gone out that day to Tilney Market, to a good colorist's shop I know, to match one of the blues that I couldn't find down here. And I'm glad I did, because I hate to think what those dogs would have done to them."

Kaab released her breath in a careful exhale. "You have them safe?" Tess nodded, pointing to a portfolio on the desk. "But they destroyed your work?"

"I'll have to start again. I'm sorry, I know you wanted the forgery quick, but it will take at least another week, maybe longer."

"Don't beg pardon. I'm glad you're safe, Tess."

She would find a way to delay Micah and Rafe. Kaab shuddered to think what Uncle Chuleb and Aunt Saabim would have said if they knew. At least the originals hadn't been caught in the destruction.

"But who was this?" Kaab said. "Did they take anything else?"

Tess shook her head. "They pawed through my dirty clothes, but they didn't take a button. Not that I have much of value, but if a thief bothers to break in, you expect him to snatch a few things just for the trouble, you know? I worried that it might have something to do with you, Kaab. You were so secretive about this job."

Kaab considered and rejected the idea. "I don't believe so. My commission is . . . unusual. And secret, yes, but there are only a very few people who would understand what the numbers mean. What about Ben's things?"

Tess jumped to her feet and walked to the shuttered window. She looked as though she wanted to hit something but was sure the blow would hurt her more than whatever she struck.

"Went through them, too," she said finally. "Just like they went through my things. There wasn't much. This isn't—this shouldn't be about him."

"Why not?"

"Because if it's his murderer, he already got Ben! And if it's someone from Riverside, I'm still in my fortnight of mourning. They wouldn't touch me. They should have respect for the dead."

Kaab could now see how grief and lack of sleep had agitated Tess. But she couldn't understand how someone would let such base emotions cloud their reason in a dangerous situation. She rolled her eyes. "Perhaps they should, but not everyone honors the gods who gave us life. You need a protector now. Or these people might come back and do worse."

Like steal my family's charts, she thought, but had the good sense not to say.

But this only made Tess angrier. "Didn't you hear? I'm in mourning! I won't dishonor Ben like that "

"Would you rather die? Or lose your home?"

Tess smacked the shutter behind her, which rattled ominously on rusted hinges. "Ben was my protector and I loved him, but he was no saint. I know he was up to something when he died. Maybe that's what whoever it was who came thought too. But if that's so, then they came up dry. And that's probably the end of it."

"It might not be," Kaab said. "You're connected to him. What if they come back?"

"Then I'll get my own pretty dagger and tell those bastards to leave me alone."

"You can't mean that."

"You know all about how I live in Riverside? A rich foreign Trader girl like you?"

"You're not safe! Tess—it is very dangerous here."

Tess's eyes were twin volcanoes, spitting smoke. "I won't have some wide-eyed foreigner coming in here with a borrowed sword and pretending she knows Riversiders better than I do. You learn to survive, or you die. I survive. I don't need your help."

"*My* help? I would help you if I could. Of course! But as you say, I'm no Local. My family has influence, but not in the way that you need. Ben is gone. Open your eyes, Tess! You need a new protector. Or are you too proud of your murderous Riverside to see the truth about it?"

Kaab knew that she shouldn't have said it. But it was said, and it was true, and pride—her own vice—kept her from apologizing.

It came as no surprise when Tess pointed to the door. No surprise, but for how much it hurt her.

"Get the hell out of here before I change my mind about your precious forgeries. Don't come back until I send for you."

"Tess—"

Tess turned her back. "Go."

In the increasingly drunken, festival atmosphere of the Old Market after the foreigner's latest, breathtaking fight, no one was inclined to take overmuch offense at a jarred elbow or a carelessly trod-upon foot. This was to the benefit of the man moving like driftwood through the crowd, bobbing in its eddies and lazy currents. He munched on a meat pie and apologized to everyone who he bumped with his conspicuously oversize, badly weighted sword. And somehow every bump, every heartfelt apology with an accent at once identifiably from the country and impossible to place more precisely, pushed him closer to the crowd that surrounded his redheaded quarry. She was the forger they called Tess the Hand, until recently under the protection of a rent boy named Ben. A young fellow who had made himself dangerous to the woman that this man served.

The bumbling man with the awkward blade had not seemed so foolish when he stepped neatly behind Ben in the open streets of the Hill and plunged his dagger between Ben's ribs. Nor when he had searched his person, removed his jacket, and dumped the body into the river.

Tess the Hand was alive. But only because the man wanted to make sure of what she did and didn't know. His employer would demand that. He didn't think Tess knew where Ben had gone the night the young man had made the fatal mistake of under-estimating his employer. To gain entry to a certain well-guarded house, Ben had carried a picture that he sent up to the swordsman's employer. It had to have been drawn by Tess. The swordsman had been ordered to make sure that no copies of it existed, and that any who knew what they looked like be silenced quickly and efficiently.

Silence, in this case, might have meant death. But in all his years of service, Ben was the first man his mistress had ever ordered her swordsman to kill. He would certainly kill, if necessary, even a woman. But killing was merely the most certain method of silencing someone, not always the most efficient.

"What's missing, Tess?"

"Maybe you dropped them."

"Who'd steal some stupid piece of paper?"

"Is it a big job, Tess? Something from the Hill?"

"Ah, come on, give us a hint at least!"

"I can't say a word," said Tess quite loudly. "Except that it's my head if I don't find those sketches!"

The swordsman bumped heavily into a plump man staring despondently at the foam dregs clinging to the bottom of his tankard of beer. His apologies carried him within a few feet of Tess. He peered at her with as much curiosity as the rest of the crowd, but when he saw the bag she had left open beside her, he forgot himself for a moment and stilled. That bag had not been in her rooms five days ago. Which meant that it quite possibly could have contained the sketches that his mistress had sworn him to find and destroy.

It also meant that someone else in this crowd could have taken them before he had his chance.

Automatically, he adjusted the weight of his sword. He looked around, scanning the crowd more deliberately for signs of any pickpockets or clandestine swordsmen like himself. He found at least eight of the former. One of the latter he knew by reputation, and he would have had opportunity to talk to them. But did Applethorpe work for anyone who might take an interest in his employer's affairs?

The swordsman re-collected himself and slouched again into the boorish country bravo. He hung back in the crowd. He waited for an opportunity to reveal itself while he contemplated how to present this latest development to his mistress. She would not be pleased.

He did not concern himself with his momentary lapse in demeanor. It did not occur to him that someone else might have noticed.

65 hours earlier

Diane, Duchess Tremontaine, returned late from a small ladies' supper hosted by Sarah, Lady Perry, who had spent most of it being insufferable about her daughter's recent betrothal. Josephine Perry was small and dark and had no conversation to speak of, but she was, nevertheless, to marry Rupert Vernay, Lord Filisand's horse-mad heir—the very one Diane had hoped her own daughter, Honora, would catch if she were clever. Honora was a lost cause, run away with a minor nobleman named Campion and breeding little heirs in the country somewhere, and everyone knew it.

If that were not enough, there were the saffron hares. Lady Perry had had the effrontery to serve Diane's own signature dish—though the desired sunset-gold color had shaded distinctly to orange due to the injudicious use of turmeric.

Every eye at the table had watched Diane as she took a delicate bite.

The duchess had smiled with a cruel sincerity. "Delicious! It is so lovely to see hares coming back into fashion at everyone's tables. And adding the spices of far-off Uru does turn them a most delightful shade! A unique recipe, Sarah; you must get your cook to send it to me."

That had been the only triumph of the night. Her dress had been, of necessity, made over from one she had worn to last year's MidWinter balls. Trust flighty Aurelia Halliday to mention how much she had enjoyed seeing Diane dance at them and then look boldly and obviously around the table to see if anyone else had noticed the dig.

Even the Duke Tremontaine had not been spared.

Eager to repay Diane's comment about the hares, Lady Perry had said, "Diane, I pray you will not think me indiscreet, but I feel we are such friends that I cannot fail to voice my concern. Is the duke quite well? I only ask because Lord Filisand mentioned, during one of our little family gatherings here—Josephine and young Rupert are so enamored that they can't bear to spend more than a few days apart, and who are we to deny our children the happiness of young love, I'm sure *you* of all parents understand my sentiments—well, dearest Filisand said that your husband has been looking quite peaked at Council meetings lately. He even slept through a vote, and only woke to the applause when it passed!"

The ladies tittered. The duchess smiled graciously.

"Of course, we all understand that sleep may elude us from time to time for one reason or another"—Lady Aurelia snorted and tried to turn it into a sneeze—"but to hear that the dear duke has been looking off-color, and has even come late to several meetings, appearing flushed and breathless, well, that is quite another matter, and I wanted to set dear Filisand's mind at ease by being able to report to him that Duke William is quite well, I hope?"

Diane prided herself on her control and poise and grace. But Lady Perry at full gloat would have tried Humility herself. Still, Diane had maintained a chilly, polite concern.

"How very kind of Lord Filisand," Diane had merely replied. "You may certainly tell him that the duke is in excellent health, and hopes that young Rupert's streak of gambling on losing horses will soon come to an end. One so hates to think of Lord Filisand having a moment's anxiety on any subject, dear man."

A little broad, perhaps, but effective. Lady Perry had not ventured anything more for the rest of the night.

But while the dinner had ended in stalemate instead of the threatened rout, Diane could not rest. When Tilson opened the door of Tremontaine House for her, she glanced at the clock. Nearly midnight. She could wait until morning, but her agitation was such that she felt it best to find her husband immediately. She had known that he had arrived late to two recent sessions of Council. She had not mentioned it to him because she had deemed the infractions minor. She had doubted that it would give rise to comment. But she had not counted on Lady Perry's uncanny nose for trouble.

"Has my lord retired for the night?" she asked her maid.

Lucinda curtsied, her head bowed. "Yes, madam."

Perhaps, had Lady Perry not spent an entire evening politely poking Diane's tenderest spots with blunted knives, Diane would have noticed Lucinda's brief hesitation before answering such a simple question. But her preoccupation with her husband was such that Diane determined to rouse him and impress upon him once again the importance of this tax meeting tomorrow, and of his standing on the Council. And when she felt sure that he was hers again, she would make love to him.

She dismissed her maid and passed through the door to her inner salon alone.

She knew before she put her hand on the door that connected their rooms. The door was not thick, but neither were the sounds he made quiet. She knew. And yet she strode to the door and put her hand on the knob. Not with any intention of turning it. But, perhaps, to make it real.

The duchess felt suddenly cold, chilled to the bone. She grabbed a throw rug from the end of her bed, wrapped it around herself. Then she took one of the light, gilded chairs and placed it, silently and carefully, next to the door and listened to the sounds of her husband and his young lover. She listened until they were finished. She considered asking someone, a footman, when the secretary had arrived that day, how long he had been with the duke. It was a silly notion, immediately dismissed. They had been together for many hours, of course. Almost certainly as many hours as she had been away from the house.

Soon enough the pair began to talk. She recognized the tone in her husband's voice, the velvet warmth of a man well sated, exhausted, and content.

"God, what's the hour, Rafe?"

"Just past midnight. Why, should I leave?"

"Never. I order you to stay with me for the next century, at least."

A young laugh, a momentary shuffle of sheets and limbs and sloppy kisses. "Won't you tire of me, my lord?"

"I'm more likely to tire of air than I am to tire of you. Look at that, will you?"

"I can hardly take my eyes off it, Will."

"You make me feel twenty years younger. But I *must* sleep. I have that blasted Council meeting tomorrow. Something to do with those chocolate traders that Diane has interested herself in. She says the vote will be central to improving our financial situation."

"Ah, that," said the boy, in the tone of one who has already had an earful. "Don't you find it . . . odd that the duchess has interested herself to such a degree in trade? I hadn't thought that a pastime of your set, in general."

"Diane has always been unusual. Forward-thinking."

"But your properties? Surely better to manage those than dabble in obscure trade agreements."

William sighed. "Diane says that in these changing times, it pays to diversify our interests."

"But, Will, how does that make any sense at all? I remember seeing a property of yours; we passed through with my father when we were going to Kingsport. Highcombe, I believe it was called. One of the jewels of Tremontaine. And my own father said that it was a pity you nobles didn't take more to renting out your properties, because a man with money would pay a good deal to live in such impressive and agreeable surroundings."

A pause. Diane's grip on the edge of her chair tightened another fraction.

"You speak wisely, love. I grew up in Highcombe, and the idea of another man living there even for a few years is difficult for me. But we might easily come out of our current difficulties, as far as I understand them, with the rent it generates. I'm afraid, though, that Diane—"

"Hell's bells, Will, if you tell me what Diane says one more time I will stop your mouth with my—"

"Sweet one, I might die of ecstasy if you do that, and no matter what you say, I must survive until this meeting tomorrow."

The boy laughed. "Just as well. Even my stamina has limits. But I still think you should ask your Diane about Highcombe." He laughed again. "Watch my own father put in a bid! Well, he might have if not for the cost of my sister's dowry and trousseau."

Diane released her grip on the edge of her chair with deliberate effort. Her fingers ached like an old woman's. Like someone who had been holding too much, for too long. She had a sensation of weightlessness, the vertigo of an accustomed weight slipping away. It was the duke, it was her William, so famously content in his marriage. So content at such great effort. Could he fail her now? For this presumptuous new lover who so blithely encouraged him to pursue a trail he must not follow? The duke's initial interest in bringing Rafe to Highcombe had been easily deflected. But William could not be allowed to even guess the real reason for her reluctance to visit—let alone to rent. The real reason was breathtaking enough that even she attempted not to think of it directly for very long.

Quite simply, she had mortgaged Highcombe.

And if she could not push through these tax breaks for the Balams, she would not be able to maintain her payments on the loans she had taken to invest in the unmitigated disaster of the *Everfair*. And if she could not pay her loans, her collateral would be seized. Her collateral, the jewel of the Tremontaine country holdings and William's childhood home: Highcombe and its lands. Their position in society would never recover from such a public shame. Nor would her standing with William. She stood to lose everything.

It was, quite possibly, the most terrifying sensation she had experienced in seventeen years.

She moved from the door, so that the lovers' conversation quickly faded to murmurs and sighs. Many years ago, she had installed a panel in the wall beside her vanity, cleverly disguised by gilt moldings of holly sprays and a green man. It swung outward silently, revealing another, smaller device. This required three keys to open, turned in a specific order, a specific number of times. When this was done, Diane looked at the sparse contents. A modest leather purse, cracked with age and disuse. A small brooch of tarnished copper embossed with a trefoil and a healer's staff, characteristic of certain Northern country hospitals. And a newer addition, carefully placed to the right of the others. She stared at this object for a long time, until the noises from the room behind her subsided into silence. She locked it all away again, satisfied.

William was aware of the importance of the meeting tomorrow. He wouldn't fail her in that. And when they had navigated this turn in the river, she would find a way to cow that meddlesome secretary. She would find a way to make the Duke Tremontaine hers again, and to renew the fortunes of their house.

Kaab meandered through the crowd with her two mugs of beer, ostensibly making her way to Tess, but really watching for anyone who seemed unduly interested in the drama of Tess's "lost" forgeries. She spotted a pair of boys who were eyeing her bag as if it contained two dozen sweet tamales, but Kaab doubted that they had the wherewithal for murder, thievery, *and* blackmail. *Give them a few years,* she thought in Tess's wry, nasal accent, and laughed shortly.

As she stood there, sipping absently from both mugs and accepting condolences and congratulations and advice with a general air of befuddlement and woefully inadequate grammar, she caught something. A man, who had a moment before seemed as blandly normal as the rest of those in the outer ring surrounding Tess, froze. He adjusted his weight. He pushed back his sword. He transformed through this and a dozen other subtle rearrangements from a tourist wearing a sword he had no idea how to use to a swordsman or a spy, reassessing new information. Then he twitched again and the impression faded so quickly that someone else might have decided it had been her imagination. Kaab, however, had not been raised to waste either time or opportunity. She moved purposefully back to Tess, and when she had come close enough she tripped slightly and spilled some beer on her vest.

"God's blood," she swore, as Tess had instructed her.

"Hey, save me some, will you? Don't leave it all on your shirt!" Tess was doing that thing again, where she didn't shout but her voice could be heard across the square. Everyone laughed. Including her quarry. Kaab bumped into him lightly as she approached Tess. Tess's gaze flicked to him and then back at Kaab, who nodded slightly.

They clinked their mugs and settled on the steps at the edge of the portico.

"Now?" Tess whispered.

"Now."

It would have fooled most observers. Kaab would have to get Tess to teach her the trick when all of this was over. Tess reached down with her left hand, fished in her bag with her right, and when she came up, her left was clutching two slightly dirty sketches of a compass watch hung on a heavy chain—almost a locket, but not quite.

A hard-eyed serving girl at the Maiden's Fancy paused on her way with a fresh beer delivery and clucked her tongue so hard the sound bounced off the stone. "Don't tell me you *dropped* them, Tess!"

"Well, what do you want me to tell you, Rosalie?" Tess blushed and stuffed them back into the bag at her feet. She gave the impression of haste while taking a full twenty seconds, just in case anyone interested had missed the papers' miraculous reappearance.

"That someone called Tess the Hand ought not be such a butterfingers. How you ever spent so much as an evening serving beer at the Three Dogs is a wonder to me."

Tess made a sour face. "Why do you think I found myself a trade that better suits my talents?"

Rosalie just laughed at that. "Lucky you!"

The man Kaab had noticed earlier didn't reveal his interest in such an obvious way as before, but it was clear enough now that she knew what to look for. She reached for Tess's mug, abandoned on the steps during the sleight of hand over the sketches, and leaned in to hand it to her.

"One last fight should be enough," she murmured. "Watch him so that you can draw him later."

"Got it."

Vincent Applethorpe, her savior and her challenger, was sitting on the lip of the fountain, tossing and catching a brass minnow. He caught Kaab looking and nodded politely. The thrill of their hunt combined with the excitement of a challenge from one who might truly teach her something about this delicate dance of swordsmanship made her forget her exhaustion. Kaab was, at once, ready to fight again.

"Well then," she said. She started to stand, but Tess stopped her with a hand on her arm. Kaab nearly jumped from her skin.

"Wait," Tess said.

"What is it?"

"Applethorpe—do you trust him? I don't want you to die for this, Kaab."

"I won't die! I'm Ixkaab—"

"Balam, first daughter of a first daughter, yes I heard that. But you're still bleeding, for the Land's sake!"

Kaab looked down at her shoulder, where one of her earlier opponents had scored first blood before she found the rules of challenge could include a simple yield. She felt surprised to see that Tess was right. The flow had mostly stopped. It wasn't any great wound. But she was so touched by Tess's concern that she didn't say anything. She just brushed the flyaway hair that framed Tess's sweaty forehead and smiled.

"I'll be fine, my sunset maize flower. This man is honorable. You will see. But for now you must let me go."

She did love it when Tess blushed. She didn't love it so much when she lost that sparking connection of Tess's hand on her bare arm. But she turned as though she did not mind at all. And by the time she had crossed the chalked line of the fighting ring, she mostly didn't. Vincent awaited her, blades drawn, a cocky smile unsheathed.

"Fight as dirty as you want, Mistress Balam," he said. "I'll still best you."

"Fight well," Kaab said, "and it will be an honor to lose to you."

They tapped their blades in the ritual salute.

And they began.

30 hours earlier

Kaab had never learned to sleep well in the cold, even covered by extra mantles and furs. Her nose began to feel like a foreign appendage, so much colder than the rest of her that she often woke unable to feel it. Whenever Traders from the great mountain lakes complained about the heat of her home, she would think in wonder that their noses must be made of jade.

So she was once again only drowsing in fits, and dreaming thin smears of images that dissipated instantly upon opening her eyes, when someone rapped softly upon her door.

"What is it?"

"Mistress Ixkaab," said the voice of one of their Local servants. "A woman has come to see you. She refuses to leave. I thought to ask your aunt, but if you would like—"

Kaab leaped from her sleeping mat and rushed to open the door.

"Who is she?"

The gatekeeper gaped like a monkey to see Kaab clad only in the simple knee-length blouse that she used for sleeping.

"A City girl, Mistress Ixkaab." He spoke to the floor rather than risking another look. "A Riverside girl, if I'm any judge of the accent. I would have turned that sort away immediately, but she said that she knew you, and that she had business of a . . . delicate kind with you."

Kaab winced and wanted to laugh. Her reputation had so preceded her that this servant had violated protocol and approached her directly. Either he thought that Tess was her latest paramour or integral to some secret Balam business—and after all, either way, he would not be entirely wrong.

"You did well to come here first," said Kaab. "I'll get dressed."

Her female cousins slept in the quarters to either side of her; they would surely hear every word she said if she held the conversation in here. She hurriedly tied on a skirt, fastened it with her shortest belt, and laced on her sandals as minimal protection against the persistent mud. Her hair she left down, like a young girl.

When she was ready, the servant led her down the stairs, through the garden and toward the west gate, the one most commonly used by servants. She felt grateful for this, because it was the farthest away from the family quarters and made it less likely that her aunt or uncle would wake and hear something suspicious.

Tess was waiting by the gate, with the Kinwiinik servant who shared night guard duty. She was clutching her cloak tightly around her, but she still shivered. She jerked when Kaab came into view and then wiped her eyes. Kaab wanted to run to her, but she knew she couldn't in front of these servants, however discreet they might be. Instead Kaab walked up calmly and greeted the second gatekeeper in Kindaan. Then she pulled a handful of cacao beans from her pocket. They were of very high quality, no small bribe. She gave half to each of the men.

"I appreciate your service," she said, "and your silence on this delicate matter."

The Local eyed the beans as if she had handed him some chia seeds, but the Kinwiinik elbowed him hard in the side and they both bowed to her.

"Of course, Mistress Ixkaab," said the Kinwiinik. "Perhaps you would like to converse with the lady in the gatehouse?"

The tiny observation room, a Local invention, was built into the top of the wall. It would not offer perfect seclusion, but it was fine for their purposes. She thanked the man sincerely and turned at last to Tess. The forger followed Kaab with a trust that was as heartbreaking as it was baffling, given how they had ended their last conversation.

"What happened?" Kaab asked, when they were finally alone in the tower. Tess sat in the chair facing the compound, while Kaab had the view of the darkened street, which framed Tess's drawn face and red eyes.

"You keep saying that Ben was killed deliberately. For a reason."

"I think it likely," Kaab said. "Because of the kind of knife wound I saw that day."

Tess nodded, too many times. She glanced up at Kaab, wiped her eyes again, and began to rock back and forth in the seat. Her hands, Kaab noticed, were stained a peculiar shade of cerulean blue. A shade she recognized, because it was the color the learned scribes of her people used to paint the night sky in their codices. Kaab wished she could touch those hands, kiss them. But she stayed where she was.

"They came back," Tess said at last. "I was in this time. Napping. They didn't go into the bedroom, far as I know. But when I woke up, someone had left me a package. On my desk. Even locked the fucking door behind them!"

Tess started to shake again. Kaab felt the hardness coming on her, the stillness of the sacred rock pools of her home, the steadiness of Xamanek, the north star. She had felt this a few times before, but never in conversation, never with another person. The stillness was too great for even surprise. She would stop whoever had killed Ben, and whoever was threatening Tess. She did not make a vow; she did not hone her determination with rage or with fear. She simply knew, and in her knowledge she would be implacable.

"What was in the package, Tess?"

Tess jerked at the change in Kaab's voice. She peered at her for a long moment. But whatever she saw there, or heard, seemed to give her confidence. Tess reached beneath her shawl and pulled out a simple bundle wrapped in brown paper and twine. From this she removed two objects. The first, a red-and-green-striped jacket, familiar, and well worn. The second was a drawing, in a fair hand, of Tess herself at her desk. The details were telling: Tess in her nightgown, her hair disheveled, one knee brought up beneath her as she worked. Whoever drew this had done it from life and had been watching her without her knowledge for some time. On a sudden suspicion, Kaab lifted the jacket again. She turned it over.

The bloodstain blended somewhat with the red stripes, but it was unmistakable. As was the hole where the dagger had gone in.

"This was Ben's," Kaab said.

"He loved the ugly thing. But it wasn't on his body. And it wasn't with his clothes when I sorted them after. We figured someone had stolen it."

"Someone had."

Tess laughed, high and disbelieving. But she sounded steadier. She reached out and gripped Kaab's hand. "They went through his things, that first time. They just threw around my drawers and bodices, but they were careful with his things. They cut the linings of his vests. Like they thought he might have hidden something there. Something small, like one of my drawings."

"And you know what they were looking for."

"I don't . . . I might." Her wide mouth was a grim, pale line. "Right before he died, Ben showed me a locket. He said his father had given it to him and it would make him rich. He had me draw it for him, and then he went off, and the next time I saw him he was dead. I didn't think about it like that. What kind of a locket would get a man killed? But maybe this one could, what do I know?"

"Do you still have the drawing you made?"

"I gave it to Ben. And there wasn't anything on him when those clam women found him. Maybe they took it. But probably not."

"I think," Kaab said, taking the stillness inside her and making of it a weapon, "that you have the right of it. This locket is probably what lies behind these threats. They must want to find out if you know something."

"I don't know anything!"

"But you might have made extra drawings. You didn't, right?"

Tess shook her head. "I didn't. Ben didn't give me time."

"So my plan," said Kaab, "is to make one. It is to make several. And it is to find you a new protector. I . . ." She swallowed. She could do this. "I apologize for my rudeness before, Tess. I'm only concerned for you. I hope that you'll agree with me. You need a new protector now. It can't wait."

Tess embraced her. "I know. I'm sorry I yelled at you. I'm sorry I kicked you out. You are something, you know that? I don't know what I would have done if I couldn't have come here."

Kaab held her for a very long time and tried, from within her stillness, not to think about what its unexpected presence meant.

Applethorpe knew how to fight. Kaab recognized some of his stances and moves as infinitely more refined relatives of the ones that she had learned on the ship. But he fought with a smoothness and a balance that she associated with the most highly trained warriors of the Kinwiinik or the Tullan: a dance of violence that worshiped the sacred water within each human, the only possible nourishment of the gods.

She was hopelessly outclassed from the first moment their blades touched. And she had never enjoyed a fight more in her life. When she was a child, the boys would play the ball game with her, and they would let her practice with sticks to mimic the moves of the dagger and the short ax. But by the time she was ten, the boys were firmly sequestered in their studies and she in hers. Even a woman dedicated to the service only needed to learn defensive fighting. She had trained diligently in the dagger, and on rare occasions she had revealed a temperament for it—a capacity for stillness, for the fine control of the passions of her head- and liver-spirits. What gave her so much trouble in her daily life was her greatest strength in a battle. But that night they embraced in the gatehouse, Tess had helped her find her stillness.

And she found it again, now, with the slash and parry, the feint and jab, every desperate block she made with muscles that pumped vinegar instead of blood. Every gasp from burning lungs that must be her last, if she weren't saved by some fierce instinct that made her spin into his feint instead of stepping west into the blow. Even the tough soles of her bare feet—surely smeared by now with the omnipresent Local street filth—felt bruised and cut by so many hard landings on broken cobblestones. And Applethorpe fought with passion and grace and brutality and not even a hint of awareness of anything beyond of the range of his two blades, and hers.

Outside the circle, there was fear; there was confusion and doubt and hatred and jealousy and pain. Outside the circle was a cage stretching to infinity. Inside the circle, there were no straight lines. Everything curved, took a longer, unexpected path, discovered unexpected affinities. There was a greeting among her people: *I am the other you.* In this backwater across the North Sea, she had discovered a woman who held the key to her stillness. She had discovered a man whose skill with the blade would have made him a great warrior even in Binkiinha. She had discovered herself and her curved reflections.

She was about to lose, she realized. Her exhausted muscles were flagging, while Vincent was relentless. For all that the match was supposed to be in sport, these were real blades. He could kill her, as that other man nearly had. She waited for the fear, but the line curved to one side and turned into something else. Its opposite.

Kaab was not afraid to die here.

So she dropped her sword.

Even Vincent hesitated. For a fraction of a second, but it was enough. Kaab saw her opening and took it. The fluid moves that she'd had drilled into her from childhood came as though from the sky and not her own memory. She flowed forward and disarmed him of his dagger in a gesture that felt as natural as breathing but that she could not recall having used before. She bent away from his sword and went in again, so close to his neck she could see the vein throbbing—

And was stopped, with perfect poise, with his long blade on her own delicate vein.

"Yield," he said. A bead of sweat rolled into his hairline.

"Be Tess's protector," Kaab said.

"King's blood, girl, you're mad!"

The depth of the stillness flowed away from her: She could hear the crowd again, feel the heat and how close she was to passing out. But just a little remained.

Kaab grinned. "You'll do it then?"

Applethorpe sheathed his sword. He bent to retrieve his dagger.

Someone shouted, "Do it, Vince! You're the best of the lot."

"But be careful, Tessie doesn't want you—she's got a taste for the foreign spices, am I right?"

That last speaker groaned as someone splashed him with beer dregs. "Mind your manners, Pip! Or did you not just pass two hours winning bets on the back of this nice foreign lady?"

Vincent shook his head, but Kaab knew. "I have better places to go," he said.

"But you want to, anyway."

"Damned if I know why."

"You want to teach me the sword. You want to know about my stillness, and how I fight with the dagger."

"I—that was like nothing I've seen before."

"So you'll protect Tess."

"I will. Long enough for you to learn what I can teach you."

"And I you."

Kaab held out her hand, in the custom of these people. The crowd quieted. Waiting.

The cheer that went up when Applethorpe walked over and shook her hand easily covered what Kaab wished to say to him in private. Vincent gave her a speculative glance and nodded.

5 hours earlier

Diane left the luncheon early, pleading a slight indisposition. It was a pretext she knew would be badly received by the hostess—the Dragon Chancellor's wife was sensitive to any slight while her husband's mistress quickened with his child—and yet it seemed, everything considered, the best of bad options.

The duchess's swordsman had taken it upon himself to send her an urgent message, informing her that her husband had not yet left his chambers. It was true that she had indicated to Reynald that she would trust him with duties that did not generally fall under the purview of a house swordsman. Still, she wondered at his boldness.

The contents of the letter would not normally be cause for concern, let alone a message that encouraged her to excuse herself from polite company. But if William had not yet left his chambers, if he were still in the arms of that Fenton brat, then he could not possibly be in attendance at the meeting of the Council of Lords, taking place at this moment in the Old City. Even if he had left just after Reynald had sent the note. William had missed the reading of proposed amendments to the tax on foreign chocolate. He had missed the debate, whose points they had so painstakingly rehearsed. He had missed the *vote* (if Davenant had allowed it to take place at all, after such a gross breach of procedure). He had missed the entire affair, and he certainly would not be allowed to introduce further amendments for debate if he could not trouble himself to attend their discussion.

Everything that she had promised to the Balams. Her perfect plan to rescue Tremontaine—and Highcombe—from the disaster of the *Everfair*. The financial reprieve that would save her from the ultimate ignominy of letting bankers repossess an ancient family estate.

William had thrown it away for a tryst with a student. And Rafe Fenton was no brilliant star, no future scholar of renown. No, this Master Fenton was belligerent and ill-mannered, cunning and duplicitous. She even suspected he was using her own William to buy his way through his examination!

So the duchess pleaded indisposition and consoled herself with the fact that she looked pale enough that the ladies present might even believe her.

Reynald caught up with her carriage not far from the Davenant townhouse.

"I regret to have brought you such distressing news, madam."

"Since you decided to meddle, I wonder that you did not do so when it might have averted disaster."

Reynald, whose demeanor toward her had shifted these last weeks to be at once more deferential and more familiar, seemed caught off guard. She supposed he had been expecting praise.

"I was away performing other duties in your service," he said. "I sent that message as soon as I returned to the house."

She imagined that he had wasted time contemplating every potential advantage of the action. But she did not see any benefit to saying so. Any earlier would have only given her an illusion of possibility. At least now she knew the scope of the disaster she must confront.

"And how have you fared with those other duties, Reynald?"

Her swordsman shrugged, which she could not recall any other servant having done in her presence in almost twenty years. Before that day, even Reynald never had. "Well as might be expected. I have watched his trull for over a week, madam. I don't think she knows anything about that business. She might have drawn the picture that he gave you, but I think she did so in ignorance, and is no threat to us."

She let the "us" go unchallenged. "Are you sure?"

He paused. "Not quite."

"Then tell me when you are. One way or another."

"Are you ordering me to kill her?"

Were she another woman, in another place, Diane might have slapped him. "I am asking for security, for which service I employ you. How you go about the business is your own concern. And Reynald, since you have so generously added messenger to your list of duties, please go ahead to Tremontaine House and tell his lordship's manservant that Lord Davenant sends word from the

Council Hall to enquire—to enquire anxiously after the duke's health."

Reynald bowed without so much as a quirked shoulder blade and hurried ahead. By the time she arrived, she had given their people sufficient time to relay the message to his lordship of Tremontaine. The duchess mounted the great stairs, while Lucinda vainly attempted to interest her in the difficult repairs of a gown, and Duchamp in some pressing issues regarding the dinner menu.

She paused before the door to his chambers. "Is my husband in?" she asked, as though the thought had only just occurred to her.

Duchamp and Lucinda and the three footmen behind them did not respond immediately.

Duchamp stepped forward. "I have heard he isn't well, madam. The Dragon Chancellor enquired after his health."

"What distressing news," she said. "We must send for his physician. Is he in his bed?"

The door opened and Rafe stumbled through. Dressed, as far as it went, but his greasy black hair hung in tangled locks down his back, and his clothes were rumpled as if they'd last been laundered weeks before. William looked a little better, as though his man had dressed him, but only to run from a fire.

"Oh," the duchess said. "They told me you weren't well, William. The Dragon Chancellor asked after your health. Did you fall ill during the meeting?"

William blanched. "That . . . Dearest Diane. You must believe me, I had no idea—"

She watched him choke on his own excuses and wished her petty revenge tasted like anything other than ashes. "Why, Master Fenton," she said mildly. "I am surprised to see you here. Did you forget something in my husband's library?"

Rafe blushed a brilliant ruby, breathless with rage, but she merely smiled. He would say nothing to her if he wanted to see her husband again. And clearly they would sacrifice a great deal to be with one another.

"No? In that case, would you see him out, Tilson? And do be so good as to report to me when you return tomorrow, Fenton. I have employment for you, if the duke can spare you from your labors."

How Rafe took this, she did not bother to learn. The footman Tilson was as good at his job as Reynald was at his.

"Diane," William tried again, "I was asleep. Duchamp said he knocked but I didn't hear—"

"We can discuss it over dinner, my dear." She looked up at him sadly and then down at the floor. He reached for her, and she sidestepped his embrace. She had never done that before.

"Darling, I'll make it up to you. I'll take the carriage to Davenant's house right now. I'll explain everything. . . ."

He seemed to realize, then, how useless his explanations would sound to a man like the Dragon Chancellor.

"I'll see you at dinner," she repeated, and left him.

Later, alone in her chambers, she laid upon her desk a blank sheet of paper and a fresh quill. She would write to Lady Davenant, recently returned from her country estates at Rendellfield, and inquire after her health. Would she be sufficiently recovered from her journey to receive a caller two days hence?

What Diane would not write, but what she knew, was that in two days Lord Davenant, Dragon Chancellor of the Council of Lords, Master of the Exchequer, and a man who more than once had made it clear that he regretted the duchess's inflexible fidelity to her husband, would also be at home. She had not made up her mind on how precisely to proceed, but the example of young

Fenton had forcibly reminded her that there were many paths to influence. Perhaps the attentions of a powerful man who had admired her for so long were worth cultivating in a spirit more open to unprecedented possibilities.

It was a fairy tale, they said—a Riverside fairy tale. The fair maiden Tess needed a protector, and so the foreign princess had fought every pretender until she found the one Riverside swordsman who was honest and true. That last fight had been the best of the day, went the judgment of the crowd. The princess had lost honorably, and Vincent Applethorpe had made the Riversiders proud.

"And it's a true Riverside fairy tale," Two-Ply Max was saying for the third time to the crowd at the Maiden's Fancy, "because I just won enough brass minnows off of these fools to buy me a barrel at the Three Dogs!"

Rosalie took his empty mug and handed him a fresh one. "How about paying your rent with it, you drunk!"

"Get off it, Rosalie! Where would you be without us drunks, a barmaid like you?"

"In my own tavern, collecting tips instead of pinches!"

Everyone laughed, especially the fair maiden and her foreign princess. The two were leaning against each other, drinking pints and telling stories. The forger's bag was at her side again, but one dramatic gesture pushed it over, a little more toward the shadows. No one seemed to notice. But several people did.

"I'm off, then," said Applethorpe, to the disappointment of his friends, old and new. He'd come to Riverside a fiery boy, full of steel and promise. When he had disappeared a few years ago, everyone assumed he had been killed. They were glad to see him turn up again, older, more sober—and with a fighting style that left the knowledgeable ones with questions.

"Where've you been training? You were good before, Vince, but that was . . ."

Vincent smiled and did not answer. "I have some business of my own to attend to, ladies, but I'll be back in a few days." He looked up and projected his voice. "And that means the rest of you louts had best leave these two be, because they are under my protection."

The foreign lady objected to this. "Tess! *She* is under your protection."

"Why can't you be?" He seemed genuinely curious.

"Because I'm under my own protection."

"Fair enough," he said. "Just Tess, then." He walked off without another word.

That man will steal something from Tess, she had said, as they shook hands. *When he does, please follow him.*

Sure enough, the man who Vincent had initially pegged as a poor country neophyte, new in Riverside and with just enough knowledge of the sword to stick himself with it, stumbled near Tess's bags as Vincent made his farewells. The boor picked himself up and apologized to everyone nearby. He seemed harmless, but Vincent had watched his hands. He had stolen the papers, just as Kaab said he would.

Kaab, who had watched this with great satisfaction, turned to Tess. She held the forger's blue-stained hands.

"Will you give me a prize?" she asked. Kaab had learned some of these people's stories during her lessons at home. She knew what the prince sometimes won from the maiden.

Tess was staring at her lips. "What prize, Kaab?"

Kaab tried to think of something clever to say, but all she found were love poems in languages that Tess couldn't understand. So instead she bent forward and kissed her. And then she stopped thinking in any language at all.

The cheering and hollering and lip-smacking of a crowd rewarded by young love followed Vincent as he left the square in pursuit of the thief. His quarry moved quickly once out on the empty streets, heading over the Bridge and then up to the Hill. That didn't surprise Vincent, since the thief was almost certainly a swordsman of some ability. And skilled swordsmen—reasonable ones, not fools lovesick for a pair of dark eyes and impossible dagger work—liked the living on the Hill.

But it shocked him when he realized that he was standing beside Tremontaine House. And that the thief had nodded to the guards and walked inside. He felt cold, like he was in the ring and a chance mistake had cost him everything.

Tess and Kaab had somehow made themselves a very powerful enemy. And they didn't even know it.

Episode Six

A FAIR HAND

Patty Bryant and Racheline Maltese

There were certain things that happened every year, as regular as clockwork. In the springtime, farmers planted their crops, the University prepared for its exams, the City's streets turned to mud, and—far more important than any of that, at least in the steward Duchamp's mind—Tremontaine held its annual Swan Ball.

Whisper the word "ball," and a noblewoman's mind fills with thoughts of silk dresses and violin music, rich sauces poured over roast meats, and sweets of airy meringue and heavy cream. But to Duchamp, steward of the Tremontaine household, a ball meant one thing: work.

Duchamp was no longer a young man. But the Tremontaine ball was his responsibility, and always had been. Duchamp had been overseeing the Swan Ball since before the current duchess had even married into the family. He knew exactly what it took to host a successful ball. The duchess relied on him to meticulously oversee the household staff as they fetched and unpacked the family's traditional swan-shaped decorations from the attics, laundered the drapes and hangings, waxed the floors, polished the silver, and replaced a vast array of candles so that the guests could actually see the result of the Tremontaine family retainers' labors. But even that was an incomplete list.

Before cleaning the silver, one had to find the silver. There were always a few pieces missing. Spoons in particular had a habit of disappearing into bodices to be sold down in Riverside by ladies' maids. Just last month, a serving bowl painted with a scene of unnatural congress between a large waterfowl and some maiden of myth had vanished entirely. All for the best, really; the vivid colors of webbed feet on virgin flesh had improved no one's appetite.

Duchamp remembered when Tremontaine had promptly bought new silver. In Duke William's father's day, when Duchamp was an under-footman, the old duke had spent lavishly and never counted the cost. So his son had inherited his father's considerable debts along with the obligation to keep up tradition. It was a blessing that the son's pretty young wife had turned out to have a streak of practicality, even if Duchamp sometimes mourned the days of heedless glamour. Instead, the old steward made do, mixing and matching the family's various sets of tableware, replacing what was missing with pieces that looked close enough. Surely not so dissimilar that any of the guests would notice.

Maybe he'd put fewer candles in the dining room this year.

And silver wasn't the only place corners were being cut. No one had been brought in to fix the wobbly leg on the clavier. Just last week, two parlor maids and an under-cook had been dismissed—supposedly for minor infractions, but more likely to have fewer servants to keep. At least there'd be no more dismissals until after the ball. They'd have enough trouble preparing for it with the staff as reduced as it was now; any less and there would be no hope of pulling off such a grand event in the style that the City expected.

* * *

"Again," Applethorpe said, beating the side of Kaab's blade with his own.

Ixkaab Balam retreated to a *garde*. At least she no longer dropped her weapon when he did that. The secret was a loose grip; if she held on tightly, her own strength worked against her, concentrating the force of the sword master's attempts to disarm her rather than letting it dissipate. Her nature argued against such a tactic. When attacked, she wanted to fight back, to launch forward, not to meekly allow his attack to flow through her.

She extended her arm, pointing the tip of her sword toward Applethorpe, and walked around the circle of their training grounds. It was within the shell of an abandoned building, nothing more than weeds and a few piles of red bricks, completely open to the sky. A pair of matching mutts nosed at a trash heap in one corner. Applethorpe had tried to run them off when they'd first arrived, but animals in Riverside weren't dissuaded by a loud voice and stomped foot. He had not deigned to threaten them with his sword.

Kaab abruptly feinted north, then south, and then made an earnest strike low and back to the north, below Applethorpe's ribs and into his soft organs. Or rather, such was her intention; instead Applethorpe parried easily, and Kaab tripped on the uneven ground. The muddier of the two dogs barked, a sound that reminded her of mocking laughter.

The blade seemed to have grown heavy as a boulder since this morning; Kaab sighed and dropped her arm. She longed for her obsidian dagger, whose weight was barely noticeable no matter how long she practiced, but Applethorpe had refused to let her use it. "You rely on it too much," he had said when she'd protested. "What's the point in practicing with a sword if you're not going to use it?"

Kaab turned away from him, intending to walk off her frustration. The dog barked again, and she made a sharp, threatening noise in the back of her throat. She didn't want any witnesses to her humiliation, not even a dog. It ignored her, so she bent over, looking for a stone to throw.

The flat of Applethorpe's blade hit the back of her thighs.

"Ow!" She leaped away. She'd had worse, and often, during her training back home in Binkiinha. It was the indignity that she resented; it was a long time since Ixkaab Balam had been a novice at anything.

"You can't leave just because I blocked you."

"I wasn't leaving. I am taking a break," she said. "Besides, this isn't an actual fight." She wished it was. She might not have the skills to beat him—yet—but at least then he wouldn't correct her like a child. She gestured with her sword at the shell of the building in a manner that didn't directly threaten Applethorpe but still showed less respect than was appropriate. "No one with any sense would fight here."

"I've fought here."

"Why?" Kaab looked skeptically at their surroundings.

"Things happen." Applethorpe shrugged, a carefully controlled motion; the rest of his body remained as still as a reed, the way it always did when his sword was drawn. Kaab couldn't help but be annoyed by that also. Everything about him made her feel inadequate.

She'd had enough of failing at swords for the day. "The man you replaced as Tess's protector," she said, deliberately keeping her voice casual. "Ben. Did you know he'd been stabbed?"

Applethorpe paused long enough to make it clear that he'd noticed her redirection of the conversation, then obliged her by answering, "Many people end up stabbed in Riverside."

"This wasn't any bar fight. Whoever did it was an expert."

He sheathed his sword. Even that small movement had the grace of a jaguar. But dressed in the bright colors and hodgepodge styles that Riversiders were partial to, Applethorpe looked like an acrobat. From what Kaab understood of how this city used swordsmen, she supposed he *was* a sort of performer. But his would be a deadly show, far from all surface and no substance.

"How do you know?"

"It was done from behind, with a thin blade. It went between the ribs and up." Kaab mimed a stabbing motion with her free hand. "Fast, and not too much blood."

"And you suspect it was done by the fellow you had me follow? The one who stole Tess's drawings in the tavern?"

Kaab hesitated. She wasn't sure how much to tell this man. She was used to working alone. But what was the point in having him protect Tess if he wasn't trustworthy? If she wanted to make any progress in the matter of Ben's death and what it meant, she must share what she knew with someone here in Riverside, someone close to Tess. Tess was a forger. But the trouble her friend was in seemed to be more than anyone would take for mere forgery.

Kaab nodded. "The man you followed to the house of Tremontaine, yes. Did you learn his name?"

"I did not. He disappeared indoors before I could find out."

"Well." Kaab liked the way this was going. She had his interest, now. And he was quick to understand. "Someone broke into Tess's rooms last week, probably looking for those drawings . . . and they left behind Ben's fancy jacket, the one he died in."

Applethorpe's eyebrows went up. "Why would someone at Tremontaine House want to kill a Riverside pretty-boy? And what do the drawings have to do with it?"

"I wish I knew."

"If you're right, then it may be serious." He drew again, indicating that the time for conversation was over. "And therefore it's all the more important that you learn how to use a sword."

Kaab groaned and let her own blade remain at her side. "You're a very difficult teacher." She was beginning to like Applethorpe. Not the way she liked Tess, of course. But his smug assurance of his own superiority, his dry humor, his cool assessment of danger . . . he was someone she might come to think of as a friend, here in this cold, strange city so far from home.

"That's because I'm not a teacher," he said. "Just a swordsman." He reached out and tapped her blade with his own. "Come on; a little longer and then we'll switch. I want you to teach me that twisting thing you do with a dagger."

That sent enough energy to her arms to bring her sword back up into a defensive position. "And then we duel?" she asked, without any real hope he'd agree.

Unsurprisingly, he shook his head. "You're not ready for a real duel."

"I won many duels here, when I chose a protector for Tess last week!"

"Because you were fighting drunk bravos who only wanted a few minutes' amusement in the marketplace. I'm trying to teach you more than how to show off to an audience. So you can fight not just with a few tricks you've memorized, but with your whole self, for your whole life." He gave that graceful shrug again. "At least, you could if you'd concentrate."

Kaab ignored that last comment, struck by the suggestion that a swordsman was never not engaged. "So I am already fighting, even without a challenge?"

Applethorpe gave her a long look. "Aren't you? As far as I can tell, Mistress Balam, you've always been fighting."

Rafe knew how to look as though he didn't completely despise the situation in which he found himself. He'd perfected the art as a child, although sometime in his adolescence he'd lost the self-discipline required to employ it regularly. All he had to do was set his back teeth at the right angle, and the tension in his jaw would give the impression that he was faintly smiling rather than grimacing in disgust.

Just now he was fighting a losing battle to keep his teeth from sliding out of that wonderfully deceptive angle. He sat at a gilded secretary in the Tremontaine library as the Duchess Tremontaine lounged on a nearby settee, her languid ease a pointed contrast to Rafe's tense posture. Supposedly she was talking him through writing invitations to the Tremontaine annual ball in her low, melodious voice, but since he obviously could handle such a simple task on his own, he assumed she was actually there to irritate him.

When Rafe had agreed to become her husband's secretary, he had imagined himself writing speeches, researching political issues, attending important meetings—not doing a task that any scribbling lackey could do. But the duchess had insisted that she needed help, and Will—sweet, kind, guilty Will, the Duke Tremontaine—had asked Rafe to be kind to her, and now here he was, wondering what had become of his life. In addition, he suspected that the duchess knew he was sleeping with her husband, enthusiastically and often, but she'd shown not a single flicker of jealousy. This uncertainty made the skin on the back of his neck itch, and being alone with her wasn't helping.

The duchess discreetly cleared her throat, and he looked up, hoping for a change in topic—but she only said, "The Lindleys next. Although keep theirs aside after you've written it."

"May I ask why?"

"Do you remember your birthday parties as a child? Surely you must, being still so young." She smiled as she said it, and her voice carried a friendly hint of laughter, but Rafe still recognized the insult.

His fingers tightened on the quill, but he managed to keep his own voice bland. "Yes. Of course."

"Tell me, did you invite only the children you liked?"

"It's not a good party if you don't enjoy the company," Rafe said.

"Oh, you dear child. You still have so very much to learn. Parties are politics, you see, like everything else. Would you think poorly of me if I admitted that I rather enjoy that aspect of them?"

"No, madam," Rafe said automatically, hating himself for it.

"You're a sweet boy. You see, the Lindleys are bores and think themselves better than they are. Particularly old Lord Horn. And yet, much like the odious Duke of Karleigh—we'll discuss him later—we must still invite them." She lifted one shoulder in an urbane shrug. "But that doesn't mean we shouldn't make them worry. They can get their invitation next week. Don't you agree?"

Rafe nodded, wishing that he had never asked. What a pointless game. Dresses and invitations and gifts, endlessly discussed and exchanged and analyzed, all to score points off someone else in the same small circle of noble society, and just so that person could throw themselves into returning the insult next season.

The duchess rapped at the arm of his chair with her closed

fan. "Woolgathering?" she asked. "I suppose that is natural at University; what would anyone expect when you gather a crowd of lively young boys into a stuffy room and ask them to debate philosophical principles? But you must focus now. This is an important household, and you are assigned important tasks."

Rafe had a vision of himself showing the relative importance of party invitations and natural philosophy by throwing the invitations into the hearth, dashing the black inkpot over the duchess's pale blue silk, and storming out of the house, never to return. He could do it. He moved his hands to the arms of his chair, his muscles tensing to shove himself to his feet, ready to smash this opportunity and all it required of him to pieces. But . . . there was his exam to think of, with his chances of starting his school. And, irritating as it was to admit, there was Will. He drew another clean sheet of paper toward himself.

Hours later, Rafe stood at the window of the library and watched the invitations being carried out. Footmen proceeded in multiple directions, some on horseback and some on foot, all dressed in the green-and-gold livery of Tremontaine. It was a dramatic show of wealth and influence, and Rafe felt oddly uplifted, knowing that he was a part of this vivid swirl of power, that it was his actions that had sent this cavalry on its way, his words they carried.

Except they weren't his words. They were the duchess's words, even if they were written in his hand. Rafe was no more an important part of the whole than the stable boy who fed the horses or the maid who mended the embroidery on the footmen's coats. He turned from the window without waiting to see the last of the parade and caught sight of the duchess in the doorway. She had been watching him, her face still and without emotion, but as soon as their gazes met, she produced a smile. "You don't look well," she said sympathetically. "A headache?"

"Yes," Rafe muttered. "I think I'll go and lie down upstairs for a bit."

The duchess made a perfect moue of concern. "Do. I'll have a cold compress sent up. I'm sure William wouldn't want you overworked."

Startled, Rafe stared at her. Her eyes were gray and flawless as a locked safe. Was it possible that she didn't know? That she had only been upset before because Will had missed a Council meeting? Surely not even an empty-headed social butterfly like Diane could be that oblivious. Besides, how likely was it that she cared about import tariffs, of all things? Even Rafe's father found tariffs boring, and he was a man who got the greatest pleasure in life out of double-entry bookkeeping. No, the duchess must know. She simply chose to pretend otherwise.

Still, Rafe felt better once he'd turned a corner of the hallway and was out of her view.

I hope I will be able to come home in a day or two—

No, she'd said that in an earlier letter, and then it hadn't been a day or two or even three. Micah crossed out the line and tried again.

I promise I'll come back next week, as soon as—

No, she'd said that before too. Micah didn't like to lie. Or not do her tasks. The problem was that now she had too many tasks: those she was starting to feel bad about neglecting at home on the farm now that the season was changing, and those at the University. She was so close to figuring out the answer to the great question of how distances worked over the round earth! Not to finish would be like having a bug bite and not scratching it. Aunt Judith had always said that scratching bites only made them worse, but Micah never had been able to stop herself.

Micah wondered what Aunt Judith would say about her life at University, with its tomato pies and playing cards for money, and if she would have a tip to keep away the rats Micah sometimes saw in the alley behind Rafe's building. She missed Aunt Judith, even though she probably wouldn't approve of Micah's new friends or all the time she spent on calculations. *And what's the use of that?* her aunt had said when Micah had tried to explain ratios to her back on the farm. *It doesn't put seeds in the ground nor food on your plate, does it?* At the time, Micah had been tremendously annoyed, but now the memory just made her feel lonely.

Was it selfish of her to stay here when her family needed her for planting season? Rafe needed her too, though. He said that finding the right numbers was very important, much more important than planting rhubarb or peas, and that no one else could do it. But was it more important than her family? Micah felt unwell even asking such a question.

Micah had never realized that there were so many things to learn or that the world contained so many fascinating puzzles. Rafe had taken her to the University library yesterday, and Micah had had to hold on to his sleeve to stop herself from running down the aisles, pulling books and scrolls and loose pages off every shelf. There was so much to read in that one room that it would take her years to go through all of it. And that was just mathematics; there were other subjects she could study, if she wanted: history and rhetoric and medicine, logic and law and other languages, vast horizons of new ideas, expanding every day she stayed here. Sometimes she was sure she could feel her brain growing to contain it all. How could she give this up to go back to the farm, where there was nothing new to learn?

Micah pushed the letter aside and dropped her face into her hands, sighing loudly. If only she could do both things! It wasn't fair that she had to choose. Back home she'd always known what she should do, even if she didn't always want to do it. Now both sides seemed like the right thing, and she could only pick one. She scrubbed at her face one last time, put her shoulders back, and looked at the letter.

I must stay at the University until I finish the calculations for Rafe. It is Very Important. I miss you all very much and will come home as soon as I can but if I am not home before Bessie has her next calf do not forget to check that she is in the barn at night and give her lots of wheat until the calf is ready to come out. It is my turn to pick a name and I have picked the name Trigonometry because it is a very pretty word. Please please do not forget or let Cousin Seth pick the name because he named the last calf. Love, Micah.

Kaab was on her way home to Uncle Chuleb and Aunt Saabim. It wasn't a terribly long walk from Riverside to the Kinwiinik Traders' quarter, but her thighs were aching, her arms were sore, and her head was filled with everything she didn't yet know: about fighting, about this city and the many smaller cities it contained, and about whoever had killed Ben. Her arms felt like ship's ballast weighing down her shoulders, and when she raised a hand to wipe the sweat from her face, sharp pain shot through her muscles.

If she were to be set upon right now, she wasn't sure she'd even be able to draw her sword. Its weight on her hip was normally reassuring, but today it was a burden, another reminder of everything she didn't know and everything she hadn't yet achieved.

Applethorpe had worked her past the point of exhaustion over the last few days, saying that it was not how well she fought at her best but how well she fought at her worst that would keep her alive. Kaab had woken before dawn day after day to join him down in Riverside. He then worked her well into the night, insisting that she practice despite the bruises from missed parries, the burn of overexerted muscles, and the lack of sleep. She did have to admit that eventually the aches and pains had transformed into a new stamina and rock-hard muscles, but it was difficult to be grateful when she was still burningly aware of how much Applethorpe's skill exceeded her own: Despite all the training and all of her own knowledge, she hadn't been able to best him once.

Her mood wasn't helped by a nagging sense that whatever her aunt Ixsaabim and uncle Chuleb would say about her scarcity around the family compound would not be laced with wild enthusiasm. Although Kaab felt certain that her efforts to improve her skills and understand more about the workings of this strange city were worthwhile, she wasn't at all sure that Saabim and Chuleb would see matters that way; she worried they would accuse her of shirking her duties. So as much as she hated to do so, Kaab was prepared to be contrite. Or, well, she was prepared to seem contrite. Actual contrition was another matter entirely.

As she entered the Kinwiinik enclave, the foreignness of the City gave way to familiar sights and sounds. The roof of the Balam family compound rose like a temple above the buildings that surrounded it, towering over them physically the way the Balam towered over the other Traders in status and importance, but there were enough other Kinwiinik families to have created a little piece of home in this foreign territory.

Even those who spoke the Local language here did so with

Kinwiinik rhythms and accents, making that tongue their own. Kaab passed compounds whose outer walls were decorated with murals in the bright colors and angular style of home, a heartwarming sight after the muted shades of Local houses. She caught a brief whiff of steamed corn and smoked chiles, and felt her belly growl. She closed her eyes to take a deeper breath, but just then someone shouted her name, and she spun on her heel to see a ball bouncing toward her from a gang of children. Normally she would have kicked it back—well, perhaps after showing off a bit by bouncing it from knee to hip—but today she was too tired and merely stepped aside. Little Ahjuub groaned in disappointment, then raced past her after the ball.

Across the street, the elder auntie Ixnoom greeted her with a wry smile at the children's antics. She had run one of the Balam family's warehouses before retiring and now dedicated most of her time to gardening. There was a potted plant on her doorstep that Kaab recognized as passion fruit, a plant she hadn't seen since leaving Binkiinha.

"Isn't it too cold to grow passion fruit here?" she asked, keeping her voice respectful as she questioned an elder. It was good to speak Kindaan again, after days spent among people who didn't understand it. Kaab was fluent in the Locals' language, but there was no language like her own, the language of her childhood games, of her mother's prayers, of her first awkward flirtations, the language that required no thought or hesitation, whose every shade of meaning and poetic allusion and piece of slang was as obvious and clear to her as the water in a mountain lake.

Ixnoom nodded and gently stroked a leaf with one wrinkled finger. "It's never produced a fruit, not one, and even its flowers are few and far between." Then she looked up at Kaab, a twinkle of amusement in her dark eyes. "But it hasn't died yet either! May we all do so well here."

Kaab passed on with a polite smile, stepping around the decrepit donkey and matching decrepit cart belonging to Ahaak. A cat sunned itself on top of the low wall surrounding the family's compound. Cats were rare in their homeland, and this one in particular held herself like the goddess Ixchel, beautiful and queenly; it seemed out of place adorning the household of one of the lesser Traders.

Kaab felt at home here. But then, she was beginning to feel the same thing about Riverside. The two neighborhoods, though so different, shared a similar vibrancy, an inescapable energy. Neither of them were truly where she belonged, but they were beginning to feel like places she could be happy.

She was glad to reach the Balam family compound after the bustle of the streets. But once she had passed through the doors, she found the house startlingly still. There were no women in the courtyard chatting as they ground corn into flour or wove on their small looms, nor any men guarding the door or tending to the family's animals. No children shrieked and ran from spot to spot. The quiet was unnatural. Kaab drew her sword—surprised at the new instinct that made her go for it over her dagger even with her aching shoulders—but kept it low as she crept down the first passageway and past the now-empty banquet hall.

She reached her uncle's office without breaking the silence and found most of the household there, gathered in a tight circle around Ixsaabim and Chuleb. Their two heads were bent together, studying something Chuleb held in his hands, while the cousins and elders and a few of the bolder servants tried to peer over their shoulders.

Kaab let her sword fall to her side, but didn't sheathe it. "What's going on?"

The murmur of worried and excited conversation broke off at the sound of her voice. People turned toward her, and she saw several pairs of eyes drop down to her weapon and widen in surprise. Someone giggled nervously.

At least her aunt Ixsaabim smiled kindly on seeing her. "We could ask you the same thing. Breaking and entering, little bee?"

Kaab hastily sheathed her sword and unbuckled the belt, her motions clumsy from embarrassment. "I do live here."

"Do you? We haven't been sure lately," Saabim said good-naturedly, but Kaab didn't miss the mild scolding.

She quickly changed the topic, jerking her chin toward the paper Chuleb had passed to a widowed aunt. "What have I missed?"

Chuleb was silent, as though he were considering not sharing the news with her. That hesitation was worse than any yelling, any punishment; being shut out from the work of her family even for a few seconds made her fiercely regret having toiled so hard to avoid them for days. She had neglected her vow to prove herself a first daughter, loyal and industrious, when she had already been given a second chance.

Thankfully, Chuleb did not force her to ask again. After a pause long enough to make his point, he answered, "It seems we have been invited to the Duchess Tremontaine's ball."

Kaab blinked wordlessly, as she struggled to switch gears to focus on her family's concerns after all the intrigue and exhaustion of Riverside. Realizing that she had been silent too long, Kaab blurted, "Why would she invite us?"

"I believe she wishes to do business with us."

Kaab remembered the duchess's odd visit to Chuleb's study,

the half-spoken questions and evasive answers cloaked in elaborate politeness. So this was what had come of it! Still: "That explains nothing," she said. "Does the Batab invite the farmers in his fields to his banquets, or his wife let the gardeners place flowers in her hair? What is the real reason the duchess invited us?"

"That," Chuleb chided, "is what we were discussing when you came stalking in here flaunting that sword. It is not the way of the Balam to rush in with weapons drawn." He looked at her more closely, and she saw sympathy displace the disappointment in his expression. She must look terrible, Kaab thought wryly, to make his eyes soften in that way. "Has something happened, Niece? Did you have a reason to fear this house was in danger?"

She didn't, of course. True, the silent, empty house had spooked her. In Riverside she had seen the marks of an expert stabbing on a man's corpse, and she was besotted with a girl who was being stalked by an unknown danger. But there was no reason to suspect those matters had anything to do with the Balam.

"Maybe I could find out," she said, hoping to distract from her preoccupation, "why the duchess invited her potential business partners to her exclusive party on the Hill."

Chuleb frowned, wary but intrigued. "How?"

She wasn't actually sure. But better to try something and see if it worked than admit to ignorance. "Let me see the invitation," she said, pleased at the cool confidence of her voice.

It had been slowly making its way from hand to hand throughout the family. Aunt Saabim handed it over with a teasing, "Expecting a secret message? Invisible ink, perhaps? Or a code that escaped the notice of the rest of us?"

Kaab frowned and made a show of turning the invitation over carefully in her hands, examining the phrasing and the loops of the oddly sparse Xanamwiinik letters. Was this the duchess's own hand? Kinwiinik nobles never did their own writing; they employed scribes for that.

"Do they have scribes here?" she asked suddenly.

"They call them secretaries," piped up one of her young male cousins. The Local word snagged on a memory.

"I know the Tremontaine duke's secretary. I've already won his trust," she said proudly, if not entirely accurately. She had no idea if this handwriting belonged to Rafe, but even if the Tremontaines had multiple secretaries to write their invitations, surely Rafe would know about it. "The oldest son of the Fenton family, the one I have been following because of—" She broke off, aware of the eyes on her. She couldn't say because of his interest in the mysteries of moving across the sea; that was a situation she wanted to keep closely guarded, hoping it would come to nothing. She shrugged sheepishly and looked embarrassed. "Because of his lovely hair. And his eyes . . ." Had they been blue? Green? *Chee,* she couldn't remember. "Like jewels!" she finished, figuring that was a safe enough comparison.

One of her distant uncles laughed. "I had heard you preferred women, little bee! If you have changed your tastes, be careful. Do not let a son of this land besmirch your honor."

Kaab managed to maintain her smile by force of will. "Of course, Great Uncle."

"Yes," said Saabim slowly, exchanging a look with her husband. "The oldest son of the Fenton family. His mother's been bragging to everyone about her son's new place in the duke's household. Information from him could be very useful."

Chuleb nodded stiffly. He was still frowning, but Kaab suspected he was actually pleased. "You have our permission to see what he knows. But be subtle, Niece. Bring no drawn swords into this matter."

Kaab grinned. "Rafe wouldn't know subtle if it hit him over the head. This will be an easy task." She schooled her voice to formality and put her hand over her heart. Like a good first daughter, she said, "Thank you, Uncle, Aunt. I will solve this mystery for you."

The Inkpot was not the best place to work on her calculations, but then neither were Rafe's rooms. Although Rafe had told Micah that his rooms at the University were private, there were always people coming and going, insisting on talking about things that were very important to them but weren't very important to Micah; she suspected they might not have been very important at all. Even Rafe did that sometimes. He was insistent on how the world should be, and when it didn't match his ideas, it made him upset. Which just meant that he talked even more.

Worse than having extra people in Rafe's rooms talking at her while she was working was when the extra people wanted to sleep there. It made sense because that's what students' rooms were for, but Micah wished they wouldn't. After all, they weren't *their* rooms, and they tended to snore and drool and sometimes fall asleep right on top of Micah's few belongings. Of course, they weren't Micah's rooms either. And Rafe's friends were like her: They had nowhere else to go.

So when she was very, very annoyed by Rafe's friends and couldn't be polite any longer, she went to the Inkpot. Sometimes when she was writing letters home she got tomato pie smeared on the paper, but at least her family would know that she was eating well.

Her table was jostled, and Micah looked up with a frown. But it wasn't a stranger who had pulled out the seat across from her—it was Kaab, the nice foreign lady.

"Do you have the charts for me?" Micah asked, then remembered to say hello.

Kaab sank into the chair stiffly, like Uncle Amos when his joints were bothering him. "No, not yet. My family is concerned, because they're very useful to us. What if you took them home, and then we needed to check on some detail about the stars in their courses? But don't worry, we're making you a copy of your own. As soon as it's done, I'll bring it to you." She leaned forward to look at Micah's papers. "What are these notes?"

"It's mathematics."

"Yes, I see." Kaab peered at Micah's work, though it was upside down to her. "And how are your calculations today?"

Micah blinked at her. Kaab always asked about that, though she didn't really listen to the answer. Kaab really didn't like numbers, even though she liked the things numbers were for. Micah thought that most people were like that a little, but Kaab was like that a lot.

"They're numbers," Micah said. "They don't change."

Kaab smiled. "Do you know where Rafe is?"

Micah shook her head. "No, I don't. If he were nearby, we would be able to hear him."

The smile turned to a grin.

"I'm going to keep calculating," Micah said, turning her attention back to her papers. "Rafe will show up eventually."

Rafe did. He came through the door of the Inkpot in midsentence, gesticulating wildly and walking backward to keep his attention on the friends following him rather than where he was going. He bumped into another student and briefly interrupted himself to apologize before picking up where he'd left off. Micah knew that meant he wasn't talking about his Big Ideas. If he was talking about the Big Ideas, he wouldn't have even noticed the collision. The people following him—Joshua and another student—weren't entirely listening, but Rafe didn't realize it, or perhaps he didn't care. Micah wasn't sure. Being Rafe was apparently very different from being her.

Kaab raised a hand to catch Rafe's attention, but Rafe had already noticed Micah and was pointing at her. "And this, Henry, is Micah. I discovered him, and he has been invaluable to my project; he has a facility for numbers and a dedication to his labors that we should all strive to emulate. Also, he made Volney furious, which is a reward all its own."

"Doctor Volney was wrong," Micah pointed out, not for the first time. She was sick of people talking about it. Anyone could have seen Volney's mistake, if only they'd looked closely enough.

"Do we have to get into this again?" Kaab asked, and Micah was glad that she wasn't the only one who was bored with Volney.

"Ah, Kaab! I'm so glad to see you. Allow me to introduce you to my friends." Rafe turned to Joshua and Henry. "This is Ixkaab Balam. She's a Kinwiinik princess," he said in a manner that even Micah could tell meant he was showing off. She was about to ask Kaab if she really was a princess, because Micah had heard that kings and queens were evil and so maybe their daughters were too, but before she could, Rafe sat in the chair next to Kaab and leaned toward her.

"Have you decided you want to study at the University too? I'd be happy to show you around. Don't trust these two." He pointed at Joshua and Henry with his thumb as they found chairs of their own. "They'd only want to get you alone so they could try to seduce a woman of your beauty and sophistication."

Joshua rolled his eyes and Henry blushed, but Kaab just shook her head. "I don't have enough time."

Rafe scoffed. "All you have is time! Whenever I see you, you're exploring here or in Riverside or the gods know where else, while I'm stuck doing petty secretarial work and desperately trying to get some of the antiquated bats who run this place to examine me so I can finally call myself a Master of Natural Science."

Kaab tilted her head to one side, amused by Rafe's rant. "I'm learning. I thought you would encourage that."

"I do, I do, but what are you learning? Street names? Where to find the best shopping? There's more to the world than that, Kaab!" Rafe pounded his fist on the table, making Micah's chocolate cup wobble. "You could be helping Micah here with his calculations! No one in this whole city knows as much about navigation as you do, and instead of teaching us you're off prancing about the town!"

Micah's eyes darted back and forth between them. Kaab had pursed her lips and would probably laugh at Rafe soon. But Micah didn't think Rafe would mind, because Kaab laughed at him often. Micah liked to watch them, although she didn't quite understand their friendship.

"I'm not done prancing yet," Kaab said. "Next I go to the Hill."

"Oh. No. You shouldn't do that." Rafe slouched back in his chair, making a face. "I've been exploring the Hill lately myself, and I don't like it at all."

"You don't mind the Hill, pigeon," Joshua said. "You just mind the work."

Rafe shrugged, smiling slightly. "There are some benefits." He said it like he had a secret, which meant it was about his duke. Which wasn't a secret at all. Micah wasn't sure why everyone kept pretending that it was.

"I must go to the Hill," Kaab repeated.

"But why? The Hill will never appreciate you the way I do, my dearest Ixkaab. Let me buy you ale—or chocolate, if you prefer, although the stuff they sell here is utter dreck—and then you and I can talk to Micah about—"

"Because my family was invited to the party, of course. Are not you their secretary? You must have seen our name on the invitations."

He paused with his hand half-raised to call a server, his eyebrows drawing down in confusion. "What party?"

"The Tremontaine ball!" Kaab threw up her hands in frustration. "There cannot be so many parties that you have forgotten."

"Ah yes. As a matter of fact, I was asked to help the duchess with a few small matters—"

"You're writing invitations?" Joshua asked, his voice incredulous. "I know I advised you to take the job, but, pigeon, I never imagined he would ask you to stoop so low."

"It was one day—" Rafe began, but Micah had an important question and raised her voice over both of them.

"What's a ball?"

"It's a party," Kaab answered after an awkward moment of silence, since Rafe was frowning fiercely and Joshua was focused on him, his gaze sympathetic. Henry was still staring at Kaab and then quickly looking away and pretending that he hadn't been.

"Why didn't the duchess write her own invitations? Doesn't she know how to write?" Micah asked.

"Well, she does, but—"

"Does she have bad handwriting?"

"It shows how important she is," Kaab explained. "She pays a secretary to write her letters for her, because she has many more letters than you or I do."

Micah thought about that and then nodded. It made sense. "What will the party be like?"

"This is what I also want to know," Kaab said, turning to Rafe.

He groaned but dropped his hands from his face. "Don't ask me. I'm sick of talking about this ball already, and it's still days away. Writing the invitations would have been terrible enough, but the duchess babbled at me the entire time about every single detail. Which flowers should she buy? What color should her dress be? What songs will the musicians play, and should two violinists be enough, or must she have three? And the rest of the household is going crazy. You're entirely right about her using it to show how important she is. Why do we even have nobility? What antiquated purpose do they serve?" He turned his face toward the ceiling. "Did I go to University for this?"

"It will get better, pigeon," Joshua murmured, squeezing Rafe's shoulder.

Kaab ignored his tragic expression. "Why were the Balam invited? And what does one wear to balls on the Hill? My family has never attended a noble's ball before."

"No, no, no, no, no!" Rafe groaned. "Not you too! I like you. Don't clutter up that brilliant mind with ribbons and lace, I beg of you. It's bad enough that I've been reduced to a secretary; don't make me a fashion consultant too."

Micah was worried at the way Rafe was shouting and flinging his arms about, but Kaab smiled and put her dark hand over Rafe's pale, nail-bitten one. "I like you too. And I believe you will not let me go to the ball looking like a stupid peasant."

Rafe sighed loudly, but his shoulders slumped and he nodded.

"My cousin Dinah talks a lot about fashion," Micah said. "She could help. But I don't think she's ever been to a ball. What happens at them?"

"I know a Dinah," Joshua said musingly. "But this Dinah is very familiar with balls. She has this trick where she takes four of them and puts them—"

"Joshua! Not in front of a lady!" Henry shouted. Kaab glanced at him, surprised, and he turned beet red and stared hard at the tabletop, adding quietly, "It isn't proper."

Rafe held up his hands in a placating gesture. He answered Micah's question first, which made her smile. "A ball is just a fancy party with dancing. People wear very expensive clothes and eat a lot of expensive food and talk to one another about nothing except the clothes and the food, and never about anything worthwhile like mathematics or natural philosophy or history."

"What type of food?" she asked. "And how much?"

"Two hundred pounds of potatoes," Joshua said, ticking each item off on his fingers, "ninety-nine loaves of bread, eight thousand tomato pies, three eels, an entire boar—"

"Wait, wait!" Micah scrabbled for a fresh sheet of paper. "I have to write it down; it's too many to remember."

"He's making it up, Micah," Rafe said, irritation showing in his voice.

"Then what do you eat at balls?"

"I don't know! They didn't make me write their shopping lists too. And anyway, it doesn't matter."

"You must know something of what food is served," Kaab said in a calm, soothing way that Micah found reassuring after all of the shouting. "I'm sure Micah would be grateful for an answer, and I would be also."

Rafe snorted, but Kaab's steady gaze made him look aside. "Apparently it is traditional for this ball to have a swan theme. Swans are on the Tremontaine family crest, you know, and the duchess is very proud of herself for finding ever new and inventive ways to incorporate swans into the ball each year. She was almost as tedious on this subject as she was on the dress. There will be pastries shaped like swans, and baked swans' eggs, and cold swan pie. There will be a swan of ice, floating upon the punch bowl. But what she's most proud of is her plan for a swan-shaped pudding, made of blackberries and wine." He rolled his eyes. "It sounds utterly unappetizing to me. I advise you to eat well before arriving."

"Are there vegetables?" Micah asked.

"There must be, I suppose."

Micah shuffled through her papers, looking for the letter she had struggled to write to her family. Once she found it, she handed it to Rafe and asked, "Turnips?"

He looked at the letter and frowned, not understanding, then shrugged. "Only if she can make a swan out of turnips."

"You can! I know you can!" She wriggled with excitement at her new idea. "The duchess needs to meet my cousin Reuben."

"I don't think the duchess—"

"He carves turnips. He's very good at it—he can make houses, or faces, or little cows. We do it every Last Night, and put candles in them for the dead. I'm sure he could make swans! If the duchess bought them for her party, she would pay a lot, and then it wouldn't even matter so much that I'm here and not there helping them. So I could stay and learn more about straight lines and spheres. If I go home now, I'll never find out what the lines do!" Micah stood and leaned over the table toward Rafe. "You must tell the duchess."

"She doesn't want my menu advice. I don't think she likes me very much."

"What about the duke? He's your boyfriend!"

Rafe sighed. "Yes, that would be why she doesn't like me very much, thank you."

"She needs swan turnips and I can get them. This is very important!" Micah shouted when she saw that Rafe was about to explain to her why it really wasn't important after all and she should just listen to him. "I know more about turnips than you do. My cousin will be at the market tomorrow. Will you come with me and tell him about the ball and the duchess and also help him understand why I have to figure out the lines?"

"Yes," Kaab answered. "Yes, he will. But first, he will tell me what one wears to a ball. And why the duchess would want my family to be there."

Rafe looked at Joshua. "Why did I take this job?" he moaned.

"Think of your school, pigeon," Joshua said. "Focus on that."

Kaab returned home in a gloomy mood. All hope was not lost, but she certainly didn't feel as though she'd solved the mystery as she'd promised. Part of the difficulty had been Micah and her belief in Tremontaine's need for turnips, but Rafe had seemed grateful for the distraction. Presumably because he didn't like his job, but Kaab couldn't be sure. Could he be protecting Tremontaine from her inquiries? Did he know something about Ben's death? Or about Diane's interest in the Balam family?

The Balam household had returned to its normal activities, and she found Aunt Saabim in the kitchen, going over her own menus for the coming week with the cook. "Ah, little bee," Saabim said, straightening up and putting a hand to her lower back. "Come, sit, and tell me what you have learned."

Kaab settled on the floor next to her aunt. It was a difficult manner of sitting when wearing the Local clothing; the long skirt bound her legs and added to her irritation. Finally managing to arrange herself into a position that was tolerable, she flung an exasperated hand toward the menus waiting by Saabim's north side. "I might as well have stayed here. They kept talking about food, no matter how many other questions I asked."

"If they talked about it so much, perhaps it is important to them," Saabim said mildly. "Tell me what they said."

"I don't think so." Kaab switched her ankles from one side to the other but was no more comfortable. "It was a conversation about turnips. Micah's people sell turnips and she wanted to sell some to the duchess, but Rafe didn't think she wanted any."

Saabim hummed thoughtfully. "Did Rafe say what the duchess is planning on serving?"

"He mentioned birds—"

"What kind?"

"Swans. Swans of ice, swans of cake, swans of pudding."

Saabim exchanged a meaningful look with the cook. "But no actual swans, correct, ma'am?" the cook asked. "And what spices in the pudding?"

"Did you want recipes?" Kaab was beginning to understand Rafe's hostility toward the frivolity of balls in general, and this one in particular.

"No," Saabim said. "Did he mention anything else?"

"Swans' eggs." Again the significant look, the comprehending nods. "What?" Kaab asked. "What am I missing?"

"Ice, cakes, puddings," said the cook. "These are the things one serves when one does not wish to spend a great deal at the market. Nothing more than flour and sugar and a cold storage room. This menu of the duchess's . . . it is not impressive. Instead, it strives to hide a lack of wealth. I'd wager that even the eggs will be nothing more than goose eggs, chopped up to disguise their size."

Kaab was sure the older woman had been introduced to her

at one point, but she'd forgotten her name, and couldn't ask now without appearing rude. She bowed her head to the cook thankfully, her mind racing. "If the duchess has no money, is that why she's trying to make a deal with Uncle?"

"Perhaps," Saabim said. "We need more information to be sure. I will keep an eye out at the ball for further indications of financial troubles, and you should do the same. Your uncle and I had already begun to suspect that such was the case. While you were busy"—and she delicately emphasized the word, making Kaab flush and look away—"we received word that the reduced tariffs she promised us will not be forthcoming soon. Her husband the duke somehow failed to attend the Council meeting where the matter was to be discussed! There is something very strange going on with that family, and if she wants our assistance, she will have to prove that she has something more to offer than empty promises and party invitations." Saabim huffed out a breath of air. "Now, did Rafe tell you anything about clothing?"

"He said they wear the same things to a ball that they wear for every day, just more elaborate and made of more expensive fabrics. And never the same one twice."

Saabim frowned. "Xamanek's light! Then I suppose that none of the Local outfits we already have will do. But a week isn't enough time to order new ones for everyone. What will we wear?"

"Why not wear our own clothes?" Kaab suggested. "The Locals seemed impressed with them at our banquet."

"Those were City merchants," Saabim said. "The nobles are very different. Even if this duchess is willing—or desperate enough—to break tradition to do business with us, I doubt she and her guests would find our anklets and nose rings anything but shocking—let alone the length of your uncle's skirt!" She chuckled, but then looked grave. "No, this is a delicate matter. I will have to discuss it with Chuleb and the elder cousins." She gathered the menus from the floor and handed them to the cook, then climbed to her feet. But before she left the room, she put a hand on Kaab's shoulder. "Thank you. This is useful knowledge you have gathered for us. Your mother would be proud."

It was only because she was so tired, Kaab told herself, that she felt the sting of tears in her eyes.

Returning to the North Market brought a certain relief. While Rafe had never liked it—as the son of a merchant he resented being expected to waste his life on trays of bread and tins of spices—he knew it. His family was wealthy enough that they hadn't needed to attend to the marketing themselves, but his father had insisted on it. He'd always said that there was no substitute for hands-on knowledge, for the innate skill at haggling and trading and making deals that could only come from being raised in the midst of a bustling market.

Rafe had avoided coming here as much as he could since he'd been at University, but everyone there ended up in North Market eventually; there was no way to escape the need to sell and to buy, to scrape and to hustle. Even Micah, normally only good with numbers, understood it instinctively. In the end, everyone needed turnips.

"Now, you both need to let me do the talking," said Micah, turning to Rafe and then to Kaab. They flanked him like a wildly mismatched honor guard through the crowded lanes.

"Then why are we here?" Kaab asked.

"Details," Micah said. "I need you to do the details."

Once they'd found his cousin Reuben's stall, Micah waited

patiently, letting him serve the current customers. Kaab plucked a turnip from the pile on the wooden boards and turned it over in her hands, apparently unfamiliar with the purple-and-cream-colored vegetable, and Micah told her several facts about it that the boy probably thought were very interesting. He seemed calm now that he was actually here, despite his worry and desperate strategizing the previous night.

Finally Reuben greeted them. His voice was a mix of surprise, concern, and—most of all—curiosity: Rafe and Kaab likely seemed strange companions.

"I'm not here to go home, but I wrote you a letter," Micah said, holding it out to his imposing cousin. "But then I found out something better than what was in the letter so I came to tell you in person."

Reuben smiled, tired and fond. "What could be better than a letter from you?" He pulled a stool out from behind himself and sat down, apparently willing to spend some time with them despite it being midmorning, the best time for selling vegetables. A man who would do that didn't seem likely to demand Micah's immediate return, which eased Rafe's worries. They were so close to solving the problem of navigation that he couldn't afford to lose Micah now.

"The Duchess Tremontaine is having a ball," Micah began seriously.

Reuben laughed, not unkindly. "Don't tell me living in the City has made you take a fancy to parties? You used to not even like it when Judith's sister and her little ones came to stay for Year's End."

"No, listen to me. The duchess needs turnips. She needs carved turnips, ones that look like swans. You could do that! No one can carve turnips like you! And because she's a duchess she'll pay lots of money for them. You should go to her immediately."

"Micah, the duchess don't need our turnips. She's got her own lands, and they produce plenty. Besides, someone like me can't go to a duchess without an introduction."

"I know that. Rafe can introduce you," Micah said, tugging Rafe forward as though Reuben might not have noticed him. "He works for her!"

"Is that so?" Reuben didn't seemed particularly impressed, which made Rafe like him even more.

"I'm the Duke Tremontaine's secretary now," he explained. "But I'm still helping Micah at University. Truly, we all expect great discoveries from him. So we appreciate your letting him stay."

"That true, boy?" Reuben asked Micah.

"Micah is very happy at the University," Kaab said, trying to be helpful.

"I just like solving things," Micah said. "And I've solved this. We have to sell the duchess your turnips."

"Micah, Tremontaine has this ball every year. Even if they wanted to serve turnips, which I doubt, they'd have ordered them weeks or even months ago. They plan that party very far in advance, just like we plan the plantings. I'm glad that you're thinking of your family, even with all your new friends, but I think we'll manage without providing turnips for this ball."

Micah's shoulders slumped. "Are you sure, Cousin?"

"If you're not coming home yet, you're not coming home yet. I'll make sure everyone reads this letter." Reuben reached across the stall's front and thumped Micah's shoulder in a friendly fashion. "Hey, why not go to the ball yourself? Then you could write us all about it. Your cousin Dinah'll pine away from jealousy."

The joke wasn't unkind. Not to Micah anyway. But Rafe could see the consequences of it rushing toward him. In the hopes of distracting Micah, he offered to buy a few turnips. "As a thank you for your time," he added.

"If you like," Reuben said agreeably, "but if you'll take my advice, we're getting past the season for turnips. Let me show you our green cabbage instead."

"No, no, turnips will do," Rafe said, and began selecting turnips from the stall somewhat frantically. He was going to have to at least pretend that he was going to show them to the duchess for Micah's sake, although he might actually even go through with it. Just to annoy her.

"Can I come to the ball with you, Rafe?" Micah asked.

Damn. Rafe laughed incredulously, causing Kaab to glance at him with raised eyebrows, but Micah pressed the issue.

"You heard my cousin say I should. If I go I can learn more about how it works and what your duchess needs—"

"She's not my duchess."

Kaab snickered. "No, but Tremontaine is your duke."

Rafe pointedly didn't answer. "Micah, I can't invite anyone to the ball. It's not my place."

"Why not?" Kaab asked. "You wrote the invitations. Write one more, for Micah."

"I wrote them at the duchess's direction!"

"You don't even like her," Kaab said. "So why follow her orders?"

"I work for her husband, not her. Not that she respects that!"

"And you don't respect the fact that he's her husband, not yours," Kaab said.

Micah stopped dead still in the center of the crowd and put his hands over his ears. "Stop yelling!"

Rafe was very tempted to keep going, but he reluctantly let his perfect witty retort slide away and put up his palms to show the boy that he was calm.

Micah kept his hands over his ears. "You should help me. I play cards even when I don't want to, just so you can buy tomato pies and beer."

"I have a job now. I don't need you to do that anymore. You should focus on your studies."

"But I did it. So you should help me."

"I agree," Kaab said. "Help Micah go to the ball if he wants to. What's so wrong with wanting to go to a ball?"

"You should know better," Rafe said, fighting to keep his voice from rising once again. Micah's hands had only just begun to lower. "Both of you."

Kaab bristled. "Don't speak to me like a child."

"What do you even do?" He rounded on her, his voice low but angry. The crowd began to give them a greater berth, not wanting to be involved. "Micah attends University, at least. What do you do all day? You still haven't brought those charts you promised us! As far as I can tell, all you do is bother me with stupid questions about what you should wear to the ball and what everyone's eating."

"The turnips are important," Micah said softly.

"No, they're not!" Rafe clutched at his hair, nearly tearing it out in his frustration. "This whole City is made up of children," he went on, yelling at no one in particular. "All anyone talks about is food and parties and clothes. It's bad enough that I've already wasted days of my valuable time on this damn ball, so that people can giggle and flirt and wear pretty clothes. Gods damn it, am I the only one who cares about knowledge anymore? Who sees these shallow, idle entertainments for what they are?"

"You shout about flirting?" Kaab said, putting her hands on her hips. "How are you any better? You wouldn't have this secretary job if you hadn't flirted with the duke first."

That dart found its target. "That's not true," Rafe said. Kaab smirked. "Or rather it was. At first. But that's not the point. This is not an idle amusement that I can toss away on writing a fraudulent invitation for a scholar who shouldn't even want to go to a ball."

Kaab scoffed. "Fine. You need not worry about these idle amusements. I will help Micah get in."

"Really?" Micah asked. He was clearly distressed by the fight, his hands clenched into fists and his shoulders hunched.

"Yes. We'll go together," Kaab said firmly, taking hold of Micah's elbow.

"Do whatever you want," Rafe said. "I don't want to hear about it."

"I am happy to not tell you things." Kaab was clearly angry, but she maintained her control as she led Micah away.

Rafe wished he could be as calm. Now that his outburst was over, he was already beginning to regret it. Joshua knew him well enough to know that Rafe's rantings weren't always meant to be taken seriously, but Micah and Kaab weren't as familiar with him. Of course, it wasn't his fault that he'd exploded. He was dealing with a year's delay in becoming a Master, a noble lover with an unsettling wife, a society occasion he dreaded but wasn't sure he'd be able to avoid, the shallowness of an entire City, and now unreasonable demands that would require him to compromise his own sense of honor. Anyone would have shouted, surely.

Well, he'd find a way to apologize to them later.

"Tell Tess what you need," Kaab said, pushing Micah forward.

Micah hesitated. She didn't like asking strangers for favors, but

Kaab had promised that Tess wouldn't mind. Tess wasn't what Micah had expected from a Riversider. Cousin Reuben had told her never to go to Riverside because the people who lived there were dangerous, and Rafe had said the same thing, but Tess looked nice. She was plump with red hair braided back from her face, and she wore a plain dress with ink stains on her sleeve; that made Micah feel better. Micah's clothes usually had ink stains on them too, though at least they didn't show on the black robes she wore at the University.

"I need an invitation to a party, please," Micah said. "I mean, a ball. The one that Rafe's duchess is holding soon."

Tess smiled. "I can do that for you. Invitations are easy, at least as long as you have a real one to copy from."

Micah's hopes plummeted, but Kaab patted her on the shoulder and pulled a letter from her pocket. "Don't worry, I've got the one the duchess sent to my family." She handed it to Tess, who flipped it open and began studying it. The paper was much thicker than what Micah used for her own letters and was a brighter white too. "I'll need it back, though I doubt she'll have forgotten about us by the time we show up at her door."

Tess nodded, distracted. She held the letter up toward the window and examined the way the light shone through the paper. "I've got good matches for the paper and ink on hand. This shouldn't take me very long. If you have the time to wait, I'll do it right now."

Kaab smiled. "We have plenty of time. I would be honored to watch you work."

Tess's cheeks turned pink. "Oh, it's nothing, really. . . ."

"No, it's fascinating." Kaab moved closer to Tess. "You're so skilled."

Micah sighed. Why were they talking so much? Tess spread

the invitation out on a bare table near the window, while Kaab sat down next to her. She was so close that occasionally her arm bumped against Tess's, which didn't seem helpful for writing, and their voices dropped almost to whispers, punctuated by giggles. Micah didn't see anything funny about paper and ink.

She decided to ignore them and studied the rest of Tess's apartment. It was somewhat like Rafe's rooms, but much bigger and with fewer people, which was nice. It was much brighter, too, both because of the large windows and because of a full-length mirror that reflected their light despite a spider web of cracks in its bottom corner. Silk and velvet scarves were tacked to the walls, hiding the peeling paint with bright blue and purple patterns. There were overlapping rugs on the floor, soft enough for Micah's shoes to sink into them.

The most interesting thing, though, was a desk not far from Tess's worktable. It had all sorts of drawers and shelves, and every surface was covered in paper of different weights and sizes, bottles of ink and sticks of wax in a rainbow of colors, dozens of quills and penknives for sharpening them. Micah opened one drawer to discover a pile of seals, made of wood and terra-cotta and one of iron. She closed that drawer and opened the one below it, which was stuffed full of tiny glass bottles and released a strong stinging smell that made her flinch back and cough.

"Those are my perfumes," Tess said, looking over at the sound. "For when I need to forge a love letter."

Micah didn't understand why anyone would want a made-up love letter. Other people's feelings were confusing enough; why make it even more complicated?

"By the way, who are you?" Tess asked. Micah wondered how Tess had forgotten her name. It wasn't a long or complicated name.

It wasn't even foreign, and, anyway, Tess could remember Kaab's name just fine. But to be polite, Micah introduced herself again.

Tess laughed and gestured at the new invitation she was writing. "Yes, but the Duchess Tremontaine wouldn't invite Micah, the turnip girl pretending to be a University boy, to her ball. So who do you want to be on the invitation?"

"I'm not pretending to be at the University. I am there," she said, going through the pile of papers on top of the desk. One of them was so strange that it caught her attention: a round circle thickly scattered with what appeared to be randomly sized dots. Each dot was labeled with symbols from a language Micah didn't recognize and numbers that she did. She held up the paper, turned it sideways and upside down, but still couldn't make sense of it. "What is this?"

"Don't mess with Tess's work," said a deep voice behind her.

Micah dropped the paper and spun around, finding herself face-to-face with a tall, dark-haired man who hadn't been there before. "I'm sorry!"

"Don't scare her, Applethorpe," Kaab said, getting up from Tess's side. She picked the paper up from where it had drifted to the floor and handed it back to Micah. "This is for you, actually. It's the star chart I was telling you about. I had Tess make a copy, so that way my uncle will still have his, and you'll have yours, and everyone will be happy." Kaab leafed through the pile of papers and pulled out several other sheets that looked very similar to the one in Micah's hands. "Here, here, and here. Take them home and study them very closely."

"What about that one?" Micah asked, pointing at a similar-looking chart in the pile.

"Oh, no, no." Kaab rolled it up before Micah could get a good look at it and tucked it into a pouch at her side. "This one is my uncle's. I have to take it back to him. You just use those ones I gave you."

Micah looked at the charts. "But I can't read any of it! Tell me what this means." She pointed to one of the symbols next to a dot; it looked like a human face that had been squished into a square.

"It's the name of the star. I could translate for you, but I'm sure you have different names for them. Focus on the numbers; I had Tess write those in your fashion." She looked at Tess. "Right? You did make the changes I asked for?"

Tess nodded, then glanced quickly at Micah before looking away again.

"I've never seen anything like these," Micah said, fascinated despite her confusion. "I don't know how to use them."

Kaab shrugged. "They're stars. Other than that, you'll have to figure it out yourself, because I don't know what it means either." She continued poking through the papers on Tess's desk, tucking away other star charts that must also have belonged to her uncle. She stopped at a pencil sketch of a piece of jewelry and stared at it for a moment, then held it up to Tess. "Is this what I think it is?"

Tess nodded silently, and Applethorpe moved closer. Micah hurriedly stepped away, but he only took the drawing from Kaab and studied it.

"The locket and chain were gold, I'd say," Tess said, "and the little chips round the edge were diamonds. The bird was done up in gems too."

Micah looked at the paper again since everyone else seemed to think it was very important, but it only looked like an oval locket on a chain—with a swan at its center and a balanced pattern of lines and curlicues behind it that was really quite satisfying. If it were real, and not just a drawing, Micah would have wanted to touch it. She turned her attention back to her new charts. She was beginning to figure them out: If the dots were stars, then these six dots here must be the Cockerel, a constellation her uncle had taught her to find in the night sky. Therefore the numbers must be . . . no, she didn't understand it yet.

Kaab set the locket sketch back on the desk and turned to Micah. "Don't worry about that," she said, which was fine because Micah wasn't worried. "Tell me who you want to be at the ball."

"I want to be myself," she said. "Who else could I be?"

"Micah, the real Micah, can't go to the ball. So we'll just make you into someone who does go to balls at Tremontaine House. We need to do more than just make you your own invitation; we have to make it so that if the duchess sees you, she believes she might have invited you."

"That seems like lying."

Kaab exchanged a glance and a small smile with Applethorpe. "Think of it like a feint instead. A little trick, to make everyone look away. Besides, it's no different from telling everyone you're a boy."

Micah shook her head. "I don't do that. Everyone thinks I'm a boy. I don't tell them otherwise, but that's not lying."

Tess laughed. "That's splitting a fine hair."

"Why do you do it, by the way?" Kaab asked. "Do you want to be a boy?"

"No, I don't mind being a girl. But people bother boys less; that's what Cousin Reuben says."

Tess smiled. "Cousin Reuben's a wise man. But what do you do when you've got your cycles?"

"Rags," Micah said. "Like anyone."

"Even at the University?" Tess tilted her head to one side. "I thought the students lived all crammed together, like birds in a nest. Someone must notice."

"Rafe's really busy. And dramatic. And messy. He doesn't pay attention to things like rags."

Kaab snorted. "Of course he doesn't. Does he pay attention to anything other than himself?"

"I don't mind," Micah said. "No one notices everything. I'd rather he noticed my calculations than my blood."

Applethorpe laughed with approval, and Micah decided that maybe he wasn't as scary as she'd thought. "Well, you'll have to stay a boy for a little longer," he said. "Noble girls don't go to parties on their own. At least not until they're widows, and you're a little young for that."

Kaab nodded. "It is the same in my country. What kind of boy do you want to be, Micah?"

Micah bit her lip and thought hard. "I want to be things that are true," she decided. "I am good with crops. I like mathematics. I go to the University. I am not from the City. I have a big family."

"How about a rich merchant?" Tess suggested, looking at Kaab. "Merchants aren't so very different from farmers, so she should be able to pull it off."

Kaab shook her head. "No, the Tremontaine ball isn't a ball that merchants go to. My family will be the first Trading family to ever attend."

"Why not take her with you? She could be your maid or something."

Micah liked that idea. It would be much less scary with Kaab there to tell her what to do. But she didn't think it would fool the duchess. Micah looked nothing like Kaab and didn't speak her language. "That won't work," she said.

Applethorpe took Micah by the shoulders and studied her for several seconds, then pronounced, "Minor country nobility."

Kaab narrowed her eyes in thought. "Will that work? Back home, the nobles all know each other."

"Trust me. There's always someone's second cousin or uncle once removed or discreetly reared by-blow at these sorts of things. Their family trees are too complicated for even the nobles to keep track of everyone. Besides, look at her. Everyone has a dozen forgettable relatives that look exactly like her."

Kaab turned to Micah. "It's not so different from the truth. A big family in the country . . . I suppose if you're minor enough nobility, you might even have helped on the farm. Does that sound like something you can do?"

Micah nodded.

Kaab clapped her hands together and grinned. "Now to the fun part! Let's get you some new clothes."

Rafe found himself left alone in the marketplace with a great deal of annoyance and nothing to do with it. He could have headed to the University, of course, to contemplate Micah's table of artificial numbers. He could have found Joshua and complained, or other friends who would let him dispel his irritation in a round of cards or a beer or two. But those were sensible occupations, and he wasn't in the mood for sensible. Instead he remembered that Will had an appointment nearby at his tailor's.

Durham's had pride of place in the center of Threadneedle Row. A large window in the front displayed several items of clothing, their cut elaborate and colors exquisite. Rafe imagined that he would be the first scholar ever to pass over its threshold.

He pushed open the heavy oak door, setting off a small bell, and was greeted by the calming masculine scents of lavender and citron. A gentleman lounged in a leather armchair drawn close to the window's light, idly perusing a broadsheet as he waited for his appointment, or perhaps simply using the space as his own private club.

A clerk emerged from the back. "Yes?" he asked imperiously, one eyebrow raised.

Rafe hated introducing himself as a secretary, but he had no other excuse for being here. Let them make what they would of his scholar's robe and long hair.

"I will inform the duke of your presence." The clerk disappeared into the back, leaving Rafe to loiter awkwardly. He told himself he belonged here as much as any man did. If he had stayed with his family and gone into business, he would be buying clothes from fine establishments like this one, or close to it. Of course, his current garments gave no hint of the status he'd so proudly rejected; his scholar's robe covered most of the wrinkled clothes he wore, but was itself fraying at the hem and in need of laundering. Rafe couldn't suppress the sense that his presence was improper. *This is what working on the Hill has done to me,* he thought savagely.

The clerk returned and ushered him back to a fitting room where Will waited, smiling broadly, dispelling Rafe's lingering fear that he might be turned away.

"Rafe! I'm so glad to see you. What a wonderful surprise."

Will wore unfinished breeches, the lining showing and a flurry of loose threads emerging from the seams, and had on nothing but his shirtsleeves. Rafe had seen him naked before, but he was somehow more compelling in this half-dressed state, slivers of pale skin visible at his neck and wrist, the shape of his body a shadow glimpsed through the linen.

Here, deep in the heart of all Durham's formality, there was only Will, a mortal man like Rafe, nothing more. But nothing less, either. It was more intimate than Rafe had expected, especially once Will sent away the clerk and tailor. He let Will take his hand and draw him close, then kiss him without words.

This was what Rafe needed after his fight with Micah and Kaab. Someone who understood him; the simple physical pleasure of human contact. When they parted, Rafe let his forehead sink to Will's shoulder.

"Are you all right?" Will asked. "You seem upset, my dear."

Rafe sighed. "It's been a trying day. No—*days*. Your wife has had me writing invitations to her ball. She didn't even let me compose them myself, but dictated every word, as though I couldn't be trusted to address a noble."

"She doesn't have a secretary of her own right now. I'm sure she only meant to help."

"No." Rafe shrugged out of Will's embrace and stepped away. "She was trying to irritate me—I'm certain of it. She wanted to waste my time and keep me from my real work."

"But why would Diane do that?" Will's expression suddenly changed. "You . . . you don't think she knows about us, do you?"

In fact, Rafe did, but when confronted with Will's obvious horror at the idea, he found himself unable to say so. He waved a hand as though unconcerned. "And what if she does? It's only an affair; there's nothing for her to be bothered by."

"I'm not sure I see it that way," Will said softly. "And I am certain that Diane won't either."

"Why shouldn't she? I know your marriage was arranged, so you can't tell me she considers herself in *love* with you! I'm glad that you two seem to have found some measure of camaraderie in your years together, but surely she understands the realities of married life by now."

Will avoided his gaze, staring off toward the bones of a waist-coat that was folded over the back of a chair. It was made of a vivid crimson clearly intended to pair with the more muted burgundy of the half-finished breeches he was wearing. He gave no answer.

A suspicion began to grow in Rafe's mind. "You *have* had affairs before, haven't you?"

"Well, no, actually I haven't," Will said, still looking away. "And neither has the duchess, if you're wondering. I am sure of her," he added stoutly, his voice firm in support of his wife.

The last thing Rafe wanted to hear right now was his lover praising his wife. This was an unforeseen disaster. He, Rafe Fenton, saddled with an inexperienced lover and a sure to be jealous wife! And yet . . . Will was, if new to this game, not unskilled. Far from it. And there was something compelling about the idea of being his first. Well, not his *first* exactly, but the first of a sort. The first to seduce the steadfastly loyal Duke Tremontaine from the arms of that grasping, irritating wife of his . . .

Rafe found himself drifting back toward Will. Will's shirt was warm and soft beneath his hands as he moved them across Will's chest. "Never mind," Rafe said, done with the topic. "I'm sure she suspects nothing. We've been very discreet."

They kissed; Will's mouth was hot and sweet, and Rafe couldn't seem to get enough. "I like you in these clothes," he said, his lips brushing Will's jaw. "Red is a good color for you."

Will smiled, his long fingers pulling Rafe's hair from its queue. "Shall I buy you an outfit as well? You will need something to wear to the ball, you know."

Rafe didn't want to talk about the ball, so he kissed him again.

Words soon grew unimportant, and they might have gone further than kissing had not the tailor bustled in, a coat in one hand and a bundle of lace in the other.

Rafe broke away from Will and fled quickly, his face hot. The tailor certainly knew now, which meant nothing, but it deepened his conviction that the duchess did too, and was far less amused.

The four of them—Micah and Kaab and Tess and the man called Applethorpe, too—left Tess's rooms and followed her through the winding streets of Riverside. She led them to a house that looked much like her own, a large building that had been fancy once, when it had been younger and cleaner and had glass in all its windows. Now it was a bit scary and leaned crookedly over the narrow alley like a gargoyle. They entered through a back door and went up a flight of stairs with no windows or lanterns to light the way; at the top, Tess pounded on a door and waited through the click and rattle of multiple locks being undone.

But after all of that, the door swept open to reveal a shop. Micah thought it was odd to have a shop hidden up a flight of stairs with no signs marking the way. How would anyone find it? But otherwise it seemed to be normal, if a bit messy. There were racks of clothes filling most of the space, and piles of more clothes on every surface, and a few shelves displaying odds and ends like pocket watches and hatpins and jewelry. A group of girls was sitting in a circle, working with needles and thread on handkerchiefs. At first Micah thought they were doing embroidery, but a closer look showed just the opposite: They were picking out monogrammed letters to make plain, unadorned handkerchiefs. That was odd too.

The oldest of the girls—a woman, really—stood and greeted

Tess with an embrace. "This is Madeline," Tess said to Micah and Kaab. "Though her place is called Vanessa's."

Everyone seemed to have two names lately. Even Micah herself did now, since according to her new invitation she was Thomas Abney.

"You want some toast and cheese?" Madeline asked. "I'll do it for you all for five, which is a better price than Jenny offers. I can also find you some wine, but it'll be ten for a bottle of the good stuff."

"Is this a cookshop, too?" Micah asked.

Madeline laughed. "Of course. Anything you want, duck, I'll get it for you—at the right price. I even got beds in the back if you need a place to sleep."

Micah shook her head. "I already have a place to stay, thank you."

"No food for us, Madeline," Tess said. "We're looking for an outfit for Micah, here. Something fancy, like what a noble would wear to a ball."

Madeline cocked her hip to one side and planted a fist on it. She was a tiny woman, shorter than Micah, even, with bright black eyes and dark hair piled in a bun high on her head. "Wellll, we're a bit short on ladies' finery right now, but—"

"Not a problem," Tess said. "Micah's a young man for this one."

Madeline did not seem confused by this. She looked at Micah, measuring with her eyes.

"I'll take that wine you offered," Applethorpe said.

The small woman grinned up at him. "I knew you would, Vincent."

That settled, Madeline began to show off clothes to Tess. Doublets, scarves and hats, breeches and trousers and shiny black boots—the two of them went through dozens of pieces, Madeline holding them up just long enough for Tess to shake her head and then tossing them aside. Some of the clothes seemed brand new, and others were so old that their dyes had faded to brown or gray. Kaab was watching closely, but it seemed to be Tess who was in charge here.

Applethorpe settled on a trunk to observe, dangling his bottle of wine loosely in one hand. No one seemed much interested in what Micah thought of the clothes, so she took a seat next to him. He offered her the bottle, but she refused; she preferred chocolate but was afraid to ask Madeline for any. She didn't know how much it would cost, and she didn't want to waste her money if she needed to buy clothes for the ball.

"Look at this one!" Madeline crowed, holding up a coat of emerald silk with gold piping on the seams. "I just acquired it, but I'll sell it to you, Tess. The lining's torn, but that won't show when your boy is wearing it."

"No, no! That's not right at all." Tess began to paw through another pile of clothes. "Micah's the younger son of a country noble. Not long in the City, and certainly not with the money for silk. Besides, it's too fashion-forward." She pulled out a cream-colored doublet with a pattern of diamonds in brown thread. "Now, this is what we want. Good, old-fashioned doublet his father probably wore in *his* first season. What do you have that matches?"

"There's a pair of loose breeches in a lovely brown velvet some-where in here—also out of fashion, but perhaps that's all the better. Fine quality. I'll let you have them both for twenty silver."

"Silver?" Tess shouted. "I'll give you twenty brass minnows, and that's more than they're worth."

"Ten silver, then, and I'll throw in a good linen shirt."

"Micah already has a shirt. Three."

Micah stopped paying attention. The numbers seemed random to her, and she didn't understand how Tess could make them change just by arguing about it. "What do you think?" she asked Applethorpe.

He nodded thoughtfully. "Brown's a good choice. It'll keep you from standing out. Best way to keep anyone from noticing the holes in your story is to keep them from noticing you in the first place." He turned to Kaab. "And what will you be wearing, Mistress Balam? You'd draw attention in any color."

Kaab sighed and picked up a cotton petticoat that Tess had tossed aside earlier. "I don't know. I am told that normally one has a new costume made to order, but there isn't time for that."

"I could fit you with a good dress," Madeline said. She dropped a stack of clothes into Micah's arms and showed her where she could duck between several lines of hanging clothes to try them on. "I got plenty. What color you want?"

"No," Applethorpe said firmly. "That'll do for Micah, but Kaab has much to lose if someone recognizes their discards from last season. Or the dress that went missing when it was supposed to be put into storage."

"They have more clothes than they can keep track of, up on the Hill." Madeline said, waving a red skirt. "This is good fabric. Sturdy weave, nice small stitching . . ."

"But if we wear old clothes, even good ones, won't people notice?" Kaab asked. "We must be impressive."

"I can make you impressive, dearie. As long as you got a good base to work with, you can do anything."

Micah emerged clumsily from behind the hanging clothes. The doublet was so tight that she felt like she couldn't breathe, but she liked the way the velvet felt under her fingers.

Tess came up to her and tried to tug up the vest, stopping when the seams creaked alarmingly. "Well, at least it's the right length," she said. "We can open the sides and add some extra fabric."

Micah was thankful when Tess nodded and said she could change back into her old clothes. When she emerged again, once more in her old shirt, breeches, and scholar's robe, the others were gathered around a shelf of hats and trinkets.

"What is this?" Kaab pointed to a woman's showy four-cornered hat ornamented with an ostrich plume. "I thought you didn't wear feathers here?"

Madeline shrugged. "They're in one season and then out the next. Why? You got some feathers to work with?"

"Many. And our feathers are much better than this." Kaab reached out to stroke the plume, which Micah had to admit did look rather ratty.

"Are they?" Tess drawled. "Then why not wear your wonderful feathers, but in our styles?"

"Why not . . ." Kaab laughed and hugged Tess swiftly. "You are brilliant! We have such beautiful things, we could just rearrange them: put on our jade and gold as you Locals do; wear a nose ring as a brooch, let us say. What else . . . ? Our mantles." She sketched a large rectangle in the air. "They are woven, with bright colors and complex designs. Is there anything like that in your fashions here?"

"Sounds like a shawl to me." Madeline dug through a nearby pile and produced a damask example, draping it around her shoulders and striking a pose.

Kaab grinned. "Excellent!" She looked to Applethorpe. "What do you think? You know these nobles better than any of us—they hire swordsmen all the time. Will this work?"

Applethorpe nodded slowly. "If you wear their clothes, they'll think you failed because they're not as new or stylish as the ones they wear. If you wear your own clothes, they'll think you failed because you're too stupid to learn our ways. But this . . . it isn't one thing or the other." He smiled. "Yes, I think you'll beat them at their own game. Or maybe even make them play yours."

Episode Seven

THE SWAN BALL

Joel Derfner

Diane, Duchess Tremontaine, shining in powder-blue silk, hears with satisfaction the graceful sound of her own laughter pealing through the ballroom like cool rain falling on crystal bells. If everything were falling to wrack and ruin around her, she would nonetheless laugh in just this particular, melodious way, simply to keep up appearances, but in this case she is expressing what she genuinely feels. For Karleigh is not here.

The Duke of Karleigh has not come to the ball!

So light is her heart that, if she were a different sort of woman, she would execute a twirl.

A *very* different sort of woman.

Lord Asper Lindley steps over to her, a splendid concoction of self-confidence and green brocade. He deposits his plate on the table beside a magnificent pile of bright silver spoons. The plate is heaped with the tiny curved necks and heads of pastry swans, which he proceeds to nibble one by one.

"Why, Asper, can it be that my little swan pastries have found favor with your discerning tastes?"

He gives her a lazy smile. There is pastry cream in the corner of his mouth. "Yes, Madam Duchess. But how could they not? One does so enjoy disjointing swans, even the flour and cream ones."

"Then keep eating, please, as many as you like. I'm sure dear Nicholas is too busy these days with Council matters for the possible results of your pastry consumption to bother him." There. An instant too long to return her smile. She has struck home. He will think twice next time he wishes to comment on her gown in the manner he did at Lady Galing's party earlier in the season.

Over his shoulder, she sees the Dragon Chancellor attempting to keep the corners of his mouth from rising, and she floats over to him. "Gregory!" She has forgotten how very handsome he is, with his deep green eyes and the dun hair falling over his brow. "Why have you not asked to lead me in the dance yet this evening?"

"Because," says Lord Davenant with a short bow, "I'm quite certain your beauty would cause me to stumble from inattention and tread on your foot, at which point I would have to hurl myself into the river in despair."

She places a hand on his arm. "I dare say I would be so distracted by the perfection of your features I would fail to notice." She is not entirely dissembling. Her hand is still on his arm.

This ball, upon which so very much depends, is proving a stunning success. Very little holds the nobility's attention like the glittering of jewels in candlelight as the women on whose necks and wrists they hang spin in the dance, the strains of the violins wafting above the crowd, adorning the air with exquisite melody, the heat and crush of the City's finest aristocracy drinking and eating and dancing and fanning and, above all else, whispering about one another. The smoke and mirrors with which she has given the proceedings the appearance of a luxury she cannot afford have aroused none of the comments she has feared they might inspire.

And the Duke of Karleigh, thank the good gods, is at home with a head cold.

Meanwhile, another much-desired guest is making his presence known. The head of the Balam Trading family has come after all, along with many of his colorful compatriots. She wasn't at all sure he'd accept her invitation; it wasn't as though any of these foreigners ever socialized on the Hill. But he has accepted both the invitation and the challenge, and seems to be enjoying both equally.

"Duchess," says Master Ahchuleb Balam, arriving at her side and bowing with exactly the correct degree of deference, "may I congratulate you on a spectacular evening?"

"Why, sir, if the evening is indeed a spectacular one—an assertion whose merit I am of course in no position to evaluate—then it is due entirely to your presence and that of your people." And to the absence of the Duke of Karleigh.

Diane glows with pleasure in the light of the flames flickering around them as they exchange increasingly intricate flatteries. Finally come the words she has been so desperate to hear from him: "The manner in which I have heard my Kinwiinik colleagues remark upon your hospitality suggests to me that, when I broach the matter to them again, I will find them eager to accept your proposal."

Diane smiles. "I leave the matter, sir, entirely in your hands. A letter from you would be a delight no matter what news it bore."

She does not mention the fact that moments earlier she heard Lord Galing say that, having met and been thoroughly charmed by the Kinwiinik here—so picturesque!—he's beginning to suspect the chocolate import tariffs might be the slightest bit excessive; by the end of the evening she will have no trouble persuading him to lower them. She feels as if a great weight, a dark mass of onyx that has lain heavy upon her for months, were disintegrating into so much dandelion seed and scattering on a refreshing breeze. She has dealt with the terrible threat posed by her disgusting, chiseling visitor of three weeks earlier, the disaster of the *Everfair* is all but behind her, and for the first time in a very long while the ease of her breath is achieved without any effort whatsoever.

The duchess turns to take in the room, the swirling couples, the reflection of candlelight in faceted precious stones, the bright hiss of silk, the sweet scent of iced cakes, and her smile is ethereal. She has secured her position once more—and Tremontaine's—and the road ahead will be strewn with violets and lilies.

Suddenly, as if from far away, she hears a low, faint rattling. She frowns. Such a noise has no place in a ballroom—but no, it is definitely there, and not only that but growing steadily louder. She flushes. "Are you quite sure you're well?" says Davenant.

"The room is somewhat close, don't you think?" she says, snapping open her fan. The rattling grows louder, and louder still, then resolves itself finally, inexplicably, into the sound of a carriage hurrying down a country road, closer, closer. She glances around, but she seems to be the only one in the room to hear it. It grows louder and louder, rumbling, advancing, thundering, until it crowds all other sound out of her ears. The room darkens, and in place of the supremely elegant gathering there are two girls, a maid and a mistress, riding in a traveling coach, giggling about the possibilities they believe the future holds, and then all of a sudden rearing horses, the shouts of men, the clash of swords, the scent of fear, rage, opportunity, and blood, blood, oh, blood, and she thinks she will faint, and she sinks toward the ground—

—and Diane, Duchess Tremontaine, wakes with a gasp, her heart wild to escape her breast, her mind whirling, spinning, clanging, and she sees after a moment's disorientation that she is not in her ballroom after all, she is in her bedchamber, because the ball has yet to take place, the ball is tonight, and Karleigh, Karleigh will be there, and if he offends the Kinwiinik deeply enough that they refuse her proposal, then she will have rescued herself from the fire only to be cast into the sea.

And now, reader, let us take advantage of our position outside the tale, first to allow a span of hours to pass unremarked (unremarked by us, that is; to be sure, the men and women with whom we concern ourselves are about their business, bemoaning their woes, cherishing their secret hopes) and then, once we return, to flit rather than to linger, to glance rather than to gaze, to visit our heroes—for who among us is not the hero of his own story?—unseen and undetected as they ready themselves for the ball.

Here we see Ixkaab, first daughter of a first daughter of the Balam, a thousand and a thousand miles from her home, as with a thrill of transgression and pride she places in her ears the silver earplugs her uncle has lent her, of a quality and craftsmanship denied her on her native shores, where to appear in greater luxury than members of the royal house is punishable by exile. She adds golden bracelets studded with precious stones and a circlet of jade and pearl upon her brow, one such as might be donned for a solemn occasion by the daughter of the Batab, Ruler of the Territories, and finally knots a headdress of stiff cloth, modest in comparison with that of her aunt Ixsaabim but nonetheless resplendent with a shower of green quetzal feathers surrounded by the brilliant red of the macaw. She and the members of the household wear these adornments tonight to show the strength and power of their people, the honor of the Traders' House of Balam of the Kinwiinik, but she herself finds an additional inner comfort in the pomp. She is terrified, as she has been for some time, that she will be discovered to have revealed the secret she has been told she must not give away, but this fear has just been overshadowed by an even greater one: They have had news this day of a disaster at home that could spell their doom and the doom of their entire people. Her aunt steps up behind her, and they regard each other in the glass, each thinking of danger and of Ixmoe, sister to one, mother to the other, who awaits them both, if their understanding of the cosmos is correct—and who is to say it is not?—in the houses beneath the earth.

Here we have Rafe Fenton, son of a different sort of trader, a City merchant's reluctant heir, sorely vexed; we shall see the cause soon enough, but let it be enough for now to say that, of two things he desires with equally burning fervor, each seems to put the other out of his grasp, and vexed more sorely still because, at least at present, he is making what he feels is the coward's choice. He too regards himself in the glass, splendid in claret velvet, and his face clouds like the sky before a storm that does not intend all it touches to survive. With an oath and a cry he tears open the soft doublet, slashed with black, and casts it to the floor along with the new stockings and the breeches; should you harbor any faith that the red silk ribbon for the hair flowing down his back is to be spared a similar fate, I advise you to gird yourself for disappointment. Now he attires himself, though he knows it will offend—or perhaps because he knows it will offend—in a manner much more befitting the man he wishes to be. The sight that confronts him when he turns back to the glass, though far less comely, pleases him far more.

Here is a girl named Micah, nervous about the evening ahead—as it happens, not nearly as nervous as she would be if she truly understood its character—rehearsing the words and phrases her friends have taught her to say should she be confronted with the need to speak. She is irked by the fit of the clothes she has consented to put on for the evening, more constricting than the scholar's robe to which she has grown accustomed, but that is nothing compared with the madness to which she feels she is being driven by the mathematical mystery that evades her indefatigable efforts to solve it. In the meanwhile, she looks forward to the evening ahead as an opportunity to assuage the guilt she feels at having abandoned her family for so long by doing them, perhaps, a great service involving a humble vegetable.

Here are Tess, known to some as the Hand, and Vincent Applethorpe—we may speak of them together in Riverside rather than individually, as they are, while vital to their own tales, ancillary to ours. The one is attempting, without much success, to stave off a feeling of dread that has been growing in her since the death of her former protector, a fear that whatever malevolent force led him to his end has not yet abandoned its machinations in her life; I am sorry to inform you, reader, that events to come will prove that fear warranted. The other, who has arranged to attach himself to the large train of one of the brightly glittering families who will soon sweep up the Tremontaine House steps, buckles on a sword that he hopes will remain undrawn by the time he sees his bed. Whether that hope is to be met or dashed—well, you must permit the storyteller to retain a modicum of mystery; it is, weak though it be, the only power he has.

Here we see William Alexander Tielman, Duke Tremontaine, bedecked in a red deeper than the great ruby that shines among a circle of diamonds on his hand, feeling for the first time in years—and who, if the duke believes it to be the first time ever, could withhold forgiveness?—the thrill that renders men children in the face of love, if love indeed it be, that leaves them helpless and jolly even as all they have built threatens, whether they know it or not, to topple around them and leave them standing amid the wreckage of their lives.

And here, at last, we see, wide awake, Diane, Duchess Tremontaine, architect of the evening that is to come. Unlike her husband, she is all too aware of the destruction that looms over them, and perhaps by nightfall she will have come a great deal closer to averting it. There is another doom, however, far worse and more grim, that hangs over her head. She believes she has dispatched it, but she is mistaken, and whether she will escape it or be reduced to ashes in its conflagration is not at the moment within my ken.

These, then, are some of the men and women who may cross one another's paths this night. Who is to say which of them will be hero to another, which villain, and which—

Ah, but the guests have begun to arrive.

In pairs they come, for the most part, over the course of an hour or two, borne in gilded carriages that bespeak opulence more than comfort, preceded down the dark cobblestone avenue by the clacking hooves of their high-necked horses, bay and chestnut and dapple gray. Some come alone and some in families, for such an opportunity to show marriageable girls to their advantage is not to be wasted. Some come beset by envy, others by spite; some come determined to find the furnishings ostentatious and the food inferior, some dreading the degree by which their own houses and entertainments will fail to shine as brightly as those that await them tonight. Some even come, curious as it is, to enjoy themselves for the evening.

But they all come.

For their hostess is an intriguing woman, a woman with a gift for mystery, and no one wants to wake up tomorrow morning to be informed by someone else what wonders the Duchess Tremontaine wrought at this year's Swan Ball.

Rafe descended the imposing Tremontaine stairs, his black, wrinkled scholar's robe brushing each dark step resentfully as he went, his face like doom.

The visiting Doctor Hugh McDonough was even now holding forth in the Great Lecture Hall on the properties of angles in irregular solids. Rafe's friend Joshua was there, sitting under the high vaulted ceiling and the stained glass representations of the hunting of the royal stag in the windows, growing more enlightened by the sentence. Henry and Thaddeus too. And he, Rafe Fenton, so very noble in his aspirations, so pure in his love of scholarship, so single-minded in his impassioned pursuit of the truth, where was he?

He was going to a *party*.

He had no need to examine himself again in a glass to be aware of the sneering contempt on his own face. Well, he deserved that sneer. Only a short time since, he'd been a man ablaze with the fire of discovery, a man on the threshold of proving his most deeply held convictions about the cosmos. What was he now? A fribble, a mincing girl aflutter with her first love, or what she believed was love. And being ordered around by his lover's wife, spending his time writing her *party invitations*. Invitations! When there was an unfinished book on his desk the pages of which would revolutionize natural science as nobody had done since Rastin! And instead he had reduced himself to this.

But he was hardly the only one to blame. Who did Will think he was, so casually to require Rafe to disregard the ambition toward which he had bent himself for years? Rafe was no tenant farmer, no jerking marionette to dance at the pleasure of his master, no—

And then, as he reached the bottom of the stairs, he saw Will walking through the entrance hall from the library to the ballroom, pale against the red velvet he wore and the richly wooded rooms through which he passed.

Rafe inhaled sharply, stopped short. Will turned, and at the sight of his face, Rafe felt the roiling inside him grow inexplicably more violent. He wanted to strike the man, he wanted to kiss him, to wrap him in his embrace, to tangle his fingers in his yellow hair, to caress every part of him not covered by clothing, to spit in his face.

Will's deep blue eyes, bright when first he turned, clouded as they traveled from Rafe's face to his body, taking in the rumpled, frayed University robe his secretary had chosen to wear to such a sparkling event. His voice was damask over steel. "Did the clothes I sent you not suit you?"

"No," said Rafe, just as quiet but cold, as cold as the snows of Arkenvelt, "they did not. I found they were cut to fit your dog better than me."

Will actually had the gall to look confused. "What?"

And in that moment, Rafe was pierced by the undeniable truth: his belief that the duke valued the same things as he did had been a gross error. Here was a dilettante, a coxcomb to whom fashion was so important he'd given Rafe clothing that matched exactly the color of his own jacket and the damned ruby on his finger. And his promise to urge the University Board of Governors to reconsider its vote on the matter of Masters' examinations—no doubt worth less than the breath it had cost him to make. Rafe would never found his school, and it was Will's fault.

Well, then. Will had snatched Rafe's dream from him. Rafe would pay him back in kind.

"The reason I have allowed you to toy with me as if I were your plaything eludes me." Should he leave the ball entirely, go to hear McDonough? His stomach twisted at the thought. No; better to make the duke suffer. "I have said I would attend this event as your secretary, and I am not a man to break my word. But rest assured, sir, that after this I will trouble your house no longer. You will not see me again."

There.

"I don't understand what you're talking about," said the duke. God, he was maddening! Why did he *refuse* to comprehend?

"William." Diane's voice as she approached was cool as chased silver. "Have our guests incurred your displeasure, that you neglect them so?"

Rafe looked up at the stream of aristocrats flowing by, each more foolish and plumped up than the last, all bedizened in useless frippery that mocked every principle he held dear. An elegant man under a mop of red hair gave him a languorous smile that implied volumes. Good. Lithe, the man was, of an age with Will, and handsome in emerald green slashed with silver. Rafe raised a careful eyebrow that implied volumes of its own.

"I'll attend to our guests," said Will, and there was a note of distance in his voice, "the very instant I understand why Rafe is wearing his scholar's rags when perfectly suitable clothing was provided him."

Diane's eyes, veiled, gave away nothing.

"Don't worry, Fenton," she said, and even through his fury her voice sounded to him like a blade all the more dangerous for its beauty. She turned to Will. "Darling," she said, "we ourselves can barely keep up with all the ridiculous rules by which we order our lives here on the Hill. You can hardly expect your secretary to understand them." She smiled at Rafe, a generous smile, compassionate, and oh, how he hated her.

He schooled his expression to utter blankness. "Forgive me my intrusion, madam." He turned and stalked toward the ballroom, Will's pursuing footsteps echoing in his ear.

The redhead would be more interesting company tonight.

Diane permitted herself, as her husband went off, a very small smile; after all, neither he nor his snake of a lover could see it.

"Duchess!"

The smile vanished as if it had never been. Karleigh had arrived.

She turned to the door and swept toward him and his wife in a thoroughly convincing transport of joy. "Frederick! Helena!" She took their hands, Helena's white as milk and Karleigh's whiter, and her voice was the softest thick wool on a cold day. "Thank the good gods you've come! I can't tell you how utterly dreary the evening has been without you!"

"Who's been blathering such nonsense?" said the duke. "Any man who could describe an evening spent at Tremontaine House as dreary ought to be apprehended at once and packed off to the madhouse. Now: Tell us what the Swan is to be this year."

"I would," said the duchess, "but I've quite forgotten myself." The duke harrumphed.

"Diane, you are stunning." Helena adjusted the lace at her pink taffeta sleeves. "With anyone else I would apologize for such a cliché, but in your presence I absolve myself, as you long ago rendered any other response impossible."

"Pish," said Diane. "Helena, it is you who put stunning to shame. Those exquisite puffs at the neckline, and that pearl! It is heaven." She regarded the duke. "And you, Frederick. I'm shocked my way to you wasn't blocked by a crowd of pretty young things vying for your favors. That doublet puts Helena and me *both* to shame." It was a hideous object, white with black braiding at the shoulders and sleeves embroidered in a blue that reminded her of something out of the sickroom. It would have looked foolish on a man half Karleigh's age—had he been old-fashioned enough as to wear it. What had Helena had been thinking, letting him out of the house in it?

"You see, Helena?" said Karleigh, his tone so gruff with victory it bordered on the uncivil. "I *told* you it flattered me." Ah, so Helena had done her best. "Now, Diane, where do you think I got it?"

By the Seven Hells. He was going to make her guess. "Frederick, I'm hopeless at such games, so I believe I'll avoid your trap altogether and simply insist that your wife tell me."

"We're quite proud of it," said Helena quickly. "People think he must have had it from—"

"People think I must have had it from Wickers," said Karleigh—really, he had always been a boor, but to interrupt one's wife!—"when in fact I had it from the hand of a crone who traced her lineage all the way back to one of Queen Amelia's ladies! The woman died shortly thereafter, childless, friendless, and alone, but what does that matter when she was able to do *this* before she went?" He stepped back and spread his arms wide to offer an unhappily full view of the garment.

"Her joy in having provided you with such perfection," said Diane, unable to help herself, "was, I'm quite certain, more than comfort enough for her in her final hours." Helena failed to keep from appearing wounded, but honestly, what could she expect?

Karleigh, appraising the crowd, gave a gasp that would have done him credit on the stage. "Good gods," he said. "Is that Latimer? I shall have to spend the evening avoiding him."

"He will be disconsolate," said Diane. "What crime has he committed, so to fall from your favor?"

"He told me last week he couldn't join me for a simple game of Constellations because he had to entertain some sort of foreign grandee from Erland—I don't know, someplace ridiculous like that. How *humiliating* for him. I'd rather serve chocolate to a good, honest local charwoman any day than to the king of a nothing country with no blood. He may wear linen and lace, but I guarantee you, go back far enough in Latimer's line and you'll find a haberdasher."

Diane harbored no doubt in her breast whatsoever that Karleigh would keel over in a fit of apoplexy before he served chocolate to a charwoman, but on the subject of foreigners and their failings the duke was not to be gainsaid. She glanced around. The Kinwiinik had yet to arrive. She was safe for now, at least. "What punishment," she said, "could be worse than to be cast out of your good graces? Now, both of you, come with me. If you stray from my side at any point during the evening, I vow I shall take to my bed at once and perish before sunrise." And, pulling gaily at the ducal pair, she wafted into the ballroom.

Micah froze.

A lot of people, Rafe had said.

She had assumed that meant twelve, or even twenty!

But here were—her eyes darted around, taking in twenty, forty, eighty, until the crowd of people became uncountable, too many, too many people.

And the noise. Voices buzzing, humming, chattering, music bellowing, heels hitting the floor over and over, all of it combining to create a roaring onslaught that filled the room and seemed to pierce her eardrums, just as the whirling, the candles reflected in reflections of reflections, the gowns of pink giving way to lavender to blue to pale yellow to pink again assaulted her eyes, and she couldn't move.

She had come here planning something—what was it?—something to help her aunt and uncle, something to do with turnips—

There was a door, a small door, nearby—if she could just *move*—yes, yes, and her feet were taking her toward it as fast as she could go, and she was in another room, and thank the gods, it was small, much smaller, but everything was still people and noise, noise and people, but there, there was a window with a blue curtain, yes, she ducked behind it and finally, yes, it was dark and, if not quiet, at least quieter, and she began rocking back and forth and grabbed the thick edge of the curtain as she rocked and rubbed it between her fingers, the softness of the heavy velvet sweet against her skin, and as she huddled here, nothing was moving, and she could begin to breathe again.

The imposing entry hall of the house of Diane, Duchess Tremontaine, thought Kaab as she stepped through the front door, was a grand thing indeed.

Its black-and-white-checkerboard marble floor had been laid, its sweeping staircase erected, its high walls painted and gilded with one purpose: to intimidate. Kaab suspected that for any number of the other guests it performed its office admirably, but she was from the great coastal city of Binkiinha, whose chief temple alone could contain multiples of this curiously designed hall.

When she entered the ballroom itself, however, her breath was, if not taken away, then—suspended for a moment. Innumerable mirrors glittered on every wall behind innumerable candles, still greater hosts of candles flickered next to the food, reflected in the endless heaps of magnificent silver on the tables scattered around the perimeter of the room, dark green ivy swept the walls and windows in such profusion that the house seemed to be transforming before her eyes into a living garden, men in servants' livery wove, unobtrusive, through the crowd, bearing shining trays of cakes in the shape of swans, or stood self-effacingly beside large mounds of pastries, and nobles everywhere wound paths around one another, talking, laughing, flirting, fanning, dancing heat into the air.

The Kinwiinik, however, presented no mean spectacle themselves. In their deep jewel-colored Local doublets, jackets, and gowns, they blazed against the pastel silks and brocades and lace of the Xanamwiinik aristocracy. The Kinwiinik were dripping with gold and flashes of jade, sporting feathers the like of which this city had never seen: iridescent quetzal, bright green cotinga tail feathers, the neck feathers of the yellow guacamaya, sweeping, graceful, at once fierce and gentle, besting the Xanamwiinik at their own displays.

As Aunt Saabim and Uncle Chuleb approached the duchess to greet their hostess, Kaab caught sight of Vincent Applethorpe in the crowd, his sword hanging at his side, intent on his quarry. She breathed a small sigh of relief. She was so unsettled by the news from home, she didn't trust herself to bend sufficient attention to finding the man who threatened the woman she—well, the woman she cared for.

The letter had arrived late in the morning, as Kaab had been— ugh—playing with some cousin's baby, and Auntie Saabim and Uncle Chuleb had been bickering, the thick smells of maize boiling with lime and sweet atole wafting from the kitchen, telling them that the afternoon meal was almost upon them.

"No, my morning star," sighed Saabim in the tone of voice that meant *I am willing to be patient with you, but if you persist in your obstinacy, that state of affairs is going to change very soon.* "I am quite sure I wish to go to the ball." She knelt on a reed mat, attending to the large packet of dispatches brought by the ship that had arrived from home the previous day. "I am pregnant, not stricken with the wasting disease."

"It would be far better to behave as if you were stricken with the wasting disease," said her young husband, his lips tight. "What if something happens there to hurt the baby? What if your headdress is not protection enough for your head-spirit from the night air?" He made a warding sign to the bright jade statue of Chaacmul in the niche altar on the south wall, offerings of fragrant cacao beans and fruit at its feet.

"Your uncle," said Saabim to Kaab, as if air occupied the space where Chuleb stood, "knows much more about bearing a child than I do." Kaab covered her mouth to avoid snickering. Saabim put a hand on her swollen belly to adjust her wide belt, embroidered with leaping jaguars, and opened another letter from the packet.

"Understandable, of course. I can hardly be considered an expert; I've only borne a few of them. Before his time, of course."

"Uncle is jealous," ventured Kaab, and Chuleb gave her a dire glower, his cheeks dark in the late-morning sun. "He's worried some ant-egg-skinned lord will catch your eye and spirit you away."

Saabim stood up suddenly. "Ekchuah guide us!" Horror was rigid in her face.

"What is it?" Chuleb was at her side in an instant. But Saabim simply continued to pore over the long, folded sheet of fig-tree paper she held in her steady hands. Kaab felt as she always did when Ahkin's priestess revealed what she had read of the family's fortunes in the book of days. Her head felt light and her liver heavy, and she couldn't quite breathe.

Finally, Saabim dropped the letter on the floor. The blood-red and charcoal-black glyphs on the page seemed to darken the room.

"Awful news from home," Saabim said, her dark eyes grim.

Kaab's aunt was as prone to understatement as an eagle to flight; if even she was calling the news awful, then it must be truly unspeakable.

"The Batab, Ruler of the Territories, is besotted with his latest wife, a daughter of the Cocom family." Chuleb's brow lifted. "A *third* daughter, at that." A derisive puff of air escaped Kaab's nose. "They have taken advantage of his infatuation to petition him to cancel our monopoly on this continent and open the trade routes to them."

Kaab's eyes met Chuleb's, and each saw fear. "Why not tell us that the Locals have discovered how to read the mysteries of the Four Hundred Siblings and are preparing to sail to our home-land while you're at it?" Chuleb kept his voice steady. "I could hardly think of anything worse." Kaab's stomach clenched as if it were full of hot pitch. So far her aunt and uncle knew nothing of her slip with Rafe and Micah, who were now terribly interested in discovering precisely that information. She must make sure it stayed that way.

"Then your imagination fails you," said Saabim, "for that is nothing compared to the rest. It seems that a Kinwiinik woman living in Tultenco became involved with a Tullan noble." Would she glance in Kaab's direction? No; her aunt spared her that embarrassment at least. "There was a dispute, and she killed him."

No one spoke. The slap of tortilla dough on the griddle and the low murmur of servants' chatter sounded from the kitchen, as if this changed nothing.

"The Tullan," Saabim finally continued, "executed her immediately, of course. They sent a delegation to Binkiinha to demand reparations. As soon as they arrived, the delegation began talking war."

Calamity.

A canceled monopoly would topple the Balam family from its prominence among the Traders of Binkiinha; a war with the Tullan Empire might see the Kinwiinik all enslaved or food for the crows before it was over, or led to the sacrificial altar. Of course the gods must be fed with the precious water that flowed through human veins, but no one in the civilized world seemed to believe them quite as undernourished as the Tullan.

"*Now* may Ekchuah guide us," said Kaab softly. But there was only so much assistance the god who moved in the deep could render his children.

Kaab could do nothing about the situation at home from the great Tremontaine ballroom, however, where Uncle Chuleb and Aunt Saabim (Kaab had known all along that there was no stopping her) were now leading the rest of the Kinwiinik company toward the Duchess Tremontaine—a figure of ivory resplendent in pale blue—to pay their respects.

All around, the fine nobles of the City stared at them. And then the whispers began, and the murmurs: shocked, amused, admiring, curious, impressed . . . There was no question but that the Kinwiinik Traders, in their gold and jade, their silver and pearls, their vivid feathered headdresses, had made a splendid debut entrance into the Duchess Tremontaine's annual Swan Ball.

Having greeted the duchess, the elders of the family moved aside to allow Kaab to do the same. "Permit me to present," said Chuleb, "my niece, Ixkaab, first daughter of the first daughter of the House of Balam."

"It is a great pleasure to meet you, Duchess." Kaab bowed with her hand on her heart, brown against the smooth yellow silk of her embarrassingly low-cut bodice. The duchess could not possibly recognize her; at their last meeting, Kaab had played the part of an unlettered servant, and people see, as her mother had often said, only what they expect to see.

But the sea-gray eyes in the face before her glittered. "And yet," breathed the Duchess Tremontaine, "is it possible we may have met before? For surely I have seen your face, so striking, so bold. . . ."

Kaab swallowed. "I do not think so." She must be very careful with this woman. "For I have not been very long in your stunning City."

Diane sighed, a puff of regret tinged with self-incrimination. "I'm sure you're right, then." she said. "And the girl I'm thinking of had nothing of your bearing, your elegance."

Kaab bowed her head. "You are too affectionate—no, excuse me, too kind."

The duchess smiled. The effect was startling: the gray ice turned warm, like kind, sheltering shadows on a hot summer's day. "I would like to be both. I wish to be a good, good friend to you and your people. And to know you better in particular, Mistress Balam, if I may."

Kaab returned the smile, meeting charm with charm. In a graceful, confiding motion, Diane snapped open her fan, a confection of blue and gold. Kaab's eyes flicked automatically to the lady's slender ivory wrist.

And saw the locket.

The duchess was wearing the locket around her wrist, hanging from the worked gold chain of a bracelet.

The same locket Ben had brought back from his father's deathbed, the same locket that Tess had copied so vividly on paper, an oval of gold ringed with diamonds, a jeweled swan resting, majestic, at the center.

Kaab and Tess had thought the locket gone forever, lying perhaps in the riverbed since the night poor Ben went uptown on the mysterious errand he had said would make his fortune.

Evidently, they had been wrong.

"I am inspired," said Kaab carefully, "by the lovely . . . arm necklace? No—the bracelet! On your wrist."

Was that a split second of alarm in the duchess's eyes? "You like it?" she said coolly. "I assure you, it is nothing. A trinket. But," she shrugged, "an old family heirloom. I wear it out of sentiment." Just as at their last meeting: A nervous person always speaks too much. The duchess regained her footing. "Nothing, certainly, compared to the splendid jewels that adorn you and your family."

So that was the game.

Kaab opened her mouth to make her next move—what it was she would not be able to say until it left her mouth; she was playing by instinct—but was forestalled.

Close by, there was a voice, pitched in a confiding murmur,

but obliviously loud enough for those nearby to hear: "This is a new low. To see Tremontaine fawning over foreign tradesmen." She jerked her head to the west to see a sneering older man in a white doublet looking at her askance. "Much less inviting them to a *ball* with the rest of us."

Diane's smile as she turned her head to look at him was beautiful. She nodded to the Kinwiinik. "Please do excuse me. I must attend to my other guests."

"Of course," said Kaab. This was exactly what she would have done in Diane's place. Neutralize him before he offended the guests. A footman walking past with a tray of iced swan cakes obligingly cleared the path by stumbling—a thing Kaab had not expected to see in the home of the duchess—and when he recovered his balance, her hostess turned and glided off like a swan herself.

Kaab was beginning to like this woman.

Damn Karleigh. And damn Helena for being unable to restrain him. If Diane could have avoided inviting him at all, she would have done so, but such an open slight offered without provocation would have been deeply insulting and probably begun a series of hostilities for which she had at the moment neither the energy nor the patience. And so she had invited him and hoped for the best.

Fond hope. His attitude toward foreigners, a relic left over from a less enlightened age, was too strong a point of pride with him not to find expression. Only the girl had overheard Karleigh's insult, though she was a sharp one; her performance two weeks earlier as a lowly servant had been masterly. Ahchuleb Balam's attention had been elsewhere when Karleigh spoke, or at least seemed to be. But if Diane failed to contain the threat the duke presented, she might not be so lucky next time. And if the Kinwiinik refused the agreement she had proposed, then Highcombe would be lost, Tremontaine's finances would never recover from the disaster of the *Everfair*, and—well, it did not bear consideration.

"Frederick! Helena!" she said, sweeping up to the pair. "I would be a poor hostess indeed, if I saw you bereft of punch and failed to rectify my error immediately!"

"Never mind that, Diane," he said, stiff as ironwood. "What I can't for the life of me determine is why you invited—"

"Duchess," said Helena quickly, "you haven't by any chance remembered Frederick's weakness for iced cakes?"

She took Helena's tiny hand in her own and applied the gentlest of pressure. Helena would interpret the gesture correctly as an expression of support and gratitude. This would be much easier with an ally. "How could you even think I would forget such a crucial detail? Both of you, please, come with me at once."

It didn't take her long to guide them to the room of tables groaning with food—a room empty of Kinwiinik, at least for the moment. "All is here for your delectation." She made a grand sweep of her hand, indicating not just the cakes, the faint perfume of roses drifting from their icing, but also the filled pastry, the tender swan meat in citrus sauce—well, duck meat, but call it swan meat and who would be the wiser?—so much food even the assembled crowd would be hard-pressed to consume it all.

Out of the corner of her eye she spied—ah yes, a piece of luck indeed. "Sarah, I insist you come here at once and discuss with Karleigh the matter with which you were holding us all spellbound at last week's dinner: your researches into the history of your family coat of arms and the questions raised by your discovery of the old escutcheon in the east wing of your home."

There. That, she thought as the doleful Lady Perry approached them, would hold him for at least twenty minutes, and with Helena's cooperation perhaps twice that. And then Diane would find something else to occupy his attention. Not only that, but Diane's instincts about pastel at the beginning of the season had been unerring; in her light green gown Sarah Perry looked not just ill but actually like someone three days dead whom her family had unaccountably neglected to bury. Yet another triumph.

She turned and glided back into the ballroom, awhirl with dancing couples.

The clavier player looked at the violinist and rolled his eyes.

"I know what it is!" Andrew said quietly, as if seized with sudden inspiration, his hands moving over the delicate keys of the instrument in front of him. "He took up the viol only after a failed attempt at a career on the stage." Jack turned a page. Andrew, for his part, played without a score. If he never heard the Boyce sarabande again after this season—a likelihood, the way people thought about music here on the Hill, fashionable one moment and worthy only of the trash heap the next—he'd be grateful; he certainly didn't need to look at the sheet music to get the notes right.

Jack sniggered, his fingers moving deftly on the neck of the violin. "No, no! He's actually gone deaf, but since he never learned another trade he's just hoping nobody will notice." Andrew hated playing with violinists who couldn't talk as they fiddled. The music popular this season was less than inspired, to put it politely, and conversation allayed the tedium.

And there went the E in the third octave. "Damn this clavier. There's another key stuck. How old is this thing, anyway?" He sighed and peered over at the violist. "He's really a spy from

Cham. He's only been masquerading as a violist this whole time."
God, the harmonies in this piece were predictable. Here came the
cadence again. Tonic, subdominant, dominant, tonic, as if Boyce
were showing off something he'd invented. Ugh.

"Ah," said Jack. "Modulation coming up in three measures."
His bow bobbed up and down in the air almost by itself. "Bet you
my hat he flats the leading tone."

"I wouldn't take that bet in a million years. It's too bad you're
not doubling him. You could just play louder and drown him out.
Here it comes." Andrew shut his eyes, cringed in anticipation, and
winced when the modulation came. "Maybe he thinks we're actually playing in C-sharp?"

"He couldn't read the accidentals in C-sharp if his life depended
on it."

In fact, the musician about whom the two of them were
speaking played his instrument no worse than either of the two
of them played theirs, and occasionally better; Andrew was the
most sought-after clavier player on the Hill not because he was
the best, but because his shoulders filled his doublet so very effec-
tively. But just three days ago Jack, released earlier than expected
from a rehearsal because the soprano was too drunk for further
work to do them any good, had opened the door to the small and
dingy rooms he rented with the offending violist to find him in
bed with Robert, their next-door neighbor. Even this breach might
have been forgivable—the violist had been up until that moment,
if not Jack's sun, then perhaps his moon, or at the very least a not
inconsequential star, and Jack was a reasonable man—but Robert,
instead of being naked like a decent person as the violist took his
pleasure, had been wearing Jack's breeches. And as a result, Jack
was now, as the saying went, pulling his plow unyoked. This gave

Andrew, who had been disappointed in love, an opportunity for which he had been hoping for quite some time.

And Andrew was not a man to let an opportunity pass him by.

"This experimental science," the redheaded noble was saying, "sounds fascinating." He took Rafe's hand and held it closer to the light reflected from the mirror towering on the wall behind them. "Why don't you tell me about it while I gaze at your beautiful fingers?"

"Oh," said Rafe lazily, "one man's fascination is another man's tedium." Even he knew better than to engage in an actual description of his work in such a moment. "I do, however, offer you leave to make free of my fingers."

Rafe knew this game like he knew his own body, had played it from a youngling, up until a few weeks ago. A breath of flattery, a honeyed sigh, a hollow endearment, and before long they would have found release with each other in an upstairs bedroom, or outside behind a hedge, or perhaps they would be in the redheaded nobleman's own home, anywhere rather than scuttling around this insipid ball avoiding Will. The duke might have denied him his Master's robe, but there was another art of which Rafe had already long been master, for which a robe was, in the end, but a hindrance.

And yet the single-minded focus with which he usually practiced that art eluded him, ruined by an unwonted sense of distraction. He started at the sound of a squeak from behind him. "Now, Horn," a high-bred Hill voice drawled—gods, these mindless nobles!—"this fellow has a job to do. You wouldn't want to deprive the other guests of the delicacies on his tray just for fifteen minutes of pleasure with him, now, would you?"

"Thank you, milord," said the squeaker, presumably the servant whose peace was being troubled.

"Nonsense, Halliday," said another mindless noble, this one elderly and irritated. "I'm far more interested in the delicacies he's carrying on his backside."

"Now you're being silly. There is a more than acceptable Ruthven red in the salon. Come join me in a glass, and we can make a wager on what tonight's Swan will be."

"Hmph. As you wish."

Could these ninnies *hear* themselves? Rafe longed to talk to Will, to huddle away in a corner with him and discuss solids or velocity or the orbits of the spheres. Something that *mattered*.

He shook his head. No need to think of Will. The languid redhead in front of him was the proper object of his attention.

"Rafe!" called a voice from his right, and he looked over to see Will coming toward him, brushing past a table draped in dark ivy. "Please, let's talk this through."

"Forgive me," he said to the redhead, his voice strangling. "We will see each other very soon, I'm sure." And with that he was away.

The redhead gave a smirking bow as Tremontaine came up to him. The duke looked at him for a moment without saying a word. "Damn him!" he muttered then, and continued after Rafe.

Micah had been breathing steadily for several minutes now. She thought she might be safe coming out from behind the curtain. *Remember the artificial numbers if you start getting anxious,* she thought. *And remember what Tess said.* She peeked out, saw no one looking, and stepped from behind the curtain to find herself before some kind of roasted bird and a big tower with thirty-four pastries on it. There were seventeen people in this room. Seventeen was a lot, but not more than she could handle, especially now that she had known to expect them. She took one of the pastries and bit into it. It was no tomato pie, but it wasn't bad. A little bit of meat, some asparagus.

"Now, who might you be?" Whoops. Make that eighteen people. She turned around to see a pale woman behind her with dark hair and funny teeth. The woman kept talking but Micah felt another flutter of panic, so she began calculating. *The fourth key of 1,024 is four. The seventh key of 343 is three. The eleventh key of . . .*

By the time she was calm again, the woman was looking at her, not saying anything, starting to get the "I'm confused" expression, and Micah began feeling an intense pressure; the woman must have said something she expected a response to. Micah fought the urge to duck back behind the curtain. She could do this. "Fascinating," she tried. "Why don't you tell me more about that?" She held her breath. Tess had better have been right.

"Well," said the woman, looking to either side and lowering her voice, "you didn't hear it from me, but Lord Humphrey said . . ."

Micah's eyes widened. Could this actually be working? This woman was doing just what Tess had said people would!

"Tell you what, sweetheart," Kaab's friend had said the previous day in Madeline's shop when they had been there to get clothes. "Do me a favor and say this: 'Fascinating. Why don't you tell me more about that?'"

It seemed weird, but Tess knew a lot more about how people acted than Micah did. "Fascinating. Why don't you tell me more about that?" Micah had repeated obediently.

"Good. Now say, 'I'm really more interested in what *you* think.'"

"I'm really more interested in what *you* think."

"There. Those are the only two things you'll have to say all evening."

Kaab, Vincent, and Madeline all laughed. Micah didn't get the joke. "Huh?"

"It's very simple," said Madeline, reaching out and stroking her hair before she could shy away. To Micah's surprise, it felt strangely soothing, almost like when Aunt Judith did it. "People love to talk about themselves. All you have to do is never stop inviting them to do it."

This sounded interesting. "What do you mean?"

"It might not work at the University," said Tess. "I'm sure they spend all their time talking about how many natural scientists can dance on a rutabaga's ass or something. But the people at this party won't be like that. So when you're in conversation with anybody, if they stop talking and you're not sure what to do, just say, 'Fascinating. Why don't you tell me more about that?' And if at some point they ask you a question you don't know how to answer, just say, 'I'm really more interested in what *you* think.' Those two sentences will get you through the entire evening."

Micah was dubious. "Are you sure?"

"Sweetheart, they've gotten friends of mine through years of peddling their asses to men on the Hill who have no right to their thoughts about anything. It should last you for one party."

But the words of the woman with the funny teeth in front of her brought her back to the ball. ". . . can't wait to see what Tremontaine will do for the Swan?" Did the woman expect an answer?

All right. If it had worked once, she might as well try it again. "I'm really more interested in what *you* think," said Micah, and the woman, amazingly, was off again. But just after she started talking, Micah saw somebody walk by the open door to the room with skin the same light-brown color as Kaab's. He was dressed like everybody else, but his clothes were brighter and there were feathers on his head. Which meant he was probably Kinwiinik. Which meant . . .

"Well, milk a chicken and call her a cow!"

The woman with the funny teeth stopped in the middle of a sentence. "Pardon me?"

Micah opened her mouth to explain that Cousin Reuben said that all the time when he had ideas that he thought should have been obvious, though he didn't have ideas very often, but then she realized that it would involve saying something other than the two sentences she knew she could get away with, and besides, every second she stood with this woman was a second farther away from the bliss and relief of enlightenment.

"Good-bye," said Micah, not wanting to be impolite, and turned around and walked out of the room. Yes, there was danger everywhere. But now she was on a mission.

The "music" was driving Kaab mad.

She regarded the men sawing away with sticks at strings on wooden clubs they held under their chins, men blowing into flutes of metal, a man sitting at a huge wooden box moving his hands all over the front part of it. They looked bored.

Xamanek's light! The ant-egg people's insipid food was one thing, the swaddling clothes they wrapped themselves in and the shoes with which the women hobbled their feet another, but this clickety-clackety, tweedly-weedly *noise* was beyond belief. And just look at them all, standing around, talking, dancing, as if they didn't notice, as if they even *liked* it! Amazingly, many of the Kinwiinik—even Chuleb and Saabim—were smiling and moving their heads slightly in time to the noise. She turned away and considered the mounds of silver on the table nearby. At least none of her people were dancing.

"Kaab!"

She turned to see Micah. "Ah, my small lordling," she said. "How are you experiencing the ball?"

"Fine," said Micah, and pointed. "I need to talk to him."

Micah was pointing to Chuleb, in deep conversation with two Local men. Kaab's brow wrinkled. "What is your need to speak with my uncle?"

"Navigation!" said Micah, and Kaab felt her heart clutch. "It's still driving me crazy, and whenever I ask you about it, you always say you can't help because it's the Kinwiinik men who know about navigation. Well, he's a Kinwiinik man, right? So I'm going to go explain what I've been trying to figure out and ask what I'm doing wrong, and he'll tell me!"

Kaab's veins throbbed. "I do not think that would be a good idea," she said, very carefully. "He is a busy man, and he certainly would not—"

"Come with me!" said the girl, her eyes afire. "We can talk to him together! We'll tell him the whole story, how you gave me the star charts and how it's been so frustrating and then he'll explain and it'll all finally make sense!"

And Kaab would be disgraced, out of the service for good, destined to cook and clean in Uncle Chuleb's house for the rest of her life. And help look after babies.

"No. You cannot." Her tongue was wood in her mouth.

"Why not?"

"Micah, *do not*—"

Someone grabbed Kaab's left arm and she whirled around. But this was not the place to assume a fighting stance. She relaxed her legs and removed her hand from the obsidian dagger at her belt.

"Your *feathers* are *impressive*." The man who stood before her now was an ill-favored fellow despite his elegant costume: reedy, his leering face pocked, his voice nasal enough to make her eyeballs itch, his gray hair stringy. To Kaab's horror, he reached up and touched the quetzal feathers on her headdress, and she jerked her head back. He was staring down her front the whole time, even as he made her one of the Locals' little bows.

"I have the honor of introducing myself: Horace Lindley, Lord Horn, very much at your service." She gritted her teeth. Micah had wandered off and was probably halfway to Chuleb by now, but Kaab didn't dare offend one of the ant-egg lords.

"As I was saying—your costume! Such a delight. And that lovely necklace, especially the bit right there . . ." The man's rude fingers reached now for the gold that hung on her breast, clearly interested in the one more than the other.

Before his hand could achieve its aim, she had her dagger out, pointed at the juncture of his breeches. "I counsel you," she said coldly, "not to continue what you have begun."

He raised an eyebrow and gave her a greasy smile. "Oh, you're a feisty one, aren't you? If you defend your titty's virtue like a boy, let's see how you fancy this instead . . ." To her amazement, even with her blade pointed right at his jewels, the mad old nobleman started reaching his other hand around for her backside.

What was she going to do? Stab him in the middle of the Tremontaine ballroom? Unwise. But if he actually touched her, she honestly wasn't sure she'd be able to keep from harming him physically. So she took the only other option open to her.

Kaab turned and fled.

* * *

"There you are." The redhead's voice was silk. "I feared you'd been spirited away."

"No," said Rafe. "I find the continued interruptions of our acquaintance quite tedious, in fact, but there's a certain person I greatly desire to avoid. I'm sure you understand that sort of thing." The corners of his mouth turned up very slightly, and the redhead laughed.

"Many's the man I've greatly desired to avoid at many a party," he said. "I'm not in the least offended." He spoke to a passing footman without releasing Rafe's gaze. "Two cakes, from that tower of them over there."

"Of course, my lord."

They picked up the conversation where they had left off. And yet Rafe was mystified. The excitement he ordinarily felt in this situation—the skill, the subtlety of the game, the end a foregone conclusion, the only thing in question the path the two of them took to get there—felt muffled somehow. For the Land's sake, it had only been a few weeks since the last time. He couldn't be out of practice. He frowned.

"Oh," said the redhead, "you are of a different opinion?"

What had the man been saying? No matter; the words themselves were irrelevant. "Let us say rather that I am still considering the question." Rafe offered an indolent smile. "When it comes to the matter under discussion, that is. On other matters I am . . . quite firm."

"I will keep that in mind, in case I find myself in a position later to make use of the information." Why, why did this not feel the same?

"No, Halliday," said a querulous voice off to Rafe's left, "it was sewn by an old bat who traced her lineage back to one of Queen

Amelia's lady's maids!" The voice, when Rafe glanced its way, proved to come from an old man in a doublet that should never have been imagined, much less cut and sewn. "And now Diane is forcing me to show it off to these foreign nobodies. As if I desired their approval. It's insulting, I tell you."

"I don't know about that, Karleigh," said the other noble, a young man of some gravity, tall, dark, perhaps not quite as vapid as the others in the room. "I find their presence intriguing. Yes, they're foreign nobodies who probably do not belong at the Tremontaine ball. But the duchess has her little whimsies. And without the Traders we wouldn't have chocolate."

"Bah. They don't even know how to drink it." God, how could Will stand to have such people in his house? "My haberdasher's supplier was at one of their parties. What kind of lout puts *spices* in chocolate?"

A twitching servant carrying a huge stack of empty glasses elbowed him in the ribs. "I'm terribly sorry, sir. Please forgive me."

"Hardly. Do that again, you wretch, and it'll mean your post." A moment, as the unfortunate man scurried off. "Good god, Halliday, what is the world coming to if even Tremontaine can't get good help?"

By the Seven Hells, this was gruesome. If only Will knew how Rafe felt, if only he truly understood!

If only pigs could fly.

"But I believe," said the redhead, "that we were talking about your fingers."

"Yes," said Rafe, miserable. "Please continue."

Alas for Rafe, he did.

Fortune, it seemed, was smiling upon Diane.

Between the two of them, she and Helena had managed to keep

Karleigh distracted the entire evening. After tearing him away from Basil Halliday before he could work himself into a foam over the Traders, they had finally settled him into a game of Constellations with Humphrey Devize, the slowest talker on the Hill, and Richard Perry, the most voluble, so she could spend, if her luck held, the better part of an hour untroubled by worry on that score.

Which gave her room, finally, to deal with her husband.

It was one thing for William to make that tedious man his secretary, to invite him to the Swan Ball—and how predictably pretty little Rafe Fenton had played the spoiled child who wished to sit at the grown-ups' table while refusing to follow the grown-ups' rules!—but for William to follow his love around like a puppy desperate for tenderness while *visibly ignoring her* was . . . well, it would be foolish to say "unforgivable," because Diane de Tremontaine had never forgiven anyone for anything in her life. Suffice it to say, however, that she kept very accurate score. And this was a serious loss.

As the Dragon Chancellor joined her near a window draped with so much ivy one could barely see out of it, she noticed William on the way toward her in that shocking red—naturally he had scorned to wear the pastel she'd advised—and settled in an instant upon an equal loss to inflict in return.

"Gregory!" she said. "Why have you not asked to lead me in the dance yet this evening?" Her voice faltered, very slightly, as she reached the end of the sentence. Something felt strange.

"Because," said Davenant, and the strange feeling continued, "I'm quite certain your beauty would cause me to stumble from inattention and tread on your foot, at which point I would have to hurl myself into the river in despair."

As William drew close enough for her to be within his field of vision, she stepped a hair closer to Davenant than propriety dictated and placed a hand on his arm. "I dare say," she said clearly, keeping her eyes on her husband's face as he approached, "I would be so distracted by the perfection of your features I would fail to notice."

And William walked right past her.

His head did not turn a fraction.

Because, of course, he was following the noxious Rafe.

Rage blossomed in her. It was invisible to her guests, of course, who saw only the magnificent smile she bestowed on the Dragon Chancellor.

"Duchess," said Master Ahchuleb Balam at her side, bowing, "may I congratulate you on a spectacular evening?"

There was that strange feeling again. Mixed with her fury, it was quite unsettling. "Why, sir, if the evening is indeed a spectacular one—an assertion whose merit I am of course in no position to evaluate—then it is due entirely to your presence and that of your people." She felt as if she were saying words that had been chosen for her by someone else.

She felt light-headed, as if she were being supported by nothing more solid than the sound of the music. "The manner in which I have heard my Kinwiinik colleagues remark upon your hospitality," he said, "suggests to me that, when I broach the matter to them again, I will find them eager to accept your proposal."

"I leave the matter, sir," she said, helpless, "entirely in your hands. A letter from you would be a delight no matter what news it bore."

The foreigner's brow furrowed. "You look," he responded, "if you will forgive my saying such a thing, more than a little pale. May I bring you a cooling drink?"

"You are kind," she said, fighting to stay steady, "but I assure you it is of no matter." Out of the corner of her eye she saw Karleigh coming out of the card salon, much too soon. So much for Devize and Perry. "If you will excuse me," she said, and began to waft toward Karleigh, grateful to have something on which to focus her attention.

Grateful? To Karleigh?

Wonders, apparently, would never cease.

Sapperton was a nervous person by temperament, and the situation into which he had been thrust this evening had multiplied that nervousness tenfold.

He was an under-cook, after all, not a footman. He belonged in the kitchen.

"Just think of it!" his wife had said, a vexing touch of awe in her voice. "You'll be able to see all the fancy things people are wearing, listen to the fancy things they talk about!"

Sapperton would have been happy not to know what anybody was wearing or what anybody talked about if it had meant he didn't have to worry that he was going to cause some sort of disaster. Because if he did, Duchamp would have his head. And he was *terrified* of the steward, who had somehow managed to make "Sapperton" into a word that struck terror into his kidneys. The fit into which Duchamp had flown when the previous cook had sent up a cake with three tiers rather than four was a thing of legend; many of the kitchen staff claimed that the woman's whimpering ghost still haunted the pantry, though Sapperton himself had never seen her. And so tonight he was going to do as he was bidden. "Every single other kitchen servant is playing above his usual role tonight," the steward had said, "so I don't see why I should issue you a special dispensation." Then he had turned and started shouting at Daisy for telling him they'd run out of duck to mix with the goose in the swan pastry.

Sapperton had acquitted himself admirably, however, all evening—had stumbled once or twice, yes, but had dropped nothing, insulted no one, placed nothing on the wrong table.

Unfortunately, none of that was what he was worried about, or, rather, his worries about those things were all eclipsed by his worry about the task that lay before him now.

He was to carry in the Tremontaine Swan.

The Swan was the highlight of every year's ball. In fact, said Duchamp, fully half the conversation of the evening was usually the guests' speculation about what the duchess would bring out as the Swan this year.

One year it had been marzipan. One year spun sugar. One year chocolate. Last season, in a particular coup, it had been a giant swan sculpted out of ground swan's liver, which everybody had said was delicious, though Sapperton had his doubts. Nevertheless, every year, apparently, when it was revealed at the height of the ball, the Swan was the cynosure of every eye in the room.

And tonight he was one of four lackeys carrying it in.

He stood before it along with the others: a great molded pudding made of red wine and blackberries. It rose to an astonishing four feet, adorned with brilliants, sheltering tiny cygnets made of sugar, with a bright necklace around its sinuous neck that ended in a ruby half the size of his fist.

The four of them gathered, one at each corner, and Alfred counted aloud. "Three, two, one, up!"

His heart in his throat, Sapperton lifted.

* * *

It is true, reader, that this year's Swan Ball, as Diane had hoped, would be talked about for weeks afterward, if not longer. Alas for the duchess, however, the reason for this was not at all the one she had had in mind.

Our heroes—for who by now can say that any of our characters is not a hero?—began a strange convergence. Rafe, chased by the redhead and fleeing William, bound finally for the former's bed, William pursuing Rafe and ignoring his wife, Micah pursuing Chuleb and ignoring Kaab, Kaab pursuing Micah and fleeing Lord Horn, old Lord Horn pursuing Kaab: They had all been moving through the crowd as quickly as they could, each intent on a goal. Andrew, the clavier player on the make, continued to play, and Sapperton and the other servants had just entered with the Swan.

And then Vincent Applethorpe—you do remember him, I'm certain: the swordsman friend of Tess the forger?—took a step forward. He had finally seen the man in search of whom he had come to the ball, a swordsman in the Tremontaine green and gold, lurking along the far wall. A man he had last seen in Riverside, without the livery, stealing the dummy sketch that Kaab and Tess had dropped in his path; a man he had then followed, at their bidding, to the gates of Tremontaine House.

So yes, Vincent Applethorpe took a step forward. And that step put him, as it happened, in Micah's path, forcing her to turn her course. This gave the enterprising Kaab the opportunity, which she seized, to keep Micah from revealing to Chuleb what Kaab wished to remain hidden. She did this by putting her foot out six inches.

This caused a great many things to happen.

Micah very considerately tripped over Kaab's foot and fell headlong into Rafe, who himself fell to the floor, his limbs entangled with those of the redheaded noble. Kaab's pursuer, since she had stopped to trip Micah, ran headlong into her, with the result that she toppled over on top of Micah, Rafe, and the redhead. The obstacle created thereby was too much for both Lord Horn and for Duke William, both of whom collapsed on top of the others in a heap.

Matters might have ended there. But Kaab's fine obsidian dagger, not firmly enough replaced in her belt after her encounter with the lecherous Lord Horn, had flown out as she fell and now sailed in a beautiful arc toward the musicians. Andrew's eyes were not on his instrument, not on the dancers, but on Jack, and when his friend's face filled with alarm, he had not the time to interpret it before the hilt of the weapon hit him on the back of the head, causing him to lose his balance and kick out so as to keep from falling down.

Unfortunately, his foot collided with the clavier, the legs of which the duchess had been told many times needed to be replaced. The instrument collapsed in a spectacular fashion, with a deafening crash of wood and discordant strings, causing the excitable Sapperton to emit a quiet shriek of terror and, more important for our purposes, to release his hold on the Swan, throwing the other men off-balance. Had the magnificent Swan even been capable of lifting its own fourth corner, it would have found doing so beneath its dignity, and so, unable to stay afloat on a sea of nothing, it fell, all red wine and blackberries, on top of Lord Karleigh and his white coat.

Well, it had *begun* the evening as white.

For a moment, complete silence reigned in the ballroom. And in that silence, Lord Karleigh growled a growl such as had never been heard before in Tremontaine House. The growl turned into a roar, and the roar finally clarified itself into speech.

"Well, Duchess," he said, "this is what comes of polluting a ball by filling it with people without family or breeding."

Lord Basil Halliday, paling next to him, seized his arm and alternated between patting it and smacking his shoulder in a vain attempt to quiet him. Karleigh brushed Halliday off and looked down at Ixkaab Balam. "I'd wager you don't know your father's name, girl. If you even know your mother's."

Kaab scrambled to her feet, her hand flying to where her dagger should have been; when it found nothing, she looked to her aunt for her cue. This time the silence lasted, it seemed, for an eternity. It was finally broken by Ixsaabim Balam, her voice ice.

"The girl you insult, sir, is Ixkaab Balam, first daughter of Ixmoe Balam, first daughter of Ixtopob Balam, first daughter of Ixchukwapl Balam, first daughter from a line of first daughters descended from queens who ruled empires more vast than your imagination can compass. You are fortunate indeed that I will not permit her to begrime herself by cutting the verminous tongue out of your mouth." She turned to Diane. "I see my people and I are not welcome here. We will discommode you no longer."

She called a word in her language, incomprehensible to most in the room. But the Kinwiinik all put down their glasses or plates, most of them gratefully, as they found the food unspeakably bland, and came to stand with Ixsaabim. Another word, and they all left as one.

Diane, Duchess Tremontaine, who had over the course of her life rescued herself from more dangers than one could easily count, who was mistress of herself in all circumstances, who knew what people wanted and what they feared as clearly as if it had been written on their brows, saw at once that there was one way, and one way only, out of the quandary in which she now found herself.

She fainted.

Ixsaabim, Kaab realized as she walked home next to her in the quiet, was smiling.

They had been grievously insulted in front of every person of rank in the City, and Saabim was *happy.*

"What," she said, "can my wise aunt possibly have to be happy about?"

"Little bee, if you have to ask that question, then perhaps you don't belong in the service after all." Kaab was glad it was too dark for Saabim to see her blush. "I am happy for two reasons. First, the duchess has been mortified in front of us at her own party. The embarrassment of one's opponent is an extraordinarily useful tool."

"Yes," she said. "And second?"

"I am also happy because I now know what business she is about."

"I don't understand."

"She is, as you yourself have pointed out, a very dangerous woman, with a subtle mind. She could have been up to anything in proposing the partnership she brought to us, and you can be sure that she does not give a cacao bean in a hurricane for the Kinwiinik in any way other than our ability to further her own aims. Before tonight, I had no idea what those aims were."

"And now you do?"

"Come, little bee. You are more observant than this. There were signs of it all over that ball. Tell me, why were all the candles either in front of mirrors or next to silver?"

"So that . . ." Her mother, Kaab thought, ashamed, had raised her better! And then she had it and smiled in the dark. "So that the reflected light would hide the fact that there were not more of them."

A pause. "Yes." Saabim's voice was pleased. "And why was there so much needless silver on the tables?"

Now that she understood, it was easy. "To make us believe the house is drowning in silver, when in fact every piece she owned was on display."

"And the pastries?"

She thought a moment. "A great deal of pastry combined with a great many vegetables and very little meat."

"And the fowl in that hideous orange sauce?"

"Similarly: gallons of sauce hiding meat of dubious origins."

"The ivy filling the room?"

"Plants are very inexpensive when one has country estates."

"And the arrangements of those silly little cakes?"

"Towering shelved structures, empty on the inside, to create the illusion that there were four times as many as there were."

"And why were the servants so awkward?"

Kaab had to think a moment. Oh, that was clever. "Because most of them were pressed into service from other duties. Otherwise there would have been too few for the crowd."

"Yes. The duchess is desperately in need of funds. And so it becomes clear that her proposal is most likely an honest one: She sees us as a way of making money, and understands that she must offer us something in return. And we will accept her proposal, if she has the audacity to renew it."

They walked in silence for a time.

"You are a good girl, Kaab. Ixmoe would be proud of you."

Kaab had to work quite hard not to cry.

"That really was a masterful faint, earlier this evening," said the Dragon Chancellor, running a hand along her delicate jawline.

"I was quite pleased with it," answered the Duchess Tremontaine. "I perfected it long ago, and was beginning to think I would never need it." She twirled an idle finger in his hair and left it there. They were in Davenant's bedchamber, naked, beneath a silk-and-feather counterpane. Desperate at the ruination of her plans for the chocolate empire, she had decided to make the first move, by granting him a favor he had long desired and she had until now denied him and, in fact, every man who had similarly importuned her. It was not guaranteed to pay off. But timidity had never availed her anything. She was unsure how she felt about what she had just done for the first time.

For a while, they exchanged pleasantries of the sort traditionally spoken after the congress in which they had been engaged.

And then, when she had worked her way around to it, she said: "I find myself at an utter loss as to an appropriate response when next I see the Duke of Karleigh."

"I imagine that for some time it will be quite difficult for you to see him at all, even if he is standing in front of you."

She sighed. Careful, now. "I suppose so. But what would give me the greatest satisfaction is unlikely to remedy the insult to the Kinwiinik. Who knows what the rules of honor in their world demand in the face of such an insult? You saw the way they all wheeled and left the ball together, like a flock of—of starlings." A silence she could not read. "I am invited for chocolate at the always delightful Lady Perry's next week."

"My sympathies."

"Mmmm." She licked the tip of his ear. "Indeed. Fortunately, she keeps an excellent grade of the stuff. But should they take it into their heads to interfere with our supply of chocolate—well, it gives me horrors."

"Ah."

"I imagine that a suitable gesture could be made. An indication that Karleigh's boorishness is unacceptable to the rest of us."

"Such as?"

"There must be . . . a tax of some kind on the importers of chocolate, no?"

"Yes," he said. "A particularly high one, for which we have to thank our fathers, who were leery of allowing in anything the Land itself does not produce."

"Or perhaps they wanted to ensure that such a stimulating treat remained out of reach of all but themselves."

The Dragon Chancellor chuckled. "In which case, it was a dismal failure."

"Just so." Diane edged herself up on one elbow, letting her curls fall across his mouth. "So why not reduce it, as a token of good-will?"

"An interesting idea." He was silent for a while. "But ultimately unworkable." He tickled her nose with the end of her own hair. "I fear there is, alas, nothing to be done about that." If he had been a more observant man, he would have noticed her slight stiffening and then, after a pause, the fraction of an inch she moved away from him.

"Oh?" Nor was he well enough acquainted with her to know how dangerous this tone of voice was.

"It has to do with infernal Council politics. Ask William to explain it, if he manages to remember he's on the Council in the first place." Diane gave a small laugh. "Your beauty empties my head; I am unable to think clearly enough to do it myself." She smiled at him, as if to show that she appreciated the compliment. "Besides, there are so many things we can discuss that are so much more pleasant."

"You're right, of course. For instance: Did you see Lord Perry and young Sophronia Latimer tonight? All those longing glances. Sarah looked as if she'd bitten into a lemon."

"Yes," he said solemnly, "but Sarah *always* looks as if she's bitten into a lemon." The conversation continued in this vein, light and friendly. She would find another way to achieve her aim. She always did.

And in the meantime, on the tally she kept always in mind, she added a black mark by Davenant's name.

The Duchess Tremontaine and the Dragon Chancellor, however, do not draw our tale to its close; there is one more scene to play, reader, in another location, before you and I retire for the night. Would that our heroes were fortunate enough to be able to do the same!

But they, alas, must continue their stories until they reach the end, whether for good or ill not even I have been given to know.

His breath is hot against Rafe's neck, his whimpers satisfying a hunger Rafe has forgotten he had. This has been their desire all evening, this the goal to which the path has taken such a very long time to tread, pale skin against paler, calf against thigh, teeth on earlobe, fingers on chest, moaning, as the one fills the other and is filled in turn, the sweet pain of a hand pulling long hair in ecstasy, Hells, he's missed this, and why on earth has Rafe spent so much time so angry when the force to quench the fire of his need has stood before him all night, and Rafe quickens, greedy, faster and faster still, and then freezes, a small sound barely escaping his mouth, the agony of his release prompting the other to join him, and when the fog of desire has dissipated, Rafe turns to behold his companion, a thumb tracing the outline of his face.

"Was that worth the trouble you took this evening?" he asks with a smile, his voice low.

"I'm not quite sure," says Will. "Let's try again, and then I'll know for certain."

Episode Eight

A CITY WITHOUT CHOCOLATE

Malinda Lo

A ll across the City, from the seamiest shadows of the river-wet docks to the elegant terraces of the Hill's grandest mansions, apple blossoms in great white cascades are blooming. Snowy petals blushed with palest pink drift across the cobblestones of the Middle City, shedding their sweet fragrance in a promise of imminent summer. In a blink, it seems, the chill of early spring has turned into soft golden warmth, but the residents of the City have not appeared to notice. Instead of throwing off the last dregs of winter and turning their faces up to the sky and the sun, they huddle indoors, grouchy and dispirited, complaining about the lack of that most invigorating drink, chocolate.

For almost a month now—since shortly after the Duchess Tremontaine's infamous ball to which the Kinwiinik chocolate Traders wore their jewel-toned feathers (which became instantly fashionable, even as the ball itself ended in a fiasco of epic proportions)—the stores of chocolate in the City have been dwindling. According to those in the know (most assume the news traveled from the Kinwiinik Traders to the Middle City chocolate-house owners to their increasingly irritable patrons), a long-awaited shipment was sunk in a storm, the ship lost at sea and the sailors, tragically, drowned. A new shipment is expected (the chocolate-house owners hasten to assure their patrons), but due to variable weather across the North Sea, no one knows precisely when it will arrive.

For Jeremiah Clarkson, owner of Clarkson's, the Middle City's finest chocolate emporium, this uncertainty has led to drastic measures. At first, he raised the price of chocolate, which had the desired effect for a brief period of time: fewer patrons paid more, which meant his income stream remained level and his supplies did not decline as quickly. But as the shortage dragged into a second week, and then a third, Clarkson resorted to watering down his chocolate and hoping that his patrons would not notice. Unfortunately, they did, and he was forced to reveal the truth of the matter: There was no more chocolate in the City for him to buy.

On this fine day, as Clarkson gazed gloomily into his empty stockroom before opening shop, he wondered for the first time how long he could manage to keep his business afloat. He would have to close if he couldn't find a substitute for chocolate. He had heard that the nobles on the Hill had begun to drink something called vanilla cream instead of chocolate, but vanilla was so expensive he would have to find a cheaper substitute before he could sell it to his patrons. He had also heard that some intrepid University students had fermented a new brew made of crushed nuts, which they called amandyne and which they claimed recreated the flavor and stimulating effect of chocolate. The idea intrigued him. Clarkson resolved to take a trip to the University area, where he was friendly with one of the few chocolate shop owners—chocolate being a luxury to most students—to try some of this amandyne himself.

* * *

The Duchess Tremontaine lifted the porcelain cup from its saucer and took a particularly satisfying sip of bitter chocolate. It was the finest in the City, kept under lock and key by the cook, and was flavored with Kinwiinik spices that the duchess had personally requested from the Balam family. The cup was a beauty, too: one from a set of twelve given to Diane by her husband, each hand-painted with a different blooming rose. This one Diane especially loved because the thorns in the pink rose's stem were rendered with such exquisite detail it seemed as if one could easily prick a finger when touching the cup itself.

The duchess set the cup back into its matching saucer, relishing the lingering taste of chocolate on her tongue, and glanced out the window. She always enjoyed the view from her private retreat at the highest point of Tremontaine House. Diane's writing desk was situated so that she could look out the windows as she handled her private correspondence, providing her with a lofty vantage point suitable to her station and matched to her ambition. It was in this room that she had conceived of the plan that would finally engineer the outcome she desperately needed: The Balams would have their tariff relaxed, and she would receive her cut of their increased profit, thus mitigating the disaster of the *Everfair*. Her previous efforts with her husband and with Gregory, Lord Davenant, had not resulted in immediate success, but she was certain that this time would be different. None had ever dared to do what she had orchestrated, but she was not one to allow tradition to dictate her desires.

It was quite simple, in the end. The City loved chocolate, but the Balams controlled the entire supply. Diane had suggested that the Balams send their most trusted envoy to the private residence of the Dragon Chancellor with a message, dictated secretly by the duchess to appeal to Gregory's ego. First, the Balams' latest chocolate shipment had been tragically lost at sea; second, the Balams viewed this as an opportunity to renegotiate the terms of their trade with the City, in preparation for the imminent arrival of the next shipment. Diane had suspected that Gregory would be initially flummoxed by such a request—these things simply were not done—but if he wanted to keep his title of Dragon Chancellor, he would be highly motivated to make sure the City (and all the persnickety nobles on the Hill) continued to get their chocolate. In order to further persuade him, the temporary (albeit false) chocolate shortage would quickly demonstrate how much the City needed the Kinwiinik's goods, not to mention their goodwill. If the City wanted to continue to enjoy chocolate, the Council simply had to acquiesce to the Balams' entirely rational demands and address the tariff.

Initially, Ahchuleb of the Balams had been hesitant to do as she suggested, but Diane had a hunch that his wife—who had so elegantly put the Duke of Karleigh in his place after his insulting behavior at the Swan Ball—had seen the wisdom of Diane's new plan. It had the added benefit of making the duchess and the Balams equal partners in this task, rather than keeping them beholden to Diane's secret machinations. Yes, the duchess mused, equality—or at least the appearance of such, because she was certain that no envoy of theirs would have a chance of succeeding without her coaching—made a solid foundation for future profit.

Now she only needed to update the Balams on the latest developments. She picked up the pen and squared off the thin sheet of paper that she had ordered her swordsman, now also her personal agent, Reynald, to purchase for her from one of the Middle City stationers. It was not the thick, embossed stationery the duchess was accustomed to using for Tremontaine business, but that was deliberate. She began to write.

> *Dear Sir and Madam,*
>
> *You may have already heard of the growing panic among those on the Hill regarding the recent decline in availability of that most precious of commodities, your own very fine chocolate. The shortage has traveled from the Middle City chocolate shops, whose sad owners I trust you are not finding too importunate, up the Hill, and into the drawing rooms of many of my noble friends, taking the matter from one of minor inconvenience to other mortals, to a perfect crisis among the City's nobility.*
>
> *The Dragon Chancellor, as I predicted, has not shared your envoy's request with the other Councilors. I am certain this is because he is on the verge of presenting your request to the Council of Lords as his own idea. Given the deprivation that all the Councilors have been enduring of late, I believe they will be quite ready to follow the Dragon Chancellor's direction, especially once rumors that I have leaked to the Merchants' Confederation come to light. Neither the Council of Lords nor the Dragon Chancellor will wish to be unmasked as weaklings at your mercy (though they are), and I am certain your goods will shortly be welcomed back into the City under much more generous terms than in the past.*
>
> *I thank you for your partnership in this endeavor, and*

I trust that my efforts to increase the popularity of vanilla
have recompensed you at least a small amount for the
short-term sacrifice you are making in chocolate profits.
I remain,
Your friend, who wishes you nothing but well.

Diane read over the letter several times before folding and seal-ing it with a plain wax stamp. Satisfied, she rang for the servant and asked her to send up Reynald.

The chocolate in her cup had gone cool while she wrote, but she drank the last few drops of it anyway. She enjoyed the slightly sandy texture on her tongue and thought of how far those tiny grains had traveled. She had been intrigued by the hints of distant lands that the Balam family had brought with them to her ball last month. Those feathers they had worn sug-gested birds of some size, with plumage of such brilliant colors. Several of the duchess's friends had asked her if she knew how to acquire similar feathers for their summer hats, but Diane did not wish to trouble the Balams with such frivolous demands—at least, not while she and they were engaged in these particular business matters. Perhaps later, when this was all resolved and the Balams' chocolate stores were once more opened to the City merchants, then Diane would acquire for herself a number of Kinwiinik feathers and wear them to great acclaim, perhaps at the theater.

The door opened, and the swordsman entered. "My lady," Reynald said, bowing.

Diane picked up the sealed letter and held it out to him. "Have this delivered to the Trader Ahchuleb of the Balams in the Kinwiinik compound. Discreetly, mind you."

"Of course, madam." He crossed the room and took the letter from her, moving silently as a cat on the soft rug.

After he left, Diane moved to the window seat and opened the glass to the warm early summer air. Below, the Tremontaine gardens looked pristine, lush with newly budded foliage and swelling roses in pink and peach and crimson. The gardener had done an excellent job of maintaining the grounds, given the cost-cutting measures the duchess had implemented. Then again, labor was cheap, and there had been just the right amount of rain this year. The river was especially pretty today, the water sparkling beneath the warm sunlight. Diane watched a ship float decorously out of sight toward the merchants' docks. She couldn't make out the details of the flag, but it was not a Balam ship. All their ships, as agreed, were docked in port, awaiting her order to unload. Everything was proceeding according to plan, although she regretted that she had been forced to take this action. It would have been so much simpler if Lord Davenant had acquiesced to her wishes. It was a pity. He was a charming man, and she'd had quite a lovely time with him after the ball. Besides Davenant's own talents, there was a certain novelty in being with a man other than her husband. For one thing, he was so much more eager than Tremontaine these days. Diane had not realized how much she missed that. Now that the Hill was so desperate for chocolate, Davenant would soon see how foolish he had been to deny Diane. And once he gave her what she wanted, she would be perfectly willing to give him what he wanted.

A fair trade, the duchess thought, especially when his desires lined up so neatly with her own.

* * *

Gregory, Lord Davenant, set down his cup of vanilla cream and pinched the bridge of his nose as the headache that had throbbed behind his eyes all morning swelled. He had drunk his last cup of chocolate the previous afternoon, and it had been comprised of the leavings at the bottom of the chocolate tin.

Across from him, his wife rattled her cup in its saucer and pleaded, "Are you sure you can't speak to those Traders, Gregory? I'm certain they must have some chocolate hidden away that we could buy from them directly."

He raised his bleary gaze to hers and said, "You shouldn't worry yourself about this, Isabella."

"But what am I to do this afternoon when my friends arrive? Am I to serve this vanilla cream?" She gestured to her cup, which contained the sweet, milky drink that someone on the Hill—she couldn't remember who—had concocted out of desperation when their chocolate had run out. "It does nothing for conversation; it puts one to sleep!"

"Then serve some wine," he snapped, pushing his seat back.

"A lady never drinks wine in the afternoon," she said frostily.

He sighed. When had his wife become so insufferable? He couldn't remember, but he blamed it on the chocolate shortage. Or, more accurately, he blamed it on the Duchess Tremontaine. Ever since their amorous evening after her ball, his appreciation of his own wife had plummeted. He was certain the chocolate shortage was making things worse, though. She disliked the vanilla cream, fine; he disliked it too. But she was the one who invited her friends over to "take chocolate," even when there was none, so she should be the one to determine what to serve them.

"Well?" she prompted him. "What are you going to do about this chocolate shortage? You are the Dragon Chancellor, after all, and if even you cannot get me some chocolate, no one can. It makes us look like poverty-stricken wretches to not have any chocolate to serve. Have you tried Tremontaine? They must know how to get some. They know those Traders."

Indeed they do, he thought bitterly. He said to his wife, "Tremontaine is of no use. He's obsessed with the University and has no interest in trade. He barely even manages to attend any Council meetings."

"I mean his wife," Isabella said pertly. "We all know the duke is useless when it comes to business. The duchess is the one to ask. In fact, perhaps I should pay her a call—I want some of those feathers the Kinwiinik wore. They would be perfect with my gown this afternoon. Yes, I'll—"

"No, no," Gregory said hastily. The last thing he wanted was for the duchess to spend any time alone with his wife. "I'll go. You're right—it is my duty. I cannot allow the Davenant reputation to be tarnished by a lack of chocolate."

Isabella clapped her hands like a little girl. "Thank you, my dear. I know you can find me chocolate. If you could bring some home before the ladies arrive this afternoon I would be ever so grateful."

He gave her a thin smile. "Of course, Isabella. I will do my best."

If there was one advantage to the chocolate shortage, it was that few of Rafe's fellow students were alert enough to attend his oral examination. When Rafe—with Micah, Joshua, and Thaddeus in tow—arrived at Badrick Hall after gulping down a cup of disgusting amandyne, the seats were nearly empty. Typically, oral examinations were attended by a good number of fellow students, eager both to cheer on the scholar being examined and to be among the first to witness any spectacular intellectual mistakes. Legend had it that in the early days of the University, exams sometimes went on for as long as twenty-four hours, and at least one young scholar had failed to survive, felled by a deadly combination of lack of sleep and excessive use of stimulants.

But those days were long past. The University was now a civilized place, and many newly minted Fellows or Masters were launched into their careers by an exemplary performance during their oral exam. Rafe had long imagined that he would be one of those scholars, holding forth brilliantly on his theories of experimental natural philosophy, but the reality of the situation that confronted him was far less satisfying. Normally, oral exams were planned well in advance—a month or more, which left plenty of time to draw an audience—but Rafe had been given notice of his exam scarcely a week ago. Additionally, because of the short notice, only Badrick Hall had been available. It was one of the smallest and most out-of-the-way lecture halls at the University, with centuries-old benches that creaked when students so much as breathed on them and windows of dark stained glass depicting the eerie hunting of a horned figure whose long hair looped noose-like around his neck. The windows might have been of interest to some students in the School of History, but to Rafe all they did was block out most of the daylight, turning the interior into a gloomy pit of shadows that seemed to reflect the murky circumstances under which he had been granted the exam.

"At least there's no trouble finding a seat," Joshua said, his voice straining under false cheer.

"Is it usually crowded?" Micah asked.

"Well, it depends," Joshua said diplomatically.

"On what?" Micah asked.

"Oh, you know, various variables," Joshua said. "Look, there's Matthew—shall we go? Best of luck, Rafe, we'll be cheering for you!" Joshua clapped Rafe on the shoulder, nearly sending him sprawling on the steep, narrow stairs that led down past the tiered benches of the lecture hall.

Thaddeus, who seemed half asleep on his feet—a consequence of his chocolate-less state—mumbled something unintelligible and followed Joshua toward their classmate Matthew, who had claimed a seat in the center of the hall.

"You'd better sit with them," Rafe said to Micah. "I have to go down there." He pointed toward the front, where a long table was set on a low dais.

Micah looked worried. "Will you be all right?"

Rafe forced a smile. "Of course! And when I'm finished we'll go out for some tomato pie to celebrate." The thought of tomato pie seemed to cheer up Micah, but it made Rafe's stomach squeeze ominously—and not because of hunger. He wasn't sure if that amandyne had entirely agreed with him. As Micah turned along the row to join their friends, Rafe headed down the stairs. Facing the long oak table was a single, hard chair that was clearly meant for the examinee. The setting bore more than a passing resemblance to the Court of Honor as depicted in sketches sold at the market after a swordsman was called to answer for a questionable kill. As Rafe took his seat with his back to the audience, he felt distinctly as if he were about to be judged for a crime. And indeed, there was honor at stake here: the honor of Rafe's intellectual convictions, dueling with hundreds of years of received wisdom that he was convinced was nothing more than myth papered over with empty scholarly words.

Two of Rafe's three examiners were already seated at the oak table facing him: ruddy-faced Chauncey, whose bald pate gleamed despite the dim light; and gray-haired Featherstone, whose yellow-sleeved robe bore the unmistakable traces of egg yolk spilled down the front. The third examiner arrived shortly after Rafe took his seat. Rafe heard the man's labored breathing as he descended the stairs, a cane thumping alongside him. As the elderly man slid with a grunt into the empty chair at the table, Rafe recognized him. It was Doctor Archibald Lyttle, who had given a series of lectures on eclipses of the moon during Rafe's first year at the University. Lyttle's theories had been widely dismissed as the fancies of a man nearing senility, and he had retired shortly afterward. Apparently he had come out of retirement, at least temporarily.

"Now that we are all here, we can begin," Chauncey said, shuffling his papers in front of him. "This is the oral examination for Rafe Fenton, who wishes to be considered a Master of Natural Science. Doctor Theodorick de Bertel, who was originally scheduled to take part in this examination, has been taken ill. Normally we would await his recovery, but the University board has insisted that we find a replacement, and we are grateful to Doctor Lyttle for stepping in."

Chauncey's explanation made Rafe suspicious. It was all a little too facile, and Rafe wondered if the Duke Tremontaine had had something to do with this. Will had been unusually ebullient when they had last parted, assuring Rafe with a curious degree of certainty that the exam would go very well. At the time, Rafe had allowed himself to believe that Will simply was confident in Rafe's intellect, but now a worm of doubt began to worry its way into Rafe's already queasy belly.

Chauncey squinted through the Badrick Hall gloom at Rafe.

"Do you, Rafe Fenton, hereby declare your fitness to be examined as to your knowledge of the natural philosophy, so that you may represent the University as a Master of your field?"

Here was his chance to call Lyttle's presence into question, but Rafe couldn't bring himself to do it. He had waited too long, struggled against too many obstacles—his parents, who never supported his scholarly pursuits; de Bertel and all those other pompous magisters who comforted themselves with lies; even the Duchess Tremontaine, who took every opportunity to insult him. No, whether Will had orchestrated this committee or not, this was Rafe's one chance to attain his Mastership. Once this was behind him, the way would be open for him to found his school. He sat up straighter in the hard-backed chair and replied, "Yes, sir."

"Very well. We shall begin with a general overview," said Chauncey. "Please explain the intellectual history of the natural sciences, beginning with the earliest theories put forth at this University, and proceeding through their various and sundry arguments, rebuttals, and the like, to our present-day status."

Rafe knew the answer to this question inside out; it was simply a basic reiteration of the standard scholarship from Rastin through Chickering. He launched into his response with no hesitation, ignoring the growing discomfort in his stomach. He shouldn't have drunk that amandyne Joshua had thrust upon him; it was certainly no substitute for chocolate. He didn't feel any more awake; he only felt increasingly ill.

The follow-up questions posed by the committee were suspiciously simple, though toward midmorning Chauncey did begin to veer into disputed territory. He asked Rafe to explain the central thesis of Chesney's *Observations on the Nature of Heaviness and*

Lightness and the influence of the work on current theories. This led to a lengthy exegesis on the part of Lyttle about the orbit of the moon, which had nothing to do with anything but allowed him to espouse his ridiculous theory of eclipses yet again.

As Lyttle prattled on, a clammy sweat broke out on Rafe's back that he was certain was due to the amandyne rather than the exam. What was in that drink, anyway? He had purchased it near the University square at Olivey's Chocolate House, which had run out of chocolate two days ago. There had been a sour edge to the drink that reminded him slightly of the way the Balams had served their chocolate at the banquet for Kaab, but the Balam chocolate (the thought of it alone shot a pang of yearning straight through him, despite his upset stomach) had not had this effect.

"Fenton, what is your opinion on this?" Chauncey barked.

Rafe blinked; he had fallen into a sweaty stupor as Lyttle and Chauncey argued over some notion about tides. He was forced to say, "I'm sorry, sir, can you repeat the question?"

Chauncey looked grim. "What is your opinion of Chickering's theory that the earth is not fixed in place?"

Rafe felt excessively hot all over, and he had to resist the urge to clutch his stomach. This question could surely end his academic dreams if he didn't answer it correctly. Chauncey was probably the only magister in the College of Natural Science to secretly support Rafe's view of experimental science, but would he support Rafe in public? *You tend to ruin things for yourself,* Joshua had told him. Rafe took a deep breath and swallowed the acidic dregs of amandyne that had risen ominously in his throat, determined for once not to ruin things.

* * *

Jeremiah Clarkson arrived at Olivey's Chocolate House to find a sign had been tacked over the front door. It read:

NOW SERVING AMANDYNE!
BETTER THAN CHOCOLATE

Inside, the usually bustling chocolate house was nearly empty; only a few University students were slouched over books by the front window, cups of chalky liquid at their elbows. Duncan Olivey himself presided gloomily over the bar at the rear of the shop, where on happier days he would have been serving hot chocolate mixed with cream and sugar to eager patrons. Today the chocolate pots were empty, and the shop had a sour smell.

Clarkson walked through the quiet room toward the bar. "Duncan, what's this amandyne business?" he asked.

Duncan, who had stopped drinking the amandyne himself because it disagreed with his stomach, said, "Have you come here to steal what tiny bit of business I have left?"

"Is it that bad?"

"You made your chocolate last two days longer than I did."

Clarkson sighed. "Well, at least you've got this stuff here." He gestured to the pitcher of amandyne on the bar. "Can I try it?"

Duncan poured a small sample into a cup and slid it over. Clarkson raised the liquid to his nose and took a sniff. He realized that the sour odor that permeated Olivey's establishment came from this amandyne. Clarkson took a reluctant sip. The drink's color resembled milk, but it tasted nothing like it. It was faintly nutty, lukewarm, and had been sweetened with honey. It had the same slightly grainy texture as chocolate, but that was where the comparison ended.

"What do you think?" Duncan asked.

"Well, it's not very good, is it?" Clarkson said.

Duncan sighed. "It's the best I can do. The stuff is horrible." He eyed the University students, who were paying no attention to the two older men at the rear of the shop. "And between you and me, it makes people sick if they drink too much. I don't think it's going to save us."

Clarkson set down the cup of amandyne and frowned. "I was hoping this might be an option."

Duncan leaned closer to Clarkson and said in a low voice, "I've heard that this whole chocolate shortage is a lie."

"What?"

"Someone—I can't say who—informed me that the Kinwiinik have plenty in stock, but aren't selling it to our dealers."

"Why not? This is a disaster!"

"Hill politics," Duncan said cryptically.

"Who told you this?" Clarkson pressed. Duncan was a friend, but he also had a tendency to dramatize.

"If you want the information, you'll support our petition to the Dragon Chancellor," Duncan said. "The Council's hiding something. We want him to tell us the truth about the chocolate supply."

Clarkson had been a member of the Merchants' Confederation ever since he opened his chocolate house a dozen years ago, but he had never involved himself in the Confederation's backroom dealings with the Council. Perhaps now was the time. He extended his hand to Duncan. "All right, I'm in. Now tell me what's going on."

Duncan leaned forward and muttered, "The Confederation has a contact who saw a Kinwiinik warehouse that's completely full of chocolate."

* * *

Accounting had never been one of Kaab's favorite aspects of a life in the Traders' service, but checking shipping records was less arduous when accomplished outside in the courtyard beneath a blue sky. The steady burbling of the waterfall accompanied by the occasional twittering of the green-and-yellow-feathered birds that had alighted in the gum trees made the courtyard especially beautiful at this time of year. If Kaab closed her eyes while the sun warmed her dark hair, she could easily believe that she had been transported back home. She had done that often when she first arrived in the City, but as the weeks passed, she had grown to develop a surprising fondness for this backwater trading post . . . and the people who lived here.

Her thoughts flew to Tess (as they did more and more lately), ink brush in hand as she bent over her work, a few stray locks of fiery hair curling down her neck. It was only a couple of days since Kaab had last called on Tess, but it already felt like too long. The memory of her last visit brought a smile to Kaab's lips and a warm flush to her skin. She would return to Riverside today, Kaab decided, and she would bring Tess a special gift.

"Ixkaab, the next statement?" Uncle Chuleb said.

"I'm sorry, Uncle," Kaab said, wrenching herself back to the present. Her uncle had spread out the most recent shipping manifests on the reed mat, and it was Kaab's task to read the appropriate quantities out loud so he could note them down in the accounting book, where he would total everything they had in stock. Currently they were dealing with an excess of supply due to their agreement with the Duchess Tremontaine. They had learned that morning that some Local merchants suspected the Balam were holding back chocolate, which meant that Kaab's next duty would be to make sure the warehouse was secure against theft and gossip. Their warehouse manager was a loyal Kinwiinik and would not betray any Balam secrets, but that didn't mean other workers, particularly the Xanamwiinik hired on locally, might not talk. And there was a lot of chocolate to hide.

A servant emerged from the arcade near the front of the house and crossed the sun-drenched courtyard, bearing a plain white letter that he presented, with a bow, to Chuleb. He glanced at it absently and then again more sharply. "Who brought this?" he asked the servant.

"A boy, sir, likely hired on the street by someone else."

"Is he still here?"

"We paid him and he left, sir. Should I send someone after him?"

"No, that's all right." Uncle Chuleb set his brush down upon the tray at his elbow and unsealed the letter. Kaab watched as he scanned the words, eyebrows furrowing.

"What is it, Uncle?" she asked.

He handed it to her without explanation, and while she began to read the fine handwriting, he asked the servant to find Aunt Saabim. There was no signature at the end of the letter, but clearly it was from the Duchess Tremontaine.

Aunt Saabim arrived shortly, walking a bit more slowly now that she was approaching the middle of her pregnancy. "What is it, my love?" she asked with concern. Uncle Chuleb acquired a stool for her, and she sat down beside Kaab near the accounting books.

Kaab handed the letter to her aunt. "News from the Hill," Kaab explained.

After reading, Saabim said, "The duchess is a bold woman. If this letter had fallen into the wrong hands . . ."

Kaab nodded. "She is quite confident that it would not."

Aunt Saabim scrutinized the letter again. "The way she drops in the revelation that she is behind the rumors circulating among the merchants is artful. That was certainly not in our original agreement."

"The woman is a serpent," Uncle Chuleb declared. "Why are we trusting her?"

Aunt Saabim said thoughtfully, "She is making a statement to us. She is telling us that the matter is under her control. That the City is under her control. She is trying to show that she has the upper hand."

Kaab said nothing, but she privately thought it showed the duchess's weakness: a need to be perceived as powerful. In truth, the upper hand belonged to the Balam. They controlled the chocolate; the duchess did not. And their generosity in the past in agreeing to pay the tariff had been a display of their strength as well as a gesture of goodwill to the City, one of their newest trading ports. The most recent news from home, though, made it advisable for them to increase their profits. The duchess's plan, if it worked, would benefit the Balam in more ways than one.

"She had better deliver on her promises soon, because we're losing money every day we keep our goods locked up," Chuleb said. "Thanks be to Chaacmul that at least we can sell a little more vanilla during this charade."

"Do you believe she'll manage to get the tariff adjustments through?" Kaab asked. "She seems quite cocky in that letter, especially considering the debacle at her ball."

"The ball fell apart, but it wasn't her fault," Aunt Saabim pointed out.

"No, it was the fault of that stinking calabash of a man, Kar . . . Kar . . . whatever his name was," Uncle Chuleb muttered.

"The Duke of Karleigh," Kaab said, smothering a grin.

"What does your friend Rafe think?" Aunt Saabim asked. "He must know her better now that he is working for the duke."

Kaab thought back to the last time she had seen Rafe. He had been frantically preparing for his examination and hadn't seemed to have much time or inclination to consider the duchess. "I know he does not like her, but his dislike stems from . . . personal reasons." Kaab had never told her aunt and uncle about Rafe's affair with the Duke Tremontaine because she wasn't the kind of person to gossip, and it didn't seem particularly relevant. "Rafe probably has little opinion of her at all. He's not so attuned to, well, women in general."

Aunt Saabim smiled a sly smile that made Kaab wonder if she already knew about Rafe and the duke. Her aunt said, "But you are, my little bee?"

Kaab reddened. "No more than any Balam who has dedicated her life to the service of the family."

Uncle Chuleb snorted but did not mention her affair in Tultenco.

Aunt Saabim said, "I can see that you have many unspoken thoughts about the duchess. Why do you question her ability to deliver on her promise?"

"It's not that I don't believe she can do it. It's that there's something about her that I can't quite understand. It's as if she wears a shell around her all the time, hiding something beneath."

"She's hiding the crumbling Tremontaine fortune," Uncle Chuleb said. "And doing quite well, I might add."

"Yes, but it's more than that. She's hiding something personal, something that is dangerous to herself and possibly to Tremontaine." Kaab hadn't yet told her aunt and uncle about Ben Hawke's death, but now she explained that at the ball she had glimpsed a locket on the duchess's wrist—a locket that had likely been the cause of a man's death.

"How do you know this man Ben?" Aunt Saabim asked. "What are you getting yourself involved in?"

"It's nothing, Auntie," Kaab assured her hastily. "Vincent Applethorpe knew him." Her aunt and uncle had approved of her training with Applethorpe because it expanded the repertoire of skills she might use in the service.

"How is Applethorpe involved in this?" The tone of Aunt Saabim's voice suggested that she was aware that Kaab was not telling the whole truth.

"Applethorpe is the designated protector of Tess Hocking, a woman in Riverside. Ben used to be her protector, so Applethorpe is naturally concerned with how Ben died."

"And who is Tess Hocking?" Aunt Saabim pressed.

"She is . . . an artist," Kaab hedged. Aunt Saabim looked suspicious and opened her mouth to ask yet another question. Rather than allow herself to be cornered into revealing Tess's counterfeiting skills, which would open the door to the issue of *why* Kaab had developed this acquaintance with a forger, Kaab blurted out, "I am in love with her!"

Aunt Saabim raised a hand to her heart and her eyes to the sky. "Ixchel help us—it has happened again!"

"It's not like that. It's different this time," Kaab insisted, feeling her face grow warm.

Uncle Chuleb broke into a rolling laugh. "This time! This time!"

Aunt Saabim shook her head at Kaab, but she was smiling. "Now it all begins to make sense—this sword-fighting business and your trips to Riverside—they're all for this woman? Tell me more about this artist who has stolen your heart, little bee."

Somehow when Aunt Saabim spoke of these things it made Kaab feel like an inexperienced child rather than the grown woman she was. "Tess is very talented," Kaab said stiffly.

"Talented!" Uncle Chuleb chortled.

Kaab gave him a dark look, which only sent him into a fresh spasm.

Aunt Saabim patted him on the thigh. "There, there, my love, we mustn't tease our little bee so much. We are embarrassing her."

Kaab turned her attention back to the shipping manifests, lining up their edges as neatly as Tess would arrange a stack of fine paper on her desk. "Shall we get back to work?" Kaab said.

Uncle Chuleb choked down another guffaw but obliged her by picking up his brush.

Aunt Saabim set the letter from the Duchess Tremontaine on the reed mat. "All right, Ixkaab, we will stop pestering you about this young woman. But have we concluded our discussion about the duchess?"

"As much as I don't want to trust her, I think we should continue with the plan," Uncle Chuleb said. "We'll know soon enough if she is able to fulfill her promises to us."

"Agreed," Kaab said.

"Perhaps that piece of jewelry you saw, the locket she wore at the ball, is tied up with the Tremontaine fortune, little bee," Aunt Saabim mused. "She may have been pawning her jewels to pay a debt, as her financial situation is insecure, and that man Ben charged her more interest than she could afford."

Kaab did not tell her aunt that Ben had not been a pawnbroker, or that she had spent the past few weeks combing the City in search of his former clients in an altogether different business, hoping to find something that linked him to Tremontaine. Nor did she tell her aunt that all she had found were dead ends. Ben had entered the bedrooms of a few select noblemen's houses on the Hill, but none of them had anything to do with the duchess. Kaab had concluded that the next logical step was to abandon her investigation into Ben's life and to begin looking into the woman who wore the locket that may have caused his death.

Kaab did not reveal any of these plans to her aunt and uncle. Instead she said demurely, "You are probably right, Aunt Saabim. It's always about money."

The duchess was delightfully absorbed in a novel chronicling the scandalous adventures of a particularly devious lady of high fashion when there was a knock at her door. Diane closed her novel over a finger to mark her place and called, "Enter!"

Once again, it was the swordsman, Reynald. He bowed to her and held out a sealed note. "My lady, a message for you from Lord Davenant."

She set down her novel, took the note, and glanced at the seal—it was plain, not the Davenant crest. "Since you have delivered this yourself rather than passing it on to Tilson, I gather you have some further information for me?"

Reynald nodded. "When I was at Davenant House, an embassage arrived from the Merchants' Confederation. They delivered a petition to the Dragon Chancellor, demanding a full report on the chocolate shortage. Apparently, the merchants believe that the Council is lying about it. They say they have knowledge of the matter from a chocolate dealer."

"Do they indeed?" she said coolly. "How did Lord Davenant respond?"

"He kept me waiting for this, while he dictated notes to the other chancellors, madam." The swordsman sounded impatient at being forced into the role of courier.

"I see." Diane ran her fingers over the fine, thick paper on which Lord Davenant had doubtless written yet another declaration of his passion for her. She looked at Reynald, who was, like Lord Davenant, a man—and thus in possession of an ego that required tending. "I would like to know which dealer is behind these rumors. Can you find that out for me?"

Had he been a peacock he would have spread his feathers in pride. "Of course, madam," Reynald said instantly. "I will return to the Kinwiinik district and discover him."

"Good." She knew that he would not find anyone, but it would keep him occupied. He might even discover something she didn't already know.

"Would you like me to silence this person, madam?" he asked eagerly.

"I simply wish to know his identity. Can you not ascertain that from a living man?" she said. Reynald had become far too bloodthirsty lately; she couldn't allow him to develop the habit of assuming she wished him to murder everyone.

"Of course, my lady," he said quickly.

"Then go."

"Yes, my lady."

After Reynald departed, Diane unsealed the note. She had written to Davenant just that morning, and she had not expected a response so soon. His handwriting was hasty, sprawling across the thick paper, and his signature was messier than usual—owing, no doubt, to his distress over the merchants' petition. She read the brief message with a smile curling the corner of her lips. He begged to see her. He was unable to contain his longing for her. What a dear.

She folded the note and placed it in the back of her novel. She would respond, but she had left the heroine, Lady Genevieve, in quite a prickly situation at the theater, and she wished to know how it would turn out. By the end of the chapter, Lady Genevieve had taken control of the situation expertly (as Diane expected), and Diane had decided upon a course of action. She pulled a piece of Tremontaine-crested stationery from her desk and picked up a pen.

My dear Gregory, she wrote, and licked the quill with the tip of her tongue.

The Inkpot, generally a crowded and convivial gathering place for University students in search of cheap beer, decent tomato pie, and the kind of whisky so raw it tastes nearly combustible, was less lively than usual on this early summer afternoon, but not because the students had taken to the outdoors. When Rafe and his fellow students arrived at the Inkpot after his excruciating six-hour oral examination, they found a room full of sleepy scholars getting sleepier as they drank beers to chase away the lingering, indigestion-inducing taste of amandyne.

"The stuff is disgusting," said one young student who looked rather pale and sweaty, as if he had developed a winter fever.

"I've heard there's something better over at Kettlesworth Hall," said another.

"You mean in the Alchemy department?"

"Yes, you smoke it."

One student left in search of this latest mythical chocolate substitute, another slumped over in a snore, and Rafe started in on his third beer in a quarter of an hour, bought by his fellow College of Natural Science classmates who trickled in to congratulate him on becoming a Master.

"I nearly thought he was a goner when he started in on Chickering," said Joshua.

"Good on you for standing up for experimentation!" said one student, shaking Rafe's hand vigorously.

"How in the Seven Hells did you get Lyttle out of retirement?" asked another.

"Good thing you did—can you imagine de Bertel's objections?"

A round of laughter followed, while Micah said in his high-pitched voice, "Does this mean you're finished with the University?"

"I think so," Rafe said, still a bit stunned by the course of the day's events. He was a Master now! Why didn't he feel more triumphant? In fact, why did he feel as if he were about to walk off a plank into shark-infested waters?

"What will you do?" Micah sounded anxious.

Rafe shoved the panic-inducing thoughts aside. "Currently my only plan is to get roaring drunk," he said.

The door to the Inkpot flew open, and Thaddeus appeared, his eyes overly bright. "It's here!" he cried loudly, drawing the gaze of every patron in the Inkpot. "The white coat! Ah, there it is, such a creature!"

Joshua stood up. "Thaddeus, what in the Seven Hells is wrong with you?"

Thaddeus spotted their group gathered around the wooden table in the front window and broke into a beatific smile. "It is glorious!" he declared, and lurched across the floor toward them.

Rafe nearly fainted when he saw the man who had been hidden behind Thaddeus in the doorway.

"Will," he said, almost to himself. Then, pushing his chair back hastily and standing on unsteady feet, he cried, "My lord! What are you doing here?"

The Duke Tremontaine glanced around the dingy, low-ceilinged establishment, favored haunt of many a University scholar, until his blue eyes alighted on the young man swaying beside a slight boy and a table full of remnants of tomato pie. "Rafe!" William called, and made his way through the tavern.

"What are you doing here?" Rafe hissed again in shock.

"I have heard that this is where newly minted Masters celebrate their success," Will said, smiling.

Rafe gaped at him for a moment. "You heard—how did you know?"

"The University informed me, of course," Will said. "May I join you?"

Behind them, Thaddeus cried, "The beard! It's so lovely."

Rafe winced. "Are you sure you want to be here?"

"I wish to absorb the atmosphere of intellectual curiosity," Will said warmly. "Let me buy you a beer, eh?"

"What is wrong with Thaddeus?" Micah was asking.

Joshua answered, "I don't know. He's seeing something that isn't there."

Rafe glanced from the duke, who was dressed far too splendidly for the Inkpot, to his inebriated classmates, to Micah. He had the distinct feeling that this could be a disaster, but the fact that Will had come to the Inkpot on his own was . . . well, Rafe's heart was beating a bit faster than usual. He pulled a chair away from an empty table and set it beside his own. "Please," Rafe said.

The duke insisted on buying a round of beers for everyone. Rafe was thus forced to introduce him, officially, to his friends, who all (except Micah) gaped at the duke as if he wore an exotic Kinwiinik feather headdress. Rafe tried to avoid remembering the fact that Joshua and Thaddeus had heard the duke many times before, due to the cramped nature of their rooms.

Micah told him brightly, "I was at your house for the ball."

Will gave the slight boy a puzzled look. "You were?"

Rafe said quickly, "Micah here is a brilliant mathematician. You know that theory I was telling you about? Micah is helping me develop it. Micah, tell the duke about the artificial numbers."

"Oh, do you want to hear about them?" Micah said eagerly.

"Indeed I do," the duke replied.

Micah launched into an explanation, and Rafe hoped that Will would forget what Micah had said about the ball. Meanwhile, beside him Thaddeus continued to stare dreamily at something that no one else could see. Rafe whispered to Joshua, "What happened to him?"

"He went to see Clarence," Joshua said, eyeing the Duke Tremontaine nervously.

"Of Alchemy?"

"Yes."

Thaddeus suddenly turned to them and said, "You are both talking about me; I know it! And you don't understand—the leaf we smoked is a miracle—I see things now so clearly that I have never seen before!"

"What do you see, Thaddeus?" Rafe asked.

"It's beautiful," Thaddeus gushed. "Look over there—perhaps you will be able to see it—you are more open-minded than the rest of them."

Rafe decided to humor him. "I only see some other University students."

"He's a wily creature," Thaddeus said. "The coat on him—white as snow, fine as—as a lady's face powder!"

"And how are you familiar with ladies' face powder?" Joshua asked.

Thaddeus paid no attention to Joshua, continuing to describe the creature in rapturous tones so piercing that everyone at the table, including Micah and William, turned to stare.

"Er, is your friend quite all right?" Will asked Rafe.

"Pay no attention to him," Rafe said. "Did Micah tell you about the star charts?"

"Yes, it's all extremely exciting," Will responded enthusiastically.

Micah was studying Thaddeus, who was gesticulating wildly and declaring that no one believed him. "Thaddeus, tell me again—this thing you're seeing has white fur and a beard?" Micah questioned.

"Yes, yes! Can you see it? And the coat is so wonderful!"

"Like snow and powder, I remember," Micah said. "But tell me what else is it wearing?"

"Wearing? It's not wearing clothes."

"But the coat?"

Thaddeus blinked slowly, his gaze shifting to Micah's curious face. "Aha!" Thaddeus exclaimed. "No, no, this isn't a human being. You really can't see it at all, can you?"

"I'm afraid I can't," Micah said.

Thaddeus looked disappointed. He turned to Rafe. "Can *you* see it?"

Rafe grimaced. "Thaddeus, I think you might need to go home and sleep this off."

"Sleep! No! Oh, look—it's coming closer." Thaddeus scooted his chair back and his eyes followed the invisible creature as it apparently crossed the Inkpot. As Joshua buried his face in his hands, Thaddeus reached one hand out as if to stroke something in midair.

"Oh for the Land's sake, will you stop that?" Rafe snapped, hoping that Will didn't think all his friends were insane.

Thaddeus did not respond, but continued to stroke the invisible creature.

"What *is* it?" Will asked.

"It appears to be approximately five feet tall, with a white coat and a beard, and it's not a human being so I assume it's an animal," Micah said helpfully.

Joshua, face still hidden behind his hands, said flatly, "Haven't you guessed yet? It's a unicorn. He's seeing unicorns."

Rafe burst into laughter, barely managing to avoid choking on his beer. "What was in that pipe he smoked?" he asked.

"You'll have to ask Clarence," Joshua said.

Micah's eyebrows were furrowed. "But there are no such things as unicorns. I know that because I've heard of them, but my aunt told me that they are only stories." Suddenly Micah's eyes brightened, and he tugged on Thaddeus's sleeve. "Thaddeus, perhaps you're mistaken. Perhaps you're seeing a goat! A white goat. I think that in some cases goats were mistaken for unicorns."

Thaddeus slowly turned to look at Micah, blinking as if he were coming out of a daze. "A goat?" he mused. He glanced back at the invisible creature, which seemed to be situated in approximately the same location as the Duke Tremontaine. "I . . . are you a goat?"

Everyone at the table except for Thaddeus and Micah froze in horror.

Will blinked. "I'm sorry, young man. Are you addressing me?"

Thaddeus's face had begun to turn an unhealthy shade of

402   TREMONTAINE

green, and as William looked at him with concern, Thaddeus pressed his hands over his stomach. "I'm—I'm not feeling —" He jumped up and bolted from the table, clutching his belly. He barely made it outside before he doubled over in the doorway, throwing up in the street.

"Er, well, shall I buy another round?" said the duke delicately.

Rafe winced.

The Kinwiinik warehouses were nestled between the docks and the Middle City in the Traders' district, a long but easy downhill walk from Tremontaine House. Reynald was aware of about half a dozen warehouses, but he wasn't about to knock on their front doors and ask for information. He would get the lay of the land first, watching for who went where.

He decided to start at the largest warehouse, one of several managed by the Balam family. He found a convenient vantage point across the street in a shady square where children were playing around a water pump. The pump also provided cover in the form of a crowd, because it brought many Kinwiinik to the area seeking both water and community gossip. Reynald settled into a corner beneath a gum tree that peeked over the wall of a family compound and pretended to fall asleep.

He had been watching for some time before he saw a figure he recognized approach the warehouse and enter. It was the Kinwiinik girl who had fought off all those men in Riverside and then shown up at the duchess's ball with her family. Definitely a person of interest. The girl left the warehouse an hour or so later carrying a leather bag over one shoulder, and Reynald followed. She proceeded down the street and around the corner, where she disappeared—damn her—right into the Balam compound. He was about to find another place to wait when he saw someone he knew slipping into an alley across the street.

Reynald approached the alley, hand on his sword. "Aldwin?" he said in a low voice.

A beat of silence, and then the Galing house swordsman stepped out of the shadows. "What are you doing here, Reynald?"

Reynald spat on the cobblestones. "None of your business. What are you doing here?"

Aldwin gave him a dark look. "I'd wager I'm doing the same thing you're doing."

Aldwin was a good swordsman, but word had it that the Crescent Chancellor had been ordering him to take on other tasks recently, the kind of tasks that Reynald was so very skilled at. "As a matter of swordsman's courtesy," Reynald said, "I'll tell if you'll tell."

Aldwin shifted on his feet and gave a short laugh. "Very well. I'll play, but you first."

Reynald gestured toward the Balam compound. "I'm following that girl."

Aldwin nodded. "I've been following her too."

"Why?"

"She was poking around my lord's house, asking after a whore who used to visit him."

Reynald could almost feel the pieces clicking into place. "Which whore? Galing had a number of them."

Aldwin gave him a cruel grin. "He did. This one died recently. Name of Ben."

Reynald's teeth clenched. "This Kinwiinik girl's been sniffing around about Ben?"

"I think so. Talked to Titus about it too—you know, Karleigh's swordsman. The Kinwiinik girl was also at their place looking for Ben."

Reynald glanced over his shoulder at the Balam compound. No movement there, and if she had left, he was certain that Aldwin would have noticed. "Mind if I join you?" Reynald asked, stepping into the alley.

"If I mind, will that stop you?"

Reynald bared his teeth at the other swordsman.

Aldwin grunted. "Didn't think so. Just don't get in my way."

The two swordsmen leaned against opposite walls in the alley, adjusted their weapons and their expressions, and prepared to wait for Ixkaab Balam to appear.

The window of Tess's Riverside studio was open to the warm, sunny day, and as Kaab approached the building she caught a glimpse of Tess inside, her face turned down to her work. She was worrying her lower lip between her teeth, and as a curl of red hair fell over her eyes, she brushed it back with impatient, ink-stained fingers. It had been over a month since they had first kissed, and in the weeks since then Kaab had learned exactly how much she enjoyed kissing the spark-eyed, red-haired beauty. She had been in no rush to turn their kisses into anything more, because Tess had clearly been mourning Ben's death, but given the state in which she had last left Tess—rather breathlessly, she recalled with a grin—Kaab was certain that the moment for more had arrived. And Kaab, who prided herself on many things, but most especially her attentiveness to feminine desires, was determined to do this the right way.

"Tess!" Kaab called from beneath the window.

Tess looked up in surprise, then leaned out the window with a smile lighting up her face. "Kaab! I didn't expect you today."

"I've brought you something," Kaab called, gesturing to a large leather satchel slung over her shoulder.

"I'll be right there."

A few moments later the front door opened to reveal Tess in a simple blue dress with a white smock, the sleeves pushed up to reveal her dimpled wrists. Her coppery hair was coming loose from its knot, and her face was a bit flushed as she asked, "What have you brought me, Kaab?"

"A special gift from my homeland. May I come inside and prepare it for you?"

"Is it chocolate?" Tess asked with a sly grin. "I've heard it's in high demand these days."

Kaab raised a finger to her lips conspiratorially. "I know nothing about such a demand, but it would be best if we not discuss it in public."

Tess laughed and opened the door wider, gesturing up the stairs. "Come inside."

Kaab enjoyed the whiff of scent she caught as she passed Tess in the entryway: sweet roses combined with the sharper smell of ink. At the top of the stairs, Kaab noticed that the door to Vincent Applethorpe's rooms was cracked open. "Where is your protector today?" Kaab asked, proceeding into the large room that Tess used as her studio. She deposited her bag onto a wooden chair with legs carved like those of a lion.

"He wouldn't tell me, but he's been out all morning," Tess said. She went to her worktable, which was covered with neat stacks of paper and fabric, bottles of ink and brushes lined up at the ready. "Let me clear some space for you."

"What are you working on?" Kaab asked.

"Oh, I couldn't say," Tess replied with a wink. "But if you have another job for me, do let me know."

"Not at the moment, but it's always a possibility."

"Then you're not here on business?"

"No," Kaab said, and Tess met her eyes briefly and blushed. "I hope I'm not interrupting an important task?"

"Depends on what you're interrupting me for," Tess said.

Kaab wanted to kiss her right away, but she restrained herself for the moment and opened the bag on the chair. "I wanted to bring you the drink of the gods."

Tess came closer and watched curiously as Kaab laid out the tools of her trade. Two elegant, tall wooden vessels, decorated with painted and carved rims that depicted the task ahead of her. A wide, shallow bowl similarly decorated. A long, wooden instrument with several turning wheels, like a series of carved flowers stacked upon each other.

"What is that?" Tess asked, leaning over the table to touch the wheels of the instrument.

"It's a *molinillo*—I'm not sure what you would call it in your language. It will beat the liquid into a foam." Kaab demonstrated by picking up the molinillo and holding it vertically between her palms, spinning it to cause the wheels to turn.

"I guess you could call it a whisk, but I've never seen a whisk like that."

Kaab also removed several brown-paper packages, a tiny jar of honey, and a grater. "This is the chocolate," Kaab said, unwrapping one of the packages to reveal a circular tablet the color of dark earth.

"This is what everyone is so upset about up on the Hill?" Tess asked.

"Yes." Kaab broke off a small piece to release the aroma. "It smells of home," Kaab said, handing it to Tess, who held it up to her nose.

"Mmm," Tess said appreciatively. "That does smell amazing. Do you eat it?"

Kaab took the piece back, laughing. "No, no. It is a drink. There are many ways to prepare it, but today I will make it for you in a special way to honor the goddess Ixcacao and to invite blessings into your home."

The preparation of chocolate in this manner was a performance that required finesse and concentration, intended to show off both the vigor of the woman who made it and the vitality of the chocolate itself. It was much more involved than the preparation the Balams had served to their Local guests at the banquet to welcome Kaab to the City, and it required a number of specific and rare ingredients that Kaab had secretly taken from her uncle's private stores. The dried, dark red petals of the hand flower, for sweetness, which she would supplement for Tess's Xanamwiinik palate with a bit of honey. Long, thin cylinders of the pepper flower for a spicy bite. Tiny black seeds scraped from the interior of a vanilla bean for their luscious scent and rich flavor. And to bring the light, airy foam that was the true expression of chocolate's spirit, white powder ground from ritually prepared pataxte seeds.

"This is pataxte; it comes from the seeds of the *balam* tree, the jaguar tree," Kaab said, opening the last small brown package.

"Is that the same balam as your family name?" Tess asked.

"Yes. The pataxte is specially significant to my family. It is a symbol of our spirit and strength, like the jaguar it is named for. You cannot prepare chocolate in this way without it."

"I am honored that you are doing this for me," Tess said, and placed her hand on Kaab's.

Kaab's heart seemed to stop. She had not anticipated that Tess would understand—not entirely—the significance of what she was doing. But the sincerity in Tess's voice made Kaab realize how much she had missed the simple, straightforward connection she shared with women of her homeland. They would have known as soon as she arrived with these ingredients that Kaab intended to show them a special honor. The fact that Tess had somehow understood despite her foreignness made Kaab lean toward her and kiss her, and the softness of Tess's mouth was a promise of what was to come.

"First," Kaab said, taking a breath, "we need hot water."

"Hot water," Tess repeated, as if dazed. "Of course."

Tess's kitchen boasted a giant hearth as tall as a man; it must have once served the entire building that Tess's rooms were carved out of but now was only tended by Tess and, sometimes, Vincent Applethorpe. Tess made quick work of building up the fire and setting a kettle of water to heat up, while Kaab grated chocolate into one of the tall vessels, adding the hand flower, the pepper flower, the pataxte, vanilla, and honey. When the water was steaming, she poured it over the mixture and then, to Tess's astonishment, poured the contents of the vessel from shoulder height into the second vessel, which she had set on the floor.

"How did you not spill that?" Tess asked, as Kaab switched the vessels to repeat the procedure.

"I learned how to do this as a child," Kaab said with a laugh. "I haven't spilled it since I was seven."

"Why are you doing that?"

"To mix the ingredients together, and also to add air." Kaab poured the chocolate between the two vessels several more times until a layer of bubbles began to rise on top. "Chocolate is the drink of the gods, so to make it worthy of them and to invite the blessing of Ixcacao, it is important to make it light as air," Kaab explained.

"It is like drinking clouds when it is finished." She moved the chocolate vessel from the floor and set it back on the worktable, picking up the molinillo. She held it vertically in the vessel and began to spin the handle between the palms of her hands. The multiple wheels whirred through the rich liquid, soon bringing a froth to the surface.

"May I try?" Tess asked.

"If you wish. Stand here."

Tess took Kaab's place before the chocolate vessel and picked up the molinillo. "Like this?" Tess asked, beginning to whir the instrument between her hands.

Kaab moved behind Tess and slid her arms around her, adjusting Tess's hands around the molinillo so that her palms were pressed flat together. "Like this," Kaab said in Tess's ear, and moved her hands back and forth along with Tess's. The feel of Tess's body in her arms was extremely distracting, and as they spun the molinillo awkwardly, the foam began to dissipate.

"I'm not good at this." Tess made a frustrated sound.

"You must put your whole energy into it." Kaab helped her to spin the handle faster. The friction between their hands warmed them, and Kaab pressed herself closer to Tess, inhaling the scent of her skin mingled with the rich fragrance of chocolate, pepper flower, and vanilla.

Tess stopped spinning the molinillo. "I—this isn't working." She sounded flustered. She turned in Kaab's arms, and the molinillo fell against the side of the vessel. Her face was inches from Kaab's, her mouth parted. "Do you think we should—"

Kaab was tempted to abandon the chocolate preparation altogether, but certain experiences were only better when prolonged. She placed her hands on Tess's shapely hips, giving her a light caress, and stepped back. "Not yet, Tess. Let me finish the chocolate."

Tess looked disappointed. "Are you sure?"

"A woman's worth, in my land, is judged by the quality of her chocolate. I feel that it would do you a dishonor to present you with anything less than the finest of Ixcacao's treasure."

Tess took a breath and tucked a flaming curl behind her ear. "Then you should show me how to do it."

Kaab took the molinillo again. As she spun it, bubbles began to rise, frothing up on the surface of the liquid in a pale brown foam. When there was a good amount of foam, she spooned it into the wide, shallow bowl to reserve it, then continued spinning the molinillo. "My people joke that the molinillo is like a man's cock," Kaab said.

Tess had moved to the side and was leaning against the work-table, her arms crossed beneath her breasts. She caught Kaab's sarcastic tone and rolled her eyes. "Some people see male anatomy in a twig on the street."

Kaab laughed. "It's true. Men do seem fond of their twigs, don't they?"

"And the foam, I can guess, is . . ."

"Let's not think too closely on that. You know what I think? No man, regardless of the size of his twig, would require the amount of effort that preparing this chocolate foam requires." She spun the molinillo repeatedly and rhythmically, whipping it through the liquid as she spoke. "They would not last. They would be spent long before enough foam had been raised." She spooned off another dollop of light brown bubbles into the shallow dish. "It is women who require such dedication," Kaab concluded.

Tess's cheeks turned pink. "When is this drink going to be ready?"

"Very soon." Kaab had accumulated a cloudlike pile of chocolate foam in the bowl, and the liquid in the vessel was dark and rich. "Do you have two cups?"

Tess went to the kitchen and returned with two porcelain chocolate cups, one decorated with a bluebird and the other with a white dove. "They were gifts from a client," Tess explained. "I have a whole set. I didn't ask where he got them."

"Perfect," Kaab said. They were different from the cups the Kinwiinik normally used to serve chocolate, but the birds were lovely, the eyes done in bright specks of white and gold. First she poured chocolate from the vessel into each of the cups, and then she spooned a thick crown of foam on top, floating it on the liquid. She handed one of the cups to Tess and said, "May the blessings of Ixcacao bring life to your household."

"In honor of the gods," Tess said solemnly, and raised the cup to her lips and tasted the chocolate foam.

Kaab did the same and judged that she had done a passable job at raising the foam. It was bitter but not overly so, and the texture light as air. Her mother would be pleased, though her cousin Ixmaas might tease her about a certain distraction nearby that had caused the foam to be slightly softer than it should be.

"Do you like it?" Kaab asked, and was surprised to discover she was anxious that Tess might not like it at all.

"It's . . . so unusual," Tess said, and licked a bit of foam from her upper lip. "I thought it would be sweeter."

"The people on the Hill drink it with much more sugar—and cream. But that's not the way we drink it."

Tess took another sip. "It has a very intense flavor, very rich. It tastes of . . . someplace far away. A beautiful place. How amazing that this has flowers in it."

Kaab felt a sweet tug at her heart. "It tastes of my home."

Tess stepped closer. "Do you miss your home?"

"Sometimes, yes. Less now than when I first arrived."

"So there are some things you like here?"

Kaab put down her chocolate. "There are some things I like here," Kaab agreed.

"Anything in particular?" Tess prompted, not innocently at all.

Kaab circled her hands around Tess's waist, drawing her near. "Yes. I like the weather now that it's warmer."

Tess pretended exasperation and put her hand on Kaab's shoulder as if to push her away. "Well, if it's the weather you like, perhaps you'd rather go outside for a walk."

Kaab pulled her closer. "Are you sure that walking is what you'd like to do?"

"I do like walking," Tess said breathlessly. She set down her chocolate cup, too.

"So do I, but that is not what I had in mind."

"Oh, good."

They kissed standing next to the chocolate vessel, and Kaab discovered there was a distinct advantage to serving someone a cup of chocolate a moment before, because it made Tess's mouth taste especially delicious. A warm breeze from the window ruffled Tess's hair, causing the red curls to tickle Kaab's face. She wanted to unbind those locks and run her fingers through their luxurious texture, but as she raised her hands to do so a movement caught Kaab's eye, and she realized that she and Tess were standing directly in front of the window.

"Let me close the curtains," Kaab said, and briefly pulled away from Tess.

A whistle went up from across the street and someone called out Tess's name.

Tess went to the window, poked her head out, and shouted, "I'm closed for the day! Come back tomorrow!"

"I don't think you're closed!" came the voice.

Tess's face was indignant as she turned back to Kaab. "Sorry."

Kaab laughed. "It's all right. Where were we?"

Tess reached for her and placed her hands on her waist decisively, as if they were beginning a dance. "Here."

In due course they moved from the studio into Tess's bedroom, where the curtains were already drawn, and lace by lace Kaab helped Tess out of her stays, until the fullness of Tess's figure emerged beneath Kaab's hands, all soft curves and rose-scented skin. Kaab did not understand why Xanamwiinik women confined themselves beneath such tight lacings and so many petticoats, unless it was to present themselves as gifts to their lovers, a thought that did not displease her as she finally unbound Tess's hair. The curls were silken, the color as marvelous as sunset over the South Sea on a hot summer evening, and as they tumbled across the pillow, over Tess's round, freckled shoulders, over the lush weight of her breasts, Kaab felt as fortunate as one of Ixchel's handmaidens.

As Tess lay back on her bed, she was reminded of the molinillo whirring between Kaab's hands, the look of concentration on Kaab's face as she worked at a task that she loved, the foam rising in the chocolate just as heat rose on Tess's own skin. She was light as air beneath Kaab's fingers, as if somehow Kaab had turned her into the drink of the gods, decadent and rich, and Kaab was a thirsty woman.

Diane received Gregory, Lord Davenant, in the back parlor that looked out over the gardens, which had the advantage of being located near a private stairway that led up to her sitting room. He looked flushed and eager when he arrived, but he quite properly waited for the servants to leave them before he did more than express the appropriate formalities. Unfortunately, there were a lot of servants, and they showed no signs of leaving.

Diane had seated herself upon a low-backed rose chair that allowed her to arrange her dove-colored skirts to her best advantage. She was surprised to feel her cheeks warm slightly with anticipation as Davenant bent over her extended hand.

"My lady, your beauty is unparalleled this afternoon," he said.

Diane gave him a perfect, public smile. "You flatter me, Lord Davenant. I am so sorry that my husband is not at home at present. I hope you will accept my company as a poor substitute."

His color deepened as he sat across from her, attempting to appear at ease but utterly failing. Shadows beneath his eyes demonstrated either a restless night or a lack of chocolate; Diane was quite certain it was the latter.

"I am honored to be in your company at any time," Davenant said.

The footman set out a tray of vanilla cream, and Diane began to pour small cups for the two of them. "How is Lady Davenant today?" she asked as she handed him a cup.

He flinched but expertly turned it to a shrug. "She is well and sends her regards."

She sipped once at her cream before setting the cup down. "So refreshing," she murmured. It might have been improved with a liberal dash of brandy, but she preferred to keep her wits about her in the company of the Dragon Chancellor.

Finally the footman closed the door behind himself, leaving her alone with Lord Davenant, who wasted no time in breaking through their forced niceties. "That vanilla cream is fit only for a baby before bedtime. A woman as . . . accomplished . . . as yourself deserves something much more complex in flavor," he said.

She enjoyed his compliments more than she thought she would. Davenant really was rather charming. "Do you mean . . . chocolate?" she asked coyly.

A flash of irritation went across his face, but that was as Diane intended.

"I had hoped we would be able to put business aside," he said.

She allowed the expression on her face to cool. "My dear Lord Davenant, you should know better than many that business comes before pleasure."

"Is that so?" he said, giving her a measuring look that quite thrilled the duchess. Here was a man who was taking her seriously. "Very well," he said. "A score of the Merchants' Confederation members have petitioned for a detailed report on the chocolate shortage. They are suggesting that it has been purposely orchestrated."

"Are they? How shocking."

Gregory stared at her intently. "Is it? Shocking?"

"Of course," Diane said demurely. "If the shortage has been purposeful, that makes the Kinwiinik rather devious, don't you think? And I thought they were so kind, especially after what the Duke of Karleigh said to them."

"Indeed," Gregory murmured. He was still studying her, as if he could will from her an admission that she had played a part in this game, but she was a more skilled player than he.

"I am flattered that you would share this information with me, my lord," Diane said. "I wonder, what will you do about this petition? It would not do for the public to believe that the Council is unable to control these foreign Traders."

He gave a short laugh. "If I didn't know better, I'd wager you had something to do with it yourself."

"Fortunately you're not a betting man, my lord," she said silkily.

Gregory smiled a bit coldly. "Let me share another piece of information with you, my lady. The Kinwiinik have sent an envoy to me to demand that I eliminate their tariff. They say it has nothing to do with the lost shipment, but the timing seems quite suspicious to me."

"My goodness!" Diane exclaimed. "What a tangle. If you might permit me to make a suggestion?"

He clasped his hands together and leaned forward, giving her a rather pointed smile. "By all means, my lady," he said.

There was something quite thrilling about him in this moment, Diane thought; he was all teeth. "My lord, I am no expert in these matters of trade, but I feel that I do know a bit about the Kinwiinik after they graced my home with their presence. I believe that your suspicion might be correct, but obviously you must not allow anyone else to know. Perhaps if you go to the Council and suggest, on your own, relaxing or eliminating the tariff? I know all of the lords hold you in high esteem and would likely follow your command."

"If I give in to the Kinwiinik's demands, that will set a dangerous precedent," Davenant said, his face reddening. "The Council—along with the Dragon Chancellor—sets the tariff rates. I cannot cede to them, or the merchants will demand their own concessions."

"If no one on the Council knows of the Kinwiinik's request, no one will believe you've ceded to anyone. You will only be strengthening the relationship between the Kinwiinik and the City."

"Their demand is extortion," he snapped.

"My, my, such strong words. It would be so much simpler if you followed my advice, Gregory." She said his name softly, and she saw him twitch as she said it. He was like a fish on a line. One more tug, and he would do as she wished.

He moved more swiftly than she had expected and was suddenly kneeling before her, his hands gripping hers. "Diane, please, can we set this matter aside? I only want to please you in one way, now."

She pulled her hands away from him, but gently, and allowed her fingertips to caress his cheek. His eyes were not as blue as her husband's, but they were filled with much more passion. She trailed a thumb over his trembling lips, but before he could do more than lean closer to her, she had escaped his grasp and gone to stand beside the mantel. He was startled—bewildered by her sudden movement—and still kneeling as if in prayer before the seat she had vacated.

"If you want to please me, then you will agree to do something about the tariffs on chocolate," she said evenly. "Are you not the Dragon Chancellor? Is this not in your power? The entire Council trusts your decisions in these matters and will surely follow your lead. You need not share with anyone the course you followed to arrive at your decision. And the entire City will owe you their thanks for bringing an end to their chocolate deprivation—even if they don't know precisely what the favorable winds were that caused the Kinwiinik fleet to reach our harbor with fresh shipments." He rose to his feet, turning to face her. She couldn't tell if he was embarrassed or angry at her—perhaps a little of both. She added, "They may not know, but I will. And I will thank you."

He spread his hands. His face bore a strange combination of frustration and submission. "You leave me no choice."

A flush of triumph filled the duchess, but she did not allow it to show. "You've always had a choice, Gregory. I'm so pleased that you have made the right one."

He came across the room, eager for her, but she said, "First, send word to the Balams to indicate that you will consider their request. You can send word to the Council later, summoning them to an important voting session, when you return home."

He halted and then smiled faintly. "Business before pleasure."

"Pleasure after business," she corrected him. "Now, come with me."

Diane led him out of the room and opened the panel in the wall that revealed the steep, narrow staircase to her private sitting room. He followed her without question, and she removed paper and pen and ink from her desk. He sat where she told him to sit, and he wrote what she told him to write. He sealed the brief note with his signet ring, and then she handed it to the servant outside her door. It would be taken by messenger to the Balam compound immediately.

She locked the door behind her and turned to face Lord Davenant. He was still seated at her desk, watching her and waiting. She enjoyed the expression on his face immensely. She crossed the room, and he rose to his feet, but did not approach. *He has learned,* she observed. When she stood before him, she reached up with her small, delicate hands and began to untie the complicated knot of his cravat, the ruby ring on her right hand flashing bright as blood against the creamy linen and lace. She pulled the stock free, a long, narrow flag of surrender, and let it flutter to the floor. Beneath the taut skin of his throat, he swallowed. She slid her fingers up and over his neck, reaching up to cup the back of his head, drawing his face down to hers. He was a tall man, though not so tall as her husband.

The thought of William caused a sharp, sudden pain in her, as if someone had jabbed her with a needle. She banished the thought with a quick, vicious efficiency. She did not succumb to common jealousy, but she was no man's fool, and she would not stand for William's lies.

Lord Gregory Davenant did not lie to her. She could read him as easily as the novel she had left on her desk. He really was a charming man, she thought, and opened her mouth.

Evening has descended in soft rose light across the City, brushing the ancient gray towers of the University with the warmth of a maiden's first blush. From inside his chocolate shop, Duncan Olivey watches the light change, feeling a weary sense of satisfaction over the day's events. The petition has been delivered, and already his source has sent a response: The chocolate ships have been sighted. They are due to arrive any day now. *I knew it,* he thinks. He resolves to discard the remaining amandyne in his possession immediately.

Down the street from Olivey's, a motley group stumbles out of the Inkpot, supporting one another with swaying shoulders, talking and laughing as the effects of the amandyne wear off in the wake of too much beer. Three of them follow more slowly: the young Rafe Fenton, now Master Fenton of Natural Science; the Duke Tremontaine, his hand on Rafe's back; and Micah, who chatters excitedly about the problems she has noticed with a set of star charts she recently acquired.

Rafe feels the effects of the many beers he has drunk over the course of the afternoon, but the watered-down brew sold at the Inkpot is not strong enough to muffle the disquieting combination of triumph and panic that has overtaken him since completing his examination. Now he is a Master, a title he has yearned for all his life, and all he can think about is how impossibly frightening it is to be facing the next step in his dream. Now he must act—now he must start his school—and he does not have the faintest idea how he is going to do this.

The Duke Tremontaine takes Rafe's hand and squeezes it, and says in his ear, "What is bothering you? Can I help?"

Up on the Hill at the duke's home, his wife is walking in their gardens. She enjoys the drama of sunset over the river, and the evening breeze is a pleasant balm on her face. She has spent a diverting afternoon with Gregory, Lord Davenant, and she hasn't felt so young in years. She leans over the marble balustrade and pulls a stem of pink roses toward her, inhaling their perfume as the petals caress her small, pert nose. In this flattering light, she is pretty as she was at sixteen, supple-skinned and sweet as a bride on her wedding night.

The long shadow of a man with a sword on the gravel path to her left jolts her out of her reverie, and her fingers close abruptly over the rose's thorns. She hisses in pain and turns to face her swordsman. "Well? What did you discover?" she asks, forgoing any niceties. The blood wells up on her fingertip; the cut stings unpleasantly.

"My lady, I haven't figured out yet how the merchants heard that gossip about the warehouses, but I found something that I am sure you would like to know."

She raises her fingertip to her mouth and sucks at the tiny wound. "These theatrics don't become you, Reynald. Tell me what you found."

He accepts her rebuke silently. "My lady, the Kinwiinik Trader girl who was at your ball—the Balam girl—she has been trying to discover who killed Ben Hawke."

The duchess stands very still in the twilight. "Are you certain?"

"Yes, madam. She has been making inquiries about Ben at various houses on the Hill. I also followed her into Riverside and discovered that she is the lover of the woman Ben was protecting, Tess. She painted that illustration that Ben had when he came here. I believe that is why the Kinwiinik girl is seeking Ben's killer. For the sake of Tess."

The duchess licks a trace of blood from her lips. Her finger still smarts from the bite of the thorn. "She must not discover the identity of his killer," the duchess says.

"No, my lady."

The sun has disappeared over the horizon, and the sky is rapidly blackening, punctuated by countless glittering stars. Reynald is but a shadow among shadows. Tremontaine House looms above them both, its windows lighted like great golden eyes in the night. The duchess turns her back to Reynald and the house on the hill. Her heart races; her blood rushes; she hears a whistling in her ears that has nothing to do with the breeze on her face.

She says to her swordsman, "I trust you know what to do."

Episode Nine

LIES IN OUR STARS

Paul Witcover

M icah glanced up in annoyance from the welter of her papers covering the wooden table as the door to the front room of Rafe's lodgings swung open to admit a trio of laughing young men who immediately blundered into the table. Her inkpot would have spilled across her latest calculations had she not already lifted it clear, well used to such interruptions by now.

"Sorry, Micah." It was Larry, the scholar who had invited her into the lecture on geometry all those weeks ago. She supposed that, in a way, she owed her presence here to that encounter, for without it she would never have met the man who, in turn, had led her to the Inkpot, and if she had not met *that* man, she would never have encountered Rafe. It was interesting to consider how far back one might trace a series of such events before reaching the initial cause from which all subsequent effects flowed. In isolation, each seemed random, pure chance, yet when looked at in a certain way, through the clarifying lens of mathematics, they were not random at all, but rather the outcome of probabilities amenable to calculation, at least theoretically. She wondered what it would take to compile a likelies table to cover all such eventualities. First it would be necessary to—

"'Scuse me!"

Micah groaned at the interruption. "Could you be quiet for a moment, please?"

"'Scuse me, but have you seen Rafe?"

"Micah, this is Nick," said Larry, then nodded to his other companion. "And you remember Tim."

She did, from numerous card games—the man had a genuine talent for losing, and, as Rafe said happily, never seemed to tire of exercising it.

"Rafe isn't here," she said impatiently, eager to get back to work. All morning she'd been experiencing the maddening sense of fizzy excitement that she'd come to associate with a fresh leap in her understanding of a subject. The last time she'd felt this way had been in the lecture hall, listening to Doctor Volney's lesson on geometric solids; the discomfort had grown until, in a flash, she'd seen that he was wrong, and that knowledge had compelled her to challenge him. Volney hadn't appreciated it, but Rafe and his friends had been impressed.

"What kind of numbers are those?" Tim was looking at her papers—the scribbled and crossed-out calculations, the Kinwiinik navigational star charts Kaab had loaned her, her corrected and re-corrected and re-re-corrected table of artificial numbers (which, maddeningly, was still not correct!)—with an expression she'd seen often enough on the faces of her family whenever they offered a minnow for her thoughts. One of the things Micah liked best about Rafe and his University friends was that most of them didn't look baffled—or, worse, sorry to have asked—when she explained what she was thinking. Well, sooner or later they did, even Rafe. But it was still better than back on the farm, where everyone's eyes glazed over long before she got to the good stuff. Even though she missed her family. And felt guilty about not helping out with the planting. Which reminded her that she owed her uncle another letter; she hadn't written home for weeks now, since the Swan Ball. . . .

"Oh gods." Tim glanced over at Larry. "Is this stuff I should know?"

Larry was looking a bit panicky himself. Nick had already made himself scarce, disappearing into Rafe's room, where a seemingly endless chocolate-and-alcohol-fueled party had been going ever since the miraculous return of chocolate to the City had coincided with the equally if not more miraculous news that Rafe had passed his exams. And what, she wondered, would the likelies have been on that eventuality? Rafe himself had been a rare visitor during this time; his tasks at Tremontaine House were quite demanding, apparently, and his friends had taken advantage of his absence to put his vacant room to what they considered better use.

Micah did not agree. But despite these annoyances, she was gratified by this unexpected interest in her work. "Those are artificial numbers," she said.

"Artificial?" squeaked Tim. "The real ones are bad enough!"

"Oh, all numbers are artificial, if you think about it! But at the same time, they're the realest things of all," she said, warming to the subject. "Even if they don't exist in the same way as, say"—her eye went to one corner of the room, where a slumbering student whose name she couldn't recall had made a pillow from the sack of turnips Rafe had purchased from her uncle before the ball, then forgotten to bring to Tremontaine House as he'd promised, even though she'd reminded him fourteen times so far—"turnips, for example—"

"Say, isn't that Joshua?" Tim's eyes had taken on a faraway look. "Talk to you later, Micah!" He lunged away from the table.

"And there's Thaddeus!" said Larry.

Before she could say another word, he was gone, joining Thaddeus, who sat by the room's one window, engaged in earnest conversation with an Alchemy student called Clarence. With a sigh, Micah set the inkpot back down on the table. Really, would it have even mattered if the ink had spilled? Her new calculations were coming out just as muddled as the previous ones, and the ones before that. What was she missing? She felt stupid and useless . . . yet there it was inside her, stronger than ever, that buoyant, fizzy feeling, as if an answer were rising up from her depths. . . .

The door swung open again, and once again she lifted the inkpot before the new arrivals could bump into her table . . . which of course they proceeded to do even though she called a timely warning. Everyone did. It was absurd to put the table here, so close to the door. But there was no other place for it; the apartment was already crowded. There were the chaise Micah sometimes used as a bed, pallets for residents both permanent and temporary stacked in a corner, a handful of chairs, overflowing bookshelves made of wooden crates, a smaller table likewise constructed, and assorted items scavenged from the streets by Rafe, Joshua, and Thaddeus for artistic or scientific projects that never quite commenced, the remains of meals too desiccated to be of interest even to rodents, and heaps of cast-off clothing that seemed to belong to no one, as if they'd sprung up overnight like toadstools in the manure piles on the farm. She'd never imagined being able to live with so much clutter. Was it any wonder her calculations kept coming out wrong? The Inkpot was scarcely better, but at least there she could enjoy a tomato pie while working.

Coming to a decision, Micah pushed away from the table and stood. She set the cover tightly onto the inkpot and stowed it in one pocket, then gathered up the papers from the desk willy-nilly; time enough to sort them properly once she was ensconced at her favorite table, a refreshing glass of cider in front of her.

She glanced around the room. Clarence, Larry, and Thaddeus were sharing a pipe whose noxious fumes provided further inducement to depart. The chaise was occupied by a pair of students who seemed to be wrestling in slow motion underneath a blanket. The student using the sack of turnips as a pillow had turned from his left side to his right.

Micah's aunt and uncle had impressed upon her that it wasn't polite to simply get up and leave a room where others were present, so she walked over to Thaddeus.

"Thaddeus, I'm going to the Inkpot."

"Hmm? Oh, that's nice, Micah," he said, gazing at her with a look of vague disappointment, as if he'd been hoping to see something else entirely.

"If Rafe comes back, will you tell him? I don't want him to worry."

He nodded absently as the pipe came round again. The billow of greenish smoke that rose from the bowl pushed her into a coughing retreat. Meanwhile, four more students had entered the room. She wondered if there might not be some equation to predict the seemingly random movement of bodies within an enclosed space, some tipping point after which the flow of students into the interior room would reverse, without the students themselves being aware of why they felt an obscure compulsion to exit a space they had so recently been keen to enter. There was something deeply comforting in the notion that even human beings—that capricious order to which, by an accident of birth, she belonged, without ever quite belonging—were as subject to the laws of mathematics as any other bodies in motion.

Comforting in theory, anyway. But in practice anything but, because that was the very problem Rafe had given her to solve, and which eluded her at every turn. How could bodies in motion—in this case, ships—plot a true course across the curved surface of an ellipsoid—which turned out to be the true shape of the world, according to Kaab, who should know!—using Kinwiinik formulae that relied upon centuries of their people's painstaking observation of the stars and planets?

Of course, the real question was why they *couldn't*. Because theoretically they absolutely should be able to do just that. It was simple geometry. Well, maybe not simple, exactly, but simple enough for her.

Math didn't lie. It shouldn't be necessary to fudge the answers to basic problems of navigation with fixes based upon direct experience, as ship captains and navigators routinely did. That was cheating. People cheated all the time, but not numbers. That was one reason why, on the whole, she preferred numbers to people. With numbers, she knew exactly where she stood.

Or always had, until now.

And there it was again, that fizzy feeling she'd felt in Volney's lecture, with its peculiarly pleasant mix of discomfort and anticipation, like an itch that begged for scratching.

An itch she couldn't reach.

But she had to reach it. If she failed, she would disappoint Rafe, who had been so nice to her. Who believed in her. And all her time here in the City would be for nothing. She would go home a failure, and her family would smile and hug her but on the inside would think about the work she'd missed, the help she hadn't been there to give them just when they'd needed it most.

At least, she thought, she could do something about that.

On her way out, Micah paused to push the slumbering student aside—he snorted but did not wake—and retrieved the sack of turnips. Sooner or later, Rafe would show up at the Inkpot; he always did. And when he did, she would make sure that he took the turnips to Tremontaine House as he'd promised. They were not yet too old to make a favorable impression on any cook who knew a thing or two about root vegetables.

Juggling the sack and papers in her arms, Micah made her way down the stairs and out the front door. The sun shone brightly; it was a hot day, the first day that really felt like summer, even though it was technically still late spring. She stood back against the door, blinking and getting her bearings as crowds of people streamed by. It was as if the party inside had reached that tipping point she'd postulated and spilled out onto the sidewalk. And in fact the return of chocolate did seem to have put the whole City in a festive mood. Lately, everyone she saw on the streets was bursting with energy and enthusiasm; people talked loudly and gesticulated as they walked, smiling and laughing together; her aunt would have said they had a spring in their step, but to Micah it seemed much more than that, as if they were awaiting only some prearranged signal that would send them spinning about each other like the dancers at the Tremontaine ball.

She took a steadying breath and plunged into the stream.

As she walked, half swept along in the flow, shifting the sack of turnips in her arms so as to keep the jumble of papers from blocking her view, she thought again of music, and of math, which was merely another kind of music, just as music was another name for math. The notion came to her that perhaps the unheard music that orchestrated the movements all around her could be translated into math.

For an instant, she pictured herself as one of the guests at the Tremontaine ball, sweeping across the tiled ballroom floor in swift and elegant steps that traced hyperbolic patterns, which themselves could be rendered in the curves of trigonometric functions, orbiting the room like one of the planets in Rafe's heliocentric theory, the floor no longer flat beneath her feet but swollen, rounded. She felt it then, the fizzy sensation that had been announcing something all day, felt it rising up higher than it had before, but still not high enough for her to grasp with her conscious mind, though she reached for it, groping, felt it slip back through the fingers of her flimsy understanding and fall away, saw in her mind's eye its glittering effervescent after-trail bending against a dark background like the tail of a comet. Desolation scraped her insides, as if she'd lost the thing she loved most in all the world. A soft moan escaped her lips, and her feet fell out of rhythm.

"Hey, watch where you're going!"

A shoulder jostled her along with the voice, and she felt herself spun in a direction she hadn't intended to go. Before she could gather herself, someone else stumbled into her, or she into someone else; at any rate, the collision altered her trajectory again, and what was even worse, loosened her grip on the papers in her arms. They began to slide, and as she frantically tried to clutch them closer to her chest, like a shield, a third collision, the most forceful yet, knocked her off her feet. As she fell, papers and charts and tables and numbers real and artificial scattering like leaves around her, the sack of turnips flew up, and its contents, as if eager to be free, shot from the open top. For an instant, a flock of bulbous shapes in graceless tumbling flight was silhouetted in transit across the sun's blazing face.

Time froze. Or she did. The backlit shapes, smoothed in shadow, hung suspended like fruit, perfect orbs ripe for plucking. She felt as if she had grown unbelievably large, bigger than the whole world, and was gazing down upon creation as the gods themselves might see it, from an incalculable height, watching the stately, ordained dance of the planets about their central star. A fizzing kind of music filled her ears.

Then it was over. Micah was her normal size again, flat on her back, head ringing from an impact she hadn't felt, partially blinded by the sun. Blurry people shapes gathered around her making solicitous sounds she barely heard and didn't trouble to understand. Things were happening to her body; distantly, she was aware of being helped to her feet, of loose papers and turnips being thrust into her arms, which somehow accepted them.

"I'm fine," she said, or tried to say, or imagined herself saying. "I'm fine. Leave me alone, please." Meanwhile, she shoved and pushed and wriggled her way free of the crowd, propelled by pure instinct.

None of this was important. None of it mattered.

What mattered was so beautiful, so simple, so clear. A sphere. The world was a sphere, orbiting the sun in harmony with other spheres. It could never be an ellipsoid; she knew that with an utter certainty, as she knew that water was wet. The math was something to be worked out. But Rafe was right. She knew that now, utterly. Felt the rightness of it, like the sprouting of a seed, the turning of a season. She understood why her calculations kept coming out wrong, even after she'd corrected the tables.

Laughing now, her mind on fire, Micah set her papers and turnips down on the sidewalk. She stood, though she barely realized it, in front of a shop of some kind, the glass of the windowpanes reflecting her own image and that of the murmurous crowd gathering behind her. She paid no heed to either. Instead, she stooped and shuffled through the papers until she found a certain page from her table of artificial numbers. Standing, she studied it intently.

Micah gasped. A terrible new knowledge broke upon her.

If the earth was a sphere, then Kaab was wrong. The Kinwiinik were wrong. Their navigation was based on a false understanding of absolutely everything! Only pure luck had enabled them to repeatedly cross the sea without disaster. That luck couldn't hold. No ship that left port was safe, she realized. Not those of the City. Not those of the Kinwiinik. All of them, and all aboard them, were as good as sailing to their deaths.

But was she right? She had to do the math. Prove it to herself, prove it all worked with her new realization. She tucked the page under one arm, digging meanwhile in her pocket for the inkpot . . . Oh god, had it broken? No, there it was, whole and sound! She wrenched off the top and heedlessly let it fall; then, with the open inkpot cradled in the palm of one hand, she patted herself down with the other, looking for a quill. But it seemed she had neglected to bring any, damn it all. No matter!

Dipping her finger into the inkpot, Micah stepped up to the glass window and began feverishly to write.

As Rafe shouldered his way down the choked, narrow streets of the Hill in the afternoon light, the memory of the afternoon's embraces so recently shared—of the last, lingering kiss he'd snatched before parting, the sweet hint of chocolate he'd licked from Will's lips—caused his breath to catch, his legs to tremble. He scarcely saw his surroundings, paid no heed to the passersby he jostled, like some drunkard reeling home from a tavern.

Ah god, the duke had such a confounded effect on him! It was as if Will had put him under a spell . . . or, rather, Rafe thought, a curse. He had but to catch a glimpse of Will, or not even that, just to smell him, for his body to respond with a fervor he couldn't resist, had no desire to resist—on the contrary, he yearned more than anything to surrender to it. And surrender he did, repeatedly, holding nothing back, giving of himself to the very dregs. It was bliss. It was torture.

His feet had led him by habit to the booksellers' quarter, one of his favorite haunts in days gone by. Stalls filled with books, journals, and pamphlets of all kinds lined the street, and he felt a pang of nostalgia for the hours he'd spent browsing here, his only concern whether or not he would be able to convince a bookseller to give him credit. Now, thanks to the duke, he had the money . . . but his desire for books had been overwhelmed by other desires, as a small flame is blown out by a larger blaze.

"Ah, young Master Fenton!" a nearby seller called. "I've been holding some journals for you—full of numbers and lines and arrows and whatnot, just the sort of thing you like best."

"How are you, Master Brooks?" Rafe inquired politely. The man was nearly as old as the books he sold, but sharp as a knife. Rafe wondered what he wanted.

"Still breathing," Brooks said, showing three yellowed teeth in a smile. "I hear congratulations are in order. You are a Master of the University now."

"It's true," Rafe said, satisfied.

Brooks gave him a sly look. "Then perhaps you can pay your debt."

"Ah, yes. Of course. How much was that again?"

A figure was named, and Rafe took some small pleasure in conveying the amount coin by coin into Brooks's wizened hand.

The old man's eyes widened at the weight in his palm. He wasted no time tucking the money into his purse. "Let me get you those journals," he said.

Rafe waved a negligent hand. "Another time."

The prospect of reading the scientific work of others filled him with something close to despair. He'd always put the pleasures of the mind above those of the body, enjoying the latter all the more for the respite they provided from the intense, exhausting demands of the former. For years he'd flitted like a bee from flower to flower in the lush hothouse of the City while his mind, unconcerned, went about its lofty and imperious business. But now there was no separation: the Duke Tremontaine had taken possession of him, body and mind.

"Shall I hold them for you?" asked Brooks.

Rafe shrugged. "As you like," he said, and resumed his downward path.

He had given everything to the duke, and what had he received in return? He was secretary to his lover . . . and to his lover's virago of a wife. He was a Master of the University, the goal toward which he'd worked for so long . . . yet could he truly claim to have won that prize on his own merits and not thanks to the duke's influence? And as for the school he planned to build, would that, too, be less his own accomplishment than the duke's fond indulgence?

This was not the life he had wanted for himself. This was not the person he had imagined himself becoming.

It wasn't Will's fault. The man had done everything in his power to make it plain how much Rafe meant to him, how much his ideas were valued, his dreams shared. But there was a fundamental imbalance between them, one that Rafe couldn't ignore even if Will seemed content to do so.

That imbalance, like so many other things, was easy for Will to ignore. He was, after all, the head of a noble house of great antiquity. Wealth and position were his birthright; they were the very air he breathed. Rafe was a merchant's son.

What, then? Must he spend his life in thrall to a passion that demanded he play a role he had no stomach for, a role that rebuked him daily for taking the easy route, for sacrificing ambition on the altar of lust and expediency? As altars went, he supposed it wasn't too shabby, but if he were to turn a corner now and find himself face to face with the Rafe of a year ago, wouldn't that Rafe regard him with a sneer, the hard glint of contempt in his eye? And wouldn't he deserve to be so regarded?

No, he told himself for the thousandth time, he must resign his post. He must make his own way in the world. If the duke loved him as he loved the duke (*and oh*, he thought, *has it really come to love?* He blushed as if that sneering Rafe of a year ago were witness to this moment and judged it as well), then wouldn't the duke understand, and wouldn't he still come to Rafe in a manner that preserved Rafe's dignity as well as his own? Was that too much to ask?

But what if he did not come! Rafe's heart thumped hollowly, and his legs grew weak in quite another way than they had a moment ago. Never to see Will again, never to touch him . . . Tears stung his eyes. He mentally kicked the smug Rafe of a year ago bloody and senseless to the curb, then trod back and forth over him with hobnail boots a dozen times for good measure.

Ah gods, such an overwhelming effect the man had!

Rafe had descended the Hill and crossed the river to the University without even noticing it. He needed a drink. Hell, he needed a few drinks. He'd intended to go home, to change into fresh clothes, check on Micah's progress, and see whom he could coax out to the Inkpot. But now Rafe decided to make straight for that refuge.

Around the next corner he came upon not the battered Rafe of a year ago seeking revenge, but a noisy crowd gathered in front of a butcher shop. The shop's window—what he could see of it through the milling crowd—was covered in numbers and geometrical drawings, like some rogue slate board run off from a University lecture hall for an exciting life in the streets . . . only the ink used to draw upon the window had run, so that the glass almost appeared to be bleeding. The crowd laughed and hooted. A smudged paper on the sidewalk caught Rafe's eye; he snatched it up; there could be no mistaking that handwriting. Gods, what had happened? Alarmed, he hastened forward and began to push his way to the front of the crowd even as he heard a voice ring out—a voice as unmistakable as the handwriting.

"I'm telling you, we have to close the port! Don't you see? We can't let them sail! Not a single ship! We have to shut it down right now!"

Laughter crested on all sides. Then Rafe burst through.

Micah stood in front of the shop window, his hair disheveled, his eyes wild, his gesturing hands covered with black ink, as was his face, which was otherwise pale as Duchess Tremontaine's pristine ball invitations. Rafe had never seen him so worked up. He was facing two men, his attention fixed on them to the exclusion of all else.

One of these men, by his dress, was a member of the City

Watch. This gentleman had pushed back his cap and was scratching his gleaming bald head in perplexity. The other man, beardless as Micah, wore a bloodstained butcher's apron and carried a cleaver in one hand and a length of sausage in the other. The former hung seemingly forgotten at his side as he shook the latter like an admonitory finger as he spoke, much to the crowd's delight.

"What do I know of ships?" he demanded. "This is a butcher shop, not a customs office! This boy is crazy—do your duty and arrest him for defacing private property!"

"Wellll . . ." drawled the watchman, squinting his right eye as if by doing so he might suddenly bring what he was seeing into a sensible focus.

"I'm not crazy!" Micah pointed toward the window. "It's all there! Are you blind or just stupid? The numbers don't lie! We have to shut down the port!"

"Wellll . . ." repeated the watchman, squinting his left eye now.

"What seems to be the problem?" Rafe said, stepping forward.

"Rafe!" Micah turned to him, an expression of relief flooding his features. "Where have you been?" he added sharply, as though Rafe were late for an appointment.

Rafe was pretty sure that wasn't the case.

"At Tremontaine House," he said, inserting himself smoothly between Micah and the two men.

"And who might you be?" the watchman asked.

"Rafe Fenton," he answered, "Master of the University and Private Secretary to His Grace the Duke Tremontaine."

At this information, delivered in a single breath, a hush fell over the crowd. The watchman drew himself up, while the butcher let his sausage droop and his jaw hang open.

"This lad," Rafe continued smoothly, "is a University student, a protégé of the duke's. He's a mathematical genius. Arrest him? Why, we should be giving him a medal! These calculations alone—" And here he glanced theatrically toward the window, where the ink had continued to run, rendering Micah's scribbles all but meaningless.

"You see, Rafe?" Micah said urgently. "You see, don't you?"

"What is it, sir?" asked the guardsman.

"Never mind," said Rafe, collecting himself. "Very sorry to have troubled you. Apologies for the window," he added, addressing the butcher.

The man managed to close his mouth, but anything more seemed beyond him.

Rafe turned to Micah. "Gather your things and let's get out of here," he said in a low, urgent tone.

"But Rafe—"

"We'll talk in private," he said. "Please hurry."

"Yes, we must hurry!" Micah echoed, and bent to retrieve his scattered papers. The nearest members of the crowd helped; one woman handed Micah a dirt-smudged, bulging sack that he accepted with a glad cry and pressed to his chest as if it were the most precious thing in the world.

"Here now," said the watchman. "What's all this about shutting down the port?"

Micah stood, the beginnings of a reply on his face, but Rafe cut him off with a laugh. "Just a misunderstanding."

"But Rafe—" Micah began.

"Now, Micah," Rafe said, shooting him a look whose meaning he hoped would be plain, though, knowing Micah, he suspected otherwise, "it's all right. You've passed."

"Passed what?" asked the watchman blankly.

Rafe leaned forward and spoke with a confidential air. "Micah's been put up for membership in an exclusive University club that sets its proposed members certain, er, amusing but harmless public tasks to prove their interest."

"Gods help me, another stupid University prank," said the watchman, frowning.

"I hope there are no hard feelings," said Rafe. "Boys will be boys, you know!"

"But my window," said the butcher.

"Oh, the ink will wash right off," said Rafe. "It was in need of a good scrubbing anyway—look at all these streaks! Come, Micah"—he grasped Micah's arm firmly above the elbow—"let's get back to the University. The lads are waiting!" And without another word, he dragged him past the watchman and the butcher, who stood dumbly aside, and then through the crowd, which parted for them amicably, with grins and chuckles, even a few hearty thumps on the back that caused Rafe to wince, knowing how distressing such contact could be for Micah.

"Cheeky lads!"

"Well done, Micah!"

Micah bore up surprisingly well, only pulling out of Rafe's grasp once they were in the clear and had hustled down the busy street, away from the crowd they had drawn. "What club, Rafe?"

"There is no club," Rafe said, glancing at him as they walked on. "Sorry about that—I had to come up with something to get us away."

"Good," said Micah. "I wouldn't want to belong to a club like that. It's mean to make people do embarrassing things in public."

"Very mean," he said. "Look, Micah, about those calculations—"

Micah thrust the bulging sack at Rafe. "Here, hold this!"

Rafe took the sack and peeked inside. "Are these turnips?"

"Yes," said Micah, and looked up from the papers he'd been sorting through. "My uncle's turnips. You promised to take them to Tremontaine House! This is the fifteenth time I've reminded you."

"I'll take them next time for sure," he said. "But the calculations—"

"The port!" cried Micah. "We've got to shut it down, Rafe!"

"Why?"

"Didn't you see the numbers?"

"They were a bit runny," Rafe said.

"It's a sphere."

"Excuse me?"

"The world. It's a sphere. Not an egg shape. Kaab and the Kinwiinik are wrong." Micah shook a handful of papers at Rafe. "That's why I couldn't get the tables to come out right! That's why the star charts are off."

"You're sure of this?"

"I did the calculations."

"On a shop window."

"It doesn't matter where. Numbers don't lie."

"I see," said Rafe, and he felt his mind click abruptly into a higher gear. He stopped walking. "Land's sakes."

"What?" said Micah, who had also stopped.

"Your results indirectly prove my theory." He felt a stirring of pride, of confidence, that had been sorely lacking these last hours and days.

"Yes, of course. That's obvious."

"It's just a question of working out the math."

"Obviously," Micah said, rolling his eyes. "But that's not important."

"Not important?" cried Rafe. "*Not important?* Micah, it's only the single most important thing in the world!"

"No, it's not. What's important is the port."

Rafe blinked. "What are you on about?"

"The port," he said. "Every Kinwiinik ship is in terrible danger. Their whole system of navigation is based on a"—he visibly groped for the words—"faulty premise. That's why we have to shut it down. We have to save those poor sailors—Kaab's people!"

"Oh great god," Rafe groaned. He recalled how Kaab had told them all those weeks ago at the Inkpot of the star charts used by her people. If those charts were wrong, as he now knew them to be . . . "You're right! We have to get down to the docks!"

"That's what I've been trying to tell you!" Micah said crossly.

"But hang on a minute," said Rafe, feeling the gears of his mind shift again.

"We don't have a minute!"

"The Kinwiinik make the crossing regularly."

"Yes, they've been very lucky!"

"Have they?" Rafe asked. Luck was a matter of math too, and he wasn't sure anyone was that lucky.

"What do you mean?"

"Where did you get those star charts again, Micah?"

"From Tess."

He nodded. "Tess the *forger*."

"Well, really from Kaab."

"Who is sleeping with Tess. And who told us that the world was an ellipsoid. Oh sodding hell." Rafe felt sick. The star charts were forgeries, intentionally misleading fakes. Obviously. He stopped, leaning against a lamppost as black-robed students streamed around him, intent on their next class.

"What is it?" asked Micah. "Are you all right? We have to get to the docks!"

"No," he said. "We don't."

"But I just explained—"

"Kaab knows about the sphere," he interrupted. "The Kinwiinik know."

"They do? Who told them?"

"They've always known." Rafe sighed. "Don't you see it, Micah? Their knowledge of these things is ahead of ours, and they want to keep it that way. Their economy, their security depend upon it. Once this gets out . . . it will change everything."

Micah looked stricken. "So . . . Kaab lied to me?"

"Yes, I'm afraid she did," he said bitterly. "To both of us." He was a fool not to have seen it sooner, he thought. Perhaps he would have seen it, if not for his preoccupation with a certain delicious duke. . . . But now he had new information to bring him, a discovery that would change everything in the heavens and upon the earth. What a splendid gift to lay at a lover's feet!

"Friends don't lie to friends," Micah said.

Something in Micah's voice cut through Rafe's reflections. The boy was upset, near tears. "Look, Micah, she had to lie," he explained gently. "She was protecting her family, her people. Wouldn't you do the same?"

"I love my family," Micah answered without hesitation.

"Same with Kaab."

The boy considered this for a moment. "Sometimes you have to lie to protect the ones you love," he said, as if stating the conclusion to a difficult mathematical problem.

"That's right."

"So Kaab is still our friend."

"Yes, she is," said Rafe. "But she can't know that we know."

"Why not?"

Rafe shuddered to think of what the Balam family would do to protect this secret. The fact that he and Micah and Kaab were friends wouldn't matter. Even if she wanted to, she wouldn't be able to protect them. Not with the stakes so high. "It's complicated. But trust me. It's better that Kaab doesn't know. You do trust me, don't you?"

"Yes," Micah said. "Well, mostly."

Rafe ignored this. "Right now, you and I are the only ones in the City who know the truth. The first thing you have to do is write down the proof. And not on a window this time. On paper."

"I don't have any quills. Or ink."

"You can get them at the Inkpot. It's closer than home. You can work there, all right?"

"Good. I'm hungry. But what if Kaab is there?"

"Oh sodding hell," Rafe said. "Look, if we see her, we have to pretend that everything is normal. Can you do that?"

Micah frowned. "I'll try."

"If there's any talking to be done, I'll do it, understand? I'm better at that sort of thing."

"Yes, you are," Micah agreed. "Just like I'm better at math."

"Er, right," Rafe said.

"We all have our special talents. That's what Aunt Judith says."

"A very wise woman. Now let's go." Rafe pushed off from the lamppost and strode down the sidewalk.

"Rafe!" He turned to see Micah holding up the sack of turnips. "You forgot these."

Rafe grimly retraced his steps and took the sack, which he hoisted over one shoulder. "Can we go now?"

"Go where?" came the last voice he wanted to hear just then. "Can I come too?"

He turned, heart sinking into his boots. It was Kaab.

As she worked in the shell of the ruined building where she and Applethorpe practiced, every inch of Kaab's flesh sang with joy, and there was a shining at the heart of her that made her want to close her eyes and bask in its melty glow whenever she wasn't with Tess. When Tess *was* near, well, she didn't want to stop looking at her for even an instant; she begrudged every blink. Was there a more beautiful, more perfect, more delightful creature in all creation? And to think that she, Ixkaab Balam, had won the love of this treasure among women! The scent of her strawberry hair, the smooth softness of her creamy skin, the heat of her kisses, the thrilling touch of her forger's fingers, so skilled, so delicate, so wicked, and so wise . . .

The flat of Applethorpe's training blade smacked against the side of Kaab's head, hard enough to leave her seeing stars and send her own blade spinning into the dirt of the weedy yard that served as their practice ground.

"Really?" he said in a disgusted tone. "That's it. We're done for today."

"But we just started," Kaab protested, gingerly probing her scalp to see if there was any blood. There wasn't. Applethorpe didn't draw blood unless he meant to do so; she knew that well enough by now.

"No, we've just finished," he repeated. "Bad enough that you show up late for our lesson—"

"I overslept!" she said. "I told you!"

"Overslept." He snorted. "Is that what you call it? Over-something, that's for sure. Forget it, Kaab. You're in no shape for training."

"I am in the best shape," she protested, stooping to pick up her blade and assuming a garde position.

"Physically, yes. But mentally?" He shook his head. "Mentally you're still in bed with our Tess."

She rushed to deny it, because she knew Applethorpe was right. "Try again and see where I am."

"No. Love and swords make a dangerous combination, Kaab."

"You think I do not know this?"

"You know it up here." Applethorpe touched the edge of his training blade lightly to the side of his head, then brought the fist that held the blade down to his heart. "But not down here." He grinned. "Or perhaps the confusion lies farther south."

Kaab still had trouble differentiating the cardinal points used by the Xanamwiinik, but Applethorpe's meaning was crystal clear. The realization that she was blushing only made that blush intensify. But she didn't lower her blade an inch. Or her gaze.

Applethorpe matched it. "I've seen plenty of fine swordsmen lose their lives because they were dreaming of a lover's kiss or a whore's embrace when they should have been concentrating on sticking the other guy with the pointy end of a blade. When you draw your sword, you have to cut through everything that binds you to your life, Kaab. Love, hate, every emotion. Nothing else can exist but the moment, the sword in your hand, your opponent, and his sword. Do you understand me? Everything else is just a distraction. And distractions are what get you killed."

She sighed and let the point of her sword fall. If only he knew how close to home his words had cut! "I know. I cannot help it."

"Poor thing," he said with a smirk that belied the sympathy. "Well, no harm done. I don't suppose you're likely to be fighting for your life anytime soon. But I've got better things to do on a beautiful afternoon than smack around a lovesick girl who doesn't have sense enough to know when to quit. You won't improve, and my arm will just get tired. We're taking some time off, as of now. Keep practicing your forms for at least an hour every day."

"But when will we spar again?"

"We'll see," he said.

"I cannot stop being in love," she said. "It does not work that way. I would not wish it even if I could."

"I've been in love myself a time or two, believe it or not. I know what it's like."

"Is that why you left the City? A love affair gone bad?"

"Wouldn't you like to know," he said, and winked. "Now, get out of here."

Normally such cavalier treatment from Applethorpe, or anyone else, would have filled Kaab with seething resentment, but now she merely laughed, put up her training blade, buckled on her own sword, and went her merry way.

Applethorpe had been right about the afternoon: It was beautiful, even by the stingy standards of this too-cold land. The air held an actual promise of heat, if not the thing itself, and the trees lining the streets were in their full greenery at last, with flowers blooming in window boxes and the songs of birds trilling out amid the racket of horses and carts clattering over cobblestones. If she closed her eyes, she could almost imagine herself in one of the plazas of Binkiinha; all that was missing was the chattering of monkeys and the chanting of Ixchel's priestesses on the temple stairs. She felt a pang, a keen awareness of how far away that familiar and loved world was, yet the sadness normally connected to all she'd left there was less than it had been, and she knew that she had changed in her time here, and would no doubt go on changing, and there was something wonderful in that knowledge—yet sad, too, all mixed up together.

She supposed she should go home, but she knew her aunt and uncle would only put her to work at some boring task or other, and she didn't have the heart for it. Not today. She considered going back to surprise Tess, but Tess had her own work to do.

In the end, she decided to visit Rafe. She hadn't seen him since he'd taken his exam, or Micah, either, and she liked to keep regular tabs on the girl's progress with her calculations, or her lack thereof. But she hadn't gone far when she saw the two of them huddled beside a lamppost. Rafe's back was to her, but she would have recognized that lanky form anywhere, even behind the sack he carried slung over one shoulder, while Micah stood out like an inky thumb, her face smudged with dark streaks. Kaab felt a surge of affection for these quirky, wonderful people whom the gods had placed in her path, and she hurried over, eager to share this gift of a perfect afternoon.

"Can we go now?" she heard Rafe say.

"Go where?" she asked. "Can I come too?"

He turned in surprise, and the look on his face—though he immediately disguised it with a grin—told her that something was wrong. A glance at Micah confirmed it; the girl was blushing fiercely, gaze fixed on the dirty sidewalk. The fact that she clutched an armful of loose papers among which Kaab recognized Tess's star charts deepened her unease.

"We're just heading to the Inkpot," said Rafe. "Of course you can come—that is, if you don't have anything more important to do."

Two can play this game, she thought. "What could be more important than congratulating you on your good news? You are a Master now. How does it feel?"

"Oh, you know," Rafe said airily as they began to walk down the pavement. "It's a burden, of course, but one does one's best not to forget the little people who helped one to greatness."

Kaab knew a diversion when she saw it. "Speaking of burdens, what's in that sack? Books?"

"Turnips." He sighed. "Don't ask."

"And what about you, Micah?" she continued brightly, leaning around Rafe, who, she noted, had been careful to place himself between them. "How did you get so dirty? Did you fall into an inkpot?"

Micah kept her eyes on her feet. "I'm not supposed to talk."

"Whyever not?"

"Because Rafe is better at it than me. But I'm better at math."

Rafe broke in with a brittle laugh. "Micah, you take things so literally!" He turned to Kaab. "He is better at math, but sometimes one doesn't enjoy being reminded of it quite so often. After all, I am a Master now."

Micah raised her head, a confused expression on her face. "But you said—"

"Ah!" Rafe interjected with obvious relief. "Here we are!"

He ushered them into the Inkpot, looking about the noisy, smoke-filled room as if in search of a group they might join, but he didn't appear to know anyone present, for he led them to an empty table. He sat, stowing the sack of turnips at his feet. Micah perched on the bench beside him as nervously as a bird, letting the papers in her arms fall onto the tabletop.

"I will buy the drinks," Kaab offered in a cheery voice. "Will you have beer?"

Micah shook her head, gaze glued to the papers, which she had begun to arrange into some kind of order that wasn't immediately obvious to Kaab. "Cider for me. And a tomato pie. And ink and quills."

"Ink and quills?" Kaab looked at Micah, narrowing her eyes. "Micah, we are here to celebrate, not work."

"You know Micah," said Rafe. "That brain of his—always churning."

"And how is the work?" Kaab asked. "Any progress?"

"None at all," said Rafe as Micah continued sorting the papers. "Isn't that right, Micah?"

"Yes," said Micah, and then glanced up at Kaab with an expression of almost frightening intensity. "I love my family."

"Well, I hope so," said Kaab, taken aback. "They seem like good people to me."

Rafe laughed that brittle laugh again. "He's a bit homesick is all. Nothing a slice or two of tomato pie won't cure!"

While Kaab was placing her order at the counter, she took the opportunity to observe Micah and Rafe in the mirrors behind the bar. They sat with their heads close together in low, urgent conversation. Actually, Rafe was talking. Micah sat quietly, still as a statue. Rafe glanced up at Kaab, gauging her attention, and, seeing her back to him, took a handful of papers from the table and slipped them into the sack of turnips.

By now, Kaab was certain that something dire had occurred. And she had a sickening feeling that it had to do with navigation. Could it be that despite her efforts to set Micah down the wrong path, the clever girl had found her way to the truth? Kaab groaned inwardly, seeing the happy life she'd begun to build for herself here in the City snatched away—and Tess with it—all because of one stupid slip of the tongue . . . and one girl's obstinate genius.

But no—she couldn't jump to conclusions. Rafe and Micah were acting oddly, but that in itself didn't prove anything. Kaab needed more than mere suspicion. She needed proof. Because if Micah really had discovered the truth, and had shared that truth with Rafe, then Kaab would have to go to her aunt and uncle and confess everything.

The thought of it made her legs wobble. But there would be no other choice. And she didn't want to think about what would happen after that. She had no illusions about her own fate. Her exile would be permanent, her duties restricted to helping in the kitchens and the nursery. For Rafe and Micah, things would be even worse, for her family would stop at nothing to keep the Kinwiinik Traders' secret of navigation from these Xanamwiinik and preserve their own privileged seafaring and merchant position, which was precarious enough already.

Kaab could scarcely contain her anguish. What was wrong with her that she kept bringing disaster to everyone she loved? It took everything she had not to walk out of the Inkpot and keep on walking, right out of the City, disappearing into the wideness of the world, where her family would never find her. But even if that were possible, it would solve nothing. Her duty was clear. With a deep breath, she lifted the drinks that had been set before her and returned to the table.

"Here she comes," Rafe whispered. "Remember, once we're gone, go back to our rooms and wait for me to send word."

Micah nodded mutely, eyes downcast. The poor kid looked miserable. Rafe felt sorry for him. And more than that: responsible.

It was plain that Kaab suspected the truth. Rafe had been a fool to invite her along to the Inkpot. He should have made some excuse, no matter how lame, to get away from her. Not that he thought he and Micah were in immediate danger from Kaab herself. But her family was another matter. The best course of action—or so he'd feverishly worked out while Kaab stood at the bar, pretending not to be spying on them in the mirror while he pretended not to be spying on her—was to muddy the waters. Right now, Kaab didn't know how much Rafe knew, or who else might know. That meant the first order of business was to get Kaab away from Micah. Once he did so, Rafe was confident he could lose the Kinwiinik woman in the streets. Then it would be a matter of securing protection for them both.

As Kaab approached the table, she tripped—or gave a very good impression of doing so—and spilled the drinks she was carrying over Micah's papers . . . and over Micah as well. "Oh, your calculations!" she cried. "They are ruined!"

Micah stood, brushing awkwardly at his clothes. "It's all right. I remember everything. I can write it down again."

Rafe, who had been caught off guard by this maneuver, saw his chance and took it. He rose to his feet, tossing the sack of turnips—and the papers he'd made sure Kaab had seen him add to it; papers snatched at random from the pile—over his shoulder. "Good idea. We'll celebrate another time. Meanwhile, I've got something to do at home—that is, Fenton House."

"Fenton House?" Kaab repeated. "I thought you did not get along with your father."

"I don't," said Rafe. "But it's never too late to patch things up. Especially with a nice gift." He gave the sack an expressive shake.

"But those—" Micah began.

"Yes, yes," Rafe said, cutting him off. "I haven't forgotten what we talked about, and you haven't either. I'll see you both later."

And he slid away from the bench and began walking toward the door, forcing himself not to glance back over his shoulder.

"Wait!" came Kaab's voice.

He stopped and turned, relief coursing through him.

"I will come with you," she said. "I have business in that direction myself—family business." She turned to Micah. "You should come too, Micah."

"I have to go back to Rafe's," the boy said.

"We'll catch up to you later," said Rafe. "Come on, Kaab, if you're coming." And he turned again and made for the door. By the time he reached it, Kaab was at his side.

Their journey through the streets of the City, from the University to the Middle City, was one of the most unpleasant he had ever made.

"How's Tess?" asked Rafe.

"Fine, fine," said Kaab. "Are those turnips from Micah's farm?"

"Yes, what of it?"

"I thought I could bring some to our cook," Kaab said. "Introduce him to some of the better Local produce."

"Very thoughtful of you."

"Could you spare a few?"

"Sorry. These are all spoken for."

"Not even one?" Kaab leaned sideways. "Here, let me choose it myself—you can make sure I leave the best!"

"Honestly, I wish I could, but I'm afraid my father would be cross with me if I didn't bring him everything in this bag."

For a moment, it seemed to Rafe that Kaab might actually try to wrest the sack away from him. Either that or draw the obsidian dagger she always wore at her side and plunge it into his. He had never been so grateful for a crowded street in his life. At last Kaab simply shrugged and said no more.

He'd hoped to shake her, but she stuck close, following him right up to the gates of Fenton House. "Perhaps you'd like to come in," he offered politely.

"Another time," she said. "I have pressing business of my own, as I mentioned."

"A pity," he said. "Thanks for the company, anyway. Don't forget, you still owe me a drink."

"That is the least I owe you," she said.

Rafe felt her eyes upon him all the way up the walk and the stairs. He doubted a dagger would feel much more piercing. Indeed, a blade between the shoulders would be an anticlimax. He knocked; the door was opened by Loverage, an unflappable man who had served the Fentons for Rafe's whole life.

"Master Rafe," he said, raising one impeccably etched eyebrow. "We did not expect you."

"To be honest," said Rafe, slipping past him and into the coolness of the house with a feeling of immense relief, "neither did I. If anyone asks for me, tell them I'm with my father."

"I'm afraid your father is not at home," Loverage deadpanned.

"Good," said Rafe. "Neither am I."

He made straight for the kitchen and the door that opened into the alley behind the house. He feared and more than half expected to find Kaab waiting for him, but there was no one. Rafe drew a deep breath, hoisted the sack of turnips, and set off for the Hill and Tremontaine House, which, of course, had been his true destination all along.

Home, he'd said. Nor had he been lying. Wherever Will was, there was his home. He knew that now. In the moment when the enormity of Micah's discovery had washed over him, he had not thought of the advantage this knowledge might win for his family's business, but of Will, and of how Will would understand more than anyone in the world how best to use it for all people, not just the privileged few. Retracing his steps to the top of the Hill, Rafe felt, for the first time since he had agreed to Will's terms, that there was nothing false in his position. He was going to Tremontaine House not as a secretary or even as a lover, but as Rafe Fenton, the man whose discovery would change everything.

Uncle Chuleb and Aunt Saabim were sitting side by side on mats and enjoying a late afternoon chocolate in the courtyard when Kaab burst in, out of breath, desperate to speak but dreading the necessity. Aunt Saabim took one look at her and dismissed the servants with a sharp clap of her hands. After that it was just the three of them in the cool, leafy courtyard, and the birds in the trees trilling their evening songs. Kaab wished she could listen to them forever. But she knew her duty.

"Well, what is it?" prompted Uncle Chuleb.

So she told him.

"They what?" he thundered.

Kaab swallowed dryly and glanced toward Aunt Saabim for reassurance—she did not find it in her aunt's pinched expression where she sat beside her husband, hands folded over her rounded belly. There was nothing for it but to repeat the words she had composed and rehearsed under her breath as she ran home from Rafe's precious Tremontaine House on the Hill.

"I have reason to believe the Xanamwiinik have learned the mysteries of the Four Hundred Siblings and deduced, or soon will deduce, the secret of crossing the North Sea."

Uncle Chuleb sagged as if he'd been struck a blow.

"Oh, little bee," said Aunt Saabim, "what have you done?"

Kaab bit her lip. She hated lying to them, but to tell the truth about that conversation with Rafe and Micah was just as impossible now as it had been all those weeks ago. "I've done nothing," she said. "I swear it! I told you they were close to understanding. I warned you it might happen."

"Tell us everything," said Aunt Saabim.

Kaab did so, though her version of everything still left out quite a lot.

"So the Fenton boy knows," said Uncle Chuleb heavily. "By now, his wretched father knows as well."

"Not so," said Kaab. "After he entered his family compound, I circled around to the back. Rafe had already tricked me once—I wasn't going to let it happen again. Sure enough, he came out almost immediately. Believe me, Uncle, there was no time for him to speak to anyone of anything significant. Or to leave a note. He led me to that house as a ruse."

Aunt Saabim smiled. "And you did not confront him. Well done, little bee. You are learning the virtues of restraint. We will make a good Trader of you yet."

Her uncle grunted dubiously.

"I followed him to the Hill," said Kaab. "To Tremontaine House."

Another groan from her uncle. "Tremontaine House? That is a thousand times worse! Better you had slain him on the street than let him reach that viper's nest!"

"In broad daylight? In front of a hundred witnesses? It would have been suicide, Uncle."

"And would that not be an honorable death, Niece, if it protected our family?"

Kaab bowed her head. She had no answer to that.

Luckily, Aunt Saabim did. "It was clever of the Fenton boy

to split them up like that. Even if she had killed him, the mathematician Micah was still at large." She thought for a moment. "If Kaab had remained with Micah and taken care of her, would the situation have been improved?"

"No," said Uncle Chuleb. "Either way, we are doomed. Once the news gets out, those upstart Cocoms will have all the leverage they need to convince His Majesty to revoke our Trading monopoly. We shall be lucky if we are left with our heads."

This byplay gave Kaab time to gather her wits. "I think we are fortunate that Rafe went to Tremontaine House."

"Explain," said her uncle. "Because you and I must have a different understanding of the word 'fortunate.' Keep in mind that you are as close as you have ever been to ruin. Less than a breath away, Niece."

Kaab looked him in the eye. "If Rafe had told his father, that would have been the end of it. Master Fenton is a greedy, grasping knave who cares about nothing beyond the swift gratification of his desires and the advertisement of his ego. But Tremontaine? The duchess is a more subtle creature."

"A viper," her uncle repeated.

"Even a viper does not strike blindly, without cause. But the Duchess Tremontaine is not a serpent but a spider. She spins her webs, planning for the future. She will not proclaim what she knows. She will hold it to her chest as tightly as we ourselves have done for all these many years. That is to our advantage. We know already that she is willing to bargain secretly with us. In this matter too, she will be approachable."

"That is well reasoned, little bee." Aunt Saabim turned to her husband. "You must admit that she has the right of it, dear."

Uncle Chuleb gave a terse nod. "In our previous dealings with the duchess, we possessed a certain leverage. We had something she needed, and so she came to us. What is our leverage here? Enlighten me, Niece."

"I don't know," said Kaab, then quickly added: "Yet. But there is something. That murdered man I told you about—Ben Hawke."

"The one who was the protector of your Tess," said Aunt Saabim.

Kaab nodded. "Remember I told you about the locket I saw the duchess wearing at the ball—the same locket that had been in Ben's possession, and which I think may have been the cause of his death?"

Her aunt pursed her lips. "You think that may be our leverage?"

"I do," said Kaab. " I don't exactly know how. But the duchess is hiding something. I'm sure of it."

"You may be right," said Uncle Chuleb. "Still, it is a slim thread to hang our hopes upon."

"At present, there is no other," said Aunt Saabim.

Her uncle grunted. "How do you mean to uncover this secret?"

"There is only one way," said Kaab. "I will have to enter the spider's web."

Diane, Duchess Tremontaine, spread the silken folds of her dressing gown and settled softly on the cushioned window seat in the highest room of Tremontaine House, itself situated on the highest point of the Hill. From this privileged perch she gazed with satisfaction on what was, now more than ever, her city.

The sun in its lazy decline still painted the canted roofs of the big houses across the river and splashed the high, windowed facades of the old University buildings beyond them in profligate gold. The river, too, at the foot of the Hill—and thus, in a very real sense, laid at her feet—glittered as if covered with spilled coins, and the bridges joining the two halves of the City, old and new, past and future, shone like fanciful confections of glazed sugar in the waning afternoon light of a late spring day in which, or so it seemed to Diane, summer had announced itself for the first time.

She felt as sleek and contented as a well-fed cat in a sunbeam.

Her arrangement with the Kinwiinik Traders had gone through without a hitch, thanks to the efforts of Lord Davenant, the Dragon Chancellor of the Council of Lords, who lay sprawled across the daybed behind her, snoring lightly, his clothes in disarray after more recent efforts, equally successful, undertaken on her behalf. The tiresome difficulties that had preyed on her mind over the last months, since the loss of the *Everfair*, were as good as over. That dark cloud had lifted with the return of chocolate to the City, and soon, by the terms of the mutually beneficial understanding she had forged with the Traders, would follow the funds allowing her to redeem Highcombe and at last place the future of the Tremontaine family—her future—on unshakable financial ground.

In that regard, even as her gaze played appreciatively over the cityscape she knew so well but which had rarely appeared to her in a more attractive light than now, she was drafting a letter to Ahchuleb of the Balams in her mind, a letter she would write and dispatch to that shrewd foreigner once Lord Davenant—who was neither of those things, but had other virtues to recommend him—took his leave.

This was a note whose every word must find its target with the artful precision of a Riverside swordsman sparring with an opponent he one day might be called upon to dispatch in earnest.

A snort from behind her signaled her paramour's return to consciousness. Smiling, Diane rose and turned to him. He remained as she had left him, shirt open, trousers likewise; there was an urgency and passion to their coupling that had been missing from her marriage of late, and which she enjoyed very much, in the manner of a brisk walk through gardens she had once loved to lounge in—though the Dragon Chancellor had the regrettable tendency, not unlike his namesake, of falling asleep over the body of the treasure he had pursued with such fevered zeal.

Davenant returned her smile, basking in her attention, confident in his effect on her. Her effect on him was already quite visible. "Come back to bed, Diane," he growled.

"It is late, Gregory," she replied, though in fact she was tempted to give in just this once. Instead, she walked to the small marble-topped table on which the paraphernalia of chocolate preparation awaited: the kettle, brazier, spouted chocolate pots, silver grater, the set of porcelain cups hand-painted with red roses, and various spices, sugars, and creams. "We've time enough for chocolate, and then I'm afraid I must dress for dinner."

He sat up and began to make himself presentable. He had learned not to argue. Still, a petulant note crept into his voice. "Our trysts always end with chocolate."

"That is because you do not give them time to begin with chocolate, or indeed with any other refreshment," she said as she bent to her task.

"Your kiss is all the refreshment I require," he said gallantly.

She laughed. It was pleasant to banter with her lover in this mindless way, to let her hands go through the practiced motions of readying the chocolate, while beneath the surface, in the ceaselessly turning mills of her mind, she worked out what she should say to Ahchuleb Balam.

It was not that she doubted the man's word. He was, after all, a merchant, and merchants, however exotic they might appear, conducted themselves within the pettifogging constraints of written agreements. What concerned her was what had not been explicitly rendered into words: the spirit rather than the letter of the thing. A bond now existed between their houses; their interests— political, economic, social—were linked in subtle ways that went beyond the terms of the present understanding. Ever so gently, without seeming to do so, she must impress upon him (and his wife, Ixsaabim, who she knew was the real power in the family) that despite all this, theirs was not a partnership of equals. This was her city, and if the Balams forgot that, there would be a price to pay. It was the kind of challenge Diane relished.

"I do enjoy watching you prepare the chocolate," said Lord Davenant, adjusting the fall of his collar. "There is something so domestic about it. Do you prepare it for the duke as well?"

"Jealous?" she asked in turn as she poured hot water from the kettle into the chocolate pot.

"Should I be?"

"That is a strange question to ask one's lover about her husband."

"You are no happier in your marriage than I am in mine," he answered. "If only we were free to—"

Her laughter interrupted him. "I have all the freedom I require, Gregory, I assure you. As for happiness, why, only a fool expects that from marriage. I have something a good deal better, as do you."

"And that is?"

"Position," she said, and began grating the chocolate: superb stuff, a gift from Ahchuleb Balam. "But to answer your question, no, I do not prepare chocolate for the duke." Or much of anything else these days, she thought with a bitterness that surprised her.

"Then I am fortunate, indeed," he said, flushing with pleasure, "to receive such a mark of favor from your hands."

She did not bother to inform him that it was for her own sake, not his, that she was teaching herself to become adept in the preparation of chocolate in the traditional way of the Kinwiinik. Months ago, when she had been a guest in the Balams' house, she had taken particular care to observe the preparation of the chocolate that had been served to her. Such knowledge, she'd reasoned, might be turned to her advantage. In that meeting, she had been briefly wrong-footed by the fiery effects of the brew; that was a negotiating tactic she meant to adopt, even as she habituated herself to the potent mix of chili, corn, and allspice that the Kinwiinik themselves preferred, or so Ahchuleb had assured her. She would not be taken unawares again. She insisted upon preparing the drink herself, scorning the assistance of a maid, first because she found the ritual soothing, a means of focusing her thoughts, and second because she did not wish anyone else in her household to learn it.

"Are you certain you will not give the chili another try?" she asked, glancing up at him.

"My dear," he said, the flush on his clean-shaven cheeks taking on a rather different hue, "that is one experience you have given me that I do not care to repeat. I will stick with my usual sugar and cream."

"I thought you might," she said as she added these final ingredients and handed the porcelain cup to Lord Davenant, who took it gingerly, as though the thorns painted upon its sides with such realistic flair might actually draw blood.

"You always ask me nevertheless," he said, and sipped. "Why is that?"

"Because one day you may surprise me."

"You like surprises, don't you?" he said with a grin.

"That depends," she answered, and sipped from her own cup. In truth, she had come to enjoy the flavorful heat of the spices . . . and even more the chilly exercise of willpower that kept all evidence of that heat from her voice and expression, though as yet she'd been unable entirely to banish a faint sheen of sweat from her brow.

"Depends on what?"

"On who is doing the surprising."

"Perhaps I will surprise you now," he said coyly. "Throw you down and ravish you. Would you like that?"

"Try it and find out," she said, with no more expression to her voice or features than had been evident after her first sip of chocolate.

Lord Davenant assayed a smile; one side of his mouth complied. He raised the cup to his lips, drained it, and licked away the thin band of chocolate. "Another time," he said, setting the cup down upon the table. "As you said, it is late."

"Indeed."

As quickly as that, something shifted between them. She saw him out of the room as warmly as ever, but now she was not at all certain that she cared to serve him chocolate again. Or anything else, for that matter. The man was so predictable. He was already starting to bore her. He had none of William's imagination. None of his quickness of mind, his variety of interests. But she still needed the Dragon Chancellor. It was too soon to break things off. She must wait until the new tax situation had become established, so that the chancellor, spurned in love, could not revenge himself on her by reneging on his support for the deal. She must wait until she had the money in hand.

Diane sat at her desk and began drafting her letter to Ahchuleb of the Balams. Most of it she had already composed during her time with Lord Davenant. She had only to decide whether to introduce some allusion to the liaison between the girl Ixkaab and the Riverside forger known as Tess the Hand. The information had come to her from her swordsman Reynald—who, she reflected, was also in need of a reminder that theirs was not a partnership of equals.

That was the problem with employing such men. Swordsman, chancellor, or duke, sooner or later they always forgot their place.

The Balam girl was an interesting person. She had first come to Diane's notice acting the part of a servant in the Balam household; honestly, it was only because the girl had prepared chocolate for her that Diane had noticed her at all. But then Diane had learned that the girl was Ixsaabim's niece, recently arrived from across the sea. Whispers of a scandal had reached her ears, enough to convince her that Ixkaab Balam was not the innocent, enthusiastic young woman she appeared to be.

First, Kaab had cultivated the friendship of Rafe Fenton, the ambitious son of a powerful merchant family who had wormed his way into her husband's employ . . . and into his bed. Further, Kaab had sought out the friendship—and, if Reynald was to be believed, the embraces—of the Riverside forger, while taking lessons in swordplay from Vincent Applethorpe, a man whose skills with a blade Reynald had described as "formidable"—high praise indeed coming from a man whose opinion of himself brooked no rivals.

Taken together, these actions struck Diane as purposeful, threads in a web whose overall shape was not yet clear. What was clear, though, was that the Trader girl was playing a part, or rather a succession of parts. This was something Diane understood very well and respected. Here was a worthwhile adversary, not to be underestimated.

Ixkaab's ultimate purpose might be hidden, but her actions touched too closely upon the affairs of Tremontaine to be coincidence. The question was, how much did the girl know? One heard she was also asking at the back doors of certain noble houses about their masters' relations with a certain Riverside pretty-boy, lately deceased. And that was where things got tricky, because while the agreement with the Balams had solved Diane's money problems, it hadn't eliminated the other danger, the one to her position. On the contrary. There were worse things than bankruptcy in the world.

What made information valuable was not what one knew but rather how one used what one knew. This was a truth that Diane had lived and thrived by. But it could also bring her down. The knowledge she possessed about Ixkaab and Tess was a minor scandal at best. Still, properly prepared for and skillfully placed, a hint that it was Tess's forger's skills, and not mere carnal pleasures, that had brought Tess to the attention of the Balam girl might be a useful card to play should the Balams forget their place.

But not, she decided, just yet. Better to leave the matter in Reynald's hands for now. He had instructions to do nothing but report. She would watch and wait. And then, when the time was ripe, strike.

Diane smiled, flexing her slender fingers with their sleek nails against the creamy white paper on which she had been writing. The duke called this room her bower, her gentle falcon's nest. Poor William. He mistook her in that as in so many things. He was a man given to deep thoughts, and too easily satisfied with what he saw on the surface, so in love with his own depths that it did not normally occur to him to look below the surface of others.

Indeed, what were others to him, really, but mirrors that reflected his own fascinating depths? How else, she thought, to explain his dalliance with the Fenton creature? What was it William embraced with such fervent passion that his groans pierced the thickest walls of the house, causing the servants to look at her—her!—with shame and pity in their eyes, but his own distorted reflection?

But of course Rafe was no mere reflection. He was, loath as she was to admit it, an intelligent, oh-so-ambitious young man. His influence over her husband was strong and growing stronger. It was not William's body that Diane begrudged the boy; it was not even his heart.

It was his will, which had always been hers to command. She would not give that up without a fight. Not now, when she had come so far, accomplished so much. Indeed, she would not.

She sealed the letter and rang the bell to summon Lucinda, instructing her to have it delivered to the Balam residence by the usual means. Then she dressed and went down to dinner.

She waited for some time for William to join her but finally began without him.

Episode Ten

SHADOWROOT

Joel Derfner

From the manuscript of the *Almanack of Poisones*, by Eamon Malfois

Umbraradix: Al o yclept ye Shadowroot. He who falleth under the Spell of this Elixir eeth not what Others ee, heareth not what Others hear, butt liueth in a Lande of his owne haping, compa s'd rounde by wicked Men and terrible Bea tes, nor can he di tingui h Time longe pa s'd from Time that pa eth from Time yet to come. I haue witne s'd a Man in ye Thrall of ye Shadowroot come to belieue his Wyfe & Sons meant to do him a Mi chief, & thereafter did hun them as ye Southren Lande hunneth ye Northren, le t they de troy him utterlie. Ye ingle Grace offer'd by Fate and ye Gods is that ye Madne s endureth onlie when ye Poi one bee drunk con tantly, for within a Spanne of ome Weekes ye Man who cea eth to con ume it beginneth a Return unto Health. Ye foule t & mo t rare Poi on, Thanks bee unto ye good Gods, el e ye Lande w'd urely haue peri h'd long before this daye.

Tess was never more beautiful than when she slept, nor her sunset-colored hair brighter in its thick braid, running sinuously over her right shoulder before entangling itself in the bedsheet that lay bunched and casual over her and left one beautiful, pale breast exposed to the dawning light.

The morning sun left half of Kaab's face in shadow as she sat in a chair west of the bed, and she smiled. Not so many hours earlier, after all, she had found reason to concern herself particularly with that breast, along with its twin, and the results of her attention had been quite satisfactory, or even—well, perhaps best to leave it at "quite satisfactory." If tended, the warmth in her belly would tempt her to wake her lover from her slumber.

Not that that slumber was particularly restful at the moment. Tess twitched on the bed, muttering incomprehensibly. Her sleep had been troubled for some time, her head-spirit wandering farther and farther through realms invisible to the waking, but for the last three days that trouble had been growing worse; she seemed to spend more time shivering and squirming as she lay unconscious than she spent still, as if she could wriggle her way out of the grasp of whatever danger lurked in her dreams.

Tess's breath came more quickly now, shallower, her muttering louder, with an undertone of frustrated protest. Impatient. She rolled onto her side, one rounded arm dangling from the bed, the other wrapping itself in the bunched bedclothes, her hand clutching and releasing, clutching and releasing, unable to catch hold of its elusive prey.

Kaab moved back in the chair, drew her legs to her chest, put her arms around them, and squeezed to keep herself from intervening. The one time she had been unable to bear it and woken her, Tess had opened her eyes with a gasp, and it had taken many terrifying breaths for her head-spirit to return from the house of dreams. But when Kaab finally asked her what monsters, human or otherwise, had pursued her in that house, Tess remembered nothing—or so she claimed.

Kaab's lips pressed together, and her head turned of its own volition toward the west, and her homeland, and Tultenco—toward the havoc her inability to control her liver had wreaked there, and the lives lost. *Ixchel,* she begged, *do not let me bring Tess to the same end as Citlali. Allow this story to conclude more happily.*

A low moan drew her attention back east. Her lover was thrashing now, dampening the bedclothes with sweat. Kaab's teeth pressed hard into her lower lip. She was a woman of action, and she could do nothing here but wait until—

Tess screamed and her eyes flew open. "No surprise she had it in her!" she gasped.

Kaab knelt beside the bed as her lover lifted herself onto her elbows, panting, her full breasts rising and falling in sharp spasms with her breath. As the fear slowly drained from her face, her breathing steadied.

"No surprise who had what in her?" Kaab asked, as gently as she could. Tess lifted the corner of her upper lip; her eyes shone with perplexity. "What do the words mean, my maize flower? Of what did you dream?"

Tess pressed her hands together. "Buggered if I know."

Words too easily spoken, too quickly. Kaab harrumphed. "Buggery is out of the question," she said, "if you continue to keep from me what is frightening you."

Tess grunted and turned a look toward the ceiling in a gesture equal parts frustration and pleading. "Nothing. I didn't see anything."

"That is not true."

"Can we just say it's true and forget about it? It was frightening enough to see without having to talk about it." She turned her glorious neck until she was staring into Kaab's eyes. A plea, and an invitation.

Kaab stepped to the bed and sat down, finally able to embrace

Tess fiercely, to enfold her lover in the warmth of what protection she could offer, and nosed the crook of Tess's neck. She spoke in her own tongue.

"*Eyes by day, dreams by night.*"

Tess raised an eyebrow in challenge.

"Try, my maize flower. You know at least some of the words."

"Fine," Tess snapped. She identified, petulantly, the words for "day" and "night." Her eyes narrowed. "The rest of it is gibberish."

A sharp retort rose to Kaab's lips, and she held her breath for a moment to keep from releasing it. Her language was a part of her, and she hated it when Tess deliberately provoked her by refusing even to try to understand. Finally, softly, she said, "It is a saying of my people. Just because the gods do not tell us in words how to live our lives in their honor does not mean that they do not instruct us at all. They gave us eyes with which to guide ourselves during the day, upright and strong. At night, however, when our eyes are of no use to us, the gods do not abandon us. They send us dreams by which we can find the proper path forward. To disregard the messages in dreams is to dishonor the gods and our ancestors."

Tess hunched her shoulder. "*Screw* the gods and screw your ancestors! I'm not talking about this."

This was enough to drive Kaab out of bed. "Say that again, and I will—" But here she broke off, for she found she could not imagine harming the beautiful woman in front of her, the woman in whose ample flesh she had found such comfort in this cold, cold land so far from her home.

"I'm sorry," said Tess in a small voice. "I didn't mean that. Your ancestors are in you, and your gods are in them." The rich lips curved. "But there's only one of you I'm interested in screwing." It was enough. Kaab returned to her lover's side. "It's just—"

Tess gave a sigh of frustration. "By the Seven Hells, Kaab, if you understood how frightened I am when I see him . . ."

Kaab took Tess's hands, squeezed tight. "Tell me," she said, "and I vow by Xamanek's light that I will allow you to come to no harm."

A deep breath. "It's Ben," Tess said. Kaab squeezed harder, nodded encouragement. "He's leaning against that wall there, drunk, dangling that damn locket from his hand. He's wearing the jacket he died in, the green-and-red-striped one, but there's blood spreading over the front of it, and every second that passes there's less green and more red. He says, 'We're going to be rich, Tessie.' And I ask him how. And he says, 'No surprise she had it in her.' And I ask him what he means, and then he grins, this awful rictus, and by now his jacket is completely soaked in blood, and then I look down and there's blood beginning to spread on my nightgown, and I start screaming." Tess finally opened her eyes, brown as a rich field awaiting seed. "And that's when I wake up."

Kaab considered this for a moment in silence. "What *does* it mean?"

"I really *don't* know, sweetheart. He said both those things the night before he died. He told me we were going to be rich, and I asked how, and at first he wouldn't answer, but then, just before he went out, he said it was 'no surprise she had it in her.' I didn't know what he meant then, and I don't know now." She turned to Kaab, her eyes bright with fear. "And I don't want to!"

Kaab held her close. "You have no need to." Her hand moved slowly over Tess's hair, crown to neck, crown to neck, soothing, calming, just as Ixmoe had done when Kaab had awoken from nightmares as a child. Her voice gained a grim edge. "But I do. For the sake of my family." She felt Tess shudder in her arms. "Fear not, my flower. My investigation will not touch you."

"I can live with that." Tess nestled close. "As long as *other* things touch me."

A pause. "What other things might you be referring to?"

Longer. "I think you already know the answer to that." A hand on Kaab's back. Kaab's own hands, moving across an expanse of smoothest skin. She bent her lips to Tess's neck and received for her trouble a low hum.

Kaab sat up, offering herself. A reach, a sigh, fingers on arms, on bellies, on breasts. Earlobes nipped, tendons taut, eyes fluttering, and now they're lying down, their legs entangled, arms searching, toes pointing, a tongue, the taste of salt, of saliva, of salt again, of paint, ink. Fingernails digging into a wide back, soft groans, the smell of sweat and yesterday's perfume, oh gods, the air is sweet, pale skin the color of the finest, most delicious festival ant eggs, her own brown flesh, inhale, a gasp, a breath held.

"I believe," said Kaab breathlessly, "that you are correct."

And then she found a use for her tongue far more interesting than speech.

Silk.

The chocolate trickling down her throat, the blue porcelain cup that had contained it until moments before, the counterpane: all smooth as silk. Diane replaced the cup on her breakfast tray precisely. She had come to prefer the blend of spices with which the Traders turned the drink to fire, but it would not do to lose entirely her taste for the gentler flavor consumed by those on the Hill.

A knock came on her bedchamber door.

"Darling?"

It was William's voice. She sighed. Now that the arrangement with the Traders had been finalized, she had looked forward to a day or two free of care before she decided how best to deal with her husband and his toad of a lover. Rafe—she found it distasteful even to think the name—was a crawling kind of pestilence, cunning and oblivious at once, with a temper like fatwood and the political sense of a small green salad, and yet, without her understanding how, he had managed to foil her every effort to rid herself of him. She had insulted him, she had belittled him, she had transformed his work for her husband into drudgery so far beneath him it could do nothing but drive him away, but it seemed to have had the opposite effect; not only had he yet to abandon the duke, but he appeared more and more often, wandering about the house at all hours, a dreary, moping lump in his ridiculous long hair and his filthy robe and his whiny moods.

William spoke again. "Might I trouble you for a few moments of your time?"

It was far too early for civilized conversation—the clock hadn't even struck noon—but his voice was suffused with urgency, and, given his erratic behavior of late, it would probably be unwise not to receive him. The gods only knew what he might do if left to plot his own course. "Of course," she called to her husband. "Take as many moments as you like. They are all yours, after all."

She sat up, snatched *The Tyrant's Dialogue* from her bed stand—it was often convenient, she had found, to present the appearance of having been interrupted at something fascinating, so she kept books in various places around the house in which to seem engrossed—opened its thick pages, and looked up with a distracted smile as the oaken door, heavy with dignity, swung open.

"Diane, I'm sorry to disturb you at such an ungodly hour, but—"

"Not at all." She gestured serenely with the book. "The choice between *The Tyrant's Dialogue* and an actual dialogue with my husband is no choice whatsoever."

"Then listen," he said, suddenly gleeful. It was obvious he had to restrain himself from running to the bed, and she was filled with a sudden fear that he would jump onto the mattress and bounce up and down. But Rafe's poisonous effect on him, thank the gods, had not been quite so deleterious to his dignity—not yet, at any rate. He simply sat very close to her, took the book gently from her, and folded her hands in his. "I have extraordinary news. For you, for me, for Tremontaine, for the City, for the Land!"

Diane sat up, hiding her unease behind a smile alight with excitement. "What is it?" Why, he was positively *grinning*. He had to be aware how silly he must look; it was appalling that he couldn't have the decency to make at least a show of embarrassment.

She let it go. If she had been the kind of woman who allowed herself to be distracted by everything that appalled her, she would never have accomplished anything in the world.

William kissed her and sat back. She let amused forbearance play on her lips. "My noble husband, I trust that at some point you will move from telling me that you have something to tell me to actually telling me."

He ducked his head. "All right, then. It concerns trade." Her face showed mild interest. "And chocolate."

As dismay filled the pit of her stomach like lead, she clapped her hands with just the right degree of girlish joy. "*Do* tell me, William, tell me at once!" Better to get it over with so she could consider what machinations would be necessary to countervail the damage her husband's enthusiasm might do. After all she'd gone through to set up her arrangement with the Traders, was he going to knock it down—and Tremontaine with it—by upsetting the balance of the City's chocolate trade?

No. He could not be permitted to destroy the house she had gone to such lengths to shore up. Her house, now, as much as his.

He took her hands again and looked into her eyes with a joy that was almost nauseating. "To begin with, this will be nothing you don't already know and find tedious, but I suspect that in truth I am not nearly as clever as you about this sort of thing, and I must keep it straight as I go."

She pressed his fingers gently. "You are forgiven everything."

"You are too kind." To her surprise, he bent his head to kiss her fingers, an old, loving gesture of the kind that used to mark their days. As if he thought nothing had changed between them. Perhaps he did. "So. Trade in the Land has for the most part consisted of importing goods from other places and either using it or selling it on."

Oh by the Seven Hells. "Yes."

"This opens us up to vulnerabilities of all kinds, the most recent example of which is that disastrous chocolate shortage."

Diane disengaged her hands and settled back among her lacy pillows. "If you please, don't remind me. The sooner that unfortunate episode can be allowed to fade into the blessed mists of time, the better."

"But to forget it, darling, is to leave ourselves open to its repetition." The concern in his voice made her want to strangle him. "I, for one, am of the opinion that there was no small element of extortion involved. Did you not notice that as soon as Davenant persuaded the Council to reduce the tariff, a new ship landed?"

The lead in Diane's stomach began to warm, to spread like thick liquid through the rest of her body. Her husband might understand nothing beyond the edges of the truth, but that only made him all the more dangerous. "I did," she said cautiously, "but I do believe it is possible to read too much into a coincidence."

He shrugged. "Either way, wouldn't it be better to eliminate our dependence on the Traders entirely?"

Diane's heart stopped beating. She willed it to start again. "How on earth—" She felt faint. "How might we do that?"

"I'll tell you, but you must promise to listen to the end."

She raised an expressive eyebrow. "Is there something you fear I'll find objectionable?"

"Hardly. I just— Well. I've spoken to you before about Rafe and his ideas about the earth orbiting the sun."

She kept any hint of resentment out of her voice. "It all sounded most interesting, if incomprehensible. But that's the University for you."

"Rafe has a friend, a young genius by all accounts, who's taken those ideas and applied them in a completely new way to the art of navigation."

She saw at once what he intended, and the mass of lead solidified again in her stomach, cold. "You intrigue me." Her voice was steady. "Pray, go on."

"If the merchants of our city learned to navigate to far shores— to make their way even to the land of the Traders—then could they not harvest raw chocolate for themselves? And bring it back here to sell?"

And to ruin us, she thought. "Oh my," she said faintly. "What a thought!"

"Just think, Diane. It could transform commerce in the City, in the Land, in a way no one ever dreamed possible! Imagine if we opened up our borders not just to goods from other nations but to *knowledge*, to other ways of looking at the world, to—"

Diane emitted a peal of laughter she was barely able to keep free of hysteria. "William, you're magnificent, but"—you? We? What would make him more pliable? Admonish him or be on his side? Quick, quick, decide—"we mustn't get ahead of ourselves!"

"You don't think it's exciting," he said.

The look on his face was so crestfallen it filled her with a desire to slap him. For the Land's sake, he was a duke. Dukes did not *pout*.

"It's not that, not that at all." She gripped his hands on the silk counterpane. "Why, *exciting* doesn't even begin to describe the possibilities! But possibilities, darling, have two edges."

He looked away from her toward the window. "Exactly the reaction Rafe thought you'd have."

Diane turned to stone.

Finally: "Your secretary presumed to counsel Tremontaine on his relations with his wife?" She heard her voice rise on the last word. Careful, careful. She must not lose control.

"He did. And he was right."

Leave this subject at once. Tread safer ground. "My love, I cannot help thinking the way I think." She pitched her voice to apology. "Yes, the knowledge we gained might lead to phenomenal advances of all sorts, but what if not all of these advances were conducive to the good of Tremontaine?"

He shook off her hands. "The good of Tremontaine, the good of Tremontaine—*damn* the good of Tremontaine; I'm *sick* of considering the good of Tremontaine!"

A shock of red heat dimmed her vision, filled her voice with shocked incredulity. "*You're* sick of considering the good of Tremontaine?"

An awful silence.

Her vision cleared, and she saw his eyes wide, his mouth open.

At once she wiped the fury off her face, replaced it with loving concern, reached for his cheek.

He swatted her hand aside. "Fine, then," he said, and his smile was ice. "Damn the good of Tremontaine and damn you, too, Diane. Damn your politicking and your maneuvering and your cold, cold heart. For seventeen years I've acted the dutiful pawn in your game of Shesh, because you play it so much better than any of us, and it's always been to my advantage, but I swear to you, in this moment I don't give a minnow for my advantage, because there is *passion* in my life again, there is fire, and you will *not* quench it, no matter how much frost you heap on it!"

Disaster. She breathed faster so her cheeks would redden. One hand strayed to her bosom; the other grasped his shoulder. "Husband, you are not the only one in whom passion stirs at this moment." She thickened her tones. "Seeing you in such a state rouses in me—"

"Oh, yes, Diane, yes, yes, how perfect!" The bitterness in his laugh! "Cold reason cannot bend me to your will, so you feign hot fervor instead, while inside ticks the same grinding metal clockwork, lubricated with acid, that has served you for a heart since the day you were born!"

She reached a beseeching hand up to him, only to see him raise his own hand to her, poised to strike; stare at her with horror, his sides heaving; and fling himself from the bed to lope, cursing, from the room.

A great cry began deep within Diane, and all her strength was not enough to contain it. For seventeen years, she had not wept a single tear that had not been in pursuit of her goal—not since a certain dreadful day—because if she had learned one thing very, very early in her life, it was that tears availed nothing, nothing at all, and every moment spent releasing them was a moment spent running toward destruction, and that was not her path, it was not, it was *not*, and she bit into her lower lip so hard it grew paler than her cheeks, and then she bit harder and shut her eyes tight and made her hands into fists and dug her nails into her palms and drew blood and bore down with everything she had and everything she was and pressed, and pressed, and *pressed*. Finally, the almost unbearable tension surrendered just enough for her to know she had conquered once more the forces that sought to draw her down into the deep, and they were *not* invincible, she had triumphed, and she released her fingernails from her palms and her teeth from her lip and felt the blood rushing back where it belonged, under her control, and she opened her eyes and began to breathe again.

She sat quite still until for five minutes together she had been utterly, utterly calm. Then she rose, wiped the blood from her palms with a handkerchief, and rinsed them in the basin until the water ran clear.

What a fool she had been, to think safety so cheaply bought.

A hired sword of Tremontaine knew where he belonged.

Leave it to Samuel, the first swordsman, to fight the showy exhibition bouts and lead the men to swoon and the women to call for their smelling salts; he found fame and adulation gratifying. As far as Reynald was concerned, the more attention you called to yourself, the more your freedom was restricted. Unobserved, as the second swordsman, he could accomplish all sorts of things Samuel would turn up his nose at—no, scratch that—all sorts of things Samuel had probably never *heard* of.

Let the first swordsman strut about like a popinjay. Reynald preferred the shadows.

So it was to the shadows that he kept as he made his way across the old bridge under a quilt of clouds spreading slowly and silently over the scatter of stars in the twilit sky, to the place where shadows cloaked all those who sought their protection:

Riverside.

She must not discover the identity of Ben's killer, the Duchess had said of the Balam Trader girl. Her insinuation that he achieve this by means other than the sword, he could safely ignore. Political maneuvering was for the Hill. Reynald did not have the patience for it.

He kept his eyes open—his hand resting lightly on the hilt of the sword hanging from his left hip—for the dark woman dressed as a boy and carrying a sword. Ridiculous.

He strode past mewling lovers, past sauntering pickpockets, past whores fanning themselves while they flirted with the link-boys, to the house of the redheaded wench where Ixkaab Balam seemed to be found most frequently these days. But he could see from the dark, unshuttered windows that no one was there. Nor was she at the Maiden's Fancy. Nor at the Three Dogs.

Bah. The evening was lengthening. Perhaps she was in the Balam compound, where he could not go. He would return tomorrow. Reynald hastened to the establishment where his other errand took him. It was too dark by now to see the sign over the door, but the figures painted on it, he knew, had long faded past the point of recognition anyway.

The proprietor, a jolly, middle-aged man with one leg that stopped at the knee, supporting himself on a crutch, looked up to attend to the new arrival. "Greetings! And how are you this fine evening?"

Reynald held out a piece of foolscap on which was scratched

a single word. The shopkeeper, after understanding that his visitor did not intend to do him the courtesy of stepping any closer, clumped merrily over to him—a customer was a customer, after all, rude or otherwise—his free hand outstretched for the paper. When he read it, however, his brow wrinkled in confusion. "I don't understand."

At last Reynald smiled. "I think you do."

"Sir," said the proprietor, his eyes wide, "I assure you, I don't. I don't know what this means. Perhaps you misunderstand the nature of my shop." A big smile. "But you have a pleasant evening, all the same."

He turned to swing back to his counter, but before he reached his destination, the point of Reynald's blade pressed into his back, a tiny spot of blood blooming around it.

"Why don't you try that again?" The proprietor shuddered, but those who knew the second swordsman of Tremontaine well would have called his tone affable.

A long silence. Then, unwillingly, the man spat, not looking around, "Fine. But I don't want to see you in here ever again."

"What you want," said Reynald, "is none of my concern."

A little while later, he left the shop whistling, his eyes light and his step jaunty. Drawing blood always put him in a better mood.

Rafe was being driven mad by his own hair.

He kept binding it up so it would stay out of his face as he worked, the flame of the single candle on his desk dancing dim light onto the foolscap. But before you could say "sword," the ribbon would be in his left hand again, his thumb and fingers working it feverishly as his goal drew nearer and nearer, and the light on the paper, foiled by the fall of dark hair, would grow even dimmer. "Yes," he muttered to himself as the sound of his pen scratching did what little it could to fill the silence of the room, "yes, take the inverse of the opposite angle as the . . . and then multiply it by the result from the previous . . ."

For he had taken measurements of the heavenly bodies again, and he could taste success like the finest chocolate on his tongue. "No, no, not that one." He laid the ribbon down, shuffled through the pile of paper in front of him, scanning each page quickly, until he found the number he had been searching for. "And then fill in this equation with . . . yes . . . yes . . ."

His eyes grew wide as the pen scratched faster and faster, and he stopped breathing for a moment, and at last his hand was still.

"*Yes!*"

He had done it.

On the ink-smeared pages before him lay proof that Rastin was wrong, that de Bertel was wrong, that the basis for all astronomy for the last two hundred years was wrong.

The earth orbited the sun.

The sun, not this planet he and his friends trod, was the center of the world.

He leaped up, knocking his chair over. "Praise be to the gods and the demons and the Horned King!" He raised his arms high above his head, grinning, his hands fists, and danced around the room like a boy of ten who'd just won a kickball tournament. "Take *that*, Rastin!" He drew an invisible sword and, leaping forward, stabbed the air in front of him. "Take *that*, de Bertel!" The air suffered another wound. "Take *that*, Chauncey! Martin! Featherstone!" His laughter in the empty room was full and rich.

And now to tell Will. Will, who would be just as deliciously thrilled as he was, would vibrate just as much with joy, would—

An insistent knocking at the door. Rafe gave the air the coup de grâce owed a worthy opponent and tripped, bubbling, to the door.

Where Will stood in the doorway.

Without even giving Rafe time to greet him, he strode into the room, swallowed Rafe in his embrace, and kissed him, hot, fierce, as if his lips would devour the younger man's. He put his hand behind Rafe's head, his fingers clutching the scholar's hair in a fist, and held it immobile.

Finally he broke the embrace.

"I feel," said Rafe breathlessly, "that I ought to make a wry comment." Instead he returned Tremontaine's kiss, his own lips just as hungry, and walked him toward the bed, tripping against the heavy frame and falling onto the mattress, his lover heavy on top of him. Will reared, his hands on Rafe's shoulders; Rafe tried weakly to pull himself up, but neither the duke's need nor his own would permit it. A voracious coupling, this, teeth and finger-nails and lips and tongues and hair and bodies yielding to each other as they moved, the guttering candle finally dying and leaving them to surrender to the dark and to each other. Eventually, after a cry from one and a cry from the other, all was quiet and all was still.

Clouds swallowed the light of the heavens, but Rafe hardly needed light to know the shape of the cheek against which he rested his fingers.

"I await your wry comment," said the duke, his voice barely a whisper.

Rafe answered him just as softly. "Alas, my lord. I have, for perhaps the first time in my adult life, none to offer."

From The Book of Kings, by Alastair Vespas

But his hopes were not to be met. For in the following year it came to pass that King Edgar, though he had thitherto been the wisest and most reasonable of men, did fall prey to the terrible malady that was to plague him and the Land for so many long years. His dreadful illness did not have quite so dramatic an effect as the madness of his grandson, King Hilary the Stag; yet still only through the offices of Good Queen Margery did the Land survive and prosper.

The cause of Edgar's illness has long been a subject of discord among medical men. Some have said it was caused by an imperfection in his blood, while others have blamed it on an imbalance in his vital humors. The folktales of a poison called shadowroot are, of course, to be classed with rumors of a Northern wizard's curse and other like nonsense. But all are in agreement on the severity of his symptoms and the suddenness of their onset. The king began, it seems, to converse with the air, as if in front of him stood a person or, at times, an animal—most often, it seems, a stag or a bear or a crow, but in no wise only these. When those around him protested, he fell into rages from which nothing but confinement and sleep released him. He grew exceedingly suspicious of all who cherished him, whom he had formerly held dear, even his lady wife.

And now is come the time to speak of the tenderness, the bravery, the loving-kindness of Good Queen Margery. When her lord husband began to rave, she took up the reins of leadership. She ruled, capable as a king, in his stead, conducting the business of the Land, negotiating treaties, and waging war when necessary. At first the people liked not to be governed by a woman, but she turned their hearts with the continued devotion she showed Edgar even after his descent into madness was complete. She mixed his medicine every evening and administered it with her own hand, ensuring that he consumed it all, lest a lackey forget for carelessness, and it was only due to the draught's salutary effects that his illness did not strike him even more cruelly than it did. The day she died, the people went into mourning for a month.

Doubly tragic, then, was the king's recovery within a few weeks of Margery's death. With what transports of joy would his lady wife have greeted her lord's recovery, a recovery that without her ministrations would undoubtedly never have been achieved!

Kaab hated wasting her time.

The carriage rattled on down the road toward the City. The other travelers had had their fill of looking at her and were looking out the window instead. Not that there was anything to see. The countryside was barren, and the clouds overhead made it more barren still. A clap of thunder startled and irritated her in equal measure. An entire morning in the middle of nowhere, spent talking to people who stared at her, and for what? Scraps of information she already had. *Rupert Hawke, Gentleman Robber, steals your money but spares your daughter!* Yes, she already knew that. She and everybody else in Riverside. Wicked Thomas. The Farnsleigh fortune and the armored carriage. The ambassador from Arkenvelt. Nothing she hadn't heard in the Three Dogs at Ben Hawke's wake. The one woman the highwayman had ever loved, the child whose birth had killed her, the boy who had become Tess's protector. His fraught relationship with that child, cold and hot, close and far. Nothing Tess hadn't already told her.

But Xamanek's light, today she had been talking to his neighbors, the people he had lived among for decades! Tess had never met Ben's father, and the men and women in the Three Dogs hadn't seen him for twenty years; they had nothing to offer but shreds of memory. But today, the women who had lived in the rooms across the hall, his landlady, the tavern keepers—they had given her nothing better. "He kept to himself," they said, and "He wasn't one for talking."

It would be blasphemous to think Ahkin of the Waves annoyed in sympathy with her, but she felt comforted nonetheless by the lowering skies.

One barmaid had said she could tell Kaab about the Gentleman Robber, but it turned out that the only words she had were in praise of Kaab's body ("delectable" was one of them), and, while Kaab was not unappreciative of the compliment, and the girl's skin was as pale as a sweet white-corn tortilla, Tess awaited her in Riverside.

Now this was a cheerier thought. She smiled the rest of the way to the City.

The smile didn't survive the wind that hit her as she alighted from the coach. She pulled her coat around her and thrust her hands in the pockets. Tess would warm them, but in the meantime, she had a long, cold walk ahead of her.

She was halfway to Riverside before something made her stop, straighten her posture, look northwest, look southeast. Yes, there was no question about it.

She was being followed.

"No, Will."

Rafe was walking down the broad avenue in the Middle City through streets gluey with mud and air heavy with the promise of rain, Will on his left, Joshua and Micah on his right. The clouds of the previous night sliced dark jags into the noon sky, reflected in the darkness on Will's face. It was not, perhaps, the best day to go seeking a home for the school that was at last within his grasp, but Will had insisted. So why was the duke so distracted?

"My students," Rafe went on, "will follow where their curiosity leads them. But first they'll be exposed to everything. Natural Science, of course, but also the humane sciences. I want them to decide for themselves what they want to study—once they've tasted it all."

"And who, pigeon," said Joshua, "is going to teach them these humane sciences? Certainly not you."

Rafe looked at his friend. "How ghastly. No, Pilson is going to join me as soon as he dons his Master's robe."

"You mean he's *forgiven* you for that memorable evening?"

"Oh, he was quite drunk at the time," said Rafe airily. "He can hardly remember I was even there. I convinced him it was Mitford."

"How on earth did you manage that, pigeon?"

"It involved a goat," said Rafe. "The rest, I leave to your fertile imagination. But now the two of them are inseparable, which makes me doubly lucky: I have escaped both Pilson's ire and his affections."

Shadowroot

That, at least, ought to have elicited a laugh from Will, as it did from Joshua. But the older man was still just frowning morosely into space, as he'd been since they set out on this little expedition. Whatever on earth was the matter with him?

"Why do you call him 'pigeon'?" Micah asked.

"I'll tell you when you're older, love." Joshua patted the boy's arm and turned back to Rafe. "But surely, you're not going to teach them *all* of Natural Science."

Rafe bristled. "Just what, my dear boy, are you implying?" He knew exactly what Joshua was implying.

"Well," said Joshua delicately, "of course you *could*. But there might be certain subjects with which others display more . . . facility than you."

"He means math," Micah put in. "You're not very good at math, so it would be a bad idea for you to teach it."

Rafe looked to the dark heavens and quoted: "'Lo, I am compass'd round by traitor friends!'"

"No, pigeon, seriously."

"I can't simply *not teach* them math. It's the foundation on which all of Natural Science—Natural Science the way it *should* be studied— is built! What do you propose I teach them instead, how to tat lace?"

Joshua assumed an expression of exaggerated patience. "No, love. You should get somebody else to teach it."

"Who could possibly be—" Rafe stopped in his tracks. By the Seven Hells, of *course*! How could he not have seen it, when it had been staring him in the face the whole time? He grabbed Joshua's head with both hands and kissed him. "You are a genius!"

Joshua lifted his brows. "Thank you?"

But Rafe was already looking at Micah, his eyes bright. "You must come teach at my school."

"What do you mean?" asked the boy.

"Look, you've been talking ever since you got here about how you have to go back to the farm and help Reuben and Amos and Seth and Judith and Elfine the goat and Ada the cow and Flora the turnip and the gods only know how you've managed to keep them all straight, but in the end you never go back. And why is that? Because *you want to stay here*. And what I'm offering you is a way to stay here *forever*. Not just until you take your exams. And to study whatever you want to study, and correct whomever you want to correct, and no one will shout at you anymore. You have a duty to scholarship! What do you think?"

He looked over at Will, who radiated gloom. "Tell him he must do as I say," he said. But Will made no response.

Thunder rolled above their heads. Micah jumped. "I—I—"

"This one!" cried Joshua suddenly. "Pigeon, this one!"

Rafe looked around to see his friend pointing at a house so garishly tricked out it would have shamed Lord Ruthven's lady. The eaves were painted a bright red, the door more intricately carved than a woman's lace collar, the windows bedecked with a cheap and dingy pink gauze.

"Joshua," said Rafe, "it looks like a brothel."

"Exactly!" Joshua was smug. "Your students can learn a useful trade along with their Natural Science and tatting."

"What's a brothel?" asked Micah.

"I'll tell you when you're older, love."

Rafe regarded Joshua. "You know, I was mistaken about you."
"How so?"

"I used to believe fervently that you had the second-worst taste of any man I knew. I see now that denying you the victor's laurel was the height of injustice." He looked over at the duke and tried again. "My lord? What do you think?"

Will spared the gaudy abomination a brief glance. "Not grand enough." His tone was short.

"Not grand *enough*?" Rafe's hands clenched. "Not grand *enough*? I do not *want* a grand house for my school. I do not want a grand house for my school today any more than I did when you showed up at my rooms last night so unexpectedly, if delightfully. I do not want a house at all, frankly; I'd much prefer to rent a shop of some kind, the more ramshackle, the better. One has appearances to keep up. The only reason I agreed to this expedition at all was that if I didn't I was afraid you'd simply do to me again what you did this morning, but there are no feathers left in my pillow, and I hesitate to think what you'd use instead."

Will ignored Joshua's laugh and stared at Rafe, his eyes wide.

Rafe snorted. "Oh, *please*! It cannot have escaped your notice that Joshua and Micah here have male body parts. They're both quite aware of the sorts of things one does with them."

Will stopped and seized both Rafe's arms. "Can't you see that your school deserves more than that? More than that dilapidated shack?"

"Will, if you call that a dilapidated shack, why don't you just have me open the school in Tremontaine House? I'm sure the duchess would love having young minds opening all around her, flirting with the lackeys, and getting their grubby lower-class fingers in the jam."

Will's hands clutched Rafe's arms to the edge of pain. "And would that be so bad? To fill Tremontaine House with people seeking knowledge, with people *passionate* about something? Who allowed themselves to be guided by their hearts?"

"And their minds," said Micah. "I hope."

Will barreled on. "To bring *joy* into the house? What would be so very, very wrong with that?"

A brief silence. "Will," said Rafe, quietly, "what is the matter?"

Will released his lover's arms. "Nothing." He turned to start walking again. "We'd better get inside somewhere. It's going to rain soon."

This time it was Rafe who took hold of Will's arms. "That's not good enough. Try again."

"I said, nothing!"

"And I said, that's not good enough. If you won't let my wretched temper and unbridled arrogance keep you from forcing me to reveal myself to you, then I'm certainly not going to let a *mood* keep me from forcing you to do the same. *What is wrong?*"

Will turned his head away, his features contorted in anguish. Joshua took Micah's hand and dragged him off in the direction of the University.

Out of the corner of his eye, Rafe saw a passing water carrier give him and Will a curious look. Clearly, the open street was no place to talk. Rafe drew Will into the alley running alongside the garish house, muddy but empty. "Tell me," he said.

Will sighed. "It's Diane."

Rafe took a deep breath, exhaled. "Go on."

"I've hurt her terribly," he said quietly. "We had words yesterday, and mine were . . . harsh."

"From you, I suspect that means you said you liked her hair better the other way."

That won, finally, a rueful smile. "I told her she had clockwork lubricated with acid for a heart."

The sound of arguing voices floated to them from the street. Rafe whistled.

"Precisely." The relief of unburdening himself, perhaps, loosed Will's tongue. "We've never quarreled like that before, and I've certainly never stormed out and spent the night elsewhere."

"No wonder you were so enthusiastic last night. And so glum today."

Warm blue eyes rose to his. "I'm sorry, Rafe. I should have told you."

"Don't be silly," Rafe said thickly. "You just did."

Will took his hand and kissed his fingertips. "Can you forgive me?"

"I could, were there anything to forgive." Rafe leaned forward and brushed Will's lips with his own, a feather on still water. There was one thing left to do—a difficult thing, but necessary. "You must go home," he went on gently. "The Duchess Tremontaine is not a woman to be trifled with."

Will frowned. "But we're seeking a home for your school—"

"Yes, at *your* insistence. Go." Rafe couldn't believe these words were issuing from his mouth. "A wife is a very complicated thing, especially when she's a duchess. Make amends. I'm easy."

Will smiled and cocked his head. "So I've been told."

"Ah, but your information is, alas, out of date. Haven't you heard?" Rafe turned, impish, and sauntered away. He looked back over his shoulder to see Will smiling at him. "I'm in love."

A razor of silver lightning slashed the sky.

"I don't know what's wrong with you today, Micah, but I'm certainly not going to check a gift stag's horns."

Micah sat back in shock as Larry swept the entire pot of bets over the scarred table, humming merrily. She hadn't made an error like this since . . . well, she couldn't remember the last time she'd made an error like this. She eyed the cards remaining in her hand. She'd known Thaddeus didn't have the Twelve of Beasts or he'd have played it off Larry's Seven of Birds. So why in the god's names had she led the Moon, when it had been perfectly obvious that if Larry played the Comet or a Crown above eight, the hand was his?

She sighed, the sound inaudible in the din of conversation that filled the Inkpot. She couldn't help it. Cousin Reuben was going to be so upset.

But the thought of a future devoted only to math filled her with such overwhelming happiness that for a moment she was almost calm. She saw a sky full of shapes, two-dimensional, three-dimensional, floating, rotating, spinning so that every moment they connected with one another and with her in new and more glorious ways, with no sharp voices to frighten her, no one and nothing standing between her and the magnificent vision.

But first she would have to inform her family, and she would have to do it in person. Telling important news in a letter would just be rude; Rafe had said so. They depended on her, and she was going to abandon them. She owed them an apology and an explanation. And that was the problem. Aunt Judith and Uncle Amos were nice. Seth was nice, even when he was upset. But Reuben was the one who came to town, and though he was usually the nicest of all of them, he definitely wasn't happy when you said something he didn't want to hear.

"Micah? Hello?"

She looked up at Patrick. "What?"

"Your play."

She examined the cards in her hand. She tried to call up the image of her likelies tables to figure out what she should play. But now she couldn't concentrate on anything but the sound of Reuben's voice as he yelled at her. *How could you?* he would say. *You know how much we need you! We can't do the turnips without you! I won't allow it! I'm taking you back home right now.* It made her elbows itch.

She shook her head to clear it and dropped her cards on the table. "I'm sorry," she said, pushed back her chair, and ducked her way out between the Inkpot's noisy, noisy customers. Thaddeus, Larry, and Patrick called out to her, but she ignored them.

The market was crowded—people probably wanted to get their shopping done before it started to rain—and the dark sky made it feel more so. Maybe Reuben wouldn't be here, she thought hopefully as she forced herself past the red-faced fishmongers, particularly loud today, past the butcher with his knife bigger than her hand, toward her cousin's stall. No, because then he would sell fewer turnips and her family would lose money, and she didn't want that. Two dirty children were chasing each other through the crowd, snaking in and out and shouting. Maybe she could just write Aunt Judith and Uncle Amos a letter after all. Maybe—

She stopped in her tracks, her mouth and eyes wide. *"Bessie!"* she called, and ran toward the spotted cow staked nearby, her arms out.

She realized before she was halfway there that the cow wasn't Bessie. She looked enough like Bessie, still, that the sight of her filled Micah with joy or relief, or both. "What's her name?" she said to the farmer when she arrived at his stand.

"Esmeralda."

"Esmeralda's spots are the same color as Bessie's, and so are her eyes. Bessie's spots are in different places, though. Bessie has one on her nose and three on her left side and five on her right side, and your cow has one less spot in each place: none on her nose, two on her left side, and four on her right side." She talked until the farmer gave her a funny look and walked away from her to the lettuces on his table, which she knew meant he didn't want to listen anymore. If she hadn't been so worried about Reuben, she would have arranged the lettuces more neatly for him.

She sat down on a stool and began stroking the side of the cow who wasn't Bessie. Thunder pealed over her, but with her hands on Esmeralda's side she was not frightened. She sat, silent, breathing deeply, as the feel of the soft flanks against her hands began to muffle the sharpness of her anxiety with images of the farm and Aunt Judith and the turnip fields. Things that made her smile.

Esmeralda tilted her head back and stuck out her tongue, which was exactly what Bessie did when she was happy.

What Micah needed to do, she realized, was to figure out exactly what to say. It was important. She thought for a moment and breathed deeply.

"Reuben," she told Esmeralda, "I'm not coming back to the farm." No. Aunt Judith always said that when you were telling people something they wouldn't be happy to hear you should warn them first that you had bad news. "Reuben, I have bad news." Yes, that was better. You should also apologize. "I'm sorry. But I'm not coming back to the farm." Or was this not a time she should apologize? "Reuben, I have bad news. I'm not coming back to the farm." No, the apology was better. Maybe.

Esmeralda tore a mouthful of hay from the pile at her feet. Stroke, stroke, stroke.

"Rafe is giving me a job teaching at his school, and you know how much I love math." Yes, that would be good. "And I'll get to spend all my time doing math." She sped up as she spoke, all in one breath. "So I know you depend on me to help with the turnips and the planting and all the other things but I think you can do them without me and if you want, I can keep coming to visit you here and remind you of things like when it's time to plow and harvest and what to do in the rain and things and I promise you'll be okay, but Rafe says I have a duty to scholarship so I'll be happy too and it will be so wonderful!"

Was that right?

Esmeralda turned her head to look at Micah, bits of hay hanging from her lower lip, and let out a soft moo.

Micah clapped her hands and then put her arms as far around Esmeralda's middle as she could and pressed hard. So solid, so dependable.

As she made her way toward her cousin's stall, though, she began to feel anxious again. It had been so clear just a little bit earlier! *Reuben, I have bad news . . . spend all my time doing math . . . keep coming to visit you here . . .* But she remembered the time on the farm that the sheep had wandered off and how loud and frightening Reuben had been when he yelled about it. The words she'd just thought of, sitting with Esmeralda, got harder and harder to remember. Reuben was going to be so angry. Wait, was she going to include an apology or not?

She caught sight of Reuben's back and started feeling sick to her stomach. She wanted to run back to Rafe's rooms, but Joshua and somebody she didn't recognize had been there in bed making noise like the pigs did when they mated so she didn't think that would be good and anyway she had to tell Reuben, she *had* to.

"Reuben!" she said, and he scowled to see her. Oh gods. He was in a bad mood.

"Wonderful," he said. "The one person who stops is somebody I *know* doesn't want any cabbage." He bit his fingernail. "In the rain the roads back will be bad enough as it is, without my having to drive them with a cart full of unsold greens."

Micah wanted to throw up. What was she supposed to say? She had been so careful, come up with something so good. But the words stayed out of her head. Finally she couldn't bear it anymore.

"I love math more than the farm so I'm not coming back and

I know you might not like it but I have a duty to scholarship," she blurted.

Was that right? Probably not. Probably he would yell at her much worse than she had expected. Her whole body was rigid. She wanted to disappear.

And then a grin split his face, and he started laughing louder than she'd ever heard him laugh before.

Reuben wasn't mad! Her body melted and she threw her arms around him and squeezed him even harder than she'd squeezed Esmeralda.

"Micah," he said when she finally let go, "I don't understand a damn thing when you talk about numbers, but you're a great kid, and if that's what you want to do, then that's what you should do." He reached out and chucked her under her chin.

"You don't need me for the turnips?"

"You've taught us enough about growing crops to last us a lifetime. Do me a favor, though?"

The wondrous shapes entered her vision again, rotating, relating, growing, changing. *Right.* "Anything, Reuben!"

"Keep coming to visit me here? And write Aunt Judith and Uncle Amos a letter every week? It'll help us miss you less."

"Every day! I'll come every day!" And she clapped again and jumped up and down.

As she ran off, thunder slapped the sky again.

It began, finally, to rain.

Kaab was fuming. The gods showered the earth with water in Binkiinha, too, but the City seemed to see more rain in a month than her homeland did in a year, if not two. And the rain here, unlike that in her homeland, was *cold*.

She looked up and muttered a curse as a raindrop landed in her eye.

She had walked around Riverside twice by now on a meandering, circuitous route, avoiding the mud and the largest puddles, taking in the whores she passed, the pimps, the pickpockets, the ne'er-do-wells, the urchins. But she had managed neither to evade nor to identify whoever was trailing her.

As she passed a secondhand clothier's, she glanced at the reflection in the window and finally saw him, across the street now, the man who had surely broken into Tess's apartment, the man Vincent said he had seen dressed in house livery at the Swan Ball.

Tremontaine's creature.

She grunted in frustration. She was tired, and she was wet, and she had lost her morning. The gods had not created her with the patience for this.

She stopped in her tracks, turned around, and stared directly at her pursuer. His hair was plastered against his forehead, water dripping from his ears, a dangerous half smile on his face. She said nothing as she crossed the street to him, simply eyed him, imperious.

"You are following me," she said when she reached him. "Furthermore, you have been plaguing a woman whose happiness is a matter of some import to me. I am displeased."

He laughed, without amusement. "Then we have something in common. *You*, girl, have been plaguing a woman whose happiness is a matter of some import to *me*." His hand moved to the hilt of his sword.

"I do not see how I can have troubled the peace of the Duchess Tremontaine by going about my family's business." Was that a flicker of surprise on his face? "Whom do you take me for, that

I should not know your mistress? Some girl on her first mission, fresh as unpicked maize, with her eyes closed to what is around her? Or is it your own pox-ridden eyes that cannot see clearly what lies before them?"

The man's half smile blossomed into something mocking, derisive. "This," he said, "will be amusing."

He drew his sword.

Kaab didn't move a muscle, but her throat closed and her liver grew heavy with fear. The air smelled suddenly sour.

She hurled a prayer up to the gods.

Protect me, Ixchel, from the spear by day and the jaguar by night.

What had she been thinking, confronting this man? Had she expected him to slink away, chastised, and leave her and Tess in peace?

Swallowing her fear, she drew her own sword. "There are customs to be observed, are there not," she said, "when two swordsmen duel?"

This time his laugh was almost genuine. "*Two* swordsmen?"

Kaab said nothing, feeling the balance of the sword in her hand.

"Very well, then." His voice rang out above the sound of the rain pattering on the ground. "I call challenge."

From the corner of her eye Kaab saw a passerby stop, then another. They had an audience. Never mind them. Immaterial.

She assumed her stance, different from the one she had learned in her youth across the Road of the Sun, but one into which, after months of work with Applethorpe, she fell naturally. Torso turned to the side, legs bent, arm lifted, elbow crooked just so, the sword loose in her hand, her other arm relaxed behind her. They began to circle each other.

Kaab stepped forward.

✱ ✱ ✱

She lunges. He parries, makes a riposte. She parries, the clash of metal on metal.

These are easy moves, testing moves. *The first part of a duel isn't part of the duel.* Vincent's words. It's strictly for information. How strong is your opponent? What are his weaknesses? Does he favor one side? Does he give anything away?

"Not bad," says the man opposite her, and she can hear an echo of something that sounds like admiration in his voice.

She, for her part, will not waste her breath in idle talk. Not until she knows it will do her good.

She was furious when Vincent made her spend their first few lessons on *walking.* Ekchuah guide her, he didn't even allow her to draw her sword! But thanks to him the circular fighting pattern the Xanamwiinik swordsmen use is second nature now. Face him to the west, one foot, the other, again, face the south. Gods, how sweet it would feel to run directly at him, as she would at home! There is something foolish in this style of fighting. Effete.

But that does not make the blade she faces any less deadly.

He thrusts. She sweeps the tip of his sword away, dances back.

This man is taller than she is, though not by much. A few inches. But where she is lean and wiry, he is muscled. Large. It will slow him down. Light, unfortunately, on his feet. His rapier is longer than hers by, what, a handspan? Two? Which means she has to stay farther away from him to keep out of his range. But it also means that she needn't get as close to him before his weapon becomes useless. A sword whose point extends past her ear can do her no harm.

His head nods up and down, judging her balance, her strength, her guard. And wasting movement. A sneer. He's underestimating her. Good. She'll use that.

As for her, everything she needs to know she sees in his face. *Watch my eyes, damn it, not my sword,* Applethorpe kept saying. This man's eyes are narrow. Veiled. He thinks himself opaque. But Ixkaab Balam is a first daughter of a first daughter of the Kinwiinik. He can conceal nothing from her.

"You will never get what you want," she says, her voice steady.

Attack, riposte. Feint from him, the whip of a blade slashing the air, feint, thrust high inside. "Oh?" he says. "And what might that be?"

She says nothing. She will tell him when it suits her.

He thrusts again, too fast, too close. She leaps to the side, barely misses being scratched. The duel has begun in earnest. She smiles, crouches lower, hears Vincent's voice in her head: *Too low.* She rises two fingers' breadth. Circle, circle.

She has this man's measure now. He still underestimates her, but he isn't letting it make him careless. His guard is high, his parry consistent. No tells, nothing that will allow her to predict any of his next attacks. She will have to wear him down. Which means the longer the fight takes, the better. "You fight well," he says, "for a barbarian."

Her left eyebrow rises very slightly. "So do you," she says. "For a barbarian."

He smiles, slows his circling steps. She follows suit. Parry, feint, feint, feint, feint, thrust center outside, yes, parry, no, no, *no!* Xamanek's light! His riposte low inside, strike, and the sleeve stuck to her arm flowers blood.

She has been bloodied many times before in combat—single,

group. But never when she has known that every wound she took brought her closer to joining her mother in the houses beneath the earth. Tears come unbidden, unwelcome, to her eyes.

Courage begins to seep from her body along with blood. She is facing a City swordsman. He is intimately acquainted with a weapon she met for the first time not half a year ago—he is toying with her; he knows what he is about, and she does not. He has spilled the blood of countless men, wasted it without the sanction of the gods.

And now his slashes and thrusts seem to come faster, faster, sharper, and sweat mixes in her eyes along with the rain, and pain, and more of her blood. She slips in mud, goes down on one knee. She can barely breathe. Up again. He batters her, drives her back toward the wall. She is blind with terror; she is doomed; she knows even as she begins to whisper a prayer to the gods that they cannot be importuned, that Chaacmul will accept this sacrifice from their priest, that—

No.

A single word, echoing, stills the roiling she feels within.

The voice, it surprises her to note, is not Applethorpe's.

It is her own.

Despair is unworthy of you, says the voice. *Have you not stood before Ekchuah's temple to celebrate the return of the morning star? Have you not danced the Water Dance in the Batab's palace with his most distinguished warriors under the first new moon of the year?*

Are you not your mother's daughter?

She knows what to do.

She reaches for the feeling of obsidian, the cool, silent force with which she has so recently become acquainted. Impassive. Respectful. Controlled.

Strength begins to spread through her, and warmth. Her smile becomes an openmouthed grin, falling rain running over her tongue. She leaps up and back like a jaguar, facing away from the crowd of spectators that has gathered to watch someone die. Step, step, yes, there! No, not far enough, *there,* back, back, damn it, *back,* but he's moved too quickly, too quickly, too close, and he seizes her sword arm, pulls her to him, hard, what on earth is he doing, his elbow coming at her, pain pierces her face, red, blooming, vicious, she staggers back toward the side of the street.

She bends over, panting, her hand on her thigh, wipes under her nose, sees bloodied rain streaming off the back of her hand. How *dare* he? Vincent almost ended her lessons when she pulled something like this move.

A swordsman never *grabs his opponent's arm,* Applethorpe had barked, furious. *Do that and you lose the duel, and probably any hope of future contracts.* She has spent months learning the rules of combat in this *godsforsaken* Land, has paid the Xanamwiinik the *respect* of acting according to their custom. Who does her opponent think she is, a dog to be spit upon, a fool to be made mock of in the sight of the gods?

Her liver begins to move within her, to heat her limbs to tingling, to urge her to strike, now. *Now.* Leap at him, do it, do it for Citlali, for her kin executed in Tultenco, for every woman killed by a man who has claimed the right.

Yes, whispers her liver as she stokes it, and it is crimson with rage, *abandon yourself, deliver yourself to me, I will make of you an eagle, striking without thought, killing by instinct, attacking, destroying, yes, yes—*

No. Her own voice again, steady, still, rooted deep in stone. Giving herself over to her liver-spirit was exactly what led to the disaster in Tultenco, to Citlali's death and the death of her kin, to her banishment here. She has no need to call on her liver-spirit.

It is part of her.

Her opponent has shown that the ordinary rules do not apply in this fight.

This is not, then, a duel.

It is a murder.

The only question is whose.

She reaches now for actual obsidian, pulls out her dagger. A handspan of chipped stone, the hilt wrapped with rough, strong henequen rope, the blade harder than steel. More deadly.

A flash of fear in his eyes. He sees that something has changed. Does not yet know what.

She drops to a crouch. Ah yes. Her work with Vincent has rendered the Xanamwiinik fighting stance comfortable for her—but this, to this position she was born.

Now is the time to speak. "It does not occur to her, you know," she says, her voice low and clear through the rain. He cannot keep uncertainty from his eyes. Apprehension. "I speak of your duchess. You dream of her; you lust after her in the dark; you bed your lovers and thrust into them and whisper her name."

His lips press together, tight. She has struck true.

"But." Make him wait. "When you are not before her, it does not occur to her that you are alive. You are less to her than her leavings in the commode."

He has begun to tremble. Now strike home.

"If she knew how you thought of her, she would laugh harder than you have ever laughed at anything since the cursed day your mother gave you to the light."

He roars, inarticulate, wild. And she sees it, as clearly as if his skin had grown transparent as the skies; she sees him fill with rage; she sees his innards clench with the truth she has hurled. It is time.

She lets her sword fall to the ground and runs directly at him, stays low as she runs, reaches down with her empty right hand, makes it a shovel collecting mud, garbage, muck, dung, flips his sword aside with a contemptuous twist of her dagger as he is still roaring, inside his guard now, hand up, fling, and now his eyes and his face are dripping with gods know what. His sword cannot touch her, and he cannot see. He strikes out with his off fist, she leaps easily out of its way.

And now she is the one who laughs, because this is so easy. He was so arrogant, so sure of himself. Now he is blind with filth. The rain running down his face does nothing to restore his sight to him. Her impulse is to toy with him, to humiliate him. She shifts her balance to step to the south, just out of his range, where she can taunt him further.

No. A third and final time. Her own voice ringing in the obsidian chambers of her mind. Do not tempt the gods.

This is not a voice she can disobey.

So she nods. Advances, lunges with the dagger, pierces, pushes. His roaring voice breaks off, he drops his sword, falls. Blood, a great deal of it, running into the mud as Chaacmul's sky pours water on them both.

She walks over, stands just north of him, his feet stretched away from her to the south. She kneels. She has never killed before. She has come close. She has *wanted* to kill, certainly, longed to water the thirsty earth with her enemies' blood. But she has never released into the world the three spirits of any child of the gods.

She puts her dagger to his throat. Holds it steady. Draws it to the west. More blood. A sigh. Stillness.

She should say something, but no words come.

She stands, nods brusquely to the spectators, and walks in the rain toward her lover's house.

From the private correspondence of Dominick Redstone, Chair of the College of Physic, to E— L—, Master of Physic, lecturer in Thelney Hall

No, Edward, my decision is final, and the fact that I even have to remind you of that—*again*—should be an indication of how pertinacious I find your repeated requests that Sparrow be allowed to return to the University. However urgently you miss thinking about his lips as you lecture—oh, yes, I know all about that; the two of you were so obvious about it that, frankly, I'm shocked Anthony stood for it at all—he has simply gone too far. There are accepted avenues of research. He knew very well what they were. And yet he chose to study poison. *Poison*, Ed. And not just any poison— no, he wanted to study a poison that *doesn't even exist*. What a ridiculous name, "shadowroot." If he wanted to spend time poking about in dusty archives, he should have done it on his own time and not subjected the rest of us to what he found, or thought he found, or—as I suspect is truly the case—pretended to find. No, Sparrow is not coming back.

This has been an annoying note to write; please don't make me do it again. I have enough annoying notes to write as it is. Next is to Tremontaine about the examination committee matter. Gods, don't you miss the days when the University was permitted to govern its own affairs?

* * *

Thank the good god, his wife was home at last, and he could make amends!

William took Diane's hands as soon as she walked through the door. She was glowing with the very last of the storm. He kissed her, his lips hard against hers, kissed her again, more enthusiastically than was strictly sensible in front of the servants, and led her silently to the grand staircase of Tremontaine House. With a tilt of her head she granted him permission to accompany her, and as soon as he had shut the door to her sitting room behind him, he took her hands again and looked into her eyes, as blue as the sky after a summer storm.

"I dare not ask your forgiveness," he said, trembling.

She flew into his arms. "Nor should you, William!" she cried. "It is I who must ask yours!" A rueful smile touched her lips. "What a miserable creature I was yesterday. In your position I don't know that I would have come back at all, much less so soon." She clutched the front of his coat, gave it a little shake. "Please, run to the Council at once, this instant, and tell them of what Rafe's friend has discovered. It will revolutionize trade for the Land. Just think of it, Will! How spectacular it will be! My love, my love!" And she nestled her head against his broad chest and began to weep.

He held her tightly to him. Oh, oh, she was such a wonder! So gentle, after the cruelty with which he'd treated her—to think *she* could take the blame for their quarrel! He did not deserve such a wife, would never deserve such a wife, no matter how much good he did the City, the Land, or the world.

He touched the alabaster skin of her neck. "No, Diane. Simply—no. I was an impetuous fribble. Yes, we can release this information, *if* we decide *after due consideration* that it's for the good of Tremontaine—"

She pulled away from him for a moment, shook her head fiercely. "*Damn* the good of Tremontaine!" Her smile was sun through showers. "Or so I heard a man much wiser than I say not long ago."

He held her closer still for a time. Then he relaxed his embrace as with a tender hand he began to stroke her hair.

"Let's leave it alone for today," he murmured. "And perhaps for tomorrow, and the day after that. When I've calmed down enough to look at things reasonably, we'll think carefully—very carefully—about all the implications." He chuckled. "*We'll* think. How silly I am. You'll lead me through the implications, and I will follow a step behind you. You only want what is good for me, and for our land and our people, and I am a fool and an ingrate to question your judgment."

She laughed, relief bright in her voice, reached up, and took his face in her delicate hands. He leaned down and kissed her again, long, full, and moved his hand down from her head to her back. He inhaled deeply. She smelled of peaches and rain, and kindness.

"I thought—" she said, hesitant, "after yesterday, that you might not—that you would—"

"Shhh," he said, put his finger to her lips, and drew her toward her bedchamber.

When they were finished, sprawled under the coverlet in each other's arms, she rang for her maid.

Lucinda, entering almost immediately, gave a deferential curtsy and kept her eyes down. "Yes, mistress?"

"Chocolate. From the new supply." William gazed at his wife as she spoke; he was unable to stop smiling.

"Of course."

They said nothing while they waited for the chocolate, did nothing at all, in fact, other than to bask in happiness. "No, Lucinda," said Diane when her maid returned and made as if to prepare the drink. "This evening I will prepare my husband's chocolate myself."

Another curtsy. "Of course, mistress."

When Lucinda was gone, Diane stepped out of bed, put on a white linen gown, drooping lace at the collar and sleeves, and bent over the chocolate tray. God, William thought, even her back was beautiful! How on earth had he gotten so very, very lucky? She had sustained him for nigh on seventeen years, him and his house. No, he did not love her in the way that he loved Rafe. But the gratitude he felt for her was real, and, as the last of the sun pouring through the window set the dust motes to dancing in the air, that gratitude grew for a moment so powerful he almost wept.

"What," he said, "is in that little pot?" He gestured with his chin toward an unfamiliar addition to the tray.

"I know you'll think me silly, William," she said, almost embarrassed, "but I've begun to take my chocolate with some of the spices the Traders add when they drink it. A foolish affectation, but it pleases me."

"Then I hope," he said, "that you will allow it to please me as well." He felt a slight alarm flash across his face. "Not *too* much, mind you. I understand their version of chocolate to be rather full of fire."

"It is an unusual flavor, and not quite what one expects. Since you request it, however, I will add the smallest pinch of spice."

Uncapping a small box, she took a pinch of what it contained, flourished it at him, laughing, and added it to the fragrant brew.

She bent over it for a few moments, whisking, then turned, shaming the carven table with her own elegance, and walked lightly over to the bed to present him with the steaming cup.

"This," she said, "is chocolate so fine the Kinwiinik ordinarily keep it for themselves. But after our ball, they were gracious enough to send us a small supply. My lord husband, your chocolate."

He took the cup from her warm hands, held it momentarily, brought it to his lips. It smelled rich and bitter. He blew on it to cool it. Swallowed. His wife had used exactly the right amount of spice: enough to lend the flavor an extraordinary depth but not so much as to do violence to his mouth.

And if out of his vision, while her back was turned, Diane had added another ingredient to his drink, the clear contents of a small vial she had not obtained from the Kinwiinik—well, the chocolate flowed no less smoothly over his tongue for it, nor did her eyes, as he drank, shine upon him any less brightly.

Episode Eleven

GO AND TELL THE MORNING STAR

Alaya Dawn Johnson

Killing a man was easy. You took a knife, of Xanamwiinik steel or of good obsidian from the Coyoalco mines, and you pushed it with force and determination past skin and muscle and bone. You struck at the heart; you severed its spirit from the body; you let the precious liquid drain into gutters on stone streets very far from all you knew before, in a land where they did not know the gods or offer them sacrifice. You killed a man, then, with less ceremony than you used to kill turkeys at home, and you left him there, and you walked away.

Death was inevitable in the service. Kaab's mother had told her so when young Kaab had first begun to understand the implications of her destiny. Those dedicated to it had to be brave and tempered, prepared at all times to send someone's heart-spirit to pass through the houses beneath the earth, or to take that great journey themselves. Kaab had nearly vomited when she'd seen Citlali's body, the side of her head dimpled and purple like a rotten squash, that last horrible night in Tultenco. Her uncle Ahkitan had had to drag her away.

This time she had walked away on her own. That awful swordsman from Tremontaine House had died on her dagger's blade, and her hands had not so much as trembled as she sheathed it and headed home. Her aunt Saabim and uncle Chuleb had commended her for efficiently eliminating the threat that the Tremontaine swordsman had represented. They were including her in discussions of what to do about the problem of the Duchess Tremontaine. Kaab should have been happy. She was beginning to redeem herself in the eyes of her family. She had a beautiful lover. The horrible weather had finally begun to warm to a bearable temperature. And she *was* happy. Surely she was.

But she couldn't sleep. She lay on her mat with her eyes on the square of light that traveled across the ceiling as the waning moon traveled across the sky. She considered sneaking away through the west gate, past the guards who knew to expect cacao if they could be understanding about such things. She could wake Tess and they could make love and surely *then* she would be able to sleep. But she had many chores to do tomorrow, and if she stayed with Tess tonight, she would be in Riverside all morning, immoderately exhausting her head-spirit on sexual activities. No, her family came first, always. And it was of utmost importance that she continue her investigation of the Duchess Tremontaine.

It didn't appear that Rafe had said anything to his merchant father about his and Micah's discoveries about Kinwiinik navigation, but that didn't mean that he hadn't. In any case, knowing what she did about Rafe and his relationship with the Tremontaine duke, she felt quite sure that he had shared it with his lover. The Balam would need a great deal of information, a great deal of leverage, to successfully counteract any move Tremontaine might make based on their new navigational knowledge. And from what she knew of that dangerous woman, it was the duchess, not the duke, who was precisely the crack in the mortar to which they needed to apply pressure.

Not that her hunch had resulted in tangible benefits, as of yet. Which was why she had to be rested and awake with the dawn to interview the Lady Hemmynge. It was her only opportunity to speak with someone who had a firsthand connection with the duchess's past.

She could not sacrifice that for a night with Tess, however beautiful. Perhaps, though, Tess could give her some insight about Lady Hemmynge, this dowager aunt of Tremontaine, and what questions Kaab should ask. Kaab squeezed her eyes shut and hugged her knees to her chest. The thought was too sweet. She wanted to linger on it like a calabash candy; she wanted to imagine herself with a lifetime of nights and days with Tess, telling her everything and hearing everything Tess had to say. But of course she couldn't. Tess wasn't part of the family, and as a woman, she could never marry into it, as Chuleb had done. Kaab simply didn't have the freedom to share family matters with an outsider. Especially not with a foreigner.

Contemplating the hard limits of her newfound joy with Tess did not make her want to cry, of course. It was certainly not responsible for the exquisite sensitivity of her skin on the woven reed mat. The mat pricked and itched and exuded the scent of drying grass and burning mesquite, the smells of the desert where she had lain in the nights during their flight from Tultenco and stared up at the stars that would eventually guide her across the sea. The stars that Citlali had been named for.

A small shadow crossed the bar of light painting the ceiling. Something scratched the wood by the open window. Kaab jumped up and reached for her knife.

But what was crouched upon her windowsill was nothing that required a sharp edge. It was a possum, a thousand needle teeth bared and eyes like twin moons in the dark of her bedroom. Impossible—there were no possums in this foreign land. Kaab felt a fright so sharp it threatened to send her head-spirit fleeing. With effort, she fought to control her breathing, to retrieve the stillness that she used in her training with Applethorpe. The possum hissed and raised its tail.

"Xamanek guide me," she whispered, forcing the words past a throat that seemed parched and sticky, coated in hot rubber. "Oh, Ekchuah, he who has dived, he who moves in the deep—" She choked. The thing before her tossed its head and released a series of small, breathy chirps. As if it was laughing. The way Citlali had laughed that one night when Kaab asked her if she was really a shape-changer, a *nahual*, like they said. *Of course not*, Citlali had answered, the way she said things she knew were lies and wanted Kaab to know as well. *But if I were, I would be a possum, for they are small and fierce and see in the night.*

"Citlali?"

The creature froze. Their gazes met for a moment that could have swallowed Kaab's souls.

"Citlali," she repeated, "I'm sorry. I never—I didn't mean—"

She couldn't continue. The possum stayed for the space of one indrawn breath and then turned with the fluidity of liquid cinnabar and jumped from the ledge.

Kaab ran to the window. What sort of possum could jump from a height such as this? Was it hurt? But though she stared for quite a long time at the ground below, the night was quiet, and she saw no further sign of it.

* * *

At that precise moment, Diane, Duchess Tremontaine, lay alone and awake in the deep of a night that seemed to have been abandoned by any blessing of sleep. She was clad in a nightdress of ivory silk, embroidered in the style of Uru at the sleeves in a cheery blue thread that had faded to silver gray over time. Her husband had presented it to his young bride during their nuptial tour of Tremontaine lands. They had been spending the night in one of the minor holdings, a dairy and supposed country retreat in the North. Diane had felt agitated and jumpy for the whole three days they passed in that damp little manor. She had finally told her husband that she was so grateful to have fled the North to marry him, she would be happy to never return there again in her life. And so William, noting her distress and discomfort in the damp chill of the great bedroom, had presented her with this bridal gift earlier than planned. He had not removed it as they made love, she remembered. He had pushed it up and let the soft, slippery folds of it catch in the small of her back and underarms. He had begun to love her then. And perhaps even she, so young and adrift and new in her role as duchess, had loved him, too, as a rescued dog loves its new master.

The pleasure, the soft and fragrant new love of those days had faded, much as had the blue embroidery of her nightdress. She was a different person than she had been then. She was a stronger person, and a smarter one. Perhaps she was not *better*, but *better* was not a luxury that the duchess had been able to afford for a very long time.

In the hallway outside the duchess's chambers, William paced restlessly on the thick carpet. He muttered constantly to himself, a stream of description, explanation, and justification that was a grotesque parody of his normal analytical habits. Instead of documenting and theorizing on the natural world, he was attempting to reason his way through an imaginary one.

"But if the sky has been eaten by green fire . . . The gods, then, must exist as an inverse to the universal principle of the unity of things as proposed by Simeon . . . Why, of course, we humans have always had three legs. However could we balance on two?"

And so on. The clouding of his mind worsened at night. Five days after she had begun administering the contents of that dangerous packet from Riverside, some society wags were already wondering if something was not quite right with the Duke Tremontaine. Soon, Diane judged, his infirmity would become common knowledge and she could take the necessary steps. It would not do to rush the process, or for his descent to seem too overly precipitous. He still had his moments of lucidity and a disquieting ability to recognize his madness even while he lost his ability to escape from it. This intermediate stage was vexing, perhaps, and carried its own small risk here in the City, but it was necessary.

If only he would keep to his chambers. If only he would let her sleep. If only he would get on with this business of going mad somewhere she did not have to hear him and remember.

Seventeen years. She had been sixteen when they wed. So very young. She had come to him with nothing but the bloody clothes on her back, the lone survivor of an attack by a vicious highwayman as she traveled with her trousseau. They had never spent more than a few days apart ever since.

Something rattled the window. A breeze, thought Diane, and turned on her side in the middle of the wide bed. It came again. A series of raps, sharp and deliberate. She sat up and placed her neat white hands on the counterpane of a rough silk nearly the same shade. She considered calling for Reynald but then remembered that the swordsman had vanished nearly a week before and was probably dead.

It was a crow at her window, in any case. Not a human intruder, as she had feared. A large crow so black it seemed she could only see its outline by the reflection of the moonlight on its inky feathers. Even its eyes were black, like twin wells. She could see herself in them: a small figure in white, drowning in the middle of an even bigger white bed. Her heart began to pound. Her fingers bunched against the counterpane. She had no voice to call for a servant and did not know what she would say even if she could.

The crow shook its head and pecked again at the glass. *I remember you,* those eyes said. *Even when no one else does.*

The murmuring voice in the hallway grew audible again. "A carriage, you say? A highwayman? I'm afraid I don't have the stomach to hear more crow stories, but thank you for the offer. You corvids are a sanguine bunch, aren't you?"

The crow spread its wings and lifted from the ledge with a few powerful strokes. Diane fell back against the pillows. When she had recovered, she rang the bell by her bedside. She asked the night maid to send for Duchamp and waited until her steward arrived a commendably short amount of time later, somewhat disheveled, but dressed for service.

"Mistress?" he asked.

"My husband's chatter distresses me," she said shortly. "He won't calm himself. Please, prepare a sleeping draft and insist that he take it, Duchamp. The duke needs his rest if his mind is to recover from this . . . strain."

Duchamp hesitated a fraction of a second before nodding. "As you say, mistress. I'll take care of the matter. I . . ."

That hesitation again. Duchamp, Diane recalled, had been in

the duke's service since his father's days. He had known William as a young boy. Seeing William deteriorate so quickly had to be distressing for him.

She raised one pale eyebrow. "Is something the matter, Duchamp?"

"Of course not, mistress. Should I be going, or is there anything else you require?"

"Ah, there is, in fact, one small thing. By any chance, have you heard from my second swordsman? Or does it seem that Reynald has run away from us?"

Duchamp's lip curled, a reaction he did not bother to hide. "I have not, my lady. But you know swordsmen. They do not live regular lives, mistress."

Diane's expression did not change in the smallest particular. Such unnatural impassivity might be the only way that a careful observer could have divined the disquiet that this news provoked. It was not that Reynald had probably died, of course—it was that she didn't know why. But even that relaxed in the next moment, as she shrugged and feigned a yawn.

"In that case, Duchamp, could you please make it your duty to inquire—discreetly—about candidates for the position? Tremontaine can't leave itself undefended, after all."

Duchamp bowed. "Of course, mistress. Will you require anything more?"

"And . . . there has been no . . . news from the Balam household? Their members seem well?"

This question did not appear to surprise Duchamp as much as it might have. "I haven't heard anything of the sort, mistress, but I would be happy to inquire with a few of my acquaintances who have regular business with the compound."

Now it was Diane's turn to hesitate. Then she shook her head. Even Reynald would not have taken it into his head to execute the Balam girl without explicit orders. After five days, wouldn't she have heard of any harm come to the girl? But just in case the Balams were guarding the news, Diane wished for no one to make even the most casual connection between that event and the Tremontaine household. "No, there's no need. That will be all, Duchamp."

He bowed and she watched him leave. Perhaps she fell asleep, or perhaps she kept her eyes on the empty ledge of that empty window the rest of the long night and only surrendered to dreaming when the sun had risen to keep vigil.

"Are you quite sure you don't take sugar? I find it undrinkable otherwise, myself."

Kaab, uncomfortable enough in the tight stays and highly starched fabric of her nicest Local calling dress, stared down at the cup of thick chocolate in her hands. If the Lady Ernestine Hemmynge had offered her cacao-blossom honey, perhaps she would have agreed. But the sugar these Locals loved to put in their chocolate was nauseatingly sweet, and with none of the complexity of honey or the nectar of maguey used at home. So she maintained her polite smile and shook her head firmly.

"I am quite content, thank you," she repeated.

Lady Ernestine shook her head and spooned another heap of sugar into her cup. "And no cream, either? Goodness, how bitter. Though I suppose if your people invented it, you ought to know how you like to drink it."

Kaab found this bit of common sense quite surprising for a Local, and her smile lost its waxen edge. Lady Ernestine Hemmynge was as old as Kaab's aunt Ixnoom, and at least as vigorous. Her dress seemed to contain twice as much fabric as Kaab's, heavily embroidered and stiff enough to stand up on its own. Perhaps this accounted for her perfect posture as she perched on the parlor chairs, whose stiff cushions seemed to have been designed with a subtle but inexorable downward slope. Kaab found herself surreptitiously wiggling and pushing herself backward so that she didn't fall off entirely. Lady Ernestine's keen eyes surely noticed this, but she merely sipped her chocolate and pretended not to. The Locals, Kaab thought as she shifted again, had peculiar ways of asserting social dominance. The lady's eyes were a dark brown flecked with green—even in her seventh decade, she retained some of what must have been a great beauty in her youth.

"I did not know her very long or very well," said Lady Ernestine, quite abruptly. Kaab froze with her chocolate cup halfway to her lips. "I don't know what you wish to learn about Diane—the duchess, I should say—but you should know that we avoid each other, to this day.

"When I knew her as a girl, she was young and vain and I thought a little stupid. Perhaps she was just young. My niece and nephew took in so many children over the years! The North is a harsh place, and they were generous, although it meant a host of brats underfoot." She laughed shortly and shook her head. "But who was I to complain? A childless, dowerless widow, given refuge by her brother's son like yet another orphan in that Northern fastness? So there I stayed—little dreaming I would find myself back in the City again, now, after all this time, and in such fine state as this!"

Kaab nodded politely and took a sip of the chocolate. It seemed a waste of such good cacao to make it without foam, but it otherwise had a good consistency. Clearly the lady was dying to tell her own tale of rags to riches, but that was of no use to Kaab. She asked instead:

"How long did the girl stay with your nephew's family?"

The lady looked past Kaab's shoulder, toward the mullioned windows with their view of a small Middle City garden. "Six years? Seven? She was young when she wed the duke, wasn't she? Sixteen, or thereabouts. Her parents died when she was ten, I believe, and so my nephew took her in, maintaining her on the little income left from her family's mingy estate. But if young Diane felt gratitude, she never showed it! She never tired of remarking upon the remoteness of Lullingstone, the lack of Important People, the lack of True Refinement. And never tired of reminding everyone that she was a descendant of the last queen, sister of the King Killer. My niece Carla, as I recall, had resigned herself to accompanying the girl to the City for her season just to find some gentleman to take her off our hands for her beauty and lineage alone . . . I know for a fact that her dowry was small! But to our utter astonishment, one day there came a messenger with the news that the Duke Tremontaine had chosen her for his son. Sight unseen. Some nonsense about the family bloodline . . . saving us the trouble, certainly, but . . . well." The lady took a sip of chocolate and licked her lips. "Tremontaine has always had a streak of oddness."

"It doesn't sound as if you cared much for her," Kaab said carefully. Kaab couldn't say that she cared for Diane herself, but it surprised her that this woman had noticed none of the qualities that now made the duchess such a subtle and formidable political player.

Lady Ernestine replaced her cup in its saucer with a firm click and laughed shortly. "I did not. I admit now that I may have misjudged her in some way, for she certainly has performed better as Duchess Tremontaine than any of us expected. When I knew her, Diane seemed to do nothing without first considering how she might use it to make someone else feel smaller. She cultivated friends and discarded them the way you might a hat. And she was vain and irredeemably silly—you would have thought her hair was truly spun gold the way she fretted over dressing it. She would keep that poor little chambermaid of hers for hours trying to achieve the most complicated styles, just to go out to a country dinner party. When one of the neighboring girls got her own personal lady's maid, Diane insisted on finding one too. Of course, she had to choose her from among the orphans at a nearby penitent hospital, trained lady's maids not being exactly thick on the ground in Lullingstone!" Lady Ernestine chuckled throatily.

"I remember that's where the girl came from, because Diane had gone with her friend on a charitable visit—such activities were popular among young girls: begging cakes from the cook, and distributing them to the poor. She returned with this skinny, silent girl in tow. She knew nothing about being a lady's maid, of course, poor girl, but that didn't matter to Diane. She just liked having her own personal hairdresser, sewing maid, and errand girl. Well, who wouldn't?"

The woman finished her chocolate but did not ring for more. She stared far away, as if Kaab weren't even in the room, and Kaab listened, silent, almost holding her breath to keep from interrupting the memories that were flooding through her hostess. "The odd thing was," Lady Ernestine said, "how much the wretched maid was like a reverse coin of Diane. Same height, same golden hair . . . but where Diane was rosy and round, the girl was thin as hunger; where Diane was bold and demanding, the girl always kept her head down, flinching, never looking anyone in the eye." The woman smiled ruefully. "You know, I sometimes felt that Diane was too silly to even remember that other people existed the way she did. If you haven't met such people, it can be hard to describe them."

Kaab took a quick sip of chocolate to cover her surprise. Vanity, she could credit in the duchess. But silliness?

"Did she really seem that way to you?" Kaab asked, after a moment of silence. "I don't know the duchess well, of course, but still it seems to me that she is . . . much changed."

"You said in your letters that you wished to inquire about Diane—the duchess—because your family is considering entering business with her. Forgive me, child, but I have a hard time imagining how reminiscences of an old woman about a child she barely knew twenty years ago could be pertinent to your negotiations in the present. I was astonished that you had obviously inquired long enough to discover the identity of her foster family. She is hardly open about the connection."

She certainly isn't, Kaab thought with a grimace, remembering the work she had put in to identify and then find this Hemmynge woman. She nodded and smiled, as though she had not quite understood the subtext of the question.

"My family is very thorough," she said. "We always want to be very sure of those with whom we do business. We were speaking of the . . . great change in the duchess?"

Now the Lady Ernestine smiled, fully and unself-consciously, painting her face with wrinkles in skin so paper thin that it glowed translucent in the light from the window to the east. "Of course we were," she said, and laughed. "My, you would have been a far more diverting child to have in the house than that pestiferous

Diane. As for her great change . . . I expect that it must have been the disaster of her journey to the City. Even Diane couldn't have survived such horror without a little self-reflection ensuing."

Kaab set down her cup. "Her journey to the City?" It sounded familiar. Had someone else mentioned this to her, back when she first began inquiring about the duchess? Something about a robbery on the road? But she had dismissed it at the time without pressing for details—such events were common on major trade routes, even at home.

"Why . . . you don't know the story? I would have thought you did, but of course, the last generation's new scandal is this generation's old story. Well, child, I will tell you, and you may draw your own conclusions. We sent Diane Roehaven off from Lullingstone in the best carriage, with well-wishes and sighs of relief, along with her hastily sewn trousseau, what little jewelry she possessed, her lady's maid, and even a young footman with a short sword to protect them. I believe most of the journey passed uneventfully. But just a day away from the City, they were set upon by Rupert Hawke, an infamous highwayman. He was known for his brutality. Well, he murdered the footmen and the coachman and the poor maid of course, and I expect he would have murdered Diane, but she ran away and hid."

At this, Kaab had to interrupt. "Rupert Hawke, Gentleman Robber?"

Lady Ernestine gave a tiny but emphatic grimace. "You have heard of him, then?"

She still vividly recalled Ben's wake at the Three Dogs, with his old friends sharing stories of his highwayman father. "'Steals your money but spares your daughter,'" she recalled, slowly. "That was his reputation. But you say he tried to kill them all?"

"For heaven's sake, child, you can't expect those ditties they compose for the gibbet to reflect a criminal's actual behavior! He was a notorious murderer. I assure you, he killed women—and children!—when there was profit in it for him. The real crime is that he was never hanged."

Kaab judged it politic to nod meekly while she considered this new information. "As you say, my lady."

"In any case, having barely survived the attack, poor Diane made her way to the City alone, on foot, with just her blood-stained dress on her back. It caused quite a sensation at the time. Tremontaine offered a reward for the apprehension of the highwayman, but nothing ever came of it. Those bloodthirsty low-lifes protect their own." Lady Ernestine shook her head. "The new young duchess sent us brief letters for the first few years of her marriage, but we never saw or spoke to her again. Still, I always imagined that Diane must have had more to her than I thought, to survive such an ordeal."

Now *that* Kaab could imagine very well. A young Diane Roehaven, just sixteen, trekking for days along a stretch of lonely highway. She wouldn't just be determined to survive after witnessing the death of her entire party. She would become a duchess even if it meant staggering into the City on bloody feet and throwing herself upon the mercy of a man who had only seen her portrait.

It felt important. She couldn't use this story as leverage with the duchess, of course, but it seemed to expose the duchess's heart and her face. Her true self, in other words. And only by following that truth would Kaab discover a secret sufficient to manipulate her.

The duke was ill, the duchess had said. The duke would see Rafe once he had recovered, the duchess had said. For five days Rafe had stayed away, assured that the duke was in no danger but that he required absolute rest—a regimen, the duchess had heavily implied, that Rafe's presence would be sure to disrupt. Against his every desire, he had agreed to leave Will to rest without the delicious distraction of his lover. Their relationship didn't mean they had to see each other every day, now did it? Wasn't Rafe his own man? A Master of the University, busy with preparations to open his radical school, certainly did not have to importune his lover while he was ill. But he dreamed of Will on the fifth night, dreamed that he couldn't sleep on the straw-filled mattress in his University rooms (which, on top of a distinct aroma of old milk, seemed to have acquired fleas with the spring). He dreamed that a light shone through the window, so bright he could hardly see. And when he went to the window, he could see that the light was a star, a violet pendant hanging low in the sky. It wasn't really a star—it was a planet, it was a living fire that traversed the sky in the night and the underworld during the day. It was a sphere that revolved around the sun, like the earth itself.

Do you truly want to know me? it asked. *Do you truly want to follow me across the sea?*

And Rafe said, *I want the world to know you. I want to change the face of natural philosophy. I want to make my lover happy, and Will was so happy to know about you.*

And the star said, *Then you have killed him with happiness.*

Rafe woke up. He was sharing the bed, and the fleas, with Thaddeus, who had collapsed there drunk the night before and proved impossible to rouse. The sky was gray with clouds in the just-brightening dawn. Rafe couldn't find the morning star in that misting rain—he could hardly find the sun. He wasn't inclined to believe in prophetic dreams, which smacked of fireside tales. But he dressed clumsily and quickly in the dim, wet light. His stomach jumped and twisted. With hunger, he told himself, because there were no such things as portents or planets that communed with humans like gods. He counted the minnows in his pockets to see if they would be enough for a roast potato. Maybe even enough for bad Inkpot chocolate, just something to wake him up, to drown the strange bitterness that rose from his chest like indigestion after a night's drinking.

He stumbled into the front room, expecting to see Micah still sleeping on his makeshift pallet in the corner. But the boy was already awake and at work, scribbling furiously in mathematical notation so crabbed that Rafe needed a magnifying glass just to read it.

"Are you sick?" Micah asked, without looking up from his work.

Rafe froze. "Sick?" *Then you have killed him; then you have killed him with happiness.* That voice was as cold as a spring morning; it was the fire of the grave. Rafe shook his head. Will had been acting oddly in the days before the duchess dismissed Rafe. But surely he wasn't seriously ill. Surely Rafe would have heard something? Felt something?

"You don't usually wake up until two or three hours after sunrise," Micah said. "And you look sick. Are you hungover like Thaddeus?"

"Thaddeus is asleep. You can only be hungover when you're awake."

Micah's furious pen stopped its movement, and he gave Rafe a considering stare. "Really? They're discrete states?"

Rafe rubbed his chest and wondered if Micah might not be right, maybe he was coming down with something. "I make a rule never to have mathematical discussions before breakfast."

"That's silly," Micah said seriously. "I think very well before breakfast."

Rafe sighed. "In any case, I'm quite well, thank you for your concern. I'm only going to Tremontaine House. I'll be back . . . well, with any luck I won't be back tonight. You can tell me all about your progress with the spherical geometry when I return."

Micah winced. "Rafe, I wanted to tell you—"

"You can still do it, right?"

"Of course! Well, the calculations are difficult, like I told you, and I'm not sure—"

"Then tell me all about it tomorrow!"

Rafe hurried out the door before Micah could find some way to detain him. He paused for one of Tom's roast potatoes but did not stop at the Inkpot. The crowd was so large it would take at least half an hour to get his chocolate, and he found that the knots in his guts would not allow him to wait so long.

Will had been oddly distracted their last two days together. He jumped conversation topics with dizzying velocity and seemed unaware that he was doing so. At times, he had stopped speaking altogether and ignored Rafe's attempts to restart the conversation. Rafe had found it impossible to do any real secretarial work, which he had assumed was why the duchess had dismissed him. And yet, why had she refused to tell him the exact nature of the duke's illness? Sometimes fevers were known to cause delirium, but Will hadn't seemed particularly hot or feverish. He hadn't really seemed ill, when Rafe considered it—just confused. His delight at the news of their navigation discoveries had made Rafe feel as though he had finally found a good and true purpose in his life: to always be worthy of this singular man and to always make him so happy. He could not have failed already.

He entered the great house purposefully, as though he had been summoned at this early hour and had every right to be here. The gate guards just nodded at him. Once Rafe was inside, Duchamp twitched an eyebrow but otherwise extended the same bland greeting as always.

"The duke is in the library," he said.

Rafe took this as a good sign. He had been fearing the news that Will was still bedridden. The library smelled of Will—of the lavender his laundress folded into his clothes and old books left open at key pages and piled atop one another like the wooden blocks of a careless child, overlaid with the clean and fragrant smoke of a cedar wood fire.

"Will?" he called. The open study by the hearth was empty, with its comfortable chairs and cheery colored light pouring from the long stained glass windows that arced with the vaulted ceiling. How many happy hours had he and Will passed there, discussing everything from planetary motion to the curious life cycle of the silkworm? The stacks of the library were well constructed but dense and narrow. It was possible that Will hadn't heard him. He called again and then heard his name spoken by a voice rough with sleep, or distress.

Will was sitting on a banquette beneath one of the long windows on the opposite end of the room from the hearth. He still wore his sleeping gown; his knees were pulled against his chest. He regarded Rafe as he approached with that clear blue gaze, but he did not smile or reach for him or give any greeting at all.

Then you have killed him with— No. Rafe did not believe in nighttime visitations.

"Will?" he said firmly. "Are you well? Shouldn't you be in bed?"

Will pursed his lips. "They gave me something to make me

sleep. But it's worse when I dream. So I spat it out and hid here. I used to hide in the library at Highcombe, you know. It would take Mother hours to find me."

Rafe stopped, unable to go any farther. Will seemed exhausted, red-eyed and hazy. His hands were chapped and covered with faded brown ink, as though he had spilled a bottle on himself and scrubbed his hands raw trying to get it off. He didn't seem to be sick in the way that Rafe had feared. He didn't look feverish or pale or out of breath.

"Will . . . dearest, what has happened to you?"

Will sighed. "I wish you wouldn't come here, Rafe. I prefer even the crow to you. It is so painful to see you in front of me, my love, and be unable to touch you or hold you or—"

The paralysis that had gripped Rafe burned to ashes. He knelt and pulled Will into a tight embrace. At first, Will merely rested his head on Rafe's shoulder. Then he gasped and pulled back slightly. He put one chapped hand against Rafe's wet cheek.

"Rafe . . . you're really here? Truly?"

"Of course I am. Will . . . I don't . . ."

Will's sudden embrace threatened to squeeze the air from Rafe's lungs. Which was probably for the best, because it distracted him from his knotting terror.

"I thought you had abandoned me. I was so sure. Perhaps she told me so—I can't remember. I know she said that she had dismissed you."

"Your bitch of a wife," Rafe said, knowing it was unwise and relishing every syllable, "can do nothing of the sort without your permission. I would never abandon you. I will always be here, as long as you wish it."

Will shivered and put an ink-stained finger to Rafe's lips. "You must not speak of Diane that way, my love. It isn't worthy of you."

Heat rose to Rafe's cheeks, some poisonous mixture of anger and shame and futility. He broke away from Will's embrace and staggered to his feet.

"Will," he said, and could hear in the broken timbre of his voice the tears that insisted on blurring his vision. "William Tielman, you are the *Duke Tremontaine*. God, you are one of the most powerful men in the land, and yet you insist on letting that little blond nothing rule you and your affairs. She should be grateful that you deigned to pull her from obscurity all those years ago by marrying her. She shouldn't be dismissing your personal secretary and abandoning you to the library while you're ill!"

"I'm afraid that I might have told her about the nature of our relationship, Rafe. We were fighting, and I lost my judgment."

Rafe felt the distinct urge to throw something, but as the only objects near to hand were Will's beloved books, he contented himself with pulling hard on the frayed ends of his neckcloth.

"And so?" he said. "If you haven't had lovers before now, that was your prerogative, and in some manner I must pity her for her jealousy, but you are hardly doing any harm to the family. Being with me causes no scandal. If she's upset, let her cry to her maid and refrain from meddling in affairs that are none of her concern!"

Will sighed and smiled with exasperated fondness, so that for a suspended moment all of the wrongness of his aspect seemed to evaporate like dew in morning sunlight.

"I always feel more myself in your presence," he said. "It's odd. Even when I disagree with you—perhaps especially then—your very passion recalls me to myself. Perhaps that was why you visited me so often. I knew that I needed to see you. To . . . better apprehend the world. Though it seems that there is so much more in it than I ever suspected. Rafe, love, did you know that even the stars can talk?"

And then it all returned, rushing upon Rafe with the inevitability of water through a breached hull. Will might seem physically healthy, but he was desperately ill. There was something wrong with him—not just his body, but that unparalleled mind. And even in this state, Will seemed to know it. To be both on the edge of madness and heartbreakingly aware of it.

Rafe bent down and pulled Will to him.

"Never leave me, Rafe."

"Of course not, of course I won't." Rafe heard his voice as though at a distance. He sounded so calm. His skin tingled, and his own consciousness of it seemed to retreat and advance, so that he was at once a small boy being held tightly by someone much larger than himself and some grotesque stretch of skin as wide as the sea, capable of enveloping Will but not helping him.

"Come," said Rafe's voice. "Come, stand up, Will. Let's get you to bed."

"No, no . . . I told you, it's worse when I sleep—"

"My love, you must rest."

He got Will out of the library, somehow. Duchamp was waiting by the door. He had probably heard every word of their exchange. Another time, Rafe might have worried about the consequences. Now he merely said to the steward, "He needs to rest. Can you get him to his rooms?"

Duchamp held his gaze for several moments longer than strictly proper for a household servant and then nodded. "Of course, Master Fenton."

Will had been staring at something on the ceiling, but at this he looked sharply at Rafe. "Are you leaving?"

"No, I'll be right there. I have something to discuss with your wife first."

Will allowed himself to be led away, muttering, "But I won't sleep. Not until I've negotiated the treaty."

Rafe found a looking glass and rearranged his neckcloth. Duchamp wouldn't be but a moment. He checked to see if he had started to cry again, but his eyes were quite dry. His fingers felt as thick as sausages. He tried again. Eventually Duchamp returned and, without a word, gently removed Rafe's old cloth and replaced it with one of Will's, which he tied expertly.

"You don't have to do that. I know you're not a valet, Duchamp," Rafe said.

Duchamp smiled slightly. "I used to perform that duty for the duke's father, Master Fenton. I have a good enough hand at it still. Now, you wish to speak to the duchess? I'm afraid I don't recommend that."

Rafe froze. "Why not, Duchamp?"

"Because if she knows that you are here, she will forbid you to come again. And this time she will warn the gatekeepers."

They stared at each other silently, both aware of words that could not be unsaid. Duchamp was at least three times Rafe's age. An aging, loyal servant, with the family his entire life. He could see what was happening to the duke as well as Rafe could. And he did not like it either.

"Duchamp," Rafe said very carefully, "has a phyician seen the duke?"

Duchamp lowered his voice. "Yes. Two days ago. He let some blood and pronounced him physically healthy."

"But he's not healthy!"

"No," Duchamp said. "But whatever ails him was beyond that physician's expertise."

Rafe swallowed thickly. "Thank you, Duchamp. I'll go to him now. Will you tell the duchess about my visit?"

"It is my duty, Master Fenton. But I might delay doing so until she has returned from her engagement this afternoon."

Rafe clasped the older man's shoulder, breaching etiquette in a rush of gratitude and grief that he could hardly contain. Duchamp nodded. And then Rafe turned and ran, pelted up the stairs and through the carpeted hallways. He would find a way to help Will. He had to. But before the duchess exercised her control over them all and forbade him even seeing the duke, Rafe had to give his dear, sweet Will as much pleasure as he could, before even that was beyond them.

Kaab's aunt Saabim was now far enough along in her pregnancy that her feet had begun to swell, and so the younger female family members took turns massaging them with oil of cacao and the seeds of jojoba. Kaab volunteered herself for this duty the afternoon after her visit with Lady Ernestine. The last several weeks had been uncomfortably quiet at the Balam compound. Productive, certainly—and her uncle was inclined to think that the projected profits on new cacao sales might be sufficient inducement to keep the duchess quiet about the implications of any mathematical studies; why should she rock the boat now that she had what she wanted? But Kaab and Saabim weren't convinced. The Duchess Tremontaine might have no interest in navigation, and if someone else here did, she *did* have the power to suppress and discredit the results of one scholar's research, but she wouldn't do so for a short-term tax deal.

It was a warm and sunny day, not as warm as it would be at home, but tolerable, for once, to sit outdoors. Saabim sat with her back against some cushions on a straw mat they had laid out in the garden. Kaab had picked a location beside one of the small waterfalls, where three adolescent Muscovy ducks were splashing and beating their wings. It would be difficult to overhear them here.

"You have been very busy of late, Niece," her aunt said, with an upward tilt to her mouth that meant she was disposed to be understanding, but that Kaab would have to be elegant and precise in her explanation. Kaab knew the expression because her mother's interrogations had often been prefaced by that exact same smile, hard as southern soil.

Kaab took a dollop of the fragrant cacao oil from its gourd container and lifted Saabim's left foot. "I have been investigating the duchess, as we discussed."

Her aunt closed her eyes and leaned back against the cushions. Kaab, however, was no longer a young sapling, to let this fool her.

"And your investigations have led you to the Riverside district quite a bit, have they?"

Kaab ground her molars, but kept the pressure of her fingers on Saabim's instep steady. "I am training with the Local weapons. And I have a lover there. My wise aunt already knows that."

"Your wise aunt wonders if her impulsive niece will once again let her physical pleasure undermine family business."

Now Kaab's hands jerked. She hadn't forgotten the possum in her window in the middle of the night. Perhaps one had snuck on board the most recent ship. And yet, if so, where had it gone? She had asked the gardeners before she left in the morning, but they had been insistent that no possum was rooting around the gum trees. "It wasn't—what happened with Cit—the Lord Itzcoatl's wife—"

Saabim sat up and put her hand around Kaab's. "It was not

entirely your fault, little bee," she said softly. "I know that. But if you had thought of your family first, you might not have put us all in such great danger."

The richness of the cacao oil mixed with the light floral scent from Saabim's loose hair made Kaab feel twelve years old again, when her mother was pregnant with her youngest brother. She remembered the comfort of being pressed against her mother's breasts, that indefinable musk of pregnancy. And her mother would have said the same. No, her mother would have judged her more harshly.

"I swear to you, Aunt," Kaab said, "I have reflected on my actions, and I will never allow such considerations to jeopardize the family again. I am a first daughter dedicated to the service. It is my entire life. My lover in Riverside . . . she is no one for any Balam to worry about."

"And if she becomes so, despite your reasonable expectations?"

Tess's image flashed in Kaab's head: her beautiful face caught in laughter, a red curl caught in the sheen of sweat on her forehead. *And if she becomes so?*

"I would leave her, of course," Kaab said as steadily as she could manage. Her aunt merely looked at her. They were both thinking of other, occasionally necessary measures to protect the family. But surely Tess was safe from that—that possibility neither Kaab nor her aunt would tempt into existence by speaking aloud.

"And this business with the duchess," Saabim continued smoothly. "If you do not find something soon, Kaab, I think we must reconsider our plan. If the Fenton boy hasn't shared his discovery with his father, that's our luck. But I think we must consider who else we can bribe or induce to discredit Master Fenton. Whatever means we choose must be thorough. The opportunity has passed for assassination—which I suspect would have been unwise, in any case. Anyone who has even heard of his discoveries would suspect our family, and we do not have such a stable position in this land to be able to kill scions of rich trading families with impunity."

Kaab wished she never had to think about killing anyone again in her life. But such a sentiment was beneath her. She merely nodded.

"Might we wait a few more days? I just discovered a strange connection between the duchess and a highwayman . . . perhaps a reason for her to have murdered Ben, that man in Riverside. I'm not sure, Aunt, but I feel as though I am close to something. . . ."

Saabim considered this for a minute while Kaab dutifully worked the swelling from her feet. "I trust your instinct, Kaab. You may have your time."

Kaab thanked her, so relieved that only her training kept her hands from trembling.

A short time later, a guard approached their mat from the direction of the east gate.

"Lady Ixkaab, there is a Local man here to see you. His name is Rafe Fenton."

Kaab nearly dropped Saabim's right foot. They exchanged a startled glance. "Have you seen the boy recently?" Saabim asked.

Kaab shook her head. "He has been very involved with his lover, the duke. That's why I thought he must have told him, but . . ."

"If he has, nothing has come of it," Saabim finished. "Well, go see what he wants, child. We will speak again."

Kaab hurried behind the guard to the high wall of the east gate. Rafe was standing just inside the guardhouse, his normally unruly hair so wild that it seemed to give him an extra two inches of height. His eyes were red and swollen, his jacket was only half buttoned, and he seemed to have lost his neckcloth. The sight of him was so alarming that Kaab's first instinct was to embrace him. But of course she couldn't do so in front of the guards.

"What has happened, Rafe?"

He gave a short laugh so hollowed of humor that Kaab flinched. "Why, only that I told my love of my great discovery—the one you took such great pains to hide from me—and it has driven him mad."

"The d— I mean, your lover has gone mad?"

Rafe ran a hand through that mane of hair, but his fingers couldn't get past the tangles a few inches in. "He thinks the stars talk! That there is a crow that follows him through the windows and tells him ugly stories about dead bodies and highwaymen! Half the time he thinks I'm some kind of phantasm as well, and then he realizes—" He choked on a sob.

Kaab decided that the guards could think whatever they liked of her. A Balam woman dedicated to the service could not be judged by their commoner standards. She took Rafe by his elbow and led him to the nearest corner of the garden, where their conversation would not be so easily overheard.

"Rafe, why have you come here?"

"I'm not stupid, Kaab. I know why you tried so hard to stop Micah and me from discovering the truth of the stars and the earth. Your family stands to lose a great deal of money if our own navigators can travel to your home country—"

Kaab smacked her thigh. "It's not just money! How can you be so ignorant? Right now we Balam have the right to your ports. But if your people start traveling to our home, you will destabilize everything! Think of the other families, powerful and ambitious, who want these Trading rights. Or of the Tullan Empire, which wants nothing better than an excuse to attack Binkiinha and the other Kinwiinik cities. What better excuse than the obvious weakness of Binkiinha's most powerful family? If your traders succeed in navigating the North Sea, then I might never have a home to return to!"

Rafe kept very still after Kaab finished. She was breathing heavily, as though she had finished a particularly challenging bout with Applethorpe. She almost certainly shouldn't have told him all of that. Traders were instructed to discuss the politics at home in only the most general terms. But she felt that, now that they had finally admitted the nature of the conflict between them, there wasn't much point to hiding its real repercussions.

"I . . . Kaab, you must believe me, I had no idea. I only thought . . . it would be a matter of money. I never told my family, you know."

Kaab searched his face, but it was clear he was telling the truth. "But the duke," she said. "You told the duke."

"He was so happy," Rafe whispered. "He wanted to tell the world. He saw immediately . . . how revolutionary it would be."

"And so he must have told his wife," Kaab said. "And now the duke has gone mad."

Rafe started to sob again. Kaab gave up and put her arm awkwardly around his shoulders.

"I'll burn my papers," he said. "I'll encourage Micah to research turnip-growing cycles. I'll do anything, just help me find a way to save him. Don't you have your own physicians? Could one of them see the duke?"

"I suppose so," Kaab said slowly. "But they couldn't without the duchess's permission. Do you think she might . . . ?"

Rafe pulled from his pocket what looked like it had once been a rather fine neckcloth, but was now being used as a handkerchief. He blew his nose several times. "No," he said shortly. "She would sooner dance naked under the moon."

"Rafe," she said, "I am so sorry about your duke. If I think of anything that might help him, I promise I will tell you."

He gave her a small smile, still genuine. "And I find that I have lost my taste for navigational mathematics. I want to found a school, not a trading company."

The worst thing was that Kaab believed him. But if this news had already reached the duchess, any hope of stopping it with Micah and Rafe had died. The duchess would understand the implications of that discovery precisely. And if she had not yet made her play with the Balam, it was only because she was arranging the pieces on the mat to her best advantage.

Applethorpe touched the tip of his practice blade to Kaab's left shoulder gently, almost apologetically. Kaab looked down at it, startled. She had barely seen him move. She certainly hadn't seen the cut.

"Match," he said.

Kaab blinked the sweat from her eyes. She meant to walk over and shake his hand, but she found her legs folding beneath her instead. She knelt among the scraggly weeds of the exposed back end of the abandoned building that they had appropriated for their practice sessions and laid her sword and dagger in front of her.

"Was that," she panted, "better?"

Applethorpe's green gaze was considering. He said nothing, just caught his breath. That last bout had winded him as well, which Kaab took as a small sort of victory. She had known that

Applethorpe was a very good swordsman from their first match, but their subsequent training had made Kaab understand the vast abyss between very good and brilliant. She would never be his equal. But she wasn't vain enough to let that discourage her.

Applethorpe rested his sword against the wall and squatted in front of her, unmindful of the dirt and grit. "You lasted nearly one full turn of the glass," he said. "That's five minutes."

She began to feel as if she were breathing a little more air and a little less fire.

"Here," Applethorpe said, and handed her the water gourd which she had brought for the both of them. She drank, but not too quickly, and then handed it to her teacher.

"Much," he said, and then shook his head and laughed.

"What?"

"Much better. That was twice as long as you've ever lasted. I wasn't holding back, Kaab. My blades didn't touch you for nearly five minutes because you didn't let them. But then, sometimes your first kill can do that."

"Do what?"

"Make you better faster. You discover things within yourself, when your life depends on it."

"How do you know it was my first?" she asked. Applethorpe didn't respond, just looked at her sadly, as though the truth were painted on her forehead and she had forgotten to wipe it away. Perhaps men like him could always tell.

Kaab wondered if she should feel something stronger than grim satisfaction, but right now happiness felt beyond her.

"Next time," she said, "I'll last longer. Next time, I might even get through."

She expected Applethorpe to laugh or scoff at her. But that

odd, considering look in his eyes deepened, and he smiled with surprising sweetness. "You just might, my girl. When you want something, you've got an edge sharper than steel. That Tremontaine swordsman had cause to regret it! You are developing a reputation. And so now I find myself wondering just what it is you're wanting."

She thought of the possum in her window, of Citlali's blood-stained blouse in the light of the just-risen morning star, of Rafe sobbing in her arms as some force he didn't understand demolished his life—and of Tess, so beautiful and so innocent of the fabric of deceit that Kaab had woven around herself. Kaab would not endanger Tess. Not even to stay with her, if it came to that. But right now she had to do as her aunt said—think of her family first. She had to find a way to control the duchess without hurting Rafe even more. Because she had no doubt that a well-funded campaign to discredit Rafe would destroy his dream of founding a school and might even ruin Micah's prospects at the University.

Applethorpe had the face of a man thinking a hundred things he wouldn't say aloud. Kaab was sure she looked the same. Finally, he shrugged and held out a hand to help her up. "Shall we go back, then? Tess will be wondering where I've kept you."

The abandoned courtyard was a short walk from Tess's rooms. Tess must have been watching the street from her window; she ran down just as Kaab was climbing the worn porch steps. Tess threw her arms around Kaab, unmindful of the sweat and grime and undoubtedly less-than-pleasant smells that clung to her clothes after several hours of hard practice.

"Tess," Kaab murmured into Tess's miraculous sunset hair, "my maize flower—"

"Kiss me," Tess said, demonstrating.

"I'm dirty. I smell very bad—"

"You smell like yourself sweating. If I didn't like that smell, my bee, I would hardly have wanted you in my bed, now would I?"

At this Kaab kissed her wrinkled nose and pulled her into a gaudily thorough embrace. "I capitulate. I am reminded that I like the smell of your sweat as well."

"Well, in that case, how about we get upstairs already?"

Kaab had planned on bidding Tess a quick farewell and heading back home, but she found herself climbing the stairs, closing the bedroom door behind her, and cursing at the side laces of Tess's dress.

"You always yell at these laces," Tess said, easing Kaab's hands away. "I wish I knew what you were saying."

"It's very improper," Kaab said. "I wouldn't seduce you with such words."

"With what words . . . would you seduce me?"

"It is a combination of gestures and words." There. Those horrible laces undone, her lover's beautiful breasts free and glowing in the afternoon sunlight. "Gestures like . . . so . . . and words like 'my maize flower, more precious than jade, more precious than the plumes of a quetzal . . .'"

She lost her train of thought, but it was all right. Tess had begun to sweat beneath her, and she smelled as fragrant as the rain in Chaacmul's paradise.

They were resting against each other, having reached a point of mutual pleasure, when Tess shook her shoulder.

"Well?" she said. "Do you think I could?"

"Could you what?" Kaab asked.

"Come to your family's home one day. I mean, officially. Not like the last time."

Kaab looked over in alarm. "What made you think of that?"

"I just thought—you know where I live. You know how I live my life. But I know almost nothing about yours."

"My family isn't very open to outsiders, Tess."

"So I'm still an outsider?"

Kaab swallowed her emphatic *yes*. But Tess looked sour, as though she had heard it anyway.

They fell silent again, still in the other's embrace, which now felt as stiff and cold as a day-old tamale. Kaab was thinking about the duchess again, about the strangeness of the story of how she came to marry the duke. There was *something* there; she was sure of it. Some part of that story that she didn't like told. Her life since coming to the City had been spotless and scandal free. But for all that the duchess presented the facade of a perfect society hostess, Kaab felt as though she could see behind that face. No one acted so innocently as the one who had a secret to keep.

"Kaab?"

"Yes?"

"I was asking about that man you killed. The one you and Vincent say was the duke's swordsman. Are you listening at all?"

"I'm sorry, Tess," Kaab said, and turned to kiss her forehead. "I have many duties that are weighing on me."

Tess sighed. "And would you prefer to attend to them rather than stay with me?"

Kaab sat up, relieved that Tess had suggested it first. "Yes. Dear Tess, yes, that is precisely what I would prefer. I must go to Tremontaine House. I must go there in person and see what I can find. Thank you for being so underst— In fact, I might need you to forge something for me. On very short notice. My family will pay you, of course."

Tess sucked in a sharp breath. "My god, you can be cold, Kaab."

Kaab frowned. "What do you mean?"

"Oh, just go. Just go before I hit you with my inkpot. You wouldn't want me to damage *that*, not if you want my *services*."

Kaab worried a little to see Tess so angry, but she could make her happy again later. She didn't have time to decipher this unexpected intricacy of Local courtship. Not with the urgency of her duty to her family.

So she pulled on her sweaty fighting clothes, which now felt merely dirty and not potentially sexy. Tess had pulled the covers to her chin and lay with her back to Kaab. When Kaab was dressed, she went around to the other side of the bed to kiss her lover goodbye. Tess let her do it, but didn't otherwise respond. Kaab sighed.

"I . . . my maize flower, I care about you . . . you can't know how much."

"Oh just hurry up and get on with your *duties*."

Kaab sighed again and left the bedroom. She found Applethorpe cleaning his sword by the window in the outside room. The walls were not thick; he of course had heard everything. He sketched her a sardonic bow.

"If it's any consolation, I have found," he said, "that swordsmen do not make good lovers."

Kaab bristled. "I'm a great lover!"

"Ah, my girl," he said, "but loving's not just about the fucking."

The lights are low in the Balam compound. In the garden, only a few guards disturb the sleep of the herons and Muscovy ducks. The rats— or any small mammals that resemble them—know well enough to keep to the underbrush when those sandaled feet pass. The extended family and other Kinwiinik have retired to their own homes on the nearby streets of this most unusual Middle City neighborhood. If one follows the dimmed lights through the great peristyle and the smaller family courtyard, through the kitchen whose banked fires glow like the braziers at the heart of the earth, and through another short hallway, one will arrive at a peculiar structure. A square platform, raised from the ground with four steps on its east and west sides, and five on its north. Upon the platform is a small stone house. By the intricate bas-reliefs and the symbolism of the high grille that is raised on all four sides, we are given to understand that this is not a house of any human. This is a house of the gods.

Inside, the family is arranged before two small altars. One is dedicated to Ekchuah, the diving god, and patron of the southern Traders. The other is for Xamanek, the north star, he whose light guides those most intrepid followers of the great road across the sea, between the clouds. A family priest pulls the thorn of a maguey through his earlobes, spilling his precious water on the altar. He has read the book of days and deemed this night reasonably propitious for a dangerous mission. The mistress of the house follows his lead, pulling the maguey thorn through her bottom lip. If it hurts her, she does not reveal it: The Lady Ixsaabim's expression does not change by so much as a flicker of an eyelid. Once all principal members of the household have given their sacrifice, the priest recites the ritual prayer for protection for a Trader about to leave on a short but vital mission. "Perhaps I have already left for the houses beneath the earth," he says. "Perhaps I have already walked where my grandmothers have walked, where my grandfathers have walked."

Ixsaabim and her young and beautiful (some whisper too beautiful) husband Ahchuleb keep their heads respectfully bowed. Their niece Ixkaab, whose many virtues have never included decorum, winces. She then induces a few more drops of blood to fall from the fresh wound on her lip to the altar stone.

When the priest has finished, Ahchuleb turns to Ixkaab to deliver a speech of the elders. The speech is traditional, and yet one would be correct in detecting certain interpolations meant particularly for his niece.

"Do not rush where caution will serve. Do not waste the strength of your sun, of your forefathers. Be wise and respectful and always centered in your heart. Do not hide from your duty; do not hide from your road."

Ixkaab grinds her teeth but manages to keep her expression humble, her gaze averted. She will be leaving soon. She feels as if she is at the door of her own redemption, that she has arrived, at last, where she has been traveling all of her life.

"Be not moved by pity, but duty," says her uncle. "Make yourself a weapon as hard as flint, as incorruptible as jade."

Her lip throbs, and she is grateful for the pain. She will think this time. She will be hard and cool this time. She will find her stillness and she will wield it, until she returns home with what her family needs, or until she dies. In the corner of her eye, something flashes in the moonlight.

She glances south, though she knows she shouldn't, though she knows her family will see. Some kind of animal, perhaps. Smaller than a cat, larger than a rat. It freezes by the doorway for a space no longer than a second. Then those great shining eyes vanish, and tiny feet patter down the stone steps.

Kaab puts her hand over her heart and touches her forehead to the floor. "As Ekchuah dives and Xamanek lights the way, this unworthy servant will give her precious water, her blood, that our honor may grow its roots into the earth."

Her aunt and uncle and the priest nod. They are satisfied.

* * *

When he'd left the Balam compound that afternoon, Rafe had taken his time going back to his rooms at the University. He stopped first at a Middle City tavern, which had nothing to recommend it beyond being open at midday and selling only moderately overpriced beer. It was a miserable little place, frequented by typical Middle City types: clerks, warehouse managers, copyists, and secretaries of a hundred ever-more-boring stripes. Their conversation felt stuffy enough for a straw mattress and about as intellectually stimulating. He only managed to get through two tankards of red ale before the arrival of a group of boisterous Kingsport merchants forced him into the street again, not nearly drunk enough.

He made his way to the Gilded Cockatrice, the traditional home of natural philosophers, and though he normally enjoyed playing a hand or two of Constellations while arguing celestial mechanics with the more hidebound followers of his discipline, today that pastime offered no diversion. He couldn't think of any reason why the revelation of his discoveries would have provoked Will's mental breakdown, but his conviction that it had was immune to logic. He wished he had never heard of Rastin, let alone set out to disprove him. So Rafe drank alone, instead. Tankard after tankard, until he had managed to numb his memory, if not the pain itself. He found himself thinking, as he stumbled out back to relieve himself again, *Why the devil does my chest hurt this much?* And for a few glorious moments it was just that, an intellectual question, a mere physical ailment that might go away with proper treatment. And then he caught sight of his breast pocket, where he had put Will's neckcloth that Duchamp had given him just this morning (a lifetime ago, this morning), and he rested his head against the filthy alley wall and felt a pain too great for tears. He could only groan, and when even that felt beyond him, he wished for the earth to swallow him whole.

It didn't oblige, of course. So he left the Cockatrice and walked the long way back to Tremontaine House. He did not expect the men at the gate to let him in, and his expectations were confirmed (*evidentiary methods*, he thought, *must be primary to logical deduction*). They were very sorry, but the duchess had made it quite clear that he was to be denied entry. Rafe considered arguing, but it seemed pointless. Duchamp had warned him, after all. So he turned around and spent the last of his minnows on a chair home. His sense of romance might have allowed for the justice of him passing out drunk on a doorstep, but he had sobered on his long walk to Tremontaine House, and, besides, it had started to rain. It occurred to Rafe that he had perhaps always been too pragmatic for romance. But this sounded like something Will might have told him, and so he started crying in the chair, and did not stop until he had arrived at his lodgings.

Micah was still sitting at his desk, the only indication that the boy had moved since this morning the remains of a tomato pie and a neat stack of coins that generally indicated some time fleecing the unwary at Constellations.

"Now you *are* sick," Micah said by way of greeting when Rafe stumbled through the door. Rafe sank into the old armchair that he and Joshua had carried home from a street corner in Middle City and always meant to reupholster. He looked at Micah and wondered when the boy had started to seem so sure of himself.

"Sick? Not drunk?" Rafe asked. He sounded hollow. But he felt about to crack.

Micah considered this. "You smell drunk. But you look . . . I don't know, Rafe; I'm not good at these things. But there is something funny in your eyes."

Rafe laughed, because there was nothing else. "Do you know,

Micah, I think you're far more perceptive than anyone gives you credit for."

"Rafe, I've been meaning to tell you, I know that I'm supposed to be working on the geometry of spheres, which is very interesting and I will still do it, I promise, but also it's a bit difficult, and two days ago I went to Goodell's class with Joshua and he was better than Volney and showed us so much! And I have been thinking about a few of the problems from that class but as soon as I've finished them I'll get back to the spheres, I promise."

"You . . . Joshua did? Goodness, from whence arose such a sudden passion for learning? And what are you working on, Micah?"

Micah peered at Rafe and shook his head. "I'm not sure you'll understand. But it's very interesting. I think Joshua brought me because he was sorry that I saw him having sex with his boyfriend. I tried to tell him that I see animals do it all the time on the farm and I don't care but he started turning red and I realized that meant he wanted me to stop talking."

Rafe agreed that Micah had probably judged correctly. Then he stood and walked over to the desk, where Micah was working on his new problems. Rafe had a passing familiarity with Goodell's work, and while it was certainly complicated and a subject of passionate interest among the ten people at the University who truly understood it, it had no practical application whatsoever. He discovered within himself an inexpressible relief. If Micah had stopped work on the navigational problem, perhaps no one else would be harmed by this terrible knowledge that Rafe had insisted on pursuing.

"You're not mad, Rafe?"

"Why would I be mad? You're doing work you love. That's more than most of us can say."

Micah sighed. "Oh, I'm so glad. You've just been so excited about the sphere geometry. I didn't want to disappoint you."

"I'm not disappointed. In fact, I'm sure that Goodell's . . . theories are much more interesting and important. Why don't you forget about those dusty old spheres completely? Focus where your talents are truly needed?"

Micah beamed. "I think spheres are wonderful also," he said, dutifully. "But it's nice to hear you say so! If you look, you'll see that Goodell's argument for a different method of describing ecliptic rotations . . ."

Rafe let Micah rattle on for a few more minutes, but he was in no frame of mind to follow. He was thinking about Will again. He was thinking about how the duchess would never let him through the front door, but he had promised Will not to abandon him.

"Micah," he interrupted. "Do you still have the clothes you came here in?"

"My clothes? You said that they smelled of turnips and weren't fit for a University student."

Rafe grimaced. "Did I? How rude of me. You didn't throw the clothes away, did you?"

Micah shook his head. "They're in my trunk. Why do you want them?"

"To wear, it would seem."

Micah frowned up at him. "But Rafe," he said, "you're taller than me."

The clothes did have a slight odor of turnips and were distinctly short in the leg, but they had been so loose on Micah that they more or less fit Rafe. Rafe then considered his hair. No farmer would grow a mane so long and unruly. Even braided, it would mark him as a University student as clearly as his robes did. He could hide it beneath a hat, perhaps. Or he could cut it. He waited for horror at the thought, but it only brought more sadness. He was a Master of the University, but this was due to a defense so fraudulent that no scholar who knew of it would take him seriously. He had his dream of a school, but the amount of political clout and influence he needed to make a success of it was entirely dependent on his lover. His lover, the duke, who seemed to be daily losing his grip on reality. What real claim did Rafe have to the University? He had entered so full of fire, but now he felt himself made of ashes.

Still, he couldn't make himself take that final step. Surely he could salvage something from this mess? So he borrowed Joshua's cloak and headed back into the night. As long as the man at the gate didn't recognize him, he had a feeling that the cook would be willing to pretend she didn't either. He would keep his promise to Will. He wouldn't abandon him, no matter what game the duchess played. Maybe love would be enough to counteract whatever force was battering at Will's mind.

Maybe it will be enough, Rafe thought, and looked up automatically for that star that could not speak. But all he could see were clouds.

Kaab walked to the Hill wrapped in a thick cloak with a hood that shadowed her face. It was useful for the walk, but her dark clothes would have to serve as camouflage enough when she infiltrated the house. She left the cloak behind a thick box hedge that lined the wall of Tremontaine's neighbors. The damp cold hit her then, but she felt the sore perforation in her lip where the maguey needle had passed through, and she steadied. She had rope in her hand and a dagger at her waist. The stillness flowed from it like the water from a spring. She would do this, and she would do this well. Her uncle's sources had told her that the duchess would be attending a dinner party tonight and would not return until the small hours of the morning. Whatever Kaab could do, she would have to complete in that window. Even the richest houses in this city did not employ soldiers, so Kaab did not have to contend with that worry. Still, she could hardly walk to the front gate and request entrance. Instead, she had determined to go over the wall. She would have to do so quickly and discreetly—if anyone saw her, she was certain they would not look kindly upon a foreign girl breaking into a Local noble's house.

The rain beat against Kaab's exposed neck and head. It felt miserable, but she was grateful for it. No servants or casual passersby were likely to be out in this weather. She used her rope to scale the outer wall, but no such method would serve her for the house herself. Fortunately, apart from the front facade, the walls were roughly mortared, awaiting repair, and cracked mortar meant sufficient handholds. Kaab judged the wall by the kitchen and felt reasonably sure of her ability to reach the second-floor window. It would be harder in the rain, but she had done even that with her cousins on the rock walls above the cenotes in Cehtuun.

"By Xamanek's light," she muttered, and jumped to the first handhold. She slipped once, when a bit of mortar crumbled in her hand, but she recovered before she fell. Her stomach didn't even jump. She felt as her uncle had counseled her: as hard as flint, as incorruptible as jade. She pushed at the window until the old catch broke and the panes swung inward. The iron catch had made some noise bouncing on the stairwell. Kaab jumped inside and closed the window before anyone could notice the draft. She appeared to be alone.

It took some time to find the duchess's rooms. Even then,

Kaab had to wait for her maid to leave. Kaab hid herself behind a tapestry, painfully aware of how easy it would be for someone to spot her. After the maid had left, Kaab waited another half an hour. No one returned to the duchess's rooms, but she heard an odd commotion nearby. It was Rafe, she would recognize that voice anywhere, but he was whispering while another man—the duke, she assumed—asked why he was wearing such odd clothes. Then the doors shut, and their voices grew fainter. Other footsteps approached the hallway where Kaab was hiding.

"The duchess will have my head when she finds out," a woman was saying.

"You didn't recognize him, Matilda." An older man's voice. "That's all you have to say."

"Like she'll believe that!"

"I think you'll be surprised. Our duchess is a pragmatic lady, and she values your ability to make miracles in that kitchen . . ."

Their voices faded. Kaab wondered what it could possibly mean. Had Rafe been forbidden to see the duke? Was the duke truly losing his mind? She shook her head, checked the hallway again, and at last entered the duchess's rooms. She judged that she had at least two more hours before the duchess would return. Carefully, she eased the dark lantern from her belt and lit it from the scented nightlight the maid had left burning. All the heavy drapes had been pulled for the night, so Kaab felt safe to open the lantern and take a good look around her.

The outer room seemed richly appointed, but was clearly meant for receiving guests. She doubted she would find anything of use here. Kaab passed through quickly to the bedroom and then the dressing room, by way of an open door to the west. The wardrobe held a number of dresses on hooks, but draped over the vanity and two chairs were four dresses that seemed to be in the midst of reconstruction. More evidence of cost cutting, Kaab thought. Noblewomen here did not take pride in wearing their own weaving and embroidery, as her own people did. They hired others to do it for them. It made Kaab respect the duchess more, knowing that she was willing to do such work creatively. But though Kaab made a rough search of the wardrobe, she found nothing beyond the clothes it was supposed to contain. She moved on to the vanity, which also bore evidence of the duchess's direct hand. The perfume was arranged in one drawer, the ribbons in another, and there were several cabinets dedicated to her jewels. But the perfumes were arranged in such a haphazard fashion—some labeled, others unlabeled, others fallen over—that Kaab could not imagine any competent maid letting them remain in such disorder unless directly instructed to do so by her mistress.

Kaab unstoppered a few in the middle, where it seemed the finger smudges on the glass were more pronounced. Some of the smells she recognized as popular Local flowers—lavender, violet, honeysuckle—and others she didn't recognize so easily. One in particular triggered an odd itch of a memory, but she couldn't place it. Its smell was very subtle, in any case, hardly suitable for a perfume. Bemused, Kaab stoppered the jar and went through the rest of the vanity. Nothing. Unless you counted the mounting evidence for the duchess's controlling tendencies. For a noblewoman, Kaab thought, she was remarkably grudging of her servants' labor. Nothing of use in the bedroom, either, Kaab decided. So she headed to the last room of the duchess's suite.

As soon as she opened the door, she could hear quite clearly the noise of two men making love. Kaab shut it quietly behind her. *So the duke's bedroom must adjoin this private office.* Did he usually take his lovers there, so that the duchess might hear him so easily? The private office bore signs of recent and continued occupation. Tracks on the thick carpet indicated frequent use of the desk on the east side. Kaab searched the desk. She tried her best to ignore Rafe and the duke, but the frantic, pounding desperation made that difficult. They made love like two men on the eve of battle, who knew they might die the next day.

The desk held three letters, partially drafted, pertaining to social events, none of particular interest. Kaab replaced the letters and surveyed the room again. The desk overlooked a window with a view of the gardens. Then there was the wall that connected with the duke's rooms. The fibers of the carpet were flatter along that wall, tracing a path along its length. And yet it didn't appear that Diane had used the door in some time: Kaab blew a faint patina of dust from the hinges. Kaab traced the path slowly, running the tips of her fingers along the plaster and molding.

The sounds from the other room exploded and then drew back like the tide. This close to the wall and the adjoining door, Kaab could hear them with surprising clarity. After a time, the duke spoke.

"Rafe, I'm afraid I'm losing my mind."

"Don't say that."

"Why not? Shouldn't I say the truth? Isn't that what you always tell me? Not to hide behind convenient lies?"

"Don't do that, Will. Don't throw my words back at me. I don't know what I believe anymore."

"Neither do I, Rafe. The things I see . . . oh god, even now, even with you, the things that I see . . ."

"Like what? Tell me."

"I see that old crow, the one that tells me stories about these two girls. And I see a great rat with eyes like the moon and the hands of a small child. It tells me that I will be betrayed by every-thing that I have ever loved. It tells me that it can still see her now, the girl who betrayed it."

Kaab put her hand against the wall to steady herself. *A great rat with eyes like the moon and the hands of a small child.* He saw a possum? It could not be Citlali. It couldn't. But the duke sounded like the priests who would consume sacred mushrooms to have visions. Kaab heard a faint click. She looked over her shoulder, but the door was still closed. She looked back to where her hand had been.

A panel, made nearly invisible by the clever molding on the wall, had snapped out. When she pulled it back, it revealed some kind of a chest, with three holes that indicated the tricky Local locks. These had been among the first technologies that her people had imported back home, and certain nobles had quietly adopted their use. As a Trader, Kaab had been trained in how to pick them. She was far from an expert at the task, but she recognized these locks and knew that they required merely patience. The moon had moved past its zenith by the time she turned the last lock in the prescribed sequence. She was sweating, and her shoulder blades ached as though someone had stabbed her. But the chest door swung open.

There were three objects inside. Two she did not recognize or understand: a battered tin trinket imprinted with some kind of Local religious symbol on a long chain, and an empty purse of cracked and aged leather. The third was a locket. The same one that poor Ben must have brought to the duchess in his failed attempt at blackmail. Kaab pulled it out: an oval of worked gold, with a jeweled swan raised above the surface. The tiny copper hinges had greened with age. And then, because she had to know, she undid the clasp and looked inside.

A beautiful miniature painting of a young girl. Diane, just as beautiful as Lady Ernestine had said. She had changed, Kaab thought. Her jaw was stronger than that of this pale slip of a child. Her face had been painted as a generous heart, though in reality it was thinner and longer. Her forehead was wider. Her eyes held more ferocity and more humor. The coloring was the same, of course. She wondered who had commissioned the miniature, and remembered that Diane and the duke had never met before their wedding. He would have wanted to know what she looked like. Still, Kaab thought, he must have been surprised. She *resembled* the girl in this painting, yes, but she seemed fundamentally—

Kaab looked back at the eyes. The slightly impatient, wide, vividly *blue* eyes.

But the duchess—the duchess everyone knew—had gray eyes.

Kaab snapped the locket shut. Two girls in a carriage. One vain, frivolous, stupidly cruel. The other sharply intelligent, watchful, ambitious. They looked like each other. The maid was fair, Lady Ernestine had told her, and the same height and coloring as her mistress. Diane was conceited and silly, often treating people as though she had forgotten they were truly human. The girls meet a highwayman. Not just any highwayman, but Ben's father. *Rupert Hawke, Gentleman Robber, steals your money but spares your daughter.* But either he made a mistake or the Lady Ernestine was right, and his reputation for gallantry was more grandstanding than truth. However it happened, the noble lady died, and the maid said, *Well, couldn't I marry a duke? Who's to know?* And she hiked to the City with a dead woman's dress on her back. The duke must never have received the painted miniature. He believed her implicitly.

And now? Rafe was telling the duke about some kind of new mathematics. Trying to pull him from his visions. But Kaab had heard the duke's voice. He was in a profound trance, one that she doubted even a trained priest could exit easily. And only after he had stopped consuming the mushrooms, of course.

And there, flowing from her hand to her nose to her heart and face: the truth of the duchess. Kaab had smelled the tincture hidden among the perfumes in the dressing room. She had recognized the smell, because it was one of the few Local imports that had regular market value back at home. The distillate of that particular Local vine, all but prohibited here, worked better even than mushrooms for communication with the gods. Though, for that very reason, it was regarded as highly dangerous and suitable only for very experienced priests. For whatever reason, the duchess had decided to use it on her husband. The very man who had been her only source of power for the last seventeen years. She was making him go mad.

If he stopped using the tincture immediately, the visions would eventually subside. In all likelihood, he would recover. Rafe would be overjoyed. And Kaab did consider it. Indeed, she longed for it.

But Kaab had seen the duchess's heart and face. A woman who owed so much of her own strength to that of her husband would not deliberately remove that pillar of her existence without good reason. The duchess needed to be in control. And for most of her marriage, she had been. But now she must be losing that control. To be willing to take such a drastic step, the duchess must be afraid that her husband could even discover the truth about her. She wouldn't have chosen to make him go mad unless it was his reason itself that threatened her.

And so Kaab's choice was clear. She could tell Rafe about the poison. But in doing so, she would bring about the downfall of the duchess. The Balam would lose the immediate benefit of the lower taxes and suffer the long-term disaster of a powerful Local lord determined to navigate to their homeland and destabilize a volatile political situation. Or she could walk away and tell no one what she knew. She could let the poison run its course with the duke.

Because then, the only Tremontaine power left would be the duchess. And now Kaab knew her greatest secret.

"Our world is but one of many," she heard the duke say, urgently. "Our star is but one of countless millions. We are grains of sand on a beach, and each grain is a constellation . . ."

Rafe hushed him.

Kaab replaced the locket where it had been, closed the chest and the panel, and walked over to the window by the desk. The rain had stopped, at last, and the clouds had cleared. The hour was late enough that the morning star was just skimming the horizon. Kaab had to leave. The duchess would return at any moment.

"My family or my friends," Kaab whispered to the sky. The stars were silent. They had no need to give her an answer that was already in her heart.

Episode Twelve

A TALE OF TWO LADIES

Malinda Lo

Seventeen Years Earlier

Lullingstone House, a ramshackle stone manor situated a ten-minute walk from the insignificant and often extremely muddy village of Lullingstone, was hardly a place suited for a noble young lady destined to marry a duke—or so Lady Diane Roehaven often thought. At sixteen years old, she was vividly conscious of her station in life: orphaned as a child and the last of the Roehaven line; raised by the Hemmynges, a minor noble family related to her grandfather's cousin; destined by birth, if not fortune, to make a distinguished match. Her destiny had come true when a messenger from the City arrived with the news that she had been chosen to wed a distant relation who was the heir to their sprawling, ancient family.

"Tremontaine," she whispered as she gazed at herself in the black-speckled mirror hanging in her small, plainly furnished dressing room. She would become the Duchess Tremontaine, and she would never again return to this godsforsaken pile of gloomy stone and crumbling plaster. She couldn't wait to leave. "Louisa!" she called sharply. "I wish to try on my blue silk gown again. Bring it to me!"

In the far corner of the dressing room, a slight, silent figure rose from where she had been sitting on a wooden stool, needle flashing through a nightdress she was sewing for Diane. "Yes, my lady," Louisa said.

Diane examined her reflection, turning her face this way and that. She had pale white skin, unblemished but for a tiny mole on her left cheek, a small, round chin, and a nose that she deemed perfectly shaped. But Diane believed her most striking characteristic was her eyes: well proportioned, delicately lashed, and as blue as the sapphire in her mother's ring, which she always wore on her right hand. She preferred to wear blue to bring out her eye color, which was why she had chosen the blue silk—specially sent to Lullingstone by her future husband's mother as a gift— for the gown she intended to wear on the day she would first meet him.

"I shall also require a blue ribbon in my hair, Louisa."

"That will make your eyes look beautiful, my lady," Louisa said promptly. "Would you like me to find a ribbon first, or would you like to put on the gown?"

"The gown first."

Louisa carefully took the gown off the mannequin where she had draped it in order to finish the last stitching and carried it across the room. The dress had a beautiful bodice embroidered in yellow thread that gave the impression of gold at a fraction of the cost, and it had taken Louisa and a local seamstress weeks to sew. Sometimes, late at night after Diane had gone to sleep, Louisa tried the dress on herself, tempted by a desire to be the lady instead of the maid, at least for a moment. She had relished the secret thrill she felt as she peered at her reflection in the dimly lit glass, holding herself taller, imagining what it would be like if she were the one betrothed to the duke. Indeed, it had not been difficult to imagine at all, for she had been Diane's constant shadow for the last two years, waiting nearby silently as Diane took her lessons in etiquette or dancing or correspondence. Louisa had practiced her own curtsies and dance steps alone in the dark dressing room, enjoying the feel of her mistress's skirts draping luxuriously over her legs.

Now, as she helped Diane into the dress, Louisa judged that it looked better on herself. There was something pinched and avaricious about Diane's face that made the dress look ill-suited, like a crown on a beggar woman. Louisa was struck with a pang of jealousy as Diane examined herself approvingly in the mirror.

"Bring me my jewels," Diane ordered. "This gown is incomplete without them."

Diane's jewels consisted of a single parure: a sapphire-and-pearl necklace, matching earrings, and the ring that Diane was already wearing. Louisa brought the small velvet-lined box out of the wardrobe and fastened the necklace around Diane's neck. Diane was heir to other family jewels, but those were kept in trust until her wedding in the City. Here at Lullingstone, they had to make do with the few trinkets that Diane had inherited from her mother, a situation that Diane often complained about. Today she seemed content, though, and as Louisa worked a wide sky-blue ribbon into her hair, Diane preened in front of her mirror. "I will be a beautiful bride, don't you think?" she said.

"Indeed, my lady. Very beautiful." Louisa, standing slightly behind and to the right of Diane, could see herself in the speckled glass as well. They were dressed very differently—Louisa wore a faded green dress that had been a castoff of the Lullingstone housekeeper's—but they could have been sisters. They were of the same height and build, and both had blond hair, though Louisa's eyes were not blue, but the gray of winter skies over Lullingstone. When Louisa had first been hired on as Diane's maid, she had overheard Lady Ernestine, Lord Hemmynge's widowed aunt, commenting caustically that Diane must have selected Louisa because Diane was vain enough to choose a servant in her own image, but Diane had never seemed to notice their likeness.

Diane frowned at her reflection and moved a bit closer, studying something at her waist. "A thread is loose here. The embroidery is unraveling! Louisa, look at this!"

A wave of irritation rolled through Louisa, but she stepped forward and asked, "Where, my lady?"

"Right here. Don't you see it? You must have made a mistake or caught it on something when you brought it over here. Your hands have been so rough lately—you must be careful when you touch my things or you'll ruin all of them."

Louisa was fairly certain she had done no such thing. She prided herself on keeping her hands smooth despite the fact that she was a maid, but she had learned that countering Diane's claims would only lead to a sound beating at the hands of the housekeeper or, worse, the steward. She swallowed her retort and said, "Let me help you take it off, and I'll fix it."

"All right. But be careful—I don't want anything more to happen to it."

"I'll be careful, my lady."

"Oh, wait—what are you doing with the skirt? Hang it over the armchair; don't let it trail on the floor. Who knows when Mrs. Gibbs last cleaned it. This place is a mess. When I'm a duchess, my home will be spotless. You'll be able to eat off the floor."

"Of course, my lady."

"Not that anyone would eat off the floor at Tremontaine House. Goodness! Take care with that petticoat—I don't want you rumpling it."

"The petticoat will be covered, my lady."

"Every layer must be perfect, Louisa. Don't shirk your duties. After all, my husband is likely to see it eventually." Diane giggled.

Louisa began to remove the pearl pins from Diane's bodice, which was rather difficult to do while Diane worked herself into a froth over the thought of her future husband.

"God save me if he helps me out of my gown on our wedding night and the petticoats are wrinkled!"

Louisa did not point out that her husband would not be assisting Diane to undress; that was Louisa's job, to present Diane in her wedding-night finery—which was what she had been working on when Diane called her over to play dress-up.

"Oh, I hope he's not horribly ugly," Diane continued. "My uncle says that Lord William is only a few years older than I am, but that doesn't mean his face will be pleasing to me. Do you think he will be ugly?"

"I'm sure that Lord William is a handsome man," Louisa said tonelessly. "Any man in your family can only ever be handsome."

"I hope you're right. But how could you know? You're only a country girl."

Louisa tried to stifle her frustration—Diane was wriggling like a fish caught on a line—but sometimes Diane was simply too insufferable for words. It would be so easy to allow the pin between her fingers to slip a tiny bit, right there—

"Ouch! Watch what you're doing! You're poking me full of holes! You can be so clumsy! If you didn't have such a fine hand with the embroidery, you wouldn't be fit to be a lady's maid."

Louisa did not allow herself to look up at her mistress. Between her fingers the pin quivered. She had drawn blood, and a drop of it had marked the edge of the bodice.

"You're staining my gown! What have you done? My blue dress is ruined!"

Diane's screeching was followed by rapid footsteps approaching the door, and a moment later the housekeeper threw it open, demanding, "What's all this ruckus about? Is everything all right, my lady?"

"Louisa's a clumsy oaf," Diane snapped. "She pricked me with the pin and look—look! The dress is ruined and I'm wounded!"

The housekeeper came to examine the tiny dot of red on the gown's bodice. Louisa stuffed the offending pin into the cherry-red pincushion, which made her wonder if it was cherry red for a reason. The better to hide the bloodstains? The thought amused her, and she barely heard the lecture that Mrs. Gibbs was raining down upon her.

". . . surely Louisa will clean this right away," Mrs. Gibbs said to Diane.

"She'd better, or I'll find a new maid!"

Louisa knew that the idea of finding a replacement for her struck dread into Mrs. Gibbs's heart; Diane was a persnickety girl, and they were due to depart for the City within the week. There was no time to find a replacement.

"Louisa, clean this immediately," Mrs. Gibbs ordered, giving her a dark look.

"Yes, Mrs. Gibbs," Louisa said, trying not to smirk. She might only be able to prick her mistress with a pin, but she had still drawn blood, and it felt as much like a triumph as winning a duel must feel to a swordsman.

"Take care you don't dirty the gown in the wash room," Diane sniped.

Still clutching the cherry-red pincushion, Louisa squeezed it until the needles and pins bit into her hand like tiny, pointed teeth. She said, "I will do my best, my lady."

The Present Day

The Duchess Tremontaine received Wickfield, the steward of Highcombe House, in her husband's library, where she had opened the windows to the warm and rather humid summer air. She had taken the seat behind William's leather-topped desk, and she gestured for the steward to sit across from her.

Wickfield was a wiry man with salt-and-pepper hair and a face that had been weathered by a lifetime of seasons in the country. He had inherited the position from his father, and his father from his father, and so on through generations of service to the Tremontaine family. Diane considered Wickfield to be one of Tremontaine's most loyal servants, which was why she had summoned him for this particular duty. He clearly would have preferred to remain in the country, for he looked distinctly uncomfortable as he twisted his cap between his hands, glancing nervously around the luxuriously appointed room. A sheen of sweat glistened on his forehead and darkened the fabric of his collar.

The duchess said, "I have called you to the City to entrust you with a task that must remain private. I need you to prepare Highcombe for the duke. He has been unwell, and I feel that a proper rest in the country will restore him."

Wickfield looked alarmed. "The duke? Of course, I'll do anything I can to make Highcombe comfortable for him. He was such a sprightly boy. . . . I taught him to play Conkers! He is very ill?"

Diane leaned forward a tiny bit so that he would feel as if she trusted him with a secret and graced him with a sad smile. "I'm afraid so. His illness is of a delicate nature. I will not speak of it in detail, but suffice it to say that he is easily confused, and not himself these days." Diane had already heard that gossip about the duke's illness had begun to spread among servants on the Hill. It was only a matter of time before everyone on the Hill was whispering about it behind their fans, but by then William would be at Highcombe, far from anyone's prying eyes.

"I am sorry to hear it, my lady," Wickfield said. "I'm sure that some time in the country will put him to rights."

"Indeed, I do hope so. You understand, I'm sure, that it is of utmost importance that the duke be given the strictest privacy in which to recover. He is not to be bothered by any guests. If any of our friends journey to Highcombe to visit him, I'm afraid they must be turned away. Do you understand?"

"Absolutely, my lady," the steward said, nodding vigorously. "The duke needs his rest and is not to be disturbed by anyone."

Diane placed her pale, soft hand on her heart as a sign of gratitude, knowing that the gesture brought Wickfield's gaze directly to her bosom. "I knew you would understand. Thank you."

The steward flushed slightly. "Anything for—for the duke, my lady."

Diane gave him an appreciative smile. "How is your wife these days?" she said in tones of concern. "I heard she suffered from a bad bout of fever last winter. I trust she has returned to good health?"

Wickfield's color deepened. "She has recovered, my lady. Thank you for asking after her."

"Of course," Diane said graciously. "I always keep abreast of how our people are doing. You're part of Tremontaine, after all. Please tell her I am glad that she is well."

"Th-thank you, my lady."

Diane sat back in her husband's chair, her hand curving over the armrest padded in dark green velvet. "The duke will be traveling to Highcombe at the end of the week along with a nurse I've hired to tend to his needs. I'd like you to accompany them, because the duke—it pains me to say this, but as you are such a trusted and faithful servant of our household—" The duchess cut herself off as if overcome with sudden emotion and took a quick breath.

"My lady, anything for you," Wickfield said.

"Thank you, my dear Wickfield," Diane said. "I do apologize; the duke's illness has quite affected me. But with your assistance, I know he shall recover."

Wickfield looked extremely flattered. "Only tell me what you need and I will do as you ask," he said.

Diane met his gaze gravely. "You see, this nurse I've hired—she comes with the best possible references, but the duke is in such a state that I'm afraid he may not trust her. But you, an old family friend of his boyhood—he will surely trust you. I need you, Wickfield, to make sure that the duke takes his medicine every evening. It is a special tincture prepared by the best physicians at the University. The nurse, of course, shall prepare it for him every day, but if he refuses to take it, you must find a way to ensure that he takes his proper dose." Diane looked as if she were on the verge of tears as she added, "Just the other day he refused to obey the orders of the physician who came to tend to him. I had to persuade him to take his medicine as if he were a child. It has come to that."

"I understand, my lady. You need not worry; I will make sure the duke takes his medicine every day. You can rest assured I will do everything in my power to support his quick recovery."

Diane graced him with a quavering smile. "I knew I could rely on you, Wickfield. You've set my heart at ease. And you'll remember, of course, that the duke is to receive absolutely no visitors at Highcombe?"

"No visitors, my lady. I understand."

"Thank you, Wickfield."

After Wickfield left, Diane sat back in her husband's chair and fanned herself crossly; she hated the humidity. She was certain that Wickfield would do as she asked without question, but the entire operation made her anxious. She had not yet decided if she would accompany William to Highcombe herself, to be sure he was settled in properly. However, she was needed in the City to ensure the smooth commencement of her agreement with the Balams. The thought of that family, particularly their unusual daughter, made her wonder again what had befallen Reynald and whether Duchamp had made any progress on hiring a replacement swordsman. She rang the bell to call for the steward. Nothing seemed to get done around here without her intervention.

Loaded down with an unwieldy canvas sack that made her sweat under its sliding weight, Kaab approached Tess's building in Riverside with some trepidation. The last time they had parted, it had not been on the best of terms. Kaab had returned from her foray into Tremontaine House with details on the forged letter she required from Tess, and though Tess had agreed to take on the job, she had not been pleased with Kaab's refusal to explain what she was up to. In fact, Tess seemed to view Kaab's reticence as a personal insult rather than a sign of Kaab's dedication to the service of her family. Reluctantly Kaab had concluded that it was time to end things with Tess, both because of Kaab's duties and for Tess's own safety. Kaab had done her best to keep Tess mostly in the dark, but due to the nature of her forgeries, she already knew more than she should. Today, Kaab would retrieve the last forged letter, and she would bring her time with Tess to a close. Logically, her plan made sense, but it didn't make Kaab happy.

Vincent Applethorpe opened the door after Kaab rapped on it. He gave her a once-over and said, "By the look on your face, you'd rather be at the end of my sword than on this doorstep."

"Is Tess upstairs?"

He stepped back, gesturing with a flourish for her to enter. "Indeed. What do you have in that giant rucksack? A gift for your beloved?"

"A dress," Kaab said shortly.

"For Tess?"

"For me."

Vincent made a surprised sound. "And here I was shocked by the fact that you wore men's trousers! Now, I admit, I can't believe you'd wear a dress."

"You Xanamwiinik have the strangest limitations when it comes to clothing," Kaab said. Upstairs, the main studio was empty. Tess's worktable was clean but for two cloth-covered boxes stacked neatly in one corner. Even her pens had been cleared away. "Where is Tess?"

"I'm right here," Tess said from the doorway to the next room.

Kaab set the sack down and turned to see Tess casually holding a wicked-looking knife. Kaab took a step back.

Tess's mouth twisted in a mocking grin. "I'm making a beef stew. You think you and Vincent are the only people who know how to handle a blade around here?" She went back into the other room, where the sounds of vigorous chopping commenced.

Vincent said, "I beg you, please make up with her. She's been in a vicious mood for days."

Kaab sighed. "Are you going to be lurking around while I do it?"

Vincent laughed briefly. "I like a bit of theater once in a while, but out of respect for my best student, I'll leave you two lovebirds alone." He was already reaching for his hat. "Besides, I have a job across the river." At the top of the stairs he saluted her. "Best of luck to you, Ixkaab."

As Kaab reluctantly headed toward the doorway through which Tess had disappeared, she caught a whiff of a faint, vinegary odor. She paused, taking a deep breath. It was not the smell of cooking, but the stink of her own disquiet. Aunt Saabim would say it was emanating from her overfull liver in a sign of her emotional agitation. This wasn't supposed to happen to her. Kaab was superbly trained and dedicated completely to the service. She should know better than to allow her passions to rule her; had she not recently promised Aunt Saabim that she would put her family first? She squared her shoulders. There was no other choice: She had to fix the problem she had created—all the problems she had created. "Xamanek guide me," she whispered beneath her breath, and stepped into the next room.

On the long, scarred wooden table before the hearth, where a fire was burning despite the day's heat, Tess had placed a cutting board and was slicing pieces of beef off a hunk that must have been enormous to begin with, judging by the size of the pile nearby. Her hands were stained pink from the blood. She didn't look up as she explained, "One of my clients is a butcher. He paid me with a side of beef on the hottest day of the year. No one wants to eat stew in the middle of the summer, but I can't let this go to waste. When I've finished chopping this up, I'll get your letter for you."

The undercurrent of anger in Tess's voice was quite clear to Kaab, and it both pained and frustrated her. She said, "You're still angry with me, even though all I've done is be honest with you about my responsibilities to my family."

Tess jabbed at the beef with her knife. "If that's why you think I'm angry with you, you're not a very good spy. Isn't that what you do in your *service*? Or do I simply not understand your ways?"

Kaab went to her, reached for the knife, and expertly removed it from Tess's grasp. "That beef doesn't deserve to be stabbed. You might hurt yourself."

Tess glared at Kaab. "Give me back my knife."

Kaab did not give it back to her. "I'm not going to have this conversation with you while you're holding a weapon."

Tess raised one bloodied hand and smacked Kaab across the face.

Reeling in shock more than pain, Kaab dropped the knife onto the wooden floor, where it dented the floorboards and skidded beneath the table. "What was that for?" Kaab cried.

Tess went calmly to the table, crouched down, retrieved the knife, and wiped it on her apron. She went back to slicing the beef. "For treating me like a fool," Tess said crisply. "You think I don't understand how important your family business is to you, but you're wrong. I understand that we come from different worlds." She gestured to the two of them with the knife, again making Kaab recoil. "How could I not understand? How stupid do you think I am? The fact is, Ixkaab Balam, you don't trust me enough to truly share anything with me. Oh, you trust me enough to have me forge those documents for you, but you won't tell me what the documents are for. If you were an ordinary client, that would be fine, but gods help me, you're not!"

To Kaab's bafflement, Tess burst into tears. She dropped the knife onto the butcher block and wiped her forearm across her eyes. Kaab said, "Tess, I—"

"I don't want to just be a forger you hire to do a job for you. I don't want to be your good-time girl in Riverside, either. If that's all you think I am, pay me for the letter and don't come back."

Kaab gazed at her, stunned into silence. Tess, with great dignity, picked up the knife again and finished chopping up the rest of the beef. Then she swept the massive pile of it into the stew pot hanging over the kitchen fire, went to a bucket of water standing by the side of the hearth, and began to rub the blood off her hands in the water. Kaab didn't know what to do. She had prepared a brief but tender speech for the moment, intending to express her deep appreciation for Tess while delicately explaining that her family responsibilities were too great to allow them to remain together, but now the speech seemed ludicrous and hurtful. She couldn't bring herself to go through with it. Not while Tess stood there, only steps away, shoulders slumped as she scrubbed the last of the blood off her hands. The curls of her red hair, escaping from the twist on her neck, seemed to glow against her white throat. Her face was downcast, her cheeks damp from tears, and Kaab could no longer deny it: The passion she felt for Tess had risen above the desires of the flesh; her feelings for this woman had moved into her heart.

This was not like what had happened with Citlali. This was not a game played by agents from different Trading families bent on profit. This emotion she had for Tess was the kind that could change everything.

Kaab picked up the linen cloth lying on the table and brought it to Tess. "To dry your hands," Kaab said softly. She saw that Tess nearly refused to accept it, but when she did, it gave Kaab a surge of hope—something she had not known she needed. "I am sorry, Tess. You are right."

Tess raised her gaze to meet Kaab's, eyebrows raised expectantly.

"I should have known you would understand," Kaab rushed on. "I was wrong to doubt you. It is simply not the way of my people to trust outsiders. We are—how do you say it?" Kaab made a frustrated sound. She felt as if all her years of Xanam instruction had failed her. "Your language! We Kinwiinik have our habits; they are difficult to change."

Tess folded the dampened towel and tossed it onto the kitchen table. "You're set in your ways?" she said, sounding less angry than resigned.

"Yes, set in our ways. Exactly that. You must understand—we Kinwiinik are like a great ship on the sea. We can travel great distances, but we cannot turn as quickly as a one-person canoe."

A wisp of a smile tugged at Tess's mouth. "I have never been on a ship."

Kaab took a step closer to her. "We have one in the harbor. I can take you on board if you like."

Tess gave Kaab a frank look. "If I tour your ship, is that simply a way to keep me away from your family compound?"

Kaab winced. "No. It is . . . a first step? Will you be patient with us? With me?"

"All you slow-moving, shiplike Balams?"

"Yes." Kaab reached for Tess's hands, and Tess allowed her to take them. "Please be patient?"

A Tale of Two Ladies

Tess frowned, but she did not pull away. "If you want me to be patient, you'll need to give me more than a tour."

"What do you want? If I can give it to you, I will."

Tess rolled her eyes. "Not like that, Kaab. First of all, you can tell me what that forged letter you had me write was all about. I don't know who Lord Nathaniel Hemmynge is, but I definitely know who the Duke Tremontaine is. What's going on? This is dangerous business!"

"I know, and that is why I didn't want you to know more than you needed."

"You already told me that you killed the Tremontaine swordsman and that he killed Ben. Why is Tremontaine involved at all? And why am I forging a letter about the duke's bride?"

Kaab released Tess's hands and went to the window, which overlooked the courtyard where the downstairs washerwoman hung laundry to dry. The courtyard was empty, but Kaab pushed the sash closed anyway. When she turned back to Tess, the forger looked distinctly uneasy. Kaab lowered her voice and said, "My family is in a tenuous position right now. Remember those star charts I asked you to create?"

"Of course."

"I can't tell you more about them—I'm sorry, Tess, but that is a true family secret. The only thing you need to understand about them is that I was using them to mislead someone."

"That farm-girl mathematician, Micah."

"Well, both her and Rafe Fenton. Did I tell you about him? He's the duke's lover, but he's also a University scholar, and he comes from a merchant family. My family trades with them regularly— that's how I met him. Rafe is working on some theories that could be extremely bad for my family's business, and I was hoping the star charts would mislead him, but they didn't. And now the duke wants to help Rafe continue his work. I can't allow that to happen. I believe that letter you forged will convince the duchess to help me stop her husband and Rafe."

"The Duchess Tremontaine?" Tess said in surprise. "How will she stop her husband from doing anything? And why would she help you?"

"The Duchess Tremontaine," Kaab said with a glint in her eye, "is not who she says she is."

"What do you mean? Who is she?"

Kaab told her the story of the duchess's journey from the North to the City and how the carriage had been attacked by Rupert Hawke, Ben's father.

"I thought that was just a legend!" Tess cried.

"No, it was a real event. The tale says that Rupert Hawke left two girls alive, but only *one* girl arrived in the City."

"What happened to the other girl?" Tess asked.

"Exactly my question!"

"Maybe Rupert Hawke killed her?" Tess suggested, but she immediately shook her head. "Ben always said his father loved that story and that he swore he never killed any girls, ever."

"I think I know what happened," Kaab said.

"What?"

"I went to Tremontaine House the other day to search the duchess's rooms—"

"Did you break into Tremontaine House?" Tess asked. She sounded rather thrilled by the idea.

"I had to."

"We'll make a Riversider out of you yet," Tess said with a gleeful laugh. "What did you discover?"

"The locket that Ben showed you the night before he died, when he said you were going to be rich. The locket you sketched, the one that swordsman ransacked your rooms for. The locket I saw the duchess wearing on her wrist at the ball. It is, my love, a very important trinket."

Tess's hands flew to her mouth. "*She* killed him, didn't she? Or at least she had her swordsman kill him!"

"I think so, yes."

"For the locket? What was in the damn locket? I saw it, and it wasn't worth a life!"

"Last night in her rooms I found the locket in a secret cabinet, and I opened it. It contains a miniature portrait of the girl who was supposed to marry the Duke Tremontaine—and it wasn't a picture of the current duchess." Kaab took a step closer to Tess. "She's an impostor! Ben was trying to blackmail her with that information, but she had him killed. She has kept her true identity a secret for seventeen years, and she wasn't about to let a Riversider get away with knowing the truth."

"What's the truth? Who is she, if not the duchess?"

"The duchess traveled here with a maid. I believe the current duchess was that maid. After Rupert Hawke robbed the carriage, he left the two girls alive, but only one arrived in the City—the girl who became the duchess. Something happened to the other girl."

"She could've gotten lost, or—or maybe she was injured? Or maybe Rupert Hawke really did kill her, and the tale is wrong. You don't think—" Tess's rosy cheeks went white.

"I don't know," Kaab said.

"But that's—" Tess hugged her arms across her belly. "That's cold-blooded."

"People kill for things much less precious than the title of duchess and all the wealth and status it comes with. People in my homeland would certainly kill to become a Balam, if they could." Kaab paused to wipe the sweat from her forehead; the room was stiflingly hot with the window closed and the fire burning.

"What are you going to do?" Tess asked, fanning herself with her hand.

"The threat of exposing the truth about the duchess is something I can use to help my family. I'm going to Tremontaine House today, and I'm going to strike a deal to keep my family secure. I created the problem with those star charts, and it is my responsibility to solve it."

Tess looked frightened. "There's nothing I can do to prevent you from using this information, is there?"

Kaab went to Tess, cupped her face in her hands, and pressed a kiss on Tess's mouth. "Don't worry about me, my maize flower."

"How can I not?" Tess whispered.

"Then you'll come with me to visit the ship in the harbor?"

Tess laughed shortly. "You come back first, and then I'll go on that tour. A first step, you said?"

"A first step. I promise."

Seventeen Years Earlier

The monotony of the fortnight-long journey south had become like a constant sore to Louisa, trapped every day in the dim, stuffy coach with her mistress, a girl who was easily bored. They had played countless rounds of Red Hearts, a stupid, silly game deemed suitable for noble young ladies, and Louisa was finding it increasingly difficult to pretend to lose. She itched to win just once so that she could see the look on Lady Diane Roehaven's tediously irritating face, but Louisa had no wish to endure the tantrum that Diane would certainly throw if she lost. So she played the mindless card game, listened with one ear to Diane's tiresome prattle about her wedding, and gazed out the small window at the passing countryside, yearning to escape.

She hadn't truly understood how vast the Land was. Lullingstone House was so far north that, as they traveled south, the seasons began to change. When they left, the ground had been barely thawed, with the first crocuses struggling to bloom, but one afternoon when they stopped to water the horses, Louisa climbed out on stiff legs to discover that the air was warm, the trees were covered in newly budded leaves, and dainty yellow flowers blossomed on the edges of the road. Behind them, twin ruts ran like brown ribbons through the woods, green grass tufting up in the center. She could not see the end of the forest, and though she was standing beside the coach and could hear the coachman talking to the footmen, she felt as if she were alone.

Louisa knew that she would never return to Lullingstone. Even if, when they arrived in the City, her mistress decided to let her go and hire a new, more fashionable lady's maid, Louisa would not go back. This was a one-way journey for her, too, and though she had no choice but to take it, an excited thrill went through her at the thought of what was in store. When she was a child at the penitent hospital, one of the nurses who worked there had come from the City, and she often reminisced about the crowded, cobblestoned streets, where buildings pressed against one another shoulder to shoulder, the sky reduced to a narrow strip above. The nurse had particularly missed the City's great market squares, packed with vendors selling all sorts of things: fabrics from far-off lands, fresh fruits and vegetables grown especially for City dwellers, even exotic delicacies like saffron and vanilla and chocolate. Louisa had no idea what those things tasted like, but she had whispered the words to herself as if they were candies on her tongue. Later, during Diane's lessons in etiquette, housekeeping, and deportment, Louisa had often snuck away from her own tasks to secretly listen at the door, imagining herself in Diane's place. She could nearly hear the ring of porcelain chocolate cups on silver trays, the tap of heeled shoes on polished marble floors, and the luxurious rustle of silk and velvet skirts. The City called to her, and Louisa was determined to make her life there, no matter what happened.

"Louisa! Where are you? We have to move on."

Diane's shrill voice grated through the still air. Louisa turned away from the road and climbed back into the coach. "Yes, my lady," she said, and pulled the door shut.

Diane gave her a curious look. "Whatever were you doing out there? There's nothing to see, only endless trees."

The coach jerked into motion again. "I needed a breath of fresh air, my lady," Louisa said. She reached down into her bag to pull out her sewing. She was nearly finished with the nightdress and hoped to complete it by the end of the day.

"Oh, I can hardly bear how long this journey is taking," Diane moaned. "A week, and we are only halfway through! I am so eager to meet my husband and to see Tremontaine House."

"He is sure to be handsome," Louisa murmured, barely paying attention.

"It is so fitting, I think, that I am marrying the duke. Do you know what Lady Hemmynge said to me? She said that I was destined before my birth for this marriage because I am the last of the Roehaven line. My destiny is to carry on the Roehaven bloodline, Louisa. Isn't that terribly romantic?"

"Indeed, my lady," Louisa said flatly. Diane had regaled her with this family history so many times she could have repeated it word for word. Diane's self-important belief in her superiority simply due to her ancestors struck Louisa as patently ridiculous, but of course she could never voice that opinion to her mistress. The Roehavens were an offshoot of the famous Tremontaine family at the time of the kings, true, but she didn't see why their blood in particular was so special. They were still a family long rooted in the North, and in the North, everyone was related to everyone else: They all had the blood of the ancient kings in them. *I am as good as you are,* Louisa thought as Diane continued to go on about family honor and noble ancestors. *And a good deal less of an idiot.*

"Did you know I was named after the great southern queen Diane?" Diane said.

"I have heard so," Louisa said, pretending for the thousandth time to be educated by her mistress.

"She united the North and South so long ago. How funny it is that now I am traveling south in order to unite the Tremontaine family!"

"Very fitting, my lady," Louisa said.

"I am going to be a wonderful duchess," Diane said.

Louisa gritted her teeth and kept sewing.

The Present Day

The round silver tray on which the Duchess Tremontaine had laid out the duke's daily medicinal draught was a pretty thing, engraved with the Tremontaine swan floating in a serene lake, willow branches arching over it in the shape of a heart. The tray held a pressed linen napkin and a small crystal glass full of amber liquid: brandy mixed with the proper dose of tincture and sweetened with a few drops of honey. The duchess kept the tray in her private dressing room and carried it herself to her husband. This afternoon, when she swept into his bedroom, she found the duke sprawled listlessly in the wingback chair before the fire, which was burning despite the summer heat. Beads of sweat had formed on his forehead, and Diane put the tray down on a side table and reached for a handkerchief to blot his skin.

He flinched away from her. "I don't need that," he hissed. "I need my—who are you?"

He fixed a feverish gaze on her, and the distrust in it was so strong she almost took a step back. But Diane did not allow herself to be cowed. "I am your wife, and you are the Duke Tremontaine. Have you forgotten again?"

He had deteriorated significantly in the last few days, and though she had expected that, his loss of memory was a startling and unsettling development. He was becoming less and less the man she had married, and she allowed herself a moment of regret that she had been forced to this juncture. She well remembered the first time she saw him, seventeen years ago, on the day of her arrival in the City. The duke had been a gangling young man of twenty-three at the time, on the cusp of growing into the handsome maturity of adulthood. The first time he had looked at her, dirty, bruised, and nearly undone by the horrible experience on the highway, she knew that he had seen through the grime to the beauty underneath. He had always been on her side, comforting her as she told the story of what had befallen her on the journey from Lullingstone, defending her to his mother when she initially pronounced that Diane was too countrified to be a proper duchess. He had even offered her the assistance of his own valet to interview new lady's maids. He had been altogether wonderful in those early days, and she had found it quite easy to convince herself she was falling in love with him.

Perhaps it was fitting, then, to find that love ending just as quickly.

"I'm not married," the duke now said, gazing at her with frighteningly bright eyes. "You are not my wife."

The first time he had spoken such words had pained her, but no more. It was a consequence of his illness, and she found it increasingly irritating. "I am your wife," she insisted. "You are sick, my love. You must drink your medicine so that you may recover." She moved to pick up the crystal glass, but he gripped her arm with bruising force. She let out a small whimper of surprise, but he did not notice.

"Where is my love? Where is Rafe? Have you done something to him?"

She jerked her arm away from his hand. "You have no need of a secretary in your state, my lord. I have sent him away so that you may recover in peace."

"He is not my secretary," the duke said, his voice suddenly weakened. He sounded as if he were about to burst into tears.

Diane marched briskly to the side table and picked up his medicinal draught. "You must drink this, my love. It will make you feel better."

He turned away from her as a sick child might. "No. I will not take anything from you."

The flat, empty tone in his voice sounded more sane than anything he had said in days, and for a moment Diane wondered if he had guessed the truth. But that was impossible. "Very well," she said, and set the glass back on the silver tray. "I will send up some chocolate for you, then."

He said nothing.

She lifted the tray and exited his bedroom. In the corridor, the footman was trying his best to appear as if he had heard nothing. "Where is Duchamp?" Diane asked. "Bring him here." When the steward arrived minutes later, Diane handed him the silver tray. "The duke refuses to take his medicine on its own. Fix him a cup of chocolate and add the medicine, then serve it to him. Take care that he drinks it."

Duchamp took the tray from her. "Yes, my lady."

The duchess turned away from her husband's room, steadfastly ignoring the lump of regret that had lodged itself in her throat.

Seventeen Years Earlier

The coach had been traveling all day, and as daylight faded into the murky soup of dusk, Louisa set aside her sewing and took up her knitting needles. She had unraveled one of Diane's old shawls and was reusing the yarn to knit herself a lacy cape, suitable for cool spring evenings. The task was simple enough that she didn't need light to do it; her fingers fell into the steady, familiar rhythm on their own. Across from her in the coach, Diane snored lightly as she slept, the skirt of her blue silk gown taking up most of the remaining space.

That morning, Diane had insisted on wearing her new gown because she believed they would arrive in the City by the end of the day, but night was rapidly falling and there was still no sign of it. Louisa had overheard the coachman telling one of the footmen that it was unlikely they would reach the City that evening. Spring rains had washed out the road in several places over the course of their journey, and though they had now been traveling for a fortnight, they were probably at least a day behind schedule. But Diane's eagerness to show off to her husband could not be contained by such mundane things as reality. Unfortunately for Louisa, the gown had become hopelessly crumpled in the small space of the coach, and she would have to find some means of refreshing it at the next inn or she would be blamed for Diane's mistaken decision to put it on a full day too early.

The coach pulled to a sudden halt, causing Louisa to lurch forward and nearly drop her knitting. Loud voices from outside cut into the silence, and Diane moved, her skirts whispering as she sat up.

"Are we at Tremontaine House?" Diane asked in a sleepy voice.

"No," Louisa said.

One of the voices they heard—a man's voice, accented oddly to Louisa's Northern ears—was unfamiliar to her. "If you do what I ask, it might be we have an agreement," the man said, and then laughed. "But of course, we might not."

"Move aside—you're blocking the road," the coachman called. "There is no toll here to pay."

"Ah! No toll, not to the locals," the stranger said, his mocking tone sending a chill down Louisa's spine. "But a toll to *me*."

"We don't pay tolls to the likes of you," the coachman snorted.

Louisa heard the unmistakable rasp of a sword being drawn from its scabbard, and she froze in place, her fingers clenching around her knitting needles and yarn. A highwayman. There were many stories of travelers being robbed on the road to the City, but it had never occurred to her that she might be in danger.

"Who is that?" Diane whispered, reaching out to grip her forearm.

Louisa couldn't see much. Twilight made the nearby trees

melt into darkness. The coach abruptly rocked, as if someone had jumped off the footboard.

"Move aside," came a voice. It was one of the footmen. He was a young local man, eager to leave Lullingstone behind. "We have a right of passage on this road," he said, but the tremble in his voice belied his words.

The highwayman chuckled. "I see you've a short sword. Know how to use it?"

Louisa flinched at the first smack of metal on metal. It was followed by the rough scrape of boots over the dirt ground, a breathless gasp or two, a strangled yelp, and a thud like a sack of flour being tossed onto the ground. Diane trembled, shrinking down in the seat beside Louisa, who continued to sit stock-still with her eyes fixed out the window. The coach began to move again, but before they had gone more than one turn of the wheels, they jerked to a stop.

"Not so fast!" the highwayman cried, and it sounded as if he was dragging the coachman off his seat, the man's body banging against the wheels and sending the coach rocking. Louisa couldn't see what was happening, but she heard another horrific thump, accompanied by a cracking sound as if someone's limbs were being broken. A man screamed horribly, over and over again, until his voice cut off into an awful, gurgling sound. The coachman was dead—or at least incapacitated, and thus useless. That left them with but one more defender, the second footman.

He suddenly came into view through the window, holding a dagger in front of him. A sword was pressing him back, the blade a hard-edged shadow in the fading light, and at the hilt of the sword was a man with a mean grin on his face, as if he relished the sight of the footman retreating before him.

It was a brutal, unmatched battle. The footman had no real chance—his dagger was no defense against a sword—and before more than a few breaths had passed, the highwayman pierced the footman in the chest. He slumped forward over the blade, reaching out with weakening arms in an attempt to stab the highwayman, who shoved the dying man back and yanked his sword out of his chest. Blood dripped from the steel and the wound in the footman's chest.

Louisa knew she should be terrified, but instead she was overcome with an awful calm, as if what was happening outside the coach had nothing to do with her at all. How could it? It was so horrific; she had never seen anything like it. She watched the footman fall to his knees, his breath emerging in a wheezing groan, and then the highwayman said almost pleasantly, "Good night." He slashed the sword across the footman's throat with such force that his head snapped back as if on a hinge, and the footman collapsed onto his side, his body twitching.

Louisa saw the highwayman glance at the coach. He must know that someone was cowering within. Louisa became aware of Diane's death grip on her arm, and perhaps some of her mistress's breathless fear infected her at last, because as the highwayman approached the door, Louisa suddenly realized what could happen: He might kill them. In fact, he probably would. At the last second, he hesitated in front of the door. His gaze sought hers in the shadows, and she shrank away, pressing back against Diane, who trembled in fright.

The highwayman turned aside and walked toward the rear of the coach.

Louisa let out her breath, and Diane gasped, "Is he leaving?"

Judging by the sounds they heard, he was pulling their trunks down and rifling through their things. He began to sing in a horrible, off-key voice. It was a song about another highwayman, one who had hanged in a town square in the midsummer sun. Louisa peeled Diane's fingers off her arm and pulled her knitting needles free from the yarn.

"What are we going to do?" Diane whispered frantically. "He's stealing my trousseau! My sapphire necklace is in my trunk!" She grabbed for Louisa again, causing her to drop one of the knitting needles. It clattered loudly onto the wooden floor, and the highwayman stopped singing. Louisa and Diane both stopped breathing.

Louisa hastily shoved the other knitting needle up her right sleeve and fumbled around on the floor of the coach for the dropped one, but she couldn't find it. It must have rolled beneath the seat or into the crack between the door and the coach floor. It was so dark now she could barely see Diane beside her; she'd never be able to find the other needle. Her fruitless search came to a halt when the coach door was pulled open without warning, and standing before them was the ominous silhouette of the highwayman.

"What have we here?" he said in the same pleasant tone he'd used before slitting the footman's throat.

Diane screamed. She screamed and screamed and screamed, her voice so piercing it made Louisa's ears ring.

The highwayman climbed onto the coach step, his body looming over them as he leaned inside, and Louisa caught a whiff of something sour as he bypassed her entirely and dragged the screaming Lady Roehaven out of the coach. Diane's legs kicked out futilely, only landing a few hard knocks against the coach wall, which caused her to scream even louder. The highwayman shoved her onto the ground, where she knelt in a puddle of blue skirts. The only thing Louisa could think was that now the dress would be completely ruined.

"Quiet!" the highwayman shouted, but Diane did not stop

screaming. He raised his hand and cuffed her on the side of the head. It was a hard blow, and Diane crumpled inelegantly onto her side, unconscious.

The highwayman turned back to the coach and looked at Louisa. It was almost completely dark now, but she didn't need to see the expression on his face to know that if she did not obey him, he would do the same to her. Feeling the thin, hard length of her ivory knitting needle against her right forearm, Louisa began to climb out of the coach. The highwayman actually offered her his arm as she jumped from the high step onto the dirt road.

"Down," he said, pointing.

She knelt, her heart racing, while he went to Diane and turned her over roughly. The locket that Diane wore around her neck glinted in the last of the twilight. Lord Hemmynge had given it to her on the day of their departure; it was to be her gift to her future husband. She had been planning to take it off and deliver it directly to him as soon as she arrived at Tremontaine House. The chain slid through the highwayman's gloved hands, and then Diane's body jerked as the chain snapped. The highwayman bent over Diane's motionless head, brushing aside her hair almost gently, and unclasped the earrings from her ears. He lifted Diane's hands to examine them, tugging off the sapphire ring that had been her mother's.

The highwayman straightened, pocketing Diane's jewels, and turned to Louisa. She held herself very still. He came to her and squatted down, reaching out with one hand to cup her chin. His fingers were painful, digging into her throat as he turned her this way and that in the pale light of the night's first stars. "I don't have any jewelry," she said, her voice squeaking out from beneath the pressure of his hand.

"You're the maid, eh?"

"Yes."

He held her face steady, looking into her eyes. She did not flinch; she would not.

"You're braver than your mistress," he said almost conversationally. "I don't like weaklings, but you have some backbone."

Louisa's intake of breath was a stutter in her lungs. "She's a fool."

The highwayman barked a harsh laugh. "You've got a mouth on you. I like that in a girl. Most nobles are fools, never had to work a day in their lives, think they deserve everything. It's not fair. That's why I take what I want when I want it."

Oddly, Louisa found the highwayman reassuring; he was treating her like an equal, something no one had ever done before. She wasn't afraid anymore. She gazed back at the highwayman boldly. "Are you going to kill us?"

He seemed to consider the question. Finally he said, "I don't kill little girls."

Before she could ask what he did do with them, he raised his hand. "Have a nice nap, little girl."

His fist was a crushing blow to the side of her head, and she saw nothing more.

The Present Day

"My lady, Ixkaab Balam is here and is very insistent upon speaking with you directly," said Tilson.

The duchess raised her eyebrows. "The Kinwiinik girl is here?" This was surprising.

"Yes. I've put her in the east drawing room to await you," Tilson replied. "If you'd like to see her, of course."

Diane set down her embroidery. She had heard nothing of Ixkaab since Reynald's mysterious disappearance, possibly while he was shadowing Ixkaab on Diane's orders. She instantly wondered if Ixkaab's unexpected arrival at Tremontaine House had anything to do with her missing swordsman. Or perhaps it was in relation to the agreement she had recently finalized with the girl's family. At any rate, it was unusual enough to be notable. Diane stood. "I'll see her. Send in some chocolate, please."

Tilson held the door open for her as she swept through. "Yes, madam."

The east drawing room was nearly at the opposite corner of Tremontaine House from Diane's private aerie, and it had been one of the first rooms to receive Diane's touch when she married William. She had been so young then, more desperate to prove herself than she liked, and she had spent weeks contemplating which paintings to hang on the walls, poring over fabrics for the upholstery. The result was a room of understated opulence: pale gold thread upon ivory silk damask, paintings of Tremontaine ancestors sporting their heirloom jewels, the finest of Tremontaine's imported Cham porcelain displayed on the intricately carved marble fireplace mantel. It was a beautiful room, but also slightly out of style, so it was only used when unexpected guests of lower rank were visiting.

Ixkaab Balam, dressed in an amber-colored gown, was standing in front of the mantel, her head tipped up so that she could gaze at the giant landscape painting above, a bucolic scene of one of the Tremontaine country estates, including a meandering river and tiny white sheep scattered over a rolling green field.

"It's such a lovely surprise to see you," Diane said as she entered the room.

Kaab turned and curtsied awkwardly, clearly unaccustomed to wearing the voluminous skirts. "My lady," she said.

"Please sit," Diane said. "We need not stand on formalities."

As Kaab sat on one of the two matching sofas, Diane took a seat across from her, observing the two-seasons-old cut of her gown and the common style of her hair, twisted efficiently but without sophistication into a knot pinned by . . . Was that a penknife? How odd. The last time Diane had seen her had been at the Swan Ball, when Kaab had been heavily weighed down with gold bracelets and earrings in a thoroughly ostentatious display of wealth. Truth be told, Diane had found the elaborate costume delightful—much more interesting than this drab little conventional dress. The gown's severe respectability made Diane suspicious, for she knew it could not reflect the woman inside it.

"What a lovely dress," Diane said warmly. "That is a beautiful color on you. I think I had a dress that color a few seasons ago."

Kaab smirked. "I'm sure the dress looked much better on you, Duchess."

Diane caught the smirk but inclined her head graciously. The game was on, then. "You are too kind. I trust that your uncle and aunt are well?"

"Very well, thank you." After a brief pause, Kaab asked, "And how is your husband?"

For a moment Diane wondered if Kaab knew—but no. It was only a courtesy to inquire about the duke. "He is a little under the weather," Diane murmured, and decided to change the subject. "To what do I owe the unexpected pleasure of your visit?"

"I have heard an interesting tale about your arrival in this City."

"Oh, that old story?" Diane said dismissively. "It is a tragedy I prefer to put behind me." She shuddered delicately, as she had done countless times in the past to silence those who wished to revisit the drama of her journey from Lullingstone House.

"I can imagine why. It must have been terrifying. And it had to have been life changing too, to deal with such violence at a young age. You were only sixteen, is that right?"

Diane's face revealed nothing, but her gut clenched involuntarily at the memory. She pushed it aside ruthlessly. That time was over. What was Ixkaab Balam after? People always dropped the subject when she objected to talking about it, but Kaab didn't seem to have gotten the message. "I don't speak of those times anymore," Diane said. "As you can imagine, they are not pleasant memories. Tell me, is there something of concern to you or your family regarding our agreement over the chocolate?"

Kaab's hands rustled in the folds of her skirts. She adjusted her seat on the couch as if her stays were giving her trouble. "No," Kaab said firmly. "This is not about the agreement with my family. Did you know there's a tale about the highwayman who attacked your coach? His name was Rupert Hawke. Like that rhyme they say: 'Rupert Hawke, Gentleman Robber, steals your money but spares your daughter.'"

The sound of the horrible doggerel spoken in Kaab's Kinwiinik accent was so startling that Diane froze momentarily in disbelief. This was an affront to her dignity.

Kaab continued relentlessly: "Did you know that in the tale about Rupert Hawke, the attack on your coach is mentioned? In fact, the story is that he killed the driver and the footmen, but he spared two girls. One was the lady who was to become the Duchess Tremontaine. The other was her maid. But only one girl reached the City."

A dreadful apprehension rose within the duchess about Kaab's purpose here today. "The highwayman killed my maid," Diane said stiffly. "It is as simple as that. I was there!"

Kaab's face twisted into a grim smile. "So was Rupert Hawke. And he was proud of the fact that he never killed women. What happened to your maid?"

Diane felt as if she had taken the wrong turn in a maze, and Kaab's slyly insinuating tone both frightened and infuriated her. "Why would you believe the word of a confirmed criminal over my own?" Diane demanded. She was the Duchess Tremontaine. This girl had no right to challenge her.

Kaab gave her a cool look that Diane recognized as the expression of someone who was entirely confident that she had the upper hand. Diane should know; she had delivered that same glance countless times in her life. Being the recipient of it was a rather unnerving experience.

Kaab said: "You seem to think we are still playing at being ladies, as if I should take a hint from you to retreat. You are wrong, Duchess. This is not the game you think it is. You should listen to what I have to say. I don't play the game your way. If only your swordsman, Reynald, had understood that, he might be alive today. But he chose to underestimate me, which only made it easier for me to kill him."

Diane gasped. This *girl* had killed her swordsman? Diane had never heard of a woman who was able to kill a trained swordsman. If Kaab had truly killed Reynald—well, that was quite something.

At that moment the door opened, and Tilson entered bearing a silver tray laden with a chocolate pot, cups, cream, sugar, and the Kinwiinik spices that Kaab's uncle had given to Diane. He placed the tray on the low table between the two sofas, and asked, "Do you require anything more, madam?"

"No, thank you," Diane said. The footman bowed and departed. When Diane and Kaab were alone again, Diane said angrily, "You killed my swordsman?"

Kaab had the indecency to look proud. "I did. He was trying to kill me."

Diane considered Kaab. She held herself with an athletic grace that Diane now guessed was due to her sword-fighting skills, and she seemed altogether too relaxed. "Why are you here?" Diane asked warily. She did not make a move to serve Kaab any chocolate, and Kaab did not give the tray a second glance. The time for false pleasantries was long over.

"I believe that Rupert Hawke did leave two girls alive," Kaab said, "but only one of them finished the journey to the City."

Diane's fingers clenched in her lap. "Obviously. It was me."

"But who are you?" Kaab asked. Without waiting for an answer, Kaab removed a folded letter from a pocket in her unfashionable gown and held it in her right hand. "Let me tell you what I believe really happened. Seventeen years ago, Rupert Hawke attacked a coach traveling south from Lullingstone. He killed the men, but he made it a point of honor never to kill women. The coach carried two of them: Lady Diane Roehaven, who was to marry the Duke Tremontaine, and Lady Roehaven's maid. The two girls could have been sisters, except for the difference in their eye color. Lady Roehaven's eyes were blue, while Louisa's eyes were gray."

Diane found it difficult to breathe, as if a lump of something hot and bitter had lodged in the back of her throat. "That is a lie," she choked out. "My eyes are gray, not blue."

Kaab gave her a knowing smile. "They are indeed. But let me continue with my story. Rupert Hawke took everything from the coach, including a locket that contained a miniature portrait of

Lady Roehaven, but he did not kill the girls. A few days later, however, only one girl arrived in the City. She was in bad shape, with the dress on her back her only possession, but she knew all the details of Lady Diane Roehaven's life, so she had to be Diane."

The duchess remembered the panic and desperation inside herself the day she had knocked on the great, glossy door of Tremontaine House. In her weary, bedraggled state, she had almost gone to the servants' entrance, but she was to be the duchess. She entered through the front.

"The duke married this girl, who said her name was Diane. For seventeen years, the Duchess Tremontaine lived on the Hill. She became well known for her sophistication and her beauty. Years passed, and the people of the City stopped talking about the tragedy that had befallen her on her journey. She thought everyone had forgotten. But one day, not so many months ago, Rupert Hawke's son, Ben, appeared on her doorstep—your doorstep—with the same locket that contained the picture of Diane Roehaven."

The night that Ben Hawke had talked his way into Tremontaine House was a night the duchess had no desire to remember. The sight of that locket, gone for so many years she had almost forgotten it existed, had been like a knife in her gut. She had known instantly that no one could ever be allowed to see it.

"Ben was not a law-abiding man," Kaab said. "He was the son of a highwayman, and a Riversider. He intended to blackmail you, but he underestimated you. Many people underestimate you, don't they? Just as they underestimate me."

The duchess's mouth drew into a thin line. She said nothing.

Kaab seemed to find her speechlessness a fitting response and nodded. "Ben was murdered by your swordsman shortly after he brought the locket here, because he had to be silenced. No one could know that you were never the Lady Diane Roehaven. You were her maid."

At last, Kaab gave the letter in her hand to the duchess, who took it with numb fingers. It was dated seventeen years ago at Lullingstone House, and it confirmed the marriage agreement between Lady Diane Roehaven and the future Duke Tremontaine. Diane was described as "a delicate, pretty girl with blond hair and sapphire-blue eyes," and in order to assure the duke that his son's bride was who she said she was, she would arrive bearing both this letter and a locket containing her picture. The letter was signed by Lord Nathaniel Hemmynge.

The duchess remembered Lord Hemmynge well. He had been the master of Lullingstone House, and the duchess never forgot anyone who had changed her life. His decision to send Louisa with Diane to the City had altered everything. "Where did you get this?" the duchess asked, her mouth dry as the yellowed paper she held in her hand.

"It was with the girl's jewelry, which Rupert Hawke stole. When he returned to the City and learned that only one girl seemed to have survived, he kept the letter along with the locket as—how do you say it? Oh, yes: insurance for the future. He kept them until he was dying, when he gave them to his son, Ben."

Diane folded the letter but did not return it to Kaab, who was watching her closely. So it had come to this. Ben's death had not solved the problem, and now this Kinwiinik woman was holding a knife to her throat in the form of a letter. Of course, a letter could be easily destroyed, but the information in it now lived in the mind of someone much more dangerous than a common Riverside blackmailer. Diane would not underestimate her again. She asked bluntly, "What do you want from me?"

"I know that you were the maid," Kaab said. "What I don't know is what happened to the real Diane Roehaven."

Diane gave a short, bitter laugh, and said, "She was reborn."

Seventeen Years Earlier

Louisa's eyes opened. The moon was almost directly overhead and nearly full. Her head throbbed with pain, and she winced as she touched the tender lump on her temple.

The highwayman.

The memory of what had happened flooded her with terror, and she sat up so quickly she nearly fainted. For a moment the dark forest swam before her blinking eyes, the rustling leaves sounding like rushing water as the ground seemed to tip and sway. She tilted forward, her hands planting on the dirt road with a jolt that she felt all the way through her bones. A cool breeze tickled at her face, bringing with it the smell of earth and pine needles as well as the sick odor of blood and something much worse.

Her eyes finally focused. Directly in front of her, the coach's shafts lay on the ground in the moonlight. The horses were gone. He had taken them, too, likely loaded down with all of Lady Roehaven's possessions. Perched on one of the fallen shafts was a crow, its black eyes reflecting the moonlight in two tiny white dots. It seemed to be staring directly at her.

As a little girl, Louisa had been fascinated by crows. Sometimes they would roost upon the crumbling stone wall outside the penitent hospital. The crows always seemed to watch her, their hard bright eyes following her every step. The headmistress had shooed them away from her once, calling them ill omens, not safe to be lurking near a little girl. They flew off at once, but after the headmistress left, they returned. Louisa would watch them through the cracks of the shuttered dormitory window, mesmerized by the cutting points of their beaks and the light-swallowing black of their feathers. She hadn't been so close to a crow in years, and in this whispering forest, with the scent of blood and viscera thick in the air, it seemed so clearly a portent—but a portent of what, she did not know.

Louisa began to crawl toward the bird. For a moment it simply watched her, but just before she came within an arm's length it spread its wings and leaped into the air. It flew toward another lump on the ground, alighting nearby and lowering its beak toward something Louisa couldn't quite see.

It took her a moment to understand. The crow was pecking at the eyes of the dead footman.

"No!" she cried, hastening toward the body instinctively. "Shoo!"

The bird cawed as if indignant and flew up to perch on top of the coach. Louisa was now on her hands and knees beside the footman, and she became aware of something long and hard poking at her wrist. She sat back on her heels and lifted her arm. It was her knitting needle. She pulled it out of her sleeve and stared at it. The ludicrousness of her improvised weapon became appallingly clear to her. What good would it have been? A thin ivory knitting needle, wielded against a much stronger man with a sword? She had been a fool.

With a furious cry, she threw the knitting needle aside. It clanked against an object on the ground nearby, and something about the sound made her look in its direction. There on the dirt road, in a patch of clear moonlight, was a knife.

The crow cawed again, its claws scratching as it shifted on the coach roof, and Louisa became keenly aware of how alone she was in this forest. There were wild creatures out there, hidden by the trees and the night, and she had nothing to defend herself with—not even her knitting needle. She scrambled to her feet and went to pick up the knife. It was a dagger, with a leather-wrapped hilt that was a little big for her grip. It had probably belonged to the footman.

She looked back at him from her new vantage point behind the coach. The moonlight was so strong that it cast shadows, and the footman's body was half swallowed by one, but his upper half was lit up clearly. Too clearly. She saw the vicious wound that had split open his throat and the lake of blood that had pooled around him, and in horror she realized that she had crawled right through it. She held up her hands, and they were sticky with blood. The front of her dress, too, was stained dark, and the sight of the blood on her made her dizzy.

A sound behind her.

She spun around, holding the dagger in front of her in a terrified grip. There was nothing but the trees, and only ten feet away, another body: the coachman. She did not want to see how he had died.

The sound came again: a low moan.

She turned back to the footman, but he was dead; it could not be him. Beyond him, back where she had first woken up, she saw the dark shape that was Diane. Of course. Diane. She hurried back to her mistress's prone body, avoiding the footman's pool of blood and other unspeakable things. She knelt down beside Diane and put one bloodstained hand on the girl's throat. She was still alive; she would surely wake up soon.

The thought of what would happen when Diane woke up filled

Louisa with a swelling rage. The girl would be a terrified, simpering mess. She had absolutely no backbone; she would weep and shriek at every little noise in the forest, and Louisa would have to deal with her. She would have to find Diane food and drink; she would have to figure out how to get them to safety. Diane might assume that help was coming for them, but Louisa knew that they were on their own and at the mercy of whatever else came down this lonely road from the North. They would have to walk. They might be within a day's drive of the City, but who knew how long it would take for them to make that journey on foot. The one thing Louisa was certain of was that Diane would complain every step of the way. And if they had any luck left and came to a village or an inn along the way, they had no money to hire another coach or pay for lodgings or even for food. The highwayman had taken it all. They would be forced to beg for charity. No, *Louisa* would be forced to beg for charity, and then she would have to give it all to Diane.

The girl did not deserve to be a duchess. She was a selfish, vain ninny whose ancestors might have been kings, but she'd clearly inherited none of their intelligence or bravery. Even the highwayman—a common criminal—had seen that Louisa was braver than Diane. Louisa would make a much better duchess than Diane. At least she knew how to keep her wits about her. She wished the highwayman had killed Diane, too.

The dagger trembled in Louisa's hand as she glared down at the still unconscious form of her mistress. A monstrous thought came into Louisa's mind, but it was so awful she would not let herself think it. The vicious anger that accompanied it, however, filled her with a not unwelcome pleasure. Her fingers tightened around the dagger. She glanced around herself at the deep, black shadows between the trees; the unmoving silhouette of the crow atop the coach; and only one body's length away, the gaping jaw that had once been the coachman's neck.

Louisa would make a much better duchess.

She had heard every one of Diane's etiquette lessons. She knew how to address every duke and lord and lady in the City; she knew how to curtsy and how to dance with light, delicate steps, how to choose a menu for a banquet for fifty or an intimate ladies' chocolate party, and how to simper behind a fan just as well as Diane did. It wasn't fair for Diane to have been born into a noble family and for Louisa to have been born to paupers, to be forced to toil in service to a nitwit when she was a hundred times smarter, a thousand times more driven. None of it was fair, but that was why the highwayman took what he wanted when he wanted it. Perhaps Louisa should take what she wanted too.

Diane's eyelids fluttered. She was almost awake.

Louisa's skin prickled with heat, as if a fever was rising within her. The dagger was slippery in her sweaty palm, so she wrapped her other hand around the hilt to steady it. Diane's throat was bare and vulnerable in the moonlight, which shone so invitingly over her skin, spotlighting the very place the blade should go.

The crow's claws scratched again on the coach roof. The wind surged through the spring leaves like floodwater hurtling toward her. Louisa saw her life branching off from this moment like a sharp turn in the road. The path she was on led to a hard bed in a servant's cell-like room, a life of obedience to a mistress she hated, and the misery of living it. This turn in the road flipped her fate on its head and gave her a title that was not her own, but should be.

She no longer hesitated. The dagger's tip sank into the girl's small, naked throat. For a dreadful moment, breath heaved through Diane's body in a sick gurgle, and then Louisa bore down on the blade with all her strength, biting through the resistance of the girl's windpipe. Blood ran hot down Diane's neck and puddled onto the ground near Louisa's knees. Louisa cut deeper just to be sure, sawing through muscle and vein, her fingers becoming coated with her mistress's blood. Louisa did not notice that she was sobbing while she cut. She did not notice that her heart was pounding faster and faster, as if it could pump her own life into the other girl's body. She did not notice a thing until the dagger struck bone and could cut no more.

Diane never woke up.

The Present Day

The Duchess Tremontaine met Ixkaab Balam's steady gaze over the tray of untouched chocolate. She still held the letter in her hands, the letter that would condemn her in the eyes of every noble in the land. If they so much as suspected any part of the truth, the duchess would be ruined.

Ruined utterly.

The nobles' obsession with bloodlines was a moat around them, separating them from the low-born commoners who toiled in their service. No one was allowed to cross that moat. There were no bridges of merit or marriage or even of wealth. A merchant might be wealthier than all the dukes combined, but he would still never be one of them.

Louisa had been a lady's maid, born to parents she had never known, orphaned as a baby, put into service at the whim of a spoiled heiress. Louisa, as far as the Duchess Tremontaine was concerned, was dead. She had died on that road in the forest at the same moment as the real Diane Roehaven. Afterward, the one who lived changed into the dead girl's bloodied blue silk gown so that there would be no mistaking who she was. She had trudged on shaking legs for the better part of a day to the next village, where a farmer had taken pity on her and offered her space in the back of his turnip wagon going to market in the morning. Once they arrived in the City, she walked up to the Hill on her own. Her first sight of Tremontaine House nearly overwhelmed her; she had never seen a mansion so grand, and the idea that it could be hers galvanized her.

Louisa could not be allowed to be born again. She must remain buried deep beneath the duchess's skin, so deep that no one would know she had ever existed.

The duchess asked, "What do you want for your silence?"

Kaab's smile did not reach her mouth, but the duchess saw it in her eyes, a bright flash of triumph. She recognized now, in Kaab's eyes, the mark of an equal.

"An exchange," Kaab proposed. "Rafe Fenton, your husband's secretary, has been investigating certain aspects of navigation in his studies at the University. Rafe has been working with a young mathematician named Micah, and your husband has promised to help them. Their work needs to stop, and none of their discoveries can be revealed. If you stop them—and prevent the results of their work from being used—then I will not share the true story of your origins."

Diane had not forgotten about her husband's enthusiastic support for Rafe's scholarship, and she immediately understood Kaab's position. If Rafe's theories were put into action, they would be as threatening to the Balams as Kaab's knowledge of Louisa was to Diane.

"You're proposing silence for silence," Diane said.

"Yes."

"What would you have me do to stop my husband and his . . . secretary?"

"That is up to you," Kaab said. "As long as you succeed in silencing them, that is all that matters to me. All knowledge and evidence of their work must be suppressed. If you promise to do this, then I too will remain silent."

Diane smoothed her fingers over the letter that could destroy everything she had worked for her entire life. Taking care of William was no problem, given his sudden illness, but the rest of Kaab's demands required some additional thought.

"That is my offer," Kaab said. "Do you agree?"

Episode Thirteen

DEPARTURES

Ellen Kushner

Kaab considered the woman before her. Diane, Duchess Tremontaine, stood pale and composed in her silk-and-damask drawing room. Only her hands, nervously clutching the damning letter Kaab had just given her, betrayed her.

"Let me be sure I understand your proposal," Diane said. "You *and your people*—for I am not fool enough to think that you alone possess the secret of my origins; I'm sure your formidable aunt, at least, does too—you will bury that knowledge, never to see the light of day. You will swear by your gods to do this. And I in turn will swear by mine that all knowledge of navigation that would enable my people to cross the seas to your land will be equally buried."

Kaab nodded. She could be patient while the duchess played for time to think. The matter would be decided now; there was no way this woman would let Kaab leave Tremontaine House without her pledge of secrecy. Diane's need was immediate; what Kaab demanded was trivial to the duchess by comparison. The Xanamwiinik had not been able to navigate yesterday; with Diane's promise, they would not be able to navigate twenty years from now either—whereas if Kaab released the duchess's secret in the morning, by nightfall Duchess Tremontaine would be out on the street.

All Kaab had to do was wait for the duchess to accept the facts and then make sure she herself got out of Tremontaine House alive. Diane was already poisoning her husband with a merciless hallucinogen to make sure he stayed out of her way. Of course, Diane did not know that Ixkaab knew this, so it did not surprise her when the duchess attempted one last dodge: "And what makes you think that I can influence the Duke Tremontaine in these matters?"

Kaab said, "It is not the duke I am concerned with. Nobody listens to him, as well you know. In fact, his own wife makes secret pledges with the Balam Traders to share profits in chocolate to pay off her debts, and he does not know it. She uses her influence with the Council of Lords to change the import tax laws, and he does not even care. Such a woman, I think, will have no trouble making sure that some raggedy students are not heeded by the Council—and if they take their knowledge to the merchants, well, the Council is the law of the land, and can surely make it very difficult for them to implement such knowledge."

Was that a blush of pride on the pale duchess's waxen face? Did she like hearing, just once, just here, in private and alone, that another woman recognized and admired what she had done? It must be tiresome, Kaab thought, to live a life where all your strength came from making sure no one knew that you had any.

Kaab continued: "The Kinwiinik would accept this woman's pledge, and value it. They would feel safe and secure in partnership with her, and would never find it in their interests to do anything to risk removing her from her present status."

The duchess lifted her head, as if already smelling victory.

She really was a magnificent creature. Kaab had to admit that she found powerful women intoxicating. What was to prevent her, here and now, from taking this bright, pale woman in her arms to seal their bargain with one deep kiss? The duchess had flirted with her at the Swan Ball; perhaps she would be ardent, like the Tullan nobleman's wife, Citlali—

"Are you distressed, Mistress Balam?"

Too late to hide it. "I am, my lady." But not too late for riposte. "I was thinking of what happens when lovers betray one another, and covenants are not honored. It can be terrible."

"I understand." The Duchess Tremontaine held up the incriminating letter. "Then let us come to an agreement. I shall burn this letter"—quickly she threw it on the embers in the hearth—"and all memory of what it contains will go up in smoke along with it. And your people, in turn, may be assured that any discoveries in mathematics or astronomy that would enable us to navigate the curves of the earth at any great distance—for you see, Mistress Balam, my husband did indeed tell me of the new research—will be mocked, discredited, scoffed at . . . outside the University. For even you cannot credit me with any influence within *those* walls!"

The letter was curling at the edges, smoldering, about to break into flame. It didn't matter; Tess could always make another one, should the duchess be playing with this talk of University. Diane had read the forged letter carefully and suspected nothing. Kaab's lover, Tess, too, was in her way a woman of power.

The duchess turned from the hearth with a smile.

"And now, my dear, will you take chocolate?"

Tess the Hand paced her rooms in a small house in Riverside.

The swordsman Vincent Applethorpe, who shared them with

her, looked up from the letter he was trying to write to his sister in the country. People in Riverside feared Applethorpe's sword, but Vincent Applethorpe feared only the pen. Still, if she didn't hear from him regularly, dear Clem was likely to kick up a fuss. And so he dutifully wrote to her once a month, no matter what it cost him.

The large red-haired woman, clad only in a loose gown, her hair flowing out behind her like a comet's tail as she paced from desk to window and back again, picking up random things and putting them down without looking at them, only made it worse.

The ink dripped as Vincent waved his pen in the air. "In the name of all, Tess, if you don't stop that and keep still, I swear I'll—"

Tess whirled. "You swear you'll what? You're my official protector, Vincent Applethorpe. Lay just one hand on me and you'll be out of a job, which means out of a roof to lay your scabrous head—"

"Te-e-e-esssss." He drew the word out gently. If this is what True Love did to her, he wasn't at all sure he liked it. "All I'm saying is—distract yourself. Find something to do, will you?"

"What are you writing?" Tess asked. Gods, she was inquisitive. She had the demon in her, nervous about her girlfriend on the Hill. She needed distracting. And so he opened his guard, just a little.

"Letter to my sister. She worries."

Tess craned her head to see the page. "'. . . ten measures of good Helmsleigh wool,'" Tess read aloud. "'Nobles . . . pay their bills . . . a good year . . .' Vincent," she said.

He shook his head, silent.

"You're one of the best swords in Riverside. And your sister thinks you own a draper's shop?"

"She worries," he repeated doggedly.

"So," Tess said. He braced himself for whatever bitchiness her nerves would squeeze out of her. "So," she said again. "Want me to run you up some receipts to show her?"

Vincent Applethorpe laughed. She was Tess the Hand: forger of documents great and small. It had never occurred to him to ask. "Sure," he said.

They spent a merry hour squabbling about whether "Applethorpe's Fine Woolens" was better than "Vincent's Notions"—he let her win, relieved to have distracted her from thinking about Kaab. The Kinwiinik woman was even now confronting the Duchess Tremontaine about some shady business involving the death of Tess's previous protector at the hands of Reynald, the Tremontaine swordsman. Applethorpe had been ridiculously pleased when Kaab reported that she'd killed him, using the sword craft that he himself had taught her. Of course, if he'd known she'd be fighting Reynald, he could have given her a few tips. . . .

Tess was pacing again. She went to the window, looked out, craned her neck to see down the street, pushed the casement open farther, craned some more. Drew in her head, twisted her hair in one hand, pinned it up by skewering it with a paper knife, and knocked over a cracked mug full of pens.

"Look," he said, "she'll be here any minute. She's a big girl; she can take care of herself."

"You're a fool, Vincent," Tess said sharply. "It's not me she's loyal to—it's her family. That Balam trading clan. It's them she'll go to first with the news. I could be waiting all night." She sank to the floor beside him, sharing the patch of sunlight he was trying to write in. "Tell me about Tremontaine House. I want to be able to picture where she is. And how she can get out, if there's trouble."

Applethorpe nodded slowly, capped the inkpot, and put the

letter aside. "Yes. All right. I can do that." Like a village story-teller, he began: "Imagine way up at the top of the Hill, on the side overlooking the river. The gates are black iron, but curly, like lace or something. When they swing open, you're in a courtyard, neatly cobbled, with the great house waiting across it. In front of the house is a set of steps—two, really, stairs on each side, and a landing with a balcony, a stone one, in the middle."

"Do their guests go up one set and down the other?"

"I have no idea. Maybe they just like to have a choice."

"And then?"

"A great wide door. A double door. Fine-grained oak, strong as iron. Carved with swans, which is the Tremontaine crest."

Tess nodded, smiling. "Don't I know it." *That's right,* he thought. She'd faked a letter for them recently.

"And if you can get through those doors, you're in a great open hall, two stories high or more. Let's see, there's checkerboard flooring, and all sorts of crazy paintings on the wall and even the ceiling. . . ."

"What of?" Tess leaned her head against his knee, like a cat. Or a sleepy child.

"I dunno . . . gods and goddesses, I guess. The sky. But the best part is this grand stairway that leads out of it, curling up into the clouds. . . ."

He looked down. Tess was asleep in that awkward position, cheek on his knee. But her nervous hands were still at last, and her breathing was regular.

With the perfect control that made him one of the great swords of Riverside, Vincent Applethorpe reached for his pen, his ink, and his paper, and recommended writing badly spelled lies to his sister Clem, all without disturbing the woman at his side.

No, Kaab would not take chocolate with the Duchess Tremontaine today. Or ever, knowing what she did about Diane's proclivity for eliminating those who stood in her way—although at this point, her trading partners the Balam were surely exempt. Maybe.

Instead, Kaab departed by the same great doors she had entered. She stood on the steps of Tremontaine House for a moment, at the apex of the Hill, taking in the vista from the courtyard, breathing deeply, enjoying her moment of triumph.

There would be complications. People could be hurt. If he ever learned what she had done, her dear friend Rafe would never forgive her for hiding the duke's true condition from him, let alone blocking his research. But for now, for just this one perfect moment, she allowed herself to look back on the last three months since she had first arrived in this city and taken on its problems as her own.

Ixkaab Balam, first daughter of a first daughter of the Kinwiinik, had said that she would do a thing, and she had done it. The stain of her botched mission was past, and her exile would surely be recalled. She could go home across the sea where she belonged.

A carriage clattered into the yard. Kaab slipped down one side of the marble steps, crouched, and peered through the balustrade. A man got out of the carriage. His cloak bore a dragon worked in gold. A Chancellor of the Council of Lords, then. The dragon meant the exchequer, so this was— *Ah!* Kaab smiled. This was the man the duchess had persuaded to put through the relief on the Kinwiinik Traders' chocolate tax!

For a moment, Kaab considered running back up the stairs, as if newly arrived herself, to greet him and have a little fun. But then she thought that she'd probably had enough fun for one day, all things considered. The duchess was surely storming about her boudoir, tearing up tapestries with her teeth and smashing china.

The Dragon Chancellor returned to his waiting carriage. The Duchess Tremontaine was receiving no one.

From a room high in Tremontaine House, William, Duke Tremontaine, looked out on the stone courtyard.

He was used to knowing things, now. It had frightened him, at first. But he was coming to understand what he saw.

Below him, a dragon stamped and snorted in the courtyard before the house. The dragon desired his wife. William was going to have to save her, for she could not save herself.

"Diane!" he shouted, to warn her. "Diane!" He ran to the door, but it would not open. "Diane!" He pounded on it, so she could hear him. "Diane, beware the dragon!"

His steady pounding was like a heartbeat, pounding fit to burst while he cried her name: "Diane! Diane!"

"Should we open it?" he heard someone out there say.

"No. He just gets like this sometimes."

William dashed back to the window. And, lo! The dragon was retreating, pulling out of the courtyard with a clatter like horses' hooves on stone. A bright yellow bee buzzed around the corner of the house, but that did not concern him. His wife was safe for now.

"Diane!" he called again, gladly.

She did not answer. Far away in the house, he heard her weeping stormily, weeping with abandon, weeping and weeping as though her heart would break.

Kaab felt free as a bird let loose on the Feast of Xamanek after weeks in darkness. To celebrate, she left the grounds the same way she had come in the other night—was it only four days ago?—hoisting herself over the back wall. It wasn't easy in skirts, but she knotted them up with her sash. First, though, she made sure to loosen her horrible stays. And if the skirts got a little torn on the way over, well, hadn't the Duchess Tremontaine, supreme arbiter of fashion, declared that they were two seasons out of date?

She tidied herself up before she stepped out onto the broad and quiet street—but she couldn't possibly look like the well-heeled Trader who had presented herself at Tremontaine House only an hour ago. No matter. She wanted to run all the way down the Hill, speed through town like a quetzal on fire, fly over the Bridge, and hasten to the arms of her love, her ripe maize flower, the loveliest woman in the world—

But no. Duty first. Her family must know what she had achieved, and Ixkaab Balam must tell them herself.

Kaab looked around the well-groomed, wide, high-walled street of the Hill. A serving boy was coming toward her, carrying an empty delivery basket and whistling.

"Hey!" Kaab beckoned to him, and, though dubious, he came. "Good day, my friend. I am going to give you a very decent amount of money to take a message for me to Riverside."

"Riverside!" The boy eyed her and backed away. "That's no honest place, and I'm an honest man. I ain't getting involved in no skullduggery."

"It's no skullduggery." Whatever that was. Just her luck, she'd managed to find the one honest man in this city. "It's a lady," Kaab improvised swiftly. Sometimes the truth was even more believable than lies. "The mistress of my heart, sick with worry for me. I come up here to serve his lordship"—she nodded at the gates behind her—"and he used me hard." She'd heard one of the whores at the Maiden's Fancy saying it last week and marked it for later use. "But I am well, and you must show her this to prove it." She pulled the spike out of her hair. It was Tullan work, and Tess would recognize it.

Fascinated, the boy stared at the silver spike with its working of jaguars and *mecaxochitl* flowers. *He'd better not steal it.* "Why don't you go tell her yourself?"

Kaab spat—another thing she'd seen the whores do. "Why do you think? I've got my living to earn, same like you."

The boy laughed. "Will she give me a free sample, then, your friend?"

Kaab nearly hit him. But that would not be in character. "Go find out for yourself." Her Red Tess could handle this punk with both hands behind her back.

"How much?" the boy asked at last. Good, she had hooked him. She counted out some of the Local coins from the purse in her pocket, gave him directions, and saw him off down the Hill.

Xamanek's light, but it was good to be herself again! Kaab hadn't realized how much she'd missed the cocksure, capable agent of the service who had left Binkiinha nearly a year ago, on that doomed mission to Tultenco. The mistakes she'd made there had cost lives, and she had thought she, too, was doomed to severity and caution, and the gloom that went with them.

But she had done it right this time, here in this gray city on the other side of the world! And her old self was back—for now, at least. She whistled her way across the Middle City and down to the Promenade along the river, where there were fewer people to stare at her. True, one took her for a lost soul and offered her some coins to get something to eat. . . . Kaab was truly sorry no one tried to attack her as she got near the docks, since she had her obsidian knife tucked away too, and a fight right then would have suited her liver very well. But no one did.

It hadn't occurred to Kaab that her own people might not take her disheveled state with equanimity.

"Ekchuah guide me, look at you!" Aunt Ixnoom shrieked as Kaab entered the family compound.

"Filthy Xanamwiinik, what have they done to you?" growled Ahaak's son Ahpuut. "If they've offered you insult, I'll—"

"I'm fine!" Kaab laughed. "Haven't you ever seen an agent's return before?"

"What I've seen," Aunt Ixnoom fussed, "is a young lady who went out this morning in her finest amber silk come home looking like a beggar woman."

"Or worse!" Cousin Ixoen said.

Kaab took the coins from her pocket. "I'll buy a new gown," she said, "though I'd rather be done with this silly costume, and be home wearing sensible clothes! Where is my aunt Ixsaabim?"

"Lying down," Ixoen said. "The child has been kicking inside her, and she needs her rest. Don't you disturb her now."

But Aunt Ixnoom looked at her keenly. "No, Ixkaab. You go disturb her. I think that she will want to hear your news."

It seemed no one would be allowed entrance to Tremontaine House that day.

The guards at the gate were very firm about that, even though Rafe argued and pleaded, and even offered them a bribe of spices from his father's warehouse, along with extra money he didn't have.

But the guards held fast. And it wasn't just him. When, in desperation, Rafe took up a position against a wall on the other side of the street, he watched a nobleman's carriage being turned away, and then a woman in a sedan chair, and even a perfectly good knife grinder, wheeling his cart from house to house.

The Duke and Duchess Tremontaine were not to be disturbed. There was illness in the house.

Rafe glared at the guards from across the road. They could see him perfectly well, but as long as he did not approach the gates again, they were content not to chase him away.

Will! He shifted his gaze to the upstairs windows, clearly seen over the stone wall and the ironwork gate. *Will, I'm here. I promised not to leave you, and I am here, my love.*

But what good did that do his lover? What use his standing outside the gate, when he could not take Will in his arms, rock him and pleasure him and tell him everything would be all right? He might as well be on the other side of the world—west across the sea, in Kaab's country, where the chocolate grew on trees.

Rafe marched deliberately back across the street.

"I may not have made myself clear," he said. "I am the duke's personal secretary. He has entrusted urgent business to me."

"We know what kind of business you have with him. You think the whole house doesn't know?"

"Fine." Rafe squared his shoulders, a peculiar thing to do, given what he was about to say. "I'll do you, then," he declared. "Each of you in turn." The guards stared at each other and then at him. "I'll give to you the same pleasure I give the Duke Tremontaine. Maybe even more." His mouth was dry. He wasn't sure how he would summon the spit. He'd give anything for a drink right now. But he would manage. He would have to. Will was in there.

"Well," the younger guard began, but the older one cuffed the side of his head.

"Well nothing! You think we want to lose our jobs for five minutes' pleasure?"

"Ten," Rafe couldn't help muttering. "At least." He tried to smile beguilingly. "Let me in the side door. No one will see you open the gates."

The younger guard wavered. "The money," Rafe repeated. "And the blow job."

The older one guffawed. "The likes of you, paying us for the pleasure! I never thought I'd see the day!" Rafe wanted to smack him when he went on relentlessly in the same hilarious vein: "If you'd told me when I got up this morning that some fine young scholar would be offering me money for the chance to lick my balls—"

"Your loss," Rafe said, with an evenness born of desperation, "if you don't want it."

They wanted it, all right; but they didn't take it, either one of them. And that night, shaking in his bed at the memory, Rafe thought of what strange depths love was driving him to.

Tomorrow, he thought. *Tomorrow the gates will be opened. They cannot keep the world out forever. And they cannot keep me from my love.*

And that same night, Ixkaab Balam lay with her sweet lover, Tess, Tess the Hand, and there was no boundary to the bliss that they enjoyed. Stars exploded in their bodies, only to be reborn and explode again. There were long, languorous kisses, and very little sleep.

Kaab felt free. She let Tess roam where she would, and she didn't give a rat's ass if she heard herself yelling loud enough to bring the house down. She realized that she had been so bent on showing Tess how very much she desired her, and what a mistress Ixkaab Balam was of the art of love, that she had not let Tess into her own center. *Or is it even my center?* she thought dizzily. She wasn't sure she had ever felt anything quite like this before—this was total abandon, with no goal but finding out what could possibly happen next, if she let herself go in the arms—and legs and hands and—*Oh, dear Ekchuah, well are you called the Diver*—the fingers, the lips, the armpits, the warm, flexible skin, and slippery sweat of someone she trusted utterly.

"Sweetheart?" someone said, and Kaab came up out of darkness enough to realize that the foreign sounds were a word she knew.

"Mmmph?" she managed to say. A warm breast brushed her cheek.

"Sweetheart, what does *titechtlatia* mean?"

"You burn us up," Kaab said gruffly. "But it means death. It's from a poem. 'Oh giver of life, you are laughing at us. / Even jade breaks, even quetzal feathers rot. / You know us, / You burn us up. / You make us disappear from this earth.'"

"Really? I realize I should have said 'good morning' first, but I was afraid I would forget it. And anyway, I think it's well past noon." Tess handed her the cup of water she'd been reaching for, and Ixkaab drank.

"It means 'I am dead without you, bringer of life.'"

"One word, all that?"

"Sort of. It's implied. Because of the poem." Kaab started to raise herself on her elbows. "But you don't want to hear all about someone's else's litera—"

"But I do." Tess licked her eyebrow smooth. "Remember? I said I do. I want to learn about you and your people."

"Then, yes." Kaab rolled on top of her, and Tess let out a long sigh. "Here is some poetry."

But in the middle of a particularly fine verse, there were footsteps on the stairs, a key in the latch, and a voice called, "Hello? Are you still there?"

"Yes," Tess called back. "We're doing poetry!"

"Oh my. Welcome to the House of Vice," said Vincent Applethorpe. "May I come in?"

"Only if you've brought some food."

"I have brought food."

They pulled the blankets up around themselves and let him sit at the bottom of the bed, laying out a small feast of apples and ripe cheeses, fresh bread and curly new fern heads. The sun was pouring in the window when he drew back the shutters, and Kaab thought what an utterly perfect and delightful place was this Riverside, where moon-breasted women let her into their beds, and a man who taught her the sword also knew enough to know when to make himself scarce.

Micah found herself telling Doctor Goodell everything.

". . . and Rafe is my friend, so when he asked me to do his calculations of course I said yes and anyway I'd never done those types of equations before . . ."

They were sitting together in a corner of the Unequal Triangle, a tiny University tavern recently cobbled together in the little space between two jutting houses, eating tomato pie and drinking fresh milk from the country, which Richie the tavern keeper got in special for the learned doctor. Micah had forgotten how good fresh milk was. She was growing more and more attached to Doctor Goodell. Not only were his ideas interesting, but he didn't like the crust on pie, so she got to eat his, too.

". . . and then my tables were really good, and Rafe was so excited he got all drunk and said the geometry of spheres was going to change the world, but I didn't have to worry about that, which is good because I don't want to; I like the world the way it is, don't you?"

Doctor Goodell nodded. "Most of the time, I do."

"And anyway you said that the job of mathematics is to *understand* the world and not to change it. So then I stopped working on my tables because it was taking such a long time but I thought Rafe would be mad and I'd have to explain it to him but he wasn't mad, he just said not to bother, like it didn't even matter . . ."

Doctor Goodell shook some crumbs out of his gingery beard. He wasn't old, but he didn't like to waste time shaving.

". . . so now I'm wondering if my calculations were all wrong and that's why . . . But Rafe is serious about mathematics, even if he isn't about other things, so he would have told me if I'd gotten it wrong, wouldn't he?"

His thin white hand patted the back of hers absently. "You're a good girl," he said; "I wouldn't worry about it."

Micah nodded. That's what Uncle Amos said sometimes, and she always found it comforting. It meant that she didn't really understand people, but no one was mad and she didn't have to do anything about it.

"Now," Doctor Goodell said, "would you like to see a card trick?" He pulled a greasy pack of Constellation cards out of his sleeve.

Micah looked at them dubiously. "Would I have to bet?"

"Oh, no," Doctor Goodell assured her. "Just watch, and be impressed."

The day of Ixkaab Balam's visit to Tremontaine House, Diane, Duchess Tremontaine, forgot to make her husband's chocolate for him—just the way he liked it, with a faint savor of the Kinwiinik merchants' spices. More important, she forgot to give him the medicine that usually went with it.

All day long, the duke was agitated. His people could hear him pacing his room, shouting prognostications and warnings—and, plaintively, calling to his wife about the dragon. But without the Duchess Tremontaine's express permission, they knew they were not to open the door to the duke's room to anyone for any reason. And the duchess had locked herself in her own rooms, leaving the strictest orders for no one to enter the house or to disturb her by even so much as a rap on her door. Even the maid, Lucinda, was banished to the kitchens.

Finally, though, William, Duke Tremontaine, was quiet—so quiet that the staff was worried enough to convince Duchamp, his oldest, beloved servant, to break the rules and see if their master was still among the living.

His old back stiff and straight, Duchamp raised his great ring of keys and unlocked the door to his master's rooms.

Duke William lay spread out faceup on his bed. His arms were outstretched, as though fending something off—but his hands were relaxed, as though welcoming it. His chest rose and fell with regular rhythm, and his open shirt revealed a pulse beating gently at his throat.

The duke was a kind man, sensitive and considerate. But he was the highborn son of a great and noble house. Duchamp had never seen him so completely open and defenseless, even as a boy. For a long time, he gazed at his master. The duke's fair hair was tangled, his chin stubbled—and some of the pinpricks of beard glinted silver. Duke William was not yet forty-five years of age. His life had included a good marriage, a living child, a long pursuit of knowledge indulged in with a substantial library, a host of friends both here and in the country—and, now, at last, an all-consuming passion for a bright, handsome, foolish, and adoring young man. If Duke William did not recover from this illness, his years could be said to have been rich and full. It was not given to everyone to live long enough to know the aches and pains and joys of a venerable age. Some men shone like the sun, and then went out.

Duchamp breathed a blessing on William, Duke Tremontaine. Whether the man recovered or not was in hands other than his.

The duke did not stir—not even when Duchamp combed his hair back from his face, and kissed his brow, and withdrew from the room, closing the door softly behind him.

William was still asleep when the duchess entered the room early the next morning; still sprawled open-armed, as though felled in battle.

For a moment, she considered letting him sleep on. He was so peaceful, so blessedly quiet. She hated always seeing him so agitated, frightened, angry, trying so hard to make himself understood in a world where he was the only one to see what he saw, to know what he knew.

The duchess, too, stroked the fine hair back from his brow. His fair lashes fluttered, and the blue eyes opened on her face.

The duke gave a sleepy smile when he saw her. She couldn't help smiling back. "William," she said tenderly.

"You look sad," he said.

"I am sad. You've been very ill, my love."

"Yes. I know." Still he lay there, looking up at her, trusting and tranquil. "But I've slept long now, and I feel stronger."

"Good. Shall I make you some chocolate?" She hated to do it, but he seemed to be returning to himself, and that would not do.

"Just water, please. Maybe later."

The duchess paused. He seemed so calm, so relaxed and open to her, as he once had been, all the years of their marriage. Could she have him back? Was it possible? Had the medicine she had been administering to keep him from reality been medicine in truth? Could the drug, the fever, have burned the love—maybe even the memory—of Rafe Fenton clean out of him?

Diane allowed herself to take her husband's hand and kiss it. It was so much finer than Lord Davenant's hand, long and slender and soft, a scholar's hand. Davenant's was stronger, hairier, more masterful, it was true, burning with a heat she enjoyed. But William's well-known fingers, the little scar on his palm . . . so often this hand had caressed her when she was in distress, or even when she needed to pretend it. This hand had wandered everywhere, coming to know her intimately. . . .

Suddenly the duchess burned for her husband with unexpected, pure, and overwhelming lust.

"William," she said huskily. Still in her morning dress, she straddled his outspread body. His mouth tasted strange and terrible—was she just imagining it because she knew the scent so well, or had the taste of the drug so permeated him that it infused his very membranes? She kissed him hard, as though to suck it out of him. He responded with fervor, and she hiked up her petticoats, undid his trousers with fevered fingers, guiding him into her and letting him overturn her in a fluster of snowy, lacy ruffles, drive into her, then pull back to tear open her bodice and address her breasts hungrily. *Ah!* the duchess thought, transported with joy; *he is completely and utterly mine!*

She wept when she came, perfectly convinced in the moment that all would be as it had been. As the winter had turned to spring, she had redeemed her debts, confronted and defeated the last proofs of her past, corrupted the Dragon Chancellor to her ends, launched a new business venture . . . She had even allowed her beloved husband a midlife fling with a silly boy from his cherished University.

But all that was over now, she thought, lying on his chest in a pool of sweat. She ran her finger along his exquisite collarbone. "William . . ."

"Yes, my dear?"

"Shall we ring for a bath?"

"Certainly, if you like." He reached across her for the bell rope next to his bed. "But you had better let me tell them."

"Very well." It was best this way: Let the household see that he was restored to himself; let them see her lying in his arms.

With her weight on his leg, he couldn't quite reach the bell pull. She laughed, and her husband laughed too. "Here, William, let me." The feel of the crisp hair of his thigh sliding under hers . . . The duchess had gotten what she needed out of Davenant. It was time to let the chancellor go.

She gave the cord a good, sharp pull, imagining it ringing down in the servants' hall. "And would my lord like some breakfast?"

"Perhaps." She hadn't heard him sound so content in what felt like forever. "But you'd better let me tell them."

"Of course, my love." Diane smiled down at him. "Do you crave something particularly odd?" *There could be aftereffects from the drugs,* she realized. *Don't expect him to be everything he has been.* But so agreeable! She'd have him back to his role as her spokesman in Council in no time.

"Not really. It's just that I don't think my people will feel comfortable taking orders from you."

Her heart started slamming. But there was still a chance— She kept her voice steady, even light: "Really? Why not?"

"They don't know you yet," he said kindly. "Delicious as you are, I'm not sure I do, even, myself." He cupped one breast. "Though I look forward to learning more."

"William." Curse it, her voice was shaking. She had let herself fall into folly, and here was the result. "I am your wife."

"But that can't be," he said reasonably. "My wife died on the road."

She allowed herself a sliver of hope. "My poor love, you're still dreaming. I am Diane." She smiled richly and beautifully at him. "Diane de Tremontaine."

He peered curiously at her face. "You do look like her. But my Diane died on the journey. Only her maid survived."

"Her maid?" Diane said icily.

"Poor girl. My wife is dead, you see."

The duchess rose from the bed to hide her trembling.

"How do you know?"

"The black crow told me."

The black-robed scholar. Rafe. Of course. He could not possibly know the truth; even the Balam girl would not have told him—she was too clever for that. But Rafe Fenton had done all he could do to poison her William against her. As much as Diane had done with the flower of shadowroot, young Rafe had done as much and more to him, and to their marriage.

She had planned to stay in the City and attend to business for a while, while word of the duke's malaise began to circulate, so that concerned friends could even come and witness his crumbling reason. But that could not be allowed now. Even his babbling was too dangerous. William must be shipped off to the isolation of Highcombe as soon as possible. She would alert Wickfield to prepare for the journey immediately.

And Rafe Fenton . . . Diane had learned by and large to let revenge pass by; her energies were always better spent on the next victory. But for Rafe Fenton she would make an exception. William was lost to her; she would take his Rafe in exchange, and make of him something his erstwhile lover would not recognize. That would be some comfort.

"Now, my lord duke—shall I make you some chocolate?"

"You said you had tables." Rafe wanted to shake his friend, but he kept his voice even. Getting mad at Micah never produced good results. "Tables, charts, I don't know—something that lets you win at cards more than the rest of us. Remember? You told me the night we met. When we went out and you had—when I got you tomato pie for the first time. You said you kept the cards in your head, and you had a way of figuring out what was likely to come up—"

But Micah wasn't fooled. He was getting that look on his face.

"Come on, Micah . . . we're friends, right?"

"Not when you're being like this. I don't like you right now, Rafe."

"I'm sorry. I don't mean to scare you." Rafe crouched down below where his friend sat on his high stool at the table that doubled as a desk in their rooms, papers spread out before him. "It's just—I need the money, Micah!"

"What do you need more money for?" Micah said. "I paid the rent. We have food. You don't have any more school fees, and I've paid mine to Doctor Goodell for the quarter. I want to work on my equations now."

"You want to know what I need money for? I'll tell you!" Rafe lost whatever control he had left. "I need it to bribe guards who wear Tremontaine's livery, but want to protect him by locking him in his house while that wife of his destroys him! There you go, Micah: That's what I need money for! And did you understand a word of it? Of course not! I'm sure it makes less sense to you than you think your stupid magic tables make to me! But you know what? Anyone else on this turning globe knows just what I mean! And if you're really the only one who understands those tables, then I—"

But his words were interrupted by Micah's shrieks. Not that Rafe stopped shouting; he just couldn't hear himself any more.

Because Micah was crouched in the corner of the room, hands over his ears, emitting the most horrible sound: high and shrill and rhythmic. Worse than rabbits dying. Worse than a baby crying—the kind you wanted to hold upside down and slap, just to get it to stop.

Rafe stood there helplessly. With the noise, he couldn't think. But he knew perfectly well what he'd done. And because he was the cause, he couldn't soothe Micah with square roots. All he could do was stand there hating himself.

He could apologize. Not that Micah would hear him, but he could do that to try to start making amends.

"Micah." He crouched down by his friend. The screams didn't stop. "Micah, it's Rafe. Micah, I'm really, really sorry." He made the mistake of trying to pat his shoulder. The boy flailed at him, breaking his awful rhythm to shriek, "Get away from me! Don't touch me!"

"I'm sorry!" Rafe sprang back. "I'm sorry I touched you! I'm sorry I hurt you! I'm sorry I scared you! I— Micah, please stop!"

"Nice try, but not very effective, pigeon."

It was Joshua, his strong tenor somehow cutting through the shrieking thing on the floor. The door must have opened, unheard. "Whatever it was you did, Rafe, and I'm sure it was supremely stupid, I am possibly even sorrier than you are. Now, make it stop!"

Rafe waved his hands in soundless, hapless explanation.

"I see," said Joshua. "All right." He let out a huff and crouched down next to Micah. "Micah. It's me. Joshua. Micah, Rafe is sorry he was horrible to you. Rafe is a horrible person, and I'm going to make him go away now. I'm going to take Rafe away, all right? You can be by yourself for a while, until you feel better."

Miraculously, the shrieks got softer; they were almost whimpers by the time Joshua finished speaking.

"Micah—" Rafe began. But Joshua gripped his arm savagely.

"I think," his friend said, "you've said about as much to Micah as we all need for one day, don't you, pigeon? Now, come on."

Obediently, Rafe bent over and started pulling on his shoes.

That was when they became aware of the knocking at the door—the loud, insistent knock of someone who had been trying for some time to make his presence known. At the sound, loud, rapid, and aggressive, Micah's shrieks resumed.

"Master Fenton!" The voice on the other side of the door sounded worried. "Master Fenton, are you at home?"

It was Joshua who opened the door a crack. "Oh yes," Rafe heard him say. "No, I'm not him. Dear Rafe is busy murdering someone. Can you not hear the screams?"

"What the hell, Fenton?" The shout came from one of the historians across the landing. "Are you skinning a cat in there?"

"Or screwing one?"

On the floor above them, someone was pounding on their ceiling. Which did nothing to calm Micah. Or Rafe, for that matter.

Joshua closed the door, and the historians' wisecracks faded into the background. The pounding—and Micah's shrieks—did not.

The seal to the paper Joshua handed Rafe bore the swan of Tremontaine; the wax went flying as Rafe tore it open.

Master Fenton: Please come when you can.

That was all. It wasn't William's handwriting. "The messenger?"

"Gone," Joshua said. "Couldn't leave fast enough."

And, he reflected, one could say the same for Rafe.

The Duchess Tremontaine received him in her drawing room.

"Master Fenton," she said gravely. "Thank you for coming."

Rafe did none of the things that courtesy demanded: He did not bow or thank her or ask how he could help. Instead he wondered: *What is she playing at?* This was the woman who had barred the gates against him. The one who missed no chance to mock and demean him every minute he had spent at Tremontaine House trying to be Will's secretary.

Now she looked up at him from the chair she sat in, looking almost boneless with fatigue. A small and delicate woman, her fair hair caught back in a simple knot. Her dress was dove-gray, fine linen, but crossed in front with a fichu of the kind a merchant's wife might wear. In fact, she looked like his mother, when she stayed up all night when the children were sick, because *no hired help, no matter how skilled or loyal, could possibly care about my family as much as I do.*

"How is he?" Rafe asked.

"Ill," the duchess said. The bright western light was not kind to her. The skin around her eyes looked thin, and he could see little lines at their corners and at the corners of her mouth. "He slept the night before last. All the night through, and into the day." She met his eyes with her clear gray ones. "I know you came to the gates. And were denied. I just wanted him to sleep. I wanted to sleep myself. . . ." She turned her head away, but he saw the tears glinting in her eyes.

He said, "Why are you telling me this?"

The duchess looked down at her hands, bare of any ornament but her wedding rings. "Because you have the right." Her voice was so low, he had to strain to hear it.

"As his secretary? I am still, you know. He hasn't dismissed me. They should have let me in."

"I let no one in that day." The duchess rose and walked to the high double windows, which led onto the terrace over the garden, and looked out at the glory that was the early summer there. "I know you love him," she said.

Rafe was silent. He had been prepared for a fight, for sarcasm, for a careful and brutal tearing down of himself and everything he and Will were to each other. This, he was not prepared for.

"And I know you think that I do not," the duchess said. She turned back to him, her back flawlessly straight, her face in shadow. "I am not willing to argue that point with you, Master Fenton."

In that moment, Rafe saw himself as she must see him: a man, young and full of promise, nothing behind him but youth, who had walked into her safe and secure marriage, carried her true husband off into a world of promise and romance, without a thought for the woman who had given herself to him for life, borne his children, minded his household (and all his other considerable properties), and maybe even—in her own way—loved him too. A woman who might have been in considerable pain for the past few months while he and Will had found each other, though pride and position demanded she show the world nothing of it.

"However," the duchess went on, "I am hoping that you will accept my request to help him now, if you can."

"Of course!" Rafe said, before he could stop himself. "I will do anything I can. Where is he? May I see him?"

"Of course," the duchess said in turn. "I will tell them to prepare him for visitors." What did that mean, "prepare him"? Was his Will wallowing in his own filth? Painting himself like an Uruk? Or did he merely need a shave and change of neckcloth? "Meanwhile, I hope you will take chocolate with me."

Rafe sat in the chair she indicated, a velvet bergère across the low table from her. This was a woman's parlor; he'd never been in it before.

He watched in a trance of fascination as Diane's tapered, elegant hands lifted the chocolate with a set of silver tongs, scraped a generous amount into a swan-shaped pitcher, added hot water from a pot over a small burner, and whipped it all with a silver whisk. Into one cup she measured a tiny spoon's worth of reddish-brown powder from a tin.

"I have come to enjoy the Kinwiinik spices," she said. "This is my own particular blend. Would you like to try some? I warn you—it is rather strong."

"Yes," Rafe answered. How could he not? But he noticed that she gave him far less than she had given herself. And even so, the first sip went up his nose and down his throat like fire.

He felt his face flush with the heat. Politely, the duchess made no indication that she had noticed. Rafe wiped his brow with the kerchief he fortunately had in one pocket.

"Cream?" she asked with perfect civility. "I'm so turned around, I forgot to offer it before."

"Please."

The cream did something to temper the burn. But still, Rafe felt that fierce rush of tingling vigor when he drank. It was followed by a sense of well-being—of stimulation, even—like coming indoors after being caught in a rainstorm and being briskly rubbed down with a warm, dry towel. The duchess's spiced chocolate was both like and unlike the stuff he'd drunk at Kaab's family welcome banquet—oh how many hundreds of years ago? The Balams must have toned it down for their local guests. This was probably closer to what Kaab drank herself. No wonder she loved the stuff! It was like a hit of strong spirits. And here was the Duchess Tremontaine, relishing a double dose, far more than Rafe could tolerate—and, no doubt, enjoying her superiority. Well, let her, poor thing.

She offered him more, because it was rude to suggest that you begrudged a guest anything, but he politely (and honestly) refused. He was ready to see Will.

"Come, then," she said.

Rafe followed her rustling skirts through the painted corridors and up the grand staircase to the richly carpeted second story. Door after door—some of them he'd been behind, some he'd no idea what they led to. . . .

Will's room was still Will's room. It was locked from the outside, now. The guard—Rafe supposed it was a guard—opened it for them to pass through.

For a moment, Rafe just stood in the doorway, staring. How could he have forgotten exactly how beautiful Will was? There was no one on this earth with skin so fine, stretched over bones so perfectly articulated. His ears, his nose, the way his shoulders extended from the column of his neck . . . Rafe's body filled with a love so sharp and all consuming that it barely left room for his own breath.

Will sat in a high-backed carved wooden chair, looking out the window. He was dressed and clean-shaven, though his hair was a little long. Rafe saw that Will's lips were moving—his sweet and supple, curved lips—muttering something over and over as if his life depended on it. He did not turn to look at them but gripped the chair's arms with white, tight knuckles.

The last time Rafe had seen Will, holding him in the sweet sweat of his bed, Will had been afraid of going mad. He said Rafe helped bring him back to himself—

Rafe stepped forward a little. "Will?"

Still the man in the chair did not turn. But Rafe could hear what he was muttering fiercely to himself, over and over:

"Red rose, black rose . . . Black rose, red rose . . . White crow, black crow . . . Black crow, white crow . . . Red rose, black rose . . . Black rose, red rose . . ."

The pain in Rafe's center turned to a chilly calm. He was a man of reason. And his love, at heart, was too, and would be so again.

Slowly he approached the man in the chair. "Will, darling. It's me. It's Rafe."

Finally the duke turned and looked at him. The muttering didn't stop—but Rafe saw recognition in his eyes.

"Will, I'm here to help. Can you tell me what is wrong?"

Will shook his head frantically, waved Rafe away with his hand, while his lips moved, unceasing. Rafe squatted beside the chair, looking up at him steadily.

"Let me help you, Will."

Will stared at him, desperate, but did not stop: "Black rose, red rose . . . White crow, black crow . . ." As if he were ensorcelled, like some young king in a wizard's tale. Will's eyes were wild, now; Rafe could see the man in there, terrified and begging for help.

"Black crow, white crow . . . Red rose, black rose . . ."

It was intolerable. He had to make it stop. He'd go mad himself if he had to keep hearing those words over and over: "Red rose, black rose . . . Black rose, red rose . . ."

He stood and reached out one hand to take Will's shoulder, and then the other to bring him to his feet. Will clung to the arms of his chair, unwilling to rise from it. "It's all right," Rafe said softly. "Never mind." He knew the way to break the spell. He bent down himself and kissed Will on the mouth.

Will's mumbling continued under Rafe's lips, a strange and terrible sensation. Still, Rafe's blood pulsed with inconvenient desire—and communicated itself to Will. The mumbling slowed; Will's lips grew soft and conformed to his. He could feel Will's shoulders relax.

That's right, Rafe thought, *come to me.* Will's mouth pressed his, more and more insistent, and Rafe let his lips open—yes, let Will be the one to come forward, there—let Will's mouth open and the familiar taste come with it, let Will slide his tongue between them and begin to explore—

For a moment, Rafe did not understand what he was doing on the floor, his head ringing. Will stood above him, his arm still raised to strike again, shouting: "Traitor! Traitor! The rat child was right! Betrayed by everything I ever loved, just as it told me!"

"No." Rafe shook his head, lifting his arm against another attack. But the duke just went on shouting: "You stink of her! I can taste her on your mouth!"

The chocolate. Her own personal blend. She'd done it on purpose.

Rafe rolled out of the way but stayed crouched on the floor, unable to go to Will, unwilling to run to the safety of the guards.

"*That* was what it was all about—the numbers, the stars, the caresses in the library, velvet and paper and ink—the way your hair curls so sweetly just there, the ways I can make you laugh, the way you cry out when I make you come—"

"Will, no—" Rafe held his hand up like a beseeching mendicant.

"She murders with the eyes of a crow, deep in the forest, but you—here in my own house, everything we had, everything I loved was only meant to kill me with happiness!"

A spear of ice went down Rafe's back. The star he'd dreamed had said that too: *Then you have killed him with happiness.*

This was a nightmare. He stumbled to his feet. Will took a swing at him. Will was taller than he was, with a nobleman's well-tuned body. But maybe he could hold him still, if he could just slip past the windmill of Will's long arms to get near him—

Will grunted as a guard on either side took hold of his arms and wrestled him to a standstill. He strained against them as he shouted, "I am betrayed by everything I love! I am betrayed by everything I love! I am betrayed by everything I love!"

It didn't stop, in volume, pain, or rage.

"I think, Master Fenton, that you had better leave." It was the duchess's clear, cold voice, very near him. "You see how you enrage him."

Rafe staggered past her to the door, his ears ringing with accusations of betrayal.

"This is what it is like." The duchess had come out to him. She, too, leaned against the wall, companionably, beside him. Her face looked ten years older. "I cannot calm him either."

Betrayed by everything I love!

It was starting to sound like a song, just one line, repeated over and over.

"What are they doing to him?" Rafe asked her.

"Restraining him," she said bleakly. "If he does not calm himself, they will bind him to the chair. Or to the bed."

"I'd better go," Rafe said.

"Wait." The duchess put one hand on his sleeve and left it there. A fine-boned hand, tiny and perfect. Such a fragile hand, he could not move against it. And the one word: "wait." Two little things that made him powerless. Rafe looked down as she raised her face to his. She was so close. She did not speak.

One bend of his head, and he would be kissing the Duchess Tremontaine. It was almost inevitable. And he would do it, just for the pleasure of remembering how far she had held herself above him, how she had mocked and flouted him— *"Betrayed!"* Will's voice rang, muffled, through the door.

Rafe took a step back. It made no sense. He didn't even want her.

"Please," the duchess said. "If you would just grant me one more minute?"

"Betrayed!"

She shuddered. "Let us go down to the drawing room. This is too distressing."

Mutely Rafe followed her. Had he imagined that moment? She was all dignity and business now, a formal but considerate hostess. Was she playing with him? Will had said that she was brilliant with people. But Rafe had never seen it. Was he seeing it now? Was he in over his head? Had the possible kiss been a possible test? What would she want Rafe to kiss her for? To prove he was a boor so she could throw him out? To try what had so seduced her Will? Or just to show that she could make him want her, after all that? Rafe grimaced. Maybe he had imagined it. But in his years of casual couplings, he prided himself on knowing what a come-on looked like. Maybe women were different. Maybe he was overwrought.

Back in the drawing room, the Duchess Tremontaine did not ask him to sit down. "I will not keep you long," she said. "It's just that—I need your help."

"I do not seem to have been very much help so far, madam."

She did not respond. "You were his secretary. As you say, you have not been formally dismissed." She walked over to a small table, picked up a gilded paperweight, and put it down. "The duke's affairs are in disorder. Tolliver is more confused than ever. If you could help me begin to go through the duke's papers, see what has been answered and what still needs doing . . . It all falls to me, now, you see. Until he is better."

"Do you think he will be?" Rafe asked—too quick, too eager. He was a fool where Will was concerned.

"I do not know," she said gravely, looking straight at him. "His father was . . . eccentric." She shrugged delicately. "Tremontaine does have a reputation. Even our daughter behaved oddly at times."

Inherited madness. Rafe supposed that it was possible. *Oh, Will!* Rafe considered what she was asking. Far from sending him away, she was inviting him to return. He would see Will again, without hindrance. He would find a way to care for him, to heal him. He would not let them bind his Will with painful ropes or tie the knots too tightly.

"Yes," he heard himself say. "I will come. I'd like to help."

"Thank you." She gave him a small and weary smile. "You will be paid, of course. And if you need a place to live—"

He couldn't believe his luck. "I would like that," he said evenly. "To be here."

"Good." She nodded. "I will have it seen to." The duchess lifted a silver bell and rang it, and a footman appeared to show him out. "Please come in two days' time," she said. "It will take me that long to sort things out."

That surprised him, but he wasn't going to argue. Not now.

"Good," Kaab said. They were drinking at the Inkpot: Rafe, Joshua, Thaddeus, Larry, Kaab, and a big redheaded woman Kaab had introduced as Tess, whom Micah had greeted warmly, so they could do no less.

Micah was playing cards nearby. His table included a mathematician who had publicly vowed to keep playing until he figured out Micah's methods. He had, so far, been unsuccessful—and so the coins kept flowing over to Rafe. Funny kid! Micah always accounted for each minnow, knew precisely what had been spent on every single thing from bread to bathwater for the past three months, and would tell you if you let him—but he loved buying drinks for his friends.

He's so adorable, Rafe thought in a haze of warmth. Rafe had apologized handsomely to Micah for being such an ass that morning, and Micah had told him that if he ever did it again, he'd sic Cousin Reuben on him, and Reuben had a mean left hook, and Rafe had solemnly promised that if he was ever even tempted, he would just recite his square roots tables, instead, which was much better than getting mad, and now they were friends again.

"No, really," Kaab repeated. "It is good that you will be close to the duchess. We have a saying, with my people: Stay near your friends, but be even more near your— No." She shook her head. "Most inelegant. Try this: Keep your friends close, but your enemies closer."

Rafe repeated the phrase. It was a good one, and fit his circumstances neatly.

"I am sorry," Kaab said, "that your duke is not better. But at least you will be near him. I'm telling you though, Rafe"—she leaned across the table and pointed a finger at him, jabbing the air in a very rude way that was probably a gesture of affection among her people or something—"do not trust this Tremontaine woman. Not for an instant. And come back and tell us whenever you can."

"Tell you what?"

"Tell us what goes on there. We are all concerned."

"Are you allowed visitors up on the Hill?" Thaddeus asked innocently. "I'd love a tour of Tremontaine House."

Rafe grimaced. "I'll ask the duchess to give you one."

"This place is dull," Tess said suddenly. Her face was a little flushed—of course, all of theirs were. "Is this all you students do? Just drink and play cards?"

"Pretty much," Joshua drawled. "Why, what's your idea of fun?"

"Music?" Tess pushed some of her abundant hair back from her face. "Dancing? If I wanted to sit around with a bunch of drunks and gamblers, I could've stayed in Riverside!"

There was a sudden silence, while everyone looked at her.

"You didn't tell them," Tess said.

Kaab lifted her head haughtily. "I saw no need."

"Because any friend of yours would automatically be assured a welcome? Or because you honestly do not get what sort of a pit it is I live in, and how this city feels about us?" Tess stood up, rocking the table. "It doesn't matter. I'm out of here."

"Tess—wait!" Tess looked down at the foreign woman, all whipcord and braid. "I will come with you."

Tess shrugged. But Kaab's brown arm snaked around her, catching her as she turned. "No—" Kaab got that look in her eye. Rafe knew it well, and wondered what mischief she was planning. "No . . . *you* will come with *me*."

"And to where?" Tess asked—but there was the edge of a smile in her voice.

"Why . . ." Kaab grinned. "To the sea!"

"The sea? Isn't that kind of far?"

"Oh, yes. But it is so very dull here in this place."

Tess shrugged, grinning, and Kaab settled her arm around her waist, and the women left the tavern laughing.

In the darkness, black water lapped against the stone of the quay. Something above them creaked, and Tess looked around nervously. Even the linkboy froze for a moment, his golden torch casting crazy shadows on the stone.

"Go on," Kaab told him, and to Tess: "You live in Riverside, and you're scared of the docks?"

"Docks are nasty," Tess said. "No Riversider goes here. This is where the ones we don't let in come. Or the ones we kick out."

"Well, there's no one here, Tess. No one who shouldn't be. Not near Kinwiinik ships. We have guards for that." Kaab lifted her hand to her mouth and blew a gurgling whistle: a long note, up and down, then three short sharp sounds like birds' cries.

She was answered by an echoing sound, down the quay. Tess squinted and saw a lantern lifted in greeting. Promising, but still: "Great fun evenings out you take me on."

"*Heyyy-AH!*"

Kaab ducked and spun suddenly, flinging a stone low to the ground. Tess screamed.

"Just a rat," Kaab said peering into the darkness. "I nearly got him."

This is what it's gonna be like, Tess thought, as she tried to get her heart to stop slamming in her chest. *Just a rat*—she's as bad as a street urchin! Tess wondered briefly what on earth she was doing out on the docks in the middle of the night with this madwoman and why she had thought this would be fun.

The man with the lantern called something in Kindaan, and Kaab shouted something back—probably "just a rat" in her language. When they came abreast of one another, their torch showed a Kinwiinik man dressed in their own garb, not even bothering to look like a City dweller. Tess tried not to stare and then gave up, as Kaab and he talked back and forth in their own tongue. Kaab gave him something from her pouch, and he laughed and nodded. Then he went off, and they waited a moment, until they heard a long whistle from down the pier.

Kaab nodded. "Let's go." The linkboy hesitated. "You too," she said.

"I dunno . . ."

"You'll be safer with me than going back through the docks by yourself. There are rats, you know."

They made their way to a wooden pier. Against a starlit sky, Tess could make out the huge, dark shape of a ship bobbing on the water. A Kinwiinik ship. From all the way across the ocean. The torchlight picked out some of the brave paint on its side. A serpent's open mouth and some kind of bird, long feathered, running endlessly before it.

Kaab mounted the gangplank and held out her hand. "My lady."

Well, thought Tess, *it's now or never.* And it was now.

The gangplank wobbled. It smelled of seawater and tar and

fish and other things she couldn't name. Step by step up the thing in the dark, the nervous torch behind them casting wild shadows on wood and water, while Kaab supported her arm and coaxed her along.

Tess heard music then. Coming from the ship. She followed the sound, and then she was standing on solid—*deck*, she supposed. She'd never been on a deck. It felt nice, after the gangplank, anyway. The whole ship bobbed gently, but she wouldn't fall off.

"Welcome," Kaab said softly, "to the great ship of the Balam, Tess."

There, on the deck, they kissed—and when they separated, the music sounded free and clear: some kind of pipe, playing a slow air, with the sad kind of beauty that music can have. Tess saw a lone figure outlined against the starlit sky, atop the roof of a little house on the deck.

"The Kinwiinik sailors," Kaab murmured, "must keep long watches, and so they play to keep themselves awake." They were silent, listening. "Do you like it?"

"I do." Tess drew in a deep breath. She was in another world now, Kaab's world. She leaned against her lover. A shadowy man came up and offered them a bottle gourd and then withdrew. Kaab took it and drank, and offered it to her with: "Be careful. The first swallow burns."

It did, oh how it did! But the second, and the third . . . Tess felt warm and light as air. She imagined herself on the ship, just the two of them, sailing out under the stars in the middle of the sea— "This thing won't really take off, will it?" she asked suddenly.

"What?" Kaab laughed. "Oh, no; the tide's all wrong. And the stars that will guide you and me home together are yet to be born, my maize flower. So let us dance under the ones that we have now."

"Dance?"

Yes, the flute was getting faster, the music flowing like a river, and soon it was joined by a drum. And so they danced, just the two of them, on the great deck under the stars of that strange city.

At one point, Tess's hair came unbound. Kaab nestled herself under it, her head between Tess's breasts. The pipe was wild, and so they danced again and drank, and somehow there were fried tortillas, hot enough to burn your fingers, fragrant with cinnamon, and then there was a nest of blankets under the stars, and they sank down together in them.

"Sleep here," Kaab murmured. "I have arranged everything. There will be chocolate in the morning, the finest, for you."

"You really are a princess," Tess said sleepily. "With a ship of your own, and servants . . . I didn't realize."

"No," said Kaab, "you didn't. And you'll probably forget. But never mind. I keep my promises, you see, Red Tess."

The duke awoke to a great flurry around him. He had been bundled into his clothes, and now they were trying to put a great fur robe on him, as well. The room was candlelit, but everyone else was already dressed.

"The medicine," False Diane was saying, "Wickfield, every *third* day, now. No less than that, though, or he becomes agitated."

A great bear, an old god of the woods, came toward the bed. It smelled of smoke and old fires. It opened its mouth, and "Hey there," it said. "Hey there, lad." It patted his arm with its great paw.

"I don't know you!" Will struggled, but the bear held him fast, breathing in his face, growling: "What do you mean you don't know me, young William? You've known me all your life."

The bear had him by the head now, and water was falling from its eyes into his. "It's me, Will! It's Wickfield, your pal. Remember we used to catch trout together, at Highcombe?"

With the bear's tears, Will saw an orchard in spring, apple blossoms, the nodding summer heads of barley lazy in the sun, and silver trout in the stream.

"I've come to take you home, lad."

"Good," he said, and lay back, comforted. "I would like that."

Rafe couldn't wait for the sun to rise. He dressed by candlelight in his dark linen suit, his clean white shirt. He didn't shave or tie his neckcloth; he'd stop at a barber in the Middle City on the way to the Hill and let him do the honors. That would also take up time, so that he didn't arrive too early at Tremontaine House.

His room looked bare; he'd packed up most of his things already, though he wasn't bringing them with him today. Despite the duchess's promise to have everything ready for him—by which he assumed she meant his permanent living quarters—he didn't want to arrive with bags in hand.

Rafe stepped quietly into the outer room. Joshua was snoring on one pallet, Thad on the other, and Micah lay on his chaise, looking very young, younger even than he did when he was awake. Rafe paused and smiled fondly: the little card sharp! His innocence was part of what fooled the other players. He'd miss Micah, he realized, miss the way they had needed each other these last three months. It was good having someone to take care of and watch them learn things. But Rafe was taking care of Will, now—and he wasn't leaving scholarship forever, just long enough to *keep his enemy close* and make things right. He didn't know how long that would take, but he was determined; and then, when Will was better, whatever it took, they could go back to planning his school together—with a special room for Micah, to teach the rules of math.

"Rafe?" Micah's eyes opened hazily, and he peered up at Rafe's candle. "Rafe, are you going?"

Rafe nodded silently.

"So can I have your room now?"

He started to object, but then thought, *What difference does one night make?* "Sure, Micah. You can move in now."

"Good." To his surprise, Micah emerged from the covers fully clothed. "Then I'm going to walk with you partway."

Micah's motives were sometimes a mystery, but Rafe could read friendship when he saw it. And so they walked together through the silent, dew-damp, gray streets of University, Micah in his scholar's robe, and Rafe feeling naked without his.

Micah prattled cheerfully, but in a muffled tone, in deference to the hour: "I'm really happy about your room, Rafe. I'm going to keep the door closed. It's a good, thick door; you can hardly hear anything through it, because when you and your boyfriend were doing your business in there we only heard you when you were screaming really loudly, and that wasn't for very long. I'm glad, because it scared me. But Joshua wouldn't let me open the door, and now I'm glad, because it turned out you were perfectly fine. . . . So when I've got the door shut, I won't be able to hear anyone on the other side, unless they're screaming but Joshua says that's once in a lifetime and will probably never happen to him—"

Rafe stopped under a sign for used books. It wasn't like Micah to go on this way. "Micah," he said, "I know you're happy about the room. But are you sad I'm leaving?"

Micah's eyes filled with tears, and when he nodded, they ran right down his cheeks followed by new ones. "I know you have to go take care of your sick boyfriend and make money and keep your enemies close and everything, and that we'll still be friends like you said"—he ran his black sleeve over his nose—"but it won't be the *same*, and I hate that part!"

Rafe didn't know what to say. Micah was right, after all; it wouldn't be. "Things change," he said helplessly. "They just do."

Micah looked up, wiped his face with his hands. "I'm going to hug you, Rafe," he said, "and then I'm going to give you a present. And then I'm going to say good-bye. Is that all right?"

Rafe nodded, unable to speak. Micah nestled like a puppy against his chest, pressing so hard he nearly had the life squeezed out of him. He hugged Micah carefully back. Then Micah broke away and reached deep in his sleeve and pulled out a packet of painstakingly tied papers.

"What's this?"

"Don't open them!" Micah said urgently. "They're a present I've been working on for you. But don't open them until you're in your new room. Promise?"

"All right." Rafe put them in his satchel, the one Will had bought him at the fancy leather shop on Larrimer Street. "I promise, Micah."

Micah's face relaxed a little. "Good. Good-bye, then, Rafe."

And that was that.

The Tremontaine carriage was drawn up to the door. The courtyard was lit with torches, but Will could see the light of dawn just starting to break in the sky over the eastern Hill.

Wickfield's comforting presence was on one side of him, with brittle False Diane on the other. Why did she try so hard to seem whole, when she was clearly broken?

Because she must, said the crow on his shoulder.

A cloaked woman emerged from the house, carrying a bundle in her arms.

"Good," said False Diane. She put one hand on the woman's shoulder. "William, this is Thea. She will take care of you at Highcombe."

"Good day, Thea."

"You need not speak to her; she cannot answer. She is a deaf-mute."

William smiled at her foolishness. "No she's not. She is singing! Can you not hear the music?"

"No, my love, I cannot." The duchess went up on tiptoe to kiss him good-bye gently on the lips. "But I'm glad you will have music on your journey."

Kaab returned to her aunt's house in wrinkled clothing, with an unwashed face and kiss-stung lips. It was full daylight now. She and Tess had had a leisurely breakfast on the ship: sour atole and fruit tamales, and little tortillas with purple beans mashed on top, as fresh as a sea voyage could leave them, since the ship was newly arrived from Binkiinha. Tess had eaten everything with gusto, and pronounced it good, and the Caana chocolate to be heavenly.

Kaab washed as much of herself as was decent in the court-yard fountain and went upstairs to do the rest and change. Her bed looked tempting, lying there in the sunlight with its red woven coverlet . . . but with the newcome ship, there would be news, and she wanted to hear it.

She found Chuleb and Saabim in their office, sitting on the reed mat together reading dispatches, his arm around her now very large waist.

Chuleb looked up and gave her a genuine smile. Since Kaab had so neatly resolved the Tremontaine episode, her uncle was becoming downright friendly. "You have a letter, Niece!"

She took the long, folded sheet of fig-tree paper and undid the seals. The ghost scent of her father's study wafted up like incense, and her heart filled as she saw his familiar handwriting.

> *My dearest daughter, sun of my days and star of my nights, may Ekchuah guide you:*
>
> *The Tullan Empire is suddenly our dearest friend again (for now), due to . . .*

She skimmed the political details to get to the end:

> *If, then, you have been comporting yourself so as to bring honor to the Balam, as I am sure you have been, I believe, and my mother agrees with me, that it will be safe for you to return home to resume your duties here.*
>
> *I hope your exile has not been too arduous, and that you have accustomed yourself to the climate some, or that the weather has improved. Your letter about the cold made your great-mother wish to send you her jaguar-skin cloak, which I was only able to dissuade her from by telling her you would most likely be returning on the very ship it arrived on . . .*

Ah, the famous cloak! Won by her great-mother in a celebrated game of chance. Even the Balam weren't allowed to wear jaguar in public, but it was lined with double-spun wool, and so her father's mother wore it within the family compound whenever it got cold enough. Which seemed to be more and more often, Kaab recalled. How many more winters before the jaguar-skin cloak would need to find a new owner? Would she even see her great-mother before then?

> *Come soon, my darling girl. It has been very dull here without you.*

"Your face shows you have received good news," Uncle Chuleb said. "We, too, were gladdened by the Tullan agreement."

Aunt Saabim flicked his toes with a dispatch. "Don't tease the girl. So you're leaving us, are you, Ixkaab?"

"The *Wasp* is in port, you know," Chuleb said, "after a good trip north, and heading home in two or three days, laden with trade goods. That will make a nice, circular voyage for you, Niece."

"We'll have another feast," Aunt Saabim said happily, "to see you off. Good luck all around! Invite your friends, if you like; they will be welcome."

Kaab opened her mouth to say one thing and found herself saying another. "Actually," she said, "I was thinking of spending a little more time here. These Locals are an interesting lot. And, as you say, now that the tax situation is a bit more equitable, there are new markets waiting to be expanded."

"Why, Niece!" Chuleb said delightedly. "You are beginning to speak like a merchant!"

But Aunt Saabim knew her better. "Really, Ixkaab? What sort of markets were you thinking of?"

"Would you believe, Aunt"—Kaab opened her eyes wide—"that when I went down to Riverside and offered a young guide some chocolate—and very inferior stuff it was, too—he refused it, thinking it was dog excrement?"

"Shocking," said Aunt Saabim. "Certainly you must spend more time there."

Uncle Chuleb leaned forward. "And how many people would you say inhabit this Riverside?"

"Oh, many," said Kaab vaguely, and pulled a long, long, flamed-red hair off the front of her shirt.

The guards were respectful when they opened the gates to Rafe Fenton. He squared his shoulders as he crossed the courtyard and looked up at the window he thought was Will's, wondering if his lover were watching for him.

A footman who looked familiar took Rafe's cloak—he'd have to learn their names now, wouldn't he?—and another led him straight to the duke's library, where the duchess already sat, setting piles of paper in order, her gown and sleeves completely covered in a muslin pinafore. She smiled when she saw him.

"Ah, Master Fenton! Prompt to the hour. Please, sit down. I will send for chocolate. Have you broken your fast?"

In the hours that passed in the dusty, sunny room, he forgot that he disliked her. The duchess was pleasant and efficient. She had a quick understanding and did not waste time in flurries of indecision or bothersome stories, like most women. She treated Rafe with respect, even asking his opinion on several matters, nodding seriously as he explained them or offered suggestions.

When the mantel clock chimed noon, a footman appeared with a massive plate of sandwiches.

"You don't mind, do you?" the duchess asked. "I thought we were making such progress. . . ."

"Not at all," Rafe said. He stood up and stretched out his back. "If you don't object, though, I'll go and see William first. Maybe I can take him something . . . ?"

The duchess looked up at him, confused. *William?* Rafe wanted to say, cross with hunger. *Your husband, remember?* But of course he did not.

"Oh." A look of distress clouded her features. "Oh, I am so sorry!" She stood and took his hands, looking up into his face. "Oh, Master Fenton, I forgot to tell you. Oh, it is entirely unforgivable of me!"

Rafe sat down suddenly, feeling faint. "He's"—he managed to breathe out—"is he—"

"He's fine." She sat by him in a rustle of skirts. "Oh dear, now I've frightened you as well." She smiled ruefully and patted his knee. "I am so sorry. It's just that William isn't here, that's all."

"Not here? Where is he?"

"In the country," she said silkily. "The Duke Tremontaine has gone to the country for his health."

The large footman was standing there. No, there were two of them. They were all that kept him from crushing the life out of her, from shaking her till she told him where Will was.

"Where?" Rafe managed to croak out.

"Oh, Master Fenton. I'm afraid I cannot tell you that. It is very important that he not be disturbed."

Rafe stumbled to his feet, all pretense of poise and civility gone. He seized her by her delicate shoulders. "Tell me," he growled, but then the footmen were on him, one on each side while he trembled with rage between them, barely able to see as her cool voice said:

"Was I not clear? I did not hire you for a sick nurse. My husband has one of those already. And your company was very, very bad for him. I thought you recognized that on your last visit and that you would understand."

He heard his own voice shouting at her, which was odd, because he never used words like that, even when he was drunk. One of the footmen punched him in the kidney, and he gasped in pain.

"I realize now," Diane went on, "that that is not the case. It really is too bad, when we were getting on so well." She ignored Rafe's wheeze of breath. "Under the circumstances, I don't suppose I can persuade you to stay. And so I will have to ask these gentlemen to show you out."

She played me, he thought, on his knees in the street outside the gates of Tremontaine House. *She played me, and she won.* He scrabbled for his satchel. *For now.*

Only for now. At least he had her measure, now. Worse even than he had imagined. Poor Will! He could crawl, Rafe supposed, on his dust-covered knees, come back to her door, grovel, apologize, and say he would still like the position: help her with her papers, bear her abuse, let her toy with him endlessly while he struggled to find out where Will was and how to set him free.

Or he could do it another way.

He would need money, of course. Money for bribes, money for travel. Money, and allies. And an unassailable position.

Master Thelonious Fenton looked up from his desk with surprise when his son was announced. It was not often that Rafe voluntarily chose to pay him a call in his merchant offices; in fact, he could not really remember the last time it had happened.

But there was his oldest, his Rafe, standing before him, decently dressed for once, his chin barbered, coat brushed, neckcloth tied—

though still with that ridiculous long hair, and looking somewhat pale. He looked older, too. Had it really been so long?

"Father," Rafe said, "I have come to tell you that I have been thinking. And I have reconsidered. I would like very much—that is, if you still want me to, I would be willing—no, eager—to join you in working here."

Diane, Duchess Tremontaine, stood in the highest room of her great house on the Hill and surveyed her city. Tomorrow, she would pay off the very last of the money for the *Everfair* loan and look into how the chocolate trade was doing. She would make sure she had someone inside the Balam compound to keep an eye on the clever Kaab, someone far more suited to it than the hapless Reynald: There was no guarantee that the pretty girl and her kinsfolk would honor their bargain to protect Diane's secret, after all, the moment it suited them not to. And so she would begin investigation of the University, to learn who Rafe Fenton's confederates had been—clearly, Fenton had not figured out the navigational formulae on his own. It was a pity the boy had lost his temper; she'd been looking forward to having him under her thumb for a while. But she could probably get him back.

The duchess drummed her fingers on the windowsill. She would also have to find someone new to represent her in the Council of Lords. Someone young this time, she thought, and handsome and ambitious, who would value what she had to teach. She would petition the Inner Council for control of all of Tremontaine's income, and then she would have some new dresses made.

There was much to do.

AUTHOR'S NOTE

Tremontaine is a project that grew out of many brains—in particular, the cofounder of Serial Box Publishing, Julian Yap, who decided to see what would happen if people had the chance to *read* weekly episodes of an ongoing story the way they watch episodes of their favorite TV series. He asked me if I would be willing to spearhead something based on my Riverside series of novels and short stories. I agreed, as long as the new narrative took place significantly before the first Riverside novel, *Swordspoint*, so nobody messed up my timeline! Then we rounded up a team of writers to expand the boundaries of the City beyond what had been written so far, while staying true to my sense of the world.

Season One of *Tremontaine* is set fifteen years before *Swordspoint*. Sure, there are Easter eggs for those who have read the books already, but we were careful to make *Tremontaine* stand alone so that this story you're reading now could be the true beginning of anyone's journey to Riverside, the Hill, and lands only hinted at in the original books.

On SerialBox.com—or in their Serial Box app—you can not only find the e-versions of the stories, season by season, but also audio narration; and on the SerialBox.com blog, we have all the authors' notes on what it was like to write their stories every week . . . plus my own explanation of how and why my big, crazy series is being written completely out of order. Welcome!

—Ellen Kushner

ACKNOWLEDGMENTS

The writers would like to thank:

Delia Sherman, for editing us into submission with patience, grace, and style;

Michael Manning, for knowing as much about math as Micah, and a lot more about science than Rafe;

Alan Bostick, for sage instruction on betting and the connection between poker and seventeenth-century natural philosophers;

Carlos Hernandez, for composing Rafe's naughty poem on page 126, as well as his enthusiastic assistance with playing cards both real and imaginary;

Jaida Jones and **Danielle Bennett**, for filling in so charmingly over the holidays with their Riverside story "Willie Be Nimble."

Kathleen Jennings, for art painstakingly cut from black paper to show our stories' true hearts.

Our Serial Box copy editor, **Noa Wheeler**, for noble service in the face of far too many characters, and *Tremontaine*'s "show runner" and cat wrangler **Racheline Maltese**, for noble service in the face of sudden deadlines, anxious authors, and a start-up project that probably shouldn't have worked, but somehow did.

In addition:

Alaya Dawn Johnson thanks Juan Paulo Pérez Tejada Ladrón de Guevara for his linguistic help in formulating the Kinwiinik language (and for having the awesomely longest name of anyone she knows).

Joel Derfner thanks Sue Fitzpatrick for keeping Micah honest.

Malinda Lo thanks all the writers for putting up with her excessive science research and plot nitpicking, and especially Alaya, for all her Kinwiinik world building.

Paul Witcover thanks Ellen Kushner for letting us play in her world.

GRIPPING SERIAL FICTION
DELIVERED WEEKLY

Read or listen to the best original serial fiction on serialbox.com or in the Serial Box App.

Fiction that fits your life